THE RANGER

BROOKE SIVENDRA

Cover by Virtually Possible Designs

Ebook: 978-0-6480649-7-8

Print: 978-0-6480649-6-1

1

DEACON

Deacon Thomas's apartment was so silent it seemed to have a heartbeat of its own. And the silence was a reminder of everything that was missing in his life—everything that had been violently ripped away from him. Nicole. The woman he'd loved and sworn to protect. The woman he'd failed. The woman who still owned his heart and soul.

Deacon's arms shook as he leaned forward, resting his elbows on his knees. He wove the silver chain through his fingers, and the dim bedside lamp caught the metal, casting a rainbow of glittering light on the wall.

A fire burned in his heart, stealing the oxygen from his lungs. He wished it would take his memories, too. But it didn't. It never did. They stayed with him like the demons of hell.

He wondered how his chest could still burn after seven years. There shouldn't be anything left of him other than a pile of ashes. Some days he was surprised his heart continued to beat when he would've sworn it had finally given up, suffocated by the ash that seemed to pile higher every year. Whoever said time heals all wounds was a liar.

He ran his thumb across the single-diamond pendant. He had few material possessions, but this one meant everything to him. It was his last piece of her. The only piece he had.

His chest shuddered as he exhaled.

Nicole passed seven years ago to the day, and this anniversary tortured him more than any other—more than her birthday, more than their first date. The anniversary of her death was a day he struggled to find a reason to get up and to go on with life. The day guilt consumed every breath he took and every second that passed. The day he feared closing his eyes because he couldn't bear seeing her—seeing her screaming for him. Pleading for him. Their eyes meeting, as they'd done that fateful night—and every night in his dreams since —his throat seizing over and his vision blurring. He hadn't been able to move. He hadn't been able to even lift a hand while her life was taken from her one agonizing second at a time.

He heard the door open and footsteps followed. He heard it even in his state of mind because it all came down to training and repetition. Training under the ultimate warrior—James Thomas.

Deacon asked himself the same question he'd asked a million times: if Deacon had had the skill set then he had now, would he have been able to save her?

The question ate at him, mostly because he was scared of the answer—of the truth. While there were no guarantees, the Deacon Thomas of today would've had a much better chance.

He shook his head and dropped the necklace into his bedside drawer as James appeared at the threshold of Deacon's bedroom.

James didn't offer any words of condolence. He didn't tell Deacon to stop torturing himself. But he understood—better than he ever had—where Deacon's mind was and the blitzing pain it was in. And yet James, knowing that and having the love of his life almost ripped away from him, still couldn't walk away from the one relationship he should.

Deacon had always said to himself that, if he could go back in time, he wouldn't have gotten involved with Nicole at all. But some microscopic part of him wondered if he really could've ended the relationship.

Deacon stood and turned off the lamp. "Where are we going?" he asked.

"Somewhere cool."

Deacon arched a brow. "Cool? That doesn't sound like us."

James chuckled. "You can find out all kinds of things when you read client reports, like where the cool bars are in town. Because, God knows, we wouldn't have a clue."

"That is true, brother," Deacon said, picking up his pistol, wallet, and cell phone from his bedside table.

It required effort to put one foot in front of the other, but the alternative was to sleep, and that thought almost crippled him. He'd much rather drown his sorrows with a bottle of tequila and delay any possibility of seeing Nicole in his dreams.

Deacon closed the apartment door behind them and pressed the elevator button, taking them to the basement. "I assume Samuel hasn't progressed on the lead," he said, his mind switching back to work. Oddly enough, if given the choice, he would never have chosen this field, but now he was grateful for it—the intensity of the job kept Nicole's ghost from his mind better than anything else did.

"No, not yet. He will, though—assuming there is something to find," James said, drawing the car keys from his pocket as the elevator descended. They both knew Deacon wasn't driving anywhere tonight.

"Is Marianne worried?" Deacon asked. What had begun as a family of four had become a blended family that continued to expand beyond their control.

James shrugged. "Mak and I visited her today . . ." James hesitated, and Deacon felt the sideways glance, but he continued to stare straight ahead. James continued, "She seems okay. I told her we'd monitor things and keep her informed, but we don't think we need to increase her security at this point."

The elevator doors slid open and they walked toward James's car.

"She's getting big now," James said while his eyes darted around the car park, as they always did.

In a few months, Marianne and her daughter's life would change forever. And so would theirs.

"Soon we're going to have a screaming baby boy in the family," Deacon said.

James snorted. "*Marianne* is going to have a screaming baby. And she's still refusing to have a nanny—even if we do full security checks. She wants to do it on her own."

Deacon turned that over in his mind for a minute. "Well, if anyone can, it's Marianne. She's no wilting flower." He slid into the passenger seat. "You're going to be an uncle again."

James's eyes twinkled. "So are you, *brother*."

Deacon chuckled. Not by blood, but if he'd learned one thing in this life, it was family wasn't born out of blood. It was born out of loyalty.

"How is Mak dealing with all of this?" Deacon asked. He rarely asked about Mak—unless it involved her security. James and Mak's relationship was a topic that brewed tension, even to this day. Deacon wanted to scream—had screamed—at James. He'd told him it wasn't worth it, but it made no difference. Deacon prayed James didn't learn the way he had. He would never wish that on anyone, least of all James.

"She says she's good with it and she's happy I've found my family —what's left of it. They get along well, but they're at very different stages: Marianne's focused on giving her children a new life, and Mak's focused on prosecuting gangland murderers . . ." James veered out of the car park and into the streets of Manhattan.

Deacon didn't miss the way his voice lowered before it trailed off. "Did you ask for the favor from our guy inside Rikers?"

James gave a long sigh. "I half did . . ." he said, pulling a face that indicated he knew he shouldn't have.

"Half did?" Deacon asked, his lips curving up.

James shrugged. "I only asked him to get in touch if the winds blew any whispers of threats his way. I, somehow, refrained myself from asking what his prison colleagues are saying about her otherwise."

James didn't have to ask—the brothers both knew what they would be saying. They'd spent enough time with criminals to know the filthy things that came out of their mouths when a beautiful, strong, intelligent woman walked inside their walls with the balls to prosecute a gangland murderer.

"Because you don't actually want to hear it? Or because you're worried about overstepping the boundary?" Deacon asked, watching James carefully.

His lips formed a thin line, but when he turned to look at him, there was a glint in his eye. "Both; but between you and me, mostly because of the second reason."

Deacon laughed. "Your secret's safe with me."

There were power issues at play between James and Mak, and although Mak might not yet realize it, she was winning more often than she was losing—particularly because getting a man like James Thomas to release control, to compromise, was no easy task. It was one Deacon had initially thought impossible but had been surprised when he saw the small, subtle changes in James's behavior.

James pulled up at a bar not far from Thomas Security—they never went far from their headquarters unless they had to—and parked on a side street.

As they always did, they walked to the front of the line, gave a voice code, and walked in without a second glance or a weapons check. They negotiated deals with all of the venues their clients regularly frequented.

The brothers went straight to the bar, ordered two drinks—one of which would never be finished, he knew—and James pulled a box of cigars from his pocket. They did the same thing every year, and somehow the routine, and the familiarity of it, helped Deacon. It didn't take away his pain, but a small part of him always felt less alone.

Deacon's eyes traveled the bar, noting the clientele. He'd be lucky if he walked out of the club without being blinded by the rocks on their fingers or the stones draped around their necks. At one stage in their life, not too long ago in the scheme of things, they'd had nothing more than a few hundred dollars to their name. Now Deacon would wage a bet that they had as much, if not more, than the wealthiest person in the club. Of course, not all of their money had been earned through legal activities—but that was probably true for many of the bar's patrons.

Deacon raised the glass to his lips, and his taste buds reveled in the liquid so rarely consumed. He allowed himself to relinquish control on only two nights of the year—Nicole's birthday and the anniversary of her death.

"Did you ask Samuel to come out?" Deacon asked before another mouthful of burning liquid slid down the back of his throat.

James puffed on a cigar. "Like I do every year. And, like every year, he said he's too busy."

Deacon smiled. "There's something really wrong with him," he said, getting a rare, deep laugh from James.

"There's something really wrong with all of us," James joked. "I'm not complaining, though. I do want to know if this chatter about taking revenge on Marianne is just that, or if there's more to it."

"I do, too," Deacon said. The further she progressed in her pregnancy, the more danger she was in if they found her. If the offspring rebels of Saratani found out she was carrying an heir to their underground criminal organization, things could get very ugly, very fast. They'd barely managed to catch their breath from the last battle with Saratani. Deacon knew what his brother was thinking, but not saying: *There are kids involved.* Innocent children who would be sacrificed for the organization.

"One day at a time," Deacon said, knowing it was pointless to worry until they had more to go on. And if anyone could find out, Samuel could. He might be a recluse, but he was a genius recluse.

Deacon tipped the glass to his lips, checking it twice when nothing more than a drop hit his tongue. He barely remembered drinking it. James noticed and motioned to the bartender for another without a word, without judgment.

"When are we leaving for Tokyo?" Deacon asked. They still had one more favor to deliver, a result of their war with Saratani. It would hopefully be the final closure of the nightmare that'd nearly killed them all.

"Soon," James said with a nod. "I think we've stalled Haruki Tohmatsu as long as we can. I'll do another physical test on Monday, and then—if I pass—we'll make plans to go."

Deacon had become James's physical trainer over the past few months and it was the first time their roles had been reversed. James had always been fitter, always stronger. But now, Deacon could easily kick his ass, something he brought up as frequently as he could.

James read his thoughts, his lips turning into a smirk. "Get ready to be dethroned, brother. I'm coming back."

Deacon beamed a grin back at him. "Game on."

2

JAMES

James might've been fooled by the smile on Deacon's lips, and the deep rumble of his chest, but the rate he was putting the drinks away told a very different story. Before, on the anniversary of Nicole's birthday, they had been caught up in the mess of what they'd thought was Mak's security case, which turned out to be a very different story. Regardless, they hadn't been able to go out like they normally did. James wondered if Deacon was simply making up for it, getting two for one tonight, of if there was more going on. James wasn't oblivious that his own relationship with Mak brought up feelings that Deacon refused to face. James didn't blame him, though. All things considered, if Deacon only drank himself into a blind mess a couple nights a year—given what he'd been through—that was a pretty good result. James wasn't going to stop him, but he would carry him home.

James nodded to the bartender again, refilling Deacon's glass. He also asked for a menu, thinking it would be a good idea to put something in Deacon's stomach, considering it had been a few hours since they'd eaten in Samuel's office.

James brought his cigar to his lips, thinking how normal they must look to everyone else, and how far this appearance was from their reality.

His phone vibrated in his pocket and he drew it out, hiding his smile as he read the message.

Mak: Home from Rikers. Safe and sound.

Her message was the result of his request, even though Cami would've alerted him to trouble far before Mak would've. And, even though tone was difficult to interpret in text messages, he imagined her typing that with an ounce or two of mocking.

But the gangland murder case she was working on made James anxious. He wanted—*needed*—a period in their life for them just to have some degree of normalcy. A period without the threat of death looming over them. He wondered if they were ever going to be that lucky. Although everything seemed calm at the moment, he knew a security case could blow up at any time.

He typed a quick reply—*I'll call you in the morning. J*—before returning his attention to Deacon.

"Mak's home," James said simply, and Deacon nodded. James changed the subject. "Getting back to Tokyo, did you get a chance to look over the surveillance folder Samuel emailed us?"

And like that, they spent the next few hours talking business. James didn't count the drinks Deacon put away—he just let the man drown his sorrows and deal with his pain in the only way he seemed to know how. Deacon chose alcohol as his vice. The fact that he could consume the volume he was and still not succumb to his emotions was extremely worrying to James. He thought about how to approach the topic again, given that every single time he had in the past, it had resulted in blazing fights between them, to the point that Deacon told him if he brought it up again, he'd leave—he'd go out on his own. It wasn't an empty threat, James knew. Deacon might let him call the shots when it came to work, but that didn't apply to his personal life. It hadn't when Deacon and Nicole had been together, and it hadn't after her death. James had given up after that last argument, and he'd let Deacon deal with the pain the way he seemingly wanted to—or the only way he knew how—but James was finding it hard not to say something again. Deacon might appear fine to the outside world, but James knew better. When he could control his emotions, he was numb. And when he couldn't, he was in a world of pain.

That's where the brothers were different. James wouldn't have suppressed his pain; he wouldn't have buried the memories away in the deepest recess of his mind. He would've taken revenge. He would've killed every person who had a link to Nicole. And it would've been a bloody mess.

James thought over the conversation he'd had with Mak last night. He knew Deacon was going to be furious, but he had to try again. He would rather see Deacon angry with him than in the state of self-loathing he was currently in, and if his brother hated him in the morning, he'd deal with it then. Anyway, Deacon couldn't leave now, not without Samuel tracking him.

James cleared his throat, grateful for the music that concealed their conversation from anyone standing around them. "I'm going to tell you something, something you probably don't want to hear, but need to," James said, choosing his words delicately. Deacon didn't respond—there was no change in demeanor, but he did lug another mouthful of his tequila.

James continued, "Mak said something to me last night. She made me promise that if something happened to her, even if it happened because of me, I wouldn't spend the rest of my life punishing myself for it."

Deacon's hands tightened around his glass.

"She said that becoming involved with me was her choice, and that she's prepared to accept those risks because what we have together is worth it. I know—"

"You *don't* know!" Deacon said, pushing back, his anger palpable. "You don't know what it feels like. I can't just get over it and pick up my life and put it back together tomorrow."

"I'm not saying you can do that," James said, keeping his voice low, refusing to match Deacon's. "I honestly don't know what I would do if something happened to Mak—I don't think it's something I'd ever fully get past—but I do think that you need to forgive yourself for what happened. You've suffered, Deacon. You've suffered for years. You've paid your price for what happened ten times over. It's okay to move on now. Whether you want to admit it or not, it's what Nicole would want."

"It doesn't matter what she'd want. She's dead," Deacon said through gritted teeth.

James reluctantly let it drop. That was enough pushing for today, and he didn't want to attract the attention of the bar patrons. "Okay." He sighed.

Deacon finished his drink in two large mouthfuls and ordered another. For a moment James regretted having said anything, worried he'd pushed his brother too far. But Deacon had been putting away the drinks before their conversation. The night had been headed in one direction from the very beginning.

James changed the conversation back to work—to a common ground. Their partnership in the business worked well because Deacon was a much better businessman than James was, while James loved doing the dirty work. Although Deacon got his hands dirty when required, he never got the same thrill from it.

When Deacon's eyes glazed over and he stopped talking in the middle of a slurred sentence, as if he had forgotten what he was saying, James knew it was time to go home. The alcohol seemed to be hitting him hard and fast now, like a snowball that had been gathering momentum. And when his words began to become incomprehensible and his head was wobbling, James knew it was definitely time to go.

James slid his credit card across the bar and paid the tab without Deacon noticing.

"Okay, brother, let's go," James said.

Deacon looked at him with hooded eyes, gave a small sigh, then slid off the bar stool, swaying. James wrapped an arm around his shoulder, like two grown men in drunken camaraderie, and guided him toward the door.

James gave a nod to the bouncer as they passed, who eyed them with interest.

James kept them walking as Deacon said a friendly goodbye. James smiled, but there was no humor in it.

When they got to the corner, Deacon tripped on his own feet, but James kept him upright, ignoring the twinge it caused in his not yet fully healed ribs. During normal daily activity, during sex even, he no longer felt any pain. But carrying Deacon, who was no small man, was not an easy task even when James was in top condition.

James unlocked the car, helped Deacon in, and jumped into the driver's seat. He put the windows down and drove home slowly so Deacon didn't become nauseated.

Deacon's head rolled to the side, and he closed his eyes. James turned his attention back to the road, checking the mirrors for a tail. There wasn't one.

When James pulled up in his designated parking spot, he assessed the situation, wondering if he should call Cami. He didn't, though; Deacon was fiercely protective of letting anyone see his guard down, and that included Samuel and Cami. As far as James knew, he was the only person that Deacon was ever vulnerable with, and even that was rare.

James sighed and then muttered to himself, "At least we have an elevator."

He walked around the car and opened Deacon's door.

"Come on, brother. Let's get you into bed," James said as Deacon's eyelids lifted slowly, and he looked around. Nothing in his expression changed. He didn't seem surprised they were home. James wasn't sure he could see right now.

He took Deacon's arm, guiding him out of the car then slinging it over his shoulder. He kicked the door shut and shuffled them toward the elevator. James was panting when they reached it, and his confidence in his ability to pass the physical test that was to come in a few days had diminished. Deacon was going to keep the throne a while yet, but James knew he'd be fit enough to do the Tokyo job regardless.

James punched in their floor number and the doors closed.

Deacon's head flopped on James's shoulder. He stared at their reflection in the mirror, questioning whether he'd failed Deacon by not forcing him to deal with Nicole's death, regardless of his brother's threats. It had been a long time since he'd brought up Nicole—he hadn't dared after Paris, because James knew exactly what Deacon's response would've been. James had refused to talk about Paris, and Deacon refused to talk about Nicole. But perhaps a tough-love approach might've helped Deacon more forward.

"Come on," James said, trying to usher Deacon out of the elevator and toward his apartment.

James struggled to keep Deacon upright and hit the wrong code twice before getting it right. Inside, James took him straight to bed. Deacon all but fell onto the mattress, bouncing.

He took off Deacon's shoes, putting them on the floor. He went to the kitchen and grabbed two bottles of water and a packet of pain relief from Deacon's medical supply.

He went back to the bedroom to find Deacon asleep. James put the water and meds on the nightstand. He left the bedside light on, in the event Deacon needed to make an urgent dash to the bathroom, and locked the door on his way out.

James entered his own apartment, drawing out his phone as he did.

Mak answered on the second ring. "Hey."

His pulse quickened at the sound of her voice—she still managed to do that to him. And he hoped she always would. He would never take their relationship for granted, not when he knew how easily it could be lost.

"Hey," James replied, opening the fridge, searching for a late-night snack. "We're home."

"How is he?" Mak asked, the playfulness dropping from her voice.

"He's going to have a killer headache in the morning," James said, leaving it at that. "Tell me about your day."

James listened, wishing Mak were in his kitchen, telling him in person. But tonight he'd needed to be there for Deacon—and Deacon's night wasn't necessarily over. The nightmares would still come, and James knew Deacon hated for anyone to hear him screaming, which was unavoidable from James's bedroom.

If the floors weren't soundproofed, even Samuel and Cami would've heard.

3

DEACON

A hammer pounded against his skull, waking him up. He found himself dressed, in his bed, wondering how he got there. He rolled his head to look at the clock on his bedside table, immediately regretting it.

Deacon groaned, pressing his fingers to his temples and squeezing his eyes shut. He focused on his breath, giving the pain a moment to calm down. When he opened his eyes again, he found the goods his fairy godmother had left for him.

Calling James a fairy godmother would've made him laugh on any other day, but the pain was so intense that the humor eluded him.

Instead, he willed his body to move, to grab the pills and water calling his name, but the task seemed like the equivalent of running a marathon right now. He closed his eyes again, deciding that sleeping it off was a better option.

When he awoke an hour later, the hammer was still beating his skull like a pendulum and his mouth felt like it was stuffed with cotton.

He gave a long sigh and forced his body to reach for the water, shaking as he did. He pushed himself up against the headboard and gulped the contents of the first bottle down without pause. A moment later his stomach clenched, and he prayed it wasn't going to come back up. He stilled, waiting for it. His body seemed unsure, like it couldn't make a decision. He popped two pills out of the packet and swallowed them, his stomach clenching again. He groaned. It was going to be a long day, but he was thankful for one thing—to his surprise, the nightmares had stayed away.

~

Deacon felt like the world was moving in slow motion, but he knew it was just him. When he finally made it to Samuel's office, it was late morning. James and Samuel were drinking coffee, and he saw a spread of takeaway containers had been laid out in the center of the table.

James looked over his shoulder, pulling a chair out for Deacon. "Morning."

"Don't talk," Deacon said, slumping. He rested his elbows on the table and buried his face in his hands.

"Eat; you'll feel better," Samuel said.

The water and pills he'd swallowed down this morning had come back up in the shower. He doubted Samuel wanted the same to happen in his office. "Can't," Deacon said with a croaky voice.

He didn't think he'd ever felt this hungover, but he wasn't sure he'd ever been that drunk. Usually he at least remembered getting home, but his memory of the last half of last night was as blank as a freshly painted wall.

James moved next to him, apparently leaving the room. Deacon didn't raise his eyes.

I should go back to bed.

He'd tried to convince himself it was better to get up and start moving, but now that seemed like an awfully bad idea.

"Sit back," James said, startling him.

Had he fallen asleep? Deacon forced his eyes open, eying James's medical kit and the IV pole. *James has a much better idea.* Deacon thought with relief.

Deacon settled down in the chair, resting his head on the top of the backrest, and rolled up his sleeve. He felt the pinprick and then whatever drugs James was giving him run up his vein.

"You'll feel better in a bit," James said.

Deacon muttered his thanks.

At some point later, he couldn't be sure how long, Cami's voice woke him up. Deacon opened one eye and then the other.

"That's one perk of working for Thomas Security," she said and took a seat beside him.

"There has to be some perks to this job," Deacon joked hoarsely. He regretted it immediately—it had taken all of his energy. But he could see the room clearly now, and he felt reasonably confident he wasn't going to throw up on Samuel's table.

Cami patted his shoulder. "If drinking like a boozehound a few nights a year is all you do, you're doing all right."

Deacon sighed, perusing what was left of the breakfast spread. He settled on a cold toasted sandwich. He took a bite, hesitantly, and when his stomach didn't clench violently, he cautiously took another. He looked at his watch. In one hour he'd gone from death to death warmed up. Drugs were miraculous things.

"What did I miss?" Deacon asked, not wanting to talk about Nicole.

Samuel massaged his jaw. "The talk of a Saratani renaissance is growing. I've intercepted several chats and telephone calls, and I'm attempting to use the voice recognition system to match them to known identities."

Deacon took the last bite of his sandwich, which he'd all but inhaled, and then scrunched the paper bag into a ball. "If you're picking up more chatter, doesn't that mean they're not using secured devices? How skilled and resourceful are we assuming these guys are?" Deacon asked as he looked for his next snack.

"It's not these guys I'm worried about," James said. "If we're intercepting this, you can bet others are, too. Some of Saratani's practices were insane, but Eric was an extremely good businessman. The destruction of that organization has opened the door for opportunists to infiltrate and expand the space Saratani had been operating in. That means this group may soon have access to additional resources, or, more likely, they'll make deals with the wrong men and end up eliminating themselves. That would be the ideal scenario."

"What are our options for the moment?" Cami asked before stealing half of Deacon's doughnut and giving him a wink. It was in her mouth before he had time to react. On a good day—a normal day —she'd never have gotten away with that.

"Let's watch and wait," James said. "The last thing we need right now is another war. The underground is going to take action and capitalize on the new business opportunities—let's find out who does and go from there."

Deacon listened to the conversation, but his mind wasn't working fast enough to contribute anything of value.

Samuel gave a slight nod. "On another note, Deacon, I've arranged the flower delivery for next week."

"Thanks," Deacon said. Flowers, he knew, for his mother's birthday.

The hardest part of living a life on the run was saying goodbye to the people you loved. To family. To this day he didn't know exactly what his mother had been told about his disappearance. The military likely said he had been killed in action. Like James, like Cami, like Samuel, they were all "deceased" on paper, their bodies "unrecoverable." But after Samuel had come into their lives, and could safely send a bouquet of flowers without being tracked, every year he had sent an arrangement of 200 white tulips to his mother. Her favorite flower. He wouldn't risk making contact with her, but he hoped the flowers gave her hope that her son was alive and well.

His father—well, he thought bitterly, his father he cared less about.

4

JAMES

James's chest heaved as he leaned over, resting his palms on his knees. He fought back the rolling waves of nausea as he gave his body time to recover. Droplets of sweat ran down his forearms. His fitness had improved, but he was not where he wanted to be—he still had work to do before he reclaimed his throne.

Deacon wasn't training with him tonight, which was to be expected. They'd spent the remaining morning in Samuel's office before actually going to their own offices to work. Deacon had barely said a word, which wasn't surprising given his hangover, but James thought there was more going on with his brother. He'd noticed the changes in him recently—the haunted flicker in Deacon's eyes that was now less of a rare occurrence than it had been over recent years. James sensed that Deacon's mental control of his emotions was finally slipping, slowly but surely.

He knew his own relationship with Mak contributed to that, and he sometimes felt guilty because of it. He'd never wanted a relationship, but now he had one. Deacon should've had the life he had been living, and although neither of them had ever said it, James thought Deacon had to have thought the same thing more than once even though he'd never shown any bitterness toward James. Disapproval, yes—but never bitterness.

He wiped a towel over his body, removing a layer of thick sweat and went in search of his brother. He wasn't going to bring up Nicole, not after last night, but he could at least keep him company. He nodded goodbye to the staff members using the gym and went to Samuel's office. He poked his head in, but Deacon wasn't there. He rang his cell phone, but he didn't answer. He wasn't in his apartment, his office, or on the rooftop. Perhaps he didn't want to be found.

James sighed and instead returned to Samuel's office.

"Any leads on Marianne's case?" James asked as he pulled out a chair and tucked it in beneath him.

"Actually, I received a few identification matches this afternoon, but I don't know if they're going to lead us anywhere," Samuel said, his fingers fluttering over the keyboard.

James shrugged. "Let's have a look." He turned his gaze toward the wall of monitors.

The screen flickered before a man with a pissed-off gaze appeared, looking back at them. His crew cut and chiseled jawline didn't help his expression.

"This lovely man," Samuel joked, "was on the receiving end of one of the telephone calls. His name is Simon Salot. He has a string of petty crime charges, the last one dating back thirteen years. I won't assume he's cleaned up his life, but rather I believe he has simply gotten smarter about his criminal dealings."

"Any known mafia or gang associations?" James asked, studying the man's face. Nothing about him sparked a sense of familiarity.

"No, nothing yet. But like I said, the last few years he's been quiet, which means I'm going to have to dig deeper," Samuel said before changing the image.

The next one was of a woman, who looked to be about thirty years old. Like the man before her, her record was unimpressive, but she did have one identifying mark.

"Is that tattoo behind her ear significant?" James asked.

Samuel pushed his glasses up the ridge of his nose, adjusting them.

"No, not that I can tell. Number three . . ." Samuel said, loading the photograph on the screen.

James's eyebrows creased. "Which one?" he asked, looking at the surveillance shot taken in what looked to be an airport.

"Him," Samuel said, moving a cursor over the man browsing the bookstore.

The air vanished from his lungs. "Zoom in," James demanded.

He leaned forward instinctively, his eyes narrowing as his heart thundered in his chest.

"What? Who is it?" Samuel asked. His eyes widened as if he were in imminent danger.

James couldn't tear his eyes away. "Has Deacon seen this?"

"Have I seen what?" Deacon asked from behind him.

5

DEACON

It took Deacon a moment to realize what James had been looking at on the screen, and when he lifted his own eyes to it, his entire world fell apart.

"Sit down," James said, jumping up from his chair and grabbing Deacon's arm.

The room tilted and James's voice blurred in his head.

He couldn't breathe, and the blood in his veins froze, stilling his heart.

Deacon looked back at the screen, looking into the eyes of one of the men who had raped and murdered Nicole.

"Deacon," James said, a plea of sorts, but Deacon couldn't draw his gaze away.

Questions flooded his mind, sweeping it of coherency, until finally he managed to grab hold of one and voice it. "Where did you get this?" he asked, his voice hoarse.

"It's a lead from Marianne's case—the Saratani chatter," Samuel said quickly, lines forming on his forehead. Samuel looked to James, and Deacon saw the understanding sweep over the analyst.

"I didn't know," Samuel said. "I'm so sorry, Deacon. If I'd known, I would've—"

"Would've what?" Deacon asked. "There's no good way to deliver this kind of intel."

Deacon pinched the bridge of his nose, reminding himself to breathe.

I can't do this.

"I'll be back in a minute," Deacon said distantly. The chair slid back behind him, toppling over as he rushed out of Samuel's office. He took the elevator to the rooftop. He needed to breathe. He needed a minute alone without someone watching his reaction—provided Samuel didn't turn on the cameras. He hoped they'd at least give him that much privacy.

His foot was out as soon as the elevator doors pulled apart.

Breathe.

Breathe.

He paced the length of the rooftop, back and forth, relentlessly. He couldn't think; he couldn't see anything but the man's image.

Why now?

After all these years, the man's face had surfaced *now*. The pain was supposed to get easier to deal with, not worse. How long would he have to suffer for loving her?

He swiped away the tear that ran down his cheek. His heart crumbled as everything he had suppressed for so long came flowing back like a rapid river. The flashbacks came one after another—a horror movie.

His legs trembled beneath him and he all but fell onto the lounge, burying his head in his hands.

His chest shuddered as he exhaled. When the door opened behind him, he didn't look up. When the figure sat down on the couch opposite him, he still didn't raise his eyes.

"I know you think you can't deal with this," James said. "But you're wrong. You can—you just don't want to. And I don't blame you for that, but I think the only way to free yourself from your pain is to face it."

"I'll never be free from this. It's going to haunt me until the day I die," Deacon said desperately. He ran his hands through his hair—

24

hair that was finally growing back after James had shaved it—and his eyes burned with hot tears.

"You'll never forget, no, but you don't have to suffer like this. She wouldn't want this for you, Deacon. She wouldn't want you to live in hell every day."

"I told you!" he spat with sudden venom. "It doesn't matter what she wants! She's dead. And she's dead because of me." Deacon raised his bloodshot eyes to James. He was the only person in the world who Deacon could have this kind of conversation with, who he could bare his soul to.

"No," James said firmly. "She's dead because a group of violent, vehement men were trying to climb the social ladder of the underground world." He paused. "You have a choice now."

"I can't deal with this," Deacon said, the oxygen of his deep breaths fueling the fire in his chest.

"You can," James said. "I'm not suggesting you be like me and go and slaughter everyone involved. But until you face the past, I don't think you're going to deal with her death. You can't keep suppressing your emotions, Deacon. What good has it done?" James didn't wait for an answer. "None," he continued flatly. "It's only caused you more pain. I know you've asked yourself: What happened? How you were captured? What mistakes were made? Who were the men involved? Let Samuel look into it again—and *help* him this time. It will give you some answers, and maybe some closure. Lay this to rest."

Deacon shook his head angrily.

But James wasn't backing down. When he tilted his head in that analyzing way, Deacon knew he wasn't going to like whatever James was going to say. "Whether you want to face it or not," he said, more gently now, "unless you're going to stand back from Marianne's potential case, you may not have a choice if it progresses in a way we don't want it to."

"I just . . ." Deacon bit back a sigh that bordered dangerously on a cry. It was too much all at once.

James nodded, his expression softening.

Deacon wiped the tears from his eyes, inhaling deeply despite his burning lungs.

They sat there quietly for a while longer, and Deacon was grateful James knew when to stop talking.

Eventually James said, "Let's go to the gym."

Deacon didn't want to. He didn't want to do anything. He didn't want to see anyone. But he also didn't want to go back to his apartment, alone, with nothing to think about other than Nicole and the men who had ravaged her.

"Okay," Deacon said, standing on shaky legs.

James stood, and they walked side by side to the elevator.

"Did you look through the rest of the leads?" Deacon asked hesitantly, scared of the answer James would give him.

"Yes. I didn't recognize anyone else," James said, but Deacon knew he was thinking the same thing. It was likely irrelevant they didn't recognize anyone else—it just meant Samuel hadn't dug deep enough yet.

~

Deacon lifted his sweat-soaked singlet over his chest, throwing it onto the bathroom floor. James wasn't back to his peak-level of fitness, but he wasn't far off. Today's sparring match had nearly seen Deacon's ass handed to him, which hadn't happened since James's injuries. And James didn't need to say a word—the gloating was plastered all over his face.

A stream of water pummeled his face, a result of the high-pressure showerhead he so loved. He leaned forward, resting his palms on the tiled wall as the water washed him clean. It was a shame it couldn't wash away his past.

He tried to push down the bubbling memories, locking them up in the mental safe he'd formed, but he couldn't control them. He couldn't shut down his mind like he'd previously been able to. He kept seeing her bloody body, the man in the image hovering over her.

Deacon turned off the water. He needed to keep busy, to keep his mind distracted.

He towel-dried his body then dressed in sweats. He looked between his bedroom and the hallway to the lounge room. It was going to be an odd design, but why did he care? No one visited him anyway except Cami and James. Samuel was a very infrequent visitor.

He went to the lounge room first, strategizing if he pushed everything back against the walls, it would provide enough room to move his bed in and slide the couches into the bedroom.

It was going to be a physically exerting task on his own, but he welcomed that—he welcomed any form of emotional exorcism right now. If he was busy and tired, his mind might settle down.

Deacon stripped the linen from his meticulously made bed—old military habits die hard—and muttered, "Here goes," as he levered the mattress up. With a heavy grunt he flipped it onto his side, his arms straining as he fought to keep it steady. He slid it down the hallway, resting it against the wall.

He went back to his bedroom, stopping by the laundry room to grab his tool kit. He returned to his bedroom and turned on the television, needing some background noise—to eliminate the quietness of his apartment. Silence was always a reminder of what was missing.

He set about dismantling his bed as he half-listened to the news reporter and took the reports therein with a grain of salt. The media manipulated and fabricated world events to their advantage—something he knew all too well.

With his bed dismantled, he carried each post and slat to his lounge room, stacking them one upon the other. Order was always imperative. One post slipped, but he fumbled and couldn't grasp it before it crashed to the floor. Luckily, porcelain tiles were hard to chip or scratch.

He went back and forth like a robot—fully immersed in the task —and once everything was lined up he reassembled his bed and rearranged the couches in his old bedroom.

Deacon looked over his new design. It was certainly odd, but it fixed the soundproofing issue while still allowing enough sound to pass through to satisfy their concerns for security. He was done hearing the muffled cries of passion that came from James's bedroom —but their apartments were small enough that if he was being murdered and screamed his lungs out, even from his lounge room, James would still be able to hear him.

When Deacon flicked off the lights, it was after midnight. He drew the blankets up under his chin, staring into the darkness.

You might not have a choice. They were James's words, and Deacon had a feeling they were going to ring true.

He wouldn't sit out Marianne's potential case. He couldn't let the team down like that, not because of his own personal demons. He would have to face them—he just had no idea where he was going to find the strength to do that.

Go to sleep, he ordered his mind.

An hour later, it finally obeyed.

~

Blood gurgles in my throat. I'm drowning in my own blood.

Focus, Deacon. Fight.

Nicole's scream rips through the air and my eyes spring open. I can see her now. They're dragging her in, her body bound and bloody.

"No!" I scream, but the only noise that comes out is the sound of my lungs drowning. The concrete floor is sticky with my blood, and my cheek is glued to it.

"Deacon! Deacon!" Her high-pitched scream makes the men around her smile like predators.

"He's not going to save you, princess," one man says, grinning as he trails a knife up her inner thigh.

"Nicole!" I try to scream as I buck against the restraints, my mind unable to make my limbs move.

The man stops the knife between her legs, and slices away her panties.

"No! No!" I scream, my words like acid in my throat.

~

Deacon's eyes sprung open and his chest heaved, gasping for breath. He bolted upright, swinging his legs down, momentarily disoriented. He was in his new bedroom. He was safe—but she was not. And he would never forget her pleading eyes.

He fought against his sweat-soaked sheets, untangling his body from them, and went to the kitchen, turning on the lights. His legs felt weak beneath him and he steadied himself against the bench. With trembling hands, he turned on the coffee machine. He needed something to stay awake. He didn't want to go back to bed—didn't want to go back to that nightmare.

"When will this end?" he whispered.

It was the same question he'd asked himself a million times, but this time he knew the answer.

When you face it.

He poured himself some coffee and took it up to the rooftop—he wanted to be anywhere but in his empty bed. He looked at the taller buildings that towered around them. Some lights were on, and Deacon could see people moving around in their apartments. It provided a strange sense of comfort, of not being alone.

He put his headphones on, turned the music up, and drank his coffee, praying for the morning to come swiftly.

6

DEACON

For the second time in less than eight hours, he woke up to find himself drenched in sweat—but this time it hadn't been induced by nightmares. The sun beamed through the glass roof, and he couldn't believe the time when he looked at his watch. It was nearing midday. He threw the blankets off—blankets he hadn't brought up to the rooftop—and picked up his phone and coffee-stained mug, taking it all back to his apartment. He showered quickly, dressed, and went to Samuel's office.

"Morning," Deacon said, despite it being late noon.

"Slim pickings," Cami said as Deacon looked over the empty paper bags. She wasn't wrong.

"What's happening today?" Deacon asked. It was Saturday, but it really made no difference to him. Work, train, sleep. That was his routine, every day, unless he was in the field.

"Not much," Samuel said. He met Deacon's gaze. "No new leads. I'll keep working on it, but otherwise all client cases are stable. I guess we have the weekend off."

"Praise the Lord," Cami said, raising her palms to the ceiling, and Deacon smiled. "If Mak is with you today," she continued, "then I'm going to bed, and I'm not waking up until tomorrow."

While the brothers had reasonable schedules, Cami's was dependent on whatever Mak was doing. And she'd been working—a lot. Given that Cami also had to brief and debrief the teams, she was working even more hours than Mak.

"Take the weekend off," James said with a nod and then added, "I'll cover you."

Cami scoffed. "Oh, I'm sure you will. Not hard to do when you never leave your bedroom."

Deacon ignored the innuendos. Samuel seemed to, too.

"You're just jealous," James said, smirking.

"I can take care of myself," Cami said with a wink, and Samuel looked anywhere but at Cami. Deacon chuckled.

James stood and said his goodbyes.

Deacon returned his attention to Samuel. His heart begged for his mind not to speak the words, but he knew he had to do this. "Can you please show me the other leads? I know James didn't recognize any of the men, but I might."

Samuel pressed his lips together, paused, then gave a nod. His eyes were soft, barely looking at his keys as he typed.

Deacon felt Cami's eyes on him. He'd never spoken about Nicole's death with her.

"First one," Samuel said, and Deacon held his breath, shifting in his chair to look at the screens. He exhaled when he didn't recognize the man.

"Next," Deacon said, repeating the process.

One after the other, surveillance shots flashed up on the screen, but he didn't recognize any of the men.

Cami didn't say a word the entire time and Deacon wondered what she was thinking. Everyone said James was hard to read, but Deacon thought Cami was much harder. She had the best poker face of them all.

Deacon shook his head. "There were six other men who stayed there on the night of her murder, but there were also three others that came and went during the time we were held captive. None of them match your profiles."

"I'll keep digging," Samuel said. Once Samuel had found, and subsequently joined, them in Chicago, he'd insisted on at least looking at the men involved in Nicole's death from a security perspective. Deacon had refused to talk about her death, so James had given him any information he could provide, but it wasn't a lot. Samuel had few leads to follow and eventually he'd given up. Deacon hadn't wanted him to look into it then, and he didn't want him to now.

He wanted to forget the faces of Nicole's murderers, not look at them again, but refusing to deal with the situation for seven years hadn't made it easier. It felt like it was getting worse, the nightmares more intense, more suffocating, and his mind constantly thought of her. Deacon sighed, rubbing his eyes. The pain just wouldn't go away.

It should've been a long romantic weekend. Four days. Four days and they would've been back in Tokyo. The security contract they'd been working on in Tokyo had reached a boiling point, and Deacon and James had been working day and night. Once it had settled down, James told him to take a few days off, and he'd cover for him. Deacon had wanted to get out of Tokyo. Since they'd left Russia, they'd done little more than work, and he knew Nicole needed a break—a break from the reality she'd known she was entering but had nevertheless not been fully prepared for.

Leaving one life and starting another is hard. Saying goodbye and never speaking to your family or friends again is hard—even if you think the person you're leaving it for is worth it. It still breaks you. It still takes a piece of your heart that you'll never get back. And when you spend ninety percent of your time in an apartment because your boyfriend is too worried about you going out alone, it starts to get to you. And that's what had happened.

So Deacon had planned what should've been a romantic trip away: four nights at a private villa within a luxury resort. They'd run checks on the staff—domestic and security—as best they could at that time. If Samuel had been working with them, it might have been a very different story. Everything had appeared fine, and the first two nights were heaven on earth. Deacon himself hadn't realized how much he'd needed a break.

But on the third night, when the air was so still and humid, he'd heard that muffled thud—the one that only someone like him would recognize. The sound of a limp body hitting the ground.

That's when the nightmare started.

A nightmare he would never wake up from.

Samuel's cell phone rang, startling him.

"Hi, Josh," Samuel said, and Deacon and Cami's eyes met.

Why is Josh calling?

Deacon wondered if there was an issue with Marianne's security.

"Seriously?" Samuel asked, chuckling. "All right, I'll send someone over." He ended the call. "Josh is having some trouble putting together Marianne's nursery furniture. The guy can coordinate a lethal task force and install security systems, but he can't put together a bassinet."

Cami scoffed and Deacon gave a weak smile—more at the sound of Samuel's laugh than anything.

"I'll go," Deacon said. "I don't have anything to do today."

"Are you sure?" Samuel asked.

Deacon nodded. Truth be told, Deacon had never put together baby furniture either, but he had faith he could figure it out. How hard could it be?

He retrieved his kit from his bedroom and rode the elevator to the basement parking garage. He was glad he had something to do to keep his mind busy.

Marianne's apartment was a total of five blocks from their headquarters, and after arriving he entered his eight-digit security code before pulling into the underground parking garage. He parked in one of the visitor bays.

They'd secured an apartment for Marianne that rivaled the security level of Mak's. They were lucky there had been one available; they didn't need to bribe someone and pay them to move out—like they'd done to get Mak's apartment.

Deacon knocked on Marianne's door then let himself in. He was greeted by the sound of cartoons. It was a reality far from their own lives and the lives of most of their clients. Their clients tended to be older, having accrued significant wealth over the years that in turn rendered a need for Thomas Security's services. Rarely did they protect young billionaires—and the few they did, didn't have families.

Whether she sensed him or heard the door close, Kaela spun around, her head appearing over the back of the couch. She gave him a big grin.

"Hi, Deacon," she said. "Do you know what time it is?"

"What time is it, Kaela?" Deacon asked with a smile to match hers. He had no idea where this conversation was going.

"It's my favorite show! Come and watch," she said, jumping on the couch.

"Kaela, Deacon is here to work, not to watch television with you," Marianne said, appearing from the hallway. She walked with a regal air, her chin slightly elevated, her frame poised elegantly. Deacon wondered if she realized she carried herself that way. Marianne raised a manicured brow. "Don't get sucked in. She'll make you sit there for hours."

Deacon grinned. Kaela's strong personality was amusing at this age, but if she ended up anything like her father, they'd all be in trouble.

"I hear Josh is having problems," Deacon said.

Marianne gave a rare, genuine smile. "And here I thought you boys could do anything," she joked, her lake-blue eyes sparkling. Her accent—a mysterious blend of British and American tones—was stronger when she was relaxed, he noted.

Deacon shrugged. "I'll admit this is a first for us, but nonetheless, Josh is going to hear about it when he gets back to the office," he said with a wink.

Marianne smiled again and tossed her long dark hair over her shoulder. She looked years younger than she was and that was a miracle in itself—a marriage to Eric should've aged anyone well beyond their years.

"Deacon, come and watch!" Kaela interrupted, but then she pouted her lips as Marianne threw her a warning gaze.

"I'll come and watch once I'm done," Deacon said, moving in the direction of the nursery. He heard Marianne's footsteps behind him. Deacon wondered how much she really trusted them. She knew they were looking out for her, that they had her best interests at heart, but he had the sense there were deep, underlying trust issues beneath the façade. He thought she only completely trusted herself. And after living a life of lies and deceit, he didn't blame her.

"Josh," Deacon said, not hiding his grin.

"Don't start," he said, running a hand through his hair.

Deacon chuckled, knelt beside him, and looked over the organized piles of screws and bolts. Deacon picked up the instruction booklet, reviewed each page, then turned to his colleague. "You're never going to live this down."

~

Three hours later, the nursery was fully assembled, changing table and all, and Deacon and Josh stood back to admire their work. It had been time consuming, but that was where the difficulty ended.

Marianne stilled as she entered the room, her eyes glazing over for a moment before she quickly regained her composure. Deacon wondered what was going through her mind. Was she thinking about how close this had come to not happening? If her pregnancy had been discovered, and she hadn't escaped Saratani, Eric would've killed her unborn son.

"Thank you," Marianne said with a strong voice that conveyed none of the emotion Deacon had seen in her eyes a moment earlier. Her chest rose and fell, and Deacon was surprised her frame had changed little, except for the burgeoning bump at her waist.

His eyes landed on two packets she held in one hand. "What's that?"

"Oh, the wall decals arrived. I can do them later," she said, waving her hand dismissively.

Deacon turned over his palm. "We might as well finish this nursery today. What else do you need done?"

She bit her lip. "There's a chandelier to be hung . . . It's in the cupboard." She nodded to the one behind Deacon.

"No problem," he said, motioning for Marianne to pass him the two packets of decals she was still holding.

She hesitated and then gave him a smile, handing them over. He wondered what prompted the resistance.

Deacon reviewed the instructions for the wall decals and grinned at Josh. "Even you won't need help with these."

Josh's eyes were daring. "I'll do the chandelier, *pretty boy*."

Deacon's eyes flickered to Marianne. "Don't ask," he said, removing the wall decals from the packet.

"I'll leave you both to it," she said, but he didn't miss the smile in her eyes.

∿

Deacon watched as Josh made the final adjustment to the chandelier height. The baby's room was complete. Marianne had come in and made up the bassinet with bedding and had laid out the white, fluffy floor rug. He couldn't fault her organizational skills.

"Deacon, can I please have a quick word before you leave?" Marianne said, appearing beside him once more. She moved like a ghost —no wonder she'd been able to spy on her husband.

She tilted her head toward the hallway, and he followed her out, curious as to what this was about. He assumed it regarded her potential case, but unless she had doubts about Josh being her bodyguard, he couldn't see why she'd want to speak to him privately.

She walked into her bedroom and turned to face him, her poise fading for a split second before she pulled herself together. Deacon closed the door. "The list of doctors that Thomas Security screened for me . . . how well do you know them?"

Deacon's eyebrows knitted together. "They've passed all of the security checks. Is there a problem?"

She chewed on her bottom lip. "I don't know," she said, looking away.

"Marianne, what's going on?" Deacon asked, the direction of the conversation eluding him yet again.

She sighed, returning her attention to him. "There are marks on my body . . . marks that would raise questions to a doctor not from my world."

Deacon stilled. It took a moment for him to process what she was saying. Marianne had been stalling on choosing a doctor, giving the weak reason that she'd seen one just before her escape, but now Deacon understood the real reason behind her hesitation.

"They're not . . . there," she said, shifting uncomfortably. "They're on my hips and below my navel." She was looking anywhere but at him.

"Eric used to cut you?" Deacon said in a hushed voice, his stomach clenching at the realization.

"Did you really think his fetishes with a knife were excluded from the bedroom?" Bitterness rolled from her tongue. "I don't want your pity, and I don't want your sympathy, but a good doctor is going to ask questions."

Deacon spoke calmly even though he felt anything but. "I'm not giving you pity—"

"You are," she said, crossing her arms over her chest.

"No, I'm not. I'm surprised. I didn't think it extended that far," Deacon said. He shouldn't have been surprised—nothing about Eric should've surprised him—but it did. To cut a sacrifice was one thing; to cut your wife was another. Deacon found himself more amazed that she had survived what she had. The more they learned about her, the more they learned of the risks she'd taken, and of her harebrained scheme to escape with James, the braver Deacon thought she was.

"Choose your doctor, and we'll take care of it. No questions will be asked—nursing and hospital staff included," Deacon said. He'd make sure of it.

Marianne straightened her shoulders, pulling them back. Any previous sign of vulnerability was gone. "Thank you," she said.

Deacon's eyes followed her as she walked out. Why was he

surprised? He squeezed his eyes shut as his mind flashed with images of soft skin marred with knife wounds. The problem was, in that moment, he wasn't sure if he was imagining Marianne or Nicole.

"Get it together," Deacon mumbled under his breath, heading for the nursery. He picked up his kit and said goodbye to Josh.

As he walked to the living room, where the television was still playing cartoons, Deacon made sure none of the unease he felt inside showed on his face. Marianne did a good job of hiding her own emotions.

"You've been saved," she said quietly.

Deacon followed her eyes, and as he took a silent step toward the couch, peering over it, he saw Kaela asleep.

"So she does actually sleep," he joked.

"Thank you for sorting out the nursery; I appreciate it," Marianne said, her eyes meeting his, but she was again business as usual.

"Not a problem," Deacon said, slinging his bag over his shoulder. "Get some rest while she's sleeping."

"I will."

As Deacon closed the door behind him, he shook his head, trying to shake away the apprehension of unease. Everything in his life seemed to be conjuring suppressed memories of Nicole. James and Mak's relationship, Marianne's mutilations—even the nursery.

It was a reminder of the life he'd planned with Nicole.

Of a life they'd never have.

7

MARIANNE

Marianne turned down the television but left it on for some background noise. A still, quiet house reminded her of her dead husband, and those were not fond memories. Among other quirks, Eric had had a distinct love for eerily silent spaces. The only time he'd ever listened to music had been at the worship ceremonies, or before or after them. Or if he'd been connecting with the gods. But otherwise, he'd had strict instructions that their homes, wherever they were in the world, were to be silent. Marianne had broken the rules, of course, but only when he wasn't there. For the rest of the time she had played the role of the good wife—it was easier than the alternative.

She draped a light blanket over Kaela, watching her chest rise and fall, her long lashes still. She had the face of an angel, but Marianne knew her daughter was anything but. She opened the camera app on her phone, taking a photograph. She'd taken so many of Kaela when she was little, and Marianne wondered where they all were now. Her eyes glossed over—she'd never see those photographs again.

Nor would she hold Kaela's baby blanket, nor her first pair of shoes, nor the first lock of hair Marianne had cut and kept in a safe place. They were starting over now, and all Marianne had were her memories.

She wiped away a tear, not wanting Josh or anyone else watching to see her cry. She saved crying for the shower, where no one could see her.

One of her greatest fears was that her memories of Kaela's first years were going to fade. It wasn't the big moments, like the first step she took, that Marianne feared forgetting—it was all the little moments. She feared that, if she hung onto them too tightly, they would only fade away faster.

She wiped away more tears, furious for letting her guard down. She lowered her chin so any cameras couldn't see her face clearly.

It's a small price to pay.

Kaela would grow to be a strong, independent woman. One who would never know about the life her father had planned for her.

Marianne tiptoed away from Kaela toward the nursery. She leaned against the doorframe, taking a moment to admire the men's work. It was beautiful. White furniture and soft blue hues paired with elegant cream drapes that covered the window. She inhaled, craving that scent of the newborn that would soon fill the room. "I will take care of you," she whispered, cradling her bump with her hands. She would give her son the life he deserved, too. She would give both of her children that. She had no idea how she was going to do it, though —to raise two young children alone. What if she failed? What if something happened to her? There would be no one else to raise her children. She was alone in this world, and she'd never felt it more.

Her mind went back to the conversation she desperately hadn't wanted to have, but had needed to have, with Deacon.

She cringed now, wondering what Deacon thought of her—what he was imagining and what he'd report back to James and the team. She'd delayed it as long as possible, and it had seemed easier to talk to Deacon about it than James. She supposed that was because she and James were still trying to establish their relationship—whatever that would be.

The scars on her abdomen were thin, but they were all over her lower waist and hips. Marianne had often wondered if Eric had done it because he'd enjoyed it, because he enjoyed having power over her, or if he'd done it so that if any other man ever looked at her naked, they'd see the scars, not her. *Probably all three,* Marianne concluded, clenching her jaw.

In a world that supposedly cherished women—respected them— Saratani had deemed certain practices suitable, and cutting women was one of them.

It's over now, she reminded herself, hoping it truly was. She knew about the online talk of a renaissance, but she also knew if anyone could protect her, it was the Thomas brothers.

She returned to the kitchen and powered up the laptop she'd been provided with. She knew it was a security precaution, but she didn't like that they could monitor everything she looked at and everything she read. Still, she'd rather they were looking than Eric.

She reviewed the doctors' profiles again, looking over their credentials and experience. They all looked excellent and equally competent. She settled on an older man with small round glasses and a gray combover. He looked like someone's grandfather. Most of all, he looked gentle—and gentle was what she needed.

She sent the email then closed the laptop, thinking she should take Deacon's advice and get some sleep.

Deacon was an interesting man. In some ways he was very similar to James, but there was a softness to him that James didn't have.

She didn't see it as a weakness. To survive what he had, and still believe there was good in this world, indicated a strength quieter than James's, but a strength nonetheless. And he'd been through hell, she knew that for sure—because once Eric had found out who James Thomas was, and therefore Deacon Thomas, he'd created a collection of intel on Deacon and Nicole.

And Marianne had read it all.

Her chest tightened at the secret she held. If the file was placed in front of her now, she wouldn't read it—she would respect his privacy —but she hadn't known him then.

And she wasn't about to admit she knew what she did.

8

DEACON

Deacon threw his right arm hard and fast. He blocked the return hit as he danced around his opponent.

"Is that the best you've got, brother?" Deacon said, laughing through his heavy breathing.

James grunted, landing a forceful blow. Deacon blocked the next one.

They continued like that until the timer sounded and both men sat down on the bench, breathing heavily—James more so than Deacon.

"Not bad . . . but still not good enough to take the throne," Deacon said with a smirk.

"Your arrogance will be your downfall," James said, looking at his feet, finding his breath.

Deacon laughed, wiping a towel over his arms and across his chest. He was jesting his brother, but given the injuries James had sustained, the fact that he'd healed this well—and this fast—was honestly remarkable.

It had been a grueling morning, one they had started with sprints. They'd progressed to weapons training and finally finished with their sparring match. Three full hours of intense activity—and without looking at the recorded results, Deacon knew James was fit enough for the Tokyo job.

"When do you want to leave?" Deacon asked.

"Tonight. The target will be easier to hit during the week when his schedule is more reliable, and I'd like to be back by the weekend," James said, guzzling half a water bottle.

Deacon didn't need to be told why, and he was grateful he'd relocated his bed—it had solved their soundproofing issue.

"Did you sort out the issues with Marianne's doctor and medical team?" James asked.

"Yes, I had a meeting with them yesterday. They've agreed to keep their mouths shut and not react to whatever they see."

Whatever that might be, Deacon didn't want to know.

"Do you think her children are the only reason she didn't snap and kill him herself?" James asked, standing to stretch.

"Very likely," Deacon said, remembering what Marianne had told him on the night they'd rescued James—when he'd been trying to ascertain her motives. She'd told him then she'd been suicidal when she was first married to Eric. She'd have known that killing Eric would come with grave consequences, but she wouldn't have cared if she was going to take her own life anyway. But she'd said her strategy had changed when she'd found out she was pregnant with Kaela. So she'd endured Eric's madness, carefully taking steps to ensure that, when an opportunity came, she'd have the resources to capitalize on it. And she had. James Thomas wasn't the only strategist in the family.

"I think we should show her the images of the leads Samuel has discovered," Deacon said. "We don't really know who she does and doesn't know. It's very preliminary at this stage, but we shouldn't make the same mistake we made with Mak when we didn't show her the images of Lucian."

James nodded. "Good idea. I don't want to worry Marianne, but she's very resourceful. I think we need to keep her closely involved in this case. Eric mistakenly trusted her, and as you said, I don't think we know all of Marianne's secrets yet," James said with a half-grin.

Deacon's eyes flickered down to his wrist. "I'll shower, prep my kit, and head over to her apartment. You go to physio," Deacon said. They had a team of trainers and physiotherapists who helped them both condition and heal their bodies.

James nodded then said, "I think I might be sick."

Deacon chuckled and patted him on the back. "It's a long way to the top, brother."

~

Deacon packed both his and James's kits in the trunk of his car as he prepared to head over to Marianne's apartment. James was going to visit Mak after his physio session, then Deacon would pick him up en route to the airport. It was a perfectly coordinated schedule, as much of their lives were—when a case wasn't out of control.

His eyes flickered to the mirrors then across to the manila folder next to his pistol as he monitored the traffic. His mind and heart were in a constant state of tug-of-war. His mind wanted him to face the past, but his heart said no—it was too much. He couldn't take it.

But he had to remind himself this wasn't about him—this could be connected to Marianne, and therefore all of them.

He knocked, but again let himself in, given that Marianne was expecting him.

"Hello?" Deacon called when he didn't immediately see her. The television was on, but no one appeared to be watching it.

"Hi," she said, emerging from the kitchen. "I'm making some tea. Would you like a cup?"

"Sure," Deacon said. "Anything is fine."

Marianne suddenly looked toward the television. "Oh, sorry, I had that on for Kaela," she said, referencing the cartoons. She turned it down, but didn't turn it off. Deacon had come up with a number of reasons why she did that, but bet she did it for reasons similar to his own—it filled the silence.

He leaned against the kitchen island as she poured hot water into two mugs. Her hair was pulled back into a bun, highlighting her strong cheekbones. She was beautiful—exotic—in a way most women weren't.

"How are you feeling?" Deacon asked to break the silence, although it wasn't uncomfortable. Their relationship with Marianne was different than with other clients. Normally they wouldn't ask about their personal lives; they kept it strictly business. But Marianne was James's half-sister, and if James and Marianne were going to have a relationship, then they all were.

"Actually, I feel good now. I had terrible morning sickness for a long time, as you know. It was horrible," she said, shaking her head. "But now I feel fine. Just a little tired, but that's probably due more to Kaela than anything else." She gave a pointed look and Deacon smiled.

"I think she'd wear anyone out," Deacon agreed, taking the mug as she passed it to him. Her fingers brushed his and he felt a little tingle he'd not felt in a very long time, a feeling he barely recognized. He pushed it from his mind.

He took his tea to the dining table, putting the mug on a coaster. Marianne sat opposite him. He slid the manila folder across the table.

"Like I said, it's very early surveillance, but we don't know who you know and who you don't, so any information might help Samuel narrow down his searches," Deacon said, before taking a sip of his steaming hot tea.

He watched Marianne closely, aware that what she didn't say might be more interesting than what she did.

She opened the folder without hesitation. Her hands were steady and calm. She held the first image, looking over it for several seconds. "I'm usually good with faces and terrible with names," she said without looking at him, "and he doesn't look familiar."

Deacon nodded, indicating he'd heard but not wanting to converse and distract her. There were fifteen photos in total, and she shuffled them through her hands.

Deacon focused on his breath, like he did on a job—because this *was* a job. The closer she got to the photograph of Nicole's murderer —the photograph Deacon had intentionally placed last in the series, because he'd wanted to be able to take note of her normal responses to the faces on the photographs—the sooner he'd know if she was lying, even if she didn't do so explicitly.

Deacon took another sip of his tea, refusing to show any of the tension coiling around his chest. He'd been counting the photographs as she looked over them, and he'd know when she got to the one he couldn't look at himself.

She almost got away with it, but the diminutive press of her lips together gave her away. He continued drinking his tea, not reacting. When he didn't think she was going to say anything, she spoke.

"I know *of* this man," she said, meeting his eyes.

9

MARIANNE

Marianne's heart fluttered. From what she'd learned, Deacon had been in the room at the time of Nicole's death. So he must have known who the man was, but you wouldn't know it from the look on his face.   •

"He's an arms dealer that Saratani—Eric—was researching," Marianne said, choosing her words carefully.

"How do you know this?" Deacon asked, his voice calm, void of emotion.

"I saw it in one of the files in his office," she said, taking a mouthful of her own tea, using it as a distraction.

Deacon was searching her eyes, looking for what she wasn't telling him. Unfortunately for Deacon, she had a lot of experience playing this game.

"What else was in the file?" Deacon asked.

"He's based in Ukraine, or at least was at that time," Marianne said. "What is his involvement in my case?" Marianne had escaped one hell, and she would not end up in another. The man in the photograph wasn't the devil—that would be too kind of a name for him.

"He appears to be talking with some of the Saratani recruits," Deacon said.

"He's looking for me?" Marianne asked, suppressing a shiver.

"No," Deacon said, his eyes softening. "We believe he's looking to expand his business dealings."

She felt a tinge of relief but she knew better than to so easily rule out someone's intentions. Especially when it came to a man like that.

"What else do you know about him?" Deacon pressed.

Does he know I'm lying?

She hadn't expected to be confronted so directly. She'd never intended to bring up what she knew about Nicole, but now she feared lying to him. She was under their protection, and she needed to be— at least until her son was born and she could relocate.

This is bad.

If she lied and was caught, what would happen? She felt backed into a corner, and her throat tingled. She resisted the urge to scratch it.

She looked to the hallway, making sure Kaela's door was still closed.

Marianne cleared her throat, deciding she didn't have an option other than speaking the truth. "I know he's the man who murdered Nicole," she said.

Deacon's jaw set, his eyes narrowed, but when he spoke his voice was a veil over whatever he was feeling inside. "How do you know that?"

"I read it in a folder of research on you. I believe Eric started putting it together after he discovered James's identity," Marianne said.

Deacon didn't drop it. "What else was in the folder?"

Her heart raced, and she didn't know if she'd made the wrong decision, but she was too far in to turn back now.

Marianne put the photographs down. "Everything, Deacon," she said softly.

His teeth ground over one another, and the vein in his forehead pulsed.

Marianne spoke quickly, "If I'd known what was in the folder, and I'd known we'd end up in this position, I wouldn't have read it. I swear."

He nodded, standing brusquely. "Anything about the man might be helpful. James and I will be away for a few days, so please speak to Samuel about it."

He turned without another word, the door almost slamming behind him.

Her first assumptions had been correct then, she noted with a tired cynicism.

Deacon was fiercely private about what had happened.

And he hadn't dealt with her death—at all.

10

DEACON

His chest heaved and his pulse raced. He hated that Marianne knew. He hated that *anyone* knew. His fingers clenched around the steering wheel.

It's not her fault.

And it really wasn't—she hadn't been the one prying into his life. If he'd been in her position, he would've read everything in the file, too. But nonetheless, he was angry. Angry that he'd failed Nicole. Angry he hadn't been able to protect her. Angry at the men who had abused her before they'd killed her. Angry her body was disposed of —only God knows how—and he couldn't even give her the decency of a resting place. Anger. Humiliation. Regret. Self-loathing. It all simmered below the surface, occasionally spewing out like hot lava.

Minutes passed before he turned the key in the ignition.

Pull yourself together.

They were the words he repeated all the way to Mak's apartment. He dialed James's number as he approached. Deacon let the car idle in front of the building as he sat in silence. Why did he care that Marianne knew? He'd always assumed that she'd known what had happened via Eric, though admittedly he hadn't thought she'd known the intimate details.

The car door opened, pulling Deacon from his thoughts.

"How did it go?" James asked as Deacon drove away, heading toward the airport.

"Well, she recognized the same man we did," Deacon said, keeping his eyes on the road ahead.

James paused for a minute. "Really? Anyone else?"

"She said she didn't. I believe her," Deacon said, his eyes darting to the mirrors and then back to the road.

"How did she know about him?" James asked, and Deacon didn't miss neither of them were using the man's name, even though both now knew it.

Jason Blake.

"How do you think? Her mastermind of a husband had a file with all of the details, apparently. Once he worked out who you were, he went to work on me." Deacon couldn't hide the bitterness from his words—bitterness directed at Eric.

Deacon could feel James watching him, contemplating his next words.

When Deacon's cell phone vibrated in his pocket, he withdrew it. His eyes looked down for only a fraction of a second:

Marianne: Can we talk when you have a minute?

Deacon sighed, dropping the phone in his lap.

"I all but stormed out of Marianne's apartment," Deacon said, reluctantly. "I hope I didn't wake Kaela up."

"Marianne understands, Deacon," James said. "She understands our world better than anyone."

"I don't care if she understands," Deacon said harshly, but he wasn't sure if that was the truth or a lie.

"Deacon," James said sympathetically, "none of us have ever thought you were to blame for her death."

Deacon didn't respond, keeping his eyes on the road. James didn't get it—it didn't matter what they thought. At the end of the day, Nicole had been targeted because of him, and he'd failed to protect her. He took the exit to the hangar.

"And Marianne doesn't think that, either," James pressed. "If she did, she wouldn't trust you to protect her and her family."

Deacon had had enough of the conversation. "It doesn't matter what Marianne thinks," he said brusquely.

In his peripheral he saw James raise an eyebrow, but he didn't push the conversation as Deacon brought the car to a stop.

The plane's engines were purring.

He grabbed his phone, deciding to make the call before he boarded so he didn't have to think about it anymore. He walked toward the wall of the hangar while James retrieved their bags. He knew his brother was watching him—discreetly.

"Hi," Marianne said as she answered the call. Her voice was softer than usual. She didn't wait for a response. "I'm sorry; I know you're busy, but I just wanted to apologize—"

Deacon sighed—he didn't want her sympathy, nor did he want her pity. They shared that much. "It's fine, Marianne. You don't need to apologize for anything. I'm sorry I left the way I did. Did I wake Kaela?"

"No, she didn't hear a thing," Marianne said—and without seeing her in person, Deacon couldn't be sure if she was telling the truth.

"Marianne," Deacon started, searching for the words. "Nicole is a very . . . difficult subject for me to talk about. In fact, I *don't* talk about her, and I would like to keep it that way."

"I completely understand—I don't like to talk about my past either. I had no intention of ever bringing it up. I wasn't sure if I should've told you I recognized him, but I didn't want to lie to you. I want to help with this case as much as I can."

"We appreciate that," Deacon said as James looked toward him once again. "Look, just forget about it. We'll see you when we get back."

"Okay. Stay safe," Marianne said.

"We will. If you need anything, call Samuel. He'll get in touch with us if he needs to." Deacon said goodbye before hanging up.

It was time to get out of New York. He walked toward his brother.

"Let's go to Tokyo," Deacon said, once again grateful for the intensity of the job—a distraction from his tormented mind.

11

JAMES

James noted the change in his brother. He saw the softening of his features during the telephone conversation, which was interesting, and he saw the resolve in his eyes now. Deacon hated contract kills, but his brother seemed less bothered about this job than he'd been about others in the past. James figured he was grateful to have any kind of distraction, which was very telling of what was going on inside Deacon's mind.

"At least on this trip we don't have to pay Haruki Tohmatsu a visit," Deacon said.

James grinned. "The farther away we are from the man who contracted us, the better."

It was the last debt they had to pay. When Haruki had first negotiated the deal, James had thought it would be a difficult job. But, given what they'd been through recently, it seemed fairly routine.

James grabbed two bottles of water, checked his phone—smiling when he read Mak's message—*Have a SAFE trip. I love you*—and then sat opposite his brother. Mak knew he was going overseas, but that was the only detail he'd revealed to her. She certainly wouldn't like the mission of his trip, and he also didn't want her to worry. But he was coming home to her. He would make sure of it.

The plane began its taxi and soon after James watched as the Manhattan skyscrapers morphed into a miniature Lego jungle.

"So, do you know any good tattoo artists?" James asked.

Deacon's eyes snapped to his. "Say again?"

James sighed. He wasn't sure how Deacon was going to react to this conversation.

"I want to get my chest done. I want to cover Eric's artwork," James said, rolling his eyes. "Mak is reminded of her dead husband every time she looks at it." What James didn't say was when they were naked in bed together—a moment that should be intimate and beautiful—it was all tainted by his scars. And she'd stopped doing things she used to. He missed the soft brushes of her fingertips across his chest. He missed the small kisses she'd often planted there.

Deacon nodded. "What do you want to have done?" he asked.

James opened his mouth to speak, but was distracted by an incoming call on Deacon's phone.

"Samuel," Deacon said, leaning forward on his elbow. He put the call on speaker. "What's up?"

"How was Marianne when you showed her the images?" Samuel asked, his voice sounding distant. Hesitant.

Deacon bit his lip, his forehead creasing. "She seemed okay. She was worried, naturally, but she wasn't freaking out, if that's what you're asking."

"Good. Because we have a big problem . . . Someone's put a contract on Marianne and Kaela," Samuel said, and James's stomach churned. "I'm trying to find out who, but I need more time."

"What is the contract worth?" Deacon asked, rubbing the back of his neck.

Samuel cleared his throat. "Four hundred million to deliver them alive. Fifty million if one or both are dead."

James's mouth dropped to form an O. *That's what you call an incentive.* "I doubt this is a Saratani recruit, Samuel. Surely they wouldn't have that kind of money."

"I agree," Samuel said. "The rumors are already starting. The dark net is like the inside of a beehive right now—it's more alive than I've seen it in a very long time, which, of course, is very worrying."

"This is bad," Deacon said with faraway eyes.

James studied his brother for a moment, wondering if he was correctly guessing his thoughts.

Deacon continued. "Total lockdown until we get back," he said, looking at James.

James wasn't sure if the decision was made or Deacon was looking to him for confirmation, but either way, James agreed.

"I'm just worried about causing her more stress, you know, with the baby and all," Samuel said.

"She needs to know, and she wants to be informed," James said.

Deacon nodded. "And send over the additional team we've had on standby to support Josh. Tell them to initiate action protocol seven. They know what to do."

"Done," Samuel said. "I'll keep working on the contract. Someone knows who it is, and I'm damn well going to find out."

Deacon ended the call, and although he didn't say anything, an aura of tension surrounded him.

More tension than James expected.

12

MARIANNE

Marianne pulled the blanket over Kaela's shoulders and tucked the edge under the mattress. She swept the fallen hair from her daughter's forehead, her touch as light as a feather. "Good night," Marianne whispered as she planted a soft kiss on Kaela's cheek.

Movement in the hallway captured her attention, and she lifted her eyes to see Josh walk past, his phone held to his ear. It was the speed of his walk that alarmed her, and a shiver ran down her spine.

Marianne turned off Kaela's bedside lamp and went in search of Josh. She found him in the kitchen, his voice low and barely audible. He sensed Marianne immediately, nodded once, and ended the call.

"Let's talk," Josh said gently, moving toward the dining table.

Marianne sat, her hand instinctively going to her growing belly. "What is it?" she asked, making sure her voice was strong. She would not appear weak—not in front of anyone.

"Bad news, unfortunately. Samuel picked up some intelligence today. A contract has been placed, Marianne. A contract for you . . . and for Kaela."

In an instant her legs felt weightless, and she was glad she was sitting down.

"How much?" she asked, fearing the answer.

Josh's fingers tapped on the table, a sign he was stalling. He sighed. "Four hundred million, if you're both alive."

His words knocked the air from her lungs.

She'd known there would be consequences. She'd known there was a good chance someone might come for her. But four hundred million? It was the largest contract she'd ever heard of.

Josh spoke quickly now. "Deacon and James are aware. They've activated the additional security team they've had on standby. And when I say team, I mean fifty-plus men. We're on total lockdown until the brothers get back."

Marianne nodded. The lockdown didn't worry her—she didn't have a life outside these walls, after all. In fact it was inside these walls she felt safest. At some point she did have a baby to deliver, though. What would happen then?

"We're taking this one day at a time," Josh said, as if reading her thoughts.

"How long will Deacon and James be away?" Marianne asked. Deacon had said they would be for a few days, and she wondered if Josh would give her a better answer.

He shrugged. "A few days, depending."

Depending on what?

"Okay," she said, noting her hands were trembling. She tucked them underneath the table.

She was wondering what the brothers thought of the contract, and then a thought occurred to her. "When was the contract placed?"

"About twenty minutes ago," Josh said without pause.

If he wasn't lying, the only good thing that came from this was confirmation that they were keeping her informed of her case, as she'd requested.

"What can I do?" Marianne asked. She would stay strong. She would fight this—fight her past. She'd come this far and she would not crumble now. She was finally free of Eric, and she would be free of this, too.

"At this stage, not much. Samuel is going to upload a file of intelligence to your computer. He wants you to look through it. If you recognize anyone, or any of the locations, he wants to know. Anything at all."

"Sure. When will it be ready?"

Josh's lips tilted up. "I'd say he's probably already done it." He slid his chair back and moved in the direction of her laptop.

She opened her mouth, about to tell him she could get it, but he held a hand up behind his head. "I know you can, but I've got it."

Marianne smiled, but his actions made her uncomfortable. She made sure he didn't see it, though—made sure that no one saw it. Marianne knew they were always watching her, but she was also watching them. Closely.

He passed her the laptop.

Marianne straightened her shoulders as she waited impatiently for the machine to start up. Once the screen loaded, she saw there was one blue folder on the desktop—with her name on it.

She took a deep breath and double-clicked on the icon.

13

DEACON

Deacon's cell phone felt like a weight in his pocket. He thought about his phone call with Marianne, and he felt guilty. She'd seemed to be in damage control, worried that she'd upset him. He didn't like that, and he regretted the way he'd left her apartment. He hoped the phone call had eased her worries, but if it hadn't, he knew she'd no longer be thinking about it—she had something bigger to worry about.

His eyes dropped to the navigation system again, making sure he didn't miss his turn.

Neither of the brothers had voiced it, but Deacon knew they were both thinking the same thing: *The sooner we get this job done the better.*

The back of their SUV was fully loaded and Samuel had confirmed the target's location. That had never been a budding issue, though—men like Asahi Kobayashi didn't need to hide. The real issue was finding a window through which to put a bullet in his chest.

Deacon signaled at the last moment and took the exit. If someone was following them, they'd have to make a brash move—one they'd notice. Nothing.

Deacon looked ahead. Cars filled the highway, weaving in and out, but they continued to coast along at a speed that would enable them to reach their destination in ten minutes.

What is Marianne thinking?

The question plagued his mind, and he refused to look at why.

Of course Marianne would be worried. Of course she'd be scared. But she would deal with it—Deacon knew that. If she was brave enough to defy Eric, she was brave enough to handle this, too.

Unfortunately Marianne hadn't been able to provide any additional intelligence after reviewing Samuel's folder. But that didn't mean she wouldn't be of help—perhaps they just hadn't shown her the right information yet.

~

Deacon adjusted the scope, focusing on Kobayashi. The man was a sick son of a bitch. The stories they'd heard about him when they'd been living in Tokyo eliminated any guilt Deacon might've otherwise felt for the hit. The world would be a better place without this man. Sure, a younger predecessor would take his place, but Deacon knew few men who liked to chop off their victims' fingers and then force the victim to eat their dismembered digits. There was something very wrong with Kobayashi.

"Convoy approaching. Five cars. Samuel, can you get a trace?" James asked from the rooftop on the western side of the restaurant. His voice was clear in Deacon's earpiece.

"Positive. Running it now," Samuel replied.

Deacon knew Samuel was running the plates he'd been able to see through James's surveillance devices.

"Copy."

Deacon's finger was steady on the trigger, but he doubted they were going to get that lucky tonight. They would follow Kobayashi, watch his men, look at any patterns that might form, and then when an opportunity arose, they would take advantage of it. Then they would get the hell out of Tokyo before someone realized they were there. Even Haruki Tohmatsu didn't know. He'd only be aware once he heard the news of Kobayashi's death.

Deacon kept his eyes trained on the front door as the cars pulled up, one after the other. A moment later, Kobayashi appeared, shielded by his men. Twenty of them, Deacon counted with a slight shake of his head. Getting a clear shot on Kobayashi was going to be impossible—something they'd thought a probable issue—but given he'd apparently added new brawn to his security team, it was now a certainty. They were going to have to change tactics. They were going to have to get on the ground and find another way.

Kobayashi was escorted into the car in a seamless operation. Deacon grabbed his rifle, springing to his feet. He ran across three rooftops and then scaled down to the car. His pulse was elevated, but his breath was steady. James was waiting for him.

Deacon opened the door, throwing his rifle and kit to James as he launched the car into drive. The navigation system loaded itself—with a helping hand from Samuel—and Deacon kept his foot on the accelerator.

"An assumption at this stage, but I think he's going home," Samuel said.

Deacon didn't know if that was a good thing or not. If they could get past his security systems, it was a good thing; if not, they'd have a better chance of hitting him while he was moving about the city.

Deacon kept a safe distance, because the last thing they wanted to do right now was alert Kobayashi's security to a tail. One chance—that was all they were going to get. If they messed it up, they'd have to wait a long time before his security team relaxed enough to make another mistake. And mistakes equaled opportunities.

"Did you recognize any of his new team?" Deacon asked, his eyes never leaving the road.

"Only one, and I'm guessing he was hired for brute strength rather than his brain, because he doesn't have one," James said, twisting to look over his shoulder.

Deacon scoffed. "Let's hope the others were hired for the same reason."

"Nakamura is still in charge of the security team, though—that was very evident. They look to him for the answers. Judging from the few minutes of observation I had, I don't think they've been working together for all that long," James said.

"So why the additional security?" Deacon asked, more to himself than James. What had changed that Kobayashi had doubled the size of his standard security team? Did he know Haruki was planning a hit?

It was a fifteen-minute drive to Kobayashi's apartment building, and Deacon stopped one block away. Kobayashi's convoy drove into an underground parking garage, and a few minutes later, lights were turned on in the penthouse. It was one of twenty-seven properties Kobayashi owned in Tokyo, not counting the estates he owned in the countryside. Kobayashi wasn't Haruki's main rival, but he had sided with Haruki's rival, and he was getting closer to Tohmatsu turf than was deemed appropriate. Deacon couldn't assume that Kobayashi was stupid enough to know that didn't come with consequences. He was, however, obviously stupid enough to believe he could protect himself and not bear those consequences.

James's hand stifled a small yawn.

"Another hour?" Deacon asked, loosening his grip on the steering wheel but never totally relaxing. He needed to be ready to drive on a second's notice.

James nodded. "If nothing happens, we'll go back to the hotel and get some rest. I have a feeling tomorrow's going to be another long day."

Deacon agreed, and when his stomach growled, he reached into the back seat, grabbing the bag of sandwiches they'd picked up earlier. He was always hungry.

"Or not," Deacon said suddenly, his head turning back so fast he was surprised he didn't give himself whiplash. A small figure in an oversized jacket had exited the building and was headed straight for them. The fur-lined hood of the jacket shielded the face, but judging by the walk, it was a woman, and she was heading straight toward their car. The brothers instinctively slid down, despite their tinted windows. Deacon counted the seconds, raising his eyes just as she walked by their car. She seemed to look over it, her gait faltering for a second. She continued past, brushing a windswept lock from her cheek. The night was dark, but the glimmer of moonlight cast a glow that lit up her face.

"Oh my God," Deacon whispered.

"What?" James asked.

"I know where Haruki's leak is coming from," he said, still recovering from the shock. They had both been looking at her, but only from his angle had Deacon been able to see her face—or enough of it to reveal her identity.

He kept his eyes on the side mirror, watching as she walked farther into the darkness.

"James, that was Akari," Deacon said.

"No!" James said, like he'd just heard the scandal of the century, which was in fact pretty accurate, given one of Haruki's mistresses had just exited Kobayashi's building. Deacon wondered how long she'd been inside.

"What is she thinking?" James asked, wonder in his voice.

Akari knew Haruki better than most—she knew what he was capable of. Why would she betray him?

"I never saw that coming," Deacon said. Granted, they'd been out of Tokyo for a while now, but Akari had been with Haruki as long as they'd known him. She was second only to his wife.

"Me neither," James said. He looked to Deacon, raising one eyebrow, a sly grin on his lips. "You know what this means, though, right?"

Deacon, fully recovered now, scoffed. "Yeah. We accomplish the hit and then deliver this news to Haruki. He's going to be furious, but he's going to love us for it. And that's a very good place to be."

James nodded slowly. "Productive trip."

"Well, if you're going to be there a while, I've got news," Samuel's said.

"Go ahead," James said between mouthfuls of his sandwich.

"I have a name: Henry Greene. Word has it that he placed the contract," Samuel said.

Deacon's eyes darted to James, looking for any sign of recognition as his own mind drew a blank.

James gave a subtle shake of his head. "Who the hell is that?"

"That's the question, isn't it? From what I can gather, he's based in Zagreb, Croatia—or at least that's where the contract was placed."

Deacon narrowed his eyes. The contract was either placed in Croatia as a distraction, or Greene *wanted* them to know he was in Croatia. Both were bad. Deacon inhaled, expanding his lungs.

What did Greene stand to gain from a hit on Marianne and her daughter?

Saratani was all but dismantled, and unless he was a former member, which they deemed unlikely, he couldn't image why the man would place a contract like that.

"This doesn't make sense," James mumbled, and Deacon knew even though his eyes were on the building, his brother's mind had gone inward, much like his own.

"Run it past Marianne," Deacon said. "See if it rings a bell. You know who might know him?" Deacon asked, scrunching his nose as he looked at his brother.

"Biskup?"

Deacon nodded. Croatia wasn't far from Biskup's playground. There was a very good chance he'd at least heard the name.

"Let's wait before we call our good friend. I don't want to feel like we owe him anything ever again," James said, and Samuel and Deacon agreed in unison.

Samuel signed off, seeming eager to get back to work and uncover the mystery that was Henry Greene.

The brothers continued to watch the building, but all appeared quiet for the near future.

At four in the morning they called it a night.

～

"Deacon. Deacon, wake up." Nicole's voice lures my eyes open, but the pull of my slumber is too great.

"In a minute," I mumble.

"No—now. Wake up, Deacon. You need to wake up," she repeats.

I sigh, forcing my eyes open again, staring into hers. They swirl with strong emotion, but one I can't identify.

"It's time," she whispers as her lips spread into a smile, one tainted with sadness.

~

"Nicole?" Deacon gasped, bolting upright. His breath was labored and it took him more than a few seconds to get his bearings.

Hotel. Tokyo.

He grabbed his phone, his mind reeling. No missed calls, no text messages.

His eyes darted to the other bed in the room. James slept on his back, his chest rising and falling. Deacon shivered, and it wasn't from the cold. He threw off the blankets, dialing Samuel's number.

"Deacon?" Samuel answered.

"Is everything okay?" Deacon asked, his voice hushed as he closed the bathroom door behind him.

"Yes, fine. Why? What's wrong?" Samuel asked, his voice alert.

Deacon exhaled a shaky breath as he looked at his reflection in the mirror. "Nothing, just a strange dream. I'll call you in the morning," Deacon said, hanging up before Samuel could ask another question.

Deacon splashed some water over his face.

He'd seen Nicole in his dreams before, but never like that.

Wake up. Wake up from what?

Deacon grabbed the hand towel, holding it to his face.

He had no idea what Samuel thought of that phone call, but Deacon didn't care. He was more concerned that Samuel wasn't the first person he had thought to call.

In the mirror, tormented eyes stared back at him.

You've learned your lesson.

14

DEACON

Deacon tossed and turned, but as hard as he tried to push the dream from his mind, it lingered. He'd become so good at controlling his mind—he'd almost perfected the ability—but the walls he'd put up were crumbling. Fast. He buried his head underneath his pillow, closing his eyes.

Go to sleep.

His mind didn't obey.

It went back to the dream.

Deacon supposed he should be grateful Nicole's eyes weren't the pleading, tormented eyes of his normal dreams. She wasn't screaming for him to help her. They weren't in the warehouse basement.

Where had they been?

Deacon made an effort to recall every detail of the dream, but there had been nothing in the background other than light; a soft brightness he'd often experienced when flying through clouds.

Deacon sighed, fumbling for his phone, relieved to see it was almost time to get up. He threw back the covers and padded silently to the bathroom.

He caught his reflection again. Dark circles hung beneath his eyes. He needed a scalding hot shower and a strong cup of coffee. Those two things fixed a lot of problems.

Thirty minutes later, when he was sure he'd used the entire hotel's water supply, he turned off the shower, stepping out into the mist. His mind was clearer. His dream had been pushed outside the barricades of his mind. He'd won the war—for now.

He quickly dressed, aware James would be awake now and wanting the bathroom. They always shared a hotel room when they traveled—for safety reasons.

He wrapped a towel around his waist, shaved the two-day-old stubble shadowing his jaw, and fixed his hair.

James was propped up against the headboard with his phone cradled in his hands when Deacon emerged.

"You're awake early," James said with inquisitive eyes.

Deacon shrugged. "Couldn't sleep."

James eyeballed him, but Deacon didn't react. He wasn't dredging up the dream again by talking about it.

"Jump in the shower. I'm starving," Deacon said as casually as he could. He'd been starving for the last two of the four hours he'd been awake.

"Give me ten," James said, dropping his phone on the bed.

While James showered, Deacon dressed, checked his emails, and fantasized about breakfast.

James emerged from the bathroom, ready for the day. "Where do you want to go?"

"Let's get some dumplings," Deacon said with a grin.

~

Deacon eyed the plate in front of James. "Are you going to eat all of them?"

James lifted his eyes from his cell phone. "Are you seriously still hungry?"

Deacon smirked. "A ripped body like this requires fuel, brother."

James shook his head and rolled his eyes, but he didn't hide his smile. He pushed the plate forward. "Half. That's all I'm sharing. This *ripped* body of mine also requires fuel."

Deacon chuckled as he picked up his chopsticks, taking a dumpling and eating it whole.

"Okay, looks like our friend is en route to his office," James said, distracted by his cell phone once more.

Deacon took another dumpling—he had missed this authentic, street-style Japanese food.

While Kobayashi was in his high-rise building, Deacon knew they wouldn't get an opportunity—they would have to wait at least until late afternoon. Kobayashi's evening calendar rivaled that of a Manhattan socialite, and would ultimately be his downfall. There was a reason the brothers liked to stay inside their building.

James slid his chair back and looked at the diminishing plate of dumplings. "There had better be five left on that plate when I get back—otherwise order more," he said before heading toward the restrooms.

Deacon called the waiter and ordered two more plates when his cell phone rang.

"Hi, Samuel," Deacon said.

"Hi. How is brunch?" Samuel asked.

Deacon raised an eyebrow. He thought the timing of Samuel's call was no accident. And he also thought Samuel didn't give a damn about his brunch.

"Sorry about last night," Deacon said instead. "I just had a weird dream."

"What made you think something was wrong? You've never done anything like that before." The thousands of miles between them didn't hide his concern. Samuel was like that—he cared. Out of all of them, he was the most sensitive.

"I've never had a dream like that," Deacon admitted, the image of Nicole's eyes flashing in his mind. "It was of Nicole . . . She was telling me to wake up. That I needed to wake up now." Deacon shook his head, uneasiness clutching his chest. "I thought maybe something was wrong at home, but given that there wasn't, I don't think we should give the dream another thought." *Or that we should speak about it again*, was really what Deacon was saying.

Samuel obviously had other ideas. "Do you think it's a coincidence that you had this kind of dream right now, given what's happened in the past week?"

"I think I *really* don't want to talk about it," Deacon said gently, but firmly, pushing back.

"All right," Samuel said, "but think about it . . . I'll talk to you later." He hung up, and Deacon put his cell phone down just as the waiter brought over his additional orders. Perfect timing.

James sat back down, eyeing Deacon's dumplings. "When you're done," he said, "shall we go and see Saito and get this over with?"

"Sure," Deacon said, pushing the dream from his mind once more. It was easier to do with the bustling noise of the restaurant and a job to focus on. The quiet, early-morning hours were always the hardest.

Saito's security was the only contract they still had in Tokyo—it was a contract too good to give up—but it had been a while since they'd checked in with the security team in person.

Deacon's eyes flickered to his watch. It was almost noon. They had at least three hours until Kobayashi would be leaving his office.

"When do you think we should speak to Haruki about the leak?" Deacon asked.

There was a glint in James's eyes that his brother understood.

It was unfortunate for Haruki, but it was a thick layer of sugar icing on their job. Christmas had come early.

"Don't look so pleased," Deacon said, his lips quirking up.

James scoffed. "I actually pity the guy—that's going to sting. But his loss is definitely our gain."

And it was a gain they weren't above exploiting if they had to. They never knew when they'd need another favor.

∾

The afternoon had passed quickly, spent in meetings with Saito's team, and now they were driving back to the city.

Saito's contract was business as usual, thankfully.

But that had left time for his mind to wander. He thought about Samuel's intel again. If Deacon advised him to look into Nicole's case, what good would it do? He wasn't going on a murdering spree. It wasn't who he was, and he wouldn't enjoy it—Sokolov's death had proven that once again. Putting a bullet in his head should've felt sweet—it should've made Deacon happy—but it hadn't.

Hunting down Nicole's murderers would also put his life and James's in danger. He'd already lost one person to those vicious men, and he wouldn't lose someone else he loved to them. He wouldn't let them destroy the only life he'd been able to build since Nicole's death.

But the questions nagged at him.

How were we found?

What mistake did I make?

When Deacon and James had retaliated against the Russians, they hadn't been so cruel. They'd killed, of course, but they'd targeted the people involved—not the innocent wives or girlfriends of the men involved. To torture Deacon was one thing, and beating up Nicole would've been another. But to mutilate and rape her . . . It was another level completely.

"What's up?" James asked, his eyes searching Deacon's.

Deacon wondered if Samuel had told him about the dream, but he doubted it. Samuel was good like that—he usually kept their secrets to himself unless he thought it presented a security risk.

"It's nothing," Deacon said with a neutral voice. "Just thinking about our current cases."

"I'm starting to worry a little about Marianne," James admitted. "I don't like this contract—not with her so close to her due date. My first thought was to hide her somewhere remote, but she needs to be near a good hospital at the moment, especially considering the complications she apparently had with Makaela."

"Agreed," Deacon said, pushing up his sleeves while keeping one hand on the wheel. It was unusually warm in Tokyo.

"God, I wish we hadn't lost Tom—for so many reasons," James said, looking out the window, his voice distant.

Deacon knew James still harbored a lot of guilt and self-loathing for Tom's death. Tom had known he was taking a huge risk, but he'd taken it at James's expense. And he'd paid the ultimate price. Tom had worked with them a long time—he'd been as close to a friend as someone could be.

"Me too," Deacon said quietly. "Are you doubting our decision to pair Josh with Marianne?"

"Not at this stage," James said. "He's good—he's really good. The best we have besides Lenny, who isn't an option because I'm not going to pull him from Jayce Tohmatsu. I don't need that on my conscience as well. Tom was better, that's all. He'd played the game a lot longer."

"Let's see how things progress," Deacon said. Worst case, James and Deacon could take shifts—they'd certainly done it for other clients. Although, Deacon did have to wonder if he was the best person to protect Marianne right now.

He checked the navigation system again, surprised to find they were almost at their destination.

The possibilities of how tonight could turn out were endless, but one thing was for sure: for a little while, at least, Deacon's mind would be free of Nicole.

15

MARIANNE

Marianne's hand clutched her stomach, a sharp pain ripping through her. She stilled, drawing a ragged breath.

"Mommy, what's wrong?" Kaela said, stopping beside her.

The pain eased and Marianne's breath returned. She put one hand on the wall, steadying herself.

She shook her head, smiling at her daughter. "I'm fine. Please go and find your school bag."

Marianne was homeschooling Kaela until after her son was born, and even after that she planned on continuing to do so. With the current state of her case, she wouldn't dream of letting her daughter out of her sight; with all they'd been through, she couldn't imagine she ever would. She would have to look into finding in-home teachers and tutors as Kaela advanced, but for now Marianne could manage.

Marianne jumped when Josh spoke from behind her. She hadn't heard him approach. She turned to face him.

"Are you okay?" he whispered, his eyes sweeping over her as if looking for a physical injury.

"Yes, I'm fine. Just an odd pain. I'm sure it's nothing," she said, waving her hand dismissively.

Kaela came running back with her bag. The child had an endless supply of energy.

Josh gave a small nod but didn't look convinced. He disappeared in the direction he'd come from. Marianne was grateful that the apartment had a security office within it, but was even more grateful it was located in such a way that it didn't feel like they were living in her apartment. She'd gone from Eric watching her to Josh and his team doing so, but she knew which was the lesser of two evils. She wondered what they thought of her, given that they obviously knew of her past. Or thought they did.

Yes, many if not most of the awful things she'd done, she'd done out of necessity—to survive. But sometimes she'd gone along with Eric just because it was easier than getting into an argument with a madman. Some things she knew she could've stopped, and guilt plagued her for those decisions. She'd cut people, and she'd destroyed lives and families by recruiting people into the madness. She wondered what Deacon and James, and her security team, would think of her if they knew all her secrets.

She told herself it didn't matter; they had a job to do—at least that was true when it came to her security team. And as soon as she had her son, she could move out of the city, somewhere Saratani would never find her. She could live the life she'd always wanted. It would be a fresh start, and no one would know those secrets.

But right now, she had a school lesson to conduct. She sat down with Kaela and opened one of her books. If she hadn't studied as a nurse, she would've been a teacher, she thought wistfully. Not that she'd actually been able to work as a nurse—not for long anyway—not once Eric came onto the scene. It was one more thing on her list that she hated him for.

He's dead. He can't hurt you anymore.

Marianne felt like she should be happy—happy she'd won—but the feeling didn't come. The initial relief upon hearing of his death had since faded, and a feeling of something being not quite right loomed in its place.

She'd expected the Saratani resurgence, or a degree of it at least, but the contract was different. The more she thought about it, the more she was sure her instincts were correct. The contract wasn't to do with the Saratani renaissance, at least not directly—it was a personal vendetta. Eric had made sure that if he died, she'd still be punished. He'd never let her get away with betraying him.

Even in death.

~

The apartment was finally quiet, but, as always, Marianne left the television on for some background noise. The curtains were drawn despite the window glass being one-way and bulletproof—apparently. The tall, luxurious fabric of the drapes created a coziness she'd never experienced. In fact, this was her first home of her own. She'd lived in Saratani housing her entire life until she'd moved in with Eric, and to call that home her own would've been a lie. Nothing about those homes had been cozy.

"Marianne?"

She jumped again, bringing a hand to her chest as her breath hitched. "You have to stop doing that," she said.

"Sorry," Josh said, giving her a lopsided smile.

She waved her hand. "You don't need to apologize. It's just that you move around like a phantom."

"I was trained to move that way," he said pointedly, and she nodded.

Marianne should've been used to that also, and she wondered if she was so jumpy because she was in a new city, with new people around her. It was an entirely new world.

"Samuel wants to ask you a few questions," Josh said.

Josh wasn't asking, she noted. "Sure, I'll call him."

Marianne retrieved her cell phone from the dining table and pulled out one of the chairs. The phone rang only once before Samuel answered.

"Evening. How are you?" he asked.

"I'm okay. Josh mentioned you wanted to ask me some questions?" Marianne wondered again where James and Deacon were and what they were doing. There was a question that niggled at her, one she needed to know the answer to, but one she wasn't sure how to ask.

"I know that the name Henry Greene didn't mean anything to you," Samuel started, "but what about the name *Patrick* Greene?"

Marianne turned the name over, desperately wishing she could help Samuel in some way—admittedly for her own benefit. *Patrick Greene.* "I'm sorry," she finally said. "I don't recall the name. I assume he's related to Henry Greene?"

"I think so. I believe it's his eldest son," Samuel said.

Marianne frowned. "Right," she said, thoughtfully. "You don't happen to have a picture, do you?"

"Not yet. I'm working on it."

Marianne hesitated. She didn't want to lead Samuel down the wrong track, but she knew Eric better than anyone. "I think, in his final days, Eric may have made a deal."

A pause. "What kind of deal?"

"I don't know. But I know the man I was married to, and if he thought there was any chance he could lose, he would've made a backup plan. I betrayed him, and I wouldn't have put it past him to create a deal that would make me suffer, even if it wasn't directly by his hand."

Samuel was silent, and she didn't know what to make of that. "It's definitely possible . . . I'm still trying to work out the Greene family's business dealings. That will at least tell us what they have stakes in. There's something strange about this, though; Henry Greene is an alias, and an identifiable one. And that means he wants either you or someone else to know he was the one who placed the contract. He could've used any other name, but he used that one. He didn't work to hide it, and a man with that kind of money certainly has the resources to."

"What does that mean?" Marianne asked.

"We don't know yet," Samuel replied.

"How closely are Deacon and James being updated on this case?" Marianne asked.

"They are both fully informed at all times."

"Do you know when they'll be back?" Marianne asked, wondering once again if he'd tell her anything different.

"They're trying to come home as soon as possible. Why? Do you not feel comfortable with your security?" Samuel asked.

"It's not that—everything is fine. I just . . . I need to ask a question, one that is a horrible thing to ask but I need to know nonetheless." She paused. "Are James and Deacon together?" Marianne asked, easing into it.

"Yes they are."

"And if something were to happen to both of them, what would I do from there?"

"That's what you're worried about?" Samuel sounded relieved. "First, you of all people should know what it would take to eliminate one of them, let alone both of them. Second, the same provisions have been made for you and Kaela—and your son once he's born, obviously —as have been made for Mak, Cami, and myself. Depending on the case, the first step is to go into lockdown in Thomas Security. Cami and I will work the intel until we find the best solution, but it would probably involve relocating somewhere safe, somewhere unsuspecting, until the full security risk can be ascertained and provisions put in place."

"Thank you, Samuel," she said.

"What did you think would happen? You saved James's life, and while I know this is all a bit strange and new at the moment, you're also family, Marianne. Of course we would take care of you."

She had taken a chance that James would help her escape from Eric, but she hadn't honestly known what would happen after that. She'd been prepared to go on her own, hide somewhere remote and start over. She'd never expected to be welcomed into their lives in the way she had been. A normal person would probably be grateful for that, but for her . . . It left her feeling uneasy. Everyone had always wanted something from her or had used her for some form of revenge. Were they doing the same? If so, she couldn't imagine what for.

She buried her suspicions for now. "Thank you. I just wasn't sure, and I wanted to have a plan in case . . ." She trailed off. With one young child and another on the way, she had to be prepared at all times.

"Let me say this once: you leave the planning to us. I do not like it when people make plans of their own—it always ends in disaster," Samuel said.

Marianne hoped her next words were not a lie. "I will leave it to you," she said—but she knew if the time came, she would do whatever was needed to save her children.

"That's what I like to hear," he said, and it sounded like he was smiling. "I'm going to get back to this data and try and find us a face, which should create a lead of sorts. I'll be in touch as soon as I have something."

Samuel hung up without another word and Marianne's eyes flickered to the clock. It was too early to go to bed, so she settled on the couch, reading one of the books she'd had delivered—via Samuel. But after reading the same paragraph three times over, she admitted defeat. Her mind was not on the story. It was on the Thomas brothers.

What are they doing?

16

DEACON

Kobayashi paced back and forth, talking on his cell phone. Deacon wished Samuel could get a trace on the call, but they'd had no such luck. What they'd had luck with, though, was the building's security. Apparently, at some point Kobayashi had decided that taking prostitutes back to his primary residence was a bad idea. And it probably was. But an even worse idea was taking them to the apartment he'd chosen tonight—a building that Samuel had been able to breach and get them inside of. They were one floor below Kobayashi, and they watched him on his own security system.

"Call girl approaching," Samuel advised.

They had a two-hour window to complete the job. Two hours before the residents of the apartment they were currently in were due home, and two hours before the call girl would be walking back out the front door. They could try and hit Kobayashi after that, of course, but why not hit him while he was distracted and improve their chances?

We've faced worse odds.

Kobayashi wasn't the real problem—his security team was. The benefit of Samuel being able to hack the security system, though: they knew where each man stood. And that was a huge advantage.

"Call girl inside," Samuel confirmed, and Deacon noted the time on his watch.

He looked to his brother and a smile lit up his face.

"Let's do this."

They pulled their facemasks down and drew their weapons. Silently, they exited the apartment and headed toward the stairwell.

"Kobayashi and call girl in bedroom," Samuel said.

If any of the security team changed positions, Samuel would let them know. Otherwise, the brothers knew what to do.

Deacon was a step behind James, his footsteps light, his breath even. Adrenaline trickled through his veins but at no point did it threaten to seduce him. It had never been like that for him—he knew it was a very different story for his brother.

They took the stairs, using only a flashlight to guide them. They stopped at the stairwell's exit.

"Door unlocked. Good luck, boys."

James counted down from three and then pushed down on the handle, swinging the door open.

James split off to the left as Deacon darted to the right, catching his target by surprise. He delivered one blow to the head and the man went limp before Deacon carefully lowered him to the floor. The last thing they needed was the sound of a thud to capture the rest of the security team's attention.

"Target down," Deacon whispered, crouching as he ran down the hallway. His heartbeat whooshed in his ears, but his body was light and agile.

"Target down," James said in kind, his voice barely audible. James was taking the east wing of the apartment.

It was a strange floor plan and Deacon could only assume it had been two apartments that Kobayashi had developed into one larger apartment. Deacon thought he should've hired a better architect.

He paused at the corner, his ears straining. He heard the faint breath of the man no more than a few footsteps from him. He tucked his weapon into his back pocket, inhaled deeply, and then lunged around the corner, wrapping one hand around the man's mouth and the other around his neck. Deacon dragged the man away from the wall so that his kicking feet didn't raise attention. He counted the seconds as the man went still. His eyes darted to a white door to his left, which Samuel had identified as a storeroom, and hauled the man in its direction. The room was smaller than most New York closets, and the man barely fit in there, but Deacon finally got his legs inside. He closed the door and leaned forward, resting his knees and catching his breath as he waited for James's confirmation.

It was a short break—a few seconds later, Deacon was running again. Two more targets each and they'd be at Kobayashi's bedroom.

Deacon pressed his back against the wall, inching forward slowly now. The hallway opened up to the kitchen, where his next target was. Deacon's weapon was at shoulder height and his finger was steady on the trigger. He stopped, using the mirror that hung in the hallway—another bad decision on Kobayashi's part—to watch the man. He determined the best method of assault and took one step forward before a gunshot rang through the air and a high-pitched scream followed it.

"James?" Deacon asked quickly as he stormed into the kitchen, firing two bullets in to the chest of his next target. The man hadn't had time to react to the sound of the first gunshot, let alone dodge Deacon's bullets. The man's eyes went wide and then he fell forward, his head making a sickening thud as it connected with the marble island.

"Copy. Target down."

"Deacon, behind you!" Samuel's cry came, but it was too late.

Fire lit up Deacon's arm as he swiveled, loading a bullet into the man's forehead. Target number four grunted as his head snapped back.

Warm liquid ran down Deacon's arm, but he didn't stop to assess his injuries.

Finish the job.

James appeared beside him, his eyes flickering to Deacon's blood-stained hand, but he didn't stop either.

"Target on bed," Samuel said.

They pressed their backs against the wall, and James kicked open the door.

Kobayashi, in a true show of his integrity, had the naked girl in front of him, using her as a shield. He had a gun in his other hand.

"Nandeshou? Watashi wa anata ni sore o ataeru yo," Kobayashi said, the words spilling out of his mouth.

"There's nothing you can give us," James said.

Deacon fired a shot at Kobayashi's hand and the moment he dropped the weapon, and coincidentally the girl, James fired twice more. Two perfect shots.

Blood sprayed from Kobayashi's chest, creating a haunting painting on his stark white walls.

James aimed his weapon at the girl. "We know who you are, Abby. You saw nothing. Remember that, or we'll come back for you."

Mascara streaked tears ran down her red cheeks as she nodded. Her knees were pulled up to her chest, and she was shaking. It was unfortunate for her that she'd taken Kobayashi's call tonight.

Deacon turned, and they ran out of the apartment, down the stairs, and onto the street. They were parked two blocks away, and only once they were in the safety of their armored car did Deacon stop to look at his wound. James helped him pull off his sweater, but in an amazing stroke of luck, the bullet had done nothing more than gash his skin. Nothing a few stitches wouldn't fix. James grabbed a bandage from the medical kit by his feet and wrapped it up for the time being.

Deacon knew he would've left DNA evidence behind, but it didn't matter.

Nathan Wyatt was the only person with records linked to the DNA, and Samuel had doctored them all long ago. Nathan Wyatt had ceased to exist. As did the man Nicole had known. The Deacon Thomas of today was a rendition of his former self, one who had given up living, focused purely on getting through each day.

Wake up, Deacon.

Deacon finally understood Nicole's message.

17

JAMES

James pushed the needle through, pulling the skin tight. Fourth and final suture. The bullet had gotten too close, but they were lucky it had done nothing more than take a chunk of flesh out of Deacon's arm.

The jet shook as they hit a patch of turbulence and James stilled.

Deacon looked at the needle in James's finger. "I'm damn glad you finished that stitch a second ago," he said with a tired smile.

"Just call me the flying doctor service," James joked, wrapping a bandage around Deacon's bicep.

Deacon yawned and relaxed in the chair. "Do you want to place bets on how long until Haruki hears the good news?"

"Given that the police arrived not long after we left, I'd say he already knows," James said, taking a bottle of water and guzzling it down. He was relieved the job was over. It was the last favor he had to repay, the final deal with the devil—for now. He didn't like owing guys like Haruki favors, but in their world it was a necessary evil.

He was also glad it had only taken a few days and they were already en route home. Back to Mak. Back to the life he loved.

James retrieved some blankets from the cupboard and passed one to Deacon. He reclined his chair and said good night—but before he closed his eyes, he cast them toward his brother. Deacon was looking out of the window, peering into the darkness. There was a look in his eyes that James found difficult to read.

It wasn't haunted, and it wasn't sad. Thoughtful, perhaps?

While Deacon had performed perfectly at Kobayashi's apartment, James knew something was amiss. He'd noticed it first thing this morning and he noticed it now. What had happened last night?

~

James picked up three trays of coffee, delicately balancing them atop one another as he walked the block to Marianne's apartment. He took the elevator to the penthouse and stopped in at the security office first, unloading all but two coffees. He checked in with Josh, who had nothing to report—which pleased him.

He walked through the office and into Marianne's apartment, knocking despite the fact that she knew he was visiting. He still felt awkward just letting himself in.

"Come in!" she yelled out, her head appearing from the kitchen. "Hi." Her smile lit up her face and James assumed she'd inherited that from their mother—he certainly didn't think it had come from Sorin.

"Decaf," he said, passing her a coffee.

James looked around her to discover a baking lesson gone wrong. Kaela was covered in flour, and James burst into laughter.

Marianne shook her head. "Don't ask me how it happened. I went to the bathroom and came back to this."

Kaela giggled. "It was an accident," she said, but James doubted that. He hadn't spent a lot of time—any time, truthfully—around children, but Kaela had a look in her eyes that led him to believe it was only a half-truth at best.

"Do you want some of my cookies, James?" Kaela asked, nodding her head.

"Did you actually make some?" James asked, still chuckling. He could see nothing but flour.

"Yes," she said feistily. "They're in the oven." She pointed like he was an idiot.

"Oh—I see. I'd love one. When will they be ready?"

She looked to Marianne, who responded, "Ten minutes. Which is plenty of time for you to clean up in the bathroom."

Kaela hesitated, and James thought she might argue, but Marianne cast her a look that moved her feet into action. She padded down the hallway with a dramatic sigh.

"Take a seat," Marianne said, motioning to the dining table. "How was your trip?"

"Good," James said, and he didn't think Marianne expected him to elaborate any further. "How has everything been here?"

She took a sip of her coffee, and then her index finger circled the rim—anxiously, perhaps. "I wish I could be more helpful to Samuel. Even with all of the spying I did on my husband, I feel like I still don't know anything."

James shrugged. "These are very early days—we don't know who or what we're dealing with yet . . . Samuel told me about the conversation he had with you."

She cringed. "I'm sorry, but I had to ask."

"You should've asked me the moment you thought about it rather than worrying about it. You're family, and we stick together. And even if you weren't family, you did save my life, Marianne. It's the least I can do for you."

Marianne's eyes scanned the hallway, but Kaela was nowhere to be seen. He didn't know if she diverted her gaze to look for Kaela, or if she had because she was uncomfortable. He wished he could get inside Marianne's head.

"You know, I'm glad things have worked out this way," James said, looking into Marianne's eyes. He was glad to have found his half-sister—his only sibling.

"Me, too," she said, finally meeting his gaze. James thought there was another question in her eyes, but if there was, she didn't ask it. Instead, she looked back to the hallway. "It's awfully quiet down there, which is probably not good," she said with a hint of amusement.

As she pushed her chair back, she inhaled sharply, clutching her stomach. James jumped out of his seat, taking her arm, steadying her.

"What's wrong?" he asked quickly, his heart racing.

She shook her head and squeezed her eyes shut. A million questions ran through his mind, but he gave her a minute. She opened her eyes, and when she spoke, she was short of breath. "Sorry, I don't know what that was. Just a sharp pain . . . It's passed now. I'll speak to the doctor when I see him tomorrow."

James looked her over but felt helpless to give her any advice. If she had a bullet wound, he'd be able to fix it—but anything related to babies was not within the realm of his expertise.

"We'll call him now," James said. "Has this happened before?"

"Once a few days ago, but I didn't give it any more thought." She straightened herself, pulling her shoulders back.

"What about during your pregnancy with Kaela?" James asked, dropping his hand.

"No, nothing like it," she said. "Oh, I forgot about her," she said quickly, disappearing in the direction of the hallway.

James wondered whether he should be concerned or not. He had no idea, but he couldn't imagine that a sudden pain, one sharp enough to take your breath away, was a good thing. His thoughts were distracted when he heard her call, "Kaela!"

James wasn't about to forget about what just happened, but he did go to check out the latest drama.

He found Kaela in the bathroom covered in bath foam. She wore a devilish grin.

James knew he shouldn't laugh, but he couldn't help himself. He liked this kid.

~

Incoming call: Haruki Tohmatsu

They'd been waiting for the call, and James wasn't surprised it came less than twenty-four hours after the hit. James nodded to Deacon and then motioned for Samuel to put the call on speaker.

"Konnichiwa," James said, greeting the man with respect.

"Konnichiwa. I woke up to some very good news this morning. Thank you," he said with a smug voice.

Haruki was never one for small talk, and James appreciated it because he wasn't either. Unfortunately for Haruki, this good news would come with a blow that would rock his world.

"You're welcome," James said. "Are we settled?"

James knew the answer, but he wanted a verbal confirmation. It was never a good idea to assume things with a gangster. Haruki's word was as good as a contract, though.

"Of course. It's quite the relationship we've developed, don't you think?"

Deacon raised an eyebrow and James smiled. "Quite the relationship indeed. And that's why we need to tell you something. You're not going to like it, but you need to hear it."

"Go ahead," Haruki said cautiously, his jubilance diminished.

"We believe we identified the source of your leak," James said.

"I'm impressed. How is this bad, though?" Haruki asked.

"It's Akari." Silence. "I'm sorry, Haruki, but it's true. Deacon saw her leaving Kobayashi's apartment—there was no mistaking it was her. Perhaps she had another reason for being there, but I can't imagine what that would be, and I doubt you can either."

Haruki cleared his throat. "Thank you. I'll deal with it."

James had no doubts about that. Haruki would unleash a wrath on Akari so severe James himself didn't even want to think about it.

"If you boys need me, you know where to find me," Haruki said tightly. "Sayōnara."

"Goodbye," James said, but the line was already dead.

Deacon inhaled through his teeth. "That's going to get ugly."

"Akari knew who she was dealing with," James said.

"But why did she turn on him?" Deacon asked, and James knew he was right. James wondered if they'd ever find out . . . but then thought it best they didn't.

18

DEACON

Deacon jolted upright as the loud ringing of his cell phone startled him from his sleep.

I really need to change that ringtone.

He fumbled in the darkness, knocking a water bottle off his bedside table as he grabbed his phone. A call from Samuel at two in the morning never ended well.

"Good morning," Deacon said as he threw the duvet off, anticipating Samuel's next words.

"Can you please come to my office?"

"Sure," Deacon said, cradling his phone between his shoulder and ear as he pulled on the jeans he'd left beside his bed. "Give me two minutes." He threw the phone down on the bed and wrangled his arms into a sweater. He cared little that he was wearing yesterday's clothes. He'd come back and change when the sun rose.

Given Samuel's tone and lack of urgency, Deacon assumed that this was important but not life threatening.

Intel.

The question was: did it relate to his past? Or Marianne's case? It could be related to any one of their clients, but his gut instincts told him it wasn't.

Deacon slipped his sneakers on, then swirled some mouthwash around before spitting it out and locking the apartment door behind him. He wondered if Samuel had gone to bed and an alert had woken him up, or if he'd been working all night. Deacon seriously wondered when the man slept.

He opened the door to Samuel's office to find that the man was alone—another indication of impending bad news.

"Am I the only one you called?" Deacon asked.

Samuel pressed his lips together and Deacon felt like he'd been punched in the stomach. He didn't need to hear Samuel's next words to know his instincts had been correct. He took a long breath and sat down.

"What is it?" Deacon asked, surprised by how normal his voice sounded when he really just wanted to run out of this office and keep running. But that's what he'd been doing since her death. He'd been mentally running, keeping the demons at bay.

"I have some news that I don't know if you want to hear, and see, or not . . ." Samuel said, his voice tight.

"I don't want to hear it, but I think I have to, don't you?" Deacon asked impatiently, his pulse rapid.

"Yes, I do," Samuel said without hesitation, but there was a hint of something else in his eyes. Sorrow?

"Michael Sonoma," Samuel said, loading an image that Deacon didn't want to see. "That's Jason Blake's real name."

Deacon felt like he was sinking, like he was caught in a swamp and being pulled under. He forced himself to lift his gaze and look at the screen.

Invisible chains wrapped around his throat.

"He's an arms dealer. Worth millions now, but he wasn't at the time you would've met him," Samuel said.

Deacon appreciated the polite way Samuel had put it—*met him*—but there had been nothing polite about that meeting.

"Who are his business partners?" Deacon asked, crossing his arms, trying to warm his suddenly chilled bones.

"That's the interesting thing . . . I was expecting to see links to the

Russians." Samuel paused. "That is who you always thought was behind the attack, right?"

"Yes, I assumed it was Sokolov," Deacon said.

"At present, I can find no links to the Russians. They don't supply their weapons, they don't deal drugs . . . I haven't had much time, admittedly, but I can't find a connection. Now, that's not to say there wasn't one," Samuel added quickly. "This all happened quite some time ago, so it's possible the relationship went sour—look at who we're dealing with."

"But your gut instinct is that he's never been tied with the Russians?" Deacon frowned as he asked the question that Samuel didn't seem to want to answer.

"It looks that way," Samuel said.

Deacon leaned forward, rubbing the back of his neck as he looked down at his shoes.

It doesn't make sense.

At that time in his life, the only enemies Deacon had made were the Russians. Deacon didn't have enemies in the CIA—at least none that were alive. It also wasn't the kind of attack the CIA was known for. They preferred to kill quickly and leave as fast as they came, not . . . Deacon shuddered.

"I don't know what to say," Deacon said.

"I think we need to keep that door open," Samuel said.

Deacon shrugged—Samuel could keep whatever doors open that he liked.

"There's more . . ." Samuel said, and Deacon refrained from groaning. He nodded instead.

Samuel's face twisted like he was in pain. "I think I'll get you a glass of juice or something," Samuel said, sliding his seat back, but Deacon stopped him.

"Tell me," he said tightly, despite his heart screaming at him not to.

Samuel sighed. "I think I've found four more of the group."

Shock hit him like a wall and he sat back.

"It looks like they still run in the same circle, which is interesting.

And when I said I've found four of them, I should've said that I'd uncovered their identities; two are no longer with us," Samuel continued.

"Show me," Deacon said, relaxing his hands. At some point his nails had dug into his biceps.

Samuel pushed his glasses up the ridge of his nose, nervously, and loaded an additional four photographs. Deacon's eyes flittered over them, bouncing from one to the next, as bile burned the back of his throat. He had never forgotten—would never forget—their faces.

"Sonoma is the ringleader. They work for him. Two of them are related by blood," Samuel said, bouncing the cursor between the men.

Deacon stared at the screen—for how long, he didn't know. He fought with his mind, which was creating flashback after flashback of that night. He squeezed his eyes shut, but the flashbacks continued.

"Deacon?" Samuel sounded worried.

He didn't know where the strength to speak his next words came from. "Where are they now?" Deacon asked with a shaky voice.

"They seem to have bases in Serbia, Berlin, and the United Arab Emirates . . . My thoughts are that the head operations office is in Serbia."

"Is any of this intel linking back to Marianne's case?" Deacon asked.

"Not at this stage. I think our first assumptions were correct—they're trying to obtain a share of the business."

Deacon nodded. He hoped that was the case. Prayed it was.

"What do you want me to do with this information?" Samuel asked.

Deacon looked away. "I don't know," he said quietly, his body internally trembling.

~

Sleep hadn't come to him after the early-morning visit to Samuel's office, and neither had a sense of tiredness—he felt wired. But his burning throat had stayed with him regardless of how much fluid he drank. He cracked open another bottle of juice.

"We need to take Marianne to her appointment today," James said. They were assembled in Samuel's office discussing client security strategies—mostly Marianne's.

Deacon agreed. "How did the talk with her yesterday go?" He hadn't seen James last night.

"It was good," James said. "While I was there, though, she had this strange sharp pain that doubled her over. I made sure she called the doctor before I left. He asked her several questions and will do some tests today. Otherwise she says she's been feeling well."

Deacon didn't know whether to be concerned or not. "By the way, who is looking after Kaela while we take Marianne to the appointment?" Deacon asked.

"The new babysitter Marianne finally agreed to. Two of Josh's team will stay at the apartment and keep an eye on things," James said.

They had a few hours until they needed to leave Thomas Security, so they talked strategy and looked at real estate—one of Deacon's favorite things to buy, second only to cars. Their London townhouse had been exposed to far too many people, so it was time to buy a new place and rig it. A trip to London was on the cards in the not-too-distant future.

James had yet to bring up Samuel's new intel, and Deacon didn't know if that was because Samuel hadn't told him about it. Deacon thought it the most logical explanation—he had been called to Samuel's office alone, after all, and he knew full well how personal this was.

"Okay, let's go," James said, sliding his cell phone into his pocket as he stood.

They said goodbye to Samuel and took the elevator down to the basement. James still didn't bring up the intel, so Deacon assumed he either didn't know or simply didn't want to bring it up. He'd talk to him about it later—he really wasn't in the mood right now, and he wanted a clear head this afternoon. Taking Marianne to a doctor's appointment should be a low-risk job, but nonetheless, if he had to put his driving skills to the test, he wanted a focused mind.

"I was thinking if we go to London to secure that townhouse, we could stop by Paris on the way home—depending on how Marianne's case is going," James said.

"You want me to come with you?" Deacon asked, his eyes leaving the road only to get a read on James. He was amazed that James had even brought up Paris, let alone invited him to the house.

James shifted in the chair like he was uncomfortable.

"Yeah," James said, looking straight ahead.

"Sure, we can do that," Deacon said. "How long do you want to stay?"

James shrugged. "A few days, maybe. The house does need some repairs—a few of them structural. It would be good to get them done." James turned to him. "That's not why I'm asking you to come," he added quickly. "Sure, an extra set of hands would be helpful, but I just thought you might like to come . . . to see the . . ."

"I'd like to," Deacon said quickly, giving James a sympathetic smile.

James nodded and returned his attention to his phone. Deacon similarly returned to intermittently checking the mirrors while concentrating on the road ahead. He saw nothing unusual.

James rang Josh as they entered the parking garage and Deacon pulled up in front of the elevator, the car's purring engine the only noise. Josh appeared a few moments later with Marianne and five members of her security team, the other two staying at the apartment with Kaela.

Josh ushered Marianne into Deacon's car and slid in next to her while the rest of the team climbed into another car.

Deacon looked over his shoulder, greeting her. She wore a smile that could almost melt a heart as hard as his. Almost.

"Hi," she said before turning to James, but Deacon didn't miss the drop of her eyes to his bicep—the one with a bandage peeking out from the pushed-up sleeve of his sweater.

The doctor's office was no more than a ten-minute drive, and as they approached, Deacon observed Marianne's demeanor via the rearview mirror. She seemed relaxed, but given the conversation about her scars, he thought there was an element of tension she must be feeling. If so, she was hiding it well. A parking area had been reserved for them—all part of their requirements—and Deacon drove into the allocated space and turned the car off. Josh helped Marianne out of the car and Deacon led them inside with James at the rear. Their orchestration raised more than one eyebrow in the doctor's waiting room, but Marianne was the only one who looked uncomfortable about that—they were used to it.

They sat in silence until the doctor came out to greet Marianne. As per protocol, James and Deacon stood with her. They didn't go into the room but took their positions in the hallway. They knew it would look out of the ordinary—but it was better that than for an active security threat to develop without them having men on the ground.

Fifteen minutes passed before the doctor opened the door a sliver, poking his head through the gap.

"Which one of you is Deacon Thomas?"

"That's me, sir," Deacon said.

"Good. Can I please have a word?" he asked, but Deacon got the feeling it was non-negotiable.

Deacon looked to Josh, motioning him in to take Deacon's place.

The doctor opened the door wide, letting Deacon enter. The room was empty, and his heart skipped a beat.

"She's in the adjoining room with my nurse," the doctor whispered.

Deacon nodded. "How can I help you?"

The doctor visibly swallowed. "The person who cut her . . . What is the relationship between them?"

Deacon could only assume he was being asked since he was the one who had given strict instructions that nothing about the marks was to be said to Marianne. "He was her husband."

The doctor raised one eyebrow as his jaw tightened. "Was?"

"He's dead," Deacon said.

The doctor's expression relaxed. "And she's safe now?"

"Yes." Safe from Eric at least.

Deacon's eyes darted to the door as he heard Marianne's voice. He didn't want her to see or overhear this conversation.

"She has suffered immensely. If she hasn't already, she should speak to someone about what she's been through," the doctor said in a hushed, rushed voice.

"I'll ensure that," he said, and the doctor walked away from him as Deacon made a quick exit. Images of mutilated flesh flashed in his mind.

Josh returned to the waiting room.

"Everything okay?" James asked, looking straight ahead.

"It's a good thing Eric's already dead," Deacon whispered. His blood was boiling.

He felt James's eyes on him, but he didn't respond. There was nothing more to say.

Deacon thought about the doctor's recommendation. They had Mak and Maya in therapy—why hadn't they thought to do the same with Marianne? It was carelessness on their behalf that they hadn't offered it to her.

It would be a delicate conversation, but one Deacon thought should be had sooner rather than later.

19

MARIANNE

The car was silent as they drove back to her apartment, and the silence made her uneasy. James and Deacon, however, seemed completely at ease. She wished they would turn on the radio, but she didn't want to ask them to.

The doctor's appointment had gone well. She knew he'd been shocked, despite being warned, when he'd looked at her scars. She'd expected it. She'd downplayed the extent of them to Deacon—the conversation had been difficult enough, and embarrassing enough, without him truly knowing what she looked like.

Marianne rested against the headrest. Her heavy eyelids had closed despite her best attempts to keep them open. The doctor had told her that everything was going as expected and, although they had to wait for the results of a few tests, her baby boy was healthy. He'd asked her about the pains again, but given that everything looked normal, he told her not to worry too much unless it happened again. She had enough to worry about, so she pushed it from her mind.

Her hand went to her mouth, stifling a yawn. She needed to sit up before she fell asleep and ended up with her head on Josh's shoulder.

That would be embarrassing.

She forced her eyes open and her gaze drew to the rearview mirror, like a magnet was dragging it, to meet Deacon's eyes. She was surprised by the steely intensity within them. She didn't understand the look.

She quickly looked away, but her mind continued to analyze what she'd just seen. She could come up with no logical explanation. They'd barely spoken today.

When they finally drove into the parking garage, she was ushered out of the car, but not before she heard Deacon say, "I'll be back in a minute."

As she walked through the front door, Kaela came bounding up to her, running with her arms outstretched. "Mama, mama!"

Marianne knelt, letting Kaela wrap her arms around Marianne's neck. Her pregnancy made it impossible to lift her daughter now. Kaela kissed her cheek and whispered, "I missed you."

Marianne kissed her forehead. "I missed you, too." She felt Deacon's presence beside her. "I need to talk to Deacon for a moment. Will you please turn the television on? We can watch one episode of *Bubbleman* before school." Marianne wasn't above bribing her daughter, who ran off a moment later.

"Nice trick," Deacon said with a smile.

"Whatever works," she said with a guilty grin. "Is everything okay?"

Deacon's eyes flickered to the television, and he nodded toward the kitchen. He leaned against the cabinets, a casual pose. She felt herself relax.

"We've been discussing your case, for obvious reasons, but something else occurred to us." His eyes were gentle, soft now. "Both Mak and Maya have been speaking with one of our therapists since the ordeal with Saratani. We didn't initially think to offer the service to you, since you lived with Saratani your entire life. But"—he shrugged —"you've been through a lot. Perhaps more than any of us. I'm not saying we think you need to, but it's an option if you want to. Anything can be discussed during the session—it's fully confidential and nothing will ever leave that room."

Marianne was a little shocked at the proposition but not offended. "I probably should," she said thoughtfully. She probably needed a century of therapy after the years spent with Eric. "I appreciate that you thought of it, but I'd prefer not to. It's . . . difficult." She instinctively brought a hand to her throat, which suddenly felt tight, and Deacon's gaze followed.

"I understand," he said with a deep voice and eyes that searched hers. They shared an unspoken connection of tormented pasts neither wanted to face.

Deacon continued, "If you ever change your mind, let me know."

"Did you speak to a therapist after—?" Marianne stopped herself short, immediately regretting bringing up Nicole.

His jaw tightened, but he didn't shut down again. "No, I didn't. That's not to say it wouldn't have helped," he said.

She thought he was going to leave, but he lingered.

Her heart pounded in her chest as she asked the next question, worried she was going to set him off. "Because it was too painful?"

"Yes. Maybe in time I'll go myself," he said, but she didn't think he was being entirely honest.

"Maybe I'll see you there," she said, giving him an understanding smile.

Of all people, Deacon was the one she felt like she had to pretend least with. And after years of pretending, it was like a burden lifting from her shoulders.

He gave a nod and pushed off the cabinet to leave. She found herself not wanting him to. There was a fleeting hesitation in his eyes, but it vanished just as quickly as it had appeared.

"Let me know if you need anything," he said before moving toward the door, closing it behind him.

Had he not wanted to leave?

It was tempting to allow herself to believe that, but that was a dangerous path to go down. He was James's brother, in every sense except the biological, and she had no idea how James would feel about a relationship between them. But it was Deacon's heart that worried her most. How could he love another woman when he was so broken? And even if he could, could he love another woman the way he loved Nicole? Was his heart capable? She didn't think so.

She supposed none of it mattered, because if he knew of everything she'd done, she doubted he would be interested anyway.

"Mom, it's on!" Kaela yelled, and Marianne sighed, refusing to give the matter another thought. She went to the couch, to the one little person who had taught her how to love. She sat beside Kaela, tucking her into her side, and kissed the crown of her head.

She had to focus on her two children now, on being the mother she'd never had. When Marianne had discovered who her biological mother was, in all the years following, sometimes even living under the same roof, she'd never actually met her. She'd never spoken a word to her. Sorin had made sure of it. Marianne admired her, though, because through the process of spying on Eric, Marianne had learned a lot about her mother. In all the years she'd been held captive and tormented by Sorin, she'd never whispered a word about her son. Not a single word. Marianne admired that inner strength and prayed to be as strong as she had been.

She also prayed her strength would never be tested in the same way.

20

JAMES

James watched the elevators, waiting for them to open and his brother to return. He wondered what was going on and thought it likely related to the doctor's visit. When Deacon had exited that room, he hadn't been calm despite the convincing show he'd put on. Deacon had been furious. The puzzling part was that Marianne had seemed fine when she'd exited the room herself.

James created a mental list of all of the reasons why the doctor would've wanted to speak to Deacon. He was still brainstorming when the driver's door opened.

"Sorry," Deacon said, twisting in his seat as he reversed the car.

James looked at his brother. The earlier tension in his body had dissipated.

James didn't ask for an explanation but rather waited for Deacon to start the conversation.

Deacon veered between two cars, heading back to Thomas Security. "I think Marianne's scars might be more serious than she'd let on . . . if that's the right way of putting it." Utter distaste laced Deacon's words and James knew the sentiment was aimed at Eric. "The doctor asked me who did it, and when I told him her husband—her dead husband—he suggested she should be in therapy."

James frowned. "Why was this brought up in Marianne's presence? Didn't you specifically speak to the doctor about this?"

Deacon shook his head. "She was in the examination room with the nurse."

"I see," James said.

"I asked Marianne about therapy just then—it seemed best to get it over with. I told her we'd been discussing her case and hadn't thought to offer her the same therapy that Mak and Maya were receiving. I told her it was an option if she ever wanted it."

"And she doesn't?" James guessed.

"No. She did seem to consider it for a second—it wasn't a defensive brush-off—but said she would prefer not to, despite probably needing it."

James nodded. They all probably needed it.

"How was she when you left? Did she seem upset that you'd asked her?" James asked, watching his brother carefully. Something was going on with him.

"No, I think she was okay," Deacon said, his eyes straight ahead.

"Good," James said. "Hopefully Kaela liked the babysitter. We're going to need her, at least while Marianne gives birth."

"Kaela was very excited to see Marianne, but that's to be expected —they're rarely separated. Otherwise, Kaela didn't seem upset at all. I think it will work out fine," Deacon said, his gaze still remaining forward.

James stole another peek at his brother, who drove calmly beside him, and wondered if he was overanalyzing him. His gut instincts told him he wasn't.

～

James stared at the growing piles of paperwork on his desk. Everything urgent had been dealt with—he was good at putting out the fires—but truth be told, he hated doing paperwork. If it wasn't for Deacon, James knew this company would've fallen apart a long time ago. He hadn't seen his brother for a few hours, but it was nearing dinnertime, so he knew where he would likely be.

James took the stairs to Samuel's office, finding him alone. Although Samuel had multiple teams of hackers he managed, he usually coordinated with them over the internal teleconference system. Samuel didn't like to leave the building, and he preferred to only travel between his office and his apartment.

Samuel's eyes lifted as James entered. "It all seemed to go well today," he said.

"So far so good. Anything new?" James asked, taking juice from the refrigerator before sitting at the large white table. Samuel also liked white clean spaces.

"Yes, actually," Samuel said, and James raised an eyebrow. He hadn't been expecting that answer.

"You remember this man, obviously," Samuel said as he loaded a photograph on the large screen.

"Yes, he was head of security before we killed him at the worship ceremony."

"Right, his name was Frankie. Well, it turns out he's a distant cousin of Henry Greene," Samuel said, laying his hands flat on the desk.

"Well . . . that's unexpected. How distant?" James asked.

"Third cousins," Samuel said. "I can't see any business connections as yet, but it's strange, don't you think?"

"Yes," James said without pause. He churned it over in his mind. "Do we know if they were friendly?"

Samuel sighed. "I don't see any connection between the men yet, other than the biological one. Do you think it's a Saratani retaliation contract? Or do you think Marianne is correct and this is a personal vendetta from the grave, so to speak?"

"I don't honestly know, but I also don't think it matters," James said. "We just need find a way to have this contract rescinded."

Samuel nodded. "I think we should speak to Marianne about him. There's a good chance she knew him relatively well, given his close relationship with Eric. You never know—we might get lucky."

James thought it was a good idea for the reason Samuel did, but for another reason, too.

"I'm having dinner with Mak, so I'll ask Deacon if he can go over tonight and talk to her," James said, making a mental note to schedule dinner plans with Mak as soon as he left Samuel's office. Samuel nodded.

"On that note," James said, "how are you doing with the intel for Deacon's case?"

Samuel paused. "He didn't speak to you about it today?"

"No," James said, wondering if that was the reason Deacon had seemed off earlier.

Samuel's hesitation was telling. He didn't want to discuss it, and James respected that. "Give him time," Samuel said.

James nodded. He hated not being informed, but ultimately this was Deacon's case—his life—and James had to respect that.

21

DEACON

Deacon drove into the underground garage of Marianne's apartment building for the third time that day.

"Hey, Josh," Deacon said, stopping by the security office first.

Josh was shoveling food into his mouth while watching the surveillance cameras. "Hey."

Deacon could barely make out the muffled word. He smiled and waved his hand dismissively. "I'll check in when I'm done," he said before knocking on the door that led to Marianne's apartment.

Deacon entered when he heard her voice.

"You don't need to knock," she said as she walked toward him. "Just come in." The vulnerability he'd seen in her eyes earlier was gone.

"I brought over the file from Samuel," Deacon said, noting the television was on, as it always was. He didn't miss the fact that he'd never walked into her apartment to find it silent. Perhaps it was so obvious to him because his apartment was always silent—at least when he walked in it was.

Marianne moved toward the dining table. She pulled out a chair to sit but then stopped. Her cheeks blushed. "Sorry, I didn't even offer tea or coffee. I'll make some," she said, rushing toward the kitchen.

She looked embarrassed that she hadn't offered, which Deacon thought was unnecessary, but he supposed she'd played hostess for Eric and the elite criminal underworld so many times it had become second nature for her. If that was true, he liked that she was comfortable enough around him to even temporarily forget such customs.

"I'll make it," Deacon said, placing a hand on her arm, but then immediately regretting the action. He refused to further any connection between them. "Take a seat. I'll get it."

Marianne's kettle took forever to boil, but that pleased Deacon. It gave him a minute to collect himself. By the time he had made two cups of tea, he was in control again. He put her mug down on one of the coasters she'd put out and then sat opposite her.

Samuel had filled Marianne in on the details over the telephone, so she opened the folder without another word, her eyes scanning page after page of details. It was an impressive collection of results, knowing Samuel had put it together in less than one day.

"Wow, Samuel really is a stalker," she joked and Deacon grinned.

"May I ask a question?" she asked, then continued before Deacon could answer. "How big is your file on me?"

Deacon hadn't been expecting that. "Honestly, we knew very little about you. We found a photograph of you doing what looked like humanitarian work in a foreign country. We also found a photograph of you with Lucian in a shopping center. Otherwise, the rest of our intel came from real-life surveillance, such as the worship ceremony."

"I can imagine what you thought of me," Marianne said, chewing on her cheek.

"We didn't know what to think," Deacon lied.

Her eyes locked on him, and it felt like she was burning a hole into his soul.

"I don't believe you," she said.

"You know what we thought . . ." he said, gently. "We had no reason to think otherwise. You played the part incredibly well. James said when he was locked in the cell, he still couldn't work out whether or not you were lying to him, and he's very good at reading people."

"And what do you think now?" Her eyes locked on his again.

He was surprised yet again, and he wondered how on earth their conversation had gone in this direction. "We think . . ." He paused, wanting to tailor his response carefully, answering from a group perspective even though she'd said *you* on more than one occasion. Had she noticed she'd done that? "We think that you did what you needed to do to survive," he continued slowly. "You're brave and also much kinder and softer than you let on, perhaps even more so than you let us see."

She looked down. Was she embarrassed? Had he made her uncomfortable?

"What exactly does Samuel want? Everything seems to be in the folder," Marianne said.

"Forget the folder," Deacon said, nodding when she gave him an odd look. She laid her palms on top of the manila folder.

"Just talk to me about him. How long did he work for Eric?" Deacon asked.

"Samuel knows, it's—"

"Forget the folder," Deacon repeated calmly. "What do *you* remember? What was happening in your life when he came into it?"

A haze passed over her eyes like a slight breeze. "I was pregnant with Kaela," Marianne said. "Eric had always been obsessed with security, but given that he had a 'princess' on the way, he went from obsessed to paranoid. I remember the first time I met that bruin." She rolled her eyes. "I won't repeat the words that had come to my mind, because they're not very ladylike."

Deacon grinned again.

"He was referred to Eric—by whom I'm not sure. His brother also worked security, which you know," she added as an afterthought.

"How did he act toward you?" Deacon asked.

"Polite, respectful . . . I couldn't fault him in that sense. Although of course he'd have been a complete idiot to have done otherwise. The ways that Saratani respect their women are very unique, but to be verbally rude to another man's wife, especially someone with an important role, would be a very stupid thing to do."

"Did he ever mention his personal life?" Deacon asked.

She rested her chin in the palm of her hand. "He wasn't married. A few months after he started working with Eric I remember hearing whispers of a girlfriend: Ariel Koni. She was a Saratani member. He would've met her through one of the parties Eric threw." She raised an eyebrow. "I'm fully aware Eric entertained multiple women."

Deacon nodded, not surprised to hear she knew. What did surprise him was how little it seemed to bother her. He supposed it was possible she'd been grateful for it—it was less time he was with her. Cutting her.

Deacon refrained from shaking his head and forced his mind back onto the conversation.

Ariel Koni.

He wondered what would come of that name.

"How long had Ariel been in Saratani?" Deacon asked.

"I didn't know her personally, but I knew of her. She was very . . . *proud* is perhaps the word, of her commitment to Saratani. She had one of the highest recruitment rates of all the women, and Eric and the leaders loved her for that. She was invited to all of the parties and private gatherings. I think she'd been a member for six years when she and Frankie started dating."

"And they were still dating on the night of the worship ceremony?" Deacon asked.

"Yes. He dated other women, too, but she was his primary girl-friend," Marianne said, as though it was nothing unusual.

"Was she at the worship ceremony?" Deacon asked, almost certain he already knew the answer, but not wanting to put words into Marianne's mouth.

"Yes, she was there. I remember seeing her as Eric and I walked toward the stage. She was always front and center."

Marianne paused.

"Are you okay?" Deacon asked, noting he'd leaned forward. He straightened back against his chair.

"Yes, I'm fine, that night was just . . ." Her eyes dropped to the closed folder.

"I know," Deacon said. Despite the things they'd seen in their lives, that night was still horrifying to them as well. It had been pure carnage.

"Do you know what happened to her? Did she survive?" Deacon asked.

Marianne cleared her throat. "I asked Eric about her, actually, because I was worried she'd become unstable when she learned of Frankie's death. Eric told me they thought she'd died in the stampede . . . I don't know if they ever confirmed that, but I know she hadn't been seen since. There weren't any parties after that night, but she didn't turn up at any of the meetings, either." Marianne looked at Deacon. "Is it safe to assume she'd dead?"

"I wouldn't say it's safe," Deacon said. Until they had DNA evidence, it was never safe to assume that. Especially when it pertained to someone who, by Marianne's own telling, could easily become unstable.

Deacon redirected the conversation. "What about any other family besides his brother? Did he mention his parents? Did he have any children from previous relationships?"

"No, I never heard him talk about his parents, and I'm almost certain he didn't have children. He was awkward around Kaela . . . Once, she ran up to him and tugged on his hand, and I'd never seen someone look so uncomfortable. Perhaps it was because he knew both Eric and I were watching, but I don't think that's the case. I don't believe he'd spent much time around children."

Deacon nodded. "Where did he live?"

"He lived with us. Despite that, though, I didn't spend a lot of time with him. He and Eric would often retire to Eric's office after dinner to conduct business of a different nature. I was glad they were both gone—I didn't ask questions."

"What about Ariel? Do you know how she got involved with Saratani? Were any of her family members involved as well?" Deacon asked. His instincts told him not to forget about her.

"I believe she was recruited by her stepbrother . . . I forget his name . . . Stephen? He was a piece of work, that one. He was a member of the London branch, but you don't need to worry about him—he overdosed at a party."

Deacon didn't detect any penitence in her voice.

"Is any of this helpful? I don't know what you're thinking," she said, searching his eyes.

"I'm thinking of questions to ask you," he said, grinning for the third time tonight. It was a small miracle, especially given the state of his mind these past few days. "It's impossible to know if anything you tell me tonight is useful or not. Samuel will use it, and we'll go from there. It's always that way with intel, and it's the same for every case. It's usually seemingly insignificant details that break open a mystery."

Deacon's gaze dropped, noticing Marianne was rubbing the tips of her fingers together. "What are you worried about?"

She sighed. "Everything. I want this to be resolved before I have this baby, and it's probably not going to be, is it?"

"We're going to protect you and your children. You're all going to be fine," Deacon said, deliberately not answering the question. He couldn't tell her what she wanted to hear.

She searched his eyes again, and he refrained from squirming. It felt intrusive, like she could see things in him others couldn't. It made him want to run from the room, and it also made him want to drag one hand through her hair and kiss her until he was breathless.

It was time to go home.

22

DEACON

His fingers gripped the steering wheel tight as he exited Marianne's apartment building. He drove on autopilot, taking the left without thinking, heading back to Thomas Security, but his mind was spinning. Images of Nicole. Images of the warehouse. Her voice screaming for him, echoing through his soul. Marred flesh. Pleading eyes. It didn't stop. His breath shortened and his throat tingled. His eyes glanced to the rearview mirror as he changed lanes, pulling over.

His breath shuddered as he inhaled, and he stretched his fingers, releasing the tension.

Never again.

He'd promised himself he would never allow someone to be targeted because of him again. It wasn't worth it. Nicole would say the same thing if she were alive. They should've walked away and spared each other from the heartache that followed.

He checked the mirrors again.

No tail.

Deacon wondered what James would think if he knew the thought had even crossed his mind. Deacon shut down the thought as quickly as it came—it didn't matter. He would never act on it. He didn't want a relationship—he didn't deserve one. He should've died instead of Nicole.

He felt out of control, his mind refusing to shut down.

He sat quietly, focusing on his breath as his eyes moved between the car mirrors.

Another minute passed.

He didn't feel any calmer.

He drew his phone, noting the time. He wondered if he should call Emma. As Kyoji Tohmatsu had always said, *"A good fuck will clear anyone's mind."*

Deacon had met Emma in a bar one night. She was a career-driven financier who had needs like his own and didn't want commitment. It was perfect. He dialed her number.

"Hey, Daniel," Emma said, her voice husky and tantalizing. "This is a surprise . . . a good one."

Deacon cleared his throat. "I'm very glad to hear that. I'm in town for the night. Are you busy?"

She laughed. "For you? Never too busy. I just need to finish a few things up. Give me an hour?"

Deacon checked the dashboard clock. "Perfect. I'll pick you up," he said before ending the call.

He exhaled, his anxiety dropping a notch.

He drove home, had a quick shower, and packed an overnight bag. The bag made it so he could actually stay the night, shower with her, then head straight to Samuel's office in the morning. Next, he called his preferred hotel and made a reservation. They used the hotel for Thomas Security clients, so it meant he didn't have to bother with anything other than providing some advance notice.

Fifty minutes later he was waiting impatiently outside her building, counting down the minutes until she arrived. He saw her exit the front of the building, say goodbye to security, and approach his car. He got out and wrapped one arm around her waist, pulling her body hard against his. He ran one hand through her hair and kissed her until he was breathless. It was a kiss he didn't want to analyze tonight. Or ever.

"Well . . ." Her voice was low and hoarse. "Tonight is going to be fun, isn't it? What's gotten into you, Daniel?"

She smirked and his teeth grazed over her plump lower lip.

"I'm stressed. I was hoping you'd help me unwind."

Deacon's gaze darted behind her, noting the security guard watching them with discernment, but Deacon didn't give a fuck.

Emma brought her lips to his ear and whispered, "I'll make you forget about everything."

～

Deacon strolled into Samuel's office at eight in the morning, feeling like a new man. A ravenous new man.

"Morning," James and Samuel said in perfect harmony, but neither of them had the voice to make the choir. Samuel chuckled to himself, apparently finding it amusing. James looked at Samuel, simultaneously looking puzzled and amused. Samuel was a weird man, but Deacon loved him anyway.

"You really need to get out more," James joked.

Samuel scoffed. "You would hate it if I actually had a life. It would mean that I wasn't available to service you every minute of the day."

Deacon laughed, and Samuel reprimanded him. "I wouldn't be laughing if I were you. You're just as demanding."

"Come on, Samuel. You'd be bored without us," Deacon said as he took two breakfast sandwiches from the spread.

"Work up an appetite last night, did you?" James asked with a straight face, but Deacon sensed that James knew he'd been out last night, and with whom. How did he know? If Samuel knew, which was highly possible, he usually kept such matters to himself. It was possible that James had stopped by Deacon's apartment this morning only to find it empty.

"Sure did," Deacon said, not denying it.

James grinned, but there was a querying look in his eyes Deacon didn't understand. It wasn't judgment, and it wasn't concern, Deacon didn't think. He brushed it off, not giving it another thought.

"How is everything this morning?" Deacon asked.

Samuel shrugged. "Good. All cases are stable."

Deacon was pleased, but with no other issues to address, he knew he had to address his own.

He forced the words from his throat. "Samuel has new intel on four of the men that were there the night of Nicole's murder."

"That fast?" James asked.

"They were—are—still running together," Samuel said by way of explanation. The playfulness in his voice was long gone. "Two of the four are dead, but I haven't been able to find much else. It happened a long time ago, and it's hard to find leads now. Without knowing how they found you, or even who hired them for the hit, I can't work backward. Any burner phones they might've used are impossible to track now. I can't find an electronic payment of any form." He frowned, turning his hands over.

Deacon's eyes dropped to the sandwich in his hands. He should've eaten it before his stomach started churning. The effects of last night were quickly diminishing. "You need me to find a lead. That's what you're not saying, right?" Deacon asked.

"It would be more efficient," Samuel said. "I can keep digging, but uncovering leads from a cold case such as this may take months, or years. Even then I might not find what we need."

Deacon rubbed the back of his neck as his heart screamed at him, pleading for him not to do this. His throat felt like it was swelling again, closing in. But what was the alternative? If he didn't face this now, it would only be harder in the future, if he ever changed his mind. He just wanted the pain to stop. The nightmares to stop.

"Show me their faces again," Deacon said. He didn't miss how drained his voice sounded.

Four faces displayed on the screen.

Deacon took a deep breath.

Look at them.

"Tell me about this man," Samuel said, drawing circles on the image with the cursor.

"He's not the ringleader, but he was always in the warehouse. He didn't come and go."

"His name is Hugo Evans," Samuel said, looking at the photograph. "Serbia is his base, but he's been traveling to Berlin often, and he travels alone. I think he's the easiest target, and I think Berlin would be the place to hit him. He's usually there for a few days at most." He paused. "Do you want me to set an alert to let us know when he books another flight? He seems to go every few weeks."

"When was his last trip?" Deacon asked.

"Eleven days ago."

Deacon inhaled until his chest burned. Could he do this? In potentially a few days' time, could he look directly into the man's eyes? Hugo Evans had been there that fatal night, and even though he hadn't actually touched Nicole, he hadn't tried to stop the other men. He had assisted them.

Deacon's temples began to pulse, and he made a conscious effort to relax his body. He raised his eyes to the image again.

He turned to James, who had been silent the entire time. "In and out, as fast as possible. This is not a revenge killing spree; this is not retaliation. It's a means to an end, and I want it over with as fast as possible." He *needed* it over with as fast as possible.

James nodded. "This is your case. I'll stay in the shadows; that's it."

Deacon sighed. "Set the alert," he said.

23

MARIANNE

Marianne straightened the cushions and placed one hand on the edge of the couch, slowly lowering herself onto her knees. Moving around was getting harder now. She didn't remember being this big with Kaela, but perhaps she'd just forgotten. Without any photos to refer to, she tried to forget about it, refusing to shed any more tears today.

She scooped up the toys Kaela had been playing with, putting them back in the basket. Normally she would've insisted that Kaela pick them up herself, but she was finally sleeping, and Marianne didn't want to wake her.

When the floor was tidy, she made herself a cup of tea, ignoring the slight tremble in her hands.

Please, God, protect us.

It was the prayer she said every day, multiple times per day. It had worked before when she'd prayed to escape Eric, and she prayed it would work again to keep them safe from whatever challenges lay ahead. She'd always been faithful to her God, just not the gods Eric prayed to. She wasn't as foolish as he had been.

Marianne sat on the couch and closed her eyes just as her cell phone rang.

"Hi, James," she said.

"Hey, how are you?" he replied, his voice as casual as ever.

"I'm fine, thanks. I'm feeling well," she said, wondering what the purpose was for his call.

"Good. I was thinking, if you're not busy and you're feeling up for it, that we'd pick up some takeout and come over for dinner. I know being locked up in an apartment and spending a lot of time alone with your thoughts can get overwhelming, so we thought we'd keep you company for a few hours."

Do they think I'm not coping? Did someone see me wiping away my tears?

"You don't have to do that," Marianne said politely.

"You're right, we don't," James said. "We would like to, though."

She cleared her throat, wary that she was being watched now. "That would be lovely, if it's no trouble," she said.

"Marianne," James said, his tone a little sterner, "trust me, I don't do much I don't want to. If we're asking to come over, it's because we want to, not because we think we have to. This is not some kind of charity offer."

Marianne smiled despite herself. "Then that would be genuinely lovely. Who else is coming?"

"Mak, Cami, and Deacon. Samuel can't make it," James said. "We'll pick up dinner on the way and be there about seven. Does that work?"

"Sure, that's fine," Marianne said, relieved she didn't have to organize dinner. She wasn't a good cook—she'd never had to be. One of the few privileges of growing up in Saratani was they'd always had a private chef. She was learning to cook now, though, but she was a long way from cooking for guests.

"I'll see you all then," Marianne said, ending the call.

Dinner at seven would give her time to bathe Kaela and have her ready for the evening. She hoped her daughter would go to bed shortly after they ate, but she didn't think the odds were in her favor. Marianne had always entertained because it had been expected of her; Kaela, however, truly loved to entertain.

Marianne cast her eyes over her apartment and set about tidying it, making sure everything was perfect for her guests.

∼

"Mommy, they're here!" Kaela screamed as she ran toward the knock at the door.

"Kaela, please don't run while you're inside!" Marianne moved at a much slower pace than her daughter.

"Hello!" Kaela said, greeting their visitors as James opened the door.

"Hey, Kaela," he said, standing aside for the others to enter.

"Hi!" Mak said, bending down to give Kaela a hug. Marianne imagined how Eric would react if he could see them now—the thought made her smile, purely because Eric would be rolling in his grave.

"Hi, Mak. Hi, Deacon," Kaela said.

Deacon beamed a smile that made Kaela's face light up. He certainly knew how to throw the charm when he wanted to. Marianne wondered if he'd grown up in a big family, because he didn't appear to be awkward with children.

Kaela grabbed his hand and pulled him toward the television. "You didn't watch it with me last time."

Deacon looked puzzled, and Marianne stepped in to stop her, but Deacon shook his head. "It's okay," he said, following Kaela.

James watched them walk away before leaning in to kiss Marianne's cheek.

Marianne explained. "Deacon told her he'd watch her favorite show with him when he was here setting up the nursery. Be careful what you tell her, because she never forgets."

Cami grinned as she entered. "Hey, how are you? How do you manage to make pregnancy look so good?"

"I thought the same thing!" Mak said.

Marianne's cheeks heated up. "Stop it. I can barely walk at this stage—there's nothing glamorous about it," she said. In the past few weeks she'd felt increasingly bloated and uncomfortable, and knew it was showing. Marianne could see it in the mirror. Cami's compliment, however, appeared genuine. The woman was a complete puzzle to Marianne. She was warm and friendly and not at all what she'd expect from a bodyguard. And because Eric hadn't been able to, or hadn't had time to collate a file on her, Marianne knew nothing about the woman. And she gave nothing away.

Marianne ushered her guests in then went to the kitchen.

"I'll set the table," Mak said. "Where are the plates?"

"Thank you," Marianne said, not used to having anyone offer, and she pointed to a cupboard.

Mak reached up on her tiptoes. "So, how are you really doing? I hate it when James locks me up."

James arrived to hear the last sentence, and he folded his arms and leaned against the cabinet. From the look in his eyes, he was thinking about locking Mak up in a very different way. He didn't make any effort to hide his feelings, and if she were being honest, there was the slightest tinge of envy in her chest. No one had ever loved her the way James loved Mak, and her him.

Mak rolled her eyes playfully. "Make yourself useful," she said, handing him a stack of plates. He laughed as he took them and then went to set the table.

Mak turned to Marianne, back to the conversation. "Are you going stir-crazy?"

Marianne wondered what Mak would think if she told her it didn't bother her at all—she liked staying within the safe walls. "It's fine. After living with Eric, this is heaven."

The corner of Mak's lips turned up, but there was sympathy in her eyes. "I'm sure it is. I'm glad you're comfortable here, but," she added with a devilish grin, "if you ever need to escape, let me know. I'm very good at pointing guns at people now."

Marianne smiled.

"Don't bank on her," James said, appearing again without a noise. "She wouldn't even get you past Josh."

Mak shrugged. "We'll see. Let's eat, I'm hungry."

"You sound like Deacon," James said, and Mak laughed.

"Speaking of, I should rescue him," Marianne said, excusing herself. She found Kaela sitting on the couch with Deacon, resting her elbow on his knee. It warmed her heart and made her legs weak. Kaela no longer had a father figure, and that pained Marianne, even though she knew it was better than having Eric fill the role.

Marianne felt eyes watching her, and she turned to see James looking at them. He looked away just as casually.

"Kaela, dinner is ready," Marianne said.

"Five more minutes," Kaela said, not moving an inch.

"Kaela," Marianne said, using her warning voice.

Kaela puffed out a breath, her little body swaying. She was still refusing to get up, and Marianne feared she was going to throw a tantrum, embarrassing them both.

"Let's eat," Deacon said, and as soon as he stood, so did Kaela.

Marianne turned down the television and made her way to the now boisterous dining table. Kaela positioned herself next to Deacon, so Marianne sat beside Kaela.

James passed her a takeout container. "I hope this food is okay," he said. "I keep forgetting how little I know about you."

Marianne smiled. "You're asking an eight-month-pregnant woman if the food is okay? It's fine."

The table laughed and Marianne was glad they appeared comfortable. Maybe, in time, she would be too.

One by one the containers were passed around, and Marianne plated her dinner.

"So, when is this rematch happening?" Cami asked, her eyes darting between the brothers before settling on Marianne. "To see who the fittest is. Egos," she scoffed.

"The loser gets to set the date," Deacon said.

James grinned. "All right, then. Next weekend we'll see who's sitting on the throne." The look in James's eyes was pure challenge.

"Game on," Deacon said. "And by the way, Mak, who will you be betting on this time?"

James looked at Mak, a wicked grin on his lips. "Yes, Mak, who will you be betting on?" When Mak hesitated, James pinched her shoulder. "That was a second too long."

"Ouch," she said, swatting him away. "I've learned my lesson. I'm betting on you this time, James."

A look transpired between them that gave Marianne the feeling there was a hidden message in their words.

"Cami?" Deacon asked.

"Team Deacon, of course," Cami said, leaning across the table to high-five him.

"I'm Team Deacon, too," Kaela said enthusiastically.

Marianne doubted Kaela had any idea what they were talking about, but wanted to high-five. She giggled, as did the rest of the table.

Mak spoke. "Don't you laugh, Marianne. You're included in this too. Team James or Team Deacon?"

Oh, no. Marianne took to cutting Kaela's food as a distraction, and an excuse to keep her gaze down. "I'd have to see you both train first," Marianne finally said, but James was already shaking his head. She could feel Deacon's eyes on her, radiating heat through her already-warm body. Her neck tingled.

"Make your choice, Marianne. And make it carefully," James said, kicking her lightly under the table.

Cheat. "Team James," she said, and earned herself a beaming smile from her half-brother.

"That's okay," Deacon said. "It's always best to be underestimated. Isn't that what we say, James?"

James laughed, and the table fell into a comfortable silence while they ate.

Mak sighed as she leaned back in her chair, resting her hands on her stomach. When Marianne didn't think she could take another mouthful, she pushed her plate away.

Deacon perused the remnants of the food on the table, and Cami shook her head. "You're unbelievable," she said, and got a chuckle in return.

"I'll take the compliment," he said as he drew his ringing cell phone from his pocket. He hesitated for the briefest moment and excused himself, taking the call.

Marianne watched him walk toward her kitchen, one hand to his ear, the other to the back of his neck. He suddenly looked tense.

"Mommy, can I please go and wash my hands now?" Kaela asked, showing Marianne her palms.

"Sure. But don't make a mess," Marianne said, raising an eyebrow.

Kaela gave that cheeky smile that Marianne simultaneously loved and hated.

"Promise," Kaela said, sliding off her chair.

Marianne glanced sideways at James.

"I don't think you can trust her," he said. He looked like he might laugh.

Deacon returned a minute later, and Marianne didn't miss the look that passed between the brothers. It was like they could communicate without speaking. Mak didn't miss it either—Marianne noticed that much, too. But whatever was happening, James seemed completely at ease. He kissed Mak's temple and whispered in her ear again, but this time Marianne could read his lips: *We'll talk later.*

Marianne wondered if it was about her case. They'd been open with her as far as she could ascertain, but that didn't necessarily mean they were telling her everything. Marianne also knew, though, that the brothers ran an elite security company. That phone call could've meant anything.

Kaela came running back, distracting her from her thoughts, and Marianne was pleased to see she wasn't covered in bath foam.

"See. I promised," she said, and Marianne smiled.

"Do you want some dessert?" Deacon asked, and Kaela spun around so fast Marianne reached out a hand to catch her, sure that she was going to topple over.

Kaela nodded. "Yes!"

Deacon disappeared to the kitchen and came back balancing a large styrofoam container in his hands. "Mini ice creams," he said with an animated face that melted Marianne's heart.

"Thank you," Kaela said, as she selected chocolate—of course.

Deacon's phone sounded again, and he read what Marianne assumed was a text message, typed a few words, and put it back in his pocket.

Another sound, a faint vibration, caught Marianne's attention, and she realized it was James's phone. He looked at his cell phone but didn't seem to respond.

Marianne looked to Cami, who was choosing her own ice cream, appearing completely nonplussed, but Marianne sensed she knew exactly what was going on.

Marianne wrapped a napkin around the base of Kaela's ice cream cone before giving it back to her daughter, who devoured it before the container had even reached Marianne. There was a lot of ice cream left in the container, and Marianne wondered who was going to eat it all.

Cami got the conversation flowing again—and, if an outsider were looking in, Marianne thought they'd look like a happy family, or at least a happy group of friends.

But something wasn't right—she just didn't know what it was.

24

DEACON

Deacon fought the emotions that had him in an invisible chokehold. *It's time.* Time to face the past—and all Deacon wanted to do was run. But as much as he didn't want to admit it, everything Deacon had used to deal with his pain hadn't worked. He was in more pain now than he'd ever been in. Because this life, being around James and Mak, and even more so Marianne and Kaela, was a reminder of everything he'd had, wanted, and lost.

Deacon focused on the taste of his ice cream. On the incessant but cute chatter that flowed from Kaela's mouth without a break. He focused on anything except what he was about to do.

The jet was booked, and in two hours they were leaving for Berlin.

He'd tried to mentally prepare himself for this moment since the discussion in Samuel's office, but he was still fighting to control his mind.

The container of ice cream made its way back to him, and he looked over the table, but everyone shook their heads.

He took the container and put it back in the freezer, grateful for the distraction. He took a moment to lean against the counter, resting his hands on the bench, trying to get some air into his lungs.

You can do this.

You have to do this.

He exhaled as his body trembled.

He heard Marianne's voice from the dining room. "Can I make anyone tea or coffee?"

"If I eat another thing I'm going to explode," Mak replied.

Deacon lingered, hoping James was going to make an excuse to get them out of there. Right now, Deacon needed to be alone.

"We should be going, actually. Deacon and I have a teleconference we need to call in for," James said, and Deacon wanted to hug him.

Deacon took one more long, slow breath then returned to the table where everyone was cleaning up. He picked up a stack of plates and carried them to the kitchen, rinsing them and loading them into the dishwasher. The mundane task eased his mind, and his chest relaxed. He could breathe again. The dishes kept arriving and Deacon remained at his post. He'd worked in a restaurant when he was in school, doing this exact same thing. He'd lied about his age and started working when he was twelve years old to help his mom pay the bills. It felt like a lifetime ago.

"Good job," Cami said, patting his shoulder.

He turned around and whipped her with the tea towel that had been draped over his shoulder.

"Ouch!" She jumped back.

"Too slow," he said. "You're spending too much time with Mak and not enough in training."

"You're going to pay for that, Deacon Thomas," she said with a wicked grin.

"Show me how to do that!" Kaela said as she came running in.

Oh, no. He looked past her, seeing Marianne.

"Our guests have to go now," Marianne said with a hint of a smile.

Deacon knelt down to give Kaela a hug goodbye. Marianne was next in line. He leaned in to kiss her goodbye, subconsciously holding his breath.

"Please don't teach her to do that, she'll end up whipping me,"

Marianne whispered in his ear, the heat of her breath tingling his skin.

"Promise," Deacon said, but his lips lingered on her cheek a second too long.

And the woman he'd once called the Ice Queen wasn't completely unaffected. Her breath hitched, and he found himself hoping she was feeling some of whatever he was, and then mentally crucified himself for thinking that.

You've learned your lesson.

~

The silence of the jet was like a megaphone for his thoughts. He went back and forth, thinking about Nicole and her killers. He also thought about Marianne, asking himself why she had an effect on him. Although he thought her more beautiful every time he saw her, it wasn't her looks that drew him to her. He knew that, because he'd fucked countless beautiful women over the years and none of them had made him want to stay for breakfast, let alone give them another thought after he'd said goodbye.

Deacon sighed, successfully pushing those questions from his mind. At least he still had some control.

~

Deacon's breaths were shallow, his heart walloping in his chest. He could see him—the man who had aided Nicole's killers. Evans. He was dining with a woman in a restaurant. The poor woman obviously had no idea who was sitting across from her. Tonight they would do her a favor.

Deacon adjusted the lens, zooming in on their target. His eyes never strayed for the entire hour and a half the man sat at the table. He wasn't planning to shoot the man, though. Deacon was only in this position in case unexpected company arrived—or in case James, who was in the restaurant, was identified. There was no way Deacon could enter the restaurant. Evans had seen his face, and Deacon doubted he'd forgotten it.

With every second that passed, Deacon knew he was a second closer to having to face the man. The very idea of it filled him with dread.

Evans finally exited the building and crossed the street with his date. They walked past the building Deacon was positioned at and James followed discreetly behind them. Deacon watched the scene play out below him. The target didn't look over his shoulder, and he appeared to be paying no attention to his surroundings. Deacon concluded Hugo Evans felt completely safe—a good thing for them, and a very bad thing for Evans.

Deacon packed his rifle and scaled down the fire escape. He paused at the bottom, catching his breath. His anxiety was asphyxiating. He forced himself to keep moving. He kept a safe distance from James, who was himself keeping a safe distance from their target. The fact that the target was moving on foot led Deacon to believe he wasn't going far. He could see a bar ahead and wondered if that was the intended destination.

"*Target slowing down,*" James said.

Deacon slid into the shadows, wanting to disappear—physically and mentally.

"*I'm going to put a tracker on him,*" James said just before he entered the bar and went out of sight.

With no electronic schedule, and no idea of the man's itinerary for the trip, James and Deacon could do little but follow him. If they lost him, Samuel would likely find him soon enough, but they might miss their window of opportunity.

"*Samuel, confirm,*" James said.

"*Copy. The tracker is active,*" Samuel replied.

Deacon refrained from raising his eyebrows—he was impressed at how quickly James had been able to make a move.

Part of him wanted something to go wrong, for the opportunity to face the man to be taken away from him. It would ease his pain—but only for the moment. Deacon knew he had to do this.

"*Deacon?*" James asked.

"Second alley on your left, heading west," Deacon said, anticipating his next question.

A few minutes later James appeared, taking a seat next to Deacon on the steps of a fire escape.

"They've just ordered a bottle of wine. He's asking her where she's staying, so my thoughts are he's not taking her back to his hotel," James said.

"Plan A," Deacon said with a raw voice. He really needed a drink to ease his burning throat.

"Do you still want to do this?" James searched his eyes.

No. "Yes."

James gave a nod of understanding. "We have a few hours at least, I'd say, depending on how long he lasts in the bedroom. Let's get some food and head to the hotel."

Deacon pushed off the steps, wondering how he was going to force food into his stomach. Something that was normally never a problem.

~

Deacon sat in the armchair, the pumping thump of his heart the only sound he could hear. This was it. Evans was finished in the woman's bedroom, and every second that passed brought them closer together. His mind wrangled with his emotions, telling him he could still back out. He could go home and forget about it. But he didn't move.

"*Target approaching lobby.*

"*Target in elevator.*

"*Target at door.*"

Deacon raised his eyes, his finger light on the trigger. He heard the beep of the electronic lock before the door swung open and closed behind him. There was a moment before the overhead lights turned on, and Deacon wondered if that was the moment Evans realized something was wrong—the lamps had already been on.

"Oh, fuck," Evans said as his eyes met Deacon's. Evans reached for his back pocket.

"Don't even think about it," Deacon said, his voice sounding strained even to his own ears.

"You," he said with wide eyes.

"I thought you'd remember me. I certainly remember you."

The man's eyes darted all over the room—but unfortunately for him, James had stepped out of the closet and was blocking his only entrance.

"Why don't you take a seat," Deacon said, motioning to the one across from him even though he wanted the man nowhere near him.

"I prefer to stand," he said, his hand inching ever so slowly toward that back pocket.

"Have it your way," Deacon muttered as James stepped behind the man and had a syringe in his neck before Evans could even turn, let alone reach his gun.

It only took a few seconds before the man was out cold. James dragged him toward the chair and they set about tying him up. Deacon's body was trembling and, unlike his brother, who he knew would be on an adrenaline high, Deacon felt a weighty sense of fatigue settling in. He was drained from days of no sleep and apprehension so severe it was lacerating.

James administered the reversal and then stepped aside, taking a seat in the adjoining dining room where he'd have the best view and still be able to provide backup should things get out of control. Looking at the current situation, though, that wasn't Deacon's concern.

The man began to shake, a sign of the reversal taking effect, and Deacon assisted the process by dragging a knife over the man's right cheek. It gave him no thrill, but it served its purpose. Evans's eyes flew open and he bolted back against the chair. The restraints kept him safely in place.

Then came something Deacon hadn't suspected.

Begging. Pitiful begging.

"Please. Please . . . I didn't touch her. I didn't hurt her," he said.

"You didn't hurt her? Really? How do you think assisting the men that mutilated, raped, and murdered her, didn't hurt her? You sure as fuck didn't help *me*, and I *could* have helped her."

"I'd just joined the group. I didn't know what they were going to do. I was scared—I thought they'd kill me if I didn't help them." His eyes pleaded with Deacon's.

"And yet you still run with them. You're still part of the group. Do you really expect me to believe your bullshit?"

"They'll kill me if I leave. You don't get out of a group like this. Not knowing the kind of secrets I do. Ford doesn't let anyone leave."

Ford? The name didn't ring a bell.

"Ford—Ford who?"

The man looked pained.

This wasn't turning out at all how Deacon had expected.

Deacon slashed the man's other cheek and he howled, but unfortunately for him there was no one to hear him scream. Blood ran down his face, dripping from his chin.

"Are you going to kill me?" he asked.

"Yes," Deacon said, deadpan. The sooner, the better.

The man shuddered as he inhaled. "I've always hated him . . . He killed my brother."

Deacon arched a brow. "Ford? And yet, again, you still work for him."

"I told you, I don't have a choice," he said, his voice tight. "What do you want to know?"

"What is Ford's full name?"

"Tom Ford."

"What is Ford's relationship with the Russians?"

"Russians? He's not friends with the Russians."

"Who ordered the hit?" Deacon asked, struggling to keep his mind focused.

"I don't know—I honestly don't. Ford never told us . . . he just said that we'd been contracted to do it."

Deacon nodded slowly. "How do I find Tom Ford?"

"He lives in Montreal, I think. I've only seen him in group settings. The other guys might know."

Montreal?

Deacon's mind was reeling. "What does he look like?"

The man looked to the right, as if struggling to recall Ford's appearance. "Tall. Six two, six three, maybe. Short blond hair. Always wears a leather jacket. Square jaw. Green eyes. He's American."

"What else? Any tattoos? Any scars?"

He was quiet again. "No, but he has a small mole near his left ear . . . I don't know why I noticed that," he said, shaking his head. Given how quickly Evans was giving up information, and how detailed it was—provided he wasn't lying, which Deacon didn't think he was— the man really did want Ford dead. It was a name for Samuel to work off, at least.

"How much were you paid to do the hit?" Deacon asked.

"I was paid five thousand. The other guys, twenty thousand each, I think. That's what they bragged about, at least," he said, and then quickly realized it was the wrong thing to say.

Deacon had expected it, though. He knew they had no remorse— he'd seen the joy in their eyes that night—but it still felt like a baseball slamming into his gut.

"Where is your base?" Deacon asked.

"Belgrade, Serbia."

"What's the address for the headquarters?" Deacon turned the knife in his hand when Evans looked like he might stop talking.

"Zanke Stokic," he said, closing his eyes. "221."

"How did you find us in Thailand?" Deacon finally asked, fighting the urge to run from the room before Evans could answer.

"We were in Serbia when we got the call to go to Thailand. Ford said Nicholas, her brother, had given them a lead, and that we were to go to Bangkok to await further instructions."

Deacon raised his eyebrows, his eyes widening. *Nicholas?* Nicole and Nicholas had been close. He was the reason she was in Russia— she'd been visiting him when Deacon had met her. What did Ford have to gain by lying about the lead, though?

"What happened once you arrived in Bangkok?"

"I stayed back in the hotel for the first day—I had a stomach virus. The next day we left for the resort. I don't know how they traced you there . . . I really am sorry," he said desperately. "For what it's worth."

"It's worth nothing," Deacon replied coldly.

Deacon's eyes flickered to his brother. When James shook his head, indicating he had no further questions, Deacon whispered, "Say a prayer," and pulled the trigger.

Then he sat, motionless, staring at the bloody corpse in front of him.

He had only one positive thought: Evans couldn't hurt anyone else now.

25

DEACON

Deacon and James walked out of the building like they didn't have a care in the world. They strolled to their car, drove off and let Samuel's team finish doctoring the only evidence that linked them to the crime scene.

The inside of Deacon's mind was a very different story, though.

"Let's break it down on the plane," James said, and Deacon understood the message in the words that weren't said.

Concentrate. Stay alert.

They could never afford to let their guards down—to be sloppy in their surveillance. While they assumed that the risk to them in Berlin was low, it was only that: an assumption. They never knew who they could run into, and after the mess they'd caused with Saratani, anywhere in Europe presented some risk.

"*Confirming data edited. You're all clear. What's the plan now?*" Samuel asked via the earpiece, bringing Deacon back to the present, although he'd only ever slipped halfway from it. He'd learned to do that over the years—keep a watch on his environment even when his mind was in overdrive. He should've been more present, though. He pushed all thoughts of that night from his mind.

"We're going home. Please organize the jet," Deacon said.

"*Copy. Head to the airport and I'll have everything ready for you,*" Samuel replied.

Deacon concentrated on driving; as they turned onto the highway, he put his foot down on the accelerator. He felt James's eyes glance across at the dashboard, but he didn't say anything. Driving was one of the few things that gave Deacon peace.

~

Deacon kept his cell phone in his hand, waiting impatiently for Samuel's call. He'd told them to get some sleep and he'd be in touch in a few hours after he'd had a chance to work the intel. That had been five hours ago, and although Deacon's eyes had been closed and his body drained of energy, sleep hadn't come to him.

Tom Ford. Who was he? Why had he ordered such a violent attack? Or perhaps he hadn't, and his men had taken that upon themselves.

And Nicholas . . . Deacon couldn't fathom it. He couldn't imagine her own brother would betray her, but he knew he couldn't completely rule it out. *Blood doesn't always run thicker than water.*

Deacon sighed. Too many questions. Too few answers. And a silent phone. James was silent, too, but Deacon doubted he was sleeping. They'd said little since boarding—they both knew it was better to debrief with Samuel.

Another hour passed before his cell phone finally rang.

"Samuel," Deacon said, putting it on speaker.

"Where to start, huh? I've confirmed the location in Serbia, and I have a team monitoring the CCTV footage in that area. We'll put together a report of who's coming and going and analyze it from there," Samuel said, before drawing a breath.

"As for Tom Ford, I don't have anything yet. Given the description Evans provided, it's safe to say he's not the fashion designer," he joked, perhaps trying in vain to lighten the mood. Deacon didn't get it, and judging by the blank expression on James's face, he didn't either.

"Designer?" Deacon asked.

"Yes. You know, the guy who makes half the suits that are in your closets?" Samuel said.

James's brows furrowed. "How in the world do you know what kinds of suits we wear?"

"I pay attention to details," Samuel said, deadpan, before continuing on. "Forget it. Anyway, so far I can't find a Tom Ford that matches that description, and that leaves two possibilities: I haven't searched deep enough, or Tom Ford is an alias. Both are highly probable."

Deacon nodded, chewing on his cheek. "What do you think about Ford being based in Montreal, if that's correct?"

"I don't know at this stage," Samuel said. "It's interesting, for sure."

"Anything on Nicholas?" Deacon asked.

"Not yet. I'd previously looked at all of Nicole's family members but ruled them out. The thing is . . ." Samuel paused, and Deacon knew he wasn't going to like what was coming. "Given that I, as skilled as I am, couldn't find you—it makes me believe that someone had inside information."

Tension coiled around his chest. "What are you saying? That Nicole was leaking information?"

"No, that's not what I'm saying at all—not intentionally at least. Did she ever contact any family members while you were in Tokyo?"

"No," Deacon said quickly, then realized he couldn't bet his life on that. "Not that I knew of. She knew the risks, Samuel."

"I know she did, but both you and I know how hard it is to leave behind our families. You were working a lot, you had to, and she was lonely—you've admitted that yourself. One phone call home may have been all it took."

It was incomprehensible to him, but he knew he had to try and consider it. "Let's say she did. How could that call later be traced?"

"That depends on who's doing the tracing. It would take me about ten seconds. Perhaps it wasn't traced later, though. Perhaps someone was banking on her phoning home and had tapped the phone."

"Why? It still doesn't make sense."

"No, it doesn't," Samuel admitted. "I've looked through every line transaction in his bank accounts for the past fifteen years—I can't go back further than that without paper copies. I can't see any suspicious transactions. He was deeply in debt around the time of Nicole's murder, but none of those debts were eliminated after her death. He paid them all off slowly, at least the ones I can track. For him to have known that you were a wanted man, or to know who to sell the information to, he had to have contacts in the mafia. He was a bartender in Russia, and the bar he worked for was mafia owned, from what I can ascertain."

"Where is Nicholas now?" Deacon asked.

"He lives in Dallas, Texas—I have all kinds of traces on him. I'm looking at his current associates, but I can't find any connections to the Russians or Sonoma or Ford. He's still married to the same woman, and their two kids are teenagers now."

Deacon, Nicole, and James had been so careful after they'd fled Russia. Nicole knew not to call. She knew it—Deacon had told her how dangerous it was a thousand times. But Samuel was right: leaving behind your family was devastating. Especially when you spent most of your time alone.

Deacon squeezed his eyes shut. He didn't want to believe it, but it definitely was possible. And that made her death even more senseless.

Deacon took a five-second break from grinding his teeth.

"Please tell me there is no connection between Ford and Greene. Right?" Deacon thought of how intricately linked James and Mak's cases had been. He had enough guilt over Nicole's death; he didn't need to know his enemies were after Marianne in an effort to get to him.

"No, I don't think we're dealing with that sort of connection again. Your group certainly has an interest in Saratani's business dealings, but so does every crime group in Europe right now. I knew this was a potential outcome of dismantling the organization, but Eric had to be stopped, so what do you do? Deal with one problem at a time."

"Right," Deacon mused. "Let me think this over. I'll call you back." He ended the call, unable to draw his eyes from his phone. He felt James watching him, but he wasn't ready to talk. He was still trying to process the conversation with Samuel.

Deacon had tried to forget every memory of Nicole, even the good ones, because they only made the memories of Nicole's death more painful.

But now he forced his mind to go there. To the last few months they were together in Tokyo. He analyzed Nicole's behavior. He'd noticed the differences in her: the dullness in her eyes, she took frequent naps during the day, she'd started cooking more. He'd known she was trying to find ways to keep herself busy, and it was one of the reasons he'd booked the trip—in addition to wanting to spend time with her. And the more he thought about it, the more he realized Samuel could be right. Why hadn't he once asked himself if she'd contacted her family? He knew the answer immediately: because he hadn't wanted to know if she had. He hadn't wanted to think about her at all. One seemingly harmless phone call could've changed their lives forever.

James had told him one night, on their many initial arguments about Deacon and Nicole's relationship, that she would break. She wasn't cut out for the type of life they'd needed to live. It wasn't that James was bitter, but at that time in his brother's life, he'd been vehemently against relationships. Deacon had been furious, and he hadn't spoken to him for weeks—unless it was work related. It was actually after that disagreement that James had agreed to disagree and Nicole would run with them.

Deacon looked tiredly at James. "Did it occur to you that Nicole might've phoned her family, or been in contact with them in the lead up to the Thailand trip?"

"Well . . ." James had that look on his face, the one that told Deacon he was choosing his words carefully. "I wasn't sure. Initially, I thought she would, and that was one of the reasons why I was so hesitant in taking her with us. But the longer she was with us . . . well, she actually adapted better than I'd thought she was going to."

"But you still didn't rule it out?"

"I questioned it, but I had nothing to base my suspicions on," James said.

"Why didn't you say anything to me?" Deacon asked.

This time James was quick to answer. "Because you didn't want to know and you already hated yourself enough. What was I supposed to say? I told you so?" James shook his head. "Especially when I didn't know for sure. I thought she was homesick, but that was to be expected. There are levels of homesickness, though."

"What do you think now?"

He frowned. "I think she probably did."

Deacon pinched the bridge of his nose, drowning in regret. Once he answered the questions surrounding Nicole's death, he'd still have to deal with the fact that she died because of him. She was targeted and brutally murdered because she loved him. He still had to get past that, and he had no idea how he ever would.

26

MARIANNE

The high-pitched screams pierced through Marianne's dream, startling her awake.

Kaela.

Marianne bolted upright, and a twinge of pain caused her hands to clutch her ballooning baby bump. Kaela's wails continued as she cried for her father.

Marianne took a deep breath and gave the pain a moment to settle. As soon as it did, she levered herself out of bed, grabbed her silk robe from the chair in the corner, and all but ran to the next room.

Her daughter was curled up in a ball, her sobbing cries cracking Marianne's heart. Guilt consumed her like a vile disease.

"Kaela, sweetie. It's okay, it's okay. Come here," Marianne said, pulling her daughter into her arms as best she could. At this stage in her pregnancy it was a futile effort. Marianne sat down on the edge of Kaela's bed, her shuddering daughter laid across her lap. She rocked back and forth, stroking her daughter's back.

"I want my daddy. I want him to come home," she cried, and Marianne squeezed her eyes shut.

It was Marianne's fault Eric was dead. She'd *wanted* him dead.

And Marianne had to remind herself again she'd done the right thing. The only thing she could've done. But Kaela was a child; there was no way she could attempt to explain it.

You did what you had to do.

Marianne wondered how many times she'd told herself that.

"Daddy's with the angels, remember? But he loves you. You will always be his princess," Marianne whispered, but Kaela continued to sob. It was the second time she'd woken up like this in the past week alone. And tonight, like the other nights, nothing Marianne did seemed to console her. Marianne wiped a tear from her own cheek—and it wasn't a tear for Eric.

Marianne wasn't sure how long she sat there with Kaela, but eventually her daughter fell back asleep. She slid out from underneath Kaela and draped a blanket over her.

Your life will be better without him.

She could only pray that, over time, Kaela would forget her father.

Marianne tightened the sash of her robe, but it did little to extinguish the chill in her bones. A chill that felt as evil as her late husband.

She stepped into the hallway, and another clutching pain had her gripping the wall, fighting for breath. She bit her lip to stop herself from screaming, fearful of waking her daughter again.

Breathe. It'll pass.

She had to call the doctor first thing in the morning. Something wasn't right. She knew it.

Breathe.

She tried to straighten, just wanting to get back into her warm bed. She took another step forward, but the next bolt of pain had her doubled over, moaning.

Marianne began to shake. Her nails dug into the wall, her breath ragged.

Don't fall. Her eyes dropped to her legs, and by a miracle she held back the scream that threatened to roar from her throat.

Blood was gushing down her legs.

Her heart whooshed in her ears, and she experienced a level of fear she had never before experienced.

I'm going to lose him.

"Marianne?" a hushed, urgent voice called her name before light footsteps ran toward her.

She couldn't stand up, she could barely breathe. Her lungs burned—she felt like she was drowning, but her heart was pounding wildly.

"Oh, fuck!"

Marianne lifted her head as Josh wrapped an arm underneath her, taking all of her weight just as her legs gave way.

His voice sounded distant, as if he were outside the room.

"Save him, please," Marianne begged with a raspy voice.

Everything went dark.

27

DEACON

Deacon awoke, disoriented. It took him a moment to work out where he was and what had woken him. He was back in New York, and Samuel was calling.

"Hello," Deacon said with a voice that sounded as croaky as an eighty-year-old's.

"Marianne's in an ambulance. She's hemorrhaging. Get to the hospital, now. There's a team at the apartment with Kaela," Samuel said, but Deacon was already out of bed, pulling on his clothes. He grabbed his pistol and ran toward his door. He pulled it shut as James appeared from his apartment.

Deacon ran to the elevator and punched the button. James was already on the phone, talking with Josh.

"How far away? How long has she been bleeding? How much blood?" James's questions were endless, and he looked as worried as he sounded.

The elevator doors opened and they sprinted for the car. Deacon launched it into reverse and fled toward the exit gate, which opened without his pass code—Samuel was on it. Deacon pulled a hard right, sliding the car out onto the street. They were fifteen minutes from the hospital at most—Deacon intended to get there in ten.

James was on the phone the entire way, and although Deacon wanted the answers to the questions that were making his heart race, his job right now was to get them there as fast as possible.

Deacon dodged the traffic like he was playing a game of Frogger. More than one driver furiously honked at him, but his focus was only on the road ahead. The drive helped to calm his mind. What had happened? Was she going to be okay? Was the baby okay?

One step at a time.

Right now they had to get to the hospital safely so they weren't the next patients, then they had to find out exactly what was going on.

Deacon stopped at the front entrance, the car screeching to a stop, and they ran through the doors and past concerned-looking staff.

He knew when they were near Marianne because the hallway was littered with their security staff. Staff motioned toward the double doors and Deacon pushed them open, finding Josh inside the small room, pacing back and forth in bloodstained clothes.

"What's going on now?" James asked.

Josh was paler than Deacon had ever seen him. "She crashed in the ambulance. They revived her, and they're doing an emergency caesarian section."

Deacon peered through the glass but there were so many medical staff he could barely see Marianne. He looked at the monitors, reading her vitals, and felt the blood drains from his legs. She was barely alive.

"Is there another entrance?" James asked, his head scanning the room.

"No. They let me go in with Marianne when we arrived, and I performed a full security check. They kicked me out as quickly as they could and told me to wait here."

"You did well." James put a hand on Josh's shoulder before looking back at Deacon. "Come on," he said.

They walked back into the hallway and Deacon knew what James was looking for. They found it three doors down—changing rooms.

They put on scrubs, boots, masks and hairnets and ran back to the operating room, letting themselves in. A nurse approached them immediately.

"You can't be in here," she said, blocking them.

"She's our sister, we're her security team, and her life is in danger. We're staying in here," James said flatly, and the nurse shrank back a little at the sound of his voice. "Please go and help her."

The nurse opened her mouth, probably to tell them to get out, but when every monitor in the room started sending off alerts, she clearly forgot all about the brothers.

The room was in apparent chaos, although Deacon knew otherwise. Arms reached over one another and voices shouted as Marianne flatlined again.

It was agonizing to watch, and it was one of the few times in his life he felt completely helpless. Yes, he and James had medical knowledge, but they wouldn't dream of stepping into this situation.

"Get him out, get him out! We're losing her!"

James swore under his breath, and Deacon looked around the room in desperation, but there was nothing they could do to help.

Fight, Marianne.

Deacon heard the baby's cry, and then the heart monitor flatlined. Life and death.

A nurse laid Marianne's baby boy on a sterile cart.

"On three!" the doctor called and Deacon held his breath, trying to watch everything at once.

Come on, come on.

"Again! Don't you fucking die on me!" the doctor shouted, and Deacon found himself immediately and fervently liking him.

The baby was screaming now as his mother was silent. Deathly silent.

A nurse grabbed the cart, wheeling the baby toward them. Neither of the brothers moved.

"Where are you going?" James asked.

"Excuse me," she said, ignoring them. James put a hand on the cart and the lady looked like she was going to ram it into him. She wasn't stopping for anyone.

"I need to get this baby to the nursery. Get out of my way!" she said, practically screaming at them.

"I'm going with you," James said, and the nurse nodded impatiently.

Deacon looked quickly at James. "I'll stay," he said just before they disappeared. He turned his attention back to the chaos still unfolding.

"Again!"

Deacon looked at the large clock on the wall. They were on their final chances.

His stomach curdled, and he fought the urge to go and resuscitate her himself. It was excruciating not being able to do anything.

"One more time!"

Deacon's own heart paused as his eyes remained glued to the monitors.

"Three, two, one!"

The entire room was quiet, but you could almost hear the silent prayers.

Fight, Marianne.

Another second passed.

Beep. Beep. Beep.

Relief hit Deacon with so much force it nearly knocked him over.

"That's my girl! Let's get her stabilized!"

Deacon moved back against the wall, keeping out of the way of the operating room staff. He'd always had a profound respect for medical staff, but it was on occasions like this he could fully appreciate the gravity of what they did.

Deacon wasn't foolish enough to believe she was out of danger yet, but for now, her baby was alive and her heart was beating. That was good enough.

~

Deacon sat in the corner of Marianne's room in the intensive care unit. She was stable, but still unconscious. James hadn't returned, but they'd been on the phone, busy making arrangements. The nursing staff had wanted to keep the baby in the nursery, but James and Deacon had very different ideas. It had taken a lot of negotiating, but they'd arranged to have Marianne's baby brought into her room with a dedicated nurse. The baby had undergone full testing, and he appeared to be a beautiful healthy boy.

He needs you, Marianne.

Her body was perfectly still; the only sign of life was the tiny rise and fall of her chest. Her skin was so pale, so clear, he could've traced her veins with his finger.

Kaela was awake now, but Mak and Cami were keeping her entertained until the babysitter arrived. Deacon had been told they were eating chocolate for breakfast and watching cartoons. Deacon wasn't sure if Marianne would approve of their babysitting skills, but right now that didn't matter.

The nurse appeared again, no longer even bothering to glance at Deacon. She took Marianne's vitals, administered medication and fluids, and retreated from the room, although Deacon knew she wasn't far away.

He wondered what the medical staff thought. Thomas Security staff were positioned all over the hospital now, securing it as best as they could. Deacon knew the risk was low: no one from Saratani—at least no one that was still alive—knew that Marianne was pregnant, so a hospital wasn't the first place they'd be looking for her, especially since she hadn't been admitted under her real name. But still, there was always risk.

The door opened again, and James entered with three medical staff and a portable hospital bassinet. The nurses fussed around, setting up what they needed to.

James came to stand beside him. "Any change?"

"Nothing," Deacon whispered.

James nodded then smiled slightly. "Well, the kid's definitely got a set of lungs on him," James said, motioning toward the bassinet.

The nurses exited, while the baby nurse stayed a minute longer, checking the boy's vitals. "I'll be back in a minute," she said before she also left.

Deacon waited until she left the room and walked over to the bassinet.

He put his hand on its edge, looking down on the little baby boy.

He looked perfect.

The baby's eyes opened, or tried to, and he made a suckling noise with his lips.

A strange urge to pick him up and hold him overcame Deacon, but he stepped away, retreating back to his corner.

James was at Marianne's bed, holding her hand. "Don't you dare give up now," he whispered.

28

DEACON

Inside the hospital walls, night and day ceased to exist. Deacon and James rotated between six-hour shifts—one of them always present in Marianne's room. She was still unconscious, but stable enough to be moved to a room, so they made plans to have her discharged as soon as she woke up.

Staff also rotated through, each one carefully screened by Samuel. The curious baby nurse was eyeing Deacon now.

"You know, you boys can hold him if you'd like. He won't break," she said, sweeping her gray bangs aside with a hand, revealing her warm eyes. Eyes that appeared worldly and wise—and judging by her accent, she hadn't been born in America, but she'd been there long enough that Deacon couldn't work out where she had been. And he didn't ask, because he didn't want to open a window for her to return the questions.

Deacon smiled. "Don't put it past us," he joked.

Although James was very likely worried about breaking the baby, it actually wasn't the reason Deacon had resisted every urge to pick him up. It just felt wrong. He wanted Marianne to hold her baby first, before any of them did—medical staff excluded. And for now they were just calling him "baby," or "him," because he didn't have a name.

The baby nurse rocked back and forth as she bottle-fed and then burped him. After watching the staff do it every few hours for the past few days, Deacon knew if an emergency erupted, and he had to steal the baby boy from the hospital, at least he'd know how to feed him. And change him. And swaddle him.

God, I even know the terms now.

The lives they'd lived before Mak had come onto the scene seemed like years ago now.

Deacon stifled a yawn. Staying alert—or even awake—when sitting in a hospital was a challenging task. It would be so easy to rest his head back against the wall and close his eyes for a minute, but he didn't dare. Never again would he be so careless.

With the little boy fed, burped, and settled, the nurse exited the room with a smile for a few minutes, but Deacon knew she'd be back soon. He returned his attention to Marianne, willing her to wake up but her eyelids remained closed. Not a single flutter.

~

Deacon drove the long way back to Thomas Security. He'd swapped shifts with James, and he used the drive to calm his worried mind. His body ached, like he had the flu, but he knew it was just exhaustion. His body and mind were drained.

He finally brought the car to a stop in his parking bay and took the elevator straight to his apartment. He didn't want to see anyone; he didn't want to talk to anyone. He just wanted to sleep.

~

White mist surrounds me. I look to my feet, barely able to see them. I take a step forward, carefully. Where am I? I can't see, but I don't feel fear.

"Deacon," she whispers. I would recognize the voice anywhere.

"Nicole!" I move toward the echo. "Nicole!"

"I'm here," she says, materializing as the mist parts.

I freeze, and my heart stalls, refusing to beat. Her silk gown is covered in blood.

"Nicole!" I scream, running now.

She smiles as I wrap my arms around her.

Tears roll down my cheeks as her lips press against my forehead, melting my heart. I close my eyes, but the precious moment lasts only a minute.

"Nicole!" I scream, trying desperately to hold on to her as she vanishes in my arms.

～

"Nicole!" Deacon screamed, waking himself. He sat upright, shuddering as he fought to control his mind. The silk gown—it was the same one she'd been murdered in. He leaned forward, burying his face in his hands, gasping in air as the emotions he'd staved off for so many years came flooding back. And for the first time in all the years since that night, he let himself shed the tears.

"I'm so sorry," he whispered, hoping she could hear him.

～

Deacon watched the sunrise from the rooftop. He'd come up a few hours ago, unable to bear the loneliness of his apartment. He sipped his coffee, hoping the caffeine would fuel him for the day. A magnificent sunrise of vibrant orange hues lit up New York City—but Deacon stared solemnly ahead, lost in his dream. In the sound of her voice. In the feel of her touch. What wouldn't he give to hold her once more?

Despite being dressed in her bloody gown, she'd been smiling. She'd looked happy. He wanted to believe she was okay, that her soul had found peace, but he didn't.

He closed his eyes, letting the morning rays, magnified by the glass panels, warm him. He could've stayed there all day, but he knew James needed to be relieved at the hospital. Life goes on, it always does, he knew. No matter how big his problems were, or anyone else's were, the world would stop for no one.

He drank the remnants of his coffee and went back to his apartment, showered, and drove to the hospital.

"How is she?" Deacon asked James, but he already knew the answer. If there'd been a change, Samuel would've notified him.

"The same," he said. "Did you get some sleep?"

Deacon nodded. "Some. Go home," he said, and James didn't stop to think about it.

Deacon took his post by the wall, mentally preparing himself for another long day. He eyed the staff, watching them carefully. The sooner they could move Marianne, the better.

Her chest rose and fell and he wondered where she was in the realms of unconsciousness. Josh had told him Marianne's last words —*save him, please*—and he hoped she knew she was fighting for two children now, not just one.

His cell phone vibrated, and he drew it from his pocket. "Hi, Samuel," he said.

"Hey. How's things?"

"I'm fine," Deacon responded. He knew Samuel wasn't asking about Marianne. Deacon had no doubt his heart rate had been dangerously high last night, and it would've triggered an alert on his tracker. Even if Samuel wasn't actively spying on them, he knew there was little they could keep from him. He would've checked the cameras in Deacon's apartment.

"Good, because we might have a problem . . . Sonoma just boarded a flight to Manhattan. He appears to be traveling on his own, or at least I didn't identify any of his old friends with him. I don't know if we need to be concerned or if it's just a coincidence."

"We need to be concerned," Deacon said immediately. "She's been here too long, Samuel. We're going on three days."

"I know, but the doctors are still refusing to discharge her, even to another hospital. At least they were yesterday."

"Where did he board the flight?"

"Serbia. He has one stop, so he'll be landing in about sixteen hours."

The hairs on his arms bristled.

"And none of the other guys are headed to Manhattan?"

"No. I've seen—via the CCTV footage—one of them enter their headquarters in the past four hours. I don't have the current whereabouts of the others."

He could already be in New York. Anything was possible.

"Where's James? Can you connect him in on this call?" Deacon asked. They needed a second backup plan, and they needed it now.

"On it . . . James?"

"Hey," James said.

"Sonoma is en route to New York, and I don't believe it's a coincidence. We need to change our backup plan. I think we need to take Marianne and the children out of Manhattan completely."

Samuel gave James the full rundown, and Deacon heard his brother swear under his breath.

"What about Boston?" Deacon said. "We could use the house there and coordinate our own team of medical staff. It'll allow us to hide her while still being in close proximity to good medical facilities. Even if they find us there, they'd have a hell of a time getting inside. We can't secure this entire hospital, or any hospital in New York, and if she's attacked here, there's going to mass casualties of innocents and mass media coverage." It went without saying that all of the aforementioned were things they desperately needed to avoid.

"It's a good plan. I'll organize teams to go now to prepare," James said.

Deacon was looking at his feet, thinking of all the things they needed to organize, when he heard it. It was so faint he wasn't sure if he'd imagine it. He held his breath as his head snapped to the bed.

Marianne's eyelids twitched, like she was trying to open them.

"James, she's waking up. I'll call you back," Deacon said. He knew it could be hours yet, days even, but if they needed to move her, it would be a damn lot easier if she was awake.

He dropped his phone into his pocket and took her hand, squeezing it.

"Marianne. Marianne, wake up," he said, repeating it over and over. Her eyes remained closed, but he persisted. He squeezed her hand, brushing his thumb over her knuckles.

"Mm..."

There it was again—the tiniest of moans. A whisper. But he hadn't imagined it.

He kept talking to her, but Marianne didn't wake up. She didn't moan again, and her eyelids grew still. Deacon wasn't discouraged, though. This was better than they'd had in days. He dragged his chair next to her bed and wrapped his hands around hers. He didn't know if she knew he was there, of if she could feel someone holding her hand, but he hoped she knew she wasn't alone.

Wake up, Marianne.

Small, yearning cries emanated from the crib, and the baby nurse moved toward him. Deacon shook his head. "Can you let him cry for a moment?"

Marianne's eyelids fluttered as the wails grew in intensity. Deacon felt a pang of guilt—he didn't like letting the baby cry—but Marianne seemed to be responding. Her fingers squeezed around Deacon's, and he knew it was working.

The nurse put a gentle hand on the infant's chest, giving him some comfort, but letting his cries continue. After another thirty seconds, when Marianne showed no further signs of waking up, Deacon nodded to the nurse, and she picked him up.

Deacon watched as she fed him, changed him, and settled him. It really was a full-time job.

She cooed him back to sleep and excused herself. "I'm going to notify the doctors she's waking up. Page me if you need me."

"Thank you," Deacon said as he relaxed back into his chair. He thought about calling Samuel, but then Marianne squeezed his fingers again and her eyelids opened like they were being dragged up, ever so slowly.

"Hey," Deacon said with a smile. "Wake up."

After a few attempts her eyes stayed open, but a look of confusion crept into them and raged like a sandstorm.

Deacon kept talking to her, telling her he was there and her baby was waiting to meet her. Her eyes finally cleared, and he saw a flicker of recognition in her eyes. And then fear.

"What happened?" she asked, gulping in air, her eyes wide and wild.

Deacon rested a hand on her forearm, rubbing it up and down, and squeezed her hand. "Shh. Everything is okay, I promise."

"I don't remember. What happened to him?" she croaked, forcing out the words, and tears began streaming down her cheek.

"He's over there. He's a beautiful, healthy baby boy," Deacon said softly, wanting to alleviate her pain.

She began sobbing—and, without thinking, he stood over her, folding her into his chest. When her tears slowed, he pulled back, wiping her wet cheeks.

"Where is he?" she asked again, either not remembering or not comprehending that Deacon had already told her.

Deacon wasn't sure if she was strong enough to hold him, but he didn't give a damn right now—he'd support the boy with her. He walked over to the bassinet, lifted the baby as he'd watched the nurse do so often, and cradled him in his arms.

Tears dripped from Marianne's chin—tears of joy.

She held out her hands and Deacon laid the baby on her chest as she wrapped her arms around him. Deacon sat on the edge of the bed, his hands on Marianne's arms, just in case.

She kissed the top of the boy's head over and over, and whispered something to him. Deacon couldn't make out what it was, and he didn't want to know. It was a private moment between a mother and son.

She closed her eyes, resting her cheek on the crown of his head and inhaled deeply. The little boy opened his eyes, sighed, and closed them again.

Eventually, Marianne spoke. "I thought I'd lost him," she whispered, as if it were a confession.

Deacon shook his head. He wondered how much she knew, at some deep, unconscious level, but he knew there would be time to give her all the details later.

She laid the boy in her outstretched arms for a short while, looking over him, her eyes full of wonder, and then laid him back on her chest.

In that moment, he thought that Marianne deserved better. She deserved to have a husband here with her, someone to experience the joy with, someone to shed the tears of happiness with. He couldn't give her that, but he could give her something else he knew many new mothers had.

"Do you want me to take a few photos?" he asked, not sure what her response would be.

She blinked, appearing confused at first—not surprising, given what she'd been through. Deacon knew she must be feeling terribly exhausted.

"That would be nice, thank you . . . I can't imagine what I look like, though," she said, and he saw the insecurity in her eyes. Vulnerability. It was rare for Marianne to be so open.

"You look beautiful," Deacon said, and he meant every word.

"And you're a liar, Deacon Thomas," she said, beaming that enchanting smile she wore so well.

The one that tugged at his heart, wishing for things he didn't deserve.

29

JAMES

James peered through the glass, listening for any noise behind him. He didn't want to go in yet, but he wasn't sure how long he could stand at the door before a nurse caught him spying. Because spying was exactly what he was doing, and if he hadn't seen Deacon and Marianne with his own eyes, he wouldn't have believed it.

He'd been testing Deacon for weeks, putting him in situations and monitoring his actions. He'd noticed the connection between Marianne and his brother, but it was only watching them together now that he realized how deep it ran. What made it more obvious than anything else was the way Deacon looked at Marianne. It wasn't a heated, lustful gaze—it was one of deep longing.

James wondered if Deacon was aware of the extent of his feelings, though. He worried his brother's awareness of them had been buried deep in his pain.

Not wanting to interrupt them, James fled to the café and ordered a few coffees. It took several minutes, and when he returned to Marianne's room, Deacon was seated in the corner once more while the baby nurse sat on the edge of Marianne's bed.

"Hey," James said, passing Deacon a coffee as he strode toward

Marianne's bed. "I'm very glad to see you awake," he said, kissing her cheek.

"Me too," she said with a shaky voice.

"You did good," James said, dropping his eyes to the little bundle in her arms.

"At some point one of you is going to tell me what happened; Deacon continues to effectively deflect the question," she said, more strength in her voice now.

James beamed a smile. "In good time. You just need to rest. Have your doctors been in?" James asked, even though he knew the answer.

"Yes, maybe . . . I don't know how long ago," she said, frowning.

"About twenty minutes ago," Deacon said, offering no more information.

James really wanted to read the doctor's notes. They had about four more hours until they had to move her.

The door behind him opened and another medical team entered. James seized the opportunity to talk to his brother privately.

"We'll be back in a minute," James said, and when he turned, Deacon was already standing.

They stood in the small space behind the closed doors of her room, but didn't walk through the next set of doors, which led to the hallway where their men were positioned as discreetly as possible. The tiny hallway they stood in provided a conveniently private space for them.

"How is she really?" James asked.

Deacon shrugged. "She wasn't good when she woke up, but that's to be expected. She was confused, and she'd thought she'd lost the baby. She's improved dramatically over the last hour. This medical team"—he motioned toward her room—"is going to get her up and moving and assess her strength. We should have a good idea afterward of how easy it's going to be to move her."

"Good," James said. "Two teams are at the Boston house, prepping it, and we've secured a medical team—they'll be there in a few hours. I'll take Kaela; you, Marianne, and the baby will leave from here."

Deacon nodded. "Is Josh's team staying behind at the hospital?"

"Yes—let's see who comes looking for her. Do you think it's too early to show her Henry Greene's face this afternoon?" James asked. If she didn't recognize him, it would mean nothing to her. But there was a chance she might recognize him, and her reaction could be distressing. That was the last thing she needed right now.

Deacon chewed on his bottom lip. "I don't know. Let's see how she is in another hour."

"All right. Are you okay to stay? I want to head back to Thomas Security and organize a few final things," James said, speaking a half-truth.

Deacon held up his coffee. "I'm good now."

"The miracle of the coffee bean," James mused, peering through the glass once again. Marianne was standing on her own, taking small, shuffling steps around the room.

Good. Very good.

The doctors were worried about postpartum hemorrhaging and potential damage to her heart muscle from the cardiac arrests, without even considering any other side effects related to her delivery. But he knew one thing about Marianne: she was tough.

The brothers watched the medial assessment from the glass window and then accosted the medical staff as soon as they exited.

"How is she?" James asked, polite but straight to the point.

"Surprisingly good, all things considered. She's weak, but that's to be expected. Her surgical wounds are healing nicely—no infection. Her blood results from this morning are better. She needs to rest, but she also needs regular periods of mobility. Short, assisted walks every few hours at least, if she's not sleeping. I'm weaning her off all pain meds, but she can take the prescribed pills as she feels the need," he said.

The team exited to the main hallway just as both his and Deacon's phones vibrated.

Incoming call: Samuel.

30

DEACON

"Samuel," he said, beating his brother to it. James connected in on the call, which saved them putting it on speaker.

"It looks like Sonoma's team is headed to New York. The two identified men booked flights an hour ago, and they're scheduled to leave in two. They'll be in Manhattan in ten hours," Samuel said quickly. "We don't know they're coming for her, but we also don't know they're not."

"We're moving her," James and Deacon said in unison.

"I thought that would be your answer. Deacon, everything is on standby for you. James, likewise. We're ready to move at a moment's notice," Samuel said, sounding like an army commander.

"I'm going now," James said. "We don't know if anyone knows the apartment's location, so let's at least move Kaela out so Marianne isn't stressing about her. Josh will back up Deacon if he needs it."

"I'll keep you updated," Samuel said, before signing off.

Given Marianne's physical and emotional state, which was completely normal and understandable with what she'd been through, Deacon knew he had to proceed cautiously. He needed her calm and cooperative. Deacon slid his phone back into his pocket.

James put one hand on his shoulder before turning. "I'll go to Marianne's apartment. Be careful."

"You, too," Deacon said, returning to Marianne's room.

She eyeballed him as soon as he walked in. "Is something wrong?"

"No," Deacon lied. "Just our usual check-ins. The doctors are very happy with your progress."

"My heart stopped twice," she said, giving him a pointed look. "At what point were you going to tell me this?"

Deacon leaned against the end of her bed, crossing his arms over his chest. "Not the minute you woke up."

She opened her mouth to speak, but her attention was quickly stolen by the infant cradled in her arms. She brushed her fingertips over the crown of his hair, and he settled.

"Do you know what you're going to name him?" Deacon asked.

"Yes," she said softly. "His name is Theodore. *Theo*. God's gift." She gazed at her son, and her words raised so many questions in Deacon's mind, but he asked none of them.

"You must wonder about Kaela's name, right?" she asked, looking back at him.

Deacon had wondered about it a million times. "It's crossed my mind," he said, and she smiled wanly.

"I didn't know about Mak at that time. Eric had insisted upon the name, and I thought it was beautiful. When I found out the truth, my first thought was to stab him while he slept," she said with a weary smile.

Deacon didn't react.

"I'm not joking," she said, and Deacon believed her. "I really thought I might kill him. It was then I started calling her Kaela instead."

"I wouldn't have blamed you for sticking one in him while he slept," Deacon said with a grin, but he wasn't joking either.

She scoffed. "One? I wanted to slay that bastard."

A chuckle slipped through his lips.

While her mood was light, and she appeared well, Deacon made the decision to show her the photograph.

"What?" she asked, her eyes narrowing.

"I need to show you something. Samuel found a photograph of Henry Greene. Do you want to see it now, or do you want to wait?"

"Wait for what?" she asked, genuinely confused.

"Until you're feeling better."

"Show me," she said, holding out her hand. Deacon withdrew his phone, unlocked it, and loaded the photo. He sat on the edge of Marianne's bed and passed it to her.

Her forehead creased, and she pursed her lips. She recognized him.

Deacon's heart raced. This could be good.

She lowered the phone into her lap. "I never knew his name was Henry Greene," she said.

Deacon held his breath.

"I knew him as Aiden Michael . . . He's Lucian's stepbrother."

"Was he a part of Saratani?" Deacon asked.

"Not exactly," she said. "He was an advisor—a business consultant—but he never formally joined."

Deacon's mind was churning out questions faster than he could ask them. "How did you know he was Lucian's stepbrother? Was this common knowledge?"

She shook her head. "No, it wasn't. I'd met him and had dinner with him several times before I knew. I stumbled across it while spying on Eric. It was the strangest thing . . . On Eric's computer I found a diagram—a family tree. Eric was mapping Lucian's heritage. I have no idea why, and I couldn't ask him about it without him becoming suspicious. Regardless, that's how I found out, because Aiden's name was on the diagram."

Why would Eric map Lucian's heritage? For Lucian?

Nothing about that made sense.

"Interesting," Deacon said. "What else do you know about him?"

Marianne sighed. "Unfortunately, not a lot. He was based in London at that time, so I'd only met him on a few occasions. He was introduced as a business associate. It wasn't uncommon that I'd attend such dinners with Eric."

"Was Aiden married?" Deacon asked.

Marianne raised an eyebrow in apparent disgust. "No. He preferred Botoxed women who could barely keep their breasts in their dresses. He changed them as often as he changed his underwear —or one would hope."

Deacon grinned. "I see. Did he ever mention previously having a wife?"

She titled her head, thoughtfully. "No. But there was a name on the diagram, because they had a son together. I never met him, though. Why do you keep asking about a wife?"

"Because the woman he had the son with appears to be missing, and has been for many, many years. We don't know if that's because her death was left unreported, or if there's another reason."

"And you're concerned about her why, exactly?" Marianne searched his eyes.

"Curious would be a better word," Deacon said. "Do you have any thought as to why Eric would've been mapping Lucian's heritage?"

"Other than Lucian asking him to, no—not a single one," she said.

Deacon didn't have one either, and his thoughts were interrupted by Samuel's call.

"I'll be back in a minute," Deacon said, ignoring the heat of Marianne's eyes as he stepped outside the room.

"Big fucking problem," Samuel said. "Sonoma is already in Manhattan. I received a CCTV alert—he's at a café about two miles from the hospital."

Deacon's heart skipped a beat. "What? How is that possible?"

"I don't know, but I think someone boarded the flight in his place, which makes me wonder about the two friends that are supposedly still coming."

Deacon's mind had gone in exactly the same direction.

"Where's James?" Deacon asked.

"At Marianne's apartment, about to put Kaela and the babysitter into a car."

"Good. Do you have a trace on Sonoma?"

"Yes. He's on foot. Right now, he appears to be heading toward you, but it's impossible to confirm."

"I'm moving her now," Deacon said. "Alert James and the team. Oh, and by the way—Henry Greene is Lucian's stepbrother. Aiden Michael."

"What? I did not see that coming," Samuel said. "I'm on it. Get out of there, Deacon."

31

MARIANNE

Marianne breathed in the exhilarating scent of her newborn. *Theo.* She wished she could bottle it up forever.

Hey, little man.

She gazed down as he opened his eyes. He was perfect, beautiful —despite being a product of his father.

You'll be nothing like him. I'll make sure of it.

She felt the strong pull, the need, to close her eyes and go back to sleep, but she'd already missed so much of his first days that she didn't want to miss another minute.

He was tiny, smaller than Kaela had been. She wondered who had bought these clothes for him, because she knew she hadn't bought this size—she hadn't expected to deliver early.

The doors to her room, which had been so busy in the last few hours you could have mistaken them for the doors of a hotel lobby, swung open once again, and Deacon strolled in.

"Good news," he said with a charming smile. "That was your doctor. He said you're well enough to be transported to the Thomas Security hospital."

She couldn't tell if he was joking or not. "What?"

"We've set up a hospital for you, in a house we own. Now that little Theo has arrived and you're awake, we want to move you out of Manhattan to somewhere safer. A medical team is waiting there, and it's not far from a good hospital. It's the best place for you both to be. James is in a car with Kaela now—they're meeting us there."

She studied him, trying to read between the lines, but her mind was hazy. "Has something changed?"

"Yes—you've delivered your baby, and you're awake," he said. "A nurse is coming in to help you change. You need to wear something warmer."

"Why right now?" she pressed, more sure of her thoughts now.

What is he hiding?

A nurse walked in, but her demeanor indicated none of the suspicion Marianne felt. Perhaps the nurse was unaware of the urgency Marianne was feeling.

"I'll be back in five minutes," Deacon said, passing the nurse a bag that had been sitting next to his chair. Marianne hadn't even noticed it earlier.

"Can I take him?" the nurse asked. Marianne nodded, and then watched her put Theo back in his bassinet. Her arms instantly felt empty. "Now, let's see what we have here," she said, and Marianne was at least pleased to see that whoever had packed for her had done a decent job.

The nurse helped her out of her gown and into a soft bra, a sleeveless shirt and a cashmere sweater. Slowly, Marianne swung her legs over the side of the bed, as the nurse helped her pull on the matching cashmere sweatpants. She wasn't sure about being moved right now, but she immediately felt better wearing her own clothes. She should've insisted upon it hours ago when the nurse had helped her bathe. She would have, had Deacon advised her he had a set of clothes. She wondered who had packed her bags.

Not long after she was dressed, Deacon came in, pushing a wheelchair.

"I can walk a little," she said, but wondered how far she'd actually make it.

"I know, but we're going up a few floors," he said, taking her arm and gently maneuvering her into the wheelchair.

Up a few floors? Were they underground? She was confused.

The nurse laid two blankets over her legs as Josh strolled in.

"Hey, hey, hey," he said with a dazzling grin. "You look a million times better."

"Thank you," she said. Her last memory prior to waking up in the hospital was of Josh catching her outside her bedroom, with blood pouring down her legs. Marianne cringed internally. She wished he hadn't seen her like that. If he was uncomfortable, though, he didn't give a single indication he was.

To Marianne's surprise, a woman came in and picked up Theo. Judging by the way the team was coordinated, she knew the woman was part of her security even though she'd never seen her before. Josh pushed the wheelchair, and Deacon led them out. As they turned into the main hallway, Marianne recognized her security team littered about inconspicuously. They were sitting on the chairs, and standing in the adjoining hallways. Some of them she recognized, and some of them she didn't. Were there more here than normal? It was a public place, so Marianne supposed there could be more, and it wouldn't be out of the ordinary for Thomas Security.

After they passed two exit signs, Marianne asked, "Where are we going?"

"We're going the long way." Another vague, deflective response on Deacon's part.

The motion of the wheelchair made her feel faint and slightly nauseated, but she did her best to ignore it. She closed her eyes, trying to concentrate on not being sick, when she realized Deacon had moved from beside her to directly in front of her.

Her eyes sprung open, searching for Theo.

Something is wrong.

32

DEACON

"Take the next left," Samuel instructed via Deacon's earpiece. Deacon followed, not daring to ask himself how things had gotten so out of control so quickly. He was focused on only one thing now: getting Marianne and Theo to the hospital rooftop alive.

"I've lost them," Samuel said, his voice a picture of agony. *"They went into a hallway with no surveillance—"*

"They're not working alone," Deacon whispered, hoping Marianne couldn't hear him.

According to Samuel's CCTV footage, Sonoma himself was still making his way to the hospital, but some of his friends were already here. On the same floor. Coming for them.

Samuel hadn't been able to confirm how many of Sonoma's men were in the hospital, but he'd been able to identify two of them because Samuel had already had intel on them—they'd been there on the night of Nicole's murder. Deacon doubted the two men were alone; they had more friends inside the hospital—he was sure of it.

An alert had been raised when one of the security team by the elevators had been rendered unconscious. Things had spiraled out of control since then. It was only when Samuel had been able to identify the men via some of the cameras they'd installed that they knew what they were dealing with, but they still didn't have the full picture.

"I've found them!" Samuel said. *"On the east side. There's no security team between you and them, Deacon!"*

Deacon turned again, his pace quickening once more. He wondered at what point Marianne had been identified, but quickly refocused his mind. His job right now was to protect her and her son. That was all that mattered.

"Deacon, they're tracking you. Someone is tagged," Samuel said, and Deacon swore under his breath.

He saw an empty room to the left and darted in there.

He knew none of his men would have been tracked, and Marianne had been watched over without pause, so that only left one option—Theo. He grabbed the boy as gently as he could from Leah's arms and laid him on the bed. Deacon pulled a tracking detector from his back pocket and hovered it over him.

"What is going on?" Marianne demanded, her voice cutting through the silent room.

Deacon ignored her, working quickly to unwrap Theo. His pulse was drumming in his ears; they were on borrowed time and they needed to move—now. Theo started crying, and Marianne tried to stand but Josh held her down.

"Deacon!"

The device beeped. *Got it.* He pulled the tracker off the baby blanket and passed it to Leah. With a single nod, she disappeared. Deacon didn't analyze who could've placed the tracker right now, there would be time for that later—he prayed. He wrapped Theo up and handed him back to Marianne as quickly as he could. Adrenaline would give her enough strength to hold her baby, and he hoped that in his mother's arms, Theo would settle down. A crying baby would give them away in seconds.

He kneeled in front of Marianne, looking into her scared eyes. There was no point hiding the reality from her now.

"We're vacating. We're going up to the rooftop because someone is following us. I will get you both out of here. Trust me," he said.

She swallowed like she had eaten an apple whole. She nodded.

"Let's go, now," Deacon said, turning on his heels. He pulled the door ajar, just enough to peer through the opening. The hallway was clear, but he knew it wasn't going to be in about thirty seconds. Theo was beginning to calm, but they didn't have time to wait for him to quiet down completely. They had to move.

"Tracker relocated," Leah said.

Deacon took the next right, and Leah reappeared beside them. With every step, Deacon focused on his breath, refusing to panic.

Stay focused.

"Deacon!" Samuel screamed, but the warning came a split second too late.

A man stepped into their path at the end of the hallway, blocking them. Deacon reacted on instinct and drew his weapon. He fired it immediately, and the man dropped down to his knees.

Deacon had used a silencer, but they could only do so much, and the screams still followed—staff and patients came running in all directions. He hadn't wanted to terrify the entire ward, but the chaos worked in their favor. Deacon kept his eyes on the man long enough to make sure he wasn't getting back up then took the next hallway, worried someone else was coming up behind them. They were almost running now, and it was hard to hear Samuel's voice over the shouting staff and Theo's lung-burning cries. Deacon tuned it all out.

Focus.

His eyes darted constantly, looking for anyone acting unusual, anyone he recognized.

He saw the elevators ahead. Thirty feet separated them.

Deacon's eyes swept over the crowd again, and he made the call as the elevator doors opened.

"Run!" Deacon said as he sprinted toward the doors, pressing his hands against them until Marianne was inside.

As the doors closed, a familiar pair of eyes looked into his, and it took everything in Deacon to stay present and focused, to not go back to the night of Nicole's murder. The man drew his weapon, but Deacon was faster. He fired two shots, but the man didn't go down without returning fire. Deacon tensed as he prepared for the bullets to hit him, but the elevator doors closed just in time and he heard the dull *ting* of metal on metal. Deacon exhaled a shaky sigh as he turned to look over everyone, making sure there weren't any injuries.

The poor old gentleman in the back corner could hardly stand on his trembling legs.

"Sorry, sir. We'll make sure you get out of the hospital safely," Deacon said as the elevator stopped mid-descent, and then began to ascend. Samuel had taken control.

"Rooftop remains secure," Samuel said.

Deacon felt the tension ease slightly—they had been overdue for some good news.

He glanced at Marianne, who had a million question in her eyes and a crying baby in her arms. She rocked him back and forth, but Theo was about as pleased with this situation as Deacon was.

The elevator doors opened and three of Deacon's men stood like a fortress in front of them.

"Make sure the old man gets out safely," Deacon said over his shoulder as they began running down the long passage. Deacon opened the door to the helipad, and a burst of frigid air stung his face. More men moved in around them, helping Marianne and Theo into the helicopter while Deacon jumped into the pilot's seat. He went through the pre-flight checks with rapidity, Samuel already confirming the flight path, before powering up his favorite toy.

Deacon looked over his shoulder as his team fastened Marianne's belt.

"Can you can fly this?" she asked, biting her lip with worry.

He gave her his most charming smile, hoping it would calm her. "Trust me."

When everyone was strapped in, Josh closed the door, banged his palm against the glass twice, and retreated toward the rooftop door. He would go back inside and find out exactly what had happened and where the breaches had occurred—and find any of Sonoma's friends that were still inside.

Deacon focused on the control panels, brought the helicopter to a hover, then raised it up.

"*You're clear to go,*" Samuel said, his voice now coming through Deacon's headphones.

"Copy," Deacon said, easing his hand down on the controls.

They were safe.

For now.

33

JAMES

James held Kaela's hand as they stood at the window.

"Look," James said, kneeling beside her and pointing at the bright lights in the dark sky.

"They're coming!" she squealed, jumping up and down.

James laughed. "They're coming," he said, and another wave of relief washed over him. It had been a close call, too close, and he really wanted to speak to Deacon. His brother hadn't just had to get them out of the situation, he'd also had to protect them from the men who had murdered his girlfriend. One of which Deacon had put a bullet in tonight.

James wrestled against a squirming Kaela as she tried to run out to the helicopter pad. "They're coming inside," he said, but she wasn't having it. Once the propellers were still, James opened the door and let her run out. The security team looked to James, but he just shrugged his shoulders—admitting defeat.

"You're weak," one of his staff said to him as he walked past, and James grinned.

"Mommy! Mommy!" Kaela screamed all the way to the helicopter.

Leah helped Marianne down and she knelt on the ground as Kaela ran into her arms.

Kaela started crying, which James hadn't been expecting. "Don't ever leave me again," he heard her say.

Marianne pulled her daughter into her chest. "I missed you."

Leah was cradling Theo, and James was surprised how relaxed and natural she appeared.

Interesting.

"Do you want to meet your little brother?" Marianne asked, her face alive with happiness.

"Yes!" Kaela asked, clapping her hands together.

Marianne reached for Theo, and Leah laid him in her arms. While the happy family reunion was taking place, James searched out Deacon, who was completing paperwork for Samuel.

"Are you all right?" James asked.

Deacon bit his lip. "I'll be all right," he said as he signed the document and handed the clipboard to one of the team.

James recalled what he'd seen earlier at the hospital, and for the first time thought that his brother really would be all right—in time. He looked over his shoulder as the security team escorted Marianne and her children inside. "I'll debrief with Samuel. Take a shower, have something to eat, and nap for a few hours. I'll be in the office when you're ready."

"Thanks," Deacon said, following the entourage inside, but hanging back—deliberately, James thought.

Their lives were changing.

All of them.

❧

James made sure everyone was settled inside the house and that Marianne's medical team had everything they needed before retreating to the office. He'd barely closed the door before he was calling Samuel's number again. He'd lost track of how many times they'd spoken in the last twenty-four hours.

"How is Deacon?" Samuel asked.

"He's okay, I think," James said. Deacon had gone straight to one of the guest rooms, and he hadn't resurfaced. Even though the kill had been quick, without a single word being exchanged, James knew how hard it was for Deacon to look at the faces of Nicole's murderers on the screen in Samuel's office. Looking into their eyes in person would've left him more than a little rattled.

"Good. So, Josh has handed in his final report. On our team, there's a few minor injuries but nothing that requires more than a few stitches. From what he's been able to ascertain, they had nine men at the hospital. Two killed by Deacon, another three by Josh's team. The others escaped but we have some video footage of them, so at least I can work on profiling them. I've dealt with the authorities, but of course the press have picked it up. Enforcements are going to label it a drug-theft crime, so hopefully the story will fade into the horizon and never rise again."

"The four that weren't killed, were they injured?" James asked.

"Two are, and one has a gunshot to the abdomen, so if luck is on our side, the death toll might rise within the next few hours. I haven't seen any of them resurface as yet but that's to be expected. They'll lie low for a few days."

"Do we have a trace on Sonoma?"

Samuel sighed. "No. He went into the subway and never resurfaced."

James didn't like that at all. "Now, the question is, how did they find out she was there?"

"That is the ultimate mystery. We all agreed it wasn't ideal to keep her in a public place, in one ward, for so long—and we paid the price for it. It had to be someone that dealt directly with Marianne, but so far I can't find any links. I've double-checked everything on the baby nurse and she's clean. I'm widening the search, and I should have an update within the next few hours.

"Someone, somehow connected to this group or to Greene, either worked in the hospital or was visiting someone. Perhaps they heard gossip; perhaps they recognized security."

James sat on the windowsill, gazing over the manicured gardens that resembled a children's storybook maze. He had no idea who maintained them, but they were immaculate. "So, we don't have a lot to go on at the moment." It was a pitiful summary.

"That's about right," Samuel said, clearing his throat. "I am working on the Lucian-stepbrother connection, and I'm currently profiling every relative. There was a reason Eric was looking into the man's heritage. He was a madman, but he wasn't stupid. It may not be relevant to this at all, because being Lucian's stepbrother is cause enough for a retaliation hit—even without Eric making a deal with Aiden. The question is: how do we rescind this contract?"

"I'm not sure yet," James said, but keeping Marianne hidden would buy them time. "Where is Josh now?"

"He's put the team on a six-hour break, and then they'll leave for Boston."

James glanced at the solid brick wall that surrounded the property and the dark clouds that hung above.

"Let me know when they leave," James said before ending the call.

He looked up to the storm clouds settling in, glad Deacon had arrived before the bad weather. He wondered what kind of storm was raging in his brother's mind.

34

DEACON

He needed air. He needed to go outside and away from what felt like a million other people in this house, even though there were probably only fifty or so. He laced up his sneakers, grabbed his phone and pistol, and slid out into the hallway. He took the service stairs the housekeepers had used many years ago when this old mansion had actually been lived in and exited through the back door.

He wrapped his arms around his chest, protecting himself from the whistling wind, and walked through the rose gardens to the back fence. He nodded at security but kept walking, not in the mood to make small talk. If there was a security concern, they'd let him know.

He followed the dirt trail that led into the woods, and once his limbs had warmed a little, he started running. He'd run this trail a few times before and knew where he was going.

Perhaps because it was so cold, or because he'd subconsciously done it for so many years, his mind shut down. After the past twenty-four hours, silence was a welcome reprieve.

Deacon slowed down as he neared the lake. The frozen ice sparkled like facets of a diamond, and he sat on one of the large boulders, catching his breath.

The man he'd shot from the elevator had been one of Nicole's murderers—the one who had tied her up. Deacon had seen the flash of recognition in the man's eyes when he'd looked at him.

Deacon sighed, dragging his hands over his face as the image of Nicole in her bloodstained gown flashed in his mind.

Her voice, and the softness in her eyes, had been a complete contrast to her physical appearance.

It was just a dream. Forget it.

A shiver crawled up his spine, and he wrapped his arms around his waist, trying to keep warm. He tilted his head back, gazing at the clusters of dark clouds. He had to go back to the house soon.

An alert chimed on his phone. It was Josh's final report. Deacon tapped on the screen, opening it.

He read through the written report first. The fact that they'd put the tracker on Theo's blanket made him livid. He hoped they found out who was responsible for that—and soon.

Next he opened the image files. Deacon didn't recognize the man he'd shot in the hallway. He concluded he was a newer recruit to the team, or maybe he hadn't been there that night.

The report was brief, which was to be expected at this stage, but Samuel and his team would build on it over the next few hours.

The goal now was to keep Marianne safe until she was well enough to move to their next destination.

The lake glistened as the sun peered out from behind the stormy clouds. It disappeared as quickly as it had come, and if Deacon had blinked he would've missed the magical moment.

There is always a silver lining.

Those were the words his mother had always spoken to them when they'd bitched and whined as teenagers. He was still waiting to see the silver lining of Nicole's death.

He closed the report, but before he tucked the phone back into his pocket, he loaded the photographs of Marianne and Theo. He looked over them once, messaged them to her, and then deleted them —eliminating the temptation to look at them again. He jogged all the way home, arriving just as the rain began to fall.

He nodded again as he passed security, feeling more settled after his run. When he entered the house, he went straight to his favorite room: the kitchen.

They'd hired two chefs for the immediate future and Deacon was very interested to see how good they were.

"Hello," he said, stripping off his crewneck.

"What would you like to eat? I can make you anything," an elderly man asked, his wispy brown hair poking out from underneath his white chef's hat. He even had a white chef's coat to match, which amused Deacon. He supposed it was normal when catering for wealthy families, but he never thought of them in that manner. They cared less about materials things than most people; perhaps they saw life and death so often that it was easy to stay grounded in what really mattered.

"Anything?" Deacon chuckled. "That's a very dangerous thing to say to me. I'll have you cooking for the next ten hours straight." He sat down on the stool, eyeing the burgers that were cooking on the hot plate.

"One to start?" the chef asked, following his gaze.

Deacon salivated. "Please."

A laugh rumbled from the chef's throat. "I'll make it two, on the larger side."

"You're a good man," Deacon said. He helped himself to the refrigerator, pouring both a glass of juice and a glass of water, then returned to his stool.

"I thought I'd find you here," James said, sneaking up behind Deacon. "I'll have whatever he's having," he said to the chef, who nodded, flipping the burgers.

"Did I miss anything?" Deacon asked, before taking a swallow of his apple juice.

James flashed a guilty smile. "I wouldn't know. I've been hiding in the office away from the noise. It's double trouble now."

Deacon scoffed. "Yes, it is."

James had an odd look in his eye, and Deacon thought to question it, but then the chef slid a mouth-watering plate in front of him and all was forgotten. His stomach growled so loudly the chef laughed again.

James's burgers were served up a minute later, and they ate in silence.

"What's for dessert?" Deacon asked when he'd finished.

The chef gave a smile that stretched over his face, and Deacon knew they were in for a treat. He disappeared into the walk-in cooler and came back with Deacon's favorite: chocolate cake with a scoop of ice cream and berries.

"It's a damn good thing I just went for a run," he said, unable to take his eyes off the plate in front of him. "What would it take for you not to serve that to anyone else?"

The chef passed him a fork. "I can be persuaded," he joked, but the first thought to cross Deacon's mind was that Samuel had better have done his due diligence. James was likely thinking the same thing.

"I'll pay you double," James said quickly.

Once James had manipulated the chef into serving him a piece of cake also, they retreated to the office, passing a blaring television and a crying baby.

See? James mouthed.

Deacon closed the office door and swore he heard James exhale in relief.

This is going to be hilarious.

"I've read Samuel's report," Deacon said, now getting straight to business. "I don't have anything to add."

"You handled it really well, Deacon. That was . . . close," he finally said.

"Too close was what it was." *Far too close.*

"And we both know every single situation can't be controlled. You managed it better than anyone could've, especially under the circumstances," James said, and Deacon knew his brother meant that.

"The question is, what do we do from here?" Deacon asked.

"I think we lie low for the next week or so, depending on how

Marianne recovers. As soon as she's well enough, I think we should move again. The more time we can buy to figure out this contract the better."

Deacon nodded, then looked at his phone when it vibrated. "Hi, Samuel," he said.

"Hey. I have some intel for you . . . an image of Tom Ford."

Deacon had had enough for one day. He sighed. "Send it to my phone."

Deacon's finger shook as he tapped the screen, ready to look at the face of the man who had caused him so much pain.

Blond hair. Square jaw. Green eyes. Mole next to his ear.

Deacon's heart bled all over again.

~

Raindrops battered against the window pane, and the wind howled through the house. The inside of Deacon's mind wasn't much different.

Knock-knock.

"Come in," he said, not expecting Marianne to enter.

"Hi. Do you have a minute?" she asked, and it was difficult for Deacon to believe she'd just had a baby, especially under the circumstances. The whites of her eyes were clear again, and her hair was tousled high in a bun, highlighting her strong cheekbones.

"Sure, take a seat," he said, wondering where this was going. She didn't give him long to ponder it.

"I want to talk about what happened at the hospital. I asked to be kept informed of my case, and there were men in the hospital— coming for me—and you didn't tell me. Why?" she asked.

Her chin was tilted up and her shoulders were back—Deacon noted it was her defensive stance.

"I didn't tell you because you'd only just woken up that morning. I needed you calm and relaxed, not panicked. I made a judgment call like I would for any other client," Deacon said. "Yes, when it's a case like yours, it's usually advantageous to keep the client informed. In that situation, it wasn't. I didn't know how you were going to react, and although you didn't, it would've been understandable if you'd panicked and shut down. You'd just woken up a few hours earlier."

Marianne wasn't satisfied with that answer, he could tell.

"I understand that, but I don't appreciate it," she said sternly. "In the future, I want to know exactly what's going on. If something happens at this house, I want to be informed."

"It's the same for every client, Marianne. It was, and still is, the same even for Mak. Being family doesn't change anything, not in a situation like that. This is life and death, and we have to make judgment calls, and we make them. We tell all of our clients this: we make decisions, and sometimes you won't like them, but we stand by them."

She eyeballed him and time seemed to stop. He expected her to push the point, but her change of direction surprised him. "What happens after an event like this? What does the security team do?"

He knew where this was leading now. "They debrief and prepare reports." He anticipated her following question and opened Samuel's report, passing his phone to her.

She took her time reading it.

"Marianne, if you'd had Theo under different circumstances—if you'd had a routine delivery—and the breach at the hospital had happened, I probably would've told you. It's not because I think you're some wallflower who can't handle it. The exact opposite is true," he said, and that was an understatement. "But this situation was unique."

She nodded and passed his phone back. Her face softened. "Are you okay?"

"Yes—why wouldn't I be?" he asked, hoping the conversation wasn't going where he didn't want it to.

"Well, first, if those elevator doors had closed a second later you could've been killed," she said.

"It's not the first time I've been shot at," Deacon said with an arched brow.

"But not by . . ." Marianne paused and Deacon's chest tightened.

"Do you want to talk about it?" she asked quietly.

"No," Deacon said, his tone harsher than he'd intended.

Marianne stood and walked out of the room.

He didn't want to talk about Nicole. He never wanted to talk about her.

35

MARIANNE

Marianne exited the room as quickly as possible without running, and almost cleaned James up in the hallway, which was impressive in itself.

He reached out, grabbing her arms, keeping her upright. "Whoa! Where are you going in such a hurry?" he asked, grinning.

"Sorry! I didn't see you," Marianne said, still catching her breath. James had scared the shit out of her.

"Obviously," he said with a chuckle. "Is Deacon in there?"

"Yeah, though he might not be in a very good mood," she said, and he eyed her keenly.

"And why is that?"

"Because I said something I shouldn't have," she said.

His eyebrows knitted together. "What did you say?"

Marianne lowered her voice. "Deacon showed me the security report. I brought up the men at the hospital . . ."

"Yeah," he said, his eyes darting behind her, "come with me." He led her to the sunroom.

James disappeared and came back with two cups of tea.

"What happened?" he asked.

She wasn't sure if she should tell him, but James had this compelling look in his eyes that was hard to deny. She told him.

"You're right, he's going to be pissed," he said. He turned the teacup with his fingertips while he seemed to look for the right words. "In the time that has passed since Nicole's death, I've let Deacon deal with it however he wants to. Most of the time that's by suppressing every emotion surrounding her and her death. Most people who attempt that break down at some point, but he's too mentally strong for his own good . . . or he has been until now, at least."

"What do you mean?" Marianne asked, wrapping her hands around the teacup, letting it warm her.

"I wonder if I should've pushed him to talk more—maybe it would've helped," he said, shaking his head.

"Do you feel guilty for that?" Marianne asked, not sure she was reading him correctly. She also didn't miss he hadn't answered her first question.

"Some days, but I don't honestly know if it would've helped or not. I want what's best for him. I want him to be happy. Although Deacon doesn't play the victim card, I feel like he's been wronged by life. His life in the military—as a Ranger—his family and friends . . . that was all ripped away from him when we went into hiding. And then he met Nicole, and they were very happy together, then she was ripped away from him too."

"Life's not fair, is it?" she asked.

"No, it's not. But, getting back on track. Yes, he's likely going to be in a foul mood, but I like that you brought it up. I think you'll be good for him . . . for each other."

"Excuse me?" she asked, feeling her cheeks heat up when she saw the look in his eyes.

He smirked. "I've been thinking it's a good thing we haven't introduced you to anyone as our sister. That could potentially get very awkward, don't you think?"

Her mouth hung open.

"Oh, come on," James said. "Who do you think you're trying to pass this by? I'm insulted you underestimate me—that both of you do, because it is two-sided, if you haven't already figured that out. But here's the thing . . ." The playfulness dropped from his voice. "He could fall in love with you, but he doesn't want to feel that way. He'll hate himself for feeling that way, and every time he feels like he's getting too close, he'll pull back. But if he's going to find any peace, any happiness, he's going to have to face the past and push through his pain. He's tried everything else, and to be honest, I think he's in more pain now than he's ever been in."

"Why are you telling me this?" Marianne asked.

"Because I've seen the way he looks at you, particularly when I'm not around," James said, a rare softness to his voice.

"You've been spying on us?" she asked.

James shrugged. "Not exactly, just monitoring the situation."

Marianne let out a high-pitched laugh that sounded more like a cry. "That's a very interesting way of putting it."

He shrugged again—he was making no apologies.

"Have you spoken to him about me?" she asked.

His eyes turned serious. "No, because he's not ready to hear it yet. I will, though, when I think the time is right."

Marianne wondered if that day would ever come.

"Excuse me, Mommy, but I'm hungry,' Kaela said with one hand on her belly.

"So am I," James said with a grin. "Do you want something to eat?" he asked Marianne.

"Uh, sure—just something small. A sandwich, perhaps?" she said. She hadn't been very hungry since leaving the hospital.

"You don't want the burgers and chocolate cake Deacon and I had an hour ago?"

"No," she said with a slight laugh. She was already wondering how long it would take her to get her pre-baby body back. "I don't need burgers and cake."

"I'll have some," Kaela said, earning a true smile from James.

"Sit with your mom, and I'll find you something to eat," James said, and Kaela climbed onto the chair beside Marianne.

She noted the time; she needed to feed Theo soon, but it had taken her an hour to settle him, and she really didn't want to wake him just yet.

James returned carrying a tray. He looked like he was hosting high tea, an amusing thought.

He put the tray down and Marianne picked out a couple sandwiches while Kaela went straight for the iced cupcake. Among the things she'd inherited from her father was a sweet tooth. Marianne put three miniature sandwiches on her plate and gave her a look. She nodded, cunningly—a look of her own that told Marianne she'd eat them in her own time. Kaela inherited that look from her father, too, and in those moments Marianne feared raising her daughter alone without someone, a father figure, to help guide Kaela.

"Mm, mm," Kaela said, and James cracked up laughing. He seemed to find Kaela's antics highly amusing, and that's because he only had to spend hours with her at a time. By laughing at her he was encouraging her bad behavior, but Marianne didn't care—she wanted them to spend time together.

Deacon walked into the room, his stride casual and relaxed. She lifted her eyes, but they didn't meet his. He didn't look at her directly, not once, which made her uneasy. She focused on Kaela, hyper-aware of the conversation she'd just had with James. She wondered what Deacon would've thought of it.

"Just in time for round two," James said as Deacon sat between his brother and Kaela. Kaela passed him a plate and started putting things on it for him, much like Marianne had done for Kaela.

"Kaela! Deacon can choose what he wants to eat," Marianne said. "Sorry, I did that for her a minute ago."

Deacon still didn't look at Marianne, but he did chuckle. "That's okay, I'll eat anything." He looked to Kaela. "What's good?"

With a huge grin, and a mouth stuffed with food, she pointed to the cupcakes.

It was hard to see them together, especially after the conversation she'd just had with James, so Marianne looked away quickly—but she didn't miss the knowing smile on James's lips.

36

DEACON

The mechanical tick-tock of the wall clock echoed in his ears. It was as relentless as the thoughts in his mind. He felt unsettled. Uneasy. And a multitude of factors contributed to that.

Tom Ford's face loitered in his mind like an unwelcome guest. He couldn't block out the man's face, no matter how hard he tried. He hadn't even looked at the photograph a second time—he didn't need to. It was seared into his memory, for all eternity, likely.

And Marianne. His body tensed even now as he thought back to their conversation. She knew he hated talking about it, and yet she'd pushed him anyway. He rubbed the back of his neck, tilting his head to the ceiling. A strained sigh escaped his lips—a representation of exactly how he felt inside. The conversation had irked him, but interestingly, he wasn't as angry as he'd expected to be.

He shook his head, shaking the thoughts away.

Forget it. It doesn't matter.

He returned his attention to the reports on his desk. The house was quiet and while he wasn't technically on night shift—the security teams had it covered—he feared going to sleep. Feared seeing Nicole.

He opened the first folder of reports and didn't look up again until he heard Theo's cries. He listened for Marianne's footsteps in the hallway, but they didn't come. The office was actually a spare bedroom turned office, and they'd intentionally positioned it among the sleeping quarters so that security could be close at all times.

Theo's cries grew louder, but still no footsteps sounded. Deacon stood and went to check Marianne's bedroom. She wasn't there.

Odd.

He eased open the door to Kaela's room, but he could only see one small bump in the bed.

He rushed to the living room and felt the tension melt from his muscles as he saw Marianne asleep on the couch. She'd looked exhausted earlier in the night, and knowing she'd barely slept recently, not to mention she was still recovering, he wasn't surprised.

Was Theo hungry? Did he need to be changed? Deacon had no idea, but he could at least take him to Marianne so she didn't have to get up.

A dim lamp provided enough light that he didn't trip over anything, and he leaned in, lifting the upset boy into his arms.

"Hey, hey," Deacon whispered, "too loud." He laid Theo in one arm and picked up a blanket from the bassinet, not sure if Marianne would need it or not. This was way beyond his level of expertise.

He took two steps toward the door, but Theo quieted, settling in his arms. Deacon pursed his lips, not sure what to do. He didn't want to wake Marianne for nothing. Theo exhaled a whimpered sigh and then closed his eyes. Deacon held him for a few minutes, and then when he was sure Theo was asleep, he tried to place him back in the bassinet.

Theo's eyes snapped open and the crying started. Deacon picked him up quickly, and once again Theo settled.

Deacon tried to put him down again and the same thing happened.

"You're manipulating me," Deacon whispered, shaking his head softly.

He sat down in the armchair, half expecting Theo to cry again—but apparently, so long as he was in someone's arms, he was content.

His little lips pressed together, and while Deacon wasn't sure if he was smiling, it looked like it.

Five minutes. He rested his head back against the chair and closed his eyes.

~

Deacon awoke with a gasp as Theo's shrieks jolted him from his slumber. How long had he been asleep? He stood but quickly realized Theo was no longer playing around. His little cheeks were rosy red, and he wanted something, and he wanted it now. Marianne was still asleep on the couch when he entered, but Theo woke her just like he had Deacon. A glimmer of disorientation crossed over her eyes. "Sorry, I fell asleep. Has he been crying long?"

She moved to get up, but he shook his head, motioning for her to stay put. "Not long," he said, leaving it at that. He passed Theo to her. "What do you need?"

"He's probably hungry," she said.

"I'll get it," Deacon said, walking off before she could refuse. Making a bottle was one of the few things he could do, since the baby nurse had told him how to do it a million times and had written down instructions for them before they left. Deacon didn't know if Marianne had tried to breastfeed or not. It likely would be in her medical records, but he didn't consider it any of his business.

Deacon stood in front of the microwave, watching the bottle go around.

Wow. He never thought he'd be making baby bottles—at least not after Nicole had died.

He was passing the bottle back to Marianne when his phone rang: *Samuel.*

"Do you need anything else?" he asked Marianne as Theo sucked on the nipple, settling.

In that moment, the realization of how much he wanted this life —a family—hit him hard, and so did the bolt of guilt. He wanted to move on, to be happy, but Nicole was never going to get that chance —and so he didn't deserve it, either.

"No, thank you," Marianne said, looking up at him.

He dropped his gaze. "I need to take this call," he said quickly, turning his back to her and all but running from the room.

He closed the office door behind him, leaning his back against it. He squeezed his eyes shut.

That's not your life. She's a client. She's family. That's all.

He turned his attention to what he needed to be focusing on.

"Hi, Samuel," Deacon said, swiveling the black-leather desk chair and taking a seat.

"Hey. I've been working on the Nicolas lead, and I'm sorry, Deacon, but I can't find anything. I've double-checked all of Nicole's email addresses, looked at phone records . . . I have no idea how he would've known you were in Thailand. If you want the answer, I think you're going to have to speak to him yourself."

Deacon leaned his elbows on the desk, pinching the bridge of his nose.

"What do you know about him in terms of his abilities? Does he have any military or weapon training?" Deacon asked. If he was going to pay a visit to Nicholas, he wanted to go alone. He wanted James here with Marianne and the kids. They weren't far enough away from Manhattan for both of them to be gone.

"There's no formal record of training that I can find," Samuel said.

Deacon rubbed one hand over his face. "Okay. Leave it with me. I'll get back to you."

He crossed his arms over his chest, his bones cold. He leaned back in the chair, closing his eyes.

Where had everything gone so wrong?

As he forced his mind to go back to Thailand, his hands grew clammy.

That sickening thud outside the door was the first time he'd known their lives were in danger. But what signs had he missed before that night?

They'd only left the resort for one day. Deacon had chartered a boat to take them around the surrounding islands. They'd spent the morning on the boat, lying on the bow, soaking up the sun, and then jumping into the crystal-clear water to cool off. He remembered Nicole's smile, the way she threw her head back and laughed. The water glistened around her, sparkling, and he remembered thinking she was his silver lining. The only life he'd ever known had been taken away from him, but life had given him her instead.

At noon they'd docked the boat on one of the islands for lunch. Hand in hand, they'd strolled through the vendor stalls. Nicole wore a white, embroidered dress over her bikini and a floppy straw hat she'd bought from one of the vendors. He had taken so many photos of her that day, but they had all been on his phone, which had been destroyed during the attack. On the boat there had been a vivacity in her eyes, in her soul, that he hadn't seen for a long time, and it had filled him with happiness. He couldn't remember ever being that happy. They had stopped for lunch—and then, as they were walking back to the boat, they saw it. A white pergola with vines of flowers wrapping around it. A wedding chapel.

"Come on!" Nicole said, giggling as she pulled him toward it.

"It's a wedding chapel," Deacon said with confusion.

"I know it is. You told me you want to get married," she said, still laughing.

"This isn't quite what I had in mind. I was thinking of something a little more romantic. I don't even have a ring."

"Oh," she'd said, waving her hand, "who cares about that? It'll be fun. Think of it as our practice run. You can propose and do the romantic wedding later."

Her smile left him weak, and there was no way he could refuse her. "Okay, but make up a name. Any name. You can't sign the wedding papers as Nicole."

"I think I'll be . . . Maria Louisa."

Deacon laughed, shaking his head. "That's a ridiculous name."

"It's funny."

And so Maria Louisa and Jack Williams were married at 3:41 in the afternoon.

When Deacon opened his eyes, he was leaning forward, wiping the tears from his cheeks as he fought to breathe. It was the first time he'd let himself remember that day since her death.

At 3:41 they were married, and at 11:55 they were taken at gunpoint.

37

MARIANNE

The nurse sat on the end of her bed, scribbling notes in Marianne's folder. Notes Marianne would read later.

"I really can't believe how quickly you're recovering," she said. "Make sure you don't overdo it. Rest still needs to be a priority."

Marianne smiled warmly, but thought the lady was delusional. When did she think Marianne was going to have time to rest?

"And your blood results are all within their respective normal ranges," she said, scribbling her initials on the paper.

Marianne wondered again what her blood had been transfused with over the years. Eric had infused their alchemized blood with vitamins, as well as vaccinations and perhaps other things Marianne didn't even know about. Most of it would well and truly be out of her system now, except for possibly some of the longer lasting vaccinations.

She'd managed to discreetly decrease her dosages of the alchemized blood over the past several years, but she'd never been able to stop completely. It would've raised too many questions, and it would've been a sign of betrayal. Eric would have seen her façade slipping, and she'd never have been able to do what she had. One of the reasons she'd succeeded at spying on him was because he believed she was so deep in Saratani that the thought of leaving would never have occurred to her. Little did he know that she'd wanted to leave before she'd even met him; after she'd met him, she had prayed for it.

God had taken his time, but he'd answered those prayers. And as she looked around the room, at Kaela building skyscrapers on the floor, and at Theo nestled quietly in his bassinet, she finally understood why God had taken his time.

The nurse closed the folder and folded her hands in her lap. "I don't think I need to be here any longer, unless you want me to stay."

The doctor was staying, just in case, but Marianne was eager for the nurse to leave. She was a nice lady, but the fewer people around her the better. The security she had little control over, but at least they didn't invade her personal space.

"I appreciate everything you've done for me," Marianne said politely. "But I feel well. If you're happy with my recovery, I see no reason for you to stay."

"Try and get some rest. I mean that," she said.

"I will," Marianne lied. Although she had actually had a lot of sleep last night, thanks to Deacon Thomas. Marianne had awoken on the couch with a fright—Theo had been too silent. She knew he was overdue for a feeding but she couldn't hear him and she feared the worst. She'd held her breath as she'd run to her room, only to find her baby asleep in Deacon's arms. The sight had stopped her dead in her tracks, her heart tumbling in a way that made her giddy and brought tears to her eyes. She wasn't sure what chain of events had led to Deacon comforting her baby, but she knew one thing: the sight had made her legs weak in a way she'd never experienced.

The sight of Deacon with her baby, both fast asleep, was very dangerous. It made her want for something she didn't know if she could have.

Even if they tried, were they both too damaged to make it work?

Marianne hadn't seen Deacon this morning, and she wondered if last night was the reason why. Or perhaps he was busy. Although spending time with both James and Deacon was nice, Marianne was under no grand illusion—they were here to work. To protect her and her children. That was the reality.

"Mommy, look," Kaela said, pointing to her rising tower. "Look how high it is."

"I can see," Marianne said as she carefully, slowly, lowered herself onto the floor. While Theo was sleeping, she wanted to give Kaela her full attention. Marianne was worried how Kaela was going to deal with not being the center of attention every minute of every day. She'd reveled in being an only child.

"I think I'll build buildings when I'm older," she said, her little face all serious. "And then I'll live up here." She pointed to the top. The penthouse.

"You'll have a very nice view," Marianne said, wondering where her child came up with these things. At least she was ambitious.

"I'll let you live with me," she said, grinning.

Marianne turned her head to the chuckle at the doorway. James was there, leaning against the doorframe.

"Can I live with you too?" he asked.

Kaela bounced her crossed legs as she considered it. "I think you'll live here. With Mak." She pointed to the level below the penthouse.

James arched a brow, looking rather unimpressed.

Marianne smiled apologetically.

"At least I'll have Mak," he said with an amused grin. "Speaking of, I'm going back to New York for a few nights. Deacon will stay here."

"Okay. Mak called this morning, actually," Marianne said. It had been a nice gesture for her to call, but Marianne wondered if she'd called because she felt she'd had to. Marianne had never really had friends in Saratani; both Lucian and Eric had made sure of it.

"I'm thinking about bringing Mak here at some point, but we'll see..."

James didn't need to finish the sentence, and Marianne didn't blame him for thinking the way he did. He'd come so close to losing her once—she knew he wouldn't take any risk involving her if he didn't need to.

Marianne smiled. "Sure. Give it some time."

"Are we staying here for a long time, Mom?" Kaela asked.

"A little while," Marianne said vaguely. She turned back to James. "Are you leaving now?"

"No, I'll leave tonight. Deacon has the day off so he can catch some sleep. I'll leave once he's up and we've checked in with the teams. Do you need anything?"

"No," Marianne said. She had everything she needed; what she wanted, however, was a different story.

"Call me if you do," he said, and she was glad he couldn't read her thoughts. Before he disappeared, he mouthed: *Check your phone.*

Marianne nodded, wondering where her phone was. She only used it to take photos or speak to Samuel. She spotted it by Theo's changing table.

While Kaela set to work on constructing her second building, Marianne eased herself off the floor. She checked her phone, noting she had a new text message. It had been sent thirty minutes ago.

Samuel: Please call me when you're free.

While Kaela was distracted, Marianne went to the bathroom, closing the door behind her, and called Samuel.

"Hi, Marianne. Sorry to bother you; I wanted you to look at something," he said.

"Sure. What is it?" She sat on the edge of the bathtub, one that was big enough for four people.

"I sent an image to your phone."

The image was blurry, but there was no mistaking it. "That's her, that's Ariel," Marianne said. Eric's security guard's girlfriend. Marianne noticed the background. "How did you obtain the image?"

"When you mentioned she was at the front at the worship ceremony, I was hoping one of the cameras our men wore might've picked her up. I'm going to use this image as a reference, but I wanted to make sure I had the right person."

"That's definitely her." There wasn't a doubt in her mind.

"Interesting," Samuel said, and before Marianne could ask him what he meant, he continued, "I have another call. I'll talk to you soon."

Interesting.

What was interesting about a woman he supposedly hadn't run any searches on?

What is Samuel up to?

38

DEACON

Rays of evening sunlight cast a warm glow across his room as he rubbed his eyes. He looked at the clock and rolled over, burying his face underneath his pillow. He'd finally succumbed to sleep, and thankfully, his dreams had evaded him.

Five minutes.

That's what he'd told Theo, and look how well that'd turned out. Deacon groaned.

He closed his eyes until his next alarm jolted him awake.

He sighed, threw off the duvet, and walked naked to the bathroom. He showered, and combed his hair. It was still too short for his liking, and as vain as it was, he missed his full head of hair. A shaved head didn't look as good on him as it did on James, although he'd never admit it.

He examined the wound on his bicep and decided it was time for the stitches to come out. He pulled a scalpel from his kit and went back to the bathroom. With a steady hand, he sliced each stitch, pulling it through his skin. He cleaned the wound, pleased with how it had healed.

He pulled a sweater over his head, tucked his pistol into his holster, and went in search of some food.

He could hear them before he even set foot in the kitchen. Kaela was talking like her life depended on it, and Marianne slipped a word in here and there when she could.

"Evening," he said as he entered, his throat deep and husky from his sleep.

Marianne lifted her eyes, and there was an intensity in them he hadn't seen before.

She looked away quickly, which both surprised and pleased him, although it should've done neither. Theo was cradled in her arms, and Deacon would've bet his life she was fussing over him as a distraction.

"What's for dinner?" Deacon asked, concentrating on the task at hand.

"Pasta!" Kaela answered before the chef could get a word in.

He couldn't be rude and ignore them, so he walked over to the table and Kaela held out a forkful of pasta for him.

What is with this kid and feeding me?

"Kaela!" Marianne reprimanded her, but Deacon couldn't stop the chuckle that slipped through his lips.

"That's okay, you eat your dinner," Deacon said, sitting beside her. "The chef is going to bring me my own bowl."

"It's very good," Kaela said, nodding enthusiastically.

"That pleases me," he said. He was famished.

"Where have you been all day?" Kaela asked.

"Sleeping," Deacon said, pouring a glass of water and topping Marianne's and Kaela's glasses.

"All day? You're supposed to sleep at night," she said, scrunching up her face.

"I was awake all night working," Deacon said. Well, he had almost been awake all night.

A light bulb went off in Kaela's mind, and her eyes lit up. "Mommy, I worked it out."

Marianne's eyes narrowed. "Worked what out?"

"Where Deacon and Cami are going to live."

Marianne's fork paused midway to her mouth. "In your buildings? Yes, they can have their own apartments in the same building," she said quickly.

What are they talking about?

Kaela shook her head. "But they'll get lonely. Cami can live with James and Mak, because Cami and Mak are friends. And Deacon can live with us, because we'll have the big apartment on the top."

Marianne blushed, and she opened her mouth to speak, but nothing came out.

Deacon cleared his throat. Words escaped him, too. Finally he said, "I'll live with Cami, and then we can keep each other company."

Kaela pouted, seeming to think through the idea. "Okay, you can have the apartment below James and Mak."

He'd just gone from the penthouse to two floors below it. "I think Cami and I should have the apartment below yours, and James and Mak could have the third floor down."

"Okay," Kaela said, shrugging and taking another bite of her pasta.

Marianne found her voice again. "She was building with Legos today and deciding where we would all live," she said, and Deacon dared to look at her again. Her blushed cheeks had faded.

"I see," he said. The chef brought over his food, and he was grateful for the distraction. "What else did you do today?" he asked. It was easier to talk to Kaela right now. Easier for his heart.

"Um, building, and then we played in the gardens, and then we did school," she said, surprising Deacon with the full itinerary.

Then, suddenly, she slid off the dining chair. "Excuse me, I'm going to wash my hands," Kaela said.

Deacon didn't want to be alone with Marianne, but he could hardly get up mid-dinner. He looked to Marianne. "Did you do all that as well?"

"Yes, of course. It's better if she's not left unsupervised," she said jokingly, but they both knew it was the truth.

Deacon felt himself smile and he wondered how that was possible with the memories he'd been reliving. "I understand that, but there are staff here to help. They can take care of her while you rest."

"I'm fine," she said defiantly.

Deacon nodded. "Okay, then," he said. He supposed her incessant need to be independent stemmed from being under the control of Saratani—and Eric—her entire life.

"Good," she said matter-of-factly.

Kaela came running full-speed at the table. "I'm back!"

From the corner of his eyes he saw Marianne shake her head.

Deacon checked his watch. He still had half an hour until he needed to check in with security. He had nothing new to talk to James about, so if he went there early it might look like he was hiding— which would be the truth. He should've slept longer.

"Who else is going to live in our building?" Kaela asked, tapping her index finger on her cheek.

"Maybe Lucy, your babysitter, should live with you," Deacon said, although the remark was aimed directly at Marianne.

He felt hard eyes on him, but he ignored them.

Kaela shook her head thoughtfully. "No. She lives with her mom and dad."

Deacon was running out of suggestions. Other than Samuel, Kaela had already allocated everyone he wanted to live in the building.

"Maybe your mom and dad should come live with us," Kaela suggested innocently.

"My mom and dad are in heaven," Deacon said. It was a lie; both of his biological parents were alive and well. But James and Deacon Thomas's parents were deceased, conveniently.

Kaela frowned. "My dad is there, too."

Her dad was in hell, but Deacon wasn't going to tell her that. It was the first time he'd heard Kaela bring her father up, although Josh's security reports had detailed Kaela's occasional nightmares.

What was more interesting, though, was Marianne's reaction. The straightening of her shoulders, the tilting of her chin.

"Maybe my dad and your dad will be friends in heaven," Deacon said.

"I hope so." Her face lit up with a big smile, but Marianne didn't see it—her gaze was on the manicured hedges beyond the window. Deacon recognized the tortured look in her eyes. *Guilt.* It was like looking in a mirror.

He wondered how he'd ever found her so difficult to read when her thoughts were now so transparent to him—if he was reading her correctly, which he was sure he was. Maybe it was because she felt safe around him and could let her guard down. Deacon doubted she'd ever felt that way around Eric. She'd had to pretend—her life had depended on it.

He heard footsteps approach from behind, and he quickly looked down, twirling his fork in his spaghetti.

"Perfect timing," James said, taking the spare seat between Marianne and Deacon.

"Yes," Deacon said, "just letting you know, you and Mak have now been demoted another floor. Cami and I are living together below the penthouse."

Poor Samuel is going to end up without a decent view. Wait until he hears about that.

James scoffed. "Kaela, this just isn't going to work. You need to build us at least three buildings."

"I can do that," she said seriously.

They all laughed, and the sparkle returned to Marianne's eyes.

～

The propellers whipped through the air, and Deacon wrapped his arms around his chest in a feeble attempt to keep warm. A few new staff were arriving, swapping out with others who were going back to New York with James. It was an expensive exercise to transport staff in and out by helicopter, even more so when Deacon wasn't the pilot, but it sure beat the traffic on a Friday night. The days were blurring, one into another, which easily happened when you lived in the protected cocoon they were in. Every day was—hopefully—the same, and when you didn't leave the house, life was duly similar to *Groundhog Day*. That was going to change soon, though, because they were moving again. Once they were sure Marianne was well enough, they'd relocate to another house. None of the team thought it was wise to stay in one place too long, even when it was secure. Predators always found a way to kill their sitting ducks.

"I'll see you Monday," James said, picking up his overnight bag and slinging it across his shoulder.

"Have a good weekend," Deacon replied.

James greeted the arriving staff and then made sure everyone was on before jumping in himself.

The new staff joked amongst themselves as they walked toward Deacon.

"Let's go inside," Deacon said, taking them to the security quarters. He left Josh to brief them and set them up before the change of shifts in two hours. It was a seamless operation.

Deacon took the stairs back into the main house. The kitchen was empty—other than the chefs. For a fleeting moment he felt disappointed then shook his head, annoyed at himself for letting his mind go there.

He raided the kitchen for a snack and retired to the office. He left the door slightly ajar, listening to the movements in the hallway. Marianne had bathed Kaela and was putting her to bed. Theo cried softly then quieted.

The house grew silent, and it stayed like that for over an hour. It was then he forced himself to look at Nicholas's file. He'd barely opened it, though, when a knock at the door startled him.

"Come in," he said, closing the file.

"Hi. Do you have a minute?" Marianne asked. The lake-blue color of her sweater matched the color of her eyes, and he found himself lost in them for a moment.

"Sure," he said quickly. "What's up?"

She sat on the other side of the desk, one long, toned leg crossed over the other. She had silk pajama shorts on and white ankle socks.

It was a surprisingly sexy combination. He forced himself to keep his eyes on her face.

She cleared her throat. "I spoke to Samuel earlier. I reviewed a photo and confirmed it was Ariel Koni," she said, and Deacon nodded. He was aware of as much.

"*Interesting* was the word Samuel used before he hung up," she continued. "Can you tell me what's so interesting? Because, as far I was aware, Samuel didn't have any other intel on her."

Deacon leaned forward, resting his elbows on the table. "I honestly don't know. James told me you identified her, but otherwise I haven't spoken to Samuel today." Deacon refrained from smiling when she gave him a distrustful look. Instead, he called Samuel, putting it on speaker.

"Samuel? Hi. I'm here with Marianne. What's the latest on Ariel Koni?"

Marianne's eyes dropped to the phone, but Deacon's stayed on her.

"Um, I don't know, exactly. I could only identify her on a few sections of footage, but on one of them she was a few feet from an exit. I can't be sure, but I think Ariel is alive."

"And that's what you thought was interesting?" Deacon asked, purely for Marianne's benefit.

"Yes. Is that not good enough?"

Samuel sounded insulted, and Marianne gave a guilty smile.

Deacon chuckled. "No, that's good enough. Thanks, Samuel, I'll talk to you later."

"Bye," he said quickly and hung up. The speed at which Samuel had ended the call was far more interesting to Deacon than the reason for their call.

"Satisfied?" Deacon said, a hint of a smile on his lips.

"I just want to be kept informed of my case," Marianne said quietly.

"We are keeping you informed. What is this really about?" Deacon asked, putting his phone aside and giving Marianne his full attention.

She sighed, dropping her eyes. "I find it difficult to trust people. Almost everyone I've ever trusted has failed me," she said, inhaling deeply, playing with her fingers in her lap.

"I understand why you would feel that way." Deacon couldn't blame her, and only over time would she fully trust them. "We are keeping you fully informed. Sometimes leads come up that don't eventuate into anything of importance, and sometimes Samuel won't even bring them to James or me unless he has evidence. If we were to update you on every single lead, you'd be sitting in Samuel's office twenty-four/seven. I promise we're keeping you informed, but it's up to you to decide whether to believe that or not. The only time we haven't was at the hospital, and that's for reasons I've already explained."

She pursed her lips. "How does Samuel manage all of this?"

"He has help. He has multiple teams below him that do the more basic work, if you will. They provide what he calls 'admin' support, which allows him to work on the more intricate hacking work. As far as how he manages those teams, we don't really know. He vets them, hires them, and trains them. Samuel is recruiting faster than any other department, but we don't care—he gets what he needs because he performs."

"Will I ever meet him?" Marianne asked, a curious grin on her lips.

"Maybe one day. Samuel is a bit of a recluse. You'd have to go to his office to meet him," Deacon said, leaving it at that—but calling Samuel "a bit of a recluse" didn't begin to describe him.

Silence hung between them, and his mind flashed back to dinner. He looked to the half-closed door and lowered his voice. "What happened today, when Kaela mentioned Eric?" Deacon asked, knowing he was overstepping a boundary, but he didn't care. Marianne had overstepped it herself yesterday. Not that two wrongs made a right, he knew, but he'd risk that she'd be angry for asking.

"It's personal," she said pointedly. He got the message.

But then she surprised him.

"How am I supposed to feel?" She gave a sigh that bordered on a soft moan. "She doesn't understand—she doesn't know the kind of man he really was—and she can't begin to understand the life she would've led if he were alive. She's hurting because of me, because I as good as killed him myself. I took her father away from her. Even if it was for the best in the long run . . ." She trailed off, her eyes glassy as she looked away.

"You did the right thing. You know what her life would've been like if you hadn't escaped."

She eyeballed him. "I know that, logically, but the guilt comes anyway. Doesn't it?"

Deacon controlled his temper, knowing it was his fault for opening the door. "That's very different."

Her eyes penetrated deep within him, and he fought that same urge to squirm—to run.

"You're good with her, with Kaela. I'm surprised."

He smiled, grateful for the change of topic. "My stepsister had two young children when I was a teenager. She was always at my mom's house with the kids, so that helped, I suppose." The words fell from his mouth so easily, and he found he didn't regret speaking them.

Her expression softened. "Do you have any contact with your family?"

"No," Deacon said. "I don't want them to be targeted, so it's best I don't—as hard as that is."

She searched his eyes again, and he wondered what she saw. "Do they know you're alive?"

"No, they don't," he said, although he doubted they had no suspicions due to his annual deliveries of white tulips.

"You said your mom's house. Are your parents separated?" Marianne asked.

"Yes," Deacon said, relaxing into the chair, the tension from their earlier conversation fading. "My father is a gambling addict who blamed my mom for all his problems. She finally kicked him out when I was eleven, and I haven't spoken to him since." From what Samuel had learned, his father hadn't changed.

"I often wonder what Kaela will remember of the past few years

—I'm hoping very little, if anything," she said, looking toward the door. "Do you think it'll be easier for her if she forgets him? Or will that raise other issues?"

"I don't know, to be honest," he said. "I can tell you, though, I don't have any fond memories of my father. It would probably have been better if he'd left when I was younger—at least then my mother would've been happier, and as a result her children would've been happier."

"How many siblings do you have?"

"Three. Two sisters and a stepsister. I was surrounded by women, my stepfather excluded."

Marianne beamed a smile. "What do you think of him?"

"He's a good guy," Deacon said, then smiled himself. "I think I've done enough talking now."

She nodded. "That's more than I expected."

Silence passed between them, but it didn't make Deacon uncomfortable. He found himself not wanting her to leave, but knowing he should want her to.

"Is this a big operation for you?" she finally asked. "I feel like I'm taking up a lot of resources and keeping you and everyone else from their lives."

Deacon gave her a lopsided smile. "First, most of our staff and I have no life outside of work—it's not a job that's conducive to a social life. And no, it's not really a big operation. Mak has a similarly sized security team at all times—and she's only one person. It's overkill, obviously, but understandable."

That brought out a full smile. "They're good together," she said, and he thought she was testing him again.

"They are," he said. *It's just not a good idea*—and what was going on in this office right now wasn't either.

"Mommy? Mommy!" Kaela called out.

"Welcome to my life," she said with a tired chuckle.

Deacon didn't tell her how much he loved her life—how much he'd rather have hers than his.

Marianne left, and the house grew silent again. Deacon saw her slender frame pass by the half-open door. Her bedroom door clicked closed, and he leaned back in the chair, rocking it back and forth with his toes.

There was a closet between the office and Marianne's room, but otherwise she was sleeping in the next bedroom.

He shook his head, returning his Nicholas's file. He opened it, forcing himself to read every line. It didn't answer any of his questions.

He dialed Samuel's number again.

"Evening," Samuel said, his voice tense—likely irritated at Deacon interrupting his work for a second time.

"Hi, Samuel." Deacon took a deep breath. "On Monday night, once James has returned, can you please book a flight to Texas?" he asked, swallowing the bile in his throat.

39

DEACON

Apprehension clung to Deacon's skin like a shadow he couldn't lose. He kept busy, working more than he had to and staying away from Marianne as much as he could without being rude. How had they become so close? Why was he telling her things about his family? It was a mistake, his mind told him, but in his heart he didn't feel that way.

He ignored his heart. His heart had only led him to heartbreak in the past.

Deacon sneezed as he crawled through the ceiling. He was installing additional cameras, and changing some of the angles of others. There wasn't going to be a black spot in the entire house when he was done. A house that they would leave soon—hopefully within the week—but it would be beneficial whenever they used the house next. Deacon knew it was probably unnecessary, but he didn't care about unnecessary; they never did. It made him feel better, but the team was less enthusiastic, particularly because a few of them had to crawl through the ceilings with him.

His phone rang, and he wiped his hands on his jeans before taking it out of his pocket.

"Hi James," he said, clearing his throat. He wasn't only inhaling dust, he was swallowing it as well. His throat was so dry it felt like sandpaper every time he swallowed.

"Samuel has booked the charter plane to Dallas. We can bring in another security team, Deacon. I can go with you."

Deacon had been expecting this call. "One of us needs to be at the house until we know what we're dealing with and where the guys from the hospital are." Samuel still hadn't been able to confirm their locations in Manhattan or otherwise.

"The house is secure. We'll be gone one day at most," James said.

His brother was right, and Deacon also thought the risk was negligible, but he still didn't want to take the chance.

"It's not only about that. I want to do this on my own, James." And then he added, "Just like you dealt with Paris on your own."

There was a moment of pause, because there was nothing James could say and he knew it.

"Okay," James said, reluctantly. "But I'm coming back on Sunday night."

"You don't need to do that. Take the weekend off," Deacon said, shaking his head. It had taken him seven years to get to this point. A few more hours wouldn't make much difference.

"I'll see you Sunday," James said, hanging up.

Deacon sighed, tucking the phone back into his pocket. James would do what he wanted.

He looked at his wrist, noting the time. He had about twenty-four hours until he had to face his past. Face the man who more than likely had betrayed them. He knew it was the right thing to do, and it was something he should've done years ago—but knowing and doing what was right thing were two very different things.

~

Deacon and Marianne were like two ghosts in the night, barely seeing each other except for brief glimpses in the hallway or in the kitchen. She had her hands full, and he was keeping as busy as he could, holding his demons at bay. He was also avoiding her, and he wondered if she knew he was.

Sunday evening arrived and Deacon packed the final items into his kit. It was a good thing he was taking a private charter because the airline would have a few issues with his baggage contents.

His bedroom door swung open and Deacon knew it was James—anyone else would've knocked first.

"Ready?" he asked, searching Deacon's eyes.

"Ready as I'll ever be," he replied, his inhalation sounding like a soft whistle.

"I can still go with you," he said.

Deacon shook his head and gave his most assured smile. "I'll be fine."

James walked with Deacon to the garage. "Good luck," he said.

Deacon threw his bag on the passenger seat and slid into the driver's seat, waving as he reversed.

He blocked everything from his mind as he drove, focusing only on his surroundings. The drive to the airport was uneventful. The pilot had the engines running, and they took off as soon as he was strapped in. Deacon used the time to prepare himself for what he needed to do. He tried to anticipate every situation he could find himself in, and prepared physical and mental responses to them. He knew, though, life often took you on a journey, one with events you couldn't anticipate.

After mercilessly strategizing and strategizing, he closed his eyes. The rhythmic purr of the plane eased his mind. It always had—it was one of the things he loved about flying.

He awoke when the wheels bounced off the tarmac before landing evenly. He grabbed a bottle of water and guzzled it down.

A car was waiting for him, and he phoned Samuel the moment he was on the road. "Is everything in place?"

"Confirm. Are you ready to do this?" he asked. Surprisingly, Deacon didn't detect any doubt in his response.

"As ready as I'll ever be," Deacon said, ignoring the chill he couldn't seem to shake.

"I agree. Okay, the property is secure, and I've sent Nicholas's number to your phone. Make the call when you're ready."

"Thanks, Samuel. I'll speak to you soon," Deacon said.

Nicholas's family was home tonight, so they'd had to come up with another plan. While Deacon wasn't against threatening family members—it was a powerful motivational tool—he didn't actually want to follow through on the threat. He also didn't want one of them calling the police if Nicholas screamed uncontrollably, which was a very likely possibility.

He followed the GPS to the property Samuel had secured, no more than a ten-minute drive from Nicholas's home. It was a large house with expansive gardens that would act as another layer of soundproofing for whatever happened inside.

Deacon had reviewed the floor plans, courtesy of Samuel, earlier in the morning, but he did his own walk-through upon arriving. His footsteps echoed off the rich-chocolate floorboards as he took in the powerful scent of citrus. Deacon couldn't work out where it was coming from until he passed a fresh floral arrangement that was big enough for him to hide behind.

When he was familiar with the property he opened his text messages. His finger trembled as he tapped the number. He held his breath as it rang.

"Hello?"

"Nicholas?"

"Yes," the voice responded hesitantly. "Who is this?"

"I need to talk to you tonight. I'm going to send you an address, and I want you to get in your car and leave now. Make up any excuse for your wife, but make sure she believes it. Your phones are tapped, as is your house. Don't call anyone. Don't try anything."

"Who is this?" he asked in a harsh, hushed whisper.

"This is Nicole's boyfriend," Deacon said coldly.

Silence.

"Nicole is dead."

"I know—I was with her the night she died. Get in the car, Nicholas. I don't want to hurt you or your family."

"I can't trust you."

"You don't have a choice. If you don't come to me, I *will* come to you. And I promise you will regret that." Deacon was grateful for the years of training that allowed him to present a strong, flat voice regardless of whatever he was feeling inside.

There was a long pause. Then, "Send me the address."

Deacon ended the call and Samuel sent the address. He paced the kitchen, listening to every single tick-tock of the clock as he painstakingly waited for Nicholas to arrive.

"Target approaching gate . . . target entering gate . . . target at front door," Samuel said.

The front door was unlocked, as the message to Nicholas had said it would be.

"He's not holding a weapon," Samuel confirmed.

Deacon squashed down the nausea that was burning his throat. He held his weapon at shoulder height as he forced his feet forward, one in front of the other.

He paused at the corner, using a pocket mirror to observe Nicholas for a moment. He looked petrified, and Deacon thought if he didn't put him out of his misery he might end up standing in a puddle. Nicholas's head whipped around haphazardly, like a man who didn't know where to turn.

Deacon stepped around the corner, the barrel of his pistol pointed at Nicholas's chest. "Come in," he said, but Nicholas didn't move. Deacon wasn't sure if he was capable of moving.

"What do you want?" Nicholas asked in a gruff voice.

"I want to talk," Deacon said, lowering his weapon. If Nicholas was carrying a weapon, in his current state of mind his reflexes wouldn't be fast enough to draw it before Deacon could draw his own.

Deacon tilted his head toward the adjoining sitting room. Nicholas took shuffling steps toward it, his eyes never leaving Deacon's.

"Stop," Deacon said. "Turn around."

Nicholas hesitated, and Deacon raised an eyebrow. It worked.

Deacon frisked him, finding two knives and a pistol, and confiscated them all.

"Sit down," Deacon said.

Nicholas sat on the chair Deacon had set up earlier. He'd moved out the furniture and placed nothing but two metal chairs in the room—two chairs that couldn't be ruined by blood stains.

"You're surprised to see me," Deacon said, sitting. It wasn't a question. "I don't blame you. It's been a long time."

Nicholas's lips pressed into a thin line.

"It took me a long time to face Nicole's death. But now that I am in the process of doing so, I've discovered something I don't like."

Nicholas's skittish eyes bounced all over the room.

"You told someone that Nicole was in Thailand, didn't you?"

His jaw clenched, but he didn't try to deny it.

"How did you know we were there?"

Nicholas didn't answer, which Deacon had been anticipating.

"There are two ways to do this, but either way, you are going to answer me. I think you know who I am, or at least have an idea, so you know what I'm capable of. And, believe me, I've only honed my skills over the years." Deacon stared at the man, his gaze unflinching. "Now—how did you know?"

Nicholas took a second longer than Deacon liked, and blood sprayed from his nose as Deacon's fist connected with it.

Nicholas howled and grunted as he grabbed his nose, but he couldn't stop the bleeding. He leaned forward, letting it gush onto the floor.

"Next comes the scalpel," Deacon said. He wasn't joking. "Answer the fucking question!"

"My mom's email," he spat. "She told me when she logged in, she kept seeing emails that had already been marked as read, but she hadn't read them. They were emails from Amelia, our sister."

Deacon's mind flashed back to Thailand and his chest coiled with regret as he remembered. After lunch, Deacon had phoned in with James. Nicole had pointed toward an internet café and he'd nodded, keeping her in his view the entire time. She'd always loved to keep up with the news—she said it made her feel less isolated. He's assumed that's what she was doing. But perhaps she hadn't been; perhaps she had logged in to her mother's email.

"Why did you think it was Nicole?"

"I didn't at first. Mom said it—she thought it was Nicole. She said Nicole had set up the email for her, and she'd never changed the password."

He pulled his cupped hand away from his nose and another gush of blood splattered on the floor. He shook his hand and then wiped it on his jeans. He swore under his breath, using his sweater to try and clean himself up.

"What did you do with the information?" Deacon asked, his voice filled with loathing—both for the man in front of him and for himself.

"I followed her once when she was going to meet you. I saw you, but only for a few seconds, and once you were together I lost track of you both. But I saw your face—I knew you were the man the Russians wanted."

"So you sold that information, no matter the cost? She was your *sister!*"

Deacon looked on as the pathetic bastard couldn't even look at him.

"I didn't sell it! At least . . . at least not initially," he said, desperation creeping into his voice. "The Russians came to me. I owed them money. They held a knife to my wife's throat and told me they were going to kill my entire family unless I gave them information. They knew Nicole and I were close—I guess they figured she must've told me something, and if not, they were going to kill my wife as punishment for not paying my debts. Either way, they'd win. All I gave them was the email address, and I wasn't even sure if it was her." He wiped his face, smearing blood over his cheeks. "I pleaded with them to keep her safe. To bring her back to me. When they told me she got caught in the crossfire, I . . . I . . ." He looked away.

"Crossfire?" Deacon asked incredulously. He must've heard wrong.

"They told me one of the bullets hit her when they were shooting at you. She died because of you—because you were a wanted man!"

"You're right," Deacon said through clenched teeth. "She did die because of me. But you sold her to a *pack of wolves!*" He lashed out and landed a fist on Nicholas's jaw. He pulled him up by the shirt and pushed him against the wall, only stopping when Nicholas's head hit it and made a sickening thud.

Deacon released his grip, worried he'd killed him for a second.

Nicholas blinked like he was seeing stars, and he probably was. Deacon stepped back, giving his ragged breath a chance to settle.

"While I was incapacitated, they mutilated and raped her. For *hours*," Deacon said through clenched teeth. "She wasn't killed by a stray bullet—she died when her body gave up."

"Oh my God, oh my God," he heard Nicholas whisper before he started sobbing. "That's why he was smiling when he told me she'd died," he said pitifully. He wiped his wet eyes. "I didn't know they would do that to her. I didn't know."

Deacon actually believed him, but it didn't ease any of Deacon's pain—and he found it only made him angrier. "Well now you do," he said, his words like a knife to his own heart.

Nicholas leaned forward and Deacon thought he was going to be sick. Tears streaked over his bloodstained cheeks. He righted himself, shaking his head.

"Who held the knife to your wife's throat?" Deacon asked, trying to clear his mind.

"Sokolov. I'd never seen him before, not in person," Nicholas said, after taking a moment to collect himself. "What was I supposed to do? My children were upstairs," he whispered.

Deacon sat. "You don't put yourself in a situation where you owe money to men like the Russians." A strangled cry came from Deacon's throat. "I would've done anything for her. I would've given my life in a second for hers. Every day I wished they'd killed me instead."

Nicholas shook his head blankly. "I guess they lied about burying her too."

"What?" Deacon froze. "Where did they say they buried her?" It was dangerous to even hope, but Deacon did anyway. If he could find her, he could lay her to rest somewhere beautiful. She deserved that much at least.

"They said they buried her in the rice paddies not far from the warehouse they'd taken you to. He said there were two crumbling Buddha statues nearby. She's buried next to them. Or so they said."

Deacon had no idea where that warehouse was. He'd been blind-folded at the time, and he'd been unconscious when James had dragged him out.

But James knew.

It was questionable, however, if the statues would still be standing.

"Are you going to kill me?" Nicholas asked, and from the look in his eyes, Deacon thought he actually wanted him to.

"No," Deacon said. "You're going to live with this pain, just like I've had to, and will have to for the rest of my life. Your hell is just beginning. Now—get out."

Deacon pointed toward the door and somehow Nicholas managed to get to his feet.

"I'm sorry. I'm so, so sorry," he said through trembling breaths.

He followed Nicholas to the door. "If you tell anyone you saw me, I will come and kill your family—then you'll really know what it's like to have their blood on your hands."

"I won't," he said with a look of despair.

Deacon hated him, but he also believed him. He slammed the door shut.

"Target in car . . . Target at gate . . . Target has exited," Samuel said.

Deacon didn't know how long he stood with his hands pressed against the door as he fought to control his own emotions.

Her death was senseless. If she hadn't checked the email, would they have been found? But even still, how did they trace them from the island to the resort in only a few hours?

Goddamn. Deacon began to sob.

40

MARIANNE

It was impossible to say, because reading James was hard, but something was different about him today—and it wasn't only that he'd been on his phone every time she'd seen him.

His casual stride seemed tight and his eyes a little harder. And the thing that worried her most was she hadn't seen Deacon since yesterday. If he was leaving, he hadn't said goodbye—but then he hadn't needed to, either. It was also possible he was in the house and she just hadn't seen him, but she sensed that wasn't the case. Something was happening.

Unfortunately, though, having two children, one a newborn, left her with little time to analyze it further. Feeding, burping, changing diapers, and sleepless nights were hard enough to deal with, and that didn't include Kaela. She had to focus on her children, not uncovering the mysteries of the Thomas brothers. She was trying to trust them, to believe they were keeping her informed, but it was hard.

Kaela tugged on her sweater, and Theo whined in her arms.

"Mommy, I'm hungry," Kaela said.

Marianne took a calming breath. "Two minutes, Kaela. Pack up your toys and we'll ask the chefs to make lunch."

Kaela fled to the door but stopped when Marianne called after her, "You're not eating until this is cleaned up!" Marianne looked at the skyscraper at her feet. Kaela was building them an entire city.

She stifled a yawn as she rested Theo against her chest, but his whining continued. "Okay, little boy, I know you're hungry," she whispered as Kaela all but threw the Lego structure into the basket. Marianne thought to reprimand her, but didn't have the energy. At least she *was* putting the blocks away.

God, give me strength, Marianne prayed at the very moment Theo began screaming in her ear. "Shh, shh," Marianne whispered, willing her son to settle down before she ended up crying herself.

"He's so loud," Kaela said, scrunching up her nose.

"Kaela, sweetie, he's a baby. That's how he talks. He's hungry," Marianne said, relieved when the microwave beeped and the bottle was ready.

"I'm hungry, too," Kaela puffed, crossing her arms over her chest and raising her chin.

"You'll go to your room if you keep that up," Marianne said. She put the bottle in Theo's mouth and sighed with relief when he quieted. "Now, what would you like to eat?" she asked more gently to her daughter, aware Kaela was playing up out of jealously.

"Cake!" Kaela said. Marianne sighed—and her day continued much the same.

∾

It was midnight when both children were finally in bed and Marianne actually had time to shower.

In the shower she let her guard down, and the tears rolled down her cheeks. She felt like a failure today—like she wasn't capable of raising her two children alone. She'd snapped at Kaela all day, and she felt terrible.

Tomorrow will be better.

She let the warm water run over her skin, cleaning her caesarian incision. She never looked at her abdomen, she avoided it, but now she couldn't—at least not until she'd healed. She inspected it as quickly as possible and then turned off the water, carefully drying herself.

She took time to blow dry her hair, because who knew when she would have the luxury again? She was exhausted, but she'd never been a good sleeper, particularly when she was overtired. She knew what would fix it, though—a cup of herbal tea in bed.

She padded to the kitchen, jumping when she realized she wasn't alone. Her hand went to her chest, and she heaved in breaths.

"Sorry," Deacon said. "I didn't mean to scare you."

He was leaning against the cabinets, presumably waiting for the kettle to boil.

It took Marianne a second to find her voice. "You don't need to apologize."

He gave a smile, but it didn't reach his eyes.

"Are you okay?" she asked, wishing there was more light than the soft glow of the floor lamps by the table. The lamps were always on at night, she'd noticed.

"Yeah, I'm fine," he said, but the tension radiating from him said something else completely. "Do you want a cup?" His eyes dropped to the lone mug.

"Please. Thank you," she said, walking toward him, stopping two paces away.

Deacon took another tea bag from the canister and placed it in her mug. The only sound between them was the tempering rise of the kettle water.

When she lifted her gaze, she was surprised to see the heat in his eyes. Her breath caught in her throat.

"Were you here today?" she asked as casually as she could muster.

"No, I had to go and look at something. I came home a few hours ago."

The word home created misplaced feelings within her. He said it like it was their home, but it wasn't—far from it.

"Do you want to talk about it?" Marianne asked as the kettle flicked off.

Deacon poured the boiling water over the tea bags, and Marianne noticed his grazed knuckles.

"No," Deacon said, making it clearer that something was wrong.

"Did you punch something?" she asked. Even before her conversation with James, she'd realized that unless she pushed Deacon, he wouldn't open up.

He raised an eyebrow. "Yes, a boxing bag," he said, handing her one of the mugs. Their fingers touched and her pulse raced. Deacon's eyes locked on hers.

She had to remind herself to breathe. This was new to her. She'd never once felt like this with Eric, and he was the only man she'd been with. She couldn't draw her eyes away, and her heart was screaming in her chest.

"Damn," Deacon swore under his breath. He looked like he might run.

There was no denying the connection now. Not for either of them.

Marianne didn't know what to do or say. She put her mug down quickly, fearing she'd drop it.

She expected him to leave, or to tell her it was a mistake, but he seemed to be battling his own internal war.

"I should go to bed," she said, turning on her heel, forgetting all about her tea.

Deacon's arm shot out, wrapping around her waist. "Wait," he said softly.

Her skin burned where he held her, his arm strong but protective. She didn't take another step, and he didn't drop his arm.

"I don't know how to do this," he said quietly, and she turned back to him.

His inner turmoil was written all over his face. He wasn't hiding it from her, and she knew he could.

"I don't know how to let go of the pain—of my past. And if I can't do that, then I don't know how I can move forward."

Marianne turned and placed a hand on his chest. She could feel his heart beating, his rapid pulse in harmony with hers. She lifted her eyes.

"I don't know how this happened. But I want this, and that terrifies me," he said.

"What happened today? These aren't words you would've spoken to me two days ago," she said, and he looked away again.

"I'm trying to face . . ." He inhaled to take another deep breath. "I'm tired of hating myself for the past. I'm tired of the pain. And you make me forget it. When I'm with you, when I'm talking to you—those are the only times I'm not thinking about it," Deacon said, his words rushed now. "I don't know how I can move forward."

"I know what happened to her," Marianne said, meeting his eyes. "Eric's report was quite detailed." Deacon squeezed his eyes shut. "And I still think you need to forgive yourself."

"And how do I do that?" he asked, gently, not taking his pain out on her.

She sighed. "I don't know, and I can't answer that for you. I don't know how to let go of my own past, of the things I did with Eric—the things I could've stopped," she said, daring to look up, baring the shame in her eyes. He lowered his chin, his eyes softening. "I just focus on my children. On being a good mother. That's the only thing that has helped me forget—temporarily. I don't think you'll ever be free of her death," she said sadly. "Not completely."

41

DEACON

Marianne looked him dead in the eyes. "But you're a good person, Deacon. You help people every day—you risk your life to protect them. How many lives have you saved since her death?" She didn't give him time to answer. "You know, when I heard you saved the sacrifice that night, I smiled. It was one less girl's blood on my hands, because that's what it would've been," she said, seeming to shake the memories from her mind.

Deacon knew they were both hurting and had been drawn to each other through their damaged pasts. Was that all this was?

His mind screamed at him to leave, to go to his room. His heart won, though, and his feet didn't move an inch.

The corner of her lips turned up. "You look tormented," she said, and he couldn't help but smile.

Theo's cries sounded from Marianne's bedroom. Theo knew better than he did.

Marianne shook her head softly. "Relentless," she said, with a true smile now. She leaned in, and he tensed as her soft lips pressed against his check. It seemed to melt away his heartache, and he didn't want to let her go. "In good time," she said softly before stepping away from him. He let her go, but his eyes followed her from the room, and he listened as Theo's cries quieted.

He finished making his tea and went to sit on the windowsill, gazing at the moonlight, lost in his thoughts, until the moon faded into the pink-streaked morning sky.

He should regret what had transpired during the night, but he didn't.

The morning peace didn't last long. Deacon heard banging doors and footsteps running down the hallway. Kaela was well and truly awake. Deacon wondered if Marianne had slept at all last night or if she'd been awake thinking, too.

He went to his bedroom, showered, shaved, then went in search of breakfast. His self-loathing was still there; the pain was still there; the turmoil was still there, but he didn't regret opening up to Marianne, even though he felt like he should.

The only two people present in the kitchen were the chefs, so Deacon took a seat at the barstool and chatted with them while he waited. He'd devoured a full serving of eggs before he heard Kaela's voice approaching, which always preceded her arrival. She came running full speed, like a human bullet.

"Good morning!" she said, waving at Deacon and the chefs, whom she'd obviously grown friendly with.

They greeted her back enthusiastically, and Deacon helped her as she tried to climb up on the stool next to him. He made sure she was sitting on the stool properly before he let go of her arm, just as Marianne entered with Theo in her arms. Their eyes locked and Deacon felt her gaze penetrate deep within him. He looked away. He had no idea what to do from here.

"Deacon, what are you having for breakfast?" Kaela asked, and her big eyes captured his attention.

"Pancakes," he said, and her eyes widened further, if that were possible. He thought it was probably best not to tell her he'd had eggs too—she'd probably want it all and end up with a stomachache.

"Can I please have pancakes?" she asked, so politely she almost sounded wicked.

The chef winked in her direction.

"Kaela, you are going to get a rude shock when we move into our own house without these luxuries," Marianne said, raising her eyebrows.

Kaela frowned thoughtfully for a moment. She looked at the chef. "Would you like to come live with us?"

At the rate Kaela was going, Marianne would have half the house living in their apartment by the time this case was over.

The chef leaned on his elbows, talking at eye level. "I have a better idea. This afternoon, you come and see me, and I'll teach you how to make pancakes."

Kaela clapped. "Can I eat them all?"

"One," Marianne said. "You can eat one, and then you can give the rest to Josh and the nice men who are looking after us," Marianne said with a stern voice, before mouthing *thank you* to the chef.

He nodded with a knowing smile. Apparently Deacon wasn't the only one who thought Marianne needed a few hours—or more—of a reprieve.

Marianne perched herself on the edge of the stool, her long legs extending out, tucking underneath Kaela's stool. Theo rested peacefully in her arms, and despite not having a lot, if any, sleep last night, her face seemed to glow. Motherhood suited her.

"Morning," James said from behind him, and Deacon looked away, but he knew it was too late. James didn't miss anything, and Deacon sensed he'd already picked up on the connection between himself and Marianne, maybe weeks ago. The fact that James hadn't said anything, though, was interesting.

James's and Deacon's phones rang in unison and Deacon's stomach clenched. Nothing good ever came when that happened. They excused themselves to the office, and Deacon felt Marianne's eyes on him.

"Samuel," James said, putting his phone on speaker.

"We don't need to worry about finding Ariel Koni—she's resurfaced and she's back with a vengeance. I think she's the one who's been behind the Saratani resurgence this the entire time. Marianne's not with you, is she? I didn't have time to check the cameras."

"No, she's having breakfast with the kids," James said. "Why?"

"I need her to look at some text; it's in the old language. I think it's a phrase—possibly one or two sentences. I don't know what it means, but I think it's very important. This phrase was released on the dark net, and I'm assuming that it's a message."

"Where does Ariel Koni fit into this?" Deacon asked, sitting on the edge of the desk.

"This girl is as messed up as Eric," Samuel said darkly, and James lifted his eyes to Deacon's. Samuel continued, "She held a worship service last night. I don't know where—it was filmed and loaded onto the dark net—but I'm working on finding out." Samuel puffed out a tense sigh. "There are many disturbing things that happened, but two concern me most. The first thing I noticed: she was wearing a jeweled crown—the same one Marianne had been wearing at the worship ceremony. Or at least it's an exact replica. None of the properties that Marianne identified for me have been accessed since Eric's death, so I'm assuming Ariel took it sometime between the worship ceremony and the night James was captured. Ariel was dressed exactly like Marianne. She wore a dress in the same style—a Grecian draped gown with a plunging neck and high split. I mean, they would've looked like sisters standing there together. That is a message in itself."

Samuel sighed. "It's hardly the worst part, though. She performed a sacrifice ritual, and it appeared to be the same ritual Eric had been performing. I saw the ending of this one, though, which is quite horrifying. I'm not sure if it's a standard ceremony or not. Most of it was conducted in the old language, except for the ending: *We serve you, gods. Forgive us for our sins. We give you this gift, the ultimate sacrifice. Give us the power we need to fulfill your prophecies. Cerah zalû.* The chant that followed is the same passage that has been posted on the internet. I need to know what it is—I'm working with half the story here."

James rubbed one hand over his face. "This is worrying."

"I'll be back in a minute," Deacon said, forming a plan to get

Samuel what he needed as he strode out of the office and toward the kitchen.

Kaela had finished eating, which was perfect. "Kaela, I think it's time for that cooking lesson," Deacon said, giving a nod to the chefs, who caught on quickly.

"You'll be the best pancake chef in the world," one of them said, beaming a grin. Kaela jumped off the seat and ran toward them. Deacon wished he had that much energy.

Deacon turned to Marianne, tilting his head toward the hallway.

She stood quickly. "What's going on?" she whispered.

"We need you to have a look at something," he said, leading her toward the office.

'Samuel, she's here," James said as they walked in. He stood and offered his chair.

"Hi, Marianne," Samuel said before briefing her.

Deacon monitored her reaction as she listened. Her eyes never left Theo, who was still sleeping in her arms.

"Show me the text," she said to James.

He opened the file, passing the phone to her. Her hand began to tremble, but that was her only outward reaction.

"What does it say?" Deacon asked

She drew a long breath. "One sacrifice per day. That's the gift they're offering the gods." Her voice sounded strained. "Until I return with my children, one innocent sacrifice will be skinned alive and offered to the flames . . ."

It was Samuel who spoke first. Either his shock had worn off quicker for him, or he'd been expecting as much. He came in with a battle plan, which was the only thing they could do right now, because no one seemed to know what to say.

"My priority is finding Ariel, or finding out where these worship ceremonies are taking place," he said.

Deacon nodded. "The sooner we dismantle this group, the better. I agree; it's likely Ariel has been behind this the entire time."

"Is the video on my phone?" James asked.

"Yes."

"We'll watch it and call you back," James said.

Deacon knew his brother wanted to see if Marianne recognized anything in the background, anything that would give away the location.

Deacon stood beside Marianne as the video played.

Ariel stood in front of a single cross, the victim bound and bloody. Ariel stared into the camera, her lips tilting up as she chanted. She turned and ran the knife over the sacrifice, and the girl's scream echoed in the chamber. She cut her from head to toe, and then horizontally along the breastbone. Finally, she put the knife down and slid her fingers beneath the woman's skin, lifting it and peeling it back.

With the contents of the woman's chest revealed, Ariel picked up a small knife, and made a savage sawing motion. Eventually, she held up the sacrifice's heart, and then placed it atop the candelabra, lighting it up like a fireball.

"Is that a standard worship ceremony?" James asked.

Marianne looked down at the baby sleeping in her arms, and Deacon knew the answer before she said it. He saw the shame creep into her eyes.

She cleared her throat. "Yes, that's a standard worship."

The cutting part of the service they had seen before now looked like mere foreplay, and Deacon had no doubt that's what it had been for Eric—and it hadn't been limited to the ceremonies.

"Does anything in that video look familiar? Do you recognize the room?" Deacon asked, making sure his voice was neutral before he spoke.

"No," she said without looking at him. "I've never seen that room before."

James called Samuel back. "It's not familiar to Marianne. Perhaps it's a new location."

"I'll work on it. One last thing . . . The bounty has been increased. Word has spread about Theo."

Marianne pressed her lips together. Deacon had been expecting that, but he wasn't sure if Marianne had been.

"Thanks. We'll talk to you soon," James said, his eyes conveying a private message to Deacon.

We're moving. Now.

～

The house was a flurry of activity, but in one hour they were ready to depart—and once the cleaners came in, it would look like they had never been here. Exactly the way they liked it. Deacon tossed his overnight bag across his shoulder and grabbed his pistol as Marianne emerged from her room. She raised her eyes briefly, but her gaze never met Deacon's. And it hadn't met his, not once, since Marianne had watched the video.

"We're ready!" Kaela called out from the end of the hallway.

Deacon knew Josh had already taken Marianne's personal belongings, except whatever she had wanted to take on the plane. "Do you have everything?" he asked, double-checking and peering in to the room. It was empty.

"Yes, thank you," she said. Marianne had mastered the art of being polite while avoiding eye contact. He almost didn't realize she was doing it. Almost.

"Where are we going now?" Kaela asked, as if they were playing a game of musical chairs, but with houses. Deacon was glad she had no sense of any danger or threat.

"Somewhere warm," Deacon said, smiling as he thought of their destination.

When James had suggested they purchase the property there, Deacon had asked why. James's response: "Because who wants to go to the fucking desert for a holiday?"

It wasn't a tourist destination—not where their house was—so it was unlikely they'd ever run into anyone they knew. And if they did, Deacon knew they'd better start running in the other direction—fast.

Josh was in the garage waiting with James, and Deacon let him and his team buckle Marianne and the children in while he took the driver's seat. It was a short drive to the private airport, and there would be another short drive to their destination, their new temporary home. As far as a transport operation went, the risk to this one was minimal, especially considering they'd already sent cars off to create checkpoints and secure the airport.

Where they were going would be perfect. Marianne would have access to medical facilities if she needed them, in addition to their favorite doctor, who was already en route to the house as backup. But most importantly, the house was remote, its security was impenetrable, and it was big enough to accommodate all of the staff in the Boston house and more. It was almost as good as moving her in to Thomas Security.

Deacon took one more look in the rearview mirror but Marianne's eyes were cast down. Deacon pushed his thoughts aside, concentrating on the job at hand.

"All checkpoints secure. Depart when you're ready."

"Let's go," James said, and Deacon lowered his foot on the accelerator.

42

MARIANNE

Marianne closed her eyes, letting the warm sun and the scent of her newborn calm her dark mind. Kaela rambled in her ear, and she mumbled a response every now and then, pretending she was listening, but her mind was far from the present. She couldn't stop thinking about the video.

She'd cringed internally when it had begun playing. It was bloody and violent and barbaric; she'd witnessed hundreds of them. She'd hoped Eric's death would have meant the end of them, but she'd underestimated Ariel. That had been a mistake. And now more innocent people were going to be sacrificed, more often than they had been, because she'd escaped to save herself and her children. She knew that should bother her, and she knew a normal response would be guilt, but although it upset her, she would make the same decisions again. Her children came first, always.

The one thing that did concern her, though, were the thoughts of the man in the driver's seat. What did he think of her now? He'd known about the ritual ceremonies, but neither brother had seen the full service, and that was something she'd been hoping would never come out. She knew they thought she'd played along with Eric to survive, and she had, but she also hadn't done a thing to stop him.

"Wait here," Josh said.

Marianne opened her eyes. She hadn't even realized the car had stopped until he spoke.

They were ushered onto the plane by security staff. James and Deacon were the last to board, and Marianne was acutely aware of their presence despite not actually looking at them. They didn't sit with Marianne and the children but rather the teams that were accompanying them. When she stole a glance in their direction, it looked like they were having a meeting of sorts.

Marianne laid Theo in the bassinet and retrieved Kaela's iPad, selecting a movie for her to watch, and praying for a few minutes of sleep.

Kaela pulled her knees to her chest and snuggled into Marianne's side. She draped an arm around her daughter and closed her eyes. She felt the haze of sleep pulling her under.

~

"Wow, look, Mommy! Is this our new house?" Kaela asked as they approached the gates. Marianne had managed to sleep for almost all of the flight, and she'd had just enough time to feed Theo before they landed.

No one had spoken for the entire car journey except Kaela, but that wasn't unusual for this group, and Marianne didn't read anything into it. What she did read into, though, was that the property they were entering looked like a glamorized high-security prison. The realization should've made her nervous—another confirmation of the threat to their lives, if she hadn't already been aware that her old friends wanted to skin her alive and burn her for the gods, along with her children. Ultimately, though, the security made her feel safe. Marianne peered out of the windows at the barren, sandy Arizona desert. There wasn't another home as far as her eyes could see.

Deacon parked the car, and again she felt the heat of his gaze on hers. She couldn't bring herself to look into his eyes. He likely thought she felt terrible about the innocents, about the sacrifices. But while it would certainly keep her awake at night, it wasn't why she couldn't bear to look at him.

Marianne took Kaela's hand to stop her from running into the house. Parenting Kaela was an exercise in thinking ahead.

They walked through a long, silent hallway. The polished concrete floors and stark white walls reminded her of the Jordan house, but strangely, despite no one apparently living there, it didn't have the eerie, cold touch that the Jordan home had always had. Marianne had hated it there. After they'd been invaded by James and Deacon, Eric had declared they'd never return to the house, and Marianne had breathed a silent sigh of relief.

Josh showed her to the suite of rooms that was now hers. Kaela's bedroom joined hers and a bassinet and nursery furniture had already been assembled. Those at Thomas Security were masters of efficiency.

Theo sighed as Marianne laid him on her bed—she could barely believe he was asleep again—and Kaela crawled up beside him, snuggling in and closing her eyes. Marianne watched her carefully, but within a few minutes she too had fallen asleep. Marianne's chest swelled as she took a moment to just watch them. She wiped the tears away as fast as they came.

A soft knock at the door captured her attention, and when she opened it, she refrained from squeezing her eyes shut.

"Can I have a word?" Deacon asked with an arched brow.

She pulled the door shut behind her. "They're sleeping."

"Good," he said in that casual tone that hid all of his thoughts.

He opened the door across the hallway, and she wasn't surprised to see it led to another office. He waited for her to walk in first.

"What's going on?" he asked.

She played dumb. "What do you mean?"

He crossed his arms over his chest as he sat on the edge of the desk. "Okay, then . . . What are you thinking since you watched the worship video?"

Her first thought was to lie, to pretend that it had bothered her, and she was drowning in guilt and worry. But she didn't. She'd spent her life pretending, and she was tired of it. If he didn't like it—didn't like her—it was best he knew now.

She searched for the right words. "It upsets me, of course. I feel bad that more people are going to die on my behalf, but I don't regret my decision to leave. I knew this was a possibility, and I did it anyway. And I'd do it again. In a choice between others and my children, I choose my children."

He searched her eyes as her heart pounded wildly. "Destabilizing the organization and killing Eric, all of which happened because of you, has saved hundreds, maybe more, innocent lives. How many more do you think would've died over Eric's lifetime if he hadn't been stopped?"

"I don't know," she said, not even wanting to guess.

"I don't like this new development, and it's upsetting to know that innocent people are dying at Ariel's hand, but sometimes innocent people die for the betterment of this world. I'm not naïve enough to believe that innocent people haven't been killed on our missions. I don't know how many, and it's not something I allow myself to think about, because it could lead me down a very destructive path . . . I like to think of the work we do as a corrective force. But, to be honest, none of that is my primary concern. I would do anything to protect those I love. Anything."

"So would I," she said quietly. "What happens now?"

"Now that you're safe and far away from Manhattan, our priority will be to have this contract rescinded—in one way or another—and to dismantle Ariel and her little group of masterminds. The sooner we can do that the better, obviously, but we need to find them first. That may take Samuel some time."

She nodded, feeling much calmer now. She felt his eyes watching her, and her mind drifted back to last night—to the way his strong arms had wrapped around her. She wondered what he was thinking, and when she finally looked at him, he had that same tormented look in his eyes she'd seen in the kitchen. The one that told her there was an internal war raging in his mind.

His phone rang, and he sighed. Deacon looked at the number for

a second, hesitating, and then cleared his throat. "I need to take this."
He left without another word.

Marianne walked to the window, gazing out at the brick wall that surrounded the property. She wondered if the wall around Deacon's heart was just as impenetrable. Did she want to find out, risking her own in the process?

She stayed there for a while longer, unmoving, her eyes never leaving the wall.

43

DEACON

Deacon's cell phone was still ringing as he closed the bathroom door. He splashed some water on his face. "Hello?" Deacon said, his voice strained.

"Are you okay?" Samuel asked.

"Fine," Deacon lied. "What's up?"

"I think I've found it, Deacon. I've found the statues," he said, and Deacon pinched the bridge of his nose.

"They're still standing?"

"They're more stumps than statues. But I was able to identify the area based on the intel from James, and we've been using satellite surveillance to narrow down the location. There's two concrete pillar-type structures that could very easily have been the statues. I'm sure it's the correct location."

His stomach churned. It *could* be the correct location, but was she there? They'd analyzed over and over again why the Russians would've later told Nicholas about the burial location. They all agreed the most likely explanation was that it had been a trap. Nicole might well be buried there, but they'd leaked the information—probably to others as well as Nicholas—hoping it would get back to

Deacon. Hoping that, when he'd healed from his injuries, he'd go back for her body and give them another chance to capture him. If that was correct, he wondered how long they'd watched the location before realizing he wasn't coming.

Deacon heard James asking for him from the hallway. He opened the door and James entered a few seconds later, closing it behind him. Deacon put the call on speaker.

"There's one slight complication with the location," Samuel continued. "About three years ago it became controlled by one of the local gangs, and it's occupied, by the look of things. I don't think they'll be impressed if you ask them if you can start digging around for a body."

"I don't imagine we would be asking them," Deacon said.

"No, I didn't think so either. Which means you're going to have a hell of a time getting in and out of there alive."

Deacon sighed.

"There's something else to consider," Samuel said then paused.

"That she may not be there?" Deacon suggested.

"Well, yes. But also that she may not be there *alone*. Who knows who else they might've buried there?"

They'd have to pack multiple body bags—that's what Samuel was saying. They wouldn't know if they'd found her or not until DNA testing had been performed.

James spoke. "You do have DNA samples we can reference, right?"

"Yes," Samuel said without hesitation. "I have multiple medical records for her."

Deacon had no idea where Samuel had obtained them, and he didn't care. He pulled the neck of his sweater away from his throat, but it wasn't the knit that was choking him.

"I'll give you two a minute," Samuel said. "Call me when you've made a decision."

It wasn't even a decision Deacon had to make—and judging by the steely determination in James's eyes, it wasn't a decision for him, either.

"Let's go find her," James said. "Let's bring her home."

//

HUNGRY FOR MORE

The second novel of the Deacon Thomas Duet will be released late January 2018.

In the meantime, you can catch up with the characters again in *The Soul Series*.

I'm giving away the first book of this series, *The Secrets of Their Souls*, for **FREE**. All you need to do is sign up at http://brookesivendra.com/tsots-download/

Enjoy!
Brooke

ALSO BY BROOKE SIVENDRA

THE JAMES THOMAS SERIES
Escanta
Saratani
Sarquis
Lucian
Sorin
The Favour

THE SOUL SERIES
The Secrets of Their Souls (Book One)
The Ghosts of Their Pasts (Book Two)
The Blood of Their Sins (Book Three)
The Soul Series Box Set (Books One - Three)

DID YOU ENJOY THIS BOOK?

As a writer, it is critically important to get reviews.

Why?

You probably weigh reviews highly when making a decision whether to try a new author—I definitely do.

So, if you've enjoyed this book, and would love to spread the word, I would be so grateful if you could leave an honest review (as short or as long as you like) where you bought it.

Thank you so much, B.

ABOUT THE AUTHOR

Brooke Sivendra lives in Adelaide, Australia with her husband and two furry children—Milly, a Rhodesian Ridgeback, and Lara, a massive Great Dane who is fifty pounds heavier than Brooke and thinks she is a lap dog!

Brooke has a degree in Nuclear Medicine and worked in the field of medical research before launching her first business at the age of twenty-six. This business grew to be Australia's premier online shopping directory before Brooke sold it to focus on her writing.

You can connect with Brooke at any of the channels listed below and she personally responds to every comment and email.
www.brookesivendra.com
brooke@brookesivendra.com
Facebook: www.facebook.com/bsivendra
Twitter: www.twitter.com/brookesivendra
Instagram: www.instagram.com/brookesivendra

Made in the USA
Lexington, KY
22 April 2018

The Essential Jung

The Essential Jung

Selected and introduced
by Anthony Storr

Princeton University Press
Princeton, New Jersey

Published by Princeton University Press,
41 William Street, Princeton, New Jersey 08540

All Rights Reserved
Selected from *The Collected Works of C. G. Jung* (translated by
R.F.C. Hull), *The Freud/Jung Letters* (passage translated by
R.F.C. Hull), *C. G. Jung: Letters,* and *C. G. Jung: Word and Image,* all
published by Princeton University Press; and from *Memories,
Dreams, Reflections* by C. G. Jung (translated by Richard and Clara
Winston), copyright © 1961, 1962, 1963 by Random House, Inc.,
and published by Pantheon Books, New York.

Library of Congress Cataloging-in-Publication Data

Jung, C. G. (Carl Gustav), 1875–1961.
The essential Jung.

Bibliography: p. includes index.
1. Psychoanalysis-Addresses, essays, lectures.
I. Storr, Anthony. II. Title.
BF173.J6623 1983   150.19'54   82-61441
ISBN 0-691-08615-X
ISBN 0-691-02935-0

The paper used in this publication meets the minimum requirements of
ANSI/NISO Z39.48-1992 (R1997) (*Permanence of Paper*)

http://pup.princeton.edu

16 15 14 13 12 11 10

Printed in the United States of America

Contents

Note on the Text   9
Preface   11
Introduction   13

Part 1   **Jung's Early Work**   29

From "On the Psychology and Pathology of So-called Occult
  Phenomena" (1902)   29
From "School Years" *Memories, Dreams, Reflections* (1962)   32
From "Tavistock Lecture II" (1935)   33
From "A Review of the Complex Theory" (1934)   38
From "Mental Disease and the Psyche" (1928)   40
From "On the Psychogenesis of Schizophrenia" (1939)   43

Part 2   **Jung's Involvement with Freud and His Divergence
        from Freud's Theories**   45

"Psychoanalysis and Neurosis" (1916)   46
From "The Theory of Psychoanalysis" (1913)   54
From "Sigmund Freud" *Memories, Dreams, Reflections*
  (1962)   58
From "On Psychic Energy" (1928)   59

Part 3   **The Development of the Idea of the Collective
        Unconscious and of Archetypes**   65

From "Recent Thoughts on Schizophrenia" (1957)   65
From "The Structure of the Psyche" (1927/31)   66

From "On the Psychology of the Unconscious" *Two Essays on Analytical Psychology* (1917/26/43) 68

From "Confrontation with the Unconscious" *Memories, Dreams, Reflections* (1962) 71

From "The Stages of Life" (1930/1) 72

From "Confrontation with the Unconscious" *Memories, Dreams, Reflections* (1962) 74

From "Confrontation with the Unconscious" *Memories, Dreams, Reflections* (1962) 83

From "Psychological Aspects of the Mother Archetype" (1938/54) 84

Part 4 **Archetypes: Shadow; Anima; Animus; the Persona; the Old Wise Man** 87

From *Psychology and Religion* (1938/40) 88

From "The Shadow" *Aion* (1951) 91

From "The Relations between the Ego and the Unconscious" *Two Essays on Analytical Psychology* (1929) 94

From "Definitions" *Psychological Types* (1921) 97

From "The Relations between the Ego and the Unconscious" *Two Essays on Analytical Psychology* (1928) 105

From "The Syzygy: Anima and Animus" *Aion* (1951) 109

From "Confrontation with the Unconscious" *Memories, Dreams, Reflections* (1962) 118

From "The Relations between the Ego and the Unconscious" *Two Essays on Analytical Psychology* (1928) 122

From "The Phenomenology of the Spirit in Fairytales" (1945/8) 125

Part 5 **Psychological Types and the Self-regulating Psyche** 129

"Introduction" *Psychological Types* (1921) 129

"Psychological Typology" (1936) 133

From "On the Psychology of the Unconscious" *Two Essays on Analytical Psychology* (1917/26/43) 147

"The Practical Use of Dream-analysis" (1934) 168

Part 6   **The Development of the Individual**   191

"The Development of Personality" (1934)   191
From "The Aims of Psychotherapy" (1931)   210
"Conscious, Unconscious, and Individuation" (1939)   212
From "Commentary on *The Secret of the Golden Flower*"
    (1929)   226

Part 7   **Integration, Wholeness, and the Self**   229

From "Confrontation with the Unconscious" *Memories, Dreams,
    Reflections* (1962)   230
"Mandalas" (1955)   235
From *Psychology and Religion* (1938/40)   239
From *Psychology and Religion* (1938/40)   240
From "The Work" *Memories, Dreams, Reflections* (1962)   250
"Introduction to the Religious and Psychological Problems of
    Alchemy" *Psychology and Alchemy* (1944)   253
From "The Conjunction" *Mysterium Coniunctionis* (1955/6)
    287

Part 8   **Self and Opposites: God and the Problem of
            Evil**   299

From "Christ, a Symbol of the Self" *Aion* (1951)   299
From *Answer to Job* (1952)   310
From *Answer to Job* (1952)   321

Part 9   **"*Unus Mundus* and Synchronicity**   331

From "Flying Saucers: a Modern Myth of Things Seen in the
    Skies" (1958)   331
From "The Conjunction" *Mysterium Coniunctionis* (1955/6)
    334
From "On the Nature of the Psyche" (1947/54)   336
From "Synchronicity: an Acausal Connecting Principle" (1952)
    339
From *Answer to Job* (1952)   343

From "Flying Saucers: a Modern Myth of Things Seen in the Skies" (1958)   345

From letter to Father Victor White (10 April 1954)   346

Part 10   **Man and His Future**   349

"The Undiscovered Self (Present and Future)" (1957)   349

Chronology of Jung's Life and Work   405
Glossary   413
Bibliography   427
Index   437

Note on the Text

Bibliographical details of the works from which I have taken extracts – *Collected Works* (CW), *Memories, Dreams, Reflections* (MDR), *Septem Sermones ad Mortuos*, *The Freud/Jung Letters* and *Letters* – are given on pages 434–5. English and American page or paragraph numbering diverges only in the case of MDR; when quoting from this book I have given the English hardback edition's pages followed by those of the American edition.

I have been selective about my inclusion of footnotes, keeping those of Jung's which illuminate the text or which refer to sources of interest to the non-specialist reader, but omitting his and his editors' references to works which, particularly in the case of the alchemical volumes, are unobtainable by all but the most dedicated scholars. Where editors' notes have been retained, they are within square brackets. I have used the bibliographies contained in CW to fill out Jung's footnotes where appropriate.

Preface

Throughout his long life, C. G. Jung was a prolific writer, so that his Collected Works run to no less than eighteen large volumes. In addition, there are five volumes of his seminars, with one more to come—the *Zofingia Lectures*—which he gave when he was a medical student; two volumes of his letters; a separate volume of his correspondence with Freud; and his autobiography, *Memories, Dreams, Reflections.* Comparatively few people are prepared to read the whole corpus of this material, but many might welcome the opportunity to become acquainted with Jung's thought as he himself expounded it. This book is an attempt to distil the essential features of Jung's psychology as it developed during the course of his life by means of extracts from his own writings. Since Jung's way of thinking may be unfamiliar to contemporary readers, I have summarized the main features of his thought in an introduction, and I have prefaced the extracts which I have chosen with brief explanatory remarks. But, so far as is possible, I have let Jung present his ideas in his own words. My purpose has been exposition, not criticism, and it must not be assumed that I personally subscribe to everything that Jung wrote.

Anthony Storr

Introduction

Carl Gustav Jung was born on 26 July 1875 and died on 6 June 1961. The greater part of his early childhood was spent at Klein-Hüningen, near Basel, to which his family moved in 1879. Jung attended the local school from the age of six, and, in his eleventh year, was transferred to the Gymnasium in Basel. From here, he went on to study medicine at the University of Basel during the years 1895–1900. Concurrently, he read extensively in the fields of philosophy and theology.

In 1900, he moved to Zurich where he became an assistant physician to Eugen Bleuler at the Burghölzli mental hospital. He was later promoted to Senior Staff Physician. In 1902–3, he spent a term at the Salpêtrière in Paris in order to study psychopathology with Pierre Janet. During these first years in psychiatry, he wrote his MD dissertation, "On the Psychology and Pathology of So-called Occult Phenomena"; undertook experimental work in word association; and, in 1903, married Emma Rauschenbach, by whom he had a son and four daughters. In 1905, he was appointed a lecturer in the University of Zurich.

In 1907, Jung published a pioneering book on schizophrenia, *The Psychology of Dementia Praecox*, which he sent to Freud. This led to a meeting between the two men in Vienna, and to a close association between them which lasted until 1913. In 1909, Jung, in company with Freud and Ferenczi, paid his first visit to the USA, where he lectured on word-association experiments and received an honorary degree from Clark University, in Massachusetts. In the same year, Jung gave up his post at the Burghölzli in favour of his growing private practice which he conducted in his own house at Küsnacht on the Lake of Zurich. Although he travelled in various parts of the world and paid frequent visits to his country retreat in Bollingen, which was also on the Lake of Zurich, Jung continued to practise and to write in the same house in Küsnacht until his death in 1961. His last piece of writing was completed only ten days before he died.

Jung's earliest work and his later writings have more in common than is generally supposed. They are linked by the theme that mental illness is characterized by disunity of the personality, whilst mental health is manifested by unity. Jung's first study was conducted on a 15½-year-old girl who, claiming to be a medium, said that she was "controlled" by a variety of different personalities, which Jung interpreted as personifications of various unconscious parts of herself. Before Freud's concept of repression became widely employed, the term used to describe such phenomena was "dissociation"; and Jung, who at that time was as much influenced by Janet, with whom he had studied, as he was by Freud, whom he had only read, continued to think of personality as being capable of dissociation into a number of subsidiary personalities, any of which could temporarily "take over." Although Jung accepted the idea of repression in the Freudian sense of making the unacceptable unconscious, and thus inaccessible, he continued to think and write in terms of subsidiary, dissociated personalities, and it is important to bear this in mind when approaching his work. In hysteria, for example, the patient might behave as if she were two or more different persons, who were sometimes given different names and who had no cognizance of each other. Dissociation was a splitting of the personality in which the right hand did not know what the left was doing; and it followed that cure of this type of neurosis depended upon making the divided selves conscious of each other and thus creating a new unity. In schizophrenia, the personality appeared fragmented into many parts, rather than into two or three as in hysteria. Moreover, whereas the hysteric retained contact with reality by means of that part of the personality which was already being called the "ego," the schizophrenic lost contact with reality because the ego was overwhelmed by irruptions from the unconscious and became only one "voice" amongst many.

Jung's next group of studies was based upon the word-association test. A list of a hundred words is read out, and the subject is asked to respond to each with the first word that occurs to him. By timing the interval between stimulus and response, it becomes possible to show that, unknown to themselves, subjects are influenced by words which arouse emotion and slow down their responses. Often, groups of words were linked around a theme; and to such a collection of associations, Jung applied the word "complex," a term which he introduced into psychology. He regarded complexes as similar to, but lesser than, the subsidiary personalities referred to above. These experiments were important in that they demonstrated objectively, in ways which could be measured, the dynamic effects of unconscious mental contents. They will also remind the reader that Jung was trained in the natural sciences and had an accurate grasp of scientific method, although his later interests drew him into fields where scientific method cannot easily be applied.

Although Freud's writings were being eagerly discussed by the younger generation when Jung was working at the Burghölzli, psychiatry was dominated by German phenomenology. Psychiatrists were content to describe their patients' symptoms and behaviour, and to fit them into diagnostic categories, without attempting to understand them as individuals. Jung, by applying psychoanalytic ideas to the study of delusions and hallucinations, was able to demonstrate that such phenomena, hitherto dismissed as incomprehensible, could sometimes be shown to have a psychological origin and meaning. Jung remained keenly interested in schizophrenia, and was one of the first psychiatrists to attempt psychoanalytic treatment of the psychotic.

Jung was never dogmatic as to a single "cause" of schizophrenia, although he inclined to the belief that a psychological, rather than a physical, origin was probable. He was also modest in his therapeutic claims, recognizing that only a limited number of cases responded to analysis, and that partial alleviation was more common than cure. Jung considered that there were many schizophrenics who never came near a mental hospital. If such people consulted him, he was cautious and sometimes dismissed them without attempting psychotherapy. Jung was one of the first to recognize that a psychotic episode could be precipitated by analysis.

It was Jung's intimate acquaintance with the phenomena of schizophrenia which led him to postulate a "collective" unconscious. He found that delusions and hallucinations, which often seemed to be variations on similar themes, could seldom be entirely explained as products of the patient's personal history. Jung's extensive knowledge of comparative religion and of mythology led him to detect parallels with psychotic material which argued a common source: a myth-producing level of mind which was common to all men.

Jung described the collective unconscious as consisting of mythological motifs or primordial images to which he gave the name "archetypes." Archetypes are not inborn ideas, but "typical forms of behaviour which, once they become conscious, naturally present themselves *as ideas and images*, like everything else that becomes a content of consciousness." (CW 8, par. 435) Archetypes have an organizing influence on images and ideas. Archetypes are not themselves conscious, but seem to be like underlying ground themes upon which conscious manifestations are sets of variations. Their presence is felt as "numinous"; that is, of profound spiritual significance. Jung wrote:

All the most powerful ideas in history go back to archetypes. This is particularly true of religious ideas, but the central concepts of science, philosophy and ethics are no exception to this rule. In their present form they are variants of archetypal ideas, created by consciously applying and adapting these ideas to reality. For it is the function of consciousness not only to recognize and assimilate the external world through the gateway of the senses, but to translate into visible reality the world within us. [CW 8, par. 342]

Examples of archetypes as images of ideas are given in extracts which follow.

It was also Jung's study of schizophrenia which led him to formulate a different, and more general, view of psychic energy from that of Freud. Freud believed that schizophrenia, in common with other mental disturbances, was due to repression of sexuality and withdrawal of erotic interest from objects in the external world into the inner world of the subject. Jung considered that contact with the external world was maintained in other ways beside the sexual; and that the loss of contact with reality characteristic of schizophrenia could not be attributed to sexual withdrawal alone.

Because of this, he came to use the term "libido" for psychic energy in general, without limiting it to sexuality.

While Jung was still at the Burghölzli, his private practice was also growing, so that he became as familiar with the various types of neurosis as he was with schizophrenia and the other psychoses. His divergence from Freud became wider. Freud believed that neurosis invariably originated in early childhood, and that the incestuous fantasies and desires connected with the Oedipus complex were central factors. (Freud made an exception in the case of so-called "traumatic" neurosis; but this did not form a main part of his theory.) Jung thought that the cause of neurosis usually lay in the present; and that the infantile fantasies which Freud unearthed were secondary phenomena. When the natural course of a man's development through life was held up, either by misfortune or by his failure to face life's obligations, his libido became turned in upon himself and reactivated the attitudes and feelings of childhood which would normally have been left behind him. Jung believed that there was a natural and proper path of development for each individual; and that neurosis might actually be a valuable signal which indicated when, through intellectual arrogance, a false set of values or an evasion of responsibilities, a person was straying too far from his own true path. Neurotic symptoms, therefore, might be *compensatory*; part of a self-regulating mechanism whose aim was the achievement of a better balance within the psyche. Jung sometimes said of an individual: "Thank God, he became neurotic!" Just as pain might make a man realize that there was something wrong with his body, so neurotic symptoms could draw attention to psychological problems of which the individual was unaware.

The idea of self-regulation runs right through the whole of Jung's scheme of how the mind works, and largely accounts for his view of dreams. Freud considered that the majority of dreams had as their core an unacceptable wish which was striving, in the dream, to find indirect expression. He believed that the "manifest content" of a dream was merely a cloak concealing the "latent content," which was generally some repressed sexual desire of an infantile kind. Jung, on the other hand, regarded dreams as communications from the unconscious. Dreams might be couched in symbolic language which was hard to understand; but they were not necessarily concerned with wishes, nor ways of concealing the unacceptable. Most commonly, dreams were compensatory to the conscious point of view; expressions of aspects of the individual which were neglected or unrealized; or, like neurotic symptoms, warnings of divergence from the individual's proper path. Dreams from the collective level might sometimes be visions of vast significance, quite outside the range of conscious contrivance.

The idea of compensation and self-regulation also became linked with Jung's classification of "psychological types." It was Jung who introduced the terms "extravert" and "introvert" into psychology. Jung's observation of the very different ways in which Freud, Adler and he himself approached the same psychological material led him to postulate that individuals adopted differing habitual attitudes toward life which determined their interpretation of experience. The extravert's bias was toward the external world; the introvert's, toward the inner world of the psyche. Jung later proposed that the psyche operated by means of four functions: thinking, feeling, sensation and intuition. Any one of these functions could also be predominant in an individual's way of dealing with experience. For example, a man could be an introverted thinker or an extraverted intuitive or an introverted feeling type. The eight possible types are vividly described in volume 6 of the Collected Works, *Psychological Types*.

Compensation and self-regulation are integral parts of this type theory. Jung considered that habitual attitudes were nearly always carried too far, so that the thinker neglected his feelings, while the intuitive paid too little attention to the facts given by sensation. Introverts were caught up in their inner worlds; while extraverts lost themselves in the press of events. In Western man, because of the achievements of his culture, there was an especial tendency toward intellectual hubris; an overvaluation of thinking which could alienate a man from his emotional roots. Neurotic symptoms, dreams and other manifestations of the unconscious were often expressions of the "other side" trying to assert itself. There was, therefore, within every individual, a striving toward unity in which divisions would be replaced by consistency, opposites equally balanced, consciousness in reciprocal relation with the unconscious. Jung affirmed that personality was manifested by "definiteness, wholeness and ripeness". (CW 17, par. 288) He considered personality to be an achievement, not something given. Moreover, it was essentially an achievement of the second half of life. In the first half of life, a person is, and should be, concerned with emancipating himself from parents and with establishing himself in the world as spouse, parent and effective contributor. In the modern world, especially, a certain one-sidedness might be needed to fulfil these conventional demands; but, once a person had done so, then he could and should look inwards. Jung called the journey toward wholeness the "process of individuation," and it is toward the study of this process that the thrust of his later work is directed.

Jung's later writings are much concerned with alchemy. Although the ostensible purpose of alchemy was to find a way of changing base metals into gold, the early alchemists "sought not only to make gold, but *to perfect everything in its own nature*" (F. Sherwood Taylor, *The Alchemists*, London: Heinemann, 1951, p. 3). Moreover they linked change in matter with change in man, so that the alchemical "work" aimed at perfecting matter was, at the same time, a psychological process aimed at perfecting man. Some of the alchemists undoubtedly thought of their work as a meditative development of the inner personality; and this is why their writings appealed to Jung, who found parallels between the series of changes described by the alchemists and the process of individuation which he observed taking place within his patients. Individuation is essentially a spiritual journey. "Only the man who can consciously assent to the power of the inner voice becomes a personality." (CW 17, par. 308) By paying attention to the voice within, the individual achieves a new synthesis between conscious and unconscious, a sense of calm acceptance and detachment, and a realization of the meaning of life.

If the unconscious can be recognized as a co-determining factor along with consciousness, and if we can live in such a way that conscious and unconscious demands are taken into account as far as possible, then the centre of gravity of the total personality shifts its position. It is then no longer in the ego, which is merely the centre of consciousness, but in the hypothetical point between conscious and unconscious. This new centre might be called the self. [CW 13, par. 67]

Jung found that the new centre expressed itself in quaternity symbols and circular structures which he called "mandalas," the Sanskrit name applied to images of this kind which, in the East, are used for meditation. Mandalas symbolize an integrating factor. In cases where consciousness is confused, mandalas may appear as compensatory attempts at self-healing by imposing an ordered structure. The self, of which the mandala is a symbol, is the archetype of unity and totality. Jung believed that this archetype was the underlying reality manifesting itself in the various systems of monotheism. The self, therefore, is the God within; and the individual, in seeking self-realization and unity, becomes the means through which "God seeks his goal." (CW 10, par. 588) By fulfilling his own highest potential, the individual is not only realizing the meaning of life, but also fulfilling God's will.

Jung believed that only exceptional individuals reached the peaks of individual development. Individuation means parting company with the crowd; and this at first accentuates loneliness, and may seem alarming. Most human beings are content to remain safely with the majority, conforming to the conventions and beliefs shared by members of their family, church or political party. But exceptional individuals are impelled by their inner nature to seek their own path; and, although human psyches, like human bodies, share a basic structure, the individual psyche is "an endlessly varied recombination of age-old components". (MDR, p. 223/235) Jung continued to affirm that the highest ideals and values were carried by the individual, never by an ideology or the State.

Jung's major contribution to psychology, therefore, lies in the field of *adult* development. Freud and his followers were primarily interested in the earliest development of the young child, since they considered that the majority of neuroses originated in the first five years of life. Freudian analysis had as its aim the reconstruction and recall of the patient's earliest years. It was assumed that, when the repressed, infantile material had been made conscious, the patient would become free of the malign effects of his childhood and lose the neurotic symptoms which were its consequence. Freudian analysis, therefore, was, and is, primarily orientated toward the patient's past.

Jung, of course, was well aware of the importance of early childhood in determining personality development. Indeed, in cases in which it was clear that the patient's primary problem was emancipating himself from the influence of home and parents, Jung advocated proceeding along Freudian or Adlerian lines. But Jung was inclined to leave such analyses to others. The patients who interested him were those who had already freed themselves from the past sufficiently to become established in their own right; who were often successful in worldly terms; but who, in the mid-period of their lives, found that the world had become stale and unprofitable. Such people were seeking a meaning to their lives; and Jung's aim was to guide them along the path of individuation. Jungian analysis, therefore, was, and is, primarily orientated toward the patient's future.

The quest for a new synthesis of personality involves taking into account those parts of the whole which have been neglected. As pointed out above, Jung found that those who consulted him because of the emptiness of their lives were one-sided in their development: too much identified with their predominant attitude and function. Since everyone has both an extraverted and an introverted potential, and also needs all four functions (thinking, feeling, sensation and intuition) if he is to live life fully, it follows that one task of analysis is to help the patient become aware of neglected aspects of his personality. Such aspects appear in dreams; and the study of dreams became even more important in Jungian analysis than in its Freudian counterpart.

Another technique developed by Jung was that of "active imagination." Jung encouraged his patients to enter a state of reverie in which judgment was suspended but consciousness preserved. They were then enjoined to note what fantasies occurred to them, and to let these fantasies go their own way without interference. Jung encouraged his patients to draw and paint their fantasies, finding that this technique both helped the patient to rediscover hidden parts of himself and also portrayed the psychological journey upon which he was embarked. Jung was the first analyst to supplement verbal exchange in this way; and the increasing use of painting, modelling and music in therapy bears witness to Jung's prescience.

In times when so much importance is attributed to good or bad interpersonal relationships as determinants of mental health or illness, Jung's concentration upon the individual's relations with the different parts of his own psyche may seem puzzling. Jung was well aware of the importance of interpersonal relationships, but believed that it was only when the individual had come to terms with himself that satisfactory relationships with others could be achieved. Jung wrote: "Companionship thrives only when each individual remembers his individuality and does not identify himself with others." (MDR, p. 328/356)

Individuation is not the same as individualism, "which is essentially no more than a morbid reaction against an equally futile collectivism. In contrast to all this, the natural process of individuation brings to birth a consciousness of human community precisely because it makes us aware of the unconscious, which unites and is common to all mankind." (CW 16, par. 227)

Although Jung claimed that what he discovered were facts which anyone else who adopted the same technique would confirm, he was also aware that subjective factors were bound to influence his point of view. "Philosophical criticism has helped me to see that every psychology – my own included – has the character of a subjective confession ... Even when I am dealing with empirical data I am necessarily speaking about myself." (CW 4, par. 774) It may be helpful to glance at some of the influences which contributed to Jung's particular viewpoint.

For the first nine years of his life, Jung remained an only child who lived primarily in his imagination and who spent much of his time in solitary play. When he first went to school, he found that, in trying to adapt to his rural companions, he tended to become alienated from himself, as sensitive and imaginative people often do when trying too hard to "fit in." It became important to him to preserve his inner imaginative world from intrusion. In his autobiography, he describes various secret rituals by means of which he kept contact with his inner world and shielded it from others. In the "Late Thoughts" which form part of his autobiography, Jung wrote: "There is no better means of intensifying the treasured feeling of individuality than the possession of a secret which the individual is pledged to guard." (MDR, p. 315/342) In the last chapter of the same book, he wrote: "As a child I felt myself to be alone, and I am still, because I know things and must hint at things which others apparently know nothing of, and for the most part do not want to know." (MDR, p. 327/356) Jung's childhood discovery of the vital importance of remaining in touch with the inner world is one factor accounting for his emphasis on healing and the growth of personality as essentially an inner process, concentrating upon the individual's relation with the various aspects of his own psyche, rather than upon his relationships with other human beings.

From his earliest years, Jung was exposed to a great deal of discussion of religious matters. His father was a minister in the Swiss Reformed Church; two of his uncles were parsons; and there were no less than six parsons in his mother's family. Very early in his life, so Jung records, he experienced dreams and visions of a religious kind which convinced him not only that religious experience was a personal matter which might have little to do with established creeds, but also that God had a "dark" side which did not accord with the conventional Christian image of an ever-loving father. His own father was content to promulgate the teachings of his church, though Jung came to question the genuineness of his faith. He was unable, or unwilling, to discuss the doubts with which his more gifted son confronted him. Jung, therefore, found himself in the position of being unable to subscribe to the faith in which he had been reared, while at the same time continuing to think that individuals could neither be happy nor healthy unless they acknowledged their dependence upon some higher power than that of the ego. Jung himself became one of those exceptional individuals who so much interested him as patients: individuals who were compelled by their own natures to strike out on their own, abandon conventional beliefs and find what they were seeking within their own psyches. Although Jung continued to profess allegiance to what he called "the extreme left wing of Protestantism," his religious ideas became so unconventional that he gave offence to both Catholic and Protestant theologians, although some from both camps continued to find value in what Jung had to say.

Another important factor determining Jung's psychological standpoint was the period of mental upheaval through which he passed in the years of the First World War, just after his break with Freud. Although, as we shall see, Jung was never a disciple of Freud, and had carried out a good deal of original work before he had even met him, Freud was a powerful influence, and separating from him was extremely painful. It was because Jung felt that he had to be true to his own inner voice that the break occurred; for Freud's tolerance of any divergence from the "truths" which he believed he had discovered was limited. At the time of parting, Jung was thirty-eight. Jung's insistence that the mid-life period was a turning point in psychological development took origin from his own experience.

Like many solitary thinkers, Jung was always an avid reader, and, while still an adolescent, plunged into Kant and Schopenhauer. The latter's sombre view especially appealed to him. "Here at last was a philosopher who had the courage to see that all was not for the best in the fundaments of the universe." (MDR, p. 76/69) Although there are profound differences between Jung's thought and that of Schopenhauer, there are also striking similarities. Schopenhauer considered that individuals were the embodiments of an underlying Will which was outside space and time. Jung begins his autobiography by writing: "My life is a story of the self-realization of the unconscious." (MDR, p. 17/3) Schopenhauer considered that the very notion of individuality, the *principium individuationis*, is dependent on the human, subjective categories of space and time which force us to be conscious of individual objects, and prevent us from seeing the original unity of the Will of which individuals are a manifestation. Jung also believed that there was a realm outside space and time from which individuals become differentiated. Borrowing the Gnostic term, he referred to this spiritual realm transcending consciousness as the *pleroma*. "We are distinguished from the pleroma in our essence ... which is confined within time and space." *Septem Sermones ad Mortuos*, I) Whereas in the pleroma all is one and there is no differentiation between opposites like good and evil, light and darkness, time and space, or force and matter, the *principium individuationis* compels distinctiveness which is the essential characteristic of individuals. Whereas Schopenhauer's philosophy is governed by the ideal of deliverance from the bonds of individuality by means of self-denial and asceticism (an ideal which Schopenhauer himself was far from realizing), Jung's philosophy is ruled by the idea of affirmation of individuality. A man who understands and comes to terms with the different aspects of his inner being is enabled to live life more completely. Jung was also influenced by Nietzsche, who was a passionate individualist; but, whereas Nietzsche stated that God was dead, Jung rediscovered God as a guiding principle of unity within the depths of the individual psyche.

Jung's belief in the ultimate unity of all existence led him to suppose that physical and mental, as well as spatial and temporal, were human categories imposed upon reality which did not accurately reflect it. Human beings, because of the nature of thought and language, are bound to categorize things as opposites; that is, all human statements are antinomian. But these opposites may, in fact, be facets of the same reality. Through his collaboration with the physicist Wolfgang Pauli, Jung came to believe that the physicist's investigation of matter and the psychologist's investigation of the depths of the psyche might be different ways of approaching the same underlying reality. It had long been recognized that analytical psychology could never be wholly "objective," since the observer was bound to exert an effect on what he was observing by the fact of paying it attention. But the same point had also been reached in modern physics. At the subatomic level, it was recognized that it was impossible to determine a particle's momentum and its velocity at the same time. Moreover, the constituents of matter could be considered to behave as waves or particles, depending on the choice of the observer. Physicists came to realize that it was possible to look at one and the same event through two different frames of reference which, though mutually exclusive, were nevertheless complementary. The Principle of Complementarity, which became a cornerstone of modern physics, could also be applied to the mind-body problem. Perhaps mind and body were simply different aspects of a single reality as viewed through different frames of reference.

Jung claimed that there were "sufficient reasons" for believing that "the psychic lies embedded in something that appears to be of a nonpsychic nature." (CW 8, par. 437) Jung came to think of archetypes as existing in this reality outside space and time, but manifesting themselves in the individual psyche as organizers. "Archetypes, so far as we can observe and explain them at all, manifest themselves only through their ability to *organize* images and ideas, and this is always an unconscious process which cannot be detected until afterwards. By assimilating material whose provenance in the phenomenal world is not to be contested, they become visible and *psychic*." (CW 8, par. 440) One reason why Jung thought of archetypes as existing outside space and time was that he believed them responsible for what he called "meaningful coincidences," of which examples are given in the extracts which follow. Throughout his life, Jung had been impressed by clusters of significant events occurring together, and by the fact that these events might be physical as well as mental. The physical death of one individual, for example, might coincide with a disturbing dream referring to that death in the mind of another. Jung felt that such coincidences, which he considered "relatively common," demanded an explanatory principle in addition to causality. This principle he named *synchronicity*. Once again, Jung seems to have been influenced by Schopenhauer, who had postulated a link between simultaneous events which were causally unconnected. Jung's idea was that synchronicity was based on a universal order of *meaning*, complementary to causality. He thought that synchronistic phenomena were connected with archetypes which he referred to as *psychoid* factors of the collective unconscious, meaning by this that archetypes were neither physical nor mental but partaking of both realms, and able, therefore, to manifest themselves both physically and mentally simultaneously. Jung refers to the case of Swedenborg, who experienced a vision of a fire in Stockholm at the same time as an actual fire was raging. Jung considered that some change in Swedenborg's state of mind gave him temporary access to "absolute knowledge"; to an area in which the limits of space and time are transcended. Jung believed that causeless events were creative acts "as the continuous creation of a pattern that exists from all eternity, repeats itself sporadically, and is not derivable from any known antecedents." (CW 8, par. 967) The recognition of patterns of order affects human beings as *meaning*.

In Jung's view, changes in the collective unconscious, which might take centuries to complete themselves, were responsible for alterations in the way in which men viewed the world and thought about themselves. The decline in conventional Christian belief, for example, is related to the fact that the Christ-image, which excludes both evil and the feminine, can no longer symbolize wholeness for modern man. It was only in 1950 that the Pope proclaimed the Assumption of the Virgin Mary as part of divine revelation. Jung considered this as a significant step toward incorporating femininity into the image of the divine, and pointed out that the impulse to do this did not come from the ecclesiastical authorities but from the Catholic masses "who have insisted more and more vehemently on this development. Their insistence is, at bottom, the urge of the archetype to realize itself" (CW 9 ii, par. 142) and it took many years for this to be accomplished.

I hope that this brief introduction to Jung's thought will make it easier for the reader to find his way through the extracts which follow. Some may find Jung's later writings difficult or antipathetic; but Jung's valuable contributions to psychotherapy and to the understanding of individuals can be appreciated without subscribing to the whole of his system of belief.

Part 1. Jung's Early Work

Jung began his career in psychiatry in December 1900, when he was appointed as an assistant physician at the Burghölzli mental hospital in Zurich. Breuer and Freud had published their Studies on Hysteria *in 1895; and Freud's* The Interpretation of Dreams *had appeared in November 1899. But psychiatrists were still fascinated by the researches of Janet and Morton Prince into cases of "multiple personality," and it was this phenomenon which inspired Jung's first published work: his dissertation for his medical degree, "On the Psychology and Pathology of So-called Occult Phenomena." This was based on his observations during seances of a $15\frac{1}{2}$-year-old cousin, Hélène Preiswerk (called S. W. in the paper), who was reputedly a medium. She claimed to be controlled by a variety of spirits, varying from her grandfather, who was deeply serious, to a figure called Ulrich von Gerbenstein, who was flirtatious and frivolous. Jung interpreted these various figures as "unconscious personalities."*

From "On the Psychology and Pathology of So-called Occult Phenomena" CW 1, par. 77

In our account of S. W.'s case, the following condition was indicated by the term "semi-somnambulism": For some time before and after the actual somnambulistic attack the patient found herself in a state whose most salient feature can best be described as "preoccupation". She lent only half an ear to the conversation around her, answered absent-mindedly, frequently lost herself in all manner of hallucinations; her face was solemn, her look ecstatic, visionary, ardent. Closer observation revealed a far-reaching alteration of her entire character. She was now grave, dignified; when she spoke, the theme was always an extremely serious one. In this state she could talk so seriously, so forcefully and convincingly, that one almost had to ask oneself: Is this really a girl of 15½? One had the impression that a mature woman was being acted with considerable dramatic talent.

Jung goes on to compare S. W. with a case of Janet's.

CW 1, pars. 92–3

Janet conducted the following conversation with the subconscious of Lucie, who, meanwhile, was engaged in conversation with another observer:

[Janet asks:] Do you hear me? [Lucie answers, in automatic writing:] *No.*
But one has to hear in order to answer. – *Absolutely.*
Then how do you do it? – *I don't know.*
There must be someone who hears me. – *Yes.*
Who is it? – *Somebody besides Lucie.*
All right. Somebody else. Shall we give the other person a name? – *No.*
Yes, it will be more convenient. – *All right. Adrienne.*
Well, Adrienne, do you hear me? – *Yes.*

One can see from these extracts how the unconscious personality builds itself up: it owes its existence simply to suggestive questions which strike an answering chord in the medium's own disposition. This disposition can be explained by the disaggregation of psychic complexes, and the feeling of strangeness evoked by these automatisms assists the process as soon as conscious attention is directed to the automatic act. Binet remarks on this experiment of Janet's: "Nevertheless it should be carefully noted that if the personality of 'Adrienne' could be created, it was because the suggestion encountered a *psychological possibility*; in other words, disaggregated phenomena were existing there apart from the normal consciousness of the subject."* The individualization of the subconscious is always a great step forward and has enormous suggestive influence on further development of the automatisms.

*Alfred Binet, *Alterations of Personality*, tr. Helen Green Baldwin, London: 1896, p. 147.

The formation of unconscious personalities in our case must also be regarded in this light.

Returning to his own case, Jung discusses the "Origin of the Unconscious Personalities."

CW 1, pars. 132-3

As we have seen, the various personalities are grouped round two types, the grandfather and Ulrich von Gerbenstein. The grandfather produces nothing but sanctimonious twaddle and edifying moral precepts. Ulrich von Gerbenstein is simply a silly schoolgirl, with nothing masculine about him except his name. We must here add, from the anamnesis, that the patient was confirmed at the age of fifteen by a very pietistic clergyman, and that even at home she had to listen to moral sermons. The grandfather represents this side of her past, Gerbenstein the other half; hence the curious contrast. So here we have, personified, the chief characters of the past: here the compulsorily educated bigot, there the boisterousness of a lively girl of fifteen who often goes too far. The patient herself is a peculiar mixture of both; sometimes timid, shy, excessively reserved, at other times boisterous to the point of indecency. She is often painfully conscious of these contrasts. This gives us the key to the origin of the two subconscious personalities. The patient is obviously seeking a middle way between two extremes; she endeavours to repress them and strives for a more ideal state. These strivings lead to the adolescent dream of the ideal Ivenes, beside whom the unrefined aspects of her character fade into the background. They are not lost; but as repressed thoughts, analogous to the idea of Ivenes, they begin to lead an independent existence as autonomous personalities.

This behaviour calls to mind Freud's dream investigations, which disclose the independent growth of repressed thoughts.

The idea that personality was not a unity, but might contain subsidiary personalities was familiar to Jung from his own experience, since he records his surprise, at the age of twelve, at finding that he himself was two different persons.

From "**School Years**" MDR, pp. 44–6/33–4

Around this time I was invited to spend the holidays with friends of the family who had a house on Lake Lucerne. To my delight the house was situated right on the lake, and there was a boat-house and a rowing boat. My host allowed his son and me to use the boat, although we were sternly warned not to be reckless. Unfortunately I also knew how to steer a *Waidling* (a boat of the gondola type) – that is to say, standing. At home we had such a punt, in which we had tried out every imaginable trick. The first thing I did, therefore, was to take my stand on the stern seat and with one oar push off into the lake. That was too much for the anxious master of the house. He whistled us back and gave me a first-class dressing-down. I was thoroughly crestfallen but had to admit that I had done exactly what he had said not to, and that his lecture was quite justified. At the same time I was seized with rage that this fat, ignorant boor should dare to insult ME. This ME was not only grown up, but important, an authority, a person with office and dignity, an old man, an object of respect and awe. Yet the contrast with reality was so grotesque that in the midst of my fury I suddenly stopped myself, for the question rose to my lips: "Who in the world are you, anyway? You are reacting as though you were the devil only knows how important! And yet you know he is perfectly right. You are barely twelve years old, a schoolboy, and he is a father and a rich, powerful man besides, who owns two houses and several splendid horses."

Then, to my intense confusion, it occurred to me that I was actually two different persons. One of them was the schoolboy who could not grasp algebra and was far from sure of himself; the other was important, a high authority, a man not to be trifled with, as powerful and influential as this manufacturer. This "Other" was an old man who lived in the eighteenth century, wore buckled shoes and a white wig and went driving in a fly with high, concave rear wheels between which the box was suspended on springs and leather straps.

This notion sprang from a curious experience I had had. When we were living in Klein-Hüningen an ancient green carriage from the Black Forest drove past our house one day. It was truly an antique, looking exactly as if it had come straight out of the eighteenth century. When I saw it, I felt with great excitement: "That's it! Sure enough, that comes from *my* times." It was as though I had recognized it because it was the same type as the one I had driven in myself. Then came a curious *sentiment écoeurant*, as though someone had stolen something from me, or as though I had been cheated – cheated out of my beloved past. The carriage was a relic of those times! I cannot describe what was happening in me or what it was that affected me so strongly: a longing, a nostalgia, or a recognition that kept saying "Yes, that's how it was! Yes, that's how it was!"

When Jung began work at the Burghölzli mental hospital, word-association tests were used as a means of studying the way in which mental contents are linked together by similarity, contrast or contiguity in space and time. Jung transformed their use into a tool for investigating emotional preoccupations; and his researches led him to formulate the notion of the "complex," a term which he introduced.

From "Tavistock Lecture II" CW 18, pars. 97–106

First of all I want to say something about *word-association tests*. To many of you perhaps these seem old-fashioned, but since they are still being used I have to refer to them. I use this test now not with patients but with criminal cases.

The experiment is made – I am repeating well-known things – with a list of say a hundred words. You instruct the test person to react with the first word that comes into his mind as quickly as possible after having heard and understood the stimulus word. When you have made sure that the test person has understood what you mean you start the experiment. You mark the time of each reaction with a stop-watch. When you have finished the hundred words you do another experiment. You repeat the stimulus words and the test person has to reproduce his former answers. In certain places his memory fails and reproduction becomes uncertain or faulty. These mistakes are important.

Originally the experiment was not meant for its present application at all; it was intended to be used for the study of mental association. That was of course a most Utopian idea. One can study nothing of the sort by such primitive means. But you can study something else when the experiment fails, when people make mistakes. You ask a simple word that a child can answer, and a highly intelligent person cannot reply. Why? That word has hit on what I call a complex, a conglomeration of psychic contents characterized by a peculiar or perhaps painful feeling-tone, something that is usually hidden from sight. It is as though a projectile struck through the thick layer of the *persona* into the dark layer. For instance, somebody with a money complex will be hit when you say: "To buy," "to pay," or "money." That is a disturbance of reaction.

We have about twelve or more categories of disturbance and I will mention a few of them so that you will get an idea of their practical value. The prolongation of the reaction time is of the greatest practical importance. You decide whether the reaction time is too long by taking the average mean of the reaction times of the test person. Other characteristic disturbances are: reaction with more than one word, against the instructions; mistakes in reproduction of the word; reaction expressed by facial expression, laughing, movement of the hands or feet or body, coughing, stammering, and such things; insufficient reactions like "yes" or "no"; not reacting to the real meaning of the stimulus word; habitual use of the same words; use of foreign languages – of which there is not a great danger in England, though with us it is a great nuisance; defective reproduction, when memory begins to fail in the reproduction experiment; total lack of reaction.

All these reactions are beyond the control of the will. If you submit to the experiment you are done for, and if you do not submit to it you are done for too, because one knows why you are unwilling to do so. If you put it to a criminal he can refuse, and that is fatal because one knows why he refuses. If he gives in he hangs himself. In Zurich I am called in by the Court when they have a difficult case; I am the last straw.

The results of the association test can be illustrated very neatly by a diagram (Figure 5). The height of the columns represents the actual reaction time of the test person. The dotted horizontal line represents the average mean of reaction times. The unshaded columns are those reactions which show no signs of disturbance.

The shaded columns show disturbed reactions. In reactions 7, 8, 9, 10, you observe for instance a whole series of disturbances: the stimulus word at 7 was a critical one, and without the test person noticing it at all three subsequent reaction times are overlong on account of the perseveration of the reaction to the stimulus

Figure 5. Association Test

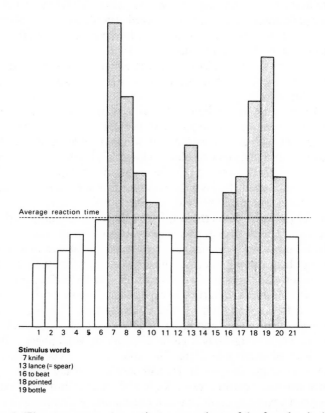

Average reaction time

1 2 3 4 5 6 7 8 9 10 11 12 13 14 15 16 17 18 19 20 21

Stimulus words
7 knife
13 lance (= spear)
16 to beat
18 pointed
19 bottle

word. The test person was quite unconscious of the fact that he had an emotion. Reaction 13 shows an isolated disturbance, and in 16–20 the result is again a whole series of disturbances. The strongest disturbances are in reactions 18 and 19. In this particular case we have to do with a so-called intensification of sensitiveness through the sensitizing effect of an unconscious emotion: when a critical stimulus word has aroused a perseverating emotional reaction, and when the next critical stimulus word happens to occur within the range of that perseveration, then it is apt to produce a greater effect than it would have been expected to produce if it had occurred in a series of indifferent associations. This is called the sensitizing effect of a perseverating emotion.

In dealing with criminal cases we can make use of the sensitizing effect, and then we arrange the critical stimulus words in such a way that they occur more or less within the presumable range of perseveration. This can be done in order to increase the effect of critical stimulus words. With a suspected culprit as a test person, the critical stimulus words are words which have a direct bearing upon the crime.

The test person for Figure 5 was a man about 35, a decent individual, one of my normal test persons. I had of course to experiment with a great number of normal people before I could draw conclusions from pathological material. If you want to know what it was that disturbed this man, you simply have to read the words that caused the disturbances and fit them together. Then you get a nice story. I will tell you exactly what it was.

To begin with, it was the word *knife* that caused four disturbed reactions. The next disturbance was *lance* (or *spear*) and then *to beat*, then the word *pointed* and then *bottle*. That was in a short series of fifty stimulus words, which was enough for me to tell the man point-blank what the matter was. So I said: "I did not know you had had such a disagreeable experience." He stared at me and said: "I do not know what you are talking about." I said: "You know you were drunk and had a disagreeable affair with sticking your knife into somebody." He said: "How do you know?" Then he confessed the whole thing. He came of a respectable family, simple but quite nice people. He had been abroad and one day got into a drunken quarrel, drew a knife and stuck it into somebody, and got a year in prison. That is a great secret which he does not mention because it would cast a shadow on his life. Nobody in his town or surroundings knows anything about it and I am the only one who by chance stumbled upon it. In my seminar in Zurich I also make these experiments. Those who want to confess are of course welcome to. However, I always ask them to bring some

material of a person *they* know and *I* do not know, and I show them
how to read the story of that individual. It is quite interesting work;
sometimes one makes remarkable discoveries.

I will give you other instances. Many years ago, when I was quite
a young doctor, an old professor of criminology asked me about
the experiment and said he did not believe in it. I said: "No,
Professor? You can try it whenever you like." He invited me to his
house and I began. After ten words he got tired and said: "What
can you make of it? Nothing has come of it." I told him he could
not expect a result with ten or twelve words; he ought to have a
hundred and then we could see something. He said: "Can you do
something with these words?" I said: "Little enough, but I can tell
you something. Quite recently you have had worries about money,
you have too little of it. You are afraid of dying of heart disease.
You must have studied in France, where you had a love affair, and
it has come back to your mind, as often, when one has thoughts
of dying, old sweet memories come back from the womb of time."
He said: "How do you know?" Any child could have seen it! He
was a man of 72 and he had associated *heart* with *pain* – fear that
he would die of heart failure. He associated *death* with *to die* – a
natural reaction – and with *money* he associated *too little*, a very
usual reaction. Then things became rather startling to me. To *pay*,
after a long reaction time, he said *La Semeuse*, though our
conversation was in German. That is the famous figure on the
French coin. Now why on earth should this old man say *La
Semeuse*? When he came to the word *kiss* there was a long reaction
time and there was a light in his eyes and he said: *Beautiful*. Then
of course I had the story. He would never have used French if it
had not been associated with a particular feeling, and so we must
think why he used it. Had he had losses with the French franc?
There was no talk of inflation and devaluation in those days. That
could not be the clue. I was in doubt whether it was money or love,
but when he came to *kiss/beautiful* I knew it was love. He was not
the kind of man to go to France in later life, but he had been a
student in Paris, a lawyer, probably at the Sorbonne. It was
relatively simple to stitch together the whole story.

Jung soon began to link the idea of complexes with that of "unconscious personalities."

From "A Review of the Complex Theory" CW 8, pars. 200–3

So far, I have purposely avoided discussing the nature of complexes, on the tacit assumption that their nature is generally known. The word "complex" in its psychological sense has passed into common speech both in German and in English. Everyone knows nowadays that people "have complexes." What is not so well known, though far more important theoretically, is that complexes can *have us*. The existence of complexes throws serious doubt on the naïve assumption of the unity of consciousness, which is equated with "psyche," and on the supremacy of the will. Every constellation of a complex postulates a disturbed state of consciousness. The unity of consciousness is disrupted and the intentions of the will are impeded or made impossible. Even memory is often noticeably affected, as we have seen. The complex must therefore be a psychic factor which, in terms of energy, possesses a value that sometimes exceeds that of our conscious intentions, otherwise such disruptions of the conscious order would not be possible at all. And in fact, an active complex puts us momentarily under a state of duress, of compulsive thinking and acting, for which under certain conditions the only appropriate term would be the judicial concept of diminished responsibility.

What then, scientifically speaking, is a "feeling toned complex"? It is the *image* of a certain psychic situation which is strongly accentuated emotionally and is, moreover, incompatible with the habitual attitude of consciousness. This image has a powerful inner coherence, it has its own wholeness and, in addition, a relatively high degree of autonomy, so that it is subject to the control of the conscious mind to only a limited extent, and therefore behaves like an animated foreign body in the sphere of consciousness. The complex can usually be suppressed with an effort of will, but not argued out of existence, and at the first suitable opportunity it reappears in all its original strength. Certain experimental investigations seem to indicate that its intensity or activity curve has a wavelike character, with a "wave-length" of hours, days, or weeks. This very complicated question remains as yet unclarified.

We have to thank the French psychopathologists, Pierre Janet in particular, for our knowledge today of the extreme *dissociability* of consciousness. Janet and Morton Prince both succeeded in producing four to five splittings of the personality, and it turned out that each fragment of personality had its own peculiar character and its own separate memory. These fragments subsist relatively independently of one another and can take one another's place at any time, which means that each fragment possesses a high degree of autonomy. My findings in regard to complexes corroborate this somewhat disquieting picture of the possibilities of psychic disintegration, for fundamentally there is no difference in principle between a fragmentary personality and a complex. They have all the essential features in common, until we come to the delicate question of fragmented consciousness. Personality fragments undoubtedly have their own consciousness, but whether such small psychic fragments as complexes are also capable of a consciousness of their own is a still unanswered question. I must confess that this question has often occupied my thoughts, for complexes behave like Descartes' devils and seem to delight in playing impish tricks. They slip just the wrong word into one's mouth, they make one forget the name of the person one is about to introduce, they cause a tickle in the throat just when the softest passage is being played on the piano at a concert, they make the tiptoeing latecomer trip over a chair with a resounding crash. They bid us congratulate the mourners at a burial instead of condoling with them, they are the instigators of all those maddening things which F. T. Vischer atributed to the "mischievousness of the object." They are the actors in our dreams, whom we confront so powerlessly; they are the elfin beings so aptly characterized in Danish folklore by the story of the clergyman who tried to teach the Lord's prayer to two elves. They took the greatest pains to repeat the words after him correctly, but at the very first sentence they could not avoid saying: "Our Father, who art not in heaven." As one might expect on theoretical grounds, these impish complexes are unteachable.

I hope that, taking it with a very large grain of salt, no one will mind this metaphorical paraphrase of a scientific problem. But even the soberest formulation of the phenomenology of complexes cannot get round the impressive fact of their autonomy, and the deeper one penetrates into their nature – I might almost say into their biology – the more clearly do they reveal their character as *splinter psyches*. Dream psychology shows us as plainly as could be wished how complexes appear in personified form when there is no inhibiting consciousness to suppress them, exactly like the hobgoblins of folklore who go crashing round the house at night. We observe the same phenomenon in certain psychoses when the complexes get "loud" and appear as "voices" having a thoroughly personal character.

In 1907, Jung published The Psychology of Dementia Praecox *(the current name for what is now called schizophrenia). He sent the book to Freud, and it was this which led to Freud's invitation to Jung to visit him in Vienna. Jung retained an interest in schizophrenia throughout his life, and wrote a paper on the condition as recently as 1957, only four years before his death.*

From "**Mental Disease and the Psyche**" CW 3, pars. 498–503

In 1907 I came before the scientific public with a book on the psychology of dementia praecox. By and large, I adopted a standpoint affirming the psychogenesis of schizophrenia, and emphasized that the symptoms (delusions and hallucinations) are not just meaningless chance happenings but, as regards their content, are in every respect significant psychic products. This means that schizophrenia has a "psychology," i.e., a psychic causality and finality, just as normal mental life has, though with this important difference: whereas in the healthy person the ego is the subject of his experience, in the schizophrenic the ego is only *one* of the experiencing subjects. In other words, in schizophrenia the normal subject has split into a plurality of subjects, or into a plurality of *autonomous complexes*.

The simplest form of schizophrenia, of the splitting of the personality, is paranoia, the classic persecution-mania of the "persécuteur persécuté." It consists in a simple doubling of the personality, which in milder cases is still held together by the identity of the two egos. The patient strikes us at first as completely normal; he may hold office, be in a lucrative position, we suspect nothing. We converse normally with him, and at some point we let fall the word "Freemason." Suddenly the jovial face before us changes, a piercing look full of abysmal mistrust and inhuman fanaticism meets us from his eye. He has become a hunted, dangerous animal, surrounded by invisible enemies: the other ego has risen to the surface.

What has happened? Obviously at some time or other the idea of being a persecuted victim gained the upper hand, became autonomous, and formed a second subject which at times completely replaces the healthy ego. It is characteristic that neither of the two subjects can fully experience the other, although the two personalities are not separated by a belt of unconsciousness as they are in an hysterical dissociation of the personality. They know each other intimately, but they have no valid arguments against one another. The healthy ego cannot counter the affectivity of the other, for at least half its affectivity has gone over into its opposite number. It is, so to speak, paralysed. This is the beginning of that schizophrenic "apathy" which can be observed in paranoid dementia. The patient can assure you with the greatest indifference: "I am the triple owner of the world, the finest Turkey, the Lorelei, Germania and Helvetia of exclusively sweet butter and Naples and I must supply the whole world with macaroni." All this without a blush, and with no flicker of a smile. Here there are countless subjects and no central ego to experience anything and react emotionally.

Turning back to our case of paranoia, we must ask: Is it psychologically meaningless that the idea of persecution has taken possession of him and usurped a part of his personality? Is it, in other words, simply a product of some chance organic disturbance of the brain? If that were so, the delusion would be "unpsychological"; it would lack psychological causality and finality, and would not be psychogenic. But should it be found that the pathological idea did not appear just by chance, that it appeared at a particular psychological moment, then we would have to speak of psychogenesis, even if we assumed that there had always been a predisposing factor in the brain which was partly responsible for the disease.

The psychological moment must certainly be something out of the ordinary; it must have something about it that would adequately explain why it had such a profound and dangerous effect. If someone is frightened by a mouse and then falls ill with schizophrenia, this is obviously not a psychic causation, which is always intricate and subtle. Thus our paranoiac fell ill long before anyone suspected his illness; and secondly, the pathological idea overwhelmed him at a psychological moment. This happened when his congenitally hypersensitive emotional life became warped, and the spiritual form which his emotions needed in order to live finally broke down. It did not break by itself, it was broken by the patient. It came about in the following way.

When still a sensitive youth, but already equipped with a powerful intellect, he developed a passionate love for his sister-in-law, until finally – and not unnaturally – it displeased her husband, his elder brother. His were boyish feelings, woven mostly out of moonshine, seeking the mother, like all psychic impulses that are immature. But these feelings really do need a mother, they need prolonged incubation in order to grow strong and to withstand the unavoidable clash with reality. In themselves there is nothing reprehensible about them, but to the simple, straightforward mind they arouse suspicion. The harsh interpretation which his brother put upon them had a devastating effect, because the patient's own mind admitted that it was right. His dream was destroyed, but this in itself would not have been harmful had it not also killed his feelings. For his intellect then took over the role of the brother and, with inquisitorial sternness, destroyed every trace of feeling, holding before him the ideal of cold-blooded heartlessness. A less passionate nature can put up with this for a time, but a highly-strung, sensitive nature in need of affection will be broken. Gradually it seemed to him that he had attained his ideal, when suddenly he discovered that waiters and suchlike people took a curious interest in him, smiling at one another understandingly, and one day he made the startling discovery that they took him for a homosexual. The paranoid idea had now become autonomous. It is easy to see the deeper connection between the pitilessness of his intellect, which cold-bloodedly destroyed every feeling, and his unshakable paranoid conviction. That is psychic causality, psycho-genesis.

In some such way – naturally with endless variations – not only does paranoia arise, but also the paranoid form of schizophrenia characterized by delusions and hallucinations, and indeed all other forms of schizophrenia. (I would not class among the group of schizophrenias those schizophrenic syndromes, such as catatonias with a rapidly lethal outcome, which seem from the beginning to have an organic basis.) The microscopic lesions of the brain often found in schizophrenia I would, for the time being, regard as secondary symptoms of degeneration, like the atrophy of the muscles in hysterical paralyses. The psychogenesis of schizophrenia would explain why certain milder cases, which do not get as far as the mental hospital but only appear in the neurologist's consulting-room, can be cured by psychotherapeutic means. With regard to the possibility of cure, however, one should not be too optimistic. Such cases are rare. The very nature of the disease, involving as it does the disintegration of the personality, rules out the possibility of psychic influence, which is the essential agent in therapy. Schizophrenia shares this peculiarity with obsessional neurosis, its nearest relative in the realm of the neuroses.

From "**On the Psychogenesis of Schizophrenia**" CW 3, pars. 539–40

Two facts have impressed themselves on me during my career as a psychiatrist and psychotherapist. One is the enormous change that the average mental hospital has undergone in my lifetime. That whole desperate crowd of utterly degenerate catatonics has practically disappeared, simply because they have been given something to do. The other fact that impressed me is the discovery I made when I began my psychotherapeutic practice: I was amazed at the number of schizophrenics whom we almost never see in psychiatric hospitals. These cases are partially camouflaged as obsessional neuroses, compulsions, phobias, and hysterias, and they are very careful never to go near an asylum. These patients insist upon treatment, and I found myself, Bleuler's loyal disciple, trying my hand on cases we never would have dreamed of touching if we had had them in the clinic, cases unmistakably schizophrenic even before treatment – I felt hopelessly unscientific in treating them at all – and after the treatment I was told that they could never have been schizophrenic in the first place. There are numbers of latent psychoses – and quite a few that are not so latent – which, under favourable conditions, can be subjected to psychological analysis, sometimes with quite decent results. Even if I am not very hopeful about a patient, I try to give him as much psychology as he can stand, because I have seen plenty of cases where the later attacks were less severe, and the prognosis was better, as a result of increased psychological understanding. At least so it seemed to me. You know how difficult it is to judge these things correctly. In such doubtful matters, where you have to work as a pioneer, you must be able to put some trust in your intuition and to follow your feeling even at the risk of going wrong. To make a correct diagnosis, and to nod your head gravely at a bad prognosis, is the less important aspect of the medical art. It can even cripple your enthusiasm, and in psychotherapy enthusiasm is the secret of success.

The results of occupational therapy in mental hospitals have clearly shown that the status of hopeless cases can be enormously improved. And the much milder cases not in hospitals sometimes show encouraging results under psychotherapeutic treatment. I do not want to appear overoptimistic. Often enough one can do little or nothing at all; or again, one can have unexpected results. For about fourteen years I have been seeing a woman, who is now sixty-four years of age. I never see her more than fifteen times in the course of a year. She is a schizophrenic and has twice spent a number of months in hospital with an acute psychosis. She suffers from numberless voices distributed all over her body. I found one voice which was fairly reasonable and helpful. I tried to cultivate that voice, with the result that for about two years the right side of the body has been free of voices. Only the left side is still under the domination of the unconscious. No further attacks have occurred. Unfortunately, the patient is not intelligent. Her mentality is early medieval, and I was able to establish a fairly good rapport with her only by adapting my terminology to that of the early Middle Ages. There were no hallucinations then; it was all devils and witchcraft.

Part 2. Jung's Involvement with Freud and His Divergence from Freud's Theories

During the years 1907–13, Jung was closely associated with Freud, and deeply influenced by him. The story of the rise and fall of their relationship can be traced and studied in The Freud/Jung Letters. *But, although Jung always acknowledged his debt to Freud, and paid tribute to his originality, he was never a whole-hearted "Freudian." For example, in his introduction to* The Psychology of Dementia Praecox, *dated July 1906, Jung writes:*

Fairness to Freud, however, does not imply, as many fear, unqualified submission to a dogma; one can very well maintain an independent judgment. If I, for instance, acknowledge the complex mechanisms of dreams and hysteria, this does not mean that I attribute to the infantile sexual trauma the exclusive importance that Freud apparently does. Still less does it mean that I place sexuality so predominantly in the foreground, or that I grant it the psychological universality which Freud, it seems, postulates in view of the admittedly enormous role which sexuality plays in the psyche. As for Freud's therapy, it is at best but one of several possible methods, and perhaps does not always offer in practice what one expects from it in theory. [CW 3, Foreword, p. 4]

And, in a letter to Freud dated 5 October 1906, Jung wrote:

What I can appreciate, and what has helped us here in our psychopathological work, are your psychological views, whereas I am still pretty far from understanding the therapy and the genesis of hysteria because our material on hysteria is rather meagre. That is to say your therapy seems to me to depend not merely on the affects released by abreaction but also on certain personal rapports, and it seems to me that though the genesis of hysteria is predominantly, it is not exclusively sexual. I take the same view of your sexual theory. [*The Freud/Jung Letters*, pp. 4–5]

Freud originally supposed that hysteria was caused by trauma, and that the trauma was both literal and sexual. By the end of 1897, however, Freud realized that the stories which his hysterical patients told him of incestuous seduction were fantasies rather than actual occurrences. Freud then postulated that the cause of neurosis was the "fixation" of the patient at an early stage of emotional development, but continued to assume that the reason for this fixation was to be found in the events of the patient's early childhood without reference to the present. Jung took a different view.

"Psychoanalysis and Neurosis" CW 4, pars. 557–75

After many years' experience I now know that it is extremely difficult to discuss psychoanalysis at public meetings and at congresses. There are so many misconceptions of the matter, so many prejudices against certain psychoanalytic views, that it is an almost impossible task to reach mutual understanding in a public discussion. I have always found a quiet conversation on the subject much more useful and fruitful than heated arguments *coram publico*. However, having been honoured by an invitation from the Committee of this Congress to speak as a representative of the psychoanalytic movement, I will do my best to discuss some of the fundamental theoretical problems of psychoanalysis. I must limit myself to this aspect of the subject because I am quite unable to put before my audience all that psychoanalysis means and strives for, and its various applications in the fields of mythology, comparative religion, philosophy, etc. But if I am to discuss certain theoretical problems fundamental to psychoanalysis, I must presuppose that my audience is familiar with the development and the main results of psychoanalytic research. Unfortunately, it often happens that people think themselves entitled to judge psychoanalysis who have not even read the literature. It is my firm conviction that no one is competent to form an opinion on this matter until he has studied the basic writings of the psychoanalytic school.

In spite of the fact that Freud's theory of neurosis has been worked out in great detail, it cannot be said to be, on the whole, very clear or easy to understand. This justifies my giving you a short abstract of his fundamental views on the theory of neurosis.

You are aware that the original theory that hysteria and the related neuroses have their origin in a trauma or sexual shock in early childhood was given up about fifteen years ago. It soon became evident that the sexual trauma could not be the real cause of the neurosis, for the simple reason that the trauma was found to be almost universal. There is scarcely a human being who has not had some sexual shock in early youth, and yet comparatively few develop a neurosis in later life. Freud himself soon realized that many of the patients who related an early traumatic experience had only invented the story of the so-called trauma; it had never occurred in reality, but was a mere creation of fantasy. Moreover, on further investigation it became quite obvious that even if a trauma had actually occurred it was not always responsible for the whole of the neurosis, although it does sometimes look as if the structure of the neurosis depended entirely on the trauma. If a neurosis were the inevitable consequence of the trauma it would be quite incomprehensible why neurotics are not incomparably more numerous than they are.

The apparently heightened effect of the shock was clearly due to the exaggerated and morbid fantasy of the patient. Freud also saw that this same fantasy activity manifested itself relatively early in bad habits, which he called infantile perversions. His new conception of the aetiology of neurosis was based on this insight, and he traced the neurosis back to some sexual activity in early infancy. This conception led to his recent view that the neurotic is "fixated" to a certain period of his early infancy, because he seems to preserve some trace of it, direct or indirect, in his mental attitude. Freud also makes the attempt to classify or to differentiate the neuroses, as well as dementia praecox, according to the stage of infantile development in which the fixation took place. From the standpoint of this theory, the neurotic appears to be entirely dependent on his infantile past, and all his troubles in later life, his moral conflicts and his deficiencies, seem to be derived from the powerful influences of that period. Accordingly, the main task of the treatment is to resolve this infantile fixation, which is conceived as an unconscious attachment of the sexual libido to certain infantile fantasies and habits.

This, so far as I can see, is the essence of Freud's theory of neurosis. But it overlooks the following important question: What is the cause of this fixation of libido to the old infantile fantasies and habits? We have to remember that almost everyone has at some time had infantile fantasies and habits exactly corresponding to those of a neurotic, yet he does not become fixated to them; consequently, he does not become neurotic later on. The aetiological secret of the neurosis, therefore, does not lie in the mere *existence* of infantile fantasies but in the so-called *fixation*. The numerous statements of neurotics affirming the existence of infantile sexual fantasies are worthless in so far as they attribute an aetiological significance to them, for the same fantasies can be found in normal individuals as well, a fact which I have often proved. It is only the fixation which seems to be characteristic.

It is therefore necessary to demand proof of the reality of this infantile fixation. Freud, an absolutely sincere and painstaking empiricist, would never have evolved this hypothesis had he not had sufficient grounds for it. These grounds are furnished by the results of psychoanalytic investigations of the unconscious. Psychoanalysis reveals the unconscious presence of numerous fantasies which have their roots in the infantile past and are grouped round the so-called "nuclear complex," which in men may be designated as the Oedipus complex, in women as the Electra complex. These terms convey their own meaning exactly. The whole tragic fate of Oedipus and Electra was acted out within the narrow confines of the family, just as a child's fate lies wholly within the family boundaries. Hence the Oedipus complex, like the Electra complex, is very characteristic of an infantile conflict. The existence of these conflicts in infancy has been proved by means of psychoanalytic research. It is in the realm of this complex that the fixation is supposed to have taken place. The extremely potent and effective existence of the nuclear complex in the unconscious of neurotics led Freud to the hypothesis that the neurotic has a peculiar fixation or attachment to it. Not the mere existence of this complex – for everybody has it in the unconscious – but the very strong attachment to it is what is typical of the neurotic. He is far more influenced by this complex than the normal person; many examples in confirmation of this can be found in every one of the recent psychoanalytic histories of neurotic cases.

We must admit that this view is a very plausible one, because the hypothesis of fixation is based on the well-known fact that certain periods of human life, and particularly infancy, do sometimes leave determining traces behind them which are permanent. The only question is whether this is a sufficient explanation or not. If we examine persons who have been neurotic from infancy it seems to be confirmed, for we see the nuclear complex as a permanent and powerful agent throughout life. But if we take cases which never show any noticeable trace of neurosis except at the particular time when they break down, and there are many such, this explanation becomes doubtful. If there is such a thing as fixation, it is not permissible to erect upon it a new hypothesis, claiming that at times during certain periods of life the fixation becomes loosened and ineffective, while at others it suddenly becomes strengthened. In these cases we find that the nuclear complex is as active and potent as in those which apparently support the theory of fixation. Here a critical attitude is justifiable, especially when we consider the oft-repeated observation that the moment of the outbreak of neurosis is not just a matter of chance; as a rule it is most critical. It is usually *the moment when a new psychological adjustment, that is, a new adaptation, is demanded.* Such moments facilitate the outbreak of a neurosis, as every experienced neurologist knows.

This fact seems to me extremely significant. If the fixation were indeed real we should expect to find its influence constant: in other words, a neurosis lasting throughout life. This is obviously not the case. The psychological determination of a neurosis is only partly due to an early infantile predisposition; it must be due to some cause in the present as well. And if we carefully examine the kind of infantile fantasies and occurrences to which the neurotic is attached, we shall be obliged to agree that there is nothing in them that is specifically neurotic. Normal individuals have pretty much the same inner and outer experiences, and may be attached to them to an astonishing degree without developing a neurosis. Primitive people, especially, are very much bound to their infantility. It now begins to look as if this so-called fixation were a normal phenomenon, and that the importance of infancy for the later mental attitude is natural and prevails everywhere. The fact that the neurotic seems to be markedly influenced by his infantile conflicts shows that it is less a matter of fixation than of the peculiar use which he makes of his infantile past. It looks as if he exaggerated its importance and attributed to it a wholly artificial value. Adler, a pupil of Freud's, expresses a very similar view.

It would be unjust to say that Freud limited himself to the hypothesis of fixation; he was also aware of the problem I have just discussed. He called this phenomenon of reactivation or secondary exaggeration of infantile reminiscences "regression." But in Freud's view it appears as if the incestuous desires of the Oedipus complex were the real cause of the regression to infantile fantasies. If this were the case, we should have to postulate an unexpected intensity of the primary incestuous tendencies. This view led Freud to his recent comparison between what he calls the psychological "incest barrier" in children and the "incest taboo" in primitive man. He supposes that a desire for real incest led primitive man to frame laws against it; while to me it looks as if the incest taboo were only one among numerous taboos of all kinds, and were due to the typical superstitious fear of primitive man – a fear existing independently of incest and its prohibition. I am able to attribute as little strength to incestuous desires in childhood as in primitive humanity. I do not even seek the reason for regression in primary incestuous or any other sexual desires. I must admit that a purely sexual aetiology of neurosis seems to me much too narrow. I base this criticism not on any prejudice against sexuality but on an intimate acquaintance with the whole problem.

I therefore suggest that psychoanalytic theory should be freed from the purely sexual standpoint. In place of it I should like to introduce an *energic viewpoint* into the psychology of neurosis.

All psychological phenomena can be considered as manifestations of energy, in the same way that all physical phenomena have been understood as energic manifestations ever since Robert Mayer discovered the law of the conservation of energy. Subjectively and psychologically, this energy is conceived as *desire*. I call it *libido*, using the word in its original sense, which is by no means only sexual. Sallust uses it exactly as we do here when he says: "They took more pleasure [*libidinem*] in handsome arms and war horses than in harlots and revelry."

From a broader standpoint libido can be understood as vital energy in general, or as Bergson's *élan vital*. The first manifestation of this energy in the infant is the nutritive instinct. From this stage the libido slowly develops through numerous variants of the act of sucking into the sexual function. Hence I do not consider the act of sucking a sexual act. The pleasure in sucking can certainly not be considered as sexual pleasure, but as pleasure in nutrition, for it is nowhere proved that pleasure is sexual in itself. This process of development is continued into adult life and is accompanied by constantly increasing adaptation to the external world. Whenever the libido, in the process of adaptation, meets an obstacle, an accumulation takes place which normally gives rise to an increased effort to overcome the obstacle. But if the obstacle seems to be insurmountable, and the individual abandons the task of overcoming it, the stored-up libido makes a regression. Instead of being employed for an increased effort, the libido gives up its present task and reverts to an earlier and more primitive mode of adaptation.

The best examples of such regressions are found in hysterical cases where a disappointment in love or marriage has precipitated a neurosis. There we find those well-known digestive disorders, loss of appetite, dyspeptic symptoms of all sorts, etc. In these cases the regressive libido, turning back from the task of adaptation, gains power over the nutritive function and produces marked disturbances. Similar effects can be observed in cases where there is no disturbance of the nutritive function but, instead, a regressive revival of reminiscences from the distant past. We then find a reactivation of the parental imagos, of the Oedipus complex. Here the events of early infancy – never before important – suddenly become so. They have been regressively reactivated. Remove the obstacle from the path of life and this whole system of infantile fantasies at once breaks down and becomes as inactive and ineffective as before. But let us not forget that, to a certain extent, it is at work all the time, influencing us in unseen ways. This view, incidentally, comes very close to Janet's hypothesis that the "parties supérieures" of a function are replaced by its "parties inférieures." I would also remind you of Claparède's conception of neurotic symptoms as emotional reflexes of a primitive nature.

For these reasons I no longer seek the cause of a neurosis in the past, but in the present. I ask, what is the necessary task which the patient will not accomplish? The long list of his infantile fantasies does not give me any sufficient aetiological explanation, because I know that these fantasies are only puffed up by the regressive libido, which has not found its natural outlet in a new form of adaptation to the demands of life.

You may ask why the neurotic has a special tendency not to accomplish his necessary tasks. Here let me point out that no living creature adjusts itself easily and smoothly to new conditions. The law of inertia is valid everywhere.

A sensitive and somewhat unbalanced person, as a neurotic always is, will meet with special difficulties and perhaps with more unusual tasks in life than a normal individual, who as a rule has only to follow the well-worn path of an ordinary existence. For the neurotic there is no established way of life, because his aims and tasks are apt to be of a highly individual character. He tries to go the more or less uncontrolled and half-conscious way of normal people, not realizing that his own critical and very different nature demands of him more effort than the normal person is required to exert. There are neurotics who have shown their heightened sensitiveness and their resistance to adaptation in the very first weeks of life, in the difficulty they have in taking the mother's breast and in their exaggerated nervous reactions, etc. For this peculiarity in the neurotic predisposition it will always be impossible to find a psychological aetiology, because it is anterior to all psychology. This predisposition – you can call it "congenital sensitiveness" or what you like – is the cause of the first resistances to adaptation. As the way to adaptation is blocked, the biological energy we call libido does not find its appropriate outlet or activity, with the result that a suitable form of adaptation is replaced by an abnormal or primitive one.

In neurosis we speak of an infantile attitude or of the predominance of infantile fantasies and wishes. In so far as infantile impressions are of obvious importance in normal people they will be equally influential in neurosis, but they have no aetiological significance; they are reactions merely, being chiefly secondary and regressive phenomena. It is perfectly true, as Freud says, that infantile fantasies determine the form and the subsequent development of neurosis, but this is not an aetiology. Even when we find perverted sexual fantasies whose existence can be demonstrated in childhood, we cannot consider them of aetiological significance. A neurosis is not really caused by infantile sexual fantasies, and the same must be said of the sexualism of neurotic fantasy in general. It is not a primary phenomenon based on a perverted sexual disposition, but merely secondary and a consequence of the failure to apply the stored-up libido in a suitable way. I realize that this is a very old view, but this does not prevent it from being true. The fact that the patient himself very often believes that his infantile fantasies are the real cause of his neurosis does not prove that he is right in his belief, or that a theory based on this belief is right either. It may look as if it were so, and I must admit that very many cases do have that appearance. At all events, it is perfectly easy to understand how Freud arrived at this view. Everyone who has any psychoanalytic experience will agree with me here.

To sum up: I cannot see the real aetiology of neurosis in the various manifestations of infantile sexual development and the fantasies to which they give rise. The fact that these fantasies are exaggerated in neurosis and occupy the foreground is a consequence of the stored-up energy or libido. The psychological trouble in neurosis, and the neurosis itself, can be formulated as *an act of adaptation that has failed*. This formulation might reconcile certain views of Janet's with Freud's view that a neurosis is, in a sense, an attempt at self-cure – a view which can be and has been applied to many other illnesses.

Here the question arises as to whether it is still advisable to bring to light all the patient's fantasies by analysis, if we now consider them of no aetiological significance. Hitherto psychoanalysis has set about unravelling these fantasies because they were considered aetiologically important. My altered view of the theory of neurosis does not affect the psychoanalytic procedure. The technique remains the same. Though we no longer imagine we are unearthing the ultimate root of the illness, we have to pull up the sexual fantasies because the energy which the patient needs for his health, that is, for adaptation, is attached to them. By means of psychoanalysis the connection between his conscious mind and the libido in the unconscious is re-established. Thus the unconscious libido is brought under the control of the will. Only in this way can the split-off energy become available again for the accomplishment of the necessary tasks of life. Considered from this standpoint, psychoanalysis no longer appears as a mere reduction of the individual to his primitive sexual wishes, but, if rightly understood, as a highly moral task of immense educational value.

Another reason for Jung's divergence from Freud was disagreement about the psychopathology of schizophrenia. Freud tried to maintain that withdrawal of sexual involvement with the external world was at the root of schizophrenic withdrawal, whereas Jung considered that schizophrenia involved a more general failure in adaptation to reality. This led to Jung's use of the word "libido" as a synonym for psychic energy in general; whereas Freud used the term to signify only sexual energy. It must be remembered that Freud had little experience of schizophrenic patients, since most such cases were to be found in mental hospitals rather than in private practice. Freud's only experience of mental hospital work was three weeks as a locum tenens (at Oberdöbling in June 1885), whereas Jung stayed at the Burghölzli from 1900 until 1909.

From "The Theory of Psychoanalysis" CW 4, pars. 271-8

THE PROBLEM OF LIBIDO IN DEMENTIA PRAECOX

In my book *Wandlungen und Symbole der Libido* I tried to furnish proof of these transgressions and at the same time to show the need for a new conception of libido which took account only of the energic view. Freud himself was forced to admit that his original conception of libido might possibly be too narrow when he tried to apply the energic view consistently to a famous case of dementia praecox – the so-called Schreber case. This case is concerned among other things with that well-known problem in the psychology of dementia praecox, the loss of adaptation to reality, a peculiar phenomenon consisting in the special tendency of these patients to construct an inner fantasy world of their own, surrendering for this purpose their adaptation to reality.

One aspect of this phenomenon, the absence of emotional rapport, will be well known to you, as this is a striking disturbance of the reality function. By dint of much psychoanalytic work with these patients we established that this lack of adaptation to reality is compensated by a progressive increase in the creation of fantasies, which goes so far that the dream world becomes more real for the patient than external reality. Schreber found an excellent figurative description for this phenomenon in his delusion about the "end of the world." He thus depicts the loss of reality in a very concrete way. The dynamic explanation is simple: we say that libido has withdrawn more and more from the external world into the inner world of fantasy, and there had to create, as a substitute for the lost world, a so-called reality equivalent. This substitute is built up piece by piece, so to speak, and it is most interesting to see out of what psychological material this inner world is constructed.

This way of looking at the displacement of libido is based on the everyday use of the term, its original, purely sexual connotation being very rarely remembered. In actual practice we speak simply of *libido*, and this is understood in so innocuous a sense that Claparède once remarked to me that one could just as well use the word "interest." The customary use of the term has developed, quite naturally and spontaneously, into a usage which makes it possible to explain Schreber's end of the world simply as a withdrawal of libido. On this occasion Freud remembered his original sexual definition of libido and tried to come to terms with the change of meaning that had quietly taken place in the meantime. In his paper on Schreber he asks himself whether *what the psychoanalytic school calls libido and conceives as "interest from erotic sources" coincides with interest in general.* You see that, putting the problem in this way, Freud asks himself the question which Claparède had already answered in practice.

Freud thus broaches the question of whether the loss of reality in schizophrenia, to which I drew attention in my "Psychology of Dementia Praecox," is due entirely to the withdrawal of erotic interest, or whether this coincides with objective interest in general. We can hardly suppose that the normal "fonction du réel" (Janet) is maintained solely by erotic interest. The fact is that in very many cases reality disappears altogether, so that not a trace of psychological adaptation can be found in these patients. (In these states reality is replaced by complex contents.) We are therefore compelled to admit that not only the erotic interest, but all interest whatsoever, has got lost, and with it the whole adaptation to reality.

Earlier, in my "Psychology of Dementia Praecox," I tried to get round this difficulty by using the expression "psychic energy," because I could not base the theory of dementia praecox on the theory of displacements of libido sexually defined. My experience – at that time chiefly psychiatric – did not permit me to understand this latter theory: only later did I come to realize its partial correctness as regards the neuroses, thanks to increased experiences in the field of hysteria and obsessional neurosis. Abnormal displacements of libido, quite definitely sexual, do in fact play a great role in these illnesses. Bùt although very characteristic repressions of sexual libido do take place in the neuroses, the loss of reality so typical of dementia praecox never occurs. In dementia praecox the loss of the reality function is so extreme that it must involve the loss of other instinctual forces whose sexual character must be denied absolutely, for no one is likely to maintain that reality is a function of sex. Moreover, if it were, the withdrawal of erotic interest in the neuroses would necessarily entail a loss of reality comparable to that which occurs in dementia praecox. But, as I said before, this is not the case.

(Another thing to be considered – as Freud also pointed out in his work on the Schreber case – is that the introversion of sexual libido leads to an investment of the ego which might conceivably produce that effect of loss of reality. It is indeed tempting to explain the psychology of the loss in this way. But when we examine more closely the various things that can arise from the withdrawal and introversion of sexual libido, we come to see that though it can produce the psychology of an ascetic anchorite, it cannot produce dementia praecox. The anchorite's whole endeavour is to exterminate every trace of sexual interest, and this is something that cannot be asserted of dementia praecox.*)

These facts have made it impossible for me to apply Freud's libido theory to dementia praecox. I am also of the opinion that Abraham's essay on this subject is theoretically untenable from the standpoint of Freud's conception of libido. Abraham's belief that the paranoid system, or the schizophrenic symptomatology, is produced by the withdrawal of sexual libido from the outside world cannot be justified in terms of our present knowledge. For, as Freud has clearly shown, a mere introversion or regression of libido invariably leads to a neurosis and not to dementia praecox. It seems to me impossible simply to transfer the libido theory to dementia praecox, because this disease shows a loss of reality which cannot be explained solely by the loss of erotic interest.

THE GENETIC CONCEPTION OF LIBIDO

The attitude of reserve which I adopted towards the ubiquity of sexuality in my foreword to "The Psychology of Dementia Praecox," despite the fact that I recognized the psychological mechanisms pointed out by Freud, was dictated by the position of the libido theory at that time. Its sexual definition did not permit me to explain functional disturbances which affect the indefinite sphere of the hunger drive just as much as that of sex solely in the light of a sexual libido theory. Freud's libido theory had long seemed to me inapplicable to dementia praecox. In my analytical work I noticed that, with growing experience, a slow change in my conception of libido had taken place. Instead of the descriptive definition set forth in Freud's *Three Essays*, there gradually took shape a genetic definition of libido, which enabled me to replace the expression "psychic energy" by "libido."

*It might be objected that dementia praecox is characterized not only by the introversion of sexual libido but also by a regression to the infantile level, and that this constitutes the difference between the anchorite and the schizophrenic. This is certainly correct, but it would still have to be proved that in dementia praecox it is regularly and exclusively the erotic interest which goes into a regression. It seems to me rather difficult to prove this, because erotic interest would then have to be understood as the "Eros" of the old philosophers. But that can hardly be meant. I know cases of dementia praecox where all regard for self-preservation disappears, but not the very lively erotic interests.

A very important divergence of view with Freud was over the question of incest. Freud, with his insistence on the literal, believed that neurosis was connected with the persistence of incestuous desires connected with the Oedipus complex. As a previous extract demonstrated, Jung believed that incestuous fantasies were not causal factors in neurosis, but became reactivated as a result of regression in the face of a failure of adaptation in the present. He also began to realize that regression might be a necessary prelude to finding a new and better adaptation. Incest, therefore, could have the symbolic significance of a new synthesis taking place within the individual which pointed toward a creative solution to his problems.

GNOSTIC
MYTHS

From "Sigmund Freud" MDR, p. 162/167

When I was working on my book about the libido and approaching the end of the chapter "The Sacrifice," I knew in advance that its publication would cost me my friendship with Freud. For I planned to set down in it my own conception of incest, the decisive transformation of the concept of libido, and various other ideas in which I differed from Freud. To me incest signified a personal complication only in the rarest cases. Usually incest has a highly religious aspect, for which reason the incest theme plays a decisive part in almost all cosmogonies and in numerous myths. But Freud clung to the literal interpretation of it and could not grasp the spiritual significance of incest as a symbol. I knew that he would never be able to accept any of my ideas on this subject.

I spoke with my wife about this, and told her of my fears. She attempted to reassure me, for she thought that Freud would magnanimously raise no objections, although he might not accept my views. I myself was convinced that he could not do so. For two months I was unable to touch my pen, so tormented was I by the conflict. Should I keep my thoughts to myself, or should I risk the loss of so important a friendship? At last I resolved to go ahead with the writing – and it did indeed cost me Freud's friendship.

In the following passage, Jung elaborates the idea that regression occurs when inner conflict prevents the individual's adaptation to the external world. He goes on to show that the unconscious contents reactivated by regression contain the germs of a new and better adaptation. (The balance of opposites and the notion of compensation which Jung touches on in the passage below will be reviewed in more detail later.)

From "**On Psychic Energy**" CW 8, pars. 60–9

FUNDAMENTAL CONCEPTS OF THE LIBIDO THEORY

Progression and Regression

One of the most important energic phenomena of psychic life is the progression and regression of libido. Progression could be defined as the daily advance of the process of psychological adaptation. We know that adaptation is not something that is achieved once and for all, though there is a tendency to believe the contrary. This is due to mistaking a person's psychic attitude for actual adaptation. We can satisfy the demands of adaptation only by means of a suitably directed attitude. Consequently, the achievement of adaptation is completed in two stages: (1) attainment of attitude, (2) completion of adaptation by means of the attitude. A man's attitude to reality is something extraordinarily persistent, but the more persistent his mental habitus is, the less permanent will be his effective achievement of adaptation. This is the necessary consequence of the continual changes in the environment and the new adaptations demanded by them.

The progression of libido might therefore be said to consist in a continual satisfaction of the demands of environmental conditions. This is possible only by means of an attitude, which as such is necessarily directed and therefore characterized by a certain one-sidedness. Thus it may easily happen that an attitude can no longer satisfy the demands of adaptation because changes have occurred in the environmental conditions which require a different attitude. For example, a feeling-attitude that seeks to fulfil the demands of reality by means of empathy may easily encounter a situation that can only be solved through thinking. In this case the feeling-attitude breaks down and the progression of libido also ceases. The vital feeling that was present before disappears, and in its place the psychic value of certain conscious contents increases in an unpleasant way; subjective contents and reactions press to the fore and the situation becomes full of affect and ripe for explosions. These symptoms indicate a damming up of libido, and the stoppage is always marked by the breaking up of the pairs of opposites. During the progression of libido the pairs of opposites are united in the co-ordinated flow of psychic processes. Their working together makes possible the balanced regularity of these processes, which without this inner polarity would become one-sided and unreasonable. We are therefore justified in regarding all extravagant and exaggerated behaviour as a loss of balance, because the co-ordinating effect of the opposite impulse is obviously lacking. Hence it is essential for progression, which is the successful achievement of adaptation, that impulse and counter-impulse, positive and negative, should reach a state of regular interaction and mutual influence. This balancing and combining of pairs of opposites can be seen, for instance, in the process of reflection that precedes a difficult decision. But in the stoppage of libido that occurs when progression has become impossible, positive and negative can no longer unite in co-ordinated action, because both have attained an equal value which keeps the scales balanced. The longer the stoppage lasts, the more the value of the opposed positions increases; they become enriched with more and more associations and attach to themselves an ever-widening range of psychic material. The tension leads to conflict, the conflict leads to attempts at mutual repression, and if one of the opposing forces is successfully repressed a dissociation ensues, a splitting of the personality, or disunion with oneself. The stage is then set for a neurosis. The acts that follow from such a condition are unco-ordinated, sometimes pathological, having the appearance of symptomatic actions. Although in part normal, they are based partly on the repressed opposite which, instead of working as an equilibrating force, has an obstructive effect, thus hindering the possibility of further progress.

The struggle between the opposites would persist in this fruitless way if the process of regression, the backward movement of libido, did not set in with the outbreak of the conflict. Through their collision the opposites are gradually deprived of value and depotentiated. This loss of value steadily increases and is the only thing perceived by consciousness. It is synonymous with regression, for in proportion to the decrease in value of the conscious

opposites there is an increase in the value of all those psychic
processes which are not concerned with outward adaptation and
therefore are seldom or never employed consciously. These
psychic factors are for the most part unconscious. As the value of
the subliminal elements and of the unconscious increases, it is to
be expected that they will gain influence over the conscious mind.
On account of the inhibiting influence which the conscious
exercises over the unconscious, the unconscious values assert
themselves at first only indirectly. The inhibition to which they are
subjected is a result of the exclusive directedness of conscious
contents. (This inhibition is identical with what Freud calls the
"censor.") The indirect manifestation of the unconscious takes the
form of disturbances of conscious behaviour. In the association
experiment they appear as complex-indicators, in daily life as the
"symptomatic actions" first described by Freud, and in neurotic
conditions they appear as symptoms.

Since regression raises the value of contents that were previously
excluded from the conscious process of adaptation, and hence are
either totally unconscious or only "dimly conscious," the psychic
elements now being forced over the threshold are momentarily
useless from the standpoint of adaptation, and for this reason are
invariably kept at a distance by the directed psychic function. The
nature of these contents is for all the world to read in Freudian
literature. They are not only of an infantile-sexual character, but
are altogether incompatible contents and tendencies, partly
immoral, partly unaesthetic, partly again of an irrational, imaginary nature. The obviously inferior character of these contents as
regards adaptation has given rise to that depreciatory view of the
psychic background which is habitual in psychoanalytic writings.*
What the regression brings to the surface certainly seems at first
sight to be slime from the depths; but if one does not stop short
at a superficial evaluation and refrains from passing judgment on
the basis of a preconceived dogma, it will be found that this "slime"
contains not merely incompatible and rejected remnants of
everyday life, or inconvenient and objectionable animal tenden-

*Somewhat after the manner of Hudibras, whose opinion is quoted by Kant
(*Träume eines Geistersehers*, III): "When a hypochondriacal wind is roaring in the
bowels, everything depends on the direction it takes. If it goes downwards, it turns
into a fart, but if it mounts upwards, it is a vision or a divine inspiration."

s, but also germs of new life and vital possibilities for the future.* This is one of the great merits of psychoanalysis, that it is not afraid to dredge up the incompatible elements, which would be a thoroughly useless and indeed reprehensible undertaking were it not for the possibilities of new life that lie in the repressed contents. That this is and must be so is not only proved by a wealth of practical experience but can also be deduced from the following considerations.

The process of adaptation requires a directed conscious function characterized by inner consistency and logical coherence. Because it is directed, everything unsuitable must be excluded in order to maintain the integrity of direction. The unsuitable elements are subjected to inhibition and thereby escape attention. Now experience shows that there is only *one* consciously directed function of adaptation. If, for example, I have a thinking orientation I cannot at the same time orient myself by feeling, because thinking and feeling are two quite different functions. In fact, I must carefully exclude feeling if I am to satisfy the logical laws of thinking, so that the thought-process will not be disturbed by feeling. In this case I withdraw as much libido as possible from the feeling process, with the result that this function becomes relatively unconscious. Experience shows, again, that the orientation is largely habitual; accordingly the other unsuitable functions, so far as they are incompatible with the prevailing attitude, are relatively unconscious, and hence unused, untrained, and undifferentiated. Moreover, on the principle of coexistence they necessarily become associated with other contents of the unconscious, the inferior and incompatible quality of which I have already pointed out. Consequently, when these functions are activated by regression and so reach consciousness, they appear in a somewhat incompatible form, disguised and covered up with the slime of the deep.

If we remember that the stoppage of libido was due to the failure of the conscious attitude, we can now understand what valuable seeds lie in the unconscious contents activated by regression. They contain the elements of that other function which was excluded by

*Though professional satiety with neurotic unrealities makes the analyst sceptical, a generalized judgment from the pathological angle has the disadvantage of being always biased.

the conscious attitude and which would be capable of effectively complementing or even of replacing the inadequate conscious attitude. If thinking fails as the adapted function, because it is dealing with a situation to which one can adapt only by feeling, then the unconscious material activated by regression will contain the missing feeling function, although still in embryonic form, archaic and undeveloped. Similarly, in the opposite type, regression would activate a thinking function that would effectively compensate the inadequate feeling.

By activating an unconscious factor, regression confronts consciousness with the problem of the psyche as opposed to the problem of outward adaptation. It is natural that the conscious mind should fight against accepting the regressive contents, yet it is finally compelled by the impossibility of further progress to submit to the regressive values. In other words, regression leads to the necessity of adapting to the inner world of the psyche.

Just as adaptation to the environment may fail because of the one-sidedness of the adapted function, so adaptation to the inner world may fail because of the one-sidedness of the function in question. For instance, if the stoppage of libido was due to the failure of the thinking attitude to cope with the demands of outward adaptation, and if the unconscious feeling function is activated by regression, there is only a feeling attitude towards the inner world. This may be sufficient at first, but in the long run it will cease to be adequate, and the thinking function will have to be enlisted too, just as the reverse was necessary when dealing with the outer world. Thus a complete orientation towards the inner world becomes necessary until such time as inner adaptation is attained. Once the adaptation is achieved, progression can begin again.

The principle of progression and regression is portrayed in the myth of the whale-dragon worked out by Frobenius, as I have shown in detail in my book *Symbols of Transformation* (pars. 307ff.). The hero is the symbolical exponent of the movement of libido. Entry into the dragon is the regressive direction, and the journey to the East (the "night sea journey") with its attendant events symbolizes the effort to adapt to the conditions of the psychic inner world. The complete swallowing up and disappearance of the hero in the belly of the dragon represents the complete withdrawal of interest from the outer world. The overcoming of the monster from within is the achievement of adaptation to the conditions of the inner world, and the emergence ("slipping out") of the hero from the monster's belly with the help of a bird, which happens at the moment of sunrise, symbolizes the recommencement of progression.

It is characteristic that the monster begins the night sea journey to the East, i.e., towards sunrise, while the hero is engulfed in its belly. This seems to me to indicate that regression is not necessarily a retrograde step in the sense of a backwards development or degeneration, but rather represents a necessary phase of development. The individual is, however, not consciously aware that he is developing; he feels himself to be in a compulsive situation that resembles an early infantile state or even an embryonic condition within the womb. It is only if he remains stuck in this condition that we can speak of involution or degeneration.

Part 3. The Development of the Idea of the Collective Unconscious and of Archetypes

Jung's deep involvement with schizophrenic patients and his endeavour to understand their psychology led him to conclude that their fantasies and delusional systems could not be explained in terms of their personal biographies.

From "**Recent Thoughts on Schizophrenia**" CW 3, par. 549

But unlike the contents of a neurosis, which can be satisfactorily explained by biographical data, psychotic contents show peculiarities that defy reduction to individual determinants, just as there are dreams where the symbols cannot be properly explained with the aid of personal data. By this I mean that neurotic contents can be compared with those of normal complexes, whereas psychotic contents, especially in paranoid cases, show close analogies with the type of dream that the primitive aptly calls a "big dream." Unlike ordinary dreams, such a dream is highly impressive, numinous, and its imagery frequently makes use of motifs analogous to or even identical with those of mythology. I call these structures *archetypes* because they function in a way similar to instinctual patterns of behaviour. Moreover, most of them can be found everywhere and at all times. They occur in the folklore of primitive races, in Greek, Egyptian, and ancient Mexican myths, as well as in the dreams, visions, and delusions of modern individuals entirely ignorant of all such traditions.

As an example of the kind of observation which led him to this conclusion, Jung quotes a particular case.

From "**The Structure of the Psyche**" CW 8, pars. 317–21

But as to whether this supra-individual psychic activity actually exists, I have so far given no proof that satisfies all the requirements. I should now like to do this once more in the form of an example. The case is that of a man in his thirties, who was suffering from a paranoid form of schizophrenia. He became ill in his early twenties. He had always presented a strange mixture of intelligence, wrong-headedness, and fantastic ideas. He was an ordinary clerk, employed in a consulate. Evidently as a compensation for his very modest existence he was seized with megalomania and believed himself to be the Saviour. He suffered from frequent hallucinations and was at times very much disturbed. In his quiet periods he was allowed to go unattended in the corridor. One day I came across him there, blinking through the window up at the sun, and moving his head from side to side in a curious manner. He took me by the arm and said he wanted to show me something. He said I must look at the sun with eyes half shut, and then I could see the sun's phallus. If I moved my head from side to side the sun-phallus would move too, and that was the origin of the wind.

I made this observation about 1906. In the course of the year 1910, when I was engrossed in mythological studies, a book of Dieterich's came into my hands. It was part of the so-called Paris magic papyrus and was thought by Dieterich to be a liturgy of the Mithraic cult.* It consisted of a series of instructions, invocations, and visions. One of these visions is described in the following words: "And likewise the so-called tube, the origin of the ministering wind. For you will see hanging down from the disc of the sun something that looks like a tube. And towards the regions westward it is as though there were an infinite east wind. But if the other wind should prevail towards the regions of the east, you will in like manner see the vision veering in that direction." The Greek word for "tube," αὐλός, means a wind-instrument, and the combination αὐλός παχύς in Homer means "a thick jet of blood." So evidently a stream of wind is blowing through the tube out of the sun.

*As the author subsequently learned, the 1910 edition was actually the second, there having been a first edition in 1903.

The vision of my patient in 1906, and the Greek text first edited in 1910, should be sufficiently far apart to rule out the possibility of cryptomnesia on his side and of thought-transference on mine. The obvious parallelism of the two visions cannot be disputed, though one might object that the similarity is purely fortuitous. In that case we should expect the vision to have no connections with analogous ideas, nor any inner meaning. But this expectation is not fulfilled, for in certain medieval paintings this tube is actually depicted as a sort of hose-pipe reaching down from heaven under the robe of Mary. In it the Holy Ghost flies down in the form of a dove to impregnate the Virgin. As we know from the miracle of Pentecost, the Holy Ghost was originally conceived as a mighty rushing wind, the πνεῦμα, "the wind that bloweth where it listeth." In a Latin text we read: "Animo descensus per orbem solis tribuitur" (They say that the spirit descends through the disc of the sun). This conception is common to the whole of late classical and medieval philosophy.

I cannot, therefore, discover anything fortuitous in these visions, but simply the revival of possibilities of ideas that have always existed, that can be found again in the most diverse minds and in all epochs, and are therefore not to be mistaken for inherited ideas.

I have purposely gone into the details of this case in order to give you a concrete picture of that deeper psychic activity which I call the collective unconscious. Summing up, I would like to emphasize that we must distinguish three psychic levels: (1) consciousness, (2) the personal unconscious, and (3) the collective unconscious. The personal unconscious consists firstly of all those contents that became unconscious either because they lost their intensity and were forgotten or because consciousness was withdrawn from them (repression), and secondly of contents, some of them sense-impressions, which never had sufficient intensity to reach consciousness but have somehow entered the psyche. The collective unconscious, however, as the ancestral heritage of possibilities of representation, is not individual but common to all men, and perhaps even to all animals, and is the true basis of the individual psyche.

Since the collective unconscious is common to all men, archetypal manifestations can be demonstrated in the normal as well as in the insane.

From "**On the Psychology of the Unconscious**" *Two Essays*, CW 7, pars. 106–9

THE PERSONAL AND THE COLLECTIVE UNCONSCIOUS

Let us take as an example one of the greatest thoughts which the nineteenth century brought to birth: the idea of the conservation of energy. Robert Mayer, the real creator of this idea, was a physician, and not a physicist or natural philosopher, for whom the making of such an idea would have been more appropriate. But it is very important to realize that the idea was not, strictly speaking, "made" by Mayer. Nor did it come into being through the fusion of ideas or scientific hypotheses then extant, but grew in its creator like a plant. Mayer wrote about it in the following way to Griesinger, in 1844:

I am far from having hatched out the theory at my writing desk. [He then reports certain physiological observations he had made in 1840 and 1841 as ship's doctor.] Now, if one wants to be clear on matters of physiology, some knowledge of physical processes is essential, unless one prefers to work at things from the metaphysical side, which I find infinitely disgusting. I therefore held fast to physics and stuck to the subject with such fondness that, although many may laugh at me for this, I paid but little attention to that remote quarter of the globe in which we were, preferring to remain on board where I could work without intermission, and where I passed many an hour as though *inspired*, the like of which I cannot remember either before or since. Some flashes of thought that passed through me while in the roads of Surabaya were at once assiduously followed up, and in their turn led to fresh subjects. Those times have passed, but the quiet examination of that which then came to the surface in me has taught me that it is a truth, which can not only be subjectively felt, but objectively proved. It remains to be seen whether this can be accomplished by a man so little versed in physics as I am.*

In his book on energetics,† Helm expresses the view that "Robert Mayer's new idea did not detach itself gradually from the traditional concepts of energy by deeper reflection on them, but belongs to those intuitively apprehended ideas which, arising in other realms of a spiritual nature, as it were take possession of the mind and compel it to reshape the traditional conceptions in their own likeness."

The question now arises: Whence this new idea that thrusts itself upon consciousness with such elemental force? And whence did it derive the power that could so seize upon consciousness that it completely eclipsed the multitudinous impressions of a first voyage to the tropics? These questions are not so easy to answer. But if we apply our theory here, the explanation can only be this: the idea of energy and its conservation must be a primordial image that was dormant in the collective unconscious. Such a conclusion naturally obliges us to prove that a primordial image of this kind really did exist in the mental history of mankind and was operative through the ages. As a matter of fact, this proof can be produced without much difficulty: the most primitive religions in the most widely separated parts of the earth are founded upon this image. These are the so-called dynamistic religions whose sole and determining thought is that there exists a universal magical power** about which everything revolves. Tylor, the well-known English investigator, and Frazer likewise, misunderstood this idea as animism. In reality primitives do not mean, by their power-concept, souls or spirits at all, but something which the American investigator Lovejoy has appropriately termed "primitive energetics." This concept is equivalent to the idea of soul, spirit, God, health, bodily strength, fertility, magic, influence, power, prestige, medicine, as well as certain states of feeling which are characterized by the release of affects. Among certain Polynesians *mulungu* – this same

---

*Robert Mayer, *Kleinere Schriften und Briefe* (Stuttgart, 1893), p. 213 (letter to Wilhelm Griesinger, June 16, 1844).
†G. F. Helm, *Die Energetik nach ihrer geschichtlichen Entwicklung* (Leipzig, 1898), p. 20.
**Generally called *mana*.

primitive power-concept – means spirit, soul, daemonism, magic, prestige; and when anything astonishing happens, the people cry out "Mulungu!" This power-concept is also the earliest form of a concept of God among primitives, and is an image which has undergone countless variations in the course of history. In the Old Testament the magic power glows in the burning bush and in the countenance of Moses; in the Gospels it descends with the Holy Ghost in the form of fiery tongues from heaven. In Heraclitus it appears as world energy, as "ever-living fire"; among the Persians it is the fiery glow of "haoma," divine grace; among the Stoics it is the original heat, the power of fate. Again, in medieval legend it appears as the aura or halo, and it flares up like a flame from the roof of the hut in which the saint lies in ecstasy. In their visions the saints behold the sun of this power, the plenitude of its light. According to the old view, the soul itself is this power; in the idea of the soul's immortality there is implicit its conservation, and in the Buddhist and primitive notion of metempsychosis – transmigration of souls – is implicit its unlimited changeability together with its constant preservation.

So this idea has been stamped on the human brain for aeons. That is why it lies ready to hand in the unconscious of every man. Only, certain conditions are needed to cause it to appear. These conditions were evidently fulfilled in the case of Robert Mayer. The greatest and best thoughts of man shape themselves upon these primordial images as upon a blueprint. I have often been asked where the archetypes or primordial images come from. It seems to me that their origin can only be explained by assuming them to be deposits of the constantly repeated experiences of humanity. One of the commonest and at the same time most impressive experiences is the apparent movement of the sun every day. We certainly cannot discover anything of the kind in the unconscious, so far as the known physical process is concerned. What we do find, on the other hand, is the myth of the sun-hero in all its countless modifications. It is this myth, and not the physical process, that forms the sun archetype. The same can be said of the phases of the moon. The archetype is a kind of readiness to produce over and over again the same or similar mythical ideas. Hence it seems as though what is impressed upon the unconscious were exclusively the subjective fantasy-ideas aroused by the physical process. Therefore we may take it that archetypes are recurrent impressions made by subjective reactions. Naturally this assumption only pushes the problem further back without solving it. There is nothing to prevent us from assuming that certain archetypes exist even in animals, that they are grounded in the peculiarities of the living organism itself and.are therefore direct expressions of life whose nature cannot be further explained. Not only are the archetypes, apparently, impressions of ever-repeated typical experiences, but, at the same time, they behave empirically like agents that tend towards the repetition of these same experiences. For when an archetype appears in a dream, in a fantasy, or in life, it always brings with it a certain influence or power by virtue of which it either exercises a numinous or a fascinating effect, or impels to action.

Jung's conception of archetypes and the collective unconscious sprang not only from his observation of patients, but from his own experience. After the break with Freud, Jung passed through a period of mental upheaval which was so intense that he decided that he was "menaced by a psychosis." Part of this upheaval was connected with Jung's need to develop his own, independent point of view.

From "Confrontation with the Unconscious" MDR, p. 165/170

After the parting of the ways with Freud, a period of inner uncertainty began for me. It would be no exaggeration to call it a state of disorientation. I felt totally suspended in mid-air, for I had not yet found my own footing. Above all, I felt it necessary to develop a new attitude towards my patients. I resolved for the present not to bring any theoretical premises to bear upon them, but to wait and see what they would tell of their own accord. My aim became to leave things to chance. The result was that the patients would spontaneously report their dreams and fantasies to me, and I would merely ask, "What occurs to you in connection with that?" or, "How do you mean that, where does that come from, what do you think about it?" The interpretations seemed to follow of their own accord from the patients' replies and associations. I avoided all theoretical points of view and simply helped the patients to understand the dream-images by themselves, without application of rules and theories.

Jung's disturbance was also connected with something which later became a cornerstone in Jung's delineation of the stages of life. In July 1913, Jung attained the age of thirty-eight; a time of life at which "mid-life crises" often occur. By this time, Jung had married and fathered a family, and had achieved professional recognition and a position in the world. His conscious attitude had been that, together with Freud, he could develop a new science of the mind which would benefit the world. Now, against his conscious will, his libido was being forced away from involvement in the external world into an exploration of the inner depths of his own psyche.

From "The Stages of Life" CW 8, pars. 772–7

The nearer we approach to the middle of life, and the better we have succeeded in entrenching ourselves in our personal attitudes and social positions, the more it appears as if we had discovered the right course and the right ideals and principles of behaviour. For this reason we suppose them to be eternally valid, and make a virtue of unchangeably clinging to them. We overlook the essential fact that the social goal is attained only at the cost of a diminution of personality. Many – far too many – aspects of life which should also have been experienced lie in the lumber-room among dusty memories; but sometimes, too, they are glowing coals under grey ashes.

Statistics show a rise in the frequency of mental depressions in men about forty. In women the neurotic difficulties generally begin somewhat earlier. We see that in this phase of life – between thirty-five and forty – an important change in the human psyche is in preparation. At first it is not a conscious and striking change; it is rather a matter of indirect signs of a change which seems to take its rise in the unconscious. Often it is something like a slow change in a person's character; in another case certain traits may come to light which had disappeared since childhood; or again, one's previous inclinations and interests begin to weaken and others take their place. Conversely – and this happens very frequently – one's cherished convictions and principles, especially the moral ones, begin to harden and to grow increasingly rigid until, somewhere around the age of fifty, a period of intolerance and fanaticism is reached. It is as if the existence of these principles were endangered and it were therefore necessary to emphasize them all the more.

The wine of youth does not always clear with advancing years; sometimes it grows turbid. All the phenomena mentioned above can best be seen in rather one-sided people, turning up sometimes sooner and sometimes later. Their appearance, it seems to me, is often delayed by the fact that the parents of the person in question are still alive. It is then as if the period of youth were being unduly drawn out. I have seen this especially in the case of men whose fathers were long-lived. The death of the father then has the effect of a precipitate and almost catastrophic ripening.

I know of a pious man who was a churchwarden and who, from the age of forty onward, showed a growing and finally unbearable intolerance in matters of morality and religion. At the same time his moods grew visibly worse. At last he was nothing more than a darkly lowering pillar of the Church. In this way he got along until the age of fifty-five, when suddenly, sitting up in bed in the middle of the night, he said to his wife: 'Now at last I've got it! I'm just a plain rascal." Nor did this realization remain without results. He spent his declining years in riotous living and squandered a goodly part of his fortune. Obviously quite a likable fellow, capable of both extremes!

The very frequent neurotic disturbances of adult years all have one thing in common: they want to carry the psychology of the youthful phase over the threshold of the so-called years of discretion. Who does not know those touching old gentlemen who must always warm up the dish of their student days, who can fan the flame of life only by reminiscences of their heroic youth, but who, for the rest, are stuck in a hopelessly wooden Philistinism? As a rule, to be sure, they have this one merit which it would be wrong to undervalue: they are not neurotic, but only boring and stereotyped. The neurotic is rather a person who can never have things as he would like them in the present, and who can therefore never enjoy the past either.

As formerly the neurotic could not escape from childhood, so now he cannot part with his youth. He shrinks from the grey thoughts of approaching age, and, feeling the prospect before him unbearable, is always straining to look behind him. Just as the childish person shrinks back from the unknown in the world and in human existence, so the grown man shrinks back from the second half of life. It is as if unknown and dangerous tasks awaited him, or as if he were threatened with sacrifices and losses which he does not wish to accept, or as if his life up to now seemed to him so fair and precious that he could not relinquish it.

Jung's "confrontation with the unconscious," as he termed it, turned out to be both extremely disturbing and highly rewarding.

From "Confrontation with the Unconscious" MDR, pp. 167–74/172–81

One fantasy kept returning: there was something dead present, but it was also still alive. For example, corpses were placed in crematory ovens, but were then discovered to be still living. These fantasies came to a head and were simultaneously resolved in a dream.

I was in a region like the Alyscamps near Arles. There they have a lane of sarcophagi which go back to Merovingian times. In the dream I was coming from the city, and saw before me a similar lane with a long row of tombs. They were pedestals with stone slabs on which the dead lay. They reminded me of old church burial vaults, where knights in armour lie outstretched. Thus the dead lay in my dream, in their antique clothes, with hands clasped, the difference being that they were not hewn out of stone, but in a curious fashion mummified. I stood still in front of the first grave and looked at the dead man, who was a person of the eighteen-thirties. I looked at his clothes with interest, whereupon he suddenly moved and came to life. He unclasped his hands; but that was only because I was looking at him. I had an extremely unpleasant feeling, but

walked on and came to another body. He belonged to the
eighteenth century. There exactly the same thing happened: when
I looked at him, he came to life and moved his hands. So I went
down the whole row, until I came to the twelfth century – that is,
to a crusader in chain mail who lay there with clasped hands. His
figure seemed carved out of wood. For a long time I looked at him
and thought he was really dead. But suddenly I saw that a finger
of his left hand was beginning to stir gently.

Of course, I had originally held to Freud's view that vestiges of
old experiences exist in the unconscious.* But dreams like this,
and my actual experiences of the unconscious, taught me that such
contents are not dead, outmoded forms, but belong to our living
being. My work had confirmed this assumption, and in the course
of years there developed from it the theory of archetypes.

The dreams, however, could not help me over my feeling of
disorientation. On the contrary, I lived as if under constant inner
pressure. At times this became so strong that I suspected there was
some psychic disturbance in myself. Therefore I twice went over
all the details of my entire life, with particular attention to
childhood memories; for I thought there might be something in my
past which I could not see and which might possibly be the cause
of the disturbance. But this retrospection led to nothing but a fresh
acknowledgment of my own ignorance. Thereupon I said to
myself, "Since I know nothing at all, I shall simply do whatever
occurs to me." Thus I consciously submitted myself to the
impulses of the unconscious.

The first thing that came to the surface was a childhood memory
from perhaps my tenth or eleventh year. At that time I had had
a spell of playing passionately with building blocks. I distinctly
recalled how I had built little houses and castles, using bottles to
form the sides of gates and vaults. Somewhat later I had used
ordinary stones, with mud for mortar. These structures had
fascinated me for a long time. To my astonishment, this memory
was accompanied by a good deal of emotion. "Aha," I said to
myself, "there is still life in these things. The small boy is still
around, and possesses a creative life which I lack. But how can I
make my way to it?" For as a grown man it seemed impossible to

*Freud speaks of "archaic vestiges."

me that I should be able to bridge the distance from the present back to my eleventh year. Yet if I wanted to re-establish contact with that period, I had no choice but to return to it and take up once more that child's life with his childish games. This moment was a turning point in my fate, but I gave in only after endless resistances and with a sense of resignation. For it was a painfully humiliating experience to realize that there was nothing to be done except play childish games.

Nevertheless, I began accumulating suitable stones, gathering them partly from the lake shore and partly from the water. And I started building: cottages, a castle, a whole village. The church was still missing, so I made a square building with a hexagonal drum on top of it, and a dome. A church also requires an altar, but I hesitated to build that.

Preoccupied with the question of how I could approach this task, I was walking along the lake as usual one day, picking stones out of the gravel on the shore. Suddenly I caught sight of a red stone, a four-sided pyramid about an inch and a half high. It was a fragment of stone which had been polished into this shape by the action of the water – a pure product of chance. I knew at once: this was the altar! I placed it in the middle under the dome, and as I did so, I recalled the underground phallus of my childhood dream. This connection gave me a feeling of satisfaction.

I went on with my building game after the noon meal every day, whenever the weather permitted. As soon as I was through eating, I began playing, and continued to do so until the patients arrived; and if I was finished with my work early enough in the evening, I went back to building. In the course of this activity my thoughts clarified, and I was able to grasp the fantasies whose presence in myself I dimly felt.

Naturally, I thought about the significance of what I was doing, and asked myself, "Now, really, what are you about? You are building a small town, and doing it as if it were a rite!" I had no answer to my question, only the inner certainty that I was on the way to discovering my own myth. For the building game was only a beginning. It released a stream of fantasies which I later carefully wrote down.

This sort of thing has been consistent with me, and at any time in my later life when I came up against a blank wall, I painted a picture or hewed stone. Each such experience proved to be a *rite d'entrée* for the ideas and works that followed hard upon it. Everything that I have written this year* and last year, "The Undiscovered Self," "Flying Saucers: A Modern Myth," "A Psychological View of Conscience," has grown out of the stone sculptures I did after my wife's death.† The close of life, the end, and what it made me realize, wrenched me violently out of myself. It cost me a great deal to regain my footing, and contact with stone helped me.

Towards the autumn of 1913 the pressure which I had felt was in *me* seemed to be moving outwards, as though there were something in the air. The atmosphere actually seemed to me darker than it had been. It was as though the sense of oppression no longer sprang exclusively from a psychic situation, but from concrete reality. This feeling grew more and more intense.

In October, while I was alone on a journey, I was suddenly seized by an overpowering vision: I saw a monstrous flood covering all the northern and low-lying lands between the North Sea and the Alps. When it came up to Switzerland I saw that the mountains grew higher and higher to protect our country. I realized that a frightful catastrophe was in progress. I saw the mighty yellow waves, the floating rubble of civilization, and the drowned bodies of uncounted thousands. Then the whole sea turned to blood. This vision lasted about one hour. I was perplexed and nauseated, and ashamed of my weakness.

Two weeks passed; then the vision recurred, under the same conditions, even more vividly than before, and the blood was more emphasized. An inner voice spoke. "Look at it well; it is wholly real and it will be so. You cannot doubt it." That winter someone asked me what I thought were the political prospects of the world in the near future. I replied that I had no thoughts on the matter, but that I saw rivers of blood.

I asked myself whether these visions pointed to a revolution, but could not really imagine anything of the sort. And so I drew the conclusion that they had to do with me myself, and decided that

*1957.
†27th November, 1955.

I was menaced by a psychosis. The idea of war did not occur to me at all.

Soon afterwards, in the spring and early summer of 1914, I had a thrice-repeated dream that in the middle of summer an Arctic cold wave descended and froze the land to ice. I saw, for example, the whole of Lorraine and its canals frozen and the entire region totally deserted by human beings. All living green things were killed by frost. This dream came in April and May, and for the last time in June, 1914.

In the third dream frightful cold had again descended from out of the cosmos. This dream, however, had an unexpected end. There stood a leaf-bearing tree, but without fruit (my tree of life, I thought), whose leaves had been transformed by the effects of the frost into sweet grapes full of healing juices. I plucked the grapes and gave them to a large, waiting crowd.

At the end of July 1914 I was invited by the British Medical Association to deliver a lecture, "On the Importance of the Unconscious in Psychopathology," at a congress in Aberdeen. I was prepared for something to happen, for such visions and dreams are fateful. In my state of mind just then, with the fears that were pursuing me, it seemed fateful to me that I should have to talk on the importance of the unconscious at such a time!

On 1st August the world war broke out. Now my task was clear: I had to try to understand what had happened and to what extent my own experience coincided with that of mankind in general. Therefore my first obligation was to probe the depths of my own psyche. I made a beginning by writing down the fantasies which had come to me during my building game. This work took precedence over everything else.

An incessant stream of fantasies had been released, and I did my best not to lose my head but to find some way to understand these strange things. I stood helpless before an alien world; everything in it seemed difficult and incomprehensible. I was living in a constant state of tension; often I felt as if gigantic blocks of stone were tumbling down upon me. One thunderstorm followed another. My enduring these storms was a question of brute strength. Others have been shattered by them – Nietzsche, and Hölderlin, and many others. But there was a demonic strength in me, and from the beginning there was no doubt in my mind that I must find the meaning of what I was experiencing in these fantasies. When I endured these assaults of the unconscious I had an unswerving conviction that I was obeying a higher will, and that feeling continued to uphold me until I had mastered the task.

I was frequently so wrought up that I had to do certain yoga exercises in order to hold my emotions in check. But since it was my purpose to know what was going on within myself, I would do these exercises only until I had calmed myself enough to resume my work with the unconscious. As soon as I had the feeling that I was myself again, I abandoned this restraint upon the emotions and allowed the images and inner voices to speak afresh. The Indian, on the other hand, does yoga exercises in order to obliterate completely the multitude of psychic contents and images.

To the extent that I managed to translate the emotions into images – that is to say, to find the images which were concealed in the emotions – I was inwardly calmed and reassured. Had I left those images hidden in the emotions, I might have been torn to pieces by them. There is a chance that I might have succeeded in splitting them off; but in that case I would inexorably have fallen into a neurosis and so been ultimately destroyed by them anyhow. As a result of my experiment I learned how helpful it can be, from the therapeutic point of view, to find the particular images which lie behind emotions.

I wrote down the fantasies as well as I could, and made an earnest effort to analyse the psychic conditions under which they had arisen. But I was able to do this only in clumsy language. First I formulated the things as I had observed them, usually in "high-flown language," for that corresponds to the style of the archetypes. Archetypes speak the language of high rhetoric, even of bombast. It is a style I find embarrassing; it grates on my nerves, as when someone draws his nails down a plaster wall, or scrapes his knife against a plate. But since I did not know what was going on, I had no choice but to write everything down in the style selected by the unconscious itself. Sometimes it was as if I were hearing it with my ears, sometimes feeling it with my mouth, as if my tongue were formulating words; now and then I heard myself whispering aloud. Below the threshold of consciousness everything was seething with life.

From the beginning I had conceived my voluntary confrontation with the unconscious as a scientific experiment which I myself was conducting and in whose outcome I was vitally interested. To-day I might equally well say that it was an experiment which was being conducted on *me*. One of the greatest difficulties for me lay in dealing with my negative feelings. I was voluntarily submitting myself to emotions of which I could not really approve, and I was writing down fantasies which often struck me as nonsense, and towards which I had strong resistances. For as long as we do not understand their meaning, such fantasies are a diabolical mixture of the sublime and the ridiculous. It cost me a great deal to undergo them, but I had been challenged by fate. Only by extreme effort was I finally able to escape from the labyrinth.

In order to grasp the fantasies which were stirring in me "underground," I knew that I had to let myself plummet down into them, as it were. I felt not only violent resistance to this, but a distinct fear. For I was afraid of losing command of myself and becoming a prey to the fantasies – and as a psychiatrist I realized only too well what that meant. After prolonged hesitation, however, I saw that there was no other way out. I had to take the chance, had to try to gain power over them; for I realized that if I did not do so, I ran the risk of their gaining power over me. A cogent motive for my making the attempt was the conviction that I could not expect of my patients something I did not dare to do myself. The excuse that a helper stood at their side would not pass muster, for I was well aware that the so-called helper – that is, myself – could not help them unless he knew their fantasy material from his own direct experience, and that at present all he possessed were a few theoretical prejudices of dubious value. This idea – that I was committing myself to a dangerous enterprise not for myself alone, but also for the sake of my patients – helped me over several critical phases.

It was during Advent of the year 1913 – 12th December, to be exact – that I resolved upon the decisive step. I was sitting at my desk once more, thinking over my fears. Then I let myself drop. Suddenly it was as though the ground literally gave way beneath my feet, and I plunged down into dark depths. I could not fend off a feeling of panic. But then, abruptly, at not too great a depth, I landed on my feet in a soft, sticky mass. I felt great relief, although I was apparently in complete darkness. After a while my eyes grew accustomed to the gloom, which was rather like a deep twilight. Before me was the entrance to a dark cave, in which stood a dwarf with a leathery skin, as if he were mummified. I squeezed past him through the narrow entrance and waded knee deep through icy water to the other end of the cave where, on a projecting rock, I saw a glowing red crystal. I grasped the stone, lifted it, and discovered a hollow underneath. At first I could make out nothing, but then I saw that there was running water. In it a corpse floated by, a youth with blond hair and a wound in the head. He was followed by a gigantic black scarab and then by a red, newborn sun, rising up out of the depths of the water. Dazzled by the light, I wanted to replace the stone upon the opening, but then a fluid welled out. It was blood. A thick jet of it leaped up, and I felt nauseated. It seemed to me that the blood continued to spurt for an unendurably long time. At last it ceased, and the vision came to an end.

I was stunned by this vision. I realized, of course, that it was a hero and solar myth, a drama of death and renewal, the rebirth symbolized by the Egyptian scarab. At the end, the dawn of the new day should have followed, but instead came that intolerable outpouring of blood – an altogether abnormal phenomenon, so it seemed to me. But then I recalled the vision of blood that I had had in the autumn of that same year, and I abandoned all further attempt to understand.

Six days later (18th December, 1913), I had the following dream. I was with an unknown, brown-skinned man, a savage, in a lonely, rocky mountain landscape. It was before dawn; the eastern sky was already bright, and the stars fading. Then I heard Siegfried's horn sounding over the mountains and I knew that we had to kill him. We were armed with rifles and lay in wait for him on a narrow path over the rocks.

Then Siegfried appeared high up on the crest of the mountain, in the first ray of the rising sun. On a chariot made of the bones of the dead he drove at furious speed down the precipitous slope. When he turned a corner, we shot at him, and he plunged down, struck dead.

Filled with disgust and remorse for having destroyed something so great and beautiful, I turned to flee, impelled by the fear that the murder might be discovered. But a tremendous downfall of rain began, and I knew that it would wipe out all traces of the dead. I had escaped the danger of discovery; life could go on, but an unbearable feeling of guilt remained.

When I awoke from the dream, I turned it over in my mind, but was unable to understand it. I tried therefore to fall asleep again, but a voice within me said, "You *must* understand the dream, and must do so at once!" The inner urgency mounted until the terrible moment came when the voice said, "If you do not understand the dream, you must shoot yourself!" In the drawer of my night table lay a loaded revolver, and I became frightened. Then I began pondering once again, and suddenly the meaning of the dream dawned on me. "Why, that is the problem that is being played out in the world." Siegfried, I thought, represents what the Germans want to achieve, heroically to impose their will, have their own way. "Where there is a will there is a way!" I had wanted to do the same. But now that was no longer possible. The dream showed that the attitude embodied by Siegfried, the hero, no longer suited me. Therefore it had to be killed.

After the deed I felt an overpowering compassion, as though I myself had been shot: a sign of my secret identity with Siegfried, as well as of the grief a man feels when he is forced to sacrifice his ideal and his conscious attitudes. This identity and my heroic idealism had to be abandoned, for there are higher things than the ego's will, and to these one must bow.

These thoughts sufficed for the present, and I fell asleep again.

The small, brown-skinned savage who accompanied me and had actually taken the initiative in the killing was an embodiment of the primitive shadow. The rain showed that the tension between consciousness and the unconscious was being resolved. Although at the time I was not able to understand the meaning of the dream beyond these few hints, new forces were released in me which helped me to carry the experiment with the unconscious to a conclusion.

This dream is typical of dreams occurring in middle life when a change in attitude is demanded. It was about this time (1913) that Jung gave up his position as lecturer (Privatdozent) *in the University of Zurich, thus abandoning his academic career. Jung felt that this sacrifice was required of him as surely as the sacrifice of Siegfried was demanded in the dream; but it nevertheless cost him a great deal to make it.*

From "**Confrontation with the Unconscious**" MDR, pp. 185–6/193–4

In the midst of this period when I was so preoccupied with the images of the unconscious, I came to the decision to withdraw from the university, where I had lectured for eight years as *Privatdozent* (since 1905). My experience and experiments with the unconscious had brought my intellectual activity to a standstill. After the completion of *The Psychology of the Unconscious* I found myself utterly incapable of reading a scientific book. This went on for three years. I felt I could no longer keep up with the world of the intellect, nor would I have been able to talk about what really preoccupied me. The material brought to light from the unconscious had, almost literally, struck me dumb. I could neither understand it nor give it form. At the university I was in an exposed position, and felt that in order to go on giving courses there I would first have to find an entirely new and different orientation. It would be unfair to continue teaching young students when my own intellectual situation was nothing but a mass of doubts.

I therefore felt that I was confronted with the choice of either continuing my academic career, whose road lay smooth before me, or following the laws of my inner personality, of a higher reason, and forging ahead with this curious task of mine, this experiment in confrontation with the unconscious. But until it was completed I could not appear before the public.

Consciously, deliberately, then, I abandoned my academic career. For I felt that something great was happening to me, and I put my trust in the thing which I felt to be more important *sub specie æternitatis*. I knew that it would fill my life, and for the sake of that goal I was ready to take any kind of risk.

Siegfried is one characteristic personification of the archetype of the hero. Hero myths are found all over the world; and, from whatever

....re they originate, show striking similarities. The archetype does not correspond to the actual manifestation produced by any particular culture; yet it underlies all manifestations produced by all cultures.

From "Psychological Aspects of the Mother Archetype" CW 9 i, par. 155

Again and again I encounter the mistaken notion that an archetype is determined in regard to its content, in other words that it is a kind of unconscious idea (if such an expression be admissible). It is necessary to point out once more that archetypes are not determined as regards their content, but only as regards their form and then only to a very limited degree. A primordial image is determined as to its content only when it has become conscious and is therefore filled out with the material of conscious experience. Its form, however, as I have explained elsewhere, might perhaps be compared to the axial system of a crystal, which, as it were, preforms the crystalline structure in the mother liquid, although it has no material existence of its own. This first appears according to the specific way in which the ions and molecules aggregate. The archetype in itself is empty and purely formal, nothing but a *facultas praeformandi*, a possibility of representation which is given *a priori*. The representations themselves are not inherited, only the forms, and in that respect they correspond in every way to the instincts, which are also determined in form only. The existence of the instincts can no more be proved than the existence of the archetypes, so long as they do not manifest themselves concretely. With regard to the definiteness of the form, our comparison with the crystal is illuminating inasmuch as the axial system determines only the stereometric structure but not the concrete form of the individual crystal. This may be either large or small, and it may vary endlessly by reason of the different size of its planes or by the growing together of two crystals. The only thing that remains constant is the axial system, or rather, the invariable geometric proportions underlying it. The same is true of the archetype. In principle, it can be named and has an invariable nucleus of meaning – but always only in principle, never as regards its concrete manifestation. In the same way, the specific appearance of the mother-image at any given time cannot be deduced from the mother archetype alone, but depends on innumerable other factors.

Part 4. Archetypes: Shadow; Anima; Animus; the Persona; the Old Wise Man

In Jung's dream about Siegfried (quoted in Part 3), it will be recalled that he was accompanied by a "small, brown-skinned savage" who initiated the killing. This figure, Jung affirms, "was an embodiment of the primitive shadow."

> By shadow I mean the "negative" side of the personality, the sum of all those unpleasant qualities we like to hide, together with the insufficiently developed functions and the contents of the personal unconscious. [CW 7, par. 103n]

The shadow is one example of an "unconscious personality" which possesses a certain measure of autonomy. The shadow might be said to be responsible for those slips of the tongue and other "mistakes" which Freud catalogues in The Psychopathology of Everyday Life; *mistakes which reveal feelings and motives which the conscious self disowns. The shadow is also often projected on to others. Examination of those attributes which a man most condemns in other people (greed, intolerance, disregard for others etc.) usually shows that, unacknowledged, he himself possesses them.*

The shadow is usually the first archetype to be encountered during analysis. In the dreams of Europeans, the shadow appears as a figure of the same sex as the dreamer; usually as dark-skinned, alien or primitive, as in Jung's own dream. Jung makes the point that making conscious the repressed tendencies and confessing the less desirable aspects of personality which the shadow portrays does not rid us of them.

From *Psychology and Religion*, CW 11, pars. 130-4

If one discounts the "statistical criminal," there still remains the vast domain of inferior qualities and primitive tendencies which belong to the psychic structure of the man who is less ideal and more primitive than we should like to be. We have certain ideas as to how a civilized or educated or moral being should live, and we occasionally do our best to fulfil these ambitious expectations. But since nature has not bestowed the same blessings upon each of her children, some are more and others less gifted. Thus there are people who can just afford to live properly and respectably; that is to say, no manifest flaw is discoverable. They either commit minor sins, if they sin at all, or their sins are concealed from them by a thick layer of unconciousness. One is rather inclined to be lenient with sinners who are unconscious of their sins. But nature is not at all lenient with unconscious sinners. She punishes them just as severely as if they had committed a conscious offence. Thus we find, as the pious Henry Drummond* once observed, that it is highly moral people, unaware of their other side, who develop particularly hellish moods which make them insupportable to their relatives. The odour of sanctity may be far reaching, but to live with a saint might well cause an inferiority complex or even a wild outburst of immorality in individuals less morally gifted. Morality seems to be a gift like intelligence. You cannot pump it into a system to which it is not indigenous.

Unfortunately there can be no doubt that man is, on the whole, less good than he imagines himself or wants to be. Everyone carries a shadow, and the less it is embodied in the individual's conscious life, the blacker and denser it is. If an inferiority is conscious, one always has a chance to correct it. Furthermore, it is constantly in contact with other interests, so that it is continually subjected to modifications. But if it is repressed and isolated from consciousness, it never gets corrected, and is liable to burst forth suddenly in a moment of unawareness. At all events, it forms an unconscious snag, blocking the most well-meant attempts.

We carry our past with us, to wit, the primitive and inferior man with his desires and emotions, and it is only with an enormous effort that we can detach ourselves from this burden. If it comes to a neurosis, we invariably have to deal with a considerably

*Widely known because of his book *Natural Law in the Spiritual World*. The quotation comes from *The Greatest Thing in the World*.

intensified shadow. And if such a person wants to be cured it is necessary to find a way in which his conscious personality and his shadow can live together.

This is a very serious problem for all those who are themselves in such a predicament or have to help sick people back to normal life. Mere suppression of the shadow is as little of a remedy as beheading would be for headache. To destroy a man's morality does not help either, because it would kill his better self, without which even the shadow makes no sense. The reconciliation of these opposites is a major problem, and even in antiquity it bothered certain minds. Thus we know of an otherwise legendary personality of the second century, Carpocrates, a Neoplatonist philosopher whose school, according to Irenaeus, taught that good and evil are merely human opinions and that the soul, before its departure from the body, must pass through the whole gamut of human experience to the very end if it is not to fall back into the prison of the body. It is as if the soul could only ransom itself from imprisonment in the somatic world of the demiurge by complete fulfilment of all life's demands. The bodily existence in which we find ourselves is a kind of hostile brother whose conditions must first be known. It was in this sense that the Carpocratians interpreted Matthew 5:25f. (also Luke 12:58f.): "Agree with thine adversary quickly, whiles thou art in the way with him; lest at any time the adversary deliver thee to the judge, and the judge deliver thee to the officer, and thou be cast into prison. Verily I say unto thee, Thou shalt by no means come out thence, till thou hast paid the uttermost farthing." Remembering the other Gnostic doctrine that no man can be redeemed from a sin he has not committed, we are here confronted with a problem of the very greatest importance, obscured though it is by the Christian abhorrence of anything Gnostic. Inasmuch as the somatic man, the "adversary," is none other than "the other in me," it is plain that the Carpocratian mode of thought would lead to the following interpretation of Matthew 5:22f.: "But I say unto you, That whosoever is angry with *himself* without a cause shall be in danger of the judgment: and whosoever shall say to *himself*, Raca, shall be in danger of the council: but whosoever shall say, Thou fool, shall be in danger of hell fire. Therefore if thou bring thy gift to the altar, and there rememberest that *thou hast aught against thyself*, leave there thy gift before the altar, and go thy way; first be reconciled to *thyself*, and then come and offer thy gift. Agree with *thyself* quickly, whiles thou art in the way with *thyself*; lest at any time *thou deliverest thyself* to the judge." From here it is but a step to the uncanonical saying: "Man, if indeed thou knowest what thou doest, thou art blessed; but if thou knowest not, thou art cursed, and a transgressor of the law." But the problem comes very close indeed in the parable of the unjust steward, which is a stumbling-block in more senses than one. "And the lord commended the unjust steward, because he had done wisely" (Luke 16:8). In the Vulgate the word for "wisely" is *prudenter*, and in the Greek text it is φρονίμως (prudently, sensibly, intelligently). There's no denying that practical intelligence functions here as a court of ethical decision. Perhaps, despite Irenaeus, we may credit the Carpocratians with this much insight, and allow that they too, like the unjust steward, were commendably aware of how to save face. It is natural that the more robust mentality of the Church Fathers could not appreciate the delicacy and the merit of this subtle and, from a modern point of view, immensely practical argument. It was also dangerous, and it is still the most vital and yet the most ticklish ethical problem of a civilization that has forgotten why man's life should be sacrificial, that is, offered up to an idea greater than himself. Man can live the most amazing things if they make sense to him. But the difficulty is to create that sense. It must be a conviction, naturally; but you find that the most convincing things man can invent are cheap and ready-made, and are never able to convince him against his personal desires and fears.

If the repressed tendencies, the shadow as I call them, were obviously evil, there would be no problem whatever. But the shadow is merely somewhat inferior, primitive, unadapted, and awkward; not wholly bad. It even contains childish or primitive qualities which would in a way vitalize and embellish human existence, but convention forbids!

Jung goes on to show that confrontation with, and at least partial acceptance of, the shadow leads on to deeper problems and further encounters with other archetypal figures.

From "**The Shadow**" *Aion*, CW 9 ii, pars. 13–19

Whereas the contents of the personal unconscious are acquired during the individual's lifetime, the contents of the collective unconscious are invariably archetypes that were present from the beginning. Their relation to the instincts has been discussed elsewhere. The archetypes most clearly characterized from the empirical point of view are those which have the most frequent and the most disturbing influence on the ego. These are the *shadow*, the *anima*, and the *animus*. The most accessible of these, and the easiest to experience, is the shadow, for its nature can in large measure be inferred from the contents of the personal unconscious. The only exceptions to this rule are those rather rare cases where the positive qualities of the personality are repressed, and the ego in consequence plays an essentially negative or unfavourable role.

The shadow is a moral problem that challenges the whole ego-personality, for no one can become conscious of the shadow without considerable moral effort. To become conscious of it involves recognizing the dark aspects of the personality as present and real. This act is the essential condition for any kind of self-knowledge, and it therefore, as a rule, meets with considerable resistance. Indeed, self-knowledge as a psychotherapeutic measure frequently requires much painstaking work extending over a long period.

Closer examination of the dark characteristics – that is, the inferiorities constituting the shadow – reveals that they have an *emotional* nature, a kind of autonomy, and accordingly an obsessive or, better, possessive quality. Emotion, incidentally, is not an activity of the individual but something that happens to him. Affects occur usually where adaptation is weakest, and at the same time they reveal the reason for its weakness, namely a certain degree of inferiority and the existence of a lower level of personality. On this lower level with its uncontrolled or scarcely controlled emotions one behaves more or less like a primitive, who is not only the passive victim of his affects but also singularly incapable of moral judgment.

Although, with insight and good will, the shadow can to some extent be assimilated into the conscious personality, experience shows that there are certain features which offer the most obstinate resistance to moral control and prove almost impossible to influence. These resistances are usually bound up with *projections*, which are not recognized as such, and their recognition is a moral achievement beyond the ordinary. While some traits peculiar to the shadow can be recognized without too much difficulty as one's own personal qualities, in this case both insight and good will are unavailing because the cause of the emotion appears to lie, beyond all possibility of doubt, in the *other person*. No matter how obvious it may be to the neutral observer that it is a matter of projections, there is little hope that the subject will perceive this himself. He must be convinced that he throws a very long shadow before he is willing to withdraw his emotionally-toned projections from their object.

Let us suppose that a certain individual shows no inclination whatever to recognize his projections. The projection-making factor then has a free hand and can realize its object – if it has one – or bring about some other situation characteristic of its power. As we know, it is not the conscious subject but the unconscious which does the projecting. Hence one meets with projections, one does not make them. The effect of projection is to isolate the subject from his environment, since instead of a real relation to it there is now only an illusory one. Projections change the world into the replica of one's own unknown face. In the last analysis, therefore, they lead to an autoerotic or autistic condition in which one dreams a world whose reality remains forever unattainable. The resultant *sentiment d'incomplétude* and the still worse feeling of sterility are in their turn explained by projection as the malevolence of the environment, and by means of this vicious circle the isolation is intensified. The more projections are thrust in between the subject and the environment, the harder it is for the ego to see through its illusions. A forty-five-year-old patient who had suffered from a compulsion neurosis since he was twenty and had become completely cut off from the world once said to me: "But I can never admit to myself that I've wasted the best twenty-five years of my life!"

It is often tragic to see how blatantly a man bungles his own life and the lives of others yet remains totally incapable of seeing how much the whole tragedy originates in himself, and how he

continually feeds it and keeps it going. Not *consciously*, of course
– for consciously he is engaged in bewailing and cursing a faithless
world that recedes further and further into the distance. Rather,
it is an unconscious factor which spins the illusions that veil his
world. And what is being spun is a cocoon, which in the end will
completely envelop him.

One might assume that projections like these, which are so very
difficult if not impossible to dissolve, would belong to the realm
of the shadow – that is, to the negative side of the personality. This
assumption becomes untenable after a certain point, because the
symbols that then appear no longer refer to the same but to the
opposite sex, in a man's case to a woman and vice versa. The source
of projections is no longer the shadow – which is always of the same
sex as the subject – but a contrasexual figure. Here we meet the
animus of a woman and the anima of a man, two corresponding
archetypes whose autonomy and unconsciousness explain the
stubbornness of their projections. Though the shadow is a motif
as well known to mythology as anima and animus, it represents
first and foremost the personal unconscious, and its content can
therefore be made conscious without too much difficulty. In this
it differs from anima and animus, for whereas the shadow can be
seen through and recognized fairly easily, the anima and animus
are much further away from consciousness and in normal
circumstances are seldom if ever realized. With a little self-
criticism one can see through the shadow – so far as its nature is
personal. But when it appears as an archetype, one encounters the
same difficulties as with anima and animus. In other words, it is
quite within the bounds of possibility for a man to recognize the
relative evil of his nature, but it is a rare and shattering experience
for him to gaze into the face of absolute evil.

*Before proceeding to what Jung has to say about the contrasexual
archetypes of animus and anima, it is necessary to outline his conception
of the* persona, *since "a compensatory relationship exists between
persona and anima."*

From "The Relations between the Ego and the Unconscious"
Two Essays, CW 7, pars. 305–9

The persona is a complicated system of relations between individual consciousness and society, fittingly enough a kind of mask, designed on the one hand to make a definite impression upon others, and, on the other, to conceal the true nature of the individual. That the latter function is superfluous could be maintained only by one who is so identified with his persona that he no longer knows himself; and that the former is unnecessary could only occur to one who is quite unconscious of the true nature of his fellows. Society expects, and indeed must expect, every individual to play the part assigned to him as perfectly as possible, so that a man who is a parson must not only carry out his official functions objectively, but must at all times and in all circumstances play the role of parson in a flawless manner. Society demands this as a kind of surety; each must stand at his post, here a cobbler, there a poet. No man is expected to be both. Nor is it advisable to be both, for that would be "queer." Such a man would be "different" from other people, not quite reliable. In the academic world he would be a dilettante, in politics an "unpredictable" quantity, in religion a free-thinker – in short, he would always be suspected of unreliability and incompetence, because society is persuaded that only the cobbler who is not a poet can supply workmanlike shoes. To present an unequivocal face to the world is a matter of practical importance: the average man – the only kind society knows anything about – must keep his nose to one thing in order to achieve anything worth while, two would be too much. Our society is undoubtedly set on such an ideal. It is therefore not surprising that everyone who wants to get on must take these expectations into account. Obviously no one could completely submerge his individuality in these expectations; hence the construction of an artificial personality becomes an unavoidable necessity. The demands of propriety and good manners are an added inducement to assume a becoming mask. What goes on behind the mask is then called "private life." This painfully familiar division of consciousness into two figures, often preposterously different, is an incisive psychological operation that is bound to have repercussions on the unconscious.

The construction of a collectively suitable persona means a formidable concession to the external world, a genuine self-sacrifice which drives the ego straight into identification with the persona, so that people really do exist who believe they are what they pretend to be. The "soullessness" of such an attitude is, however, only apparent, for under no circumstances will the unconscious tolerate this shifting of the centre of gravity. When we examine such cases critically, we find that the excellence of the mask is compensated by the "private life" going on behind it. The pious Drummond once lamented that "bad temper is the vice of the virtuous." Whoever builds up too good a persona for himself naturally has to pay for it with irritability. Bismarck had hysterical weeping fits, Wagner indulged in correspondence about the belts of silk dressing-gowns, Nietzsche wrote letters to his "dear lama," Goethe held conversations with Eckermann, etc. But there are subtler things than the banal lapses of heroes. I once made the acquaintance of a very venerable personage – in fact, one might easily call him a saint. I stalked round him for three whole days, but never a mortal failing did I find in him. My feeling of inferiority grew ominous, and I was beginning to think seriously of how I might better myself. Then, on the fourth day, his wife came to consult me ... Well, nothing of the sort has ever happened to me since. But this I did learn: that any man who becomes one with his persona can cheerfully let all disturbances manifest themselves through his wife without her noticing it, though she pays for her self-sacrifice with a bad neurosis.

These identifications with a social role are a very fruitful source of neuroses. A man cannot get rid of himself in favour of an artificial personality without punishment. Even the attempt to do so brings on, in all ordinary cases, unconscious reactions in the form of bad moods, affects, phobias, compulsive ideas, backslidings, vices, etc. The socially "strong man" is in his private life often a mere child where his own states of feeling are concerned; his public discipline (which he demands quite particularly of others) goes miserably to pieces in private. His "happiness in his work" assumes a woeful countenance at home; his "spotless" public morality looks strange indeed behind the mask – we will not mention deeds, but only fantasies, and the wives of such men would have a pretty tale to tell. As to his selfless altruism, his children have decided views about that.

To the degree that the world invites the individual to identify with the mask, he is delivered over to influences from within. "High rests on low," says Lao-tzu. An opposite forces its way up from inside; it is exactly as though the unconscious suppressed the ego with the very same power which drew the ego into the persona. The absence of resistance outwardly against the lure of the persona means a similar weakness inwardly against the influence of the unconscious. Outwardly an effective and powerful role is played, while inwardly an effeminate weakness develops in face of every influence coming from the unconscious. Moods, vagaries, timidity, even a limp sexuality (culminating in impotence), gradually gain the upper hand.

The persona, the ideal picture of a man as he should be, is inwardly compensated by feminine weakness, and as the individual outwardly plays the strong man, so he becomes inwardly a woman, i.e., the anima, for it is the anima that reacts to the persona. But because the inner world is dark and invisible to the extraverted consciousness, and because a man is all the less capable of conceiving his weaknesses the more he is identified with the persona, the persona's counterpart, the anima, remains completely in the dark and is at once projected, so that our hero comes under the heel of his wife's slipper. If this results in a considerable increase of her power, she will acquit herself none too well. She becomes inferior, thus providing her husband with the welcome proof that it is not he, the hero, who is inferior in private, but his wife. In return the wife can cherish the illusion, so attractive to many, that at least she has married a hero, unperturbed by her own uselessness. This little game of illusion is often taken to be the whole meaning of life.

The ideal individual, one might postulate, would be consistently the same whatever the circumstances. In practice, most human beings adopt attitudes in public which are different from their attitudes in private. There is a dissociation of personality into "outer" and "inner"; into "mask" and "soul." Jung affirms that, in men, the inner personality

*or soul is feminine, and represented as such by female figures in dreams
and fantasies; whereas the opposite is true for women.*
*(The words preceding "q.v." in the following passage are defined by
Jung elsewhere in "Definitions.")*

From "**Definitions**" *Psychological Types*, CW 6, pars. 797–811

48. SOUL [Psyche, personality, persona, anima]. I have been
compelled, in my investigations into the structure of the unconscious, to make a conceptual distinction between *soul* and *psyche*.
By psyche I understand the totality of all psychic processes,
conscious as well as unconscious. By soul, on the other hand, I
understand a clearly demarcated functional complex that can best
be described as a "personality." In order to make clear what I mean
by this, I must introduce some further points of view. It is, in
particular, the phenomena of somnambulism, double consciousness, split personality, etc., whose investigation we owe primarily
to the French school, that have enabled us to accept the possibility
of a plurality of personalities in one and the same individual.

[Soul as a functional complex or "personality"]
It is at once evident that such a plurality of personalities can
never appear in a normal individual. But, as the above-mentioned
phenomena show, the possibility of a dissociation of personality
must exist, at least in the germ, within the range of the normal.
And, as a matter of fact, any moderately acute psychological
observer will be able to demonstrate, without much difficulty,
traces of character-splitting in normal individuals. One has only to
observe a man rather closely, under varying conditions, to see that
a change from one milieu to another brings about a striking
alteration of personality, and on each occasion a clearly defined
character emerges that is noticeably different from the previous
one. "Angel abroad, devil at home" is a formulation of the
phenomenon of character-splitting derived from everyday experience. A particular milieu necessitates a particular *attitude* (q.v.).
The longer this attitude lasts, and the more often it is required, the
more habitual it becomes. Very many people from the educated
classes have to move in two totally different milieus – the domestic

ᵉ and the world of affairs. These two totally different _ᵒnments demand two totally different attitudes, which, depending on the degree of the ego's *identification* (q.v.) with the attitude of the moment, produce a duplication of character. In accordance with social conditions and requirements, the social character is oriented on the one hand by the expectations and demands of society, and on the other by the social aims and aspirations of the individual. The domestic character is, as a rule, moulded by emotional demands and an easy-going acquiescence for the sake of comfort and convenience; whence it frequently happens that men who in public life are extremely energetic, spirited, obstinate, wilful and ruthless appear good-natured, mild, compliant, even weak, when at home and in the bosom of the family. Which is the true character, the real personality? This question is often impossible to answer.

These reflections show that even in normal individuals character-splitting is by no means an impossibility. We are, therefore, fully justified in treating personality dissociation as a problem of normal psychology. In my view the answer to the above question should be that such a man has no real character at all: he is not *individual* (q.v.) but *collective* (q.v.), the plaything of circumstance and general expectations. Were he individual, he would have the same character despite the variation of attitude. He would not be identical with the attitude of the moment, and he neither would nor could prevent his *individuality* (q.v.) from expressing itself just as clearly in one state as in another. Naturally he is individual, like every living being, but unconsciously so. Because of his more or less complete identification with the attitude of the moment, he deceives others, and often himself, as to his real character. He puts on a *mask*, which he knows is in keeping with his conscious intentions, while it also meets the requirements and fits the opinions of society, first one motive and then the other gaining the upper hand.

[*Soul as persona*]

This mask, i.e., the *ad hoc* adopted attitude, I have called the *persona*, which was the name for the masks worn by actors in antiquity. The man who identifies with this mask I would call "personal" as opposed to "individual."

The two above-mentioned attitudes represent two collective personalities, which may be summed up quite simply under the name "personae." I have already suggested that the real individuality is different from both. The persona is thus a functional complex that comes into existence for reasons of adaptation or personal convenience, but is by no means identical with the individuality. The persona is exclusively concerned with the relation to objects. The relation of the individual to the object must be sharply distinguished from the relation to the subject. By the "subject" I mean first of all those vague, dim stirrings, feelings, thoughts, and sensations which flow in on us not from any demonstrable continuity of conscious experience of the object, but well up like a disturbing, inhibiting, or at times helpful, influence from the dark inner depths, from the background and underground vaults of consciousness, and constitute, in their totality, our perception of the life of the unconscious. The subject, conceived as the "inner object," *is* the unconscious. Just as there is a relation to the outer object, an outer attitude, there is a relation to the inner object, an inner attitude. It is readily understandable that this inner attitude, by reason of its extremely intimate and inaccessible nature, is far more difficult to discern than the outer attitude, which is immediately perceived by everyone. Nevertheless, it does not seem to me impossible to formulate it as a concept. All those allegedly accidental inhibitions, fancies, moods, vague feelings, and scraps of fantasy that hinder concentration and disturb the peace of mind even of the most normal man, and that are rationalized away as being due to bodily causes and suchlike, usually have their origin, not in the reasons consciously ascribed to them, but in perceptions of unconscious processes. Dreams naturally belong to this class of phenomena, and, as we all know, are often traced back to such external and superficial causes as indigestion, sleeping on one's back, and so forth, in spite of the fact that these explanations can never stand up to searching criticism. The attitude of the individual in these matters is extremely varied. One man will not allow himself to be disturbed in the slightest by his inner processes – he can ignore them completely; another man is just as completely at their mercy – as soon as he wakes up some fantasy or other, or a disagreeable feeling, spoils his mood for the whole day; a vaguely unpleasant sensation puts the idea into his head that he is suffering from a secret disease, a dream fills him with gloomy forebodings, although ordinarily he is not superstitious. Others, again, have only periodic access to these unconscious stirrings, or only to a certain category of them. For one man they may never have reached consciousness at all as anything worth thinking about, for another they are a worrying problem he broods on daily. One man takes them as physiological, another attributes them to the behaviour of his neighbours, another finds in them a religious revelation.

These entirely different ways of dealing with the stirrings of the unconscious are just as habitual as the attitudes to the outer object. The inner attitude, therefore, is correlated with just as definite a functional complex as the outer attitude. People who, it would seem, entirely overlook their inner psychic processes no more lack a typical inner attitude than the people who constantly overlook the outer object and the reality of facts lack a typical outer one. In all the latter cases, which are by no means uncommon, the persona is characterized by a lack of relatedness, at times even a blind inconsiderateness, that yields only to the harshest blows of fate. Not infrequently, it is just these people with a rigid persona who possess an attitude to the unconscious processes which is extremely susceptible and open to influence. Inwardly they are as weak, malleable, and "soft-centred" as they are inflexible and unapproachable outwardly. Their inner attitude, therefore, corresponds to a personality that is diametrically opposed to the outer personality. I know a man, for instance, who blindly and pitilessly destroyed the happiness of those nearest to him, and yet would interrupt important business journeys just to enjoy the beauty of a forest scene glimpsed from the carriage window. Cases of this kind are doubtless familiar to everyone, so I need not give further examples.

[Soul as anima]

We can, therefore, speak of an inner personality with as much justification as, on the grounds of daily experience, we speak of an outer personality. The inner personality is the way one behaves in relation to one's inner psychic processes; it is the inner attitude, the characteristic face, that is turned towards the unconscious. I call the outer attitude, the outward face, the *persona*; the inner attitude, the inward face, I call the *anima*. To the degree that an attitude is habitual, it is a well-knit functional complex with which the ego can identify itself more or less. Common speech expresses this very graphically: when a man has an habitual attitude to certain situations, an habitual way of doing things, we say he is quite *another man* when doing this or that. This is a practical demonstration of the autonomy of the functional complex represented by the habitual attitude: it is as though another personality had taken possession of the individual, as though "another spirit had got into him." The same autonomy that very often characterizes the outer attitude is also claimed by the inner attitude, the anima. It is one of the most difficult educational feats to change the persona, the outer attitude, and it is just as difficult to change the anima, since its structure is usually quite as well-knit as the persona's. Just as the persona is an entity that often seems to constitute the whole character of a man, and may even accompany him unaltered throughout his entire life, the anima is a clearly defined entity with a character that, very often, is autonomous and immutable. It therefore lends itself very readily to characterization and description.

As to the character of the anima, my experience confirms the rule that it is, by and large, *complementary* to the character of the persona. The anima usually contains all those common human qualities which the conscious attitude lacks. The tyrant tormented by bad dreams, gloomy forebodings, and inner fears is a typical figure. Outwardly ruthless, harsh, and unapproachable, he jumps inwardly at every shadow, is at the mercy of every mood, as though he were the feeblest and most impressionable of men. Thus his anima contains all those fallible human qualities his persona lacks. If the persona is intellectual, the anima will quite certainly be sentimental. The complementary character of the anima also affects the sexual character, as I have proved to myself beyond a doubt. A very feminine woman has a masculine soul, and a very masculine man has a feminine soul. This contrast is due to the fact that a man is not in all things wholly masculine, but also has certain feminine traits. The more masculine his outer attitude is, the more his feminine traits are obliterated: instead, they appear in his unconscious. This explains why it is just those very virile men who are most subject to characteristic weaknesses; their attitude to the unconscious has a womanish weakness and impressionability. Conversely, it is often just the most feminine women who, in their inner lives, display an intractability, an obstinacy, and a wilfulness that are to be found with comparable intensity only in a man's outer attitude. These are masculine traits which, excluded from the womanly outer attitude, have become qualities of her soul.

If, therefore, we speak of the *anima* of a man, we must logically speak of the *animus* of a woman, if we are to give the soul of a woman its right name. Whereas logic and objectivity are usually the predominant features of a man's outer attitude, or are at least regarded as ideals, in the case of a woman it is feeling. But in the soul it is the other way round: inwardly it is the man who feels, and the woman who reflects. Hence a man's greater liability to total despair, while a woman can always find comfort and hope; accordingly a man is more likely to put an end to himself than a woman. However much a victim of social circumstances a woman may be, as a prostitute for instance, a man is no less a victim of impulses from the unconscious, taking the form of alcoholism and other vices.

As to its common human qualities, the character of the anima can be deduced from that of the persona. Everything that should normally be in the outer attitude, but is conspicuously absent, will invariably be found in the inner attitude. This is a fundamental rule which my experience has borne out over and over again. But as regards its individual qualities, nothing can be deduced about them in this way. We can only be certain that when a man is identical with his persona, his individual qualities will be associated with the anima. This association frequently gives rise in dreams to the symbol of psychic pregnancy, a symbol that goes back to the *primordial image* (q.v.) of the hero's birth. The child that is to be born signifies the individuality, which, though present, is not yet conscious. For in the same way as the persona, the instrument of adaptation to the environment, is strongly influenced by environmental conditions, the anima is shaped by the unconscious and its qualities. In a primitive milieu the persona necessarily takes on primitive features, and the anima similarly takes over the *archaic* (q.v.) features of the unconscious as well as its symbolic, prescient character. Hence the "pregnant," "creative" qualities of the inner attitude.

Identity (q.v.) with the persona automatically leads to an unconscious identity with the anima because, when the ego is not differentiated from the persona, it can have no conscious relation to the unconscious processes. Consequently, it *is* these processes, it is identical with them. Anyone who is himself his outward role will infallibly succumb to the inner processes; he will either frustrate his outward role by absolute inner necessity or else reduce it to absurdity, by a process of *enantiodromia* (q.v.). He can no longer keep to his individual way, and his life runs into one deadlock after another. Moreover, the anima is inevitably projected upon a real object, with which he gets into a relation of almost total dependence. Every reaction displayed by this object has an immediate, inwardly enervating effect on the subject. Tragic ties are often formed in this way (v. *Soul-image*).

49. SOUL-IMAGE [Anima / Animus]. The soul-image is a specific *image* (q.v.) among those produced by the unconscious. Just as the *persona* (v. *Soul*), or outer attitude, is represented in dreams by images of definite persons who possess the outstanding qualities of the persona in especially marked form, so in a man the soul, i.e., anima, or inner attitude, is represented in the unconscious by definite persons with the corresponding qualities. Such an image is called a "soul-image." Sometimes these images are of quite unknown or mythological figures. With men the anima is usually personified by the unconscious as a woman; with women the animus is personified as a man. In every case where the *individuality* (q.v.) is unconscious, and therefore associated with the soul, the soul-image has the character of the same sex. In all cases where there is an *identity* (q.v.) with the persona, and the soul accordingly is unconscious, the soul-image is transferred to a real person. This person is the object of intense love or equally intense hate (or fear). The influence of such a person is immediate and absolutely compelling, because it always provokes an affective response. The *affect* (q.v.) is due to the fact that a real, conscious adaptation to the person representing the soul-image is impossible. Because an objective relationship is non-existent and out of the question, the *libido* (q.v.) gets dammed up and explodes in an outburst of affect. Affects always occur where there is a failure of adaptation. Conscious adaptation to the person representing the

soul-image is impossible precisely because the subject is unconscious of the soul. Were he conscious of it, it could be distinguished from the object, whose immediate effects might then be mitigated, since the potency of the object depends on the *projection* (q.v.) of the soul-image.

For a man, a woman is best fitted to be the real bearer of his soul-image, because of the feminine quality of his soul; for a woman it will be a man. Wherever an impassioned, almost magical, relationship exists between the sexes, it is invariably a question of a projected soul-image. Since these relationships are very common, the soul must be unconscious just as frequently – that is, vast numbers of people must be quite unaware of the way they are related to their inner psychic processes. Because this unconsciousness is always coupled with complete identification with the persona, it follows that this identification must be very frequent too. And in actual fact very many people are wholly identified with their outer attitude and therefore have no conscious relation to their inner processes. Conversely, it may also happen that the soul-image is not projected but remains with the subject, and this results in an identification with the soul because the subject is then convinced that the way he relates to his inner processes is his real character. In that event the persona, being unconscious, will be projected on a person of the same sex, thus providing a foundation for many cases of open or latent homosexuality, and of father-transferences in men or mother-transferences in women. In such cases there is always a defective adaptation to external reality and a lack of relatedness, because identification with the soul produces an attitude predominantly oriented to the perception of inner processes, and the object is deprived of its determining power.

If the soul-image is projected, the result is an absolute affective tie to the object. If it is not projected, a relatively unadapted state develops, which Freud has described as *narcissism*. The projection of the soul-image offers a release from preoccupation with one's inner processes so long as the behaviour of the object is in harmony with the soul-image. The subject is then in a position to live out his persona and develop it further. The object, however, will scarcely be able to meet the demands of the soul-image indefinitely, although there are many women who, by completely disregarding their own lives, succeed in representing their husband's soul-image for a very long time. The biological feminine instinct assists them in this. A man may unconsciously do the same for his wife, though this will prompt him to deeds which finally exceed his capacities whether for good or evil. Here again the biological masculine instinct is a help.

If the soul-image is not projected, a thoroughly morbid relation to the unconscious gradually develops. The subject is increasingly overwhelmed by unconscious contents, which his inadequate relation to the object makes him powerless to assimilate or put to any kind of use, so that the whole subject-object relation only deteriorates further. Naturally these two attitudes represent the two extremes between which the more normal attitudes lie. In a normal man the soul-image is not distinguished by any particular clarity, purity, or depth, but is apt to be rather blurred. In men with a good-natured and unaggressive persona, the soul-image has a rather malevolent character. A good literary example of this is the daemonic woman who is the companion of Zeus in Spitteler's *Olympian Spring*. For an idealistic woman, a depraved man is often the bearer of the soul-image; hence the "saviour fantasy" so frequent in such cases. The same thing happens with men, when the prostitute is surrounded with the halo of a soul crying for succour.

From "The Relations between the Ego and the Unconscious"
Two Essays, CW 7, pars. 296–301, 314–16

ANIMA AND ANIMUS

Among all possible spirits the spirits of the parents are in practice the most important; hence the universal incidence of the ancestor cult. In its original form it served to conciliate the revenants, but on a higher level of culture it became an essentially moral and educational institution, as in China. For the child, the parents are his closest and most influential relations. But as he grows older this influence is split off; consequently the parental imagos become increasingly shut away from consciousness, and on account of the restrictive influence they sometimes continue to exert, they easily acquire a negative aspect. In this way the parental imagos remain as alien elements somewhere "outside" the psyche.

In place of the parents, woman now takes up her position as the most immediate environmental influence in the life of the adult man. She becomes his companion, she belongs to him in so far as she shares his life and is more or less of the same age. She is not of a superior order, either by virtue of age, authority, or physical strength. She is, however, a very influential factor and, like the parents, she produces an imago of a relatively autonomous nature – not an imago to be split off like that of the parents, but one that has to be kept associated with consciousness. Woman, with her very dissimilar psychology, is and always has been a source of information about things for which a man has no eyes. She can be his inspiration; her intuitive capacity, often superior to man's, can give him timely warning, and her feeling, always directed towards the personal, can show him ways which his own less personally accented feeling would never have discovered. What Tacitus says about the Germanic women is exactly to the point in this respect.*

Here, without a doubt, is one of the main sources for the feminine quality of the soul. But it does not seem to be the only source. No man is so entirely masculine that he has nothing feminine in him. The fact is, rather, that very masculine men have – carefully guarded and hidden – a very soft emotional life, often incorrectly described as "feminine." A man counts it a virtue to repress his feminine traits as much as possible, just as a woman, at least until recently, considered it unbecoming to be "mannish." The repression of feminine traits and inclinations naturally causes these contrasexual demands to accumulate in the unconscious. No less naturally, the imago of woman (the soul-image) becomes a receptacle for these demands, which is why a man, in his love-choice, is strongly tempted to win the woman who best corresponds to his own unconscious femininity – a woman, in short, who can unhesitatingly receive the projection of his soul. Although such a choice is often regarded and felt as altogether ideal, it may turn out that the man has manifestly married his own worst weakness. This would explain some highly remarkable conjunctions.

It seems to me, therefore, that apart from the influence of

*Cf. Tacitus, *Germania* (Loeb Classical Library), pars. 18, 19.

woman there is also the man's own femininity to explain the feminine nature of the soul complex. There is no question here of any linguistic "accident," of the kind that makes the sun feminine in German and masculine in other languages. We have, in this matter, the testimony of art from all ages, and besides that the famous question: *habet mulier animam?* Most men, probably, who have any psychological insight at all will know what Rider Haggard means by "She-who-must-be-obeyed," and will also recognize the chord that is struck when they read Benoît's description of Antinéa.* Moreover they know at once the kind of woman who most readily embodies this mysterious factor, of which they have so vivid a premonition.

The wide recognition accorded to such books shows that there must be some supra-individual quality in this image of the anima, something that does not owe a fleeting existence simply to its individual uniqueness, but is far more typical, with roots that go deeper than the obvious surface attachments I have pointed out. Both Rider Haggard and Benoît give unmistakable utterance to this supposition in the *historical* aspect of their anima figures.

As we know, there is no human experience, nor would experience be possible at all, without the intervention of a subjective aptitude. What is this subjective aptitude? Ultimately it consists in an innate psychic structure which allows man to have experiences of this kind. Thus the whole nature of man presupposes woman, both physically and spiritually. His system is tuned in to woman from the start, just as it is prepared for a quite definite world where there is water, light, air, salt, carbohydrates, etc. The form of the world into which he is born is already inborn in him as a virtual image. Likewise parents, wife, children, birth, and death are inborn in him as virtual images, as psychic aptitudes. These *a priori* categories have by nature a collective character; they are images of parents, wife, and children in general, and are not individual predestinations. We must therefore think of these images as lacking in solid content, hence as unconscious. They only acquire solidity, influence, and eventual consciousness in the encounter with empirical facts, which touch the unconscious

*Cf. H. Rider Haggard, *She* (London, 1887), and Pierre Benoît, *L'Atlantide* (Paris, 1920; trans. by Mary C. Tongue and Mary Ross as *Atlantida*, New York, 1920).

aptitude and quicken it to life. They are in a sense the deposits of all our ancestral experiences, but they are not the experiences themselves. So at least it seems to us, in the present limited state of our knowledge. (I must confess that I have never yet found infallible evidence for the inheritance of memory images, but I do not regard it as positively precluded that in addition to these collective deposits which contain nothing specifically individual, there may also be inherited memories that are individually determined.)

An inherited collective image of woman exists in a man's unconscious, with the help of which he apprehends the nature of woman. This inherited image is the third important source for the femininity of the soul.

. . . .

Now, everything that is true of the persona and of all autonomous complexes in general also holds true of the anima. She likewise is a personality, and this is why she is so easily projected upon a woman. So long as the anima is unconscious she is always projected, for everything unconscious is projected. The first bearer of the soul-image is always the mother; later it is borne by those women who arouse the man's feelings, whether in a positive or a negative sense. Because the mother is the first bearer of the soul-image, separation from her is a delicate and important matter of the greatest educational significance. Accordingly among primitives we find a large number of rites designed to organize this separation. The mere fact of becoming adult, and of outward separation, is not enough; impressive initiations into the "men's house" and ceremonies of rebirth are still needed in order to make the separation from the mother (and hence from childhood) entirely effective.

Just as the father acts as a protection against the dangers of the external world and thus serves his son as a model persona, so the mother protects him against the dangers that threaten from the darkness of his psyche. In the puberty rites, therefore, the initiate receives instruction about these things of "the other side," so that he is put in a position to dispense with his mother's protection.

The modern civilized man has to forgo this primitive but nonetheless admirable system of education. The consequence is that the anima, in the form of the mother-imago, is transferred to the wife; and the man, as soon as he marries, becomes childish, sentimental, dependent, and subservient, or else truculent, tyrannical, hypersensitive, always thinking about the prestige of his superior masculinity. The last is of course merely the reverse of the first. The safeguard against the unconscious, which is what his mother meant to him, is not replaced by anything in the modern man's education; unconsciously, therefore, his ideal of marriage is so arranged that his wife has to take over the magical role of the mother. Under the cloak of the ideally exclusive marriage he is really seeking his mother's protection, and thus he plays into the hands of his wife's possessive instincts. His fear of the dark incalculable power of the unconscious gives his wife an illegitimate authority over him, and forges such a dangerously close union that the marriage is permanently on the brink of explosion from internal tension – or else, out of protest, he flies to the other extreme, with the same results.

From "The Syzygy: Anima and Animus" *Aion*, CW 9 ii, pars. 24–40

In the case of the son, the projection-making factor is identical with the mother-imago, and this is consequently taken to be the real mother. The projection can only be dissolved when the son sees that in the realm of his psyche there is an imago not only of the mother but of the daughter, the sister, the beloved, the heavenly goddess, and the chthonic Baubo. Every mother and every beloved is forced to become the carrier and embodiment of this omnipresent and ageless image, which corresponds to the deepest reality in a man. It belongs to him, this perilous image of Woman; she stands for the loyalty which in the interests of life he must sometimes forgo; she is the much needed compensation for the risks, struggles, sacrifices that all end in disappointment; she is the solace for all the bitterness of life. And, at the same time, she is the great illusionist, the seductress, who draws him into life with her Maya – and not only into life's reasonable and useful aspects, but into its frightful paradoxes and ambivalences where good and evil, success and ruin, hope and despair, counterbalance one another. Because she is his greatest danger she demands from a man his greatest, and if he has it in him she will receive it.

This image is "My Lady Soul," as Spitteler called her. I have suggested instead the term "anima," as indicating something specific, for which the expression "soul" is too general and too vague. The empirical reality summed up under the concept of the anima forms an extremely dramatic content of the unconscious. It is possible to describe this content in rational, scientific language, but in this way one entirely fails to express its living character. Therefore, in describing the living processes of the psyche, I deliberately and consciously give preference to a dramatic, mythological way of thinking and speaking, because this is not only more expressive but also more exact than an abstract scientific terminology, which is wont to toy with the notion that its theoretic formulations may one fine day be resolved into algebraic equations.

The projection-making factor is the anima, or rather the unconscious as represented by the anima. Whenever she appears, in dreams, visions, and fantasies, she takes on personified form, thus demonstrating that the factor she embodies possesses all the outstanding characteristics of a feminine being.* She is not an invention of the conscious, but a spontaneous product of the unconscious. Nor is she a substitute figure for the mother. On the contrary, there is every likelihood that the numinous qualities which make the mother-imago so dangerously powerful derive from the collective archetype of the anima, which is incarnated anew in every male child.

Since the anima is an archetype that is found in men, it is reasonable to suppose that an equivalent archetype must be present in women; for just as the man is compensated by a feminine element, so woman is compensated by a masculine one. I do not, however, wish this argument to give the impression that these compensatory relationships were arrived at by deduction. On the contrary, long and varied experience was needed in order to grasp

---

*Naturally, she is a typical figure in *belles-lettres*. Recent publications on the subject of the anima include Linda Fierz-David, *The Dream of Poliphilo*, and my "Psychology of the Transference." The anima as a psychological idea first appears in the 16th-cent. humanist Richardus Vitus. Cf. my *Mysterium Coniunctionis*, pars. 91ff.

the nature of anima and animus empirically. Whatever we have to say about these archetypes, therefore, is either directly verifiable or at least rendered probable by the facts. At the same time, I am fully aware that we are discussing pioneer work which by its very nature can only be provisional.

Just as the mother seems to be the first carrier of the projection-making factor for the son, so is the father for the daughter. Practical experience of these relationships is made up of many individual cases presenting all kinds of variations on the same basic theme. A concise description of them can, therefore, be no more than schematic.

Woman is compensated by a masculine element and therefore her unconscious has, so to speak, a masculine imprint. This results in a considerable psychological difference between men and women, and accordingly I have called the projection-making factor in women the animus, which means mind or spirit. The animus corresponds to the paternal Logos just as the anima corresponds to the maternal Eros. But I do not wish or intend to give these two intuitive concepts too specific a definition. I use Eros and Logos merely as conceptual aids to describe the fact that woman's consciousness is characterized more by the connective quality of Eros than by the discrimination and cognition associated with Logos. In men, Eros, the function of relationship, is usually less developed than Logos. In women, on the other hand, Eros is an expression of their true nature, while their Logos is often only a regrettable accident. It gives rise to misunderstandings and annoying interpretations in the family circle and among friends. This is because it consists of *opinions* instead of reflections, and by opinions I mean *a priori* assumptions that lay claim to absolute truth. Such assumptions, as everyone knows, can be extremely irritating. As the animus is partial to argument, he can best be seen at work in disputes where both parties know they are right. Men can argue in a very womanish way, too, when they are anima-possessed and have thus been transformed into the animus of their own anima. With them the question becomes one of personal vanity and touchiness (as if they were females); with women it is a question of *power*, whether of truth or justice or some other "ism" – for the dressmaker and hairdresser have already taken care of their vanity. The "Father" (i.e., the sum of conventional opinions) always plays a great role in female argumentation. No matter how friendly and obliging a woman's Eros may be, no logic on earth can shake her if she is ridden by the animus. Often the man has the feeling – and he is not altogether wrong – that only seduction or a beating or rape would have the necessary power of persuasion. He is unaware that this highly dramatic situation would instantly come to a banal and unexciting end if he were to quit the field and let a second woman carry on the battle (his wife, for instance, if she herself is not the fiery war horse). This sound idea seldom or never occurs to him, because no man can converse with an animus for five minutes without becoming the victim of his own anima. Anyone who still had enough sense of humour to listen objectively to the ensuing dialogue would be staggered by the vast number of commonplaces, misapplied truisms, clichés from newspapers and novels, shop-soiled platitudes of every description interspersed with vulgar abuse and brain-splitting lack of logic. It is a dialogue which, irrespective of its participants, is repeated millions and millions of times in all the languages of the world and always remains essentially the same.

This singular fact is due to the following circumstance: when animus and anima meet, the animus draws his sword of power and the anima ejects her poison of illusion and seduction. The outcome need not always be negative, since the two are equally likely to fall in love (a special instance of love at first sight). The language of love is of astonishing uniformity, using the well-worn formulas with the utmost devotion and fidelity, so that once again the two partners find themselves in a banal collective situation. Yet they live in the illusion that they are related to one another in a most individual way.

In both its positive and its negative aspects the anima/animus relationship is always full of "animosity," i.e., it is emotional, and hence collective. Affects lower the level of the relationship and bring it closer to the common instinctual basis, which no longer has anything individual about it. Very often the relationship runs its course heedless of its human performers, who afterwards do not know what happened to them.

Whereas the cloud of "animosity" surrounding the man is composed chiefly of sentimentality and resentment, in woman it expresses itself in the form of opinionated views, interpretations,

insinuations, and misconstructions, which all have the purpose
(sometimes attained) of severing the relation between two human
beings. The woman, like the man, becomes wrapped in a veil of
illusions by her demon-familiar, and, as the daughter who alone
understands her father (that is, is eternally right in everything), she
is translated to the land of sheep, where she is put to graze by the
shepherd of her soul, the animus.

Like the anima, the animus too has a positive aspect. Through
the figure of the father he expresses not only conventional opinion
but – equally – what we call "spirit," philosophical or religious
ideas in particular, or rather the attitude resulting from them.
Thus the animus is a psychopomp, a mediator between the
conscious and the unconscious and a personification of the latter.
Just as the anima becomes, through integration, the Eros of
consciousness, so the animus becomes a Logos; and in the same
way that the anima gives relationship and relatedness to a man's
consciousness, the animus gives to woman's consciousness a
capacity for reflection, deliberation, and self-knowledge.

The effect of anima and animus on the ego is in principle the
same. This effect is extremely difficult to eliminate because, in the
first place, it is uncommonly strong and immediately fills the
ego-personality with an unshakable feeling of rightness and
righteousness. In the second place, the cause of the effect is
projected and appears to lie in objects and objective situations.
Both these characteristics can, I believe, be traced back to the
peculiarities of the archetype. For the archetype, of course, exists
a priori. This may possibly explain the often totally irrational yet
undisputed and indisputable existence of certain moods and
opinions. Perhaps these are so notoriously difficult to influence
because of the powerfully suggestive effect emanating from the
archetype. Consciousness is fascinated by it, held captive, as if
hypnotized. Very often the ego experiences a vague feeling of
moral defeat and then behaves all the more defensively, defiantly,
and self-righteously, thus setting up a vicious circle which only
increases its feeling of inferiority. The bottom is then knocked out
of the human relationship, for, like megalomania, a feeling of
inferiority makes mutual recognition impossible, and without this
there is no relationship.

As I said, it is easier to gain insight into the shadow than into the anima or animus. With the shadow, we have the advantage of being prepared in some sort by our education, which has always endeavoured to convince people that they are not one-hundred-per-cent pure gold. So everyone immediately understands what is meant by "shadow," "inferior personality," etc. And if he has forgotten, his memory can easily be refreshed by a Sunday sermon, his wife, or the tax collector. With the anima and animus, however, things are by no means so simple. Firstly, there is no moral education in this respect, and secondly, most people are content to be self-righteous and prefer mutual vilification (if nothing worse!) to the recognition of their projections. Indeed, it seems a very natural state of affairs for men to have irrational moods and women irrational opinions. Presumably this situation is grounded on instinct and must remain as it is to ensure that the Empedoclean game of the hate and love of the elements shall continue for all eternity. Nature is conservative and does not easily allow her courses to be altered; she defends in the most stubborn way the inviolability of the preserves where anima and animus roam. Hence it is much more difficult to become conscious of one's anima/animus projections than to acknowledge one's shadow side. One has, of course, to overcome certain moral obstacles, such as vanity, ambition, conceit, resentment, etc., but in the case of projections all sorts of purely intellectual difficulties are added, quite apart from the contents of the projection which one simply doesn't know how to cope with. And on top of all this there arises a profound doubt as to whether one is not meddling too much with nature's business by prodding into consciousness things which it would have been better to leave asleep.

Although there are, in my experience, a fair number of people who can understand without special intellectual or moral difficulties what is meant by anima and animus, one finds very many more who have the greatest trouble in visualizing these empirical concepts as anything concrete. This shows that they fall a little outside the usual range of experience. They are unpopular precisely because they seem unfamiliar. The consequence is that they mobilize prejudice and become taboo like everything else that is unexpected.

So if we set it up as a kind of requirement that projections should be dissolved, because it is wholesomer that way and in every respect more advantageous, we are entering upon new ground. Up till now everybody has been convinced that the idea "my father," "my mother," etc., is nothing but a faithful reflection of the real parent, corresponding in every detail to the original, so that when someone says "my father" he means no more and no less than what his father is in reality. This is actually what he supposes he does mean, but a supposition of identity by no means brings that identity about. This is where the fallacy of the *enkekalymmenos* ("the veiled one") comes in.* If one includes in the psychological equation X's picture of his father, which he takes for the real father, the equation will not work out, because the unknown quantity he has introduced does not tally with reality. X has overlooked the fact that his idea of a person consists, in the first place, of the possibly very incomplete picture he has received of the real person and, in the second place, of the subjective modifications he has imposed upon this picture. X's idea of his father is a complex quantity for which the real father is only in part responsible, an indefinitely larger share falling to the son. So true is this that every time he criticizes or praises his father he is unconsciously hitting back at himself, thereby bringing about those psychic consequences that overtake people who habitually disparage or overpraise themselves. If, however, X carefully compares his reactions with reality, he stands a chance of noticing that he has miscalculated somewhere by not realizing long ago from his father's behaviour that the picture he has of him is a false one. But as a rule X is convinced that he is right, and if anybody is wrong it must be the other fellow. Should X have a poorly developed Eros, he will be either indifferent to the inadequate relationship he has with his father or else annoyed by the inconsistency and general incomprehensibility of a father whose behaviour never really corresponds to the picture X has of him. Therefore X thinks he has every right to feel hurt, misunderstood, and even betrayed.

One can imagine how desirable it would be in such cases to dissolve the projection. And there are always optimists who believe that the golden age can be ushered in simply by telling people the

*The fallacy, which stems from Eubulides the Megarian, runs: "Can you recognize your father?" Yes. "Can you recognize this veiled one?" No. "This veiled one is your father. Hence you can recognize your father and not recognize him."

right way to go. But just let them try to explain to these people that they are acting like a dog chasing its own tail. To make a person see the shortcomings of his attitude considerably more than mere "telling" is needed, for more is involved than ordinary common sense can allow. What one is up against here is the kind of fateful misunderstanding which, under ordinary conditions, remains forever inaccessible to insight. It is rather like expecting the average respectable citizen to recognize himself as a criminal.

I mention all this just to illustrate the order of magnitude to which the anima/animus projections belong, and the moral and intellectual exertions that are needed to dissolve them. Not all the contents of the anima and animus are projected, however. Many of them appear spontaneously in dreams and so on, and many more can be made conscious through active imagination. In this way we find that thoughts, feelings, and affects are alive in us which we would never have believed possible. Naturally, possibilities of this sort seem utterly fantastic to anyone who has not experienced them himself, for a normal person "knows what he thinks." Such a childish attitude on the part of the "normal person" is simply the rule, so that no one without experience in this field can be expected to understand the real nature of anima and animus. With these reflections one gets into an entirely new world of psychological experience, provided of course that one succeeds in realizing it in practice. Those who do succeed can hardly fail to be impressed by all that the ego does not know and never has known. This increase in self-knowledge is still very rare nowadays and is usually paid for in advance with a neurosis, if not with something worse.

The autonomy of the collective unconscious expresses itself in the figures of anima and animus. They personify those of its contents which, when withdrawn from projection, can be integrated into consciousness. To this extent, both figures represent *functions* which filter the contents of the collective unconscious through to the conscious mind. They appear or behave as such, however, only so long as the tendencies of the conscious and unconscious do not diverge too greatly. Should any tension arise, these functions, harmless till then, confront the conscious mind in personified form and behave rather like systems split off from the personality, or like part souls. This comparison is inadequate in so far as nothing previously belonging to the ego-personality has split off from it; on the contrary, the two figures represent a disturbing accretion. The reason for their behaving in this way is that though the *contents* of anima and animus can be integrated they themselves cannot, since they are archetypes. As such they are the foundation stones of the psychic structure, which in its totality exceeds the limits of consciousness and therefore can never become the object of direct cognition. Though the effects of anima and animus can be made conscious, they themselves are factors transcending consciousness and beyond the reach of perception and volition. Hence they remain autonomous despite the integration of their contents, and for this reason they should be borne constantly in mind. This is extremely important from the therapeutic standpoint, because constant observation pays the unconscious a tribute that more or less guarantees its co-operation. The unconscious as we know can never be "done with" once and for all. It is, in fact, one of the most important tasks of psychic hygiene to pay continual attention to the symptomatology of unconscious contents and processes, for the good reason that the conscious mind is always in danger of becoming one-sided, of keeping to well-worn paths and getting stuck in blind alleys. The complementary and compensating function of the unconscious ensures that these dangers, which are especially great in neurosis, can in some measure be avoided. It is only under ideal conditions, when life is still simple and unconscious enough to follow the serpentine path of instinct without hesitation or misgiving, that the compensation works with entire success. The more civilized, the more unconscious and complicated a man is, the less he is able to follow his instincts. His complicated living conditions and the influence of his environment are so strong that they drown the quiet voice of nature. Opinions, beliefs, theories, and collective tendencies appear in its stead and back up all the aberrations of the conscious mind. Deliberate attention should then be given to the unconscious so that the compensation can set to work. Hence it is especially important to picture the archetypes of the unconscious not as a rushing phantasmagoria of fugitive images but as constant, autonomous factors, which indeed they are.

us "Confrontation with the Unconscious," Jung encountered figures who represented superior wisdom; personifications of "intelligence and knowledge."

From "Confrontation with the Unconscious" MDR, pp. 174–8/181–5

In order to seize hold of the fantasies, I frequently imagined a steep descent. I even made several attempts to get to the very bottom. The first time I reached, as it were, a depth of about a thousand feet; the next time I found myself at the edge of a cosmic abyss. It was like a voyage to the moon, or a descent into empty space. First came the image of a crater, and I had the feeling that I was in the land of the dead. The atmosphere was that of the other world. Near the steep slope of a rock I caught sight of two figures, an old man with a white beard and a beautiful young girl. I summoned up my courage and approached them as though they were real people, and listened attentively to what they told me. The old man explained that he was Elijah, and that gave me a shock. But the girl staggered me even more, for she called herself Salome! She was blind. What a strange couple: Salome and Elijah. But Elijah assured me that he and Salome had belonged together from all eternity, which completely astounded me . . . They had a black serpent living with them which displayed an unmistakable fondness for me. I stuck close to Elijah because he seemed to be the most reasonable of the three, and to have a clear intelligence. Of Salome I was distinctly suspicious. Elijah and I had a long conversation which, however, I did not understand.

Naturally I tried to find a plausible explanation for the appearance of Biblical figures in my fantasy by reminding myself that my father had been a clergyman. But that really explained nothing at all. For what did the old man signify? What did Salome signify? Why were they together? Only many years later, when I knew a great deal more than I knew then, did the connection between the old man and the young girl appear perfectly natural to me.

In such dream wanderings one frequently encounters an old man who is accompanied by a young girl, and examples of such couples are to be found in many mythic tales. Thus, according to Gnostic tradition, Simon Magus went about with a young girl whom he had picked up in a brothel. Her name was Helen, and she was regarded as the reincarnation of the Trojan Helen. Klingsor and Kundry, Lao-tzu and the dancing girl, likewise belong to this category.

I have mentioned that there was a third figure in my fantasy besides Elijah and Salome: the large black snake. In myths the snake is a frequent counterpart of the hero. There are numerous accounts of their affinity. For example, the hero has eyes like a snake, or after his death he is changed into a snake and revered as such, or the snake is his mother, etc. In my fantasy, therefore, the presence of the snake was an indication of a hero-myth.

Salome is an anima figure. She is blind because she does not see the meaning of things. Elijah is the figure of the wise old prophet and represents the factor of intelligence and knowledge; Salome, the erotic element. One might say that the two figures are personifications of Logos and Eros. But such a definition would be excessively intellectual. It is more meaningful to let the figures be what they were for me at the time – namely, events and experiences.

Soon after this fantasy another figure rose out of the unconscious. He developed out of the Elijah figure. I called him Philemon. Philemon was a pagan and brought with him an Egypto-Hellenistic atmosphere with a Gnostic colouration. His figure first appeared to me in the following dream.

There was a blue sky, like the sea, covered not by clouds but by flat brown clods of earth. It looked as if the clods were breaking apart and the blue water of the sea were becoming visible between them. But the water was the blue sky. Suddenly there appeared from the right a winged being sailing across the sky. I saw that it was an old man with the horns of a bull. He held a bunch of four keys, one of which he clutched as if he were about to open a lock. He had the wings of the kingfisher with its characteristic colours.

Since I did not understand this dream-image, I painted it in order to impress it upon my memory. During the days when I was occupied with the painting, I found in my garden, by the lake shore, a dead kingfisher! I was thunderstruck, for kingfishers are quite rare in the vicinity of Zürich and I have never since found a dead one. The body was recently dead – at the most, two or three days – and showed no external injuries.

Philemon and other figures of my fantasies brought home to me the crucial insight that there are things in the psyche which I do not produce, but which produce themselves and have their own life. Philemon represented a force which was not myself. In my fantasies I held conversations with him, and he said things which I had not consciously thought. For I observed clearly that it was he who spoke, not I. He said I treated thoughts as if I generated them myself, but in his view thoughts were like animals in the forest, or people in a room, or birds in the air, and added, "If you should see people in a room, you would not think that you had made those people, or that you were responsible for them." It was he who taught me psychic objectivity, the reality of the psyche. Through him the distinction was clarified between myself and the object of my thought. He confronted me in an objective manner, and I understood that there is something in me which can say things that I do not know and do not intend, things which may even be directed against me.

Psychologically, Philemon represented superior insight. He was a mysterious figure to me. At times he seemed to me quite real, as if he were a living personality. I went walking up and down the garden with him, and to me he was what the Indians call a guru.

Whenever the outlines of a new personification appeared, I felt it almost as a personal defeat. It meant: "Here is something else you didn't know until now!" Fear crept over me that the succession of such figures might be endless, that I might lose myself in bottomless abysses of ignorance. My ego felt devalued – although the successes I had been having in worldly affairs might have reassured me. In my darknesses (*horridas nostrae mentis purga tenebras* – "cleanse the horrible darknesses of our mind" – the *Aurora Consurgens** says) I could have wished for nothing better than a real, live guru, someone possessing superior knowledge and ability, who would have disentangled for me the involuntary creations of my imagination. This task was undertaken by the figure of Philemon, whom in this respect I had willy-nilly to

*An alchemical treatise ascribed to Thomas Aquinas.

recognize as my psychagogue. And the fact was that he conveyed to me many an illuminating idea.

More than fifteen years later a highly cultivated elderly Indian visited me, a friend of Gandhi's, and we talked about Indian education – in particular, about the relationship between guru and chela. I hesitantly asked him whether he could tell me anything about the person and character of his own guru, whereupon he replied in a matter-of-fact tone, "Oh yes, he was Shankaracharya."

"You don't mean the commentator on the Vedas who died centuries ago?" I asked.

"Yes, I mean him," he said, to my amazement.

"Then you are referring to a spirit?" I asked.

"Of course it was his spirit," he agreed.

At that moment I thought of Philemon.

"There are ghostly gurus too," he added. "Most people have living gurus. But there are always some who have a spirit for teacher."

This information was both illuminating and reassuring to me. Evidently, then, I had not plummeted right out of the human world, but had only experienced the sort of thing that could happen to others who made similar efforts.

Later, Philemon became relativized by the emergence of yet another figure, whom I called Ka. In ancient Egypt the "king's ka" was his earthly form, the embodied soul. In my fantasy the ka-soul came from below, out of the earth as if out of a deep shaft. I did a painting of him, showing him in his earth-bound form, as a herm with base of stone and upper part of bronze. High up in the painting appears a kingfisher's wing, and between it and the head of Ka floats a round, glowing nebula of stars. Ka's expression has something demonic about it – one might also say, Mephistophelian. In one hand he holds something like a coloured pagoda, or a reliquary, and in the other a stylus with which he is working on the reliquary. He is saying, "I am he who buries the gods in gold and gems."

Philemon had a lame foot, but was a winged spirit, whereas Ka represented a kind of earth demon or metal demon. Philemon was the spiritual aspect, or "meaning." Ka, on the other hand, was a spirit of nature like the Anthroparion of Greek alchemy – with which at the time I was still unfamiliar.* Ka was he who made everything real, but who also obscured the halcyon spirit, Meaning, or replaced it by beauty, the "eternal reflection."

In time I was able to integrate both figures through the study of alchemy.

The archetype of the wise old man, also called the "Mana-personality," tends to be projected upon human beings who set themselves up as leaders, secular or spiritual. This may have disastrous results, as when religious sects or political movements are led by charlatans or madmen. Alternatively, the subject may identify himself with the archetype, believing that he himself has superior wisdom. Analysts and priests, as well as politicians, sometimes succumb to this danger, referred to by Jung as "inflation."

From "The Relations between the Ego and the Unconscious" *Two Essays*, CW 7, pars. 387–90

THE MANA-PERSONALITY

The immediate goal of the analysis of the unconscious, therefore, is to reach a state where the unconscious contents no longer remain unconscious and no longer express themselves indirectly as animus and anima phenomena; that is to say, a state in which animus and anima become functions of relationship to the unconscious. So long as they are not this, they are autonomous complexes, disturbing factors that disrupt conscious control and act like true "disturbers of the peace." Because this is such a well-known fact my term "complex," as used in this sense, has passed into common speech. The more "complexes" a man has, the more he is possessed; and when we try to form a picture of the personality which expresses itself through its complexes we must admit that it resembles nothing so much as an hysterical woman

---

*[The Anthroparion is a tiny man, a kind of homunculus. He is found, for example, in the visions of Zosimos of Panopolis, an important alchemist of the third century. To the group which includes the Anthroparion belong the gnomes, the Dactyls of classical antiquity, and the homunculi of the alchemists. As the spirit of quicksilver, the alchemical Mercurius was also an Anthroparion.]

– i.e., the anima! But if such a man makes himself conscious of his unconscious contents, as they appear firstly in the factual contents of his personal unconscious, and then in the fantasies of the collective unconscious, he will get to the roots of his complexes, and in this way rid himself of his possession. With that the anima phenomenon comes to a stop.

That superior power, however, which caused the possession – for what I cannot shake off must in some sense be superior to me – should, logically, disappear with the anima. One should then be "complex-free," psychologically house-trained, so to speak. Nothing more should happen that is not sanctioned by the ego, and when the ego wants something, nothing should be capable of interfering. The ego would thus be assured of an impregnable position, the steadfastness of a superman or the sublimity of a perfect sage. Both figures are ideal images: Napoleon on the one hand, Lao-tzu on the other. Both are consistent with the idea of "the extraordinarily potent," which is the term that Lehmann, in his celebrated monograph,* uses for his definition of mana. I therefore call such a personality simply the *mana-personality*. It corresponds to a dominant of the collective unconscious, to an archetype which has taken shape in the human psyche through untold ages of just that kind of experience. Primitive man does not analyse and does not work out why another is superior to him. If another is cleverer and stronger than he, then he has mana, he is possessed of a stronger power; and by the same token he can lose this power, perhaps because someone has walked over him in his sleep, or stepped on his shadow.

Historically, the mana-personality evolves into the hero and the godlike being,† whose earthly form is the priest. How very much the doctor is still mana is the whole plaint of the analyst! But in so far as the ego apparently draws to itself the power belonging to the anima, the ego does become a mana-personality. This development is an almost regular phenomenon. I have never yet seen a fairly advanced development of this kind where at least a temporary identification with the archetype of the mana-personality did not take place. It is the most natural thing in the

*F. R. Lehmann, *Mana* (Leipzig, 1922).
†According to popular belief, the Most Christian King could cure epilepsy with his mana by the laying on of hands.

world that this should happen, for not only does one expect it oneself, but everybody else expects it too. One can scarcely help admiring oneself a little for having seen more deeply into things than others, and the others have such an urge to find a tangible hero somewhere, or a superior wise man, a leader and father, some undisputed authority, that they build temples to little tin gods with the greatest promptitude and burn incense upon the altars. This is not just the lamentable stupidity of idolaters incapable of judging for themselves, but a natural psychological law which says that what has once been will always be in the future. And so it will be, unless consciousness puts an end to the naïve concretization of primordial images. I do not know whether it is desirable that consciousness should alter the eternal laws; I only know that occasionally it does alter them, and that this measure is a vital necessity for some people – which, however, does not always prevent these same people from setting themselves up on the father's throne and making the old rule come true. It is indeed hard to see how one can escape the sovereign power of the primordial images.

Actually I do not believe it can be escaped. One can only alter one's attitude and thus save oneself from naively falling into an archetype and being forced to act a part at the expense of one's humanity. Possession by an archetype turns a man into a flat collective figure, a mask behind which he can no longer develop as a human being, but becomes increasingly stunted. One must therefore beware of the danger of falling victim to the dominant of the mana-personality. The danger lies not only in oneself becoming a father-mask, but in being overpowered by this mask when worn by another. Master and pupil are in the same boat in this respect.

In a lecture on "The Phenomenology of the Spirit in Fairytales," Jung defines the spirit (Geist) as "the principle that stands in opposition to matter." He goes on to link spirit with paternal authority and the archetype of the wise old man.

From "**The Phenomenology of the Spirit in Fairytales**" CW 9 i, pars. 396–9

SELF-REPRESENTATION OF THE SPIRIT IN DREAMS

The psychic manifestations of the spirit indicate at once that they are of an archetypal nature – in other words, the phenomenon we call spirit depends on the existence of an autonomous primordial image which is universally present in the preconscious makeup of the human psyche. As usual, I first came up against this problem when investigating the dreams of my patients. It struck me that a certain kind of father-complex has a "spiritual" character, so to speak, in the sense that the father-image gives rise to statements, actions, tendencies, impulses, opinions, etc., to which one could hardly deny the attribute "spiritual." In men, a positive father-complex very often produces a certain credulity with regard to authority and a distinct willingness to bow down before all spiritual dogmas and values; while in women, it induces the liveliest spiritual aspirations and interests. In dreams, it is always the father-figure from whom the decisive convictions, prohibitions, and wise counsels emanate. The invisibility of this source is frequently emphasized by the fact that it consists simply of an authoritative voice which passes final judgments. Mostly, therefore, it is the figure of a "wise old man" who symbolizes the spiritual factor. Sometimes the part is played by a "real" spirit, namely the ghost of one dead, or, more rarely, by grotesque gnomelike figures or talking animals. The dwarf forms are found, at least in my experience, mainly in women; hence it seems to me logical that in Ernst Barlach's play *Der tote Tag* (1912), the gnomelike figure of Steissbart ("Rumpbeard") is associated with the mother, just as Bes is associated with the mother-goddess at Karnak. In both sexes the spirit can also take the form of a boy or a youth. In women he corresponds to the so-called "positive" animus who indicates the possibility of conscious spiritual effort. In men his meaning is not so simple. He can be positive, in which case he signifies the "higher" personality, the self or *filius regius* as conceived by the alchemists.* But he can also be negative, and then

*Cf. the vision of the "naked boy" in Meister Eckhart (trans. by Evans, I, p. 438).

he signifies the infantile shadow. In both cases the boy means some form of spirit. Graybeard and boy belong together. The pair of them play a considerable role in alchemy as symbols of Mercurius.

It can never be established with one-hundred-per-cent certainty whether the spirit-figures in dreams are morally good. Very often they show all the signs of duplicity, if not of outright malice. I must emphasize, however, that the grand plan on which the unconscious life of the psyche is constructed is so inaccessible to our understanding that we can never know what evil may not be necessary in order to produce good by enantiodromia, and what good may very possibly lead to evil. Sometimes the *probate spiritus* recommended by John cannot, with the best will in the world, be anything other than a cautious and patient waiting to see how things will finally turn out.

The figure of the wise old man can appear so plastically, not only in dreams but also in visionary meditation (or what we call "active imagination"), that, as is sometimes apparently the case in India, it takes over the role of a guru.* The wise old man appears in dreams in the guise of a magician, doctor, priest, teacher, professor, grandfather, or any other person possessing authority. The archetype of spirit in the shape of a man, hobgoblin, or animal always appears in a situation where insight, understanding, good advice, determination, planning, etc., are needed but cannot be mustered on one's own resources. The archetype compensates this state of spiritual deficiency by contents designed to fill the gap. An excellent example of this is the dream about the white and black magicians, which tried to compensate the spiritual difficulties of a young theological student. I did not know the dreamer myself, so the question of my personal influence is ruled out. He dreamed *he was standing in the presence of a sublime hieratic figure called the "white magician," who was nevertheless clothed in a long black robe. This magician had just ended a lengthy discourse with the words "And for that we require the help of the black magician." Then the door*

*Hence the many miraculous stories about rishis and mahatmas. A cultured Indian with whom I once conversed on the subject of gurus told me, when I asked him who his guru had been, that it was Shankaracharya (who lived in the 8th and 9th cents.). "But that's the celebrated commentator," I remarked in amazement. Whereupon he replied, "Yes, so he was; but naturally it was his spirit," not in the least perturbed by my Western bewilderment.

suddenly opened and another old man came in, the "black magician who however was dressed in a white robe. He too looked noble and sublime. The black magician evidently wanted to speak with the white, but hesitated to do so in the presence of the dreamer. At that the white magician, pointing to the dreamer, said, "Speak, he is an innocent." So the black magician began to relate a strange story of how he had found the lost keys of Paradise and did not know how to use them. He had, he said, come to the white magician for an explanation of the secret of the keys. He told him that the king of the country in which he lived was seeking a suitable tomb for himself. His subjects had chanced to dig up an old sarcophagus containing the mortal remains of a virgin. The king opened the sarcophagus, threw away the bones, and had the empty sarcophagus buried again for later use. But no sooner had the bones seen the light of day than the being to whom they once had belonged – the virgin – changed into a black horse that galloped off into the desert. The black magician pursued it across the sandy wastes and beyond, and there after many vicissitudes and difficulties he found the lost keys of Paradise. That was the end of his story, and also, unfortunately, of the dream.

Here the compensation certainly did not fall out as the dreamer would wish, by handing him a solution on a plate; rather it confronted him with a problem to which I have already alluded, and one which life is always bringing us up against: namely, the uncertainty of all moral valuation, the bewildering interplay of good and evil, and the remorseless concatenation of guilt, suffering, and redemption. This path to the primordial religious experience is the right one, but how many can recognize it? It is like a still small voice, and it sounds from afar. It is ambiguous, questionable, dark, presaging danger and hazardous adventure; a razor-edged path, to be trodden for God's sake only, without assurance and without sanction.

Part 5. Psychological Types and the Self-regulating Psyche

At the same time that Jung was engaged in his own confrontation with the unconscious, he was also concerned with defining the difference in his approach to the problems of psychology from those adopted by Freud and Adler. How was it, he asked, that each could interpret the same material so differently? He concluded that human beings belonged to different psychological types; and, in 1921, his book Psychological Types *was first published in Zurich. The terms "extravert" and "introvert" were introduced by Jung, and are still in current use as descriptive of personality differences.*

"Introduction" *Psychological Types*, CW 6, pars. 1–7

In my practical medical work with nervous patients I have long been struck by the fact that besides the many individual differences in human psychology there are also typical differences. Two types especially become clear to me; I have termed them the introverted and the extraverted types.

When we consider the course of human life, we see how the fate of one individual is determined more by the objects of his interest, while in another it is determined more by his own inner self, by the subject. Since we all swerve rather more towards one side or the other, we naturally tend to understand everything in terms of our own type.

I mention this circumstance at once in order to avoid possible misunderstandings. It will be apparent that it is one which considerably aggravates the difficulty of a general description of types. I must presume unduly upon the goodwill of the reader if I may hope to be rightly understood. It would be relatively simple if every reader knew to which category he belonged. But it is often very difficult to find out whether a person belongs to one type or the other, especially in regard to oneself. In respect of one's own personality one's judgment is as a rule extraordinarily clouded. This subjective clouding of judgment is particularly common because in every pronounced type there is a special tendency to compensate the one-sidedness of that type, a tendency which is biologically purposive since it strives constantly to maintain the psychic equilibrium. The compensation gives rise to secondary characteristics, or secondary types, which present a picture that is extremely difficult to interpret, so difficult that one is inclined to deny the existence of types altogether and to believe only in individual differences.

I must emphasize this difficulty in order to justify certain peculiarities in my presentation. It might seem as if the simplest way would be to describe two concrete cases and to dissect them side by side. But everyone possesses both mechanisms, extraversion as well as introversion, and only the relative predominance of one or the other determines the type. Hence, in order to throw the picture into the necessary relief, one would have to retouch it rather vigorously, and this would amount to a more or less pious fraud. Moreover, the psychological reactions of a human being are so complicated that my powers of description would hardly suffice to draw an absolutely correct picture. From sheer necessity, therefore, I must confine myself to a presentation of principles which I have abstracted from a wealth of facts observed in many different individuals. In this there is no question of a *deductio a priori*, as it might appear; it is rather a deductive presentation of empirically gained insights. These insights will, I hope, help to clarify a dilemma which, not only in analytical psychology but in other branches of science as well, and especially in the personal relations of human beings with one another, has led and still continues to lead to misunderstanding and discord. For they explain how the existence of two distinct types is actually a fact that has long been known: a fact that in one form or another has struck the observer of human nature or dawned upon the brooding reflection of the thinker, presenting itself to Goethe's intuition, for instance, as the all-embracing principle of systole and diastole. The names and concepts by which the mechanisms of extraversion and introversion have been grasped are extremely varied, and each of them is adapted to the standpoint of the observer in question. But despite the diversity of the formulations the fundamental idea common to them all constantly shines through: in one case an outward movement of interest towards the object, and in the other a movement of interest away from the object to the subject and his own psychological processes. In the first case the object works like a magnet upon the tendencies of the subject; it determines the subject to a large extent and even alienates him from himself. His qualities may become so transformed by assimilation to the object that one might think it possessed some higher and decisive significance for him. It might almost seem as if it were an absolute determinant, a special purpose of life or fate that he should abandon himself wholly to the object. But in the second case the subject is and remains the centre of every interest. It looks, one might say, as though all the life-energy were ultimately seeking the subject, and thus continually prevented the object from exercising any overpowering influence. It is as though the energy were flowing away from the object, and the subject were a magnet drawing the object to itself.

It is not easy to give a clear and intelligible description of this two-way relationship to the object without running the risk of paradoxical formulations which would create more confusion than clarity. But in general one could say that the introverted standpoint is one which sets the ego and the subjective psychological process above the object and the objective process, or at any rate seeks to hold its ground against the object. This attitude, therefore, gives the subject a higher value than the object, and the object accordingly has a lower value. It is of secondary importance; indeed, sometimes the object represents no more than an outward token of a subjective content, the embodiment of an idea, the idea being the essential thing. If it is the embodiment of a feeling, then again the feeling is the main thing and not the object in its own right. The extraverted standpoint, on the contrary, subordinates the subject to the object, so that the object has the higher value. In this case the subject is of secondary importance, the subjective process appearing at times as no more than a disturbing or superfluous appendage of objective events. It is clear that the psychology resulting from these contrary standpoints must be classed as two totally different orientations. The one sees everything in terms of his own situation, the other in terms of the objective event.

These contrary attitudes are in themselves no more than correlative mechanisms: a diastolic going out and seizing of the object, and a systolic concentration and detachment of energy from the object seized. Every human being possesses both mechanisms as an expression of his natural life-rhythm, a rhythm which Goethe, surely not by chance, described physiologically in terms of the heart's activity. A rhythmical alternation of both forms of psychic activity would perhaps correspond to the normal course of life. But the complicated outer conditions under which we live and the even more complicated conditions of our individual psychic make-up seldom permit a completely undisturbed flow of psychic energy. Outer circumstances and inner disposition frequently favour one mechanism and restrict or hinder the other. One mechanism will naturally predominate, and if this condition becomes in any way chronic a *type* will be produced; that is, an habitual attitude in which one mechanism predominates permanently, although the other can never be completely suppressed since it is an integral part of the psychic economy. Hence there can never be a pure type in the sense that it possesses only one mechanism with the complete atrophy of the other. A typical attitude always means merely the relative predominance of one mechanism.

The hypothesis of introversion and extraversion allows us, first of all, to distinguish two large groups of psychological individuals. Yet this grouping is of such a superficial and general nature that it permits no more than this very general distinction. Closer investigation of the individual psychologies that fall into one group or the other will at once show great differences between individuals who nevertheless belong to the same group. If, therefore, we wish to determine wherein lie the differences between individuals belonging to a definite group, we must take a further step. Experience has taught me that in general individuals can be distinguished not only according to the broad distinction between introversion and extraversion, but also according to their basic psychological functions. For in the same measure as outer circumstances and inner disposition cause either introversion or extraversion to predominate, they also favour the predominance of one definite basic function in the individual. I have found from experience that the basic psychological functions, that is, functions which are genuinely as well as essentially different from other functions, prove to be *thinking, feeling, sensation,* and *intuition.* If one of these functions habitually predominates, a corresponding type results. I therefore distinguish a thinking, a feeling, a sensation, and an intuitive type. *Each of these types may moreover be either introverted or extraverted,* depending on its relation to the object as we have described above. In my preliminary work on psychological types I did not carry out this differentiation, but identified the thinking type with the introvert and the feeling type with the extravert. A deeper study of the problem has shown this equation to be untenable. In order to avoid misunderstandings, I would ask the reader to bear in mind the differentiation I have developed here. For the sake of clarity, which is essential in such complicated matters, I have devoted the last chapter of this book to the definition of my psychological concepts.

Psychological Types *is a long and interesting book in which Jung draws on his extensive knowledge of literature and history to demonstrate that his typology has various ancestors. In a work presenting the essentials of Jung's own thought, these historical parallels must be omitted. However, a paper of 1936 which is published as an appendix to* Psychological Types *gives a good summary of Jung's conceptions, and also mentions in passing some of his predecessors in the field.*

"Psychological Typology" CW 6, pars. 960–87

Ever since the early days of science, it has been a notable endeavour of the reflective intellect to interpose gradations between the two poles of the absolute similarity and dissimilarity of human beings. This resulted in a number of types, or "temperaments" as they were then called, which classified similarities and dissimilarities into regular categories. The Greek philosopher Empedocles attempted to impose order on the chaos of natural phenomena by dividing them into the four elements: earth, water, air, and fire. It was above all the physicians of ancient times who applied this principle of order, in conjunction with the related doctrine of the four qualities, dry, moist, cold, warm, to human beings, and thus tried to reduce the bewildering diversity of mankind to orderly groups. Of these physicians one of the most important was Galen, whose use of these teachings influenced medical science and the treatment of the sick for nearly seventeen hundred years. The very names of the Galenic temperaments betray their origin in the pathology of the four "humours." *Melancholic* denotes a preponderance of black bile, *phlegmatic* a preponderance of phlegm or mucus (the Greek word *phlegma* means fire, and phlegm was regarded as the end-product of inflammation), *sanguine* a preponderance of blood, and *choleric* a preponderance of choler, or yellow bile.

Our modern conception of "temperament" has certainly become much more psychological, since in the course of man's development over the last two thousand years the "soul" has freed itself from any conceivable connection with cold agues and fevers, or secretions of mucus and bile. Not even the doctors of today would equate a temperament, that is, a certain kind of emotional state or excitability, directly with the constitution of the blood or lymph, although their profession and their exclusive approach to human beings from the side of physical illness tempt them, more often than the layman, to regard the psyche as an end-product dependent on the physiology of the glands. The "humours" of present-day medicine are no longer the old body-secretions, but the more subtle hormones, which influence "temperament" to an outstanding degree, if we define this as the sum-total of emotional reactions. The whole make-up of the body, its constitution in the broadest sense, has in fact a very great deal to do with the psychological temperament, so much that we cannot blame the doctors if they regard psychic phenomena as largely dependent on the body. Somewhere the psyche is living body, and the living body is animated matter; somehow and somewhere there is an undiscoverable unity of psyche and body which would need investigating psychically as well as physically; in other words, this unity must be as dependent on the body as it is on the psyche so far as the investigator is concerned. The materialism of the nineteenth century gave the body first place and relegated the psyche to the rank of something secondary and derived, allowing it no more substantiality than that of a so-called "epiphenomenon." What proved to be a good working hypothesis, namely, that psychic phenomena are conditioned by physical processes, became a philosophical presumption with the advent of materialism. Any serious science of the living organism will reject this presumption; for on the one hand it will constantly bear in mind that living matter is an as yet unsolved mystery, and on the other hand it will be objective enough to recognize that for us there is a completely unbridgeable gulf between physical and psychic phenomena, so that the psychic realm is no less mysterious than the physical.

The materialistic presumption became possible only in recent times, after man's conception of the psyche had, in the course of many centuries, emancipated itself from the old view and developed in an increasingly abstract direction. The ancients could still see body and psyche together, as an undivided unity, because they were closer to that primitive world where no moral rift yet ran through the personality, and the pagan could still feel himself indivisibly one, childishly innocent and unburdened by responsibility. The ancient Egyptians could still enjoy the naïve luxury of a negative confession of sin: "I have not let any man go hungry. I have not made anyone weep. I have not committed murder," and so on. The Homeric heroes wept, laughed, raged, outwitted and killed each other in a world where these things were taken as natural and self-evident by men and gods alike, and the Olympians amused themselves by passing their days in a state of amaranthine irresponsibility.

It was on this archaic level that pre-philosophical man lived and experienced the world. He was entirely in the grip of his emotions. All passions that made his blood boil and his heart pound, that accelerated his breathing or took his breath away, that "turned his bowels to water" – all this was a manifestation of the "soul." Therefore he localized the soul in the region of the diaphragm (in Greek *phren*, which also means mind) and the heart. It was only with the first philosophers that the seat of reason began to be assigned to the head. There are still Negroes today whose "thoughts" are localized principally in the belly, and the Pueblo Indians "think" with their hearts – "only madmen think with their heads," they say. On this level consciousness is essentially passion and the experience of oneness. Yet, serene and tragic at once, it was just this archaic man who, having started to think, invented that dichotomy which Nietzsche laid at the door of Zarathustra: the discovery of pairs of opposites, the division into odd and even, above and below, good and evil. It was the work of the old Pythagoreans, and it was their doctrine of moral responsibility and the grave metaphysical consequences of sin that gradually, in the course of the centuries, percolated through to all strata of the population, chiefly owing to the spread of the Orphic and Pythagorean mysteries. Plato even used the parable of the white and black horses to illustrate the intractability and polarity of the human psyche, and, still earlier, the mysteries proclaimed the doctrine of the good rewarded in the Hereafter and of the wicked punished in hell. These teachings cannot be dismissed as the mystical humbug of "backwoods" philosophers, as Nietzsche claimed, or as so much sectarian cant, for already in the sixth century B.C. Pythagoreanism was something like a state religion throughout Graecia Magna. Also, the ideas underlying its mysteries never died out, but underwent a philosophical renaissance in the second century B.C., when they exercised the strongest influence on the Alexandrian world of thought. Their collision with Old Testament prophecy then led to what one can call the beginnings of Christianity as a world religion.

From Hellenistic syncretism there now arose a classification of man into types which was entirely alien to the "humoral" psychology of Greek medicine. In the philosophical sense, it established gradations between the Parmenidean poles of light and darkness, of above and below. It classified men into *hylikoi*, *psychikoi*, and *pneumatikoi* – material, psychic, and spiritual beings. This classification is not, of course, a scientific formulation of similarities and dissimilarities; it is a critical system of values based not on the behaviour and outward appearance of man as a phenotype, but on definitions of an ethical, mystical, and philosophic kind. Although it is not exactly a "Christian" conception it nevertheless forms an integral part of early Christianity at the time of St. Paul. Its very existence is incontrovertible proof of the split that had occurred in the original unity of man as a being entirely in the grip of his emotions. Before this, he was merely alive and there, the plaything of experience, incapable of any reflective analysis concerning his origins and his destination. Now, suddenly, he found himself confronted by three fateful factors and endowed with body, soul, and spirit, to each of which he had moral obligations. Presumably it was already decided at birth whether he would pass his life in the hylic or the pneumatic state, or in the indeterminate centre between the two. The ingrained dichotomy of the Greek mind had now become acute, with the result that the accent shifted significantly to the psychic and spiritual, which was unavoidably split off from the hylic realm of the body. All the highest and ultimate goals lay in man's moral destination, in a spiritual, supramundane end-state, and the separation of the hylic realm broadened into a cleavage between world and spirit. Thus the original, suave wisdom expressed in the Pythagorean pairs of opposites became a passionate moral conflict. Nothing, however, is so apt to challenge our self-awareness and alertness as being at war with oneself. One can hardly think of any other or more effective means of waking humanity out of the irresponsible and innocent half-sleep of the primitive mentality and bringing it to a state of conscious responsibility.

This process is called cultural development. It is, at any rate, a development of man's powers of discrimination and capacity for judgment, and of consciousness in general. With the increase of knowledge and enhanced critical faculties the foundations were laid for the whole subsequent development of the human mind in terms of intellectual achievement. The particular mental product that far surpassed all the achievements of the ancient world was science. It closed the rift between man and nature in the sense that, although he was separated from nature, science enabled him to find his rightful place again in the natural order. His special metaphysical position, however, had to be jettisoned – so far as it was not secured by belief in the traditional religion – whence arose the notorious conflict between "faith and knowledge." At all events, science brought about a splendid rehabilitation of matter, and in this respect materialism may even be regarded as an act of historical justice.

But one absolutely essential field of experience, the hun ...

psyche itself, remained for a very long time the preserve of metaphysics, although increasingly serious attempts were made after the Enlightenment to open it up to scientific investigation. They began, tentatively, with the sense perceptions, and gradually ventured into the domain of associations. This line of research paved the way for experimental psychology, and it culminated in the "physiological psychology" of Wundt. A more descriptive kind of psychology, with which the medical men soon made contact, developed in France. Its chief exponents were Taine, Ribot, and Janet. It was characteristic of this scientific approach that it broke down the psyche into particular mechanisms or processes. In face of these attempts, there were some who advocated what we today would call a "holistic" approach – the systematic observation of the psyche as a whole. It seems as if this trend originated in a certain type of biography, more particularly the kind that an earlier age, which also had its good points, used to describe as "curious lives." In this connection I think of Justinus Kerner and his *Seeress of Prevorst*, and the case of the elder Blumhardt and his medium Gottliebin Dittus. To be historically fair, however, I should not forget the medieval *Acta Sanctorum*.

This line of research has been continued in more recent investigations associated with the names of William James, Freud, and Theodore Flournoy. James and his friend Flournoy, a Swiss psychologist, made an attempt to describe the whole phenomenology of the psyche and also to view it as a totality. Freud, too, as a doctor, took as his point of departure the wholeness and indivisibility of the human personality, though, in keeping with the spirit of the age, he restricted himself to the investigation of instinctive mechanisms and individual processes. He also narrowed the picture of man to the wholeness of an essentially "bourgeois" collective person, and this necessarily led to philosophically one-sided interpretations. Freud, unfortunately, succumbed to the medical man's temptation to trace everything psychic to the body, in the manner of the old "humoral" psychologists, not without rebellious gestures at those metaphysical preserves of which he had a holy dread.

Unlike Freud, who after a proper psychological start reverted to the ancient assumption of the sovereignty of the physical constitution, trying to turn everything back in theory into instinctual processes conditioned by the body, I start with the assumption of the sovereignty of the psyche. Since body and psyche somewhere form a unity, although in their manifest natures they are so utterly different, we cannot but attribute to the one as to the other a substantiality of its own. So long as we have no way of knowing that unity, there is no alternative but to investigate them separately and, for the present, treat them as though they were independent of each other, at least in their structure. That they are not so, we can see for ourselves every day. But if we were to stop at that, we would never be in a position to make out anything about the psyche at all.

Now if we assume the sovereignty of the psyche, we exempt ourselves from the – at present – insoluble task of reducing everything psychic to something definitely physical. We can then take the manifestations of the psyche as expressions of its intrinsic being, and try to establish certain conformities or types. So when I speak of a psychological typology, I mean by this the formulation of the structural elements of the psyche and not a description of the psychic emanations of a particular type of constitution. This is covered by, for instance, Kretschmer's researches into body-structure and character.

I have given a detailed description of a purely psychological typology in my book *Psychological Types*. My investigation was based on twenty years of work as a doctor, which brought me into contact with people of all classes from all the great nations. When one begins as a young doctor, one's head is still full of clinical pictures and diagnoses. In the course of the years, impressions of quite another kind accumulate. One is struck by the enormous diversity of human individuals, by the chaotic profusion of individual cases, the special circumstances of whose lives and whose special characters produce clinical pictures that, even supposing one still felt any desire to do so, can be squeezed into the straitjacket of a diagnosis only by force. The fact that the disturbance can be given such and such a name appears completely irrelevant beside the overwhelming impression one has that all clinical pictures are so many mimetic or histrionic demonstrations of certain definite character traits. The pathological problem upon which everything turns has virtually nothing to do with the clinical picture, but is essentially an expression of character. Even the complexes, the "nuclear elements" of a neurosis, are beside the point, being mere concomitants of a certain characterological disposition. This can be seen most easily in the relation of the patient to his parental family. He is, let us say, one of four siblings, is neither the eldest nor the youngest, has had the same education and conditioning as the others. Yet he is sick and they are sound. The anamnesis shows that a whole series of influences to which the others were exposed as well as he, and from which indeed they all suffered, had a pathological effect on him alone – at least to all appearances. In reality these influences were not aetiological factors in his case either, but prove to be false explanations. The real cause of the neurosis lies in the peculiar way he responded to and assimilated the influences emanating from the environment.

By comparing many such cases it gradually became clear to me that there must be two fundamentally different general attitudes which would divide human beings into two groups – provided the whole of humanity consisted of highly differentiated individuals. Since this is obviously not the case, one can only say that this difference of attitude becomes plainly observable only when we are confronted with a comparatively well-differentiated personality; in other words, it becomes of practical importance only after a certain degree of differentiation has been reached. Pathological cases of this kind are almost always people who deviate from the familial type and, in consequence, no longer find sufficient security in their inherited instinctual foundation. Weak instincts are one of the prime causes of the development of an habitual one-sided attitude, though in the last resort it is conditioned or reinforced by heredity.

I have called these two fundamentally different attitudes *extraversion* and *introversion*. Extraversion is characterized by interest in the external object, responsiveness, and a ready acceptance of external happenings, a desire to influence and be influenced by events, a need to join in and get "with it," the capacity to endure bustle and noise of every kind, and actually find them enjoyable, constant attention to the surrounding world, the cultivation of friends and acquaintances, none too carefully selected, and finally by the great importance attached to the figure one cuts, and hence by a strong tendency to make a show of oneself. Accordingly, the extravert's philosophy of life and his ethics are as a rule of a highly collective nature with a strong streak of altruism, and his conscience is in large measure dependent on public opinion. Moral misgivings arise mainly when "other people know." His religious convictions are determined, so to speak, by majority vote.

The actual subject, the extravert as a subjective entity, is, so far as possible, shrouded in darkness. He hides it from himself under veils of unconsciousness. The disinclination to submit his own motives to critical examination is very pronounced. He has no secrets he has not long since shared with others. Should something unmentionable nevertheless befall him, he prefers to forget it. Anything that might tarnish the parade of optimism and positivism is avoided. Whatever he thinks, intends, and does is displayed with conviction and warmth.

The psychic life of this type of person is enacted, as it were, outside himself, in the environment. He lives in and through others; all self-communings give him the creeps. Dangers lurk there which are better drowned out by noise. If he should ever have a "complex," he finds refuge in the social whirl and allows himself to be assured several times a day that everything is in order. Provided he is not too much of a busy-body, too pushing, and too superficial, he can be a distinctly useful member of the community.

In this short essay I have to content myself with an allusive sketch. It is intended merely to give the reader some idea of what extraversion is like, something he can bring into relationship with his own knowledge of human nature. I have purposely started with a description of extraversion because this attitude is familiar to everyone; the extravert not only lives in this attitude, but parades it before his fellows on principle. Moreover it accords with certain popular ideals and moral requirements.

Introversion, on the other hand, being directed not to the object but to the subject, and not being oriented by the object, is not so easy to put into perspective. The introvert is not forthcoming, he is as though in continual retreat before the object. He holds aloof from external happenings, does not join in, has a distinct dislike of society as soon as he finds himself among too many people. In a large gathering he feels lonely and lost. The more crowded it is, the greater becomes his resistance. He is not in the least "with it," and has no love of enthusiastic get-togethers. He is not a good mixer. What he does, he does in his own way, barricading himself against influences from outside. He is apt to appear awkward, often seeming inhibited, and it frequently happens that, by a certain brusqueness of manner, or by his glum unapproachability, or some kind of malapropism, he causes unwitting offence to people. His better qualities he keeps to himself, and generally does everything he can to dissemble them. He is easily mistrustful, self-willed, often suffers from inferiority feelings and for this reason is also envious. His apprehensiveness of the object is not due to fear, but to the fact that it seems to him negative, demanding, overpowering or even menacing. He therefore suspects all kinds of bad motives, has an everlasting fear of making a fool of himself, is usually very touchy and surrounds himself with a barbed wire entanglement so dense and impenetrable that finally he himself would rather do anything than sit behind it. He confronts the world with an elaborate defensive system compounded of scrupulosity, pedantry, frugality, cautiousness, painful conscientiousness, stiff-lipped rectitude, politeness, and open-eyed distrust. His picture of the world lacks rosy hues, as he is over-critical and finds a hair in every soup. Under normal conditions he is pessimistic and worried, because the world and human beings are not in the least good but crush him, so he never feels accepted and taken to their bosom. Yet he himself does not accept the world either, at any rate not outright, for everything has first to be judged by his own critical standards. Finally only those things are accepted which, for various subjective reasons, he can turn to his own account.

For him self-communings are a pleasure. His own world is a safe harbour, a carefully tended and walled-in garden, closed to the public and hidden from prying eyes. His own company is the best. He feels at home in his world, where the only changes are made by himself. His best work is done with his own resources, on his own initiative, and in his own way. If ever he succeeds, after long and often wearisome struggles, in assimilating something alien to himself, he is capable of turning it to excellent account. Crowds, majority views, public opinion, popular enthusiasm never convince him of anything, but merely make him creep still deeper into his shell.

His relations with other people become warm only when safety is guaranteed, and when he can lay aside his defensive distrust. All too often he cannot, and consequently the number of friends and acquaintances is very restricted. Thus the psychic life of this type is played out wholly within. Should any difficulties and conflicts arise in this inner world, all doors and windows are shut tight. The introvert shuts himself up with his complexes until he ends in complete isolation.

In spite of these peculiarities the introvert is by no means a social loss. His retreat into himself is not a final renunciation of the world, but a search for quietude, where alone it is possible for him to make his contribution to the life of the community. This type of person is the victim of numerous misunderstandings – not unjustly, for he actually invites them. Nor can he be acquitted of the charge of taking a secret delight in mystification, and that being misunderstood gives him a certain satisfaction, since it reaffirms his pessimistic outlook. That being so, it is easy to see why he is accused of being cold, proud, obstinate, selfish, conceited, cranky, and what not, and why he is constantly admonished that devotion to the goals of society, clubbableness, imperturbable urbanity, and selfless trust in the powers-that-be are true virtues and the marks of a sound and vigorous life.

The introvert is well enough aware that such virtues exist, and that somewhere, perhaps – only not in his circle of acquaintances – there are divinely inspired people who enjoy undiluted possession of these ideal qualities. But his self-criticism and his awareness of his own motives have long since disabused him of the illusion that he himself would be capable of such virtues; and his mistrustful gaze, sharpened by anxiety, constantly enables him to detect on his fellow men the ass's ear sticking up from under the lion's mane. The world and men are for him a disturbance and a danger, affording no valid standard by which he could ultimately orient himself. What alone is valid for him is his subjective world, which he sometimes believes, in moments of delusion, to be the objective one. We could easily charge these people with the worst kind of subjectivism, indeed with morbid individualism, if it were certain beyond a doubt that only one objective world existed. But this truth, if such it be, is not axiomatic; it is merely a half truth, the other half of which is the fact that the world *also* is as it is seen by human beings, and in the last resort by the individual. There nply no world at all without the knowing subject. This, be it never so small and inconspicuous, is always the other pier supporting the bridge of the phenomenal world. The appeal to the subject therefore has the same validity as the appeal to the so-called objective world, for it is grounded on psychic reality itself. But this is a reality with its own peculiar laws which are not of a secondary nature.

The two attitudes, extraversion and introversion, are opposing modes that make themselves felt not least in the history of human thought. The problems to which they give rise were very largely anticipated by Friedrich Schiller, and they underlie his *Letters on the Aesthetic Education of Man*. But since the concept of the unconscious was still unknown to him, he was unable to reach a satisfactory solution. Moreover philosophers, who would be the best equipped to go more closely into this question, do not like having to submit their thinking function to a thorough psychological criticism, and therefore hold aloof from such discussions. It should, however, be obvious that the intrinsic polarity of such an attitude exerts a very great influence on the philosopher's own point of view.

For the extravert the object is interesting and attractive *a priori*, as is the subject, or psychic reality, for the introvert. We could therefore use the expression "numinal accent" for this fact, by which I mean that for the extravert the quality of positive significance and value attaches primarily to the object, so that it plays the predominant, determining, and decisive role in all psychic processes from the start, just as the subject does for the introvert.

But the numinal accent does not decide only between subject and object; it also selects the conscious function of which the individual makes the principal use. I distinguish four functions: *thinking, feeling, sensation*, and *intuition*. The essential function of sensation is to establish that something exists, thinking tells us what it means, feeling what its value is, and intuition surmises whence it comes and whither it goes. Sensation and intuition I call irrational functions, because they are both concerned simply with what happens and with actual or potential realities. Thinking and feeling, being discriminative functions, are rational. Sensation, the *fonction du réel*, rules out any simultaneous intuitive activity, since the latter is not concerned with the present but is rather a sixth sense for hidden possibilities, and therefore should not allow itself to be unduly influenced by existing reality. In the same way, thinking is opposed to feeling, because thinking should not be influenced or deflected from its purpose by feeling values, just as feeling is usually vitiated by too much reflection. The four functions therefore form, when arranged diagrammatically, a cross with a rational axis at right angles to an irrational axis.

The four orienting functions naturally do not contain everything that is in the conscious psyche. Will and memory, for instance, are not included. The reason for this is that the differentiation of the four orienting functions is, essentially, an empirical consequence of typical differences in the functional attitude. There are people for whom the numinal accent falls on sensation, on the perception of actualities, and elevates it into the sole determining and all-overriding principle. These are the fact-minded men, in whom intellectual judgment, feeling, and intuition are driven into the background by the paramount importance of actual facts. When the accent falls on thinking, judgment is reserved as to what significance should be attached to the facts in question. And on this significance will depend the way in which the individual deals with the facts. If feeling is numinal, then his adaptation will depend entirely on the feeling value he attributes to them. Finally, if the numinal accent falls on intuition, actual reality counts only in so far as it seems to harbour possibilities which then become the supreme motivating force, regardless of the way things actually are in the present.

The localization of the numinal accent thus gives rise to four function-types, which I encountered first of all in my relations with people and formulated systematically only very much later. In practice these four types are always combined with the attitude-type, that is, with extraversion or introversion, so that the functions appear in an extraverted or introverted variation. This produces a set of eight demonstrable function-types. It is naturally impossible to present the specific psychology of these types within the confines of an essay, and to go into its conscious and unconscious manifestations. I must therefore refer the interested reader to the aforementioned study.

It is not the purpose of a psychological typology to classify human beings into categories – this in itself would be pretty pointless. Its purpose is rather to provide a critical psychology which will make a methodical investigation and presentation of the empirical material possible. First and foremost, it is a critical tool for the research worker, who needs definite points of view and guidelines if he is to reduce the chaotic profusion of individual experiences to any kind of order. In this respect we could compare typology to a trigonometric net or, better still, to a crystallographic axial system. Secondly, a typology is a great help in understanding the wide variations that occur among individuals, and it also furnishes a clue to the fundamental differences in the psychological theories now current. Last but not least, it is an essential means for determining the "personal equation" of the practising psychologist, who, armed with an exact knowledge of his differentiated and inferior functions, can avoid many serious blunders in dealing with his patients.

The typological system I have proposed is an attempt, grounded on practical experience, to provide an explanatory basis and theoretical framework for the boundless diversity that has hitherto prevailed in the formation of psychological concepts. In a science as young as psychology, limiting definitions will sooner or later become an unavoidable necessity. Some day psychologists will have to agree upon certain basic principles secure from arbitrary interpretation if psychology is not to remain an unscientific and fortuitous conglomeration of individual opinions.

In "On the Psychology of the Unconscious," the first of the Two Essays on Analytical Psychology which constitute volume 7 of the Collected Works, Jung gives an outline of Freudian theory and Adlerian theory, and goes on to show that the psychopathology of a particular case can be interpreted equally validly from either standpoint. He then presents these two "psychologies" as examples of extraversion versus introversion; affirms that both attitudes are present in human beings; and suggests that neurosis occurs when either attitude is exaggerated. At the end of this passage, he states an important principle of Jungian thought: the psyche is self-regulating.

From "**On the Psychology of the Unconscious**" *Two Essays*, CW
7, pars. 56–92

THE PROBLEM OF THE ATTITUDE-TYPE

The incompatibility of the two theories discussed in the
preceding chapters requires a standpoint superordinate to both, in
which they could come together in unison. We are certainly not
entitled to discard one in favour of the other, however convenient
this expedient might be. For, if we examine the two theories
without prejudice, we cannot deny that both contain significant
truths, and, contradictory as these are, they should not be regarded
as mutually exclusive. The Freudian theory is attractively simple,
so much so that it almost pains one if anybody drives in the wedge
of a contrary assertion. But the same is true of Adler's theory. It
too is of illuminating simplicity and explains just as much as the
Freudian theory. No wonder, then, that the adherents of both
schools obstinately cling to their one-sided truths. For humanly
understandable reasons they are unwilling to give up a beautiful,
rounded theory in exchange for a paradox, or, worse still, lose
themselves in the confusion of contradictory points of view.

Now, since both theories are in a large measure correct – that
is to say, since they both appear to explain their material – it follows
that a neurosis must have two opposite aspects, one of which is
grasped by the Freudian, the other by the Adlerian theory. But
how comes it that each investigator sees only one side, and why
does each maintain that he has the only valid view? It must come
from the fact that, owing to his psychological peculiarity, each
investigator most readily sees that factor in the neurosis which
corresponds to his peculiarity. It cannot be assumed that the cases
of neurosis seen by Adler are totally different from those seen by
Freud. Both are obviously working with the same material; but
because of personal peculiarities they each see things from a
different angle, and thus they evolve fundamentally different views
and theories. Adler sees how a subject who feels suppressed and
inferior tries to secure an illusory superiority by means of
"protests," "arrangements," and other appropriate devices directed equally against parents, teachers, regulations, authorities,
situations, institutions, and such. Even sexuality may figure
among these devices. This view lays undue emphasis upon the

subject, before which the idiosyncrasy and significance of objects entirely vanishes. Objects are regarded at best as vehicles of suppressive tendencies. I shall probably not be wrong in assuming that the love relation and other desires directed upon objects exist equally in Adler as essential factors; yet in his theory of neurosis they do not play the principal role assigned to them by Freud.

Freud sees his patient in perpetual dependence on, and in relation to, significant objects. Father and mother play a large part here; whatever other significant influences or conditions enter into the life of the patient go back in a direct line of causality to these prime factors. The *pièce de résistance* of his theory is the concept of transference, i.e., the patient's relation to the doctor. Always a specifically qualified object is either desired or met with resistance, and this reaction always follows the pattern established in earliest childhood through the relation to father and mother. What comes from the subject is essentially a blind striving after pleasure; but this striving always acquires its quality from specific objects. With Freud objects are of the greatest significance and possess almost exclusively the determining power, while the subject remains remarkably insignificant and is really nothing more than the source of desire for pleasure and a "seat of anxiety." As already pointed out, Freud recognizes ego-instincts, but this term alone is enough to show that his conception of the subject differs *toto coelo* from Adler's, where the subject figures as the determining factor.

Certainly both investigators see the subject in relation to the object; but how differently this relation is seen! With Adler the emphasis is placed on a subject who, no matter what the object, seeks his own security and supremacy; with Freud the emphasis is placed wholly upon objects, which, according to their specific character, either promote or hinder the subject's desire for pleasure.

This difference can hardly be anything else but a difference of temperament, a contrast between two types of human mentality, one of which finds the determining agency pre-eminently in the subject, the other in the object. A middle view, it may be that of common sense, would suppose that human behaviour is conditioned as much by the subject as by the object. The two investigators would probably assert, on the other hand, that their theory does not envisage a psychological explanation of the normal man, but is a theory of neurosis. But in that case Freud would have to explain and treat some of his patients along Adlerian lines, and Adler condescend to give earnest consideration in certain instances to his former teacher's point of view – which has occurred neither on the one side nor on the other.

The spectacle of this dilemma made me ponder the question: are there at least two different human types, one of them more interested in the object, the other more interested in himself? And does that explain why the one sees only the one and the other only the other, and thus each arrives at totally different conclusions? As we have said, it was hardly to be supposed that fate selected the patients so meticulously that a definite group invariably reached a definite doctor. For some time it had struck me, in connection both with myself and with my colleagues, that there are some cases which make a distinct appeal, while others somehow refuse to "click." It is of crucial importance for the treatment whether a good relationship between doctor and patient is possible or not. If some measure of natural confidence does not develop within a short period, then the patient will do better to choose another doctor. I myself have never shrunk from recommending to a colleague a patient whose peculiarities were not in my line or were unsympathetic to me, and indeed this is in the patient's own interests. I am positive that in such a case I would not do good work. Everyone has his personal limitations, and the psychotherapist in particular is well advised never to disregard them. Excessive personal differences and incompatibilities cause resistances that are disproportionate and out of place, though they are not altogether unjustified. The Freud-Adler controversy is simply a paradigm and one single instance among many possible attitude-types.

I have long busied myself with this question and have finally, on the basis of numerous observations and experiences, come to postulate two fundamental attitudes, namely introversion and extraversion. The first attitude is normally characterized by a hesitant, reflective, retiring nature that keeps itself to itself, shrinks from objects, is always slightly on the defensive and prefers to hide behind mistrustful scrutiny. The second is normally characterized by an outgoing, candid, and accommodating nature that adapts easily to a given situation, quickly forms attachments, and, setting aside any possible misgivings, will often venture forth with careless confidence into unknown situations. In the first case obviously the subject, and in the second the object, is all-important.

Naturally these remarks sketch the two types only in the roughest outlines.* As a matter of empirical fact the two attitudes, to which I shall come back shortly, can seldom be observed in their pure state. They are infinitely varied and compensated, so that often the type is not at all easy to establish. The reason for variation – apart from individual fluctuations – is the predominance of one of the conscious functions, such as thinking or feeling, which then gives the basic attitude a special character. The numerous compensations of the basic type are generally due to experiences which teach a man, perhaps in a very painful way, that he cannot give free rein to his nature. In other cases, for instance with neurotics, one frequently does not know whether one is dealing with a conscious or an unconscious attitude because, owing to the dissociation of the personality, sometimes one half of it and sometimes the other half occupies the foreground and confuses one's judgment. This is what makes it so excessively trying to live with neurotic persons.

The actual existence of far-reaching type-differences, of which I have described eight groups† in the above-mentioned book, has enabled me to conceive the two controversial theories of neurosis as manifestations of a type-antagonism.

This discovery brought with it the need to rise above the opposition and to create a theory which should do justice not merely to one or the other side, but to both equally. For this purpose a critique of both the aforementioned theories is essential. Both are painfully inclined to reduce high-flown ideals, heroic attitudes, nobility of feeling, deep convictions, to some banal reality, if applied to such things as these. On no account should they be so applied, for both theories are properly therapeutic instruments from the armoury of the doctor, whose knife must be

---

*A complete study of the type problem is to be found in my *Psychological Types*, *Coll. Works*, Vol. 6.
†Naturally this does not include all the existing types. Further points of difference are age, sex, activity, emotionality, and level of development. My type-psychology is based on the four orienting functions of consciousness: thinking, feeling, sensation, and intuition.

sharp and pitiless for excising what is diseased and injurious. This
was what Nietzsche wanted with his destructive criticism of ideals,
which he held to be morbid overgrowths in the soul of humanity
(as indeed they sometimes are). In the hand of a good doctor, of
one who really knows the human soul – who, to use Nietzsche's
phrase, has a "finger for nuances" – both theories, when applied
to the really sick part of a soul, are wholesome caustics, of great
help in dosages measured to the individual case, but harmful and
dangerous in the hand that knows not how to measure and weigh.
They are critical methods, having, like all criticism, the power to
do good when there is something that must be destroyed,
dissolved, or reduced, but capable only of harm when there is
something to be built.

Both theories may therefore be allowed to pass with no ill
consequences provided that, like medical poisons, they are
entrusted to the sure hand of the physician, for it requires an
uncommon knowledge of the human psyche to apply these caustics
with advantage. One must be capable of distinguishing the
pathological and the useless from what is valuable and worth
preserving, and that is one of the most difficult things. Anyone
who wishes to get a vivid impression of how irresponsibly a
psychologizing doctor can falsify his subject from narrow,
pseudo-scientific prejudice, should turn to the writings of Möbius
on Nietzsche, or, better still, to the various "psychiatric" writings
on the "case" of Christ. He will not hesitate to cry a "threefold
lamentation" over the patient who meets with such "understanding."

The two theories of neurosis are not universal theories: they are
caustic remedies to be applied, as it were, locally. They are
destructive and reductive. They say to everything, "You are
nothing but . . ." They explain to the sufferer that his symptoms
come from here and from there and are nothing but this or that.
It would be unjust to assert that this reduction is wrong in a given
case; but, exalted to the status of a general explanation of the
healthy psyche as well as the sick, a reductive theory by itself is
impossible. For the human psyche, be it sick or healthy, cannot
be explained *solely* by reduction. Eros is certainly always and
everywhere present, the urge to power certainly pervades the
heights and depths of the psyche, but the psyche is not *just* the one

or the other, nor for that matter both together. It is *also* what it has made and will make out of them. A man is only half understood when we know how everything in him came into being. If that were all, he could just as well have been dead years ago. As a living being he is not understood, for life does not have only a yesterday, nor is it explained by reducing today to yesterday. Life has also a tomorrow, and today is understood only when we can add to our knowledge of what was yesterday the beginnings of tomorrow. This is true of all life's psychological expressions, even of pathological symptoms. The symptoms of a neurosis are not simply the effects of long-past causes, whether "infantile sexuality" or the infantile urge to power; they are also attempts at a new synthesis of life – unsuccessful attempts, let it be added in the same breath, yet attempts nevertheless, with a core of value and meaning. They are seeds that fail to sprout owing to the inclement conditions of inner and outer nature.

The reader will doubtless ask: What in the world is the value and meaning of a neurosis, this most useless and pestilent curse of humanity? To be neurotic – what good can that do? As much good, possibly, as flies and other pests, which the good Lord created so that man might exercise the useful virtue of patience. However stupid this thought is from the point of view of natural science, it may yet be sensible enough from the point of view of psychology, if we put "nervous symptoms" instead of "pests." Even Nietzsche, a rare one for scorning stupid and banal thoughts, more than once acknowledged how much he owed to his malady. I myself have known more than one person who owed his entire usefulness and reason for existence to a neurosis, which prevented all the critical follies in his life and *forced* him to a mode of living that developed his valuable potentialities. These might have been stifled had not the neurosis, with iron grip, held him to the place where he belonged. There are actually people who have the whole meaning of their life, their true significance, in the unconscious, while in the conscious mind is nothing but inveiglement and error. With others the case is reversed, and here neurosis has a different meaning. In these cases, but not in the former, a thorough-going reduction is indicated.

At this point the reader may be inclined to grant the possibility that the neurosis has such a meaning in certain cases, while denying it so far-reaching a purposiveness in ordinary everyday cases. What, for instance, could be the value of a neurosis in the above-mentioned case of asthma with its hysterical anxiety-states? I admit that the value is not so obvious here, especially when the case is considered from the theoretical reductive standpoint, that is, from the shadow-side of individual development.

The two theories we have been discussing evidently have this much in common: they pitilessly unveil everything that belongs to man's shadow-side. They are theories or, more correctly, hypotheses which explain in what the pathogenic factor consists. They are accordingly concerned not with a man's positive values, but with his negative values which make themselves so disturbingly conspicuous.

A "value" is a possibility for the display of energy. But in so far as a negative value is likewise a possibility for the display of energy – which can be seen most clearly in the notable manifestations of neurotic energy – it too is properly a "value," but one that makes possible useless and harmful manifestations of energy. Energy in itself is neither good nor bad, neither useful nor harmful, but neutral, since everything depends on the *form* into which energy passes. Form gives energy its quality. On the other hand, mere form without energy is equally neutral. For the creation of a real value, therefore, both energy and valuable form are needed. In neurosis psychic energy* is present, but undoubtedly it is there in an inferior and unserviceable form. The two reductive theories act as solvents of this inferior form. They are approved caustic remedies, by means of which we obtain free but neutral energy. Now, it has hitherto been supposed that this newly disengaged energy is at the conscious disposal of the patient, so that he can apply it at his pleasure. Since it was thought that the energy is nothing but the instinctual power of sex, people talked of a "sublimated" application of it, on the assumption that the patient could, with the help of analysis, canalize the sexual energy into a "sublimation," in other words, could apply it non-sexually, in the practice of an art, perhaps, or in some other good or useful activity. According to this view, it is possible for the patient, from free

*I refer the reader to my essay "On Psychic Energy," *Coll. Works*, Vol. 8.

choice or inclination, to achieve the sublimation of his instinctual forces.

We may allow that this view has a certain justification in so far as man is at all capable of marking out a definite line along which his life has to go. But we know that there is no human foresight or wisdom that can prescribe direction to our life, except for small stretches of the way. This is of course true only of the "ordinary" type of life, not of the "heroic" type. The latter kind also exists, though it is much rarer. Here we are certainly not entitled to say that no marked direction can be given to life, or only for short distances. The heroic conduct of life is absolute – that is, it is oriented by fateful decisions, and the decision to go in a certain direction holds, sometimes, to the bitter end. Admittedly the doctor has to do, in the main, only with human beings, seldom with voluntary heroes, and then they are mostly of a type whose surface heroism is an infantile defiance of a fate greater than they, or else a pomposity meant to cover up some touchy inferiority. In this overpoweringly humdrum existence, alas, there is little out of the ordinary that is healthy, and not much room for conspicuous heroism. Not that heroic demands are never put to us: on the contrary – and this is just what is so irritating and irksome – the banal everyday makes banal demands upon our patience, our devotion, perseverance, self-sacrifice; and for us to fulfil these demands (as we must) humbly and without courting applause through heroic gestures, a heroism is needed that cannot be seen from the outside. It does not glitter, is not belauded, and it always seeks concealment in everyday attire. These are the demands which, if not fulfilled, are the cause of neurosis. In order to evade them, many a man has dared the great decision of his life and carried it through, even if in the common human estimation it was a great error. Before a fate such as this one can only bow one's head. But, as I say, such cases are rare; the others are in the vast majority. For them the direction of their life is not a simple, straight line; fate confronts them like an intricate labyrinth, all too rich in possibilities, and yet of these many possibilities only one is their own right way. Who would presume – even though armed with the completest knowledge of his own character – to designate in advance that single possibility? Much indeed can be attained by the will, but, in view of the fate of certain markedly strong-willed personalities, it is a fundamental error to try to subject our own fate at all costs to our will. Our will is a function regulated by reflection; hence it is dependent on the quality of that reflection. This, if it really is reflection, is supposed to be rational, i.e., in accord with reason. But has it ever been shown, or will it ever be, that life and fate are in accord with reason, that they too are rational? We have on the contrary good grounds for supposing that they are irrational, or rather that in the last resort they are grounded beyond human reason. The irrationality of events is shown in what we call chance, which we are obviously compelled to deny, because we cannot in principle think of any process that is not causal and necessary, whence it follows that it cannot happen by chance.* In practice, however, chance reigns everywhere, and so obtrusively that we might as well put our causal philosophy in our pocket. The plenitude of life is governed by law and yet not governed by law, rational and yet irrational. Hence reason and the will that is grounded in reason are valid only up to a point. The further we go in the direction selected by reason, the surer we may be that we are excluding the irrational possibilities of life which have just as much right to be lived. It was indeed highly expedient for man to become somewhat more capable of directing his life. It may justly be maintained that the acquisition of reason is the greatest achievement of humanity; but that is not to say that things must or will always continue in that direction. The frightful catastrophe of the first World War drew a very thick line through the calculations of even the most optimistic rationalizers of culture. In 1913, Ostwald wrote:

> The whole world is agreed that the present state of armed peace is untenable and is gradually becoming impossible. It demands tremendous sacrifices from each single nation, far exceeding the expenditure for cultural purposes, yet without securing any positive values. If mankind could discover ways and means for doing away with these preparations for wars *which never take place*, together with the immobilization of a large part of the nation's manhood, at the age of maximum strength and

*Modern physics has put an end to this strict causality. Now there is only "statistical probability." As far back as 1916, I had pointed out the limitations of the causal view in psychology, for which I was heavily censured at the time.

efficiency, for the furtherance of warlike aims, and all the other innumerable evils which the present state of affairs creates, such an immense economy of energy would be effected that from this moment onwards we could look forward to a blossoming of culture hitherto undreamed of. For war, like personal combat, although the oldest of all possible means of settling contests of will, is on that very account the most inept, and entails the most grievous waste of energy. Hence the complete abolition of warfare, potential no less than actual, is the categorical imperative of efficiency and one of the supremely important cultural tasks of our day.*

The irrationality of fate, however, did not concur with the rationality of well-meaning thinkers; it ordained not only the destruction of the accumulated arms and armies, but, far beyond that, a mad and monstrous devastation, a mass murder without parallel – from which humanity may possibly draw the conclusion that only one side of fate can be mastered with rational intentions.

What is true of humanity in general is also true of each individual, for humanity consists only of individuals. And as is the psychology of humanity so also is the psychology of the individual. The World War brought a terrible reckoning with the rational intentions of civilization. What is called "will" in the individual is called "imperialism" in nations; for all will is a demonstration of power over fate, i.e., the exclusion of chance. Civilization is the rational, "purposeful" sublimation of free energies, brought about by will and intention. It is the same with the individual; and just as the idea of a world civilization received a fearful correction at the hands of war, so the individual must often learn in his life that so-called "disposable" energies are not his to dispose.

Once, in America, I was consulted by a business man of about forty-five, whose case is a good illustration of what has been said. He was a typical American self-made man who had worked his way up from the bottom. He had been very successful and had founded an immense business. He had also succeeded in organizing it in such a way that he was able to think of retiring. Two years before

*Wilhelm Ostwald, *Die Philosophie der Werte* (Leipzig, 1913), pp. 312f.

I saw him he had in fact taken his farewell. Until then he had lived entirely for his business and concentrated all his energies on it with the incredible intensity and one-sidedness peculiar to successful American business men. He had purchased a splendid estate where he thought of "living," by which he meant horses, automobiles, golf, tennis, parties and what not. But he had reckoned without his host. The energy which should have been at his disposal would not enter into these alluring prospects, but went capering off in quite another direction. A few weeks after the initiation of the longed-for life of bliss, he began brooding over peculiar, vague sensations in his body, and a few weeks more sufficed to plunge him into a state of extreme hypochondria. He had a complete nervous collapse. From a healthy man, of uncommon physical strength and abounding energy, he became a peevish child. That was the end of all his glories. He fell from one state of anxiety to the next and worried himself almost to death with hypochondriacal mopings. He then consulted a famous specialist, who recognized at once that there was nothing wrong with the man but lack of work. The patient saw the sense of this, and returned to his former position. But, to his immense disappointment, no interest in the business could be aroused. Neither patience nor resolution was of any use. His energy could not by any means be forced back into the business. His condition naturally became worse than before. All that had formerly been living, creative energy in him now turned against him with terrible destroying force. His creative genius rose up, as it were, in revolt against him; and just as before he had built up great organizations in the world, so now his daemon spun equally subtle systems of hypochondriacal delusion that completely annihilated him. When I saw him he was already a hopeless moral ruin. Nevertheless I tried to make clear to him that though such a gigantic energy might be withdrawn from the business, the question remained, where should it go? The finest horses, the fastest cars, and the most amusing parties may very likely fail to allure the energy, although it would be rational enough to think that a man who had devoted his whole life to serious work had a sort of natural right to enjoy himself. Yes, if fate behaved in a humanly rational way, it would certainly be so: first work, then well-earned rest. But fate behaves irrationally, and the energy of life inconveniently demands a gradient agreeable to itself; otherwise it simply gets dammed up and turns destructive. It regresses to former situations – in the case of this man, to the memory of a syphilitic infection contracted twenty-five years before. Yet even this was only a stage on the way to the resuscitation of infantile reminiscences which had all but vanished in the meantime. It was the original relation to his mother that mapped the course of his symptoms: they were an "arrangement" whose purpose it was to compel the attention and interest of his long-dead mother. Nor was this stage the last; for the ultimate goal was to drive him back, as it were, into his own body, after he had lived since his youth only in his head. He had differentiated one side of his being; the other side remained in an inert physical state. He would have needed this other side in order to "live." The hypochondriacal "depression" pushed him down into the body he had always overlooked. Had he been able to follow the direction indicated by his depression and hypochondriacal illusion, and make himself conscious of the fantasies which proceed from such a condition, that would have been the road to salvation. My argument naturally met with no response, as was to be expected. A case so far advanced can only be cared for until death; it can hardly be cured.

This example clearly shows that it does not lie in our power to transfer "disposable" energy at will to a rationally chosen object. The same is true in general of the apparently disposable energy which is disengaged when we have destroyed its unserviceable forms through the corrosive of reductive analysis. This energy, as we have said, can at best be applied voluntarily for only a short time. But in most cases it refuses to seize hold, for any length of time, of the possibilities rationally presented to it. Psychic energy is a very fastidious thing which insists on fulfilment of its own conditions. However much energy may be present, we cannot make it serviceable until we have succeeded in finding the right gradient.

This question of the gradient is an eminently practical problem which crops up in most analyses. For instance, when in a favourable case the disposable energy, the so-called libido,* does

*From the foregoing it will have become clear to the reader that the term "libido," coined by Freud and very suitable for practical usage, is used by me in a much wider sense. Libido for me means psychic energy, which is equivalent to the intensity with which psychic contents are charged.

seize hold of a rational object, we think we have brought about tl transformation through conscious exertion of the will. But in that we are deluded, because even the most strenuous exertions would not have sufficed had there not been present at the same time a gradient in that direction. How important the gradient is can be seen in cases when, despite the most desperate exertions, and despite the fact that the object chosen or the form desired impresses everybody with its reasonableness, the transformation still refuses to take place, and all that happens is a new repression.

It has become abundantly clear to me that life can flow forward only along the path of the gradient. But there is no energy unless there is a tension of opposites; hence it is necessary to discover the opposite to the attitude of the conscious mind. It is interesting to see how this compensation by opposites also plays its part in the historical theories of neurosis: Freud's theory espoused Eros, Adler's the will to power. Logically, the opposite of love is hate, and of Eros, Phobos (fear); but psychologically it is the will to power. Where love reigns, there is no will to power; and where the will to power is paramount, love is lacking. The one is but the shadow of the other: the man who adopts the standpoint of Eros finds his compensatory opposite in the will to power, and that of the man who puts the accent on power is Eros. Seen from the one-sided point of view of the conscious attitude, the shadow is an inferior component of the personality and is consequently repressed through intensive resistance. But the repressed content must be made conscious so as to produce a tension of opposites, without which no forward movement is possible. The conscious mind is on top, the shadow underneath, and just as high always longs for low and hot for cold, so all consciousness, perhaps without being aware of it, seeks its unconscious opposite, lacking which it is doomed to stagnation, congestion, and ossification. Life is born only of the spark of opposites.

It was a concession to intellectual logic on the one hand and to psychological prejudice on the other that impelled Freud to name the opposite of Eros the destructive or death instinct. For in the first place, Eros is not equivalent to life; but for anyone who thinks it is, the opposite of Eros will naturally appear to be death. And in the second place, we all feel that the opposite of our own highest principle must be purely destructive, deadly, and evil. We refuse to endow it with any positive life-force; hence we avoid and fear it.

As I have already indicated, there are many highest principles both of life and of philosophy, and accordingly there are just as many different forms of compensation by opposition. Earlier on I singled out the two – as it seems to me – main opposite types, which I have called introverted and extraverted. William James* had already been struck by the existence of both these types among thinkers. He distinguished them as "tender-minded" and "tough-minded." Similarly Ostwald† found an analogous division into "classical" and "romantic" types among men of learning. So I am not alone in my idea of types, to mention only these two well-known names among many others. Inquiries into history have shown me that not a few of the great spiritual controversies rest upon the opposition of the two types. The most significant case of this kind is the opposition between nominalism and realism which, beginning with the difference between the Platonic and Megaric schools, became the heritage of scholastic philosophy, where it is Abelard's great merit to have hazarded at least the attempt to unite the two opposed standpoints in his "conceptualism." This controversy has continued right into our own day, as is shown in the opposition between idealism and materialism. And again, not only the human mind in general, but each individual has a share in this opposition of types. It has come to light on closer investigation that either type has a predilection to marry its opposite, each being unconsciously complementary to the other. The reflective nature of the introvert causes him always to think and consider before acting. This naturally makes him slow to act. His shyness and distrust of things induces hesitation, and so he always has difficulty in adapting to the external world. Conversely the extravert has a positive relation to things. He is, so to speak, attracted by them. New, unknown situations fascinate him. In order to make closer acquaintance with the unknown he will jump into it with both feet. As a rule he acts first and thinks afterwards. Thus his action is swift, subject to no misgivings and hesitations.

*Pragmatism (London and Cambridge, Mass., 1907).
†Grosse Männer (Leipzig, 1910).

The two types therefore seem created for a symbiosis. The one takes care of reflection and the other sees to the initiative and practical action. When the two types marry they may effect an ideal union. So long as they are fully occupied with their adaptation to the manifold external needs of life they fit together admirably. But when the man has made enough money, or if a fine legacy should drop from the skies and external necessity no longer presses, then they have time to occupy themselves with one another. Hitherto they stood back to back and defended themselves against necessity. But now they turn face to face and look for understanding – only to discover that they have never understood one another. Each speaks a different language. Then the conflict between the two types begins. This struggle is envenomed, brutal, full of mutual depreciation, even when conducted quietly and in the greatest intimacy. For the value of the one is the negation of value for the other. It might reasonably be supposed that each, conscious of his own value, could peaceably recognize the other's value, and that in this way any conflict would be superfluous. I have seen a good number of cases where this line of argument was adopted, without, however, arriving at a satisfactory goal. Where it is a question of normal people, such critical periods of transition will be overcome fairly smoothly. By "normal" I mean a person who can somehow exist under all circumstances which afford him the minimum needs of life. But many people cannot do this; therefore not so very many people are normal. What we commonly mean by a "normal person" is actually an ideal person whose happy blend of character is a rare occurrence. By far the greater number of more or less differentiated persons demand conditions of life which afford considerably more than the certainty of food and sleep. For these the ending of a symbiotic relationship comes as a severe shock.

It is not easy to understand why this should be so. Yet if we consider that no man is simply introverted or simply extraverted, but has both attitudes potentially in him – although he has developed only one of them as a function of adaptation – we shall immediately conjecture that with the introvert extraversion lies dormant and undeveloped somewhere in the background, and that introversion leads a similar shadowy existence in the extravert. And this is indeed the case. The introvert does possess an extraverted attitude, but it is unconscious, because his conscious gaze is always turned to the subject. He sees the object, of course, but has false or inhibiting ideas about it, so that he keeps his distance as much as possible, as though the object were something formidable and dangerous. I will make my meaning clear by a simple illustration:

Let us suppose two youths rambling in the country. They come to a fine castle; both want to see inside it. The introvert says, "I'd like to know what it's like inside." The extravert answers, "Right, let's go in," and makes for the gateway. The introvert draws back – "Perhaps we aren't allowed in," says he, with visions of policemen, fines, and fierce dogs in the background. Whereupon the extravert answers, "Well, we can ask. They'll let us in all right" – with visions of kindly old watchmen, hospitable seigneurs, and the possibility of romantic adventures. On the strength of extraverted optimism they at length find themselves in the castle. But now comes the dénouement. The castle has been rebuilt inside, and contains nothing but a couple of rooms with a collection of old manuscripts. As it happens, old manuscripts are the chief joy of the introverted youth. Hardly has he caught sight of them when he becomes as one transformed. He loses himself in contemplation of the treasures, uttering cries of enthusiasm. He engages the keeper in conversation so as to extract from him as much information as possible, and when the result is meagre the youth asks to see the curator in order to propound his questions to him. His shyness has vanished, objects have taken on a seductive glamour, and the world wears a new face. But meanwhile the spirits of the extraverted youth are ebbing lower and lower. His face grows longer and he begins to yawn. No kindly watchmen are forthcoming here, no knightly hospitality, not a trace of romantic adventure – only a castle made over into a museum. There are manuscripts enough to be seen at home. While the enthusiasm of the one rises, the spirits of the other fall, the castle bores him, the manuscripts remind him of a library, library is associated with university, university with studies and menacing examinations. Gradually a veil of gloom descends over the once so interesting and enticing castle. The object becomes negative. "Isn't it marvellous," cries the introvert, "to have stumbled on this wonderful collection?" "The place bores me to extinction," replies the other with undisguised ill humour. This annoys the introvert, who secretly vows never again to go rambling with an extravert. The latter is annoyed with the other's annoyance, and he thinks to himself that he always knew the fellow was an inconsiderate egotist who would, in his own selfish interest, waste all the lovely spring day that could be enjoyed so much better out of doors.

What has happened? Both were wandering together in happy symbiosis until they discovered the fatal castle. Then the forethinking, or Promethean, introvert said it might be seen from the inside, and the afterthinking, or Epimethean, extravert opened the door. At this point the types invert themselves: the introvert, who at first resisted the idea of going in, cannot now be induced to go out, and the extravert curses the moment when he set foot inside the castle. The former is now fascinated by the object, the latter by his negative thoughts. When the introvert spotted the manuscripts, it was all up with him. His shyness vanished, the object took possession of him, and he yielded himself willingly. The extravert, however, felt a growing resistance to the object and was eventually made the prisoner of his own ill-humoured subjectivity. The introvert became extraverted, the extravert introverted. But the extraversion of the introvert is different from the extraversion of the extravert, and vice versa. So long as both were wandering along in joyous harmony, neither fell foul of the other, because each was in his natural character. Each was positive to the other, because their attitudes were complementary. They were complementary, however, only because the attitude of the one included the other. We can see this from the short conversation at the gateway. Both wanted to enter the castle. The doubt of the introvert as to whether an entry were possible also held good for the other. The initiative of the extravert likewise held good for the other. Thus the attitude of the one included the other, and this is always in some degree true if a person happens to be in the attitude natural to him, for this attitude has some degree of collective adaptation. The same is true of the introvert's attitude, although this always comes from the subject. It simply goes from subject to object, while the extravert's attitude goes from object to subject.

But the moment when, in the case of the introvert, the object overpowers and attracts the subject, his attitude loses its social character. He forgets the presence of his friend, he no longer includes him, he becomes absorbed into the object and does not see how very bored his friend is. In the same way the extravert loses all consideration for the other as soon as his expectations are disappointed and he withdraws into subjectivity and moodiness.

We can therefore formulate the occurrence as follows: in the introvert the influence of the object produces an inferior extraversion, while in the extravert an inferior introversion takes the place of his social attitude. And so we come back to the proposition from which we started: "The value of the one is the negation of value for the other."

Positive as well as negative occurrences can constellate the inferior counter-function. When this happens, sensitiveness appears. Sensitiveness is a sure sign of the presence of inferiority. This provides the psychological basis for discord and misunderstanding, not only as between two people, but also in ourselves. The essence of the inferior function is autonomy: it is independent, it attacks, it fascinates and so spins us about that we are no longer masters of ourselves and can no longer rightly distinguish between ourselves and others.

And yet it is necessary for the development of character that we should allow the other side, the inferior function, to find expression. We cannot in the long run allow one part of our personality to be cared for symbiotically by another; for the moment when we might have need of the other function may come at any time and find us unprepared, as the above example shows. And the consequences may be bad: the extravert loses his indispensable relation to the object, and the introvert loses his to the subject. Conversely, it is equally indispensable for the introvert to arrive at some form of action not constantly bedevilled by doubts and hesitations, and for the extravert to reflect upon himself, yet without endangering his relationships.

In extraversion and introversion it is clearly a matter of two antithetical, natural attitudes or trends, which Goethe once referred to as diastole and systole. They ought, in their harmonious alternation, to give life a rhythm, but it seems to require a high degree of art to achieve such a rhythm. Either one must do it quite unconsciously, so that the natural law is not disturbed by any conscious act, or one must be conscious in a much higher sense, to be capable of willing and carrying out the antithetical movements. Since we cannot develop backwards into animal unconsciousness, there remains only the more strenuous way forwards into higher consciousness. Certainly that consciousness, which would enable us to live the great Yea and Nay of our own free will and purpose, is an altogether superhuman ideal. Still, it is a goal. Perhaps our present mentality only allows us consciously to will the Yea and to bear with the Nay. When that is the case, much is already achieved.

The problem of opposites, as an inherent principle of human nature, forms a further stage in our process of realization. As a rule it is one of the problems of maturity. The practical treatment of a patient will hardly ever begin with this problem, especially not in the case of young people. The neuroses of the young generally come from a collision between the forces of reality and an inadequate, infantile attitude, which from the causal point of view is characterized by an abnormal dependence on the real or imaginary parents, and from the teleological point of view by unrealizable fictions, plans, and aspirations. Here the reductive methods of Freud and Adler are entirely in place. But there are many neuroses which either appear only at maturity or else deteriorate to such a degree that the patients become incapable of work. Naturally one can point out in these cases that an unusual dependence on the parents existed even in youth, and that all kinds of infantile illusions were present; but all that did not prevent them from taking up a profession, from practising it successfully, from keeping up a marriage of sorts until that moment in riper years when the previous attitude suddenly failed. In such cases it is of little help to make them conscious of their childhood fantasies, dependence on the parents, etc., although this is a necessary part of the procedure and often has a not unfavourable result. But the real therapy only begins when the patient sees that it is no longer father and mother who are standing in his way, but himself – i.e., an unconscious part of his personality which carries on the role of father and mother. Even this realization, helpful as it is, is still negative; it simply says, "I realize that it is not father and mother who are against me, but I myself." But *who* is it in him that is against him? What is this mysterious part of his personality that hides under the father- and mother-imagos, making him believe for years that the cause of his trouble must somehow have got into him from outside? This part is the counterpart to his conscious attitude; and it will leave him no peace and will continue to plague him until it has been accepted. For young people a liberation from the past may be enough: a beckoning future lies ahead, rich in possibilities. It is sufficient to break a few bonds; the life-urge will do the rest. But we are faced with another task in the case of people who have left a large part of their life behind them, for whom the future no longer beckons with marvellous possibilities, and nothing is to be expected but the endless round of familiar duties and the doubtful pleasures of old age.

If ever we succeed in liberating young people from the past, we see that they always transfer the imagos of their parents to more suitable substitute figures. For instance, the feeling that clung to the mother now passes to the wife, and the father's authority passes to respected teachers and superiors or to institutions. Although this is not a fundamental solution, it is yet a practical road which the normal man treads unconsciously and therefore with no notable inhibitions and resistances.

The problem for the adult is very different. He has put this part of the road behind him with or without difficulty. He has cut loose from his parents, long since dead perhaps, and has sought and found the mother in the wife, or, in the case of a woman, the father in the husband. He has duly honoured his fathers and their institutions, has himself become a father, and, with all this in the past, has possibly come to realize that what originally meant advancement and satisfaction has now become a boring mistake, part of the illusion of youth, upon which he looks back with mingled regret and envy, because nothing now awaits him but old age and the end of all illusions. Here there are no more fathers and mothers; all the illusions he projected upon the world and upon things gradually come home to him, jaded and way-worn. The energy streaming back from these manifold relationships falls into the unconscious and activates all the things he had neglected to develop.

In a young man, the instinctual forces tied up in the neurosis give him, when released, buoyancy and hope and the chance to extend the scope of his life. To the man in the second half of life the development of the function of opposites lying dormant in the unconscious means a renewal; but this development no longer proceeds via the solution of infantile ties, the destruction of infantile illusions and the transference of old imagos to new figures: it proceeds via the problem of opposites.

The principle of opposition is, of course, fundamental even in adolescence, and a psychological theory of the adolescent psyche is bound to recognize this fact. Hence the Freudian and Adlerian viewpoints contradict each other only when they claim to be generally applicable theories. But so long as they are content to be technical, auxiliary concepts, they do not contradict or exclude one another. A psychological theory, if it is to be more than a technical makeshift, must base itself on the principle of opposition; for without this it could only re-establish a neurotically unbalanced psyche. There is no balance, no system of self-regulation, without opposition. The psyche is just such a self-regulating system.

If the psyche is regarded as a self-regulating system, it follows that the attitude of consciousness is compensated by the attitude of the unconscious. In Jungian analysis, the principal, though not the only, way of discovering the attitude of the unconscious is through the study and interpretation of the patient's dreams.

Neurotic symptoms, also, can be compensatory to a distorted, one-sided conscious attitude, and may thus be valuable pointers toward a new adaptation rather than being simply disagreeable. In a discussion following one of his Tavistock Lectures, Jung says:

I am not altogether pessimistic about neurosis. In many cases we have to say: "Thank heaven he could make up his mind to be neurotic." Neurosis is really an attempt at self-cure, just as any physical disease is in part an attempt at self-cure. We cannot understand a disease as an *ens per se* any more, as something detached which not so long ago it was believed to be. Modern medicine – internal medicine, for instance – conceives of disease as a system composed of a harmful factor and a healing factor. It is exactly the same with neurosis. It is an attempt of the self-regulating psychic system to restore the balance, in no way different from the function of dreams – only rather more forceful and drastic. [CW 18, par. 389]

Jung's view of dreams as generally compensatory is clearly stated in a paper which he first read in Dresden in 1931, "The Practical Use of Dream-analysis."

"The Practical Use of Dream-analysis" CW 16, pars. 294–352

The use of dream-analysis in psychotherapy is still a much debated question. Many practitioners find it indispensable in the treatment of neuroses, and consider that the dream is a function whose psychic importance is equal to that of the conscious mind itself. Others, on the contrary, dispute the value of dream-analysis and regard dreams as a negligible by-product of the psyche. Obviously, if a person holds the view that the unconscious plays a decisive part in the aetiology of neuroses, he will attribute a high practical importance to dreams as direct expressions of the unconscious. Equally obviously, if he denies the unconscious or at least thinks it aetiologically insignificant, he will minimize the importance of dream-analysis. It might be considered regrettable that in this year of grace 1931, more than half a century after Carus formulated the concept of the unconscious, more than a century after Kant spoke of the "illimitable field of obscure ideas," and nearly two hundred years after Leibniz postulated an unconscious psychic activity, not to mention the achievements of Janet, Flournoy, Freud, and many more – that after all this, the actuality of the unconscious should still be a matter for controversy. But, since it is my intention to deal exclusively with practical questions, I will not advance in this place an apology for the unconscious, although our special problem of dream-analysis stands or falls with such an hypothesis. Without it, the dream is a mere freak of nature, a meaningless conglomeration of fragments left over from the day. Were that really so, there would be no excuse for the present discussion. We cannot treat our theme at all unless we recognize the unconscious, for the avowed aim of dream-analysis is not only to exercise our wits, but to uncover and realize those hitherto unconscious contents which are considered to be of importance in the elucidation or treatment of a neurosis. Anyone who finds this hypothesis unacceptable must simply rule out the question of the applicability of dream-analysis.

But since, according to our hypothesis, the unconscious possesses an aetiological significance, and since dreams are the direct expression of unconscious psychic activity, the attempt to analyse and interpret dreams is theoretically justified from a scientific standpoint. If successful, we may expect this attempt to give us scientific insight into the structure of psychic causality, quite apart from any therapeutic results that may be gained. The practitioner, however, tends to consider scientific discoveries as, at most, a gratifying by-product of his therapeutic work, so he is hardly likely to take the bare possibility of theoretical insight into the aetiological background as a sufficient reason for, much less an indication of, the practical use of dream-analysis. He may believe, of course, that the explanatory insight so gained is of therapeutic value, in which case he will elevate dream-analysis to a professional duty. It is well known that the Freudian school is of the firm opinion that very valuable therapeutic results are achieved by throwing light upon the unconscious causal factors – that is, by explaining them to the patient and thus making him fully conscious of the sources of his trouble.

Assuming for the moment that this expectation is justified by the facts, then the only question that remains is whether dream-analysis can or cannot be used, alone or in conjunction with other methods, to discover the unconscious aetiology. The Freudian answer to this question is, I may assume, common knowledge. I can confirm this answer inasmuch as dreams, particularly the initial dreams which appear at the very outset of the treatment, often bring to light the essential aetiological factor in the most unmistakable way. The following example may serve as an illustration:

I was consulted by a man who held a prominent position in the world. He was afflicted with a sense of anxiety and insecurity, and complained of dizziness sometimes resulting in nausea, heaviness in the head, and constriction of breath – a state that might easily be confused with mountain sickness. He had had an extraordinarily successful career, and had risen, by dint of ambition, industry, and native talent, from his humble origins as the son of a poor peasant. Step by step he had climbed, attaining at last a leading position which held every prospect of further social advancement. He had now in fact reached the spring-board from which he could have commenced his flight into the empyrean, had not his neurosis suddenly intervened. At this point in his story the patient could not refrain from that familiar exclamation which begins with the stereotyped words: "And just now, when . . ." The fact that he had all the symptoms of mountain sickness seemed highly appropriate as a drastic illustration of his peculiar impasse. He had also brought to the consultation two dreams from the preceding night. The first dream was as follows: "*I am back again in the small village where I was born. Some peasant lads who went to school with me are standing together in the street. I walk past, pretending not to know them. Then I hear one of them say, pointing at me: 'He doesn't often come back to our village.'*"

It requires no feat of interpretation to see in this dream a reference to the humble beginnings of the dreamer's career and to understand what this reference means. The dream says quite clearly: "You forgot how far down you began."

Here is the second dream: "*I am in a great hurry because I want to go on a journey. I keep on looking for things to pack, but can find nothing. Time flies, and the train will soon be leaving. Having finally succeeded in getting all my things together, I hurry along the street, only to discover that I have forgotten a brief-case containing important papers. I dash back all out of breath, find it at last, then race to the station, but I make hardly any headway. With a final effort I rush on to the platform only to see the train just steaming out of the station yard. It is very long, and it runs in a curious S-shaped curve, and it occurs to me that if the engine-driver does not look out, and puts on steam when he comes into the straight, the rear coaches will still be on the curve and will be thrown off the rails by the gathering speed. And this is just what happens: the engine-driver puts on steam, I try to cry out, the rear coaches give a frightful lurch and are thrown off the rails. There is a terrible catastrophe. I wake up in terror.*"

Here again no effort is needed to understand the message of the dream. It describes the patient's frantic haste to advance himself still further. But since the engine-driver in front steams relentlessly ahead, the neurosis happens at the back: the coaches rock and the train is derailed.

It is obvious that, at the present phase of his life, the patient has reached the highest point of his career; the strain of the long ascent from his lowly origin has exhausted his strength. He should have rested content with his achievements, but instead of that his ambition drives him on and on, and up and up into an atmosphere that is too thin for him and to which he is not accustomed. Therefore his neurosis comes upon him as a warning.

Circumstances prevented me from treating the patient further, nor did my view of the case satisfy him. The upshot was that the fate depicted in the dream ran its course. He tried to exploit the professional openings that tempted his ambition, and ran so violently off the rails that the catastrophe was realized in actual life.

Thus, what could only be inferred from the conscious anamnesis – namely that the mountain sickness was a symbolical representation of the patient's inability to climb any further – was confirmed by the dreams as a fact.

Here we come upon something of the utmost importance for the applicability of dream-analysis: the dream describes the inner situation of the dreamer, but the conscious mind denies its truth and reality, or admits it only grudgingly. Consciously the dreamer could not see the slightest reason why he should not go steadily forward; on the contrary, he continued his ambitious climbing and refused to admit his own inability which subsequent events made all too plain. So long as we move in the conscious sphere, we are always unsure in such cases. The anamnesis can be interpreted in various ways. After all, the common soldier carries the marshal's baton in his knapsack, and many a son of poor parents has achieved the highest success. Why should it not be the case here? Since my judgment is fallible, why should my conjecture be better than his? At this point the dream comes in as the expression of an involuntary, unconscious psychic process beyond the control of the conscious mind. It shows the inner truth and reality of the patient as it really is: not as I conjecture it to be, and not as he would like it to be, but *as it is*. I have therefore made it a rule to regard dreams as I regard physiological facts: if sugar appears in the urine, then the urine contains sugar, and not albumen or urobilin or something else that might fit in better with my expectations. That is to say, I take dreams as diagnostically valuable facts.

As is the way of all dreams, my little dream example gives us rather more than we expected. It gives us not only the aetiology of the neurosis but a prognosis as well. What is more, we even know exactly where the treatment should begin: we must prevent the patient from going full steam ahead. This is just what he tells himself in the dream.

Let us for the time being content ourselves with this hint and return to our consideration of whether dreams enable us to throw light on the aetiology of a neurosis. The dreams I have cited actually do this. But I could equally well cite any number of initial dreams where there is no trace of an aetiological factor, although they are perfectly transparent. I do not wish for the present to consider dreams which call for searching analysis and interpretation.

The point is this: there are neuroses whose real aetiology becomes clear only right at the end of an analysis, and other neuroses whose aetiology is relatively unimportant. This brings me back to the hypothesis from which we started, that for the purposes of therapy it is absolutely necessary to make the patient conscious of the aetiological factor. This hypothesis is little more than a hang-over from the old trauma theory. I do not of course deny that many neuroses are traumatic in origin; I simply contest the notion that all neuroses are of this nature and arise without exception from some crucial experience in childhood. Such a view necessarily results in the causalistic approach. The doctor must give his whole attention to the patient's past; he must always ask "Why?" and ignore the equally pertinent question "What for?" Often this has a most deleterious effect on the patient, who is thereby compelled to go searching about in his memory – perhaps for years – for some hypothetical event in his childhood, while things of immediate importance are grossly neglected. The purely causalistic approach is too narrow and fails to do justice to the true significance either of the dream or of the neurosis. Hence an approach that uses dreams for the sole purpose of discovering the aetiological factor is biased and overlooks the main point of the dream. Our example indeed shows the aetiology clearly enough, but it also offers a prognosis or anticipation of the future as well as a suggestion about the treatment. There are in addition large numbers of initial dreams which do not touch the aetiology at all, but deal with quite other matters, such as the patient's attitude to the doctor. As an example of this I would like to tell you three dreams, all from the same patient, and each dreamt at the beginning of a course of treatment under three different analysts. Here is the first: "*I have to cross the frontier into another country, but cannot find the frontier and nobody can tell me where it is.*"

The ensuing treatment proved unsuccessful and was broken off after a short time. The second dream is as follows: "*I have to cross the frontier, but the night is pitch-black and I cannot find the customs-house. After a long search I see a tiny light far off in the distance, and assume that the frontier is over there. But in order to get there, I have to pass through a valley and a dark wood in which I lose my way. Then I notice that someone is near me. Suddenly he clings to me like a madman and I awake in terror.*"

This treatment, too, was broken off after a few weeks because the analyst unconsciously identified himself with the patient and the result was complete loss of orientation on both sides.

The third dream took place under my treatment: "*I have to cross a frontier, or rather, I have already crossed it and find myself in a Swiss customs-house. I have only a handbag with me and think I have nothing to declare. But the customs official dives into my bag and, to my astonishment, pulls out a pair of twin beds.*"

The patient had got married while under my treatment, and at first she developed the most violent resistance to her marriage. The aetiology of the neurotic resistance came to light only many months afterwards and there is not a word about it in the dreams. They are without exception anticipations of the difficulties she is to have with the doctors concerned.

These examples, like many others of the kind, may suffice to show that dreams are often anticipatory and would lose their specific meaning completely on a purely causalistic view. They afford unmistakable information about the analytical situation, the correct understanding of which is of the greatest therapeutic importance. Doctor A understood the situation correctly and handed the patient over to Doctor B. Under him she drew her own conclusions from the dream and decided to leave. My interpretation of the third dream was a disappointment to her, but the fact that the dream showed the frontier as already crossed encouraged her to go on in spite of all difficulties.

Initial dreams are often amazingly lucid and clear-cut. But as the work of analysis progresses, the dreams tend to lose their clarity. If, by way of exception, they keep it we can be sure that the analysis has not yet touched on some important layer of the personality. As a rule, dreams get more and more opaque and blurred soon after the beginning of the treatment, and this makes the interpretation increasingly difficult. A further difficulty is that a point may soon be reached where, if the truth be told, the doctor no longer understands the situation as a whole. That he does not understand is proved by the fact that the dreams become increasingly obscure, for we all know that their "obscurity" is a purely subjective opinion of the doctor. To the understanding nothing is obscure; it is only when we do not understand that things appear unintelligible and muddled. In themselves dreams are naturally clear; that is, they are just what they must be under the given circumstances. If, from a later stage of treatment or from a distance of some years, we look back at these unintelligible dreams, we are often astounded at our own blindness. Thus when, as the analysis proceeds, we come upon dreams that are strikingly obscure in comparison with the illuminating initial dreams, the doctor should not be too ready to accuse the dreams of confusion or the patient of deliberate resistance; he would do better to take these findings as a sign of his own growing inability to understand – just as the psychiatrist who calls his patient "confused" should recognize that this is a projection and should rather call himself confused, because in reality it is he whose wits are confused by the patient's peculiar behaviour. Moreover it is therapeutically very important for the doctor to admit his lack of understanding in time, for nothing is more unbearable to the patient than to be always understood. He relies far too much anyway on the mysterious powers of the doctor and, by appealing to his professional vanity, lays a dangerous trap for him. By taking refuge in the doctor's self-confidence and "profound" understanding, the patient loses all sense of reality, falls into a stubborn transference, and retards the cure.

Understanding is clearly a very subjective process. It can be extremely one-sided, in that the doctor understands but not the patient. In such a case the doctor conceives it to be his duty to convince the patient, and if the latter will not allow himself to be convinced, the doctor accuses him of resistance. When the understanding is all on my side, I say quite calmly that I do not understand, for in the end it makes very little difference whether the doctor understands or not, but it makes all the difference whether the patient understands. Understanding should therefore be understanding in the sense of an agreement which is the fruit of joint reflection. The danger of a one-sided understanding is that the doctor may judge the dream from the standpoint of a preconceived opinion. His judgment may be in line with orthodox theory, it may even be fundamentally correct, but it will not win the patient's assent, he will not come to an understanding with him, and that is in the practical sense incorrect – incorrect because it anticipates and thus cripples the patient's development. The patient, that is to say, does not need to have a truth inculcated into him – if we do that, we only reach his head; he needs far more to grow up to this truth, and in that way we reach his heart, and the appeal goes deeper and works more powerfully.

When the doctor's one-sided interpretation is based on mere agreement as to theory or on some other preconceived opinion, his chances of convincing the patient or of achieving any therapeutic results depend chiefly upon *suggestion*. Let no one deceive himself about this. In itself, suggestion is not to be despised, but it has serious limitations, not to speak of the subsidiary effects upon the patient's independence of character which, in the long run, we could very well do without. A practising analyst may be supposed to believe implicitly in the significance and value of conscious realization, whereby hitherto unconscious parts of the personality are brought to light and subjected to conscious discrimination and criticism. It is a process that requires the patient to face his problems and that taxes his powers of conscious judgment and decision. It is nothing less than a direct challenge to his ethical sense, a call to arms that must be answered by the whole personality. As regards the maturation of personality, therefore, the analytical approach is of a higher order than suggestion, which is a species of magic that works in the dark and makes no ethical demands upon the personality. Methods of treatment based on suggestion are deceptive makeshifts; they are incompatible with the principles of analytical therapy and should be avoided if at all possible. Naturally suggestion can only be avoided if the doctor is conscious of its possibility. There is at the best of times always enough – and more than enough – unconscious suggestion.

The analyst who wishes to rule out conscious suggestion must therefore consider every dream-interpretation invalid until such time as a formula is found which wins the assent of the patient.

The observance of this rule seems to me imperative when dealing with those dreams whose obscurity is evidence of the lack of understanding of both doctor and patient. The doctor should regard every such dream as something new, as a source of information about conditions whose nature is unknown to him, concerning which he has as much to learn as the patient. It goes without saying that he should give up all his theoretical assumptions and should in every single case be ready to construct a totally new theory of dreams. There are still boundless opportunities for pioneer work in this field. The view that dreams are merely the imaginary fulfilments of repressed wishes is hopelessly out of date. There are, it is true, dreams which manifestly represent wishes or fears, but what about all the other things? Dreams may contain ineluctable truths, philosophical pronouncements, illusions, wild fantasies, memories, plans, anticipations, irrational experiences, even telepathic visions, and heaven knows what besides. One thing we ought never to forget: almost half our life is passed in a more or less unconscious state. The dream is specifically the utterance of the unconscious. Just as the psyche has a diurnal side which we call consciousness, so also it has a nocturnal side: the unconscious psychic activity which we apprehend as dreamlike fantasy. It is certain that the conscious mind consists not only of wishes and fears, but of vastly more besides; and it is highly probable that our dream psyche possesses a wealth of contents and living forms equal to or even greater than those of the conscious mind, which is characterized by concentration, limitation, and exclusion.

This being so, it is imperative that we should not pare down the meaning of the dream to fit some narrow doctrine. We must remember that there are not a few patients who imitate the technical or theoretical jargon of the doctor, and do this even in their dreams, in accordance with the old tag, *Canis panem somniat, piscator pisces.* This is not to say that the fishes of which the fisherman dreams are fishes and nothing more. There is no language that cannot be misused. As may easily be imagined, the misuse often turns the tables on us; it even seems as if the unconscious had a way of strangling the doctor in the coils of his own theory. Therefore I leave theory aside as much as possible when analysing dreams – not entirely, of course, for we always need some theory to make things intelligible. It is on the basis of theory, for instance, that I expect dreams to have a meaning. I cannot prove in every case that this is so, for there are dreams which the doctor and the patient simply do not understand. But I have to make such an hypothesis in order to find courage to deal with dreams at all. To say that dreams add something important to our conscious knowledge, and that a dream which fails to do so has not been properly interpreted – that, too, is a theory. But I must make this hypothesis as well in order to explain to myself why I analyse dreams in the first place. All other hypotheses, however, about the function and the structure of dreams are merely rules of thumb and must be subjected to constant modification. In dream-analysis we must never forget, even for a moment, that we move on treacherous ground where nothing is certain but uncertainty. If it were not so paradoxical, one would almost like to call out to the dream interpreter: "Do anything you like, only don't try to understand!"

When we take up an obscure dream, our first task is not to understand and interpret, but to establish the context with minute care. By this I do *not* mean unlimited "free association" starting from any and every image in the dream, but a careful and conscious illumination of the interconnected associations objectively grouped round particular images. Many patients have first to be educated to this, for they resemble the doctor in their insuperable desire to understand and interpret offhand, especially when they have been primed by ill-digested reading or by a previous analysis that went wrong. They begin by associating in accordance with a theory, that is, they try to understand and interpret, and they nearly always get stuck. Like the doctor, they want to get behind the dream at once in the false belief that the dream is a mere façade concealing the true meaning. But the so-called façade of most houses is by no means a fake or a deceptive distortion; on the contrary, it follows the plan of the building and often betrays the interior arrangement. The "manifest" dream-picture is the dream itself and contains the whole meaning of the dream. When I find sugar in the urine, it is sugar and not just a façade for albumen. What Freud calls the "dream-façade" is the dream's obscurity, and this is really only a projection of our own lack of understanding.

We say that the dream has a false front only because we fail to see into it. We would do better to say that we are dealing with something like a text that is unintelligible not because it has a façade – a text has no façade – but simply because we cannot read it. We do not have to get behind such a text, but must first learn to read it.

The best way to do this, as I have already remarked, is to establish the context. Free association will get me nowhere, any more than it would help me to decipher a Hittite inscription. It will of course help me to uncover all my own complexes, but for this purpose I have no need of a dream – I could just as well take a public notice or a sentence in a newspaper. Free association will bring out all my complexes, but hardly ever the meaning of a dream. To understand the dream's meaning I must stick as close as possible to the dream-images. When somebody dreams of a "deal table," it is not enough for him to associate it with his writing-desk which does not happen to be made of deal. Supposing that nothing more occurs to the dreamer, this blocking has an objective meaning, for it indicates that a particular darkness reigns in the immediate neighbourhood of the dream-image, and that is suspicious. We would expect him to have dozens of associations to a deal table, and the fact that there is apparently nothing is itself significant. In such cases I keep on returning to the image, and I usually say to my patient, "Suppose I had no idea what the words 'deal table' mean. Describe this object and give me its history in such a way that I cannot fail to understand what sort of a thing it is."

In this way we manage to establish almost the whole context of the dream-image. When we have done this for all the images in the dream we are ready for the venture of interpretation.

Every interpretation is an hypothesis, an attempt to read an unknown text. An obscure dream, taken in isolation, can hardly ever be interpreted with any certainty. For this reason I attach little importance to the interpretation of single dreams. A relative degree of certainty is reached only in the interpretation of a series of dreams, where the later dreams correct the mistakes we have made in handling those that went before. Also, the basic ideas and themes can be recognized much better in a dream-series, and I therefore urge my patients to keep a careful record of their dreams and of the interpretations given. I also show them how to work out their dreams in the manner described, so that they can bring the dream and its context with them in writing to the consultation. At a later stage I get them to work out the interpretation as well. In this way the patient learns how to deal correctly with his unconscious without the doctor's help.

Were dreams nothing more than sources of information about factors of aetiological importance, the whole work of dream-interpretation could safely be left to the doctor. Again, if their only use was to provide the doctor with a collection of useful hints and psychological tips, my own procedure would be entirely superfluous. But since, as my examples have shown, dreams contain something more than practical helps for the doctor, dream-analysis deserves very special attention. Sometimes, indeed, it is a matter of life and death. Among many instances of this sort, there is one that has remained particularly impressive. It concerns a colleague of mine, a man somewhat older than myself, whom I used to see from time to time and who always teased me about my dream-interpretations. Well, I met him one day in the street and he called out to me, "How are things going? Still interpreting dreams? By the way, I've had another idiotic dream. Does that mean something too?" This is what he had dreamed: "*I am climbing a high mountain, over steep snow-covered slopes. I climb higher and higher, and it is marvellous weather. The higher I climb the better I feel. I think, 'If only I could go on climbing like this for ever!' When I reach the summit my happiness and elation are so great that I feel I could mount right up into space. And I discover that I can actually do so: I mount upwards on empty air, and awake in sheer ecstasy.*"

After some discussion, I said, "My dear fellow, I know you can't give up mountaineering, but let me implore you not to go alone from now on. When you go, take two guides, and promise on your word of honour to follow them absolutely." "Incorrigible!" he replied, laughing, and waved good-bye. I never saw him again. Two months later the first blow fell. When out alone, he was buried by an avalanche, but was dug out in the nick of time by a military patrol that happened to be passing. Three months afterwards the end came. He went on a climb with a younger friend, but without guides. A guide standing below saw him literally step out into the air while descending a rock face. He fell on the head of his friend, who was waiting lower down, and both were dashed to pieces far below. That was *ecstasis* with a vengeance!

No amount of scepticism and criticism has yet enabled me to regard dreams as negligible occurrences. Often enough they appear senseless, but it is obviously we who lack the sense and ingenuity to read the enigmatic message from the nocturnal realm of the psyche. Seeing that at least half our psychic existence is passed in that realm, and that consciousness acts upon our nightly life just as much as the unconscious overshadows our daily life, it would seem all the more incumbent on medical psychology to sharpen its senses by a systematic study of dreams. Nobody doubts the importance of conscious experience; why then should we doubt the significance of unconscious happenings? They also are part of our life, and sometimes more truly a part of it for weal or woe than any happenings of the day.

Since dreams provide information about the hidden inner life and reveal to the patient those components of his personality which, in his daily behaviour, appear merely as neurotic symptoms, it follows that we cannot effectively treat him from the side of consciousness alone, but must bring about a change in and through the unconscious. In the light of our present knowledge this can be achieved only by the thorough and conscious assimilation of unconscious contents.

"Assimilation" in this sense means mutual penetration of conscious and unconscious, and not – as is commonly thought and practised – a one-sided evaluation, interpretation, and deformation of unconscious contents by the conscious mind. As to the value and significance of unconscious contents in general, very mistaken views are current. It is well known that the Freudian school presents the unconscious in a thoroughly negative light, much as it regards primitive man as little better than a monster. Its nursery-tales about the terrible old man of the tribe and its teachings about the "infantile-perverse-criminal" unconscious have led people to make a dangerous ogre out of something perfectly natural. As if all that is good, reasonable, worth while, and beautiful had taken up its abode in the conscious mind! Have the horrors of the World War done nothing to open our eyes, so that we still cannot see that the conscious mind is even more devilish and perverse than the naturalness of the unconscious?

The charge has recently been laid at my door that my teaching about the assimilation of the unconscious would undermine civilization and deliver up our highest values to sheer primitivity. Such an opinion can only be based on the totally erroneous supposition that the unconscious is a monster. It is a view that springs from fear of nature and the realities of life. Freud invented the idea of sublimation to save us from the imaginary claws of the unconscious. But what is real, what actually exists, cannot be alchemically sublimated, and if anything is apparently sublimated it never was what a false interpretation took it to be.

The unconscious is not a demoniacal monster, but a natural entity which, as far as moral sense, aesthetic taste, and intellectual judgment go, is completely neutral. It only becomes dangerous when our conscious attitude to it is hopelessly wrong. To the degree that we repress it, its danger increases. But the moment the patient begins to assimilate contents that were previously unconscious, its danger diminishes. The dissociation of personality, the anxious division of the day-time and the night-time sides of the psyche, cease with progressive assimilation. What my critic feared – the overwhelming of the conscious mind by the unconscious – is far more likely to ensue when the unconscious is excluded from life by being repressed, falsely interpreted, and depreciated.

The fundamental mistake regarding the nature of the unconscious is probably this: it is commonly supposed that its contents have only one meaning and are marked with an unalterable plus or minus sign. In my humble opinion, this view is too naïve. The psyche is a self-regulating system that maintains its equilibrium just as the body does. Every process that goes too far immediately and inevitably calls forth compensations, and without these there would be neither a normal metabolism nor a normal psyche. In this sense we can take the theory of compensation as a basic law of psychic behaviour. Too little on one side results in too much on the other. Similarly, the relation between conscious and unconscious is compensatory. This is one of the best-proven rules of dream-interpretation. When we set out to interpret a dream, it is always helpful to ask: What conscious attitude does it compensate?

Compensation is not as a rule merely an illusory wish-fulfilment, but an actual fact that becomes still more actual the more we repress it. We do not stop feeling thirsty by repressing our thirst. In the same way, the dream-content is to be regarded with due seriousness as an actuality that has to be fitted into the conscious attitude as a codetermining factor. If we fail to do this, we merely persist in that eccentric frame of mind which evoked the unconscious compensation in the first place. It is then difficult to see how we can ever arrive at a sane judgment of ourselves or at a balanced way of living.

If it should occur to anyone to replace the conscious content by an unconscious one – and this is the prospect which my critics find so alarming – he would only succeed in repressing it, and it would then reappear as an unconscious compensation. The unconscious would thus have changed its face completely: it would now be timidly reasonable, in striking contrast to its former tone. It is not generally believed that the unconscious operates in this way, yet such reversals constantly take place and constitute its proper function. That is why every dream is an organ of information and control, and why dreams are our most effective aid in building up the personality.

The unconscious does not harbour in itself any explosive materials unless an overweening or cowardly conscious attitude has secretly laid up stores of explosives there. All the more reason, then, for watching our step.

From all this it should now be clear why I make it an heuristic rule, in interpreting a dream, to ask myself: What conscious attitude does it compensate? By so doing, I relate the dream as closely as possible to the conscious situation; indeed, I would even assert that without knowledge of the conscious situation the dream can never be interpreted with any degree of certainty. Only in the light of this knowledge is it possible to make out whether the unconscious content carries a plus or a minus sign. The dream is not an isolated event completely cut off from daily life and lacking its character. If it seems so to us, that is only the result of our lack of understanding, a subjective illusion. In reality the relation between the conscious mind and the dream is strictly causal, and they interact in the subtlest of ways.

I should like to show by means of an example how important it is to evaluate the unconscious contents correctly. A young man brought me the following dream: "*My father is driving away from the house in his new car. He drives very clumsily, and I get very annoyed over his apparent stupidity. He goes this way and that, forwards and backwards, and manoeuvres the car into a dangerous position. Finally he runs into a wall and damages the car badly. I shout at him in a perfect fury that he ought to behave himself. My father only laughs, and then I see that he is dead drunk.*" This dream has no foundation in fact. The dreamer is convinced that his father would never behave like that, even when drunk. As a motorist he himself is very careful and extremely moderate in the use of alcohol, especially when he has to drive. Bad driving, and even slight damage to the car, irritate him greatly. His relation to his father is positive. He admires him for being an unusually successful man. We can say, without any great feat of interpretation, that the dream presents a most unfavourable picture of the father. What, then, should we take its meaning to be for the son? Is his relation to his father good only on the surface, and does it really consist in over-compensated resistances? If so, we should have to give the dream-content a positive sign; we should have to tell the young man: "That is your real relation to your father." But since I could find nothing neurotically ambivalent in the son's real relation to his father, I had no warrant for upsetting the young man's feelings with such a destructive pronouncement. To do so would have been a bad therapeutic blunder.

But, if his relation to his father is in fact good, why must the dream manufacture such an improbable story in order to discredit the father? In the dreamer's unconscious there must be some tendency to produce such a dream. Is that because he has resistances after all, perhaps fed by envy or some other inferior motive? Before we go out of our way to burden his conscience – and with sensitive young people this is always rather a dangerous proceeding – we would do better to inquire not *why* he had this dream, but what its purpose is. The answer in this case would be that his unconscious is obviously trying to take the father down a peg. If we regard this as a compensation, we are forced to the conclusion that his relation to his father is not only good, but actually too good. In fact he deserves the French soubriquet of *fils à papa*. His father is still too much the guarantor of his existence, and the dreamer is still living what I would call a provisional life. His particular danger is that he cannot see his own reality on account of his father; therefore the unconscious resorts to a kind of artificial blasphemy so as to lower the father and elevate the son. "An immoral business," we may be tempted to say. An unintelligent father would probably take umbrage, but the compensation is entirely to the point, since it forces the son to contrast himself with his father, which is the only way he could become conscious of himself.

The interpretation just outlined was apparently the correct one, for it struck home. It won the spontaneous assent of the dreamer, and no real values were damaged, either for the father or for the son. But this interpretation was only possible when the whole conscious phenomenology of the father-son relationship had been carefully studied. Without a knowledge of the conscious situation the real meaning of the dream would have remained in doubt.

For dream-contents to be assimilated, it is of overriding importance that no real values of the conscious personality should be damaged, much less destroyed, otherwise there is no one left to do the assimilating. The recognition of the unconscious is not a Bolshevist experiment which puts the lowest on top and thus re-establishes the very situation it intended to correct. We must see to it that the values of the conscious personality remain intact, for unconscious compensation is only effective when it co-operates with an integral consciousness. Assimilation is never a question of "this *or* that," but always of "this *and* that."

Just as the interpretation of dreams requires exact knowledge of the conscious status quo, so the treatment of dream symbolism demands that we take into account the dreamer's philosophical, religious, and moral convictions. It is far wiser in practice not to regard dream-symbols semiotically, i.e., as signs or symptoms of a fixed character, but as true symbols, i.e., as expressions of a content not yet consciously recognized or conceptually formulated. In addition, they must be considered in relation to the dreamer's immediate state of consciousness. I say that this procedure is advisable *in practice* because in theory relatively fixed symbols do exist whose meaning must on no account be referred to anything known and formulable as a concept. If there were no such relatively fixed symbols it would be impossible to determine the structure of the unconscious, for there would be nothing that could in any way be laid hold of or described.

It may seem strange that I should attribute an as it were indefinite content to these relatively fixed symbols. Yet if their content were not indefinite, they would not be symbols at all, but signs or symptoms. We all know how the Freudian school operates with hard-and-fast sexual "symbols" – which in this case I would call "signs" – and endows them with an apparently definitive content, namely sexuality. Unfortunately Freud's idea of sexuality is incredibly elastic and so vague that it can be made to include almost anything. The word sounds familiar enough, but what it denotes is no more than an indeterminable x that ranges from the physiological activity of the glands at one extreme to the sublime reaches of the spirit at the other. Instead of yielding to a dogmatic conviction based on the illusion that we know something because we have a familiar word for it, I prefer to regard the symbol as an unknown quantity, hard to recognize and, in the last resort, never quite determinable. Take, for instance, the so-called phallic symbols which are supposed to stand for the *membrum virile* and nothing more. Psychologically speaking, the *membrum* is itself – as Kranefeldt points out in a recent work* – an emblem of something whose wider content is not at all easy to determine. But primitive people, who, like the ancients, make the freest use of phallic symbols, would never dream of confusing the phallus, as a ritualistic symbol, with the penis. The phallus always means the creative mana, the power of healing and fertility, the "extraordinarily potent," to use Lehmann's expression, whose equivalents in mythology and in dreams are the bull, the ass, the pomegranate, the yoni, the he-goat, the lightning, the horse's hoof, the dance, the magical cohabitation in the furrow, and the menstrual fluid, to mention only a few of the thousand other analogies. That which underlies all the analogies, and sexuality itself, is an archetypal image whose character is hard to define, but whose nearest psychological equivalent is perhaps the primitive mana-symbol.

All these symbols are relatively fixed, but in no single case can we have the *a priori* certainty that in practice the symbol must be interpreted in that way.

*"Komplex und Mythos" (1950).

Practical necessity may call for something quite different. Of course, if we had to give an exhaustive scientific interpretation of a dream, in accordance with a theory, we should have to refer every such symbol to an archetype. But in practice that can be a positive mistake, for the patient's psychological state at the moment may require anything but a digression into dream theory. It is therefore advisable to consider first and foremost the meaning of the symbol in relation to the conscious situation – in other words, to treat the symbol as if it were not fixed. This is as much as to say that we must renounce all preconceived opinions, however knowing they make us feel, and try to discover what things mean for the patient. In so doing, we shall obviously not get very far towards a theoretical interpretation; indeed we shall probably get stuck at the very beginning. But if the practitioner operates too much with fixed symbols, there is a danger of his falling into mere routine and pernicious dogmatism, and thus failing his patient. Unfortunately I must refrain from illustrating this point, for I should have to go into greater detail than space here permits. Moreover I have published sufficient material elsewhere in support of my statements.

It frequently happens at the very beginning of the treatment that a dream will reveal to the doctor, in broad perspective, the whole programme of the unconscious. But for practical reasons it may be quite impossible to make clear to the patient the deeper meaning of the dream. In this respect, too, we are limited by practical considerations. Such insight is rendered possible by the doctor's knowledge of relatively fixed symbols. It can be of the greatest value in diagnosis as well as in prognosis. I was once consulted about a seventeen-year-old girl. One specialist had conjectured that she might be in the first stages of progressive muscular atrophy, while another thought that it was a case of hysteria. In view of the second opinion, I was called in. The clinical picture made me suspect an organic disease, but there were signs of hysteria as well. I asked for dreams. The patient answered at once: "Yes, I have terrible dreams. Only recently I dreamt *I was coming home at night. Everything is as quiet as death. The door into the living-room is half open, and I see my mother hanging from the chandelier, swinging to and fro in the cold wind that blows in through the open windows.* Another time I dreamt that *a terrible noise broke out in the house at night. I get up and discover that a frightened horse is tearing through the rooms. At last it finds the door into the hall, and jumps through the hall window from the fourth floor into the street below. I was terrified when I saw it lying there, all mangled."*

The gruesome character of the dreams is alone sufficient to make one pause. All the same, other people have anxiety dreams now and then. We must therefore look more closely into the meaning of the two main symbols, "mother" and "horse." They must be equivalents, for they both do the same thing: they commit suicide. "Mother" is an archetype and refers to the place of origin, to nature, to that which passively creates, hence to substance and matter, to materiality, the womb, the vegetative functions. It also means the unconscious, our natural and instinctive life, the physiological realm, the body in which we dwell or are contained; for the "mother" is also the matrix, the hollow form, the vessel that carries and nourishes, and it thus stands psychologically for the foundations of consciousness. Being inside or contained in something also suggests darkness, something nocturnal and fearful, hemming one in. These allusions give the idea of the mother in many of its mythological and etymological variants; they also represent an important part of the Yin idea in Chinese philosophy. This is no individual acquisition of a seventeen-year-old girl; it is a collective inheritance, alive and recorded in language, inherited along with the structure of the psyche and therefore to be found at all times and among all peoples.

The word "mother," which sounds so familiar, apparently refers to the best-known, the individual mother – to "my mother." But the mother-symbol points to a darker background which eludes conceptual formulation and can only be vaguely apprehended as the hidden, nature-bound life of the body. Yet even this is too narrow and excludes too many vital subsidiary meanings. The underlying, primary psychic reality is so inconceivably complex that it can be grasped only at the farthest reach of intuition, and then but very dimly. That is why it needs symbols.

If we apply our findings to the dream, its interpretation will be: The unconscious life is destroying itself. That is the dream's message to the conscious mind of the dreamer and to anybody who has ears to hear.

"Horse" is an archetype that is widely current in mythology and folklore. As an animal it represents the non-human psyche, the subhuman, animal side, the unconscious. That is why horses in folklore sometimes see visions, hear voices, and speak. As a beast of burden it is closely related to the mother-archetype (witness the Valkyries that bear the dead hero to Valhalla, the Trojan horse, etc.). As an animal lower than man it represents the lower part of the body and the animal impulses that rise from there. The horse is dynamic and vehicular power: it carries one away like a surge of instinct. It is subject to panics like all instinctive creatures who lack higher consciousness. Also it has to do with sorcery and magical spells – especially the black night-horses which herald death.

It is evident, then, that "horse" is an equivalent of "mother" with a slight shift of meaning. The mother stands for life at its origin, the horse for the merely animal life of the body. If we apply this meaning to the text of our dream, its interpretation will be: The animal life is destroying itself.

The two dreams make nearly identical statements, but, as is usually the case, the second is the more specific. Note the peculiar subtlety of the dream: there is no mention of the death of the individual. It is notorious that one often dreams of one's own death, but that is no serious matter. When it is really a question of death, the dream speaks another language.

Both dreams point to a grave organic disease with a fatal outcome. This prognosis was soon confirmed.

As for the relatively fixed symbols, this example gives a fair idea of their general nature. There are a great many of them, and all are individually marked by subtle shifts of meaning. It is only through comparative studies in mythology, folklore, religion, and philology that we can evaluate their nature scientifically. The evolutionary stratification of the psyche is more clearly discernible in the dream than in the conscious mind. In the dream, the psyche speaks in images, and gives expression to instincts, which derive from the most primitive levels of nature. Therefore, through the assimilation of unconscious contents, the momentary life of consciousness can once more be brought into harmony with the law of nature from which it all too easily departs, and the patient can be led back to the natural law of his own being.

I have not been able, in so short a space, to deal with anything but the elements of the subject. I could not put together before your eyes, stone by stone, the edifice that is reared in every analysis from the materials of the unconscious and finally reaches completion in the restoration of the total personality. The way of successive assimilations goes far beyond the curative results that specifically concern the doctor. It leads in the end to that distant goal which may perhaps have been the first urge to life: the complete actualization of the whole human being, that is, individuation. We physicians may well be the first conscious observers of this dark process of nature. As a rule we see only the pathological phase of development, and we lose sight of the patient as soon as he is cured. Yet it is only after the cure that we would really be in a position to study the normal process, which may extend over years and decades. Had we but a little knowledge of the ends toward which the unconscious development is tending, and were the doctor's psychological insight not drawn exclusively from the pathological phase, we should have a less confused idea of the processes mediated to the conscious mind by dreams and a clearer recognition of what the symbols point to. In my opinion, every doctor should understand that every procedure in psychotherapy, and particularly the analytical procedure, breaks into a purposeful and continuous process of development, now at this point and now at that, and thus singles out separate phases which seem to follow opposing courses. Each individual analysis by itself shows only one part or one aspect of the deeper process, and for this reason nothing but hopeless confusion can result from comparative case histories. For this reason, too, I have preferred to confine myself to the rudiments of the subject and to practical considerations; for only in closest contact with the everyday facts can we come to anything like a satisfactory understanding.

Part 6. The Development of the Individual

Jung of course accepted that man is a social animal, and realized that the majority of mankind are content to live in accordance with the collective, social conventions of their time. But the people who really interested him were not those who were thus adapted, but the exceptional individuals whose own nature compelled them to reject conventional ways and discover their own path. In Jung's view, "Nature is aristocratic, and one person of value outweighs ten lesser ones." (CW 7, par. 236) It is the individual who is the carrier of culture. "All the highest achievements of virtue, as well as the blackest villainies, are individual." (CW 7, par. 240) The development of individuality, the discovery of what an individual really thinks and feels and believes, as opposed to the collective thoughts, feelings and beliefs imposed on him by society, becomes a quest of vital significance.

"The Development of Personality" CW 17, pars. 284–323

In somewhat free-handed fashion the last two lines of Goethe's stanza are often quoted:

> The Highest bliss on earth shall be
> The joys of personality!

This gives expression to the view that the ultimate aim and strongest desire of all mankind is to develop that fulness of life which is called personality. Nowadays, "personality training" has become an educational ideal that turns its back upon the standardized, mass-produced, "normal" human being demanded by the machine age. It thus pays tribute to the historical fact that the great liberating deeds of world history have sprung from leading personalities and never from the inert mass, which is at all times secondary and can only be prodded into activity by the demagogue. The huzzahs of the Italian nation go forth to the personality of the Duce, and the dirges of other nations lament the absence of strong leaders.* The yearning for personality has therefore become a real problem that occupies many minds today, whereas in former times there was only one man who had a glimmering of this question – Friedrich Schiller, whose letters on aesthetic education have lain dormant, like a Sleeping Beauty of literature, for more than a century. We may confidently assert that the "Holy Roman Empire of the German Nation" has not taken much notice of Schiller as an educator. On the other hand, the *furor teutonicus* has hurled itself upon pedagogics (in the strict sense of the education of children), delved into child psychology, ferreted out the infantilism of the adult, and made of childhood such a portentous condition of life and human fate that it completely overshadows the creative meaning and potentialities of adult existence. Our age has been extravagantly praised as the "century of the child." This boundless expansion of the kindergarten amounts to complete forgetfulness of the problems of adult education divined by the genius of Schiller. Nobody will deny or underestimate the importance of childhood; the severe and often life-long injuries caused by stupid upbringing at home or in school are too obvious, and the need for more reasonable pedagogic methods is far too urgent. But if this evil is to be attacked at the root, one must in all seriousness face the question of how such idiotic and bigoted methods of education ever came to be employed, and still are employed. Obviously, for the sole reason that there are half-baked educators who are not human beings at all, but walking personifications of method. Anyone who wants to educate must himself be educated. But the parrot-like book-learning and mechanical use of methods that is still practised today is no education either for the child or for educator. People are everlastingly saying that the child's personality must be trained. While I admire this lofty ideal, I can't help asking who it is that trains the personality? In the first and foremost place we have the parents, ordinary, incompetent folk who, more often than not, are half children themselves and remain so all their lives. How could

*Since this sentence was written, Germany too has found her Führer.

anyone expect all these ordinary parents to be "personalities," and who has ever given a thought to devising methods for inculcating "personality" into them? Naturally, then, we expect great things of the pedagogue, of the trained professional, who, heaven help us, has been stuffed full of "psychology" and is bursting with ill-assorted views as to how the child is supposed to be constituted and how he ought to be handled. It is presumed that the youthful persons who have picked on education as a career are themselves educated; but nobody, I daresay, will venture to assert that they are all "personalities" as well. By and large, they suffer from the same defective education as the hapless children they are supposed to instruct, and as a rule are as little "personalities" as their charges. Our whole educational problem suffers from a one-sided approach to the child who is to be educated, and from an equally one-sided lack of emphasis on the uneducatedness of the educator. Everyone who has finished his course of studies feels himself to be fully educated; in a word, he feels grown up. He must feel this, he must have this solid conviction of his own competence in order to survive the struggle for existence. Any doubt or feeling of uncertainty would hinder and cripple him, undermining the necessary faith in his own authority and unfitting him for a professional career. People expect him to be efficient and good at his job and not to have doubts about himself and his capabilities. The professional man is irretrievably condemned to be competent.

Everyone knows that these conditions are not ideal. But, with reservations, we can say that they are the best possible under the circumstances. We cannot imagine how they could be different. We cannot expect more from the average educator than from the average parent. If he is good at his job, we have to be content with that, just as we have to be content with parents bringing up their children as best they can.

The fact is that the high ideal of educating the personality is not for children: for what is usually meant by personality – a well-rounded psychic whole that is capable of resistance and abounding in energy – is an *adult ideal*. It is only in an age like ours, when the individual is unconscious of the problems of adult life, or – what is worse – when he consciously shirks them, that people could wish to foist this ideal on to childhood. I suspect our contemporary pedagogical and psychological enthusiasm for the child of dishonourable intentions: we talk about the child, but we should mean the child in the adult. For in every adult there lurks a child – an eternal child, something that is always becoming, is never completed, and calls for unceasing care, attention, and education. That is the part of the human personality which wants to develop and become whole. But the man of today is far indeed from this wholeness. Dimly suspecting his own deficiencies, he seizes upon child education and fervently devotes himself to child psychology, fondly supposing that something must have gone wrong in his own upbringing and childhood development that can be weeded out in the next generation. This intention is highly commendable, but comes to grief on the psychological fact that we cannot correct in a child a fault that we ourselves still commit. Children are not half as stupid as we imagine. They notice only too well what is genuine and what is not. Hans Andersen's story of the emperor's clothes contains a perennial truth. How many parents have come to me with the laudable intention of sparing their children the unhappy experiences they had to go through in their own childhood! And when I ask, "Are you quite sure you have overcome these mistakes yourself?" they are firmly convinced that the damage has long since been repaired. In actual fact it has not. If as children they were brought up too strictly, then they spoil their own children with a tolerance bordering on bad taste; if certain matters were painfully concealed from them in childhood, these are revealed with a lack of reticence that is just as painful. They have merely gone to the opposite extreme, the strongest evidence for the tragic survival of the old sin – a fact which has altogether escaped them.

If there is anything that we wish to change in our children, we should first examine it and see whether it is not something that could better be changed in ourselves. Take our enthusiasm for pedagogics. It may be that the boot is on the other leg. It may be that we misplace the pedagogical need because it would be an uncomfortable reminder that we ourselves are still children in many respects and still need a vast amount of educating.

At any rate this doubt seems to me to be extremely pertinent when we set out to train our children's "personalities." Personality is a seed that can only develop by slow stages throughout life.

There is no personality without definiteness, wholeness, and ripeness. These three qualities cannot and should not be expected of the child, as they would rob it of childhood. It would be nothing but an abortion, a premature pseudo-adult; yet our modern education has already given birth to such monsters, particularly in those cases where parents set themselves the fanatical task of always "doing their best" for the children and "living only for them." This clamant ideal effectively prevents the parents from doing anything about their own development and allows them to thrust their "best" down their children's throats. This so-called "best" turns out to be the very things the parents have most badly neglected in themselves. In this way the children are goaded on to achieve their parents' most dismal failures, and are loaded with ambitions that are never fulfilled. Such methods and ideals only engender educational monstrosities.

No one can train the personality unless he has it himself. And it is not the child, but only the adult, who can achieve personality as the fruit of a full life directed to this end. The achievement of personality means nothing less than the optimum development of the whole individual human being. It is impossible to foresee the endless variety of conditions that have to be fulfilled. A whole lifetime, in all its biological, social, and spiritual aspects, is needed. Personality is the supreme realization of the innate idiosyncrasy of a living being. It is an act of high courage flung in the face of life, the absolute affirmation of all that constitutes the individual, the most successful adaptation to the universal conditions of existence coupled with the greatest possible freedom for self-determination. To educate a man to *this* seems to me no light matter. It is surely the hardest task the modern mind has set itself. And it is dangerous too, dangerous to a degree that Schiller never imagined, though his prophetic insight made him the first to venture upon these problems. It is as dangerous as the bold and hazardous undertaking of nature to let women bear children. Would it not be sacrilege, a Promethean or even Luciferian act of presumption, if a superman ventured to grow an homunculus in a bottle and then found it sprouting into a Golem? And yet he would not be doing anything that nature does not do every day. There is no human horror or fairground freak that has not lain in the womb of a loving mother. As the sun shines upon the just and the unjust, and as women who bear and give suck tend God's children and the devil's brood with equal compassion, unconcerned about the possible consequences, so we also are part and parcel of this amazing nature, and, like it, carry within us the seeds of the unpredictable.

Our personality develops in the course of our life from germs that are hard or impossible to discern, and it is only our deeds that reveal who we are. We are like the sun, which nourishes the life of the earth and brings forth every kind of strange, wonderful, and evil thing; we are like the mothers who bear in their wombs untold happiness and suffering. At first we do not know what deeds or misdeeds, what destiny, what good and evil we have in us, and only the autumn can show what the spring has engendered, only in the evening will it be seen what the morning began.

Personality, as the complete realization of our whole being, is an unattainable ideal. But unattainability is no argument against the ideal, for ideals are only signposts, never the goal.

Just as the child must develop in order to be educated, so the personality must begin to sprout before it can be trained. And this is where the danger begins. For we are handling something unpredictable, we do not know how and in what direction the budding personality will develop, and we have learned enough of nature and the world to be somewhat chary of both. On top of that, we were brought up in the Christian belief that human nature is intrinsically evil. But even those who no longer adhere to the Christian teaching are by nature mistrustful and not a little frightened of the possibilities lurking in the subterranean chambers of their being. Even enlightened psychologists like Freud give us an extremely unpleasant picture of what lies slumbering in the depths of the human psyche. So it is rather a bold venture to put in a good word for the development of personality. Human nature, however, is full of the strangest contradictions. We praise the "sanctity of motherhood," yet would never dream of holding it responsible for all the human monsters, the homicidal maniacs, dangerous lunatics, epileptics, idiots and cripples of every description who are born every day. At the same time we are tortured with doubts when it comes to allowing the free development of personality. "Anything might happen then," people say. Or they dish up the old, feeble-minded objection to "individualism." But individualism is not and never has been a natural development; it is nothing but an unnatural usurpation, a freakish, impertinent pose that proves its hollowness by crumpling up before the least obstacle. What we have in mind is something very different.

Clearly, no one develops his personality because somebody tells him that it would be useful or advisable to do so. Nature has never yet been taken in by well-meaning advice. The only thing that moves nature is causal necessity, and that goes for human nature too. Without necessity nothing budges, the human personality least of all. It is tremendously conservative, not to say torpid. Only acute necessity is able to rouse it. The developing personality obeys no caprice, no command, no insight, only brute necessity; it needs the motivating force of inner or outer fatalities. Any other development would be no better than individualism. That is why the cry of "individualism" is a cheap insult when flung at the natural development of personality.

The words "many are called, but few are chosen" are singularly appropriate here, for the development of personality from the germ-state to full consciousness is at once a charisma and a curse, because its first fruit is the conscious and unavoidable segregation of the single individual from the undifferentiated and unconscious herd. This means isolation, and there is no more comforting word for it. Neither family nor society nor position can save him from this fate, nor yet the most successful adaptation to his environ- ment, however smoothly he fits in. The development of personal- ity is a favour that must be paid for dearly. But the people who talk most loudly about developing their personalities are the very ones who are least mindful of the results, which are such as to frighten away all weaker spirits.

Yet the development of personality means more than just the fear of hatching forth monsters, or of isolation. It also means fidelity to the law of one's own being.

For the word "fidelity" I should prefer, in this context, the Greek word used in the New Testament, πίστις, which is errone- ously translated "faith." It really means "trust," "trustful loyalty." Fidelity to the law of one's own being is a trust in this law, a loyal perseverance and confident hope; in short, an attitude such as a religious man should have towards God. It can now be seen how portentous is the dilemma that emerges from behind our problem:

pious ?.

personality can never develop unless the individual chooses his own way, consciously and with moral deliberation. Not only the causal motive – necessity – but conscious moral decision must lend its strength to the process of building the personality. If the first is lacking, then the alleged development is a mere acrobatics of the will; if the second, it will get stuck in unconscious automatism. But a man can make a moral decision to go his own way only if he holds that way to be the best. If any other way were held to be better, then he would live and develop that other personality instead of his own. The other ways are conventionalities of a moral, social, political, philosophical, or religious nature. The fact that the conventions always flourish in one form or another only proves that the vast majority of mankind do not choose their own way, but convention, and consequently develop not themselves but a method and a collective mode of life at the cost of their own wholeness.

Just as the psychic and social life of mankind at the primitive level is exclusively a group life with a high degree of unconsciousness among the individuals composing it, so the historical process of development that comes afterwards is in the main collective and will doubtless remain so. That is why I believe convention to be a collective necessity. It is a stopgap and not an ideal, either in the moral or in the religious sense, for submission to it always means renouncing one's wholeness and running away from the final consequences of one's own being.

To develop one's own personality is indeed an unpopular undertaking, a deviation that is highly uncongenial to the herd, an eccentricity smelling of the cenobite, as it seems to the outsider. Small wonder, then, that from earliest times only the chosen few have embarked upon this strange adventure. Had they all been fools, we could safely dismiss them as ἰδιῶται, mentally "private" persons who have no claim on our interest. But, unfortunately, these personalities are as a rule the legendary heroes of mankind, the very ones who are looked up to, loved, and worshipped, the true sons of God whose names perish not. They are the flower and the fruit, the ever fertile seeds of the tree of humanity. This allusion to historical personalities makes it abundantly clear why the development of personality is an ideal, and why the cry of individualism is an insult. Their greatness has never lain in their abject submission *to* convention, but, on the contrary, in their deliverance *from* convention. They towered up like mountain peaks above the mass that still clung to its collective fears, its beliefs, laws, and systems, and boldly chose their own way. To the man in the street it has always seemed miraculous that anyone should turn aside from the beaten track with its known destinations, and strike out on the steep and narrow path leading into the unknown. Hence it was always believed that such a man, if not actually crazy, was possessed by a daemon or a god; for the miracle of a man being able to act otherwise than as humanity has always acted could only be explained by the gift of daemonic power or divine spirit. How could anyone but a god counterbalance the dead weight of humanity in the mass, with its everlasting convention and habit? From the beginning, therefore, the heroes were endowed with godlike attributes. According to the Nordic view they had snake's eyes, and there was something peculiar about their birth or descent; certain heroes of ancient Greece were snake-souled, others had a personal daemon, were magicians or the elect of God. All these attributes, which could be multiplied at will, show that for the ordinary man the outstanding personality is something *supernatural*, a phenomenon that can only be explained by the intervention of some daemonic factor.

What is it, in the end, that induces a man to go his own way and to rise out of unconscious identity with the mass as out of a swathing mist? Not necessity, for necessity comes to many, and they all take refuge in convention. Not moral decision, for nine times out of ten we decide for convention likewise. What is it, then, that inexorably tips the scales in favour of the *extra-ordinary*?

It is what is commonly called *vocation*: an irrational factor that destines a man to emancipate himself from the herd and from its well-worn paths. True personality is always a vocation and puts its trust in it as in God, despite its being, as the ordinary man would say, only a personal feeling. But vocation acts like a law of God from which there is no escape. The fact that many a man who goes his own way ends in ruin means nothing to one who has a vocation. He *must* obey his own law, as if it were a daemon whispering to him of new and wonderful paths. Anyone with a vocation hears the voice of the inner man: he is *called*. That is why the legends say that he possesses a private daemon who counsels him and whose mandates he must obey. The best known example of this is Faust, and an historical instance is provided by the daemon of Socrates. Primitive medicine-men have their snake spirits, and Aesculapius, the tutelary patron of physicians, has for his emblem the Serpent of Epidaurus. He also had, as his private daemon, the Cabir Telesphoros, who is said to have dictated or inspired his medical prescriptions.

The original meaning of "to have a vocation" is "to be addressed by a voice." The clearest examples of this are to be found in the avowals of the Old Testament prophets. That it is not just a quaint old-fashioned way of speaking is proved by the confessions of historical personalities such as Goethe and Napoleon, to mention only two familiar examples, who made no secret of their feeling of vocation.

Vocation, or the feeling of it, is not, however, the prerogative of great personalities; it is also appropriate to the small ones all the way down to the "midget" personalities, but as the size decreases the voice becomes more and more muffled and unconscious. It is as if the voice of the daemon within were moving further and further off, and spoke more rarely and more indistinctly. The smaller the personality, the dimmer and more unconscious it becomes, until finally it merges indistinguishably with the surrounding society, thus surrendering its own wholeness and dissolving into the wholeness of the group. In the place of the inner voice there is the voice of the group with its conventions, and vocation is replaced by collective necessities. But even in this unconscious social condition there are not a few who are called awake by the summons of the voice, whereupon they are at once set apart from the others, feeling themselves confronted with a problem about which the others know nothing. In most cases it is impossible to explain to the others what has happened for any understanding is walled off by impenetrable prejudices. "You are no different from anybody else," they will chorus, or, "there's no such thing," and even if there is such a thing, it is immediately branded as "morbid" and "most unseemly." For it is "a monstrous presumption to suppose anything of that sort could be of the slightest significance" – it is "purely psychological." This last objection is extremely popular nowadays. It stems from a curious underestimation of anything psychic, which people apparently regard as personal, arbitrary, and therefore completely futile. And this, paradoxically enough, despite their enthusiasm for psychology. The unconscious, after all, is "nothing but fantasy." We "merely imagined" so and so, etc. People think themselves magicians who can conjure the psyche hither and thither and fashion it to suit their moods. They deny what strikes them as inconvenient, sublimate anything nasty, explain away their phobias, correct their faults, and feel in the end that they have arranged everything beautifully. In the meantime they have forgotten the essential point, which is that only the tiniest fraction of the psyche is identical with the conscious mind and its box of magic tricks, while for much the greater part it is sheer unconscious *fact*, hard and immitigable as granite, immovable, inaccessible, yet ready at any time to come crashing down upon us at the behest of unseen powers. The gigantic catastrophes that threaten us today are not elemental happenings of a physical or biological order, but psychic events. To a quite terrifying degree we are threatened by wars and revolutions which are nothing other than psychic epidemics. At any moment several millions of human beings may be smitten with a new madness, and then we shall have another world war or devastating revolution. Instead of being at the mercy of wild beasts, earthquakes, landslides, and inundations, modern man is battered by the elemental forces of his own psyche. This is the World Power that vastly exceeds all other powers on earth. The Age of Enlightenment, which stripped nature and human institutions of gods, overlooked the God of Terror who dwells in the human soul. If anywhere, fear of God is justified in face of the overwhelming supremacy of the psychic.

But all this is so much abstraction. Everyone knows that the intellect, that clever jackanapes, can put it this way or any other way he pleases. It is a very different thing when the psyche, as an objective fact, hard as granite and heavy as lead, confronts a man as an inner experience and addresses him in an audible voice, saying, "This is what will and must be." Then he feels himself called, just as the group does when there's a war on, or a revolution, or any other madness. It is not for nothing that our age calls for the redeemer personality, for the one who can emancipate himself from the inescapable grip of the collective and save at least his own soul, who lights a beacon of hope for others, proclaiming that here is at least *one* man who has succeeded in extricating himself from that fatal identity with the group psyche. For the group, because of its unconsciousness, has no freedom of choice, and so psychic activity runs on in it like an uncontrolled law of nature. There is thus set going a chain reaction that comes to a stop only in catastrophe. The people always long for a hero, a slayer of dragons, when they feel the danger of psychic forces; hence the cry for personality.

But what has the individual personality to do with the plight of the many? In the first place he is part of the people as a whole, and is as much at the mercy of the power that moves the whole as anybody else. The only thing that distinguishes him from all the others is his vocation. He has been called by that all-powerful, all-tyrannizing psychic necessity that is his own and his people's affliction. If he hearkens to the voice, he is at once set apart and isolated as he has resolved to obey the law that commands him from within. "His *own* law!" everybody will cry. But he knows better: it is *the* law, *the* vocation for which he is destined, no more "his own" than the lion that fells him, although it is undoubtedly this particular lion that kills him and not any other lion. Only in this sense is he entitled to speak of "his" vocation, "his" law.

With the decision to put his way above all other possible ways he has already fulfilled the greater part of his vocation as a redeemer. He has invalidated all other ways for himself, exalting his law above convention and thus making a clean sweep of all those things that not only failed to prevent the great danger but actually accelerated it. For conventions in themselves are soulless mechanisms that can never understand more than the mere routine of life. Creative life always stands outside convention. That is why, when the mere routine of life predominates in the form of convention and tradition, there is bound to be a destructive outbreak of creative energy. This outbreak is a catastrophe only when it is a mass phenomenon, but never in the individual who consciously submits to these higher powers and serves them with all his strength. The mechanism of convention keeps people unconscious, for in that state they can follow their accustomed tracks like blind brutes, without the need for conscious decision. This unintended result of even the best conventions is unavoidable but is no less a terrible danger for that. For when new conditions arise that are not provided for under the old conventions, then, just as with animals, panic is liable to break out among human beings kept unconscious by routine, and with equally unpredictable results.

Personality, however, does not allow itself to be seized by the panic terror of those who are just waking to consciousness, for it has put all its terrors behind it. It is able to cope with the changing times, and has unknowingly and involuntarily become a *leader*.

All human beings are much alike, otherwise they could not succumb to the same delusion, and the psychic substratum upon which the individual consciousness is based is universally the same, otherwise people could never reach a common understanding. So, in this sense, personality and its peculiar psychic make-up are not something absolutely unique. The uniqueness holds only for the *individual* nature of the personality, as it does for each and every individual. To become a personality is not the absolute prerogative of the genius, for a man may be a genius without being a personality. In so far as every individual has the law of his life inborn in him, it is theoretically possible for any man to follow this law and so become a personality, that is, to achieve wholeness. But since life only exists in the form of living units, i.e., individuals, the law of life always tends towards a life individually lived. So although the objective psyche can only be conceived as a universal and uniform datum, which means that all men share the same primary, psychic condition, this objective psyche must nevertheless individuate itself if it is to become actualized, for there is no other way in which it could express itself except through the individual human being. The only exception to this is when it seizes hold of a group, in which case it must, of its own nature, precipitate a catastrophe, because it can only operate unconsciously and is not assimilated by any consciousness or assigned its place among the existing conditions of life.

Only the man who can consciously assent to the power of the inner voice becomes a personality; but if he succumbs to it he will be swept away by the blind flux of psychic events and destroyed. That is the great and liberating thing about any genuine personality: he voluntarily sacrifices himself to his vocation, and consciously translates into his own individual reality what would only lead to ruin if it were lived unconsciously by the group.

One of the most shining examples of the meaning of personality that history has preserved for us is the life of Christ. In Christianity, which, be it mentioned in passing, was the only religion really persecuted by the Romans, there rose up a direct opponent of the Caesarean madness that afflicted not only the emperor, but every Roman as well: *civis Romanus sum*. The opposition showed itself wherever the worship of Caesar clashed with Christianity. But, as we know from what the evangelists tell us about the psychic development of Christ's personality, this opposition was fought out just as decisively in the soul of its founder. The story of the Temptation clearly reveals the nature of the psychic power with which Jesus came into collision: it was the power-intoxicated devil of the prevailing Caesarean psychology that led him into dire temptation in the wilderness. This devil was the objective psyche that held all the peoples of the Roman Empire under its sway, and that is why it promised Jesus all the kingdoms of the earth, as if it were trying to make a Caesar of him. Obeying the inner call of his vocation, Jesus voluntarily exposed himself to the assaults of the imperialistic madness that filled everyone, conqueror and conquered alike. In this way he recognized the nature of the objective psyche which had plunged the whole world into misery and had begotten a yearning for salvation that found expression even in the pagan poets. Far from suppressing or allowing himself to be suppressed by this psychic onslaught, he let it act on him consciously, and assimilated it. Thus was world-conquering Caesarism transformed into spiritual kingship, and the Roman Empire into the universal kingdom of God that was not of this world. While the whole Jewish nation was expecting an imperialistically minded and politically active hero as a Messiah, Jesus fulfilled the Messianic mission not so much for his own nation as for the whole Roman world, and pointed out to humanity the old truth that where force rules there is no love, and where love reigns force does not count. The religion of love was the exact psychological counterpart to the Roman devil-worship of power.

The example of Christianity is perhaps the best illustration of my previous abstract argument. This apparently unique life became a sacred symbol because it is the psychological prototype of the only meaningful life, that is, of a life that strives for the individual realization – absolute and unconditional – of its own particular law. Well may we exclaim with Tertullian: *anima naturaliter christiana!*

The deification of Jesus, as also of the Buddha, is not surprising, for it affords a striking example of the enormous valuation that humanity places upon these hero figures and hence upon the ideal of personality. Though it seems at present as if the blind and destructive dominance of meaningless collective forces would thrust the ideal of personality into the background, yet this is only a passing revolt against the dead weight of history. Once the revolutionary, unhistorical, and therefore uneducated inclinations of the rising generation have had their fill of tearing down tradition, new heroes will be sought and found. Even the Bolsheviks, whose radicalism leaves nothing to be desired, have embalmed Lenin and made a saviour of Karl Marx. The ideal of personality is one of the ineradicable needs of the human soul, and the more unsuitable it is the more fanatically it is defended. Indeed, the worship of Caesar was itself a misconceived cult of personality, and modern Protestantism, whose critical theology has reduced the divinity of Christ to vanishing point, has found its last refuge in the personality of Jesus.

Yes, this thing we call personality is a great and mysterious problem. Everything that can be said about it is curiously unsatisfactory and inadequate, and there is always a danger of the discussion losing itself in pomposity and empty chatter. The very idea of personality is, in common usage, so vague and ill-defined that one hardly ever finds two people who take the word in the same sense. If I put forward a more definite conception of it, I do not imagine that I have uttered the last word. I should like to regard all I say here only as a tentative attempt to approach the problem of personality without making any claim to solve it. Or rather, I should like my attempt to be regarded as a description of the psychological problems raised by personality. All the usual explanations and nostrums of psychology are apt to fall short here, just as they do with the man of genius or the creative artist. Inferences from heredity or from environment do not quite come off; inventing fictions about childhood, so popular today, ends – to put it mildly – in unreality; explanations from necessity – "he had no money," "he was a sick man," etc. – remain caught in externals. There is always something irrational to be added, something that simply cannot be explained, a *deus ex machina* or an *asylum ignorantiae*, that well-known sobriquet for God. The problem thus seems to border on the extrahuman realm, which has always been known by a divine name. As you can see, I too have had to refer to the "inner voice," the vocation, and define it as a powerful objective-psychic factor in order to characterize the way in which it functions in the developing personality and how it appears subjectively. Mephistopheles, in *Faust*, is not personified merely because this creates a better dramatic or theatrical effect, as though Faust were his own moralist and painted his private devil on the wall. The opening words of the Dedication – "Once more you hover near me, forms and faces" – are more than just an aesthetic flourish. Like the concretism of the devil, they are an admission of the objectivity of psychic experience, a whispered avowal that this was what *actually happened*, not because of subjective wishes, or fears, or personal opinions, but somehow quite of itself. Naturally only a numskull thinks of ghosts, but something like a primitive numskull seems to lurk beneath the surface of our reasonable daytime consciousness.

Hence the eternal doubt whether what appears to be the objective psyche is really objective, or whether it might not be imagination after all. But then the question at once arises: have I imagined such and such a thing on purpose, or has it been imagined by something in me? It is a similar problem to that of the neurotic who suffers from an imaginary carcinoma. He knows, and has been told a hundred times before, that it is all imagination, and yet he asks me brokenly, "But why do I imagine such a thing? I don't want to do it!" To which the answer is: the idea of the carcinoma has imagined itself in him without his knowledge and without his consent. The reason is that a psychic growth, a "proliferation," is taking place in his unconscious without his being able to make it conscious. In the face of this interior activity he feels afraid. But since he is entirely persuaded that there can be nothing in his own soul that he does not know about, he must relate his fear to a physical carcinoma which he knows does not exist. And if he should still be afraid of it, there are a hundred doctors to convince him that his fear is entirely groundless. The neurosis is thus a defence against the objective, inner activity of the psyche, or an attempt, somewhat dearly paid for, to escape from the inner voice and hence from the vocation. For this "growth" is the objective activity of the psyche, which, independently of conscious volition, is trying to speak to the conscious mind through the inner voice and lead him towards wholeness. Behind the neurotic perversion is concealed his vocation, his destiny: the growth of personality, the full realization of the life-will that is born with the individual. It is the man without *amor fati* who is the neurotic; he, truly, has missed his vocation, and never will he be able to say with Cromwell, "None climbeth so high as he who knoweth not whither his destiny leadeth him."

To the extent that a man is untrue to the law of his being and does not rise to personality, he has failed to realize his life's meaning. Fortunately, in her kindness and patience, Nature never puts the fatal question as to the meaning of their lives into the mouths of most people. And where no one asks, no one need answer.

The neurotic's fear of carcinoma is therefore justified: it is not imagination, but the consistent expression of a psychic fact that exists in a sphere outside consciousness, beyond the reach of his will and understanding. If he withdrew into the wilderness and listened to his inner life in solitude, he might perhaps hear what the voice has to say. But as a rule the miseducated, civilized human being is quite incapable of perceiving the voice, which is something not guaranteed by the current shibboleths. Primitive people have a far greater capacity in this respect; at least the medicine-men are able, as part of their professional equipment, to talk with spirits, trees, and animals, these being the forms in which they encounter the objective psyche or psychic non-ego.

Because neurosis is a developmental disturbance of the personality, we physicians of the soul are compelled by professional necessity to concern ourselves with the problem of personality and the inner voice, however remote it may seem to be. In practical psychotherapy these psychic facts, which are usually so vague and have so often degenerated into empty phrases, emerge from obscurity and take visible shape. Nevertheless, it is extremely rare for this to happen spontaneously as it did with the Old Testament prophets; generally the psychic conditions that have caused the disturbance have to be made conscious with considerable effort. But the contents that then come to light are wholly in accord with the inner voice and point to a predestined vocation, which, if accepted and assimilated by the conscious mind, conduces to the development of personality.

Just as the great personality acts upon society to liberate, to redeem, to transform, and to heal, so the birth of personality in oneself has a therapeutic effect. It is as if a river that had run to waste in sluggish side-streams and marshes suddenly found its way back to its proper bed, or as if a stone lying on a germinating seed were lifted away so that the shoot could begin its natural growth.

The inner voice is the voice of a fuller life, of a wider, more comprehensive consciousness. That is why, in mythology, the birth of the hero or the symbolic rebirth coincides with sunrise, for the growth of personality is synonymous with an increase of self-consciousness. For the same reason most heroes are characterized by solar attributes, and the moment of birth of their greater personality is known as illumination.

The fear that most people naturally have of the inner voice is not so childish as might be supposed. The contents that rise up and confront a limited consciousness are far from harmless, as is shown by the classic example of the temptation of Christ, or the equally significant Mara episode in the Buddha legend. As a rule, they signify the specific danger to which the person concerned is liable to succumb. What the inner voice whispers to us is generally something negative, if not actually evil. This must be so, first of all because we are usually not as unconscious of our virtues as of our vices, and then because we suffer less from the good than from the bad in us. The inner voice, as I have explained above, makes us conscious of the evil from which the whole community is suffering, whether it be the nation or the whole human race. But it presents this evil in an individual form, so that one might at first suppose it to be only an individual characteristic. The inner voice brings the evil before us in a very tempting and convincing way in order to make us succumb. If we do not partially succumb, nothing of this apparent evil enters into us, and no regeneration or healing can take place. (I say "apparent," though this may sound too optimistic.) If we succumb completely, then the contents expressed by the inner voice act as so many devils, and a catastrophe ensues. But if we can succumb only in part, and if by self-assertion the ego can save itself from being completely swallowed, then it can assimilate the voice, and we realize that the evil was, after all, only a semblance of evil, but in reality a bringer of healing and illumination. In fact, the inner voice is a "Lucifer" in the strictest and most unequivocal sense of the word, and it faces people with ultimate moral decisions without which they can never achieve full consciousness and become personalities. The highest and the lowest, the best and the vilest, the truest and the most deceptive things are often blended together in the inner voice in the most baffling way, thus opening up in us an abyss of confusion, falsehood, and despair.

It is naturally absurd for people to accuse the voice of Nature, the all-sustainer and all-destroyer, of evil. If she appears inveterately evil to us, this is mainly due to the old truth that the good is always the enemy of the better. We would be foolish indeed if we did not cling to the traditional good for as long as possible. But as Faust says:

> When we the good things of this world attain
> We call the better all a lie and sham.

A good thing is unfortunately not a good forever, for otherwise there would be nothing better. If better is to come, good must stand aside. Therefore Meister Eckhart says, "God is not good, or else he could be better."

There are times in the world's history – and our own time may be one of them – when good must stand aside, so that anything destined to be better first appears in evil form. This shows how extremely dangerous it is even to touch these problems, for evil can so easily slip in on the plea that it is, potentially, the better! The problems of the inner voice are full of pitfalls and hidden snares. Treacherous, slippery ground, as dangerous and pathless as life itself once one lets go of the railings. But he who cannot lose his life, neither shall he save it. The hero's birth and the heroic life are always threatened. The serpents sent by Hera to destroy the infant Hercules, the python that tries to strangle Apollo at birth, the massacre of the innocents, all these tell the same story. To develop the personality is a gamble, and the tragedy is that the daemon of the inner voice is at once our greatest danger and an indispensable help. It is tragic, but logical, for it is the nature of things to be so.

Can we, therefore, blame humanity, and all the well-meaning shepherds of the flock and worried fathers of families, if they erect protective barriers, hold up wonder-working images, and point out the roads that wind safely past the abyss?

But, in the end, the hero, the leader, the saviour, is one who discovers a new way to greater certainty. Everything could be left undisturbed did not the new way demand to be discovered, and did it not visit humanity with all the plagues of Egypt until it finally is discovered. The undiscovered vein within us is a living part of the psyche; classical Chinese philosophy names this interior way "Tao," and likens it to a flow of water that moves irresistibly towards its goal. To rest in Tao means fulfilment, wholeness, one's destination reached, one's mission done; the beginning, end, and perfect realization of the meaning of existence innate in all things. Personality is Tao.

As analysis proceeds, and the individual becomes more aware of the compensatory activity of the unconscious, he may lose his symptoms, become relatively well adapted, and feel no need to pursue any further development of his personality. However, many of Jung's patients wanted, or felt compelled, to go beyond the point of "adaptation."

From "**The Aims of Psychotherapy**" CW 16, pars. 81–4

The human psyche is a thing of enormous ambiguity. In every single case we have to ask ourselves whether an attitude or a so-called *habitus* is authentic, or whether it may not be just a compensation for its opposite. I must confess that I have so often been deceived in this matter that in any concrete case I am at pains to avoid all theoretical presuppositions about the structure of the neurosis and about what the patient can and ought to do. As far as possible I let pure experience decide the therapeutic aims. This may perhaps seem strange, because it is commonly supposed that the therapist has an aim. But in psychotherapy it seems to me positively advisable for the doctor not to have too fixed an aim. He can hardly know better than the nature and will to live of the patient. The great decisions in human life usually have far more to do with the instincts and other mysterious unconscious factors than with conscious will and well-meaning reasonableness. The shoe that fits one person pinches another; there is no universal recipe for living. Each of us carries his own life-form within him – an irrational form which no other can outbid.

All this naturally does not prevent us from doing our utmost to make the patient normal and reasonable. If the therapeutic results are satisfactory, we can probably let it go at that. If not, then for better or worse the therapist must be guided by the patient's own irrationalities. Here we must follow nature as a guide, and what the doctor then does is less a question of treatment than of developing the creative possibilities latent in the patient himself.

What I have to say begins where the treatment leaves off and this development sets in. Thus my contribution to psychotherapy confines itself to those cases where rational treatment does not yield satisfactory results. The clinical material at my disposal is of a peculiar composition: new cases are decidedly in the minority. Most of them already have some form of psychotherapeutic treatment behind them, with partial or negative results. About a third of my cases are not suffering from any clinically definable neurosis, but from the senselessness and aimlessness of their lives. I should not object if this were called the general neurosis of our age. Fully two thirds of my patients are in the second half of life.

This peculiar material sets up a special resistance to rational methods of treatment, probably because most of my patients are socially well-adapted individuals, often of outstanding ability, to whom normalization means nothing. As for so-called normal people, there I really am in a fix, for I have no ready-made philosophy of life to hand out to them. In the majority of my cases the resources of the conscious mind are exhausted (or, in ordinary English, they are "stuck"). It is chiefly this fact that forces me to look for hidden possibilities. For I do not know what to say to the patient when he asks me, "What do you advise? What shall I do?" I don't know either. I only know one thing: when my conscious mind no longer sees any possible road ahead and consequently gets stuck, my unconscious psyche will react to the unbearable standstill.

This further development of personality was named by Jung "the process of individuation." It is the central concept of his psychology, and his major original contribution.

"Conscious, Unconscious, and Individuation" CW 9 i, pars. 489–524

The relation between the conscious and the unconscious on the one hand, and the individuation process on the other, are problems that arise almost regularly during the later stages of analytical treatment. By "analytical" I mean a procedure that takes account of the existence of the unconscious. These problems do not arise in a procedure based on suggestion. A few preliminary words may not be out of place in order to explain what is meant by "individuation."

I use the term "individuation" to denote the process by which a person becomes a psychological "in-dividual," that is, a separate, indivisible unity or "whole."* It is generally assumed that consciousness is the whole of the psychological individual. But knowledge of the phenomena that can only be explained on the hypothesis of unconscious psychic processes makes it doubtful whether the ego and its contents are in fact identical with the "whole." If unconscious processes exist at all, they must surely belong to the totality of the individual, even though they are not components of the conscious ego. If they were part of the ego they would necessarily be conscious, because everything that is directly related to the ego is conscious. Consciousness can even be equated with the relation between the ego and the psychic contents. But unconscious phenomena are so little related to the ego that most people do not hesitate to deny their existence outright. Nevertheless, they manifest themselves in an individual's behaviour. An attentive observer can detect them without difficulty, while the

*Modern physicists (Louis de Broglie, for instance) use instead of this the concept of something "discontinuous."

observed person remains quite unaware of the fact that he is betraying his most secret thoughts or even things he has never thought consciously. It is, however, a great prejudice to suppose that something we have never thought consciously does not exist in the psyche. There is plenty of evidence to show that consciousness is very far from covering the psyche in its totality. Many things occur semiconsciously, and a great many more remain entirely unconscious. Thorough investigation of the phenomena of dual and multiple personalities, for instance, has brought to light a mass of material with observations to prove this point. (I would refer the reader to the writings of Pierre Janet, Théodore Flournoy, Morton Prince, and others.)

The importance of such phenomena has made a deep impression on medical psychology, because they give rise to all sorts of psychic and physiological symptoms. In these circumstances, the assumption that the ego expresses the totality of the psyche has become untenable. It is, on the contrary, evident that the whole must necessarily include not only consciousness but the illimitable field of unconscious occurrences as well, and that the ego can be no more than the centre of the field of consciousness.

You will naturally ask whether the unconscious possesses a centre too. I would hardly venture to assume that there is in the unconscious a ruling principle analogous to the ego. As a matter of fact, everything points to the contrary. If there were such a centre, we could expect almost regular signs of its existence. Cases of dual personality would then be frequent occurrences instead of rare curiosities. As a rule, unconscious phenomena manifest themselves in fairly chaotic and unsystematic form. Dreams, for instance, show no apparent order and no tendency to systematization, as they would have to do if there were a personal consciousness at the back of them. The philosophers Carus and von Hartmann treat the unconscious as a metaphysical principle, a sort of universal mind, without any trace of personality or ego-consciousness, and similarly Schopenhauer's "Will" is without an ego. Modern psychologists, too, regard the unconscious as an egoless function below the threshold of consciousness. Unlike the philosophers, they tend to derive its subliminal functions from the conscious mind. Janet thinks that there is a certain weakness of consciousness which is unable to hold all the psychic processes together. Freud, on the other hand, favours the idea of conscious factors that suppress certain incompatible tendencies. Much can be said for both theories, since there are numerous cases where a weakness of consciousness actually causes certain contents to fall below the threshold, or where disagreeable contents are repressed. It is obvious that such careful observers as Janet and Freud would not have constructed theories deriving the unconscious mainly from conscious sources had they been able to discover traces of an independent personality or of an autonomous will in the manifestations of the unconscious.

If it were true that the unconscious consists of nothing but contents accidentally deprived of consciousness but otherwise indistinguishable from the conscious material, then one could identify the ego more or less with the totality of the psyche. But actually the situation is not quite so simple. Both theories are based mainly on observations in the field of neurosis. Neither Janet nor Freud had any specifically psychiatric experience. If they had, they would surely have been struck by the fact that the unconscious displays contents that are utterly different from conscious ones, so strange, indeed, that nobody can understand them, neither the patient himself nor his doctors. The patient is inundated by a flood of thoughts that are as strange to him as they are to a normal person. That is why we call him "crazy": we cannot understand his ideas. We understand something only if we have the necessary premises for doing so. But here the premises are just as remote from our consciousness as they were from the mind of the patient before he went mad. Otherwise he would never have become insane.

There is, in fact, no field directly known to us from which we could derive certain pathological ideas. It is not a question of more or less normal contents that became unconscious just by accident. They are, on the contrary, products whose nature is at first completely baffling. They differ in every respect from neurotic material, which cannot be said to be at all bizarre. The material of a neurosis is understandable in human terms, but that of a psychosis is not.*

*By this I mean only certain cases of schizophrenia, such as the famous Schreber case (*Memoirs of My Nervous Illness*) or the case published by Nelken ("Analytische Beobachtungen über Phantasien eines Schizophrenen," 1912).

This peculiar psychotic material cannot be derived from the conscious mind, because the latter lacks the premises which would help to explain the strangeness of the ideas. Neurotic contents can be integrated without appreciable injury to the ego, but psychotic ideas cannot. They remain inaccessible, and ego-consciousness is more or less swamped by them. They even show a distinct tendency to draw the ego into their "system."

Such cases indicate that under certain conditions the unconscious is capable of taking over the role of the ego. The consequence of this exchange is insanity and confusion, because the unconscious is not a second personality with organized and centralized functions but in all probability a decentralized congeries of psychic processes. However, nothing produced by the human mind lies absolutely outside the psychic realm. Even the craziest idea must correspond to something in the psyche. We cannot suppose that certain minds contain elements that do not exist at all in other minds. Nor can we assume that the unconscious is capable of becoming autonomous only in certain people, namely in those predisposed to insanity. It is very much more likely that the tendency to autonomy is a more or less general peculiarity of the unconscious. Mental disorder is, in a sense, only one outstanding example of a hidden but none the less general condition. This tendency to autonomy shows itself above all in affective states, including those of normal people. When in a state of violent affect one says or does things which exceed the ordinary. Not much is needed: love and hate, joy and grief, are often enough to make the ego and the unconscious change places. Very strange ideas indeed can take possession of otherwise healthy people on such occasions. Groups, communities, and even whole nations can be seized in this way by psychic epidemics.

The autonomy of the unconscious therefore begins where emotions are generated. Emotions are instinctive, involuntary reactions which upset the rational order of consciousness by their elemental outbursts. Affects are not "made" or wilfully produced; they simply happen. In a state of affect a trait of character sometimes appears which is strange even to the person concerned, or hidden contents may irrupt involuntarily. The more violent an affect the closer it comes to the pathological, to a condition in which the ego-consciousness is thrust aside by autonomous contents that were unconscious before. So long as the unconscious is in a dormant condition, it seems as if there were absolutely nothing in this hidden region. Hence we are continually surprised when something unknown suddenly appears "from nowhere." Afterwards, of course, the psychologist comes along and shows that things had to happen as they did for this or that reason. But who could have said so beforehand?

We call the unconscious "nothing," and yet it is a reality *in potentia*. The thought we shall think, the deed we shall do, even the fate we shall lament tomorrow, all lie unconscious in our today. The unknown in us which the affect uncovers was always there and sooner or later would have presented itself to consciousness. Hence we must always reckon with the presence of things not yet discovered. These, as I have said, may be unknown quirks of character. But possibilities of future development may also come to light in this way, perhaps in just such an outburst of affect which sometimes radically alters the whole situation. The unconscious has a Janus-face: on one side its contents point back to a preconscious, prehistoric world of instinct, while on the other side it potentially anticipates the future – precisely because of the instinctive readiness for action of the factors that determine man's fate. If we had complete knowledge of the ground plan lying dormant in an individual from the beginning, his fate would be in large measure predictable.

Now, to the extent that unconscious tendencies – be they backward-looking images or forward-looking anticipations – appear in dreams, dreams have been regarded, in all previous ages, less as historical regressions than as anticipations of the future, and rightly so. For everything that will be happens on the basis of what has been, and of what – consciously or unconsciously – still exists as a memory-trace. In so far as no man is born totally new, but continually repeats the stage of development last reached by the species, he contains unconsciously, as an *a priori* datum, the entire psychic structure developed both upwards and downwards by his ancestors in the course of the ages. That is what gives the unconscious its characteristic "historical" aspect, but it is at the same time the *sine qua non* for shaping the future. For this reason it is often very difficult to decide whether an autonomous manifestation of the unconscious should be interpreted as an *effect* (and therefore historical) or as an *aim* (and therefore teleological and anticipatory). The conscious mind thinks as a rule without regard to ancestral preconditions and without taking into account the influence this *a priori* factor has on the shaping of the individual's fate. Whereas we think in periods of years, the unconscious thinks and lives in terms of millennia. So when something happens that seems to us an unexampled novelty, it is generally a very old story indeed. We still forget, like children, what happened yesterday. We are still living in a wonderful new world where man thinks himself astonishingly new and "modern." This is unmistakable proof of the youthfulness of human consciousness, which has not yet grown aware of its historical antecedents.

As a matter of fact, the "normal" person convinces me far more of the autonomy of the unconscious than does the insane person. Psychiatric theory can always take refuge behind real or alleged organic disorders of the brain and thus detract from the importance of the unconscious. But such a view is no longer applicable when it comes to normal humanity. What one sees happening in the world is not just a "shadowy vestige of activities that were once conscious," but the expression of a living psychic condition that still exists and always will exist. Were that not so, one might well be astonished. But it is precisely those who give least credence to the autonomy of the unconscious who are the most surprised by it. Because of its youthfulness and vulnerability, our consciousness tends to make light of the unconscious. This is understandable enough, for a young man should not let himself be overawed by the authority of his parents if he wants to start something on his own account. Historically as well as individually, our consciousness has developed out of the darkness and somnolence of primordial unconsciousness. There were psychic processes and functions long before any ego-consciousness existed. "Thinking" existed long before man was able to say: "I am conscious of thinking."

The primitive "perils of the soul" consist mainly of dangers to consciousness. Fascination, bewitchment, "loss of soul," possession, etc. are obviously phenomena of the dissociation and suppression of consciousness caused by unconscious contents. Even civilized man is not yet entirely free of the darkness of primeval times. The unconscious is the mother of consciousness. Where there is a mother there is also a father, yet he seems to be unknown. Consciousness, in the pride of its youth, may deny its father, but it cannot deny its mother. That would be too unnatural, for one can see in every child how hesitantly and slowly its ego-consciousness evolves out of a fragmentary consciousness lasting for single moments only, and how these islands gradually emerge from the total darkness of mere instinctuality.

Consciousness grows out of an unconscious psyche which is older than it, and which goes on functioning together with it or even in spite of it. Although there are numerous cases of conscious contents becoming unconscious again (through being repressed, for instance), the unconscious as a whole is far from being a mere remnant of consciousness. Or are the psychic functions of animals remnants of consciousness?

As I have said, there is little hope of our finding in the unconscious an order equivalent to that of the ego. It certainly does not look as if we were likely to discover an unconscious ego-personality, something in the nature of a Pythagorean "counter-earth." Nevertheless, we cannot overlook the fact that, just as consciousness arises from the unconscious, the ego-centre, too, crystallizes out of a dark depth in which it was somehow contained *in potentia*. Just as a human mother can only produce a human child, whose deepest nature lay hidden during its potential existence within her, so we are practically compelled to believe that the unconscious cannot be an entirely chaotic accumulation of instincts and images. There must be something to hold it together and give expression to the whole. Its centre cannot possibly be the ego, since the ego was born out of it into consciousness and turns its back on the unconscious, seeking to shut it out as much as possible. Or can it be that the unconscious loses its centre with the birth of the ego? In that case we would expect the ego to be far superior to the unconscious in influence and importance. The unconscious would then follow meekly in the footsteps of the conscious, and that would be just what we wish.

Unfortunately, the facts show the exact opposite: consciousness succumbs all too easily to unconscious influences, and these are often truer and wiser than our conscious thinking. Also, it frequently happens that unconscious motives overrule our conscious decisions, especially in matters of vital importance. Indeed, the fate of the individual is largely dependent on unconscious factors. Careful investigation shows how very much our conscious decisions depend on the undisturbed functioning of memory. But memory often suffers from the disturbing interference of unconscious contents. Moreover, it functions as a rule automatically. Ordinarily it uses the bridges of association, but often in such an extraordinary way that another thorough investigation of the whole process of memory-reproduction is needed in order to find out how certain memories managed to reach consciousness at all. And sometimes these bridges cannot be found. In such cases it is impossible to dismiss the hypothesis of the spontaneous activity of the unconscious. Another example is intuition, which is chiefly dependent on unconscious processes of a very complex nature. Because of this peculiarity, I have defined intuition as "perception via the unconscious."

Normally the unconscious collaborates with the conscious without friction or disturbance, so that one is not even aware of its existence. But when an individual or a social group deviates too far from their instinctual foundations, they then experience the full impact of unconscious forces. The collaboration of the unconscious is intelligent and purposive, and even when it acts in opposition to consciousness its expression is still compensatory in an intelligent way, as if it were trying to restore the lost balance.

There are dreams and visions of such an impressive character that some people refuse to admit that they could have originated in an unconscious psyche. They prefer to assume that such phenomena derive from a sort of "superconsciousness." Such people make a distinction between a quasi-physiological or instinctive unconscious and a psychic sphere or layer "above" consciousness, which they style the "superconscious." As a matter of fact, this psyche, which in Indian philosophy is called the "higher" consciousness, corresponds to what we in the West call the "unconscious." Certain dreams, visions, and mystical experiences do, however, suggest the existence of a consciousness in the unconscious. But, if we assume a consciousness in the unconscious, we are at once faced with the difficulty that no consciousness can exist without a subject, that is, an ego to which the contents are related. Consciousness needs a centre, an ego to which nething is conscious. We know of no other kind of consciousness, nor can we imagine a consciousness without an ego. There can be no consciousness when there is no one to say: "*I* am conscious."

It is unprofitable to speculate about things we cannot know. I therefore refrain from making assertions that go beyond the bounds of science. It was never possible for me to discover in the unconscious anything like a personality comparable with the ego. But although a "second ego" cannot be discovered (except in the rare cases of dual personality), the manifestations of the unconscious do at least show *traces of personalities*. A simple example is the dream, where a number of real or imaginary people represent the dream-thoughts. In nearly all the important types of dissociation, the manifestations of the unconscious assume a strikingly personal form. Careful examination of the behaviour and mental content of these personifications, however, reveals their fragmentary character. They seem to represent complexes that have split off from a greater whole, and are the very reverse of a personal centre of the unconscious.

I have always been greatly impressed by the character of dissociated fragments as personalities. Hence I have often asked myself whether we are not justified in assuming that, if such fragments have personality, the whole from which they were broken off must have personality to an even higher degree. The inference seemed logical, since it does not depend on whether the fragments are large or small. Why, then, should not the whole have personality too? *Personality need not imply consciousness. It can just as easily be dormant or dreaming.*

The general aspect of unconscious manifestations is in the main chaotic and irrational, despite certain symptoms of intelligence and purposiveness. The unconscious produces dreams, visions, fantasies, emotions, grotesque ideas, and so forth. This is exactly what we would expect a dreaming personality to do. It seems to be a personality that was never awake and was never conscious of the life it had lived and of its own continuity. The only question is whether the hypothesis of a dormant and hidden personality is possible or not. It may be that all of the personality to be found in the unconscious is contained in the fragmentary personifications mentioned before. Since this is very possible, all my conjectures would be in vain – unless there were evidence of much less fragmentary and more complete personalities, even though they are hidden.

I am convinced that such evidence exists. Unfortunately, the material to prove this belongs to the subtleties of psychological analysis. It is therefore not exactly easy to give the reader a simple and convincing idea of it.

I shall begin with a brief statement: in the unconscious of every man there is hidden a feminine personality, and in that of every woman a masculine personality.

It is a well-known fact that sex is determined by a majority of male or female genes, as the case may be. But the minority of genes belonging to the other sex does not simply disappear. A man therefore has in him a feminine side, an unconscious feminine figure – a fact of which he is generally quite unaware. I may take it as known that I have called this figure the "anima," and its counterpart in a woman the "animus." In order not to repeat myself, I must refer the reader to the literature.* This figure frequently appears in dreams, where one can observe all the attributes I have mentioned in earlier publications.

Another, no less important and clearly defined figure is the "shadow." Like the anima, it appears either in projection on suitable persons, or personified as such in dreams. The shadow coincides with the "personal" unconscious (which corresponds to Freud's conception of the unconscious). Again like the anima, this figure has often been portrayed by poets and writers. I would mention the Faust-Mephistopheles relationship and E. T. A. Hoffmann's tale *The Devil's Elixir* as two especially typical descriptions. The shadow personifies everything that the subject refuses to acknowledge about himself and yet is always thrusting itself upon him directly or indirectly – for instance, inferior traits of character and other incompatible tendencies.

The fact that the unconscious spontaneously personifies certain affectively toned contents in dreams is the reason why I have taken over these personifications in my terminology and formulated them as names.

*Psychological Types, Def. "soul" (CW 6); "The Relations between the Ego and the Unconscious," Part II, ch. 2 (CW 7); Psychology and Alchemy, Part II (CW 12). Cf. also "Concerning the Archetypes . . ." (CW 9 i).

Besides these figures there are still a few others, less frequent and less striking, which have likewise undergone poetic as well as mythological formulation. I would mention, for instance, the figure of the hero* and of the wise old man,† to name only two of the best known.

All these figures irrupt autonomously into consciousness as soon as it gets into a pathological state. With regard to the anima, I would particularly like to draw attention to the case described by Nelken.** Now the remarkable thing is that these figures show the most striking connections with the poetic, religious, or mythological formulations, though these connections are in no way factual. That is to say, they are spontaneous products of analogy. One such case even led to the charge of plagiarism: the French writer Benoît gave a description of the anima and her classic myth in his book *L'Atlantide*, which is an exact parallel of Rider Haggard's *She*. The lawsuit proved unsuccessful; Benoît had never heard of *She*. (It might, in the last analysis, have been an instance of cryptomnesic deception, which is often extremely difficult to rule out.) The distinctly "historical" aspect of the anima and her condensation with the figures of the sister, wife, mother, and daughter, plus the associated incest motif, can be found in Goethe ("You were in times gone by my wife or sister"), as well as in the anima figure of the *regina* and *femina alba* in alchemy. The English alchemist Eirenaeus Philalethes ("lover of truth"), writing about 1645, remarks that the "Queen" was the King's "sister, mother, or wife."†† The same idea can be found, ornately elaborated, in Nelken's patient and in a whole series of cases observed by me, where I was able to rule out with certainty any possibility of literary influence. For the rest, the anima complex is one of the oldest features of Latin alchemy.

When one studies the archetypal personalities and their behaviour with the help of the dreams, fantasies, and delusions of patients,*** one is profoundly impressed by their manifold and unmistakable connections with mythological ideas completely

---

Symbols of Transformation, Part II (CW 5).
†Cf. "The Phenomenology of the Spirit in Fairytales" (CW 9 i).
**See note [page 214] above.
††*Ripley Reviv'd; or, An Exposition upon Sir George Ripley's Hermetico-Poetical Works* (1678), trans. into German in 1741 and possibly known to Goethe.
***For an example of the method, see *Psychology and Alchemy*, Part II (CW 12).

unknown to the layman. They form a species of singular beings whom one would like to endow with ego-consciousness; indeed, they almost seem capable of it. And yet this idea is not borne out by the facts. There is nothing in their behaviour to suggest that they have an ego-consciousness as we know it. They show, on the contrary, all the marks of fragmentary personalities. They are masklike, wraithlike, without problems, lacking self-reflection, with no conflicts, no doubts, no sufferings; like gods, perhaps, who have no philosophy, such as the Brahma-gods of the *Samyutta-nikāya*, whose erroneous views needed correction by the Buddha. Unlike other contents, they always remain strangers in the world of consciousness, unwelcome intruders saturating the atmosphere with uncanny forebodings or even with the fear of madness.

If we examine their content, i.e., the fantasy material constituting their phenomenology, we find countless archaic and "historical" associations and images of an archetypal nature.* This peculiar fact permits us to draw conclusions about the "localization" of anima and animus in the psychic structure. They evidently live and function in the deeper layers of the unconscious, especially in that phylogenetic substratum which I have called the collective unconscious. This localization explains a good deal of their strangeness: they bring into our ephemeral consciousness an unknown psychic life belonging to a remote past. It is the mind of our unknown ancestors, their way of thinking and feeling, their way of experiencing life and the world, gods and men. The existence of these archaic strata is presumably the source of man's belief in reincarnations and in memories of "previous existences." Just as the human body is a museum, so to speak, of its phylogenetic history, so too is the psyche. We have no reason to suppose that the specific structure of the psyche is the only thing in the world that has no history outside its individual manifestations. Even the conscious mind cannot be denied a history reaching back at least five thousand years. It is only our ego-consciousness that has forever a new beginning and an early

---

*In my *Symbols of Transformation*, I have described the case of a young woman with a "hero-story," i.e., an animus fantasy that yielded a rich harvest of mythological material. Rider Haggard, Benoît, and Goethe (in *Faust*) have all stressed the historical character of the anima.

end. The unconscious psyche is not only immensely old, it is also capable of growing into an equally remote future. It moulds the human species and is just as much a part of it as the human body, which, though ephemeral in the individual, is collectively of immense age.

The anima and animus live in a world quite different from the world outside – in a world where the pulse of time beats infinitely slowly, where the birth and death of individuals count for little. No wonder their nature is strange, so strange that their irruption into consciousness often amounts to a psychosis. They undoubtedly belong to the material that comes to light in schizophrenia.

What I have said about the collective unconscious may give you a more or less adequate idea of what I mean by this term. If we now turn back to the problem of individuation, we shall see ourselves faced with a rather extraordinary task: the psyche consists of two incongruous halves which together should form a whole. One is inclined to think that ego-consciousness is capable of assimilating the unconscious, at least one hopes that such a solution is possible. But unfortunately the unconscious really is unconscious; in other words, it is unknown. And how can you assimilate something unknown? Even if you can form a fairly complete picture of the anima and animus, this does not mean that you have plumbed the depths of the unconscious. One hopes to control the unconscious, but the past masters in the art of self-control, the yogis, attain perfection in *samādhi*, a state of ecstasy, which so far as we know is equivalent to a state of unconsciousness. It makes no difference whether they call our unconscious a "universal consciousness"; the fact remains that in their case the unconscious has swallowed up ego-consciousness. They do not realize that a "universal consciousness" is a contradiction in terms, since exclusion, selection, and discrimination are the root and essence of everything that lays claim to the name "consciousness." "Universal consciousness" is logically identical with unconsciousness. It is nevertheless true that a correct application of the methods described in the Pāli Canon or in the *Yoga-sūtra* induces a remarkable extension of consciousness. But, with increasing extension, the contents of consciousness lose in clarity of detail. In the end, consciousness becomes all-embracing, but nebulous; an infinite number of things merge into an indefinite whole, a state in which subject and object are almost completely identical. This is all very beautiful, but scarcely to be recommended anywhere north of the Tropic of Cancer.

For this reason we must look for a different solution. We believe in ego-consciousness and in what we call reality. The realities of a northern climate are somehow so convincing that we feel very much better off when we do not forget them. For us it makes sense to concern ourselves with reality. Our European ego-consciousness is therefore inclined to swallow up the unconscious, and if this should not prove feasible we try to suppress it. But if we understand anything of the unconscious, we know that it cannot be swallowed. We also know that it is dangerous to suppress it, because the unconscious is life and this life turns against us if suppressed, as happens in neurosis.

Conscious and unconscious do not make a whole when one of them is suppressed and injured by the other. If they must contend, let it at least be a fair fight with equal rights on both sides. Both are aspects of life. Consciousness should defend its reason and protect itself, and the chaotic life of the unconscious should be given the chance of having its way too – as much of it as we can stand. This means open conflict and open collaboration at once. That, evidently, is the way human life should be. It is the old game of hammer and anvil: between them the patient iron is forged into an indestructible whole, an "individual."

This, roughly, is what I mean by the individuation process. As the name shows, it is a process or course of development arising out of the conflict between the two fundamental psychic facts. I have described the problems of this conflict, at least in their essentials, in my essay "The Relations between the Ego and the Unconscious." A special chapter, however, is the *symbolism* of the process, which is of the utmost importance for understanding the final stages of the encounter between conscious and unconscious, in practice as well as in theory. My investigations during these last years have been devoted mainly to this theme. It turned out, to my own great astonishment, that the symbol formation has the closest affinities with alchemical ideas, and especially with the conceptions of the "uniting symbol," which yield highly significant parallels. Naturally these are processes which have no meaning in the initial stages of psychological treatment. On the other hand, more difficult cases, such as cases of unresolved transference, develop these symbols. Knowledge of them is of inestimable importance in treating cases of this kind, especially when dealing with cultured patients.

How the harmonizing of conscious and unconscious data is to be undertaken cannot be indicated in the form of a recipe. It is an irrational life-process which expresses itself in definite symbols. It may be the task of the analyst to stand by this process with all the help he can give. In this case, knowledge of the symbols is indispensable, for it is in them that the union of conscious and unconscious contents is consummated. Out of this union emerge new situations and new conscious attitudes. I have therefore called the union of opposites the "transcendent function." This rounding out of the personality into a whole may well be the goal of any psychotherapy that claims to be more than a mere cure of symptoms.

In his commentary on The Secret of the Golden Flower,* *the ancient Taoist text which first aroused Jung's interest in alchemy, Jung points out that the process of individuation is a path followed by the few rather than by the many.*

From "**Commentary on *The Secret of the Golden Flower*"** CW 13, pars. 16–18

It would also be a great mistake to suppose that this is the path every neurotic must travel, or that it is the solution at every stage of the neurotic problem. It is appropriate only in those cases where consciousness has reached an abnormal degree of development and has diverged too far from the unconscious. This is the *sine qua non* of the process. Nothing would be more wrong than to open this way to neurotics who are ill on account of an excessive pre-dominance of the unconscious. For the same reason, this way of development has scarcely any meaning before the middle of life

Richard Wilhelm and C. G. Jung, The Secret of the Golden Flower: a Chinese Book of Life, tr. Cary F. Baynes, London and New York: new edition, 1962.

(normally between the ages of thirty-five and forty), and if entered upon too soon can be decidedly injurious.

As I have said, the essential reason which prompted me to look for a new way was the fact that the fundamental problem of the patient seemed to me insoluble unless violence was done to one or the other side of his nature. I had always worked with the temperamental conviction that at bottom there are no insoluble problems, and experience justified me in so far as I have often seen patients simply outgrow a problem that had destroyed others. This "outgrowing," as I formerly called it, proved on further investigation to be a new level of consciousness. Some higher or wider interest appeared on the patient's horizon, and through this broadening of his outlook the insoluble problem lost its urgency. It was not solved logically in its own terms, but faded out when confronted with a new and stronger life urge. It was not repressed and made unconscious, but merely appeared in a different light, and so really did become different. What, on a lower level, had led to the wildest conflicts and to panicky outbursts of emotion, from the higher level of personality now looked like a storm in the valley seen from the mountain top. This does not mean that the storm is robbed of its reality, but instead of being in it one is above it. But since, in a psychic sense, we are both valley and mountain, it might seem a vain illusion to deem oneself beyond what is human. One certainly does feel the affect and is shaken and tormented by it, yet at the same time one is aware of a higher consciousness looking on which prevents one from becoming identical with the affect, a consciousness which regards the affect as an object, and can say, "I *know* that I suffer." What our text says of indolence, "Indolence of which a man is conscious, and indolence of which he is unconscious, are a thousand miles apart," holds true in the highest degree of affect.

Now and then it happened in my practice that a patient grew beyond himself because of unknown potentialities, and this became an experience of prime importance to me. In the meantime, I had learned that all the greatest and most important problems of life are fundamentally insoluble. They must be so, for they express the necessary polarity inherent in every self-regulating system. They can never be solved, but only outgrown. I therefore asked myself whether this outgrowing, this possibility of further psychic development, was not the normal thing, and whether getting stuck in a conflict was pathological. Everyone must possess that higher level, at least in embryonic form, and must under favourable circumstances be able to develop this potentiality. When I examined the course of development in patients who quietly, and as if unconsciously, outgrew themselves, I saw that their fates had something in common. The new thing came to them from obscure possibilities either outside or inside themselves; they accepted it and grew with its help. It seemed to me typical that some took the new thing from outside themselves, others from inside; or rather, that it grew into some persons from without, and into others from within. But the new thing never came exclusively either from within or from without. If it came from outside, it became a profound inner experience; if it came from inside, it became an outer happening. In no case was it conjured into existence intentionally or by conscious willing, but rather seemed to be borne along on the stream of time.

Part 7. Integration, Wholeness, and the Self

The goal toward which the individuation process is tending is "Wholeness" or "Integration": a condition in which all the different elements of the psyche, both conscious and unconscious, are welded together. The person who achieves this goal possesses "an attitude that is beyond the reach of emotional entanglements and violent shocks – a consciousness detached from the world." (CW 13, par. 68)

Individuation, in Jung's view, is a spiritual journey; and the person embarking upon it, although he might not subscribe to any recognized creed, was nonetheless pursuing a religious quest.

By paying careful attention to the unconscious, as manifested in dream and fantasy, the individual comes to change his attitude from one in which ego and will are paramount to one in which he acknowledges that he is guided by an integrating factor which is not of his own making.

This integrating factor, expressed by the emergence of quaternity or mandala symbols, is named the Self; an archetype which not only signifies union between the opposites within the psyche, but "is a God-image, or at least cannot be distinguished from one." (CW 9 ii, par. 42) Jung states:

> Unity and totality stand at the highest point on the scale of objective values because their symbols can no longer be distinguished from the *imago Dei*. Hence all statements about the God-image apply also to the empirical symbols of totality. [CW 9 ii, par. 42]

If we turn to Jung's autobiography, we find that, as he began to emerge from his period of "confrontation with the unconscious," he went through a period of drawing mandalas.

From "**Confrontation with the Unconscious**" MDR, pp. 186–9/195–7

It was only towards the end of the First World War that I gradually began to emerge from the darkness. Two events contributed to this. The first was that I broke with the woman who was determined to convince me that my fantasies had artistic value; the second and principal event was that I began to understand mandala drawings. This happened in 1918–19. I had painted the first mandala in 1916 after writing the *Septem Sermones*: naturally I had not, then, understood it.

In 1918–19 I was in Château d'Oex as Commandant de la Région Anglaise des Internés de Guerre. While I was there I sketched every morning in a notebook a small circular drawing, a mandala, which seemed to correspond to my inner situation at the time. With the help of these drawings I could observe my psychic transformations from day to day. One day, for example, I received a letter from that aesthetic lady in which she again stubbornly maintained that the fantasies arising from my unconscious had artistic value and should be considered art. The letter got on my nerves. It was far from stupid and therefore dangerously persuasive. The modern artist, after all, seeks to create art out of the unconscious. The utilitarianism and self-importance concealed behind this thesis touched a doubt in myself, namely, my uncertainty as to whether the fantasies I was producing were really spontaneous and natural, and not ultimately my own arbitrary inventions. I was by no means free from the bigotry and hubris of consciousness which wants to believe that any half-way decent inspiration is due to one's own merit, whereas inferior reactions come merely by chance, or even derive from alien sources. Out of this irritation and disharmony within myself there proceeded, the following day, a changed mandala: part of the periphery had burst open and the symmetry was destroyed.

Only gradually did I discover what the mandala really is: "Formation, Transformation, Eternal Mind's eternal recreation."* And that is the self, the wholeness of the personality, which if all goes well is harmonious, but which cannot tolerate self-deceptions.

---

*Goethe, *Faust*, Part Two, trans. by Philip Wayne (Penguin Classics, 1959), p. 79.

1. *Jung's first painting of a mandala, 1916*

2. *Mandala painting by Jung, 1927*

3. *Mandala painting by Jung, 1928*

My mandalas were cryptograms concerning the state of the self which were presented to me anew each day. In them I saw the self – that is, my whole being – actively at work. To be sure, at first I could only dimly understand them; but they seemed to me highly significant, and I guarded them like precious pearls. I had the distinct feeling that they were something central, and in time I acquired through them a living conception of the self. The self, I thought, was like the monad which I am, and which is my world. The mandala represents this monad, and corresponds to the microcosmic nature of the psyche.

I no longer know how many mandalas I drew at this time. There were a great many. While I was working on them, the question arose repeatedly: What is this process leading to? Where is its goal? From my own experience, I knew by now that I could not presume to choose a goal which would seem trustworthy to me. It had been proved to me that I had to abandon the idea of the superordinate position of the ego. After all, I had been brought up short when I had attempted to maintain it. I had wanted to go on with the scientific analysis of myths which I had begun in *Symbols of Transformation*. That was still my goal – but I must not think of that! I was being compelled to go through this process of the unconscious. I had to let myself be carried along by the current, without a notion of where it would lead me. When I began drawing the mandalas, however, I saw that everything, all the paths I had been following, all the steps I had taken, were leading back to a single point – namely, to the mid-point. It became increasingly plain to me that the mandala is the centre. It is the exponent of all paths. It is the path to the centre, to individuation.

During those years, between 1918 and 1920, I began to understand that the goal of psychic development is the self. There is no linear evolution; there is only a circumambulation of the self. Uniform development exists, at most, only at the beginning; later, everything points towards the centre. This insight gave me stability, and gradually my inner peace returned. I knew that in finding the mandala as an expression of the self I had attained what was for me the ultimate. Perhaps someone else knows more, but not I.

Some years later (in 1927) I obtained confirmation of my ideas about the centre and the self by way of a dream. I represented its essence in a mandala which I called "Window on Eternity." The picture is reproduced in *The Secret of the Golden Flower* (Fig. 3). A year later I painted a second picture, likewise a mandala, with a golden castle in the centre. When it was finished, I asked myself, "Why is this so Chinese?" I was impressed by the form and choice of colours, which seemed to me Chinese, although there was nothing outwardly Chinese about it. Yet that was how it affected me. It was a strange coincidence that shortly afterwards I received a letter from Richard Wilhelm enclosing the manuscript of a Taoist-alchemical treatise entitled *The Secret of the Golden Flower*, with a request that I write a commentary on it. I devoured the manuscript at once, for the text gave me undreamed-of confirmation of my ideas about the mandala and the circumambulation of the centre. That was the first event which broke through my isolation. I became aware of an affinity; I could establish ties with something and someone.

In remembrance of this coincidence, this "synchronicity," I wrote underneath the picture which had made so Chinese an impression upon me: "In 1928, when I was painting this picture, showing the golden, well-fortified castle, Richard Wilhelm in Frankfurt sent me the thousand-year-old Chinese text on the yellow castle, the germ of the immortal body."

"Mandalas" CW 9 i, pars. 713–18

The Sanskrit word *mandala* means "circle" in the ordinary sense of the word. In the sphere of religious practices and in psychology it denotes circular images, which are drawn, painted, modelled, or danced. Plastic structures of this kind are to be found, for instance, in Tibetan Buddhism, and as dance figures these circular patterns occur also in Dervish monasteries. As psychological phenomena they appear spontaneously in dreams, in certain states of conflict, and in cases of schizophrenia. Very frequently they contain a quaternity or a multiple of four, in the form of a cross, a star, a square, an octagon, etc. In alchemy we encounter this motif in the form of the *quadratura circuli*.

In Tibetan Buddhism the figure has the significance of a ritual instrument (*yantra*), whose purpose is to assist meditation and

CELTIC
CROSS

concentration. Its meaning in alchemy is somewhat similar, inasmuch as it represents the synthesis of the four elements which are forever tending to fall apart. Its spontaneous occurrence in modern individuals enables psychological research to make a closer investigation into its functional meaning. As a rule a mandala occurs in conditions of psychic dissociation or disorientation, for instance in the case of children between the ages of eight and eleven whose parents are about to be divorced, or in adults who, as the result of a neurosis and its treatment, are confronted with the problem of opposites in human nature and are consequently disoriented; or again in schizophrenics whose view of the world has become confused, owing to the invasion of incomprehensible contents from the unconscious. In such cases it is easy to see how the severe pattern imposed by a circular image of this kind compensates the disorder and confusion of the psychic state – namely, through the construction of a central point to which everything is related, or by a concentric arrangement of the disordered multiplicity and of contradictory and irreconcilable elements. This is evidently an *attempt at self-healing* on the part of Nature, which does not spring from conscious reflection but from an instinctive impulse. Here, as comparative research has shown, a fundamental schema is made use of, an archetype which, so to speak, occurs everywhere and by no means owes its individual existence to tradition, any more than the instincts would need to be transmitted in that way. Instincts are given in the case of every newborn individual and belong to the inalienable stock of those qualities which characterize a species. What psychology designates as archetype is really a particular, frequently occurring, formal aspect of instinct, and is just as much an *a priori* factor as the latter. Therefore, despite external differences, we find a fundamental conformity in mandalas regardless of their origin in time and space.

The "squaring of the circle" is one of the many archetypal motifs which form the basic patterns of our dreams and fantasies. But it is distinguished by the fact that it is one of the most important of them from the functional point of view. Indeed, it could even be called the *archetype of wholeness*. Because of this significance, the "quaternity of the One" is the schema for all images of God, as depicted in the visions of Ezekiel, Daniel, and Enoch, and as the representation of Horus with his four sons also shows. The latter suggests an interesting differentiation, inasmuch as there are occasionally representations in which three of the sons have animals' heads and only one a human head, in keeping with the Old Testament visions as well as with the emblems of the seraphim which were transferred to the evangelists, and – last but not least – with the nature of the Gospels themselves: three of which are synoptic and one "Gnostic." Here I must add that, ever since the opening of Plato's *Timaeus* ("One, two, three . . . but where, my dear Socrates, is the fourth?") and right up to the Cabiri scene in *Faust*, the motif of four as three and one was the ever-recurring preoccupation of alchemy.

The profound significance of the quaternity with its singular process of differentiation extending over the centuries, and now manifest in the latest development of the Christian symbol,* may explain why *Du* chose just the archetype of wholeness as an example of symbol formation. For, just as this symbol claims a central position in the historical documents, individually too it has an outstanding significance. As is to be expected, individual mandalas display an enormous variety. The overwhelming majority are characterized by the circle and the quaternity. In a few, however, the three or the five predominates, for which there are usually special reasons.

Whereas ritual mandalas always display a definite style and a limited number of typical motifs as their content, individual mandalas make use of a well-nigh unlimited wealth of motifs and symbolic allusions, from which it can easily be seen that they are endeavouring to express either the totality of the individual in his inner or outer experience of the world, or its essential point of reference. Their object is the *self* in contradistinction to the *ego*, which is only the point of reference for consciousness, whereas the self comprises the totality of the psyche altogether, i.e., conscious *and* unconscious. It is therefore not unusual for individual mandalas to display a division into a light and a dark half, together with their typical symbols. An historical example of this kind is Jakob Böhme's mandala, in his treatise *Forty Questions concerning the Soul*. It is at the same time an image of God and is designated

---

*[Proclamation of the dogma of the Assumption of the Virgin, in 1950.]

as such. This is not a matter of chance, for Indian philosophy, which developed the idea of the self, Atman or Purusha, to the highest degree, makes no distinction in principle between the human essence and the divine. Correspondingly, in the Western mandala, the *scintilla* or soul-spark, the innermost divine essence of man, is characterized by symbols which can just as well express a God-image, namely the image of Deity unfolding in the world, in nature, and in man.

The fact that images of this kind have under certain circumstances a considerable therapeutic effect on their authors is empirically proved and also readily understandable, in that they often represent very bold attempts to see and put together apparently irreconcilable opposites and bridge over apparently hopeless splits. Even the mere attempt in this direction usually has a healing effect, but only when it is done spontaneously. Nothing can be expected from an artificial repetition or a deliberate imitation of such images.

As we saw earlier, Jung regarded the individuation process as a kind of religious quest. Jung thought that a religious attitude was natural to man, and that modern man who found himself unable to subscribe to one or other of the orthodox faiths was at risk of substituting something inferior like the worship of the State. "When the god is not acknowledged, egomania develops, and out of this mania comes sickness." (CW 13, par. 55) Above the door of his house, Jung had carved a sentence attributed to the Delphic Oracle (translated into Latin): "Vocatus atque non vocatus, deus aderit," that is, "Invoked or not invoked, the god will be present."

It is not a matter of indifference whether one calls something a "mania" or a "god." To serve a mania is detestable and undignified, but to serve a god is full of meaning and promise because it is an act of submission to a higher, invisible, and spiritual being. [CW 13, par. 55]

In the lectures which he gave at Yale in 1937, Jung defines what he means by "religion."

From *Psychology and Religion*, CW 11, pars. 6–9

In speaking of religion I must make clear from the start what I mean by that term. Religion, as the Latin word denotes, is a careful and scrupulous observation of what Rudolf Otto* aptly termed the *numinosum*, that is, a dynamic agency or effect not caused by an arbitrary act of will. On the contrary, it seizes and controls the human subject, who is always rather its victim than its creator. The *numinosum* – whatever its cause may be – is an experience of the subject independent of his will. At all events, religious teaching as well as the *consensus gentium* always and everywhere explain this experience as being due to a cause external to the individual. The *numinosum* is either a quality belonging to a visible object or the influence of an invisible presence that causes a peculiar alteration of consciousness. This is, at any rate, the general rule.

There are, however, certain exceptions when it comes to the question of religious practice or ritual. A great many ritualistic performances are carried out for the sole purpose of producing at will the effect of the *numinosum* by means of certain devices of a magical nature, such as invocation, incantation, sacrifice, meditation and other yoga practices, self-inflicted tortures of various descriptions, and so forth. But a religious belief in an external and objective divine cause is always prior to any such performance. The Catholic Church, for instance, administers the sacraments for the purpose of bestowing their spiritual blessings upon the believer; but since this act would amount to enforcing the presence of divine grace by an indubitably magical procedure, it is logically argued that nobody can compel divine grace to be present in the sacramental act, but that it is nevertheless inevitably present since the sacrament is a divine institution which God would not have caused to be if he had not intended to lend it his support.†

Religion appears to me to be a peculiar attitude of mind which could be formulated in accordance with the original use of the word

---

The Idea of the Holy, tr. John W. Harvey, Oxford: fourth impression 1926.
†*Gratia adiuvans* and *gratia sanctificans* are the effects of the *sacramentum ex opere operato*. The sacrament owes its undoubted efficacy to the fact that it is directly instituted by Christ himself. The Church is powerless to connect the rite with grace in such a way that the sacramental act would produce the presence and effect of grace. Consequently the rite performed by the priest is not a *causa instrumentalis*, but merely a *causa ministerialis*.

religio, which means a careful consideration and observation of certain dynamic factors that are conceived as "powers": spirits, daemons, gods, laws, ideas, ideals, or whatever name man has given to such factors in his world as he has found powerful, dangerous, or helpful enough to be taken into careful consideration, or grand, beautiful, and meaningful enough to be devoutly worshipped and loved. In colloquial speech one often says of somebody who is enthusiastically interested in a certain pursuit that he is almost "religiously devoted" to his cause; William James, for instance, remarks that a scientist often has no creed, but his "temper is devout."*

I want to make clear that by the term "religion"† I do not mean a creed. It is, however, true that every creed is originally based on the one hand upon πίστις, that is to say, trust or loyalty, the experience of the *numinosum* and on the other hand upon faith and confidence in a certain experience of a numinous nature and in the change of consciousness that ensues. The conversion of Paul is a striking example of this. We might say, then, that the term "religion" designates the attitude peculiar to a consciousness which has been changed by experience of the *numinosum.*

In part 2 of Psychology and Alchemy *Jung described a series of dreams dreamed by a young scientist who had no religious belief at the level of consciousness, but who was compelled by his experience in analysis to adopt a religious attitude. The series of dreams discussed ended with a mandala in the shape of a "world clock," to which Jung refers in the following passage.*

From *Psychology and Religion*, CW 11, pars. 138–49

If we allow ourselves to draw conclusions from modern mandalas we should ask people, first, whether they worship stars, suns, flowers, and snakes. They will deny this, and at the same

---

*"But our esteem for facts has not neutralized in us all religiousness. It is itself almost religious. Our scientific temper is devout." *Pragmatism,* London: Longmans, 1907, p. 14.
†"Religion is that which gives reverence and worship to some higher nature [which is called divine]." Cicero, *De inventione rhetorica,* II, 53, 161. For "testimony given under the sanction of religion on the faith of an oath" cf. Cicero, *Pro Coelio,* 55.

time they will assert that the globes, stars, crosses, and the like are symbols for a *centre in themselves*. And if asked what they mean by this centre, they will begin to stammer and to refer to this or that experience which may turn out to be something very similar to the confession of my patient, who found that the vision of his world clock had left him with a wonderful feeling of perfect harmony. Others will confess that a similar vision came to them in a moment of extreme pain or profound despair. To others again it is the memory of a sublime dream or of a moment when long and fruitless struggles came to an end and a reign of peace began. If you sum up what people tell you about their experiences, you can formulate it this way: They came to themselves, they could accept themselves, they were able to become reconciled to themselves, and thus were reconciled to adverse circumstances and events. This is almost like what used to be expressed by saying: He has made his peace with God, he has sacrificed his own will, he has submitted himself to the will of God.

A modern mandala is an involuntary confession of a peculiar mental condition. There is no deity in the mandala, nor is there any submission or reconciliation to a deity. The place of the deity seems to be taken by the wholeness of man.*

When one speaks of man, everybody means his own ego-personality – that is, his personality so far as he is conscious of it – and when one speaks of others one assumes that they have a very similar personality. But since modern research has acquainted us with the fact that individual consciousness is based on and surrounded by an indefinitely extended unconscious psyche, we must needs revise our somewhat old-fashioned prejudice that man is nothing but his consciousness. This naïve assumption must be confronted at once with the critical question: *Whose* consciousness? The fact is, it would be a difficult task to reconcile the picture I have of myself with the one which other people have of me. Who is right? And who is the real individual? If we go further and consider the fact that man is also what neither he himself nor other people know of him – an unknown something which can yet be proved to exist – the problem of identity becomes more difficult

*For the psychology of the mandala, see my commentary on *The Secret of the Golden Flower*.

still. Indeed, it is quite impossible to define the extent and the ultimate character of psychic existence. When we now speak of man we mean the indefinable whole of him, an ineffable totality, which can only be formulated symbolically. I have chosen the term "self" to designate the totality of man, the sum total of his conscious and unconscious contents.* I have chosen this term in accordance with Eastern philosophy, which for centuries has occupied itself with the problems that arise when even the gods cease to incarnate. The philosophy of the Upanishads corresponds to a psychology that long ago recognized the relativity of the gods.† This is not to be confused with a stupid error like atheism. The world is as it ever has been, but our consciousness undergoes peculiar changes. First, in remote times (which can still be observed among primitives living today), the main body of psychic life was apparently in human and in nonhuman objects: it was projected, as we should say now.** Consciousness can hardly exist in a state of complete projection. At most it would be a heap of emotions. Through the withdrawal of projections, conscious knowledge slowly developed. Science, curiously enough, began with the discovery of astronomical laws, and hence with the withdrawal, so to speak, of the most distant projections. This was the first stage in the despiritualization of the world. One step followed another: already in antiquity the gods were withdrawn from mountains and rivers, from trees and animals. Modern science has subtilized its projections to an almost unrecognizable degree, but our ordinary life still swarms with them. You can find them spread out in the newspapers, in books, rumours, and ordinary social gossip. All gaps in our actual knowledge are still filled out with projections. We are still so sure we know what other people think or what their true character is. We are convinced that certain people have all the bad qualities we do not know in ourselves or that they practise all those vices which could, of course, never be our own. We must still be exceedingly careful not to project our own shadows too shamelessly; we are still swamped with projected illusions. If you imagine someone who is brave

*See *Psychological Types*, Def. 51 (CW 6).
†Concerning the concept of the "relativity of God," see *Psychological Types* (CW 6), pars. 412ff.
**This fact accounts for the theory of animism.

enough to withdraw all these projections, then you get an individual who is conscious of a considerable shadow. Such a man has saddled himself with new problems and conflicts. He has become a serious problem to himself, as he is now unable to say that *they* do this or that, *they* are wrong, and *they* must be fought against. He lives in the "House of the Gathering." Such a man knows that whatever is wrong in the world is in himself, and if he only learns to deal with his own shadow he has done something real for the world. He has succeeded in shouldering at least an infinitesimal part of the gigantic, unsolved social problems of our day. These problems are mostly so difficult because they are poisoned by mutual projections. How can anyone see straight when he does not even see himself and the darkness he unconsciously carries with him into all his dealings?

Modern psychological development leads to a much better understanding as to what man really consists of. The gods at first lived in superhuman power and beauty on the top of snow-clad mountains or in the darkness of caves, woods, and seas. Later on they drew together into one god, and then that god became man. But in our day even the God-man seems to have descended from his throne and to be dissolving himself in the common man. That is probably why his seat is empty. Instead, the common man suffers from a hybris of consciousness that borders on the pathological. This psychic condition in the individual corresponds by and large to the hypertrophy and totalitarian pretensions of the idealized State. In the same way that the State has caught the individual, the individual imagines that he has caught the psyche and holds her in the hollow of his hand. He is even making a science of her in the absurd supposition that the intellect, which is but a part and a function of the psyche, is sufficient to comprehend the much greater whole. In reality the psyche is the mother and the maker, the subject and even the possibility of consciousness itself. It reaches so far beyond the boundaries of consciousness that the latter could easily be compared to an island in the ocean. Whereas the island is small and narrow, the ocean is immensely wide and deep and contains a life infinitely surpassing, in kind and degree, anything known on the island – so that if it is a question of space, it does not matter whether the gods are "inside" or "outside." It might be objected that there is no proof that consciousness is nothing more than an island in the ocean. Certainly it is impossible to prove this, since the known range of consciousness is confronted with the unknown extension of the unconscious, of which we only know that it exists and by the very fact of its existence exerts a limiting influence on consciousness and its freedom. Wherever unconsciousness reigns, there is bondage and possession. The immensity of the ocean is simply a comparison; it expresses in allegorical form the capacity of the unconscious to limit and threaten consciousness. Empirical psychology loved, until recently, to explain the "unconscious" as mere absence of consciousness – the term itself indicates as much – just as shadow is an absence of light. Today accurate observation of unconscious processes has recognized, with all other ages before us, that the unconscious possesses a creative autonomy such as a mere shadow could never be endowed with. When Carus, von Hartmann and, in a sense, Schopenhauer equated the unconscious with the world-creating principle, they were only summing up all those teachings of the past which, grounded in inner experience, saw the mysterious agent personified as the gods. It suits our hypertrophied and hybristic modern consciousness not to be mindful of the dangerous autonomy of the unconscious and to treat it negatively as an absence of consciousness. The hypothesis of invisible gods or daemons would be, psychologically, a far more appropriate formulation, even though it would be an anthropomorphic projection. But since the development of consciousness requires the withdrawal of all the projections we can lay our hands on, it is not possible to maintain any non-psychological doctrine about the gods. If the historical process of world despiritualization continues as hitherto, then everything of a divine or daemonic character outside us must return to the psyche, to the inside of the unknown man, whence it apparently originated.

The materialistic error was probably unavoidable at first. Since the throne of God could not be discovered among the galactic systems, the inference was that God had never existed. The second unavoidable error is psychologism: if God is anything, he must be an illusion derived from certain motives – from will to power, for instance, or from repressed sexuality. These arguments are not new. Much the same thing was said by the Christian missionaries who overthrew the idols of heathen gods. But whereas the early missionaries were conscious of serving a new God by combating the old ones, modern iconoclasts are unconscious of the one in whose name they are destroying old values. Nietzsche thought himself quite conscious and responsible when he smashed the old tablets, yet he felt a peculiar need to back himself up with a revivified Zarathustra, a sort of alter ego, with whom he often identifies himself in his great tragedy *Thus Spake Zarathustra*. Nietzsche was no atheist, but his God was dead. The result of this demise was a split in himself, and he felt compelled to call the other self "Zarathustra" or, at times, "Dionysus." In his fatal illness he signed his letters "Zagreus," the dismembered god of the Thracians. The tragedy of *Zarathustra* is that, because his God died, Nietzsche himself became a god; and this happened because he was no atheist. He was of too positive a nature to tolerate the urban neurosis of atheism. It seems dangerous for such a man to assert that "God is dead": he instantly becomes the victim of inflation.* Far from being a negation, God is actually the strongest and most effective "position" the psyche can reach, in exactly the same sense in which Paul speaks of people "whose God is their belly" (Phil. 3:19). The strongest and therefore the decisive factor in any individual psyche compels the same belief or fear, submission or devotion which a God would demand from man. Anything despotic and inescapable is in this sense "God," and it becomes absolute unless, by an ethical decision freely chosen, one succeeds in building up against this natural phenomenon a position that is equally strong and invincible. If this psychic position proves to be absolutely effective, it surely deserves to be named a "God," and what is more, a spiritual God, since it sprang from the freedom of ethical decision and therefore from the mind. Man is free to decide whether "God" shall be a "spirit" or a natural phenomenon like the craving of a morphine addict, and hence whether "God" shall act as a beneficent or a destructive force.

However indubitable and clearly understandable these psychic events or decisions may be, they are very apt to lead people to the false, unpsychological conclusion that it rests with them to decide whether they will *create* a "God" for themselves or not. There is

*Concerning the concept "inflation," see "The Relations between the Ego and the Unconscious" (CW 7), pars. 227ff.

ıestion of that, since each of us is equipped with a psychic
ᴜɪᴄᴩᴏsition that limits our freedom in high degree and makes it
practically illusory. Not only is "freedom of the will" an
incalculable problem philosophically, it is also a misnomer in the
practical sense, for we seldom find anybody who is not influenced
and indeed dominated by desires, habits, impulses, prejudices,
resentments, and by every conceivable kind of complex. All these
natural facts function exactly like an Olympus full of deities who
want to be propitiated, served, feared and worshipped, not only
by the individual owner of this assorted pantheon, but by
everybody in his vicinity. Bondage and possession are synonymous. Always, therefore, there is something in the psyche that
takes possession and limits or suppresses our moral freedom. In
order to hide this undeniable but exceedingly unpleasant fact from
ourselves and at the same time pay lip-service to freedom, we have
got accustomed to saying apotropaically, "*I have* such and such a
desire or habit or feeling of resentment," instead of the more
veracious "Such and such a desire or habit or feeling of resentment
has me." The latter formulation would certainly rob us even of the
illusion of freedom. But I ask myself whether this would not be
better in the end than fuddling ourselves with words. The truth
is that we do not enjoy masterless freedom; we are continually
threatened by psychic factors which, in the guise of "natural
phenomena," may take possession of us at any moment. The
withdrawal of metaphysical projections leaves us almost defenceless in the face of this happening, for we immediately identify with
every impulse instead of giving it the name of the "other," which
would at least hold it at arm's length and prevent it from storming
the citadel of the ego. "Principalities and powers" are always with
us; we have no need to create them even if we could. It is merely
incumbent on us to *choose* the master we wish to serve, so that his
service shall be our safeguard against being mastered by the
"other" whom we have not chosen. We do not *create* "God," we
choose him.

Though our choice characterizes and defines "God," it is always
man-made, and the definition it gives is therefore finite and
imperfect. (Even the idea of perfection does not posit perfection.)
The definition is an image, but this image does not raise the
unknown fact it designates into the realm of intelligibility,

otherwise we would be entitled to say that we had created a God. The "master" we choose is not identical with the image we project of him in time and space. He goes on working as before, like an unknown quantity in the depths of the psyche. We do not even know the nature of the simplest thought, let alone the ultimate principles of the psyche. Also, we have no control over its inner life. But because this inner life is intrinsically free and not subject to our will and intentions, it may easily happen that the living thing chosen and defined by us will drop out of its setting, the man-made image, even against our will. Then, perhaps, we could say with Nietzsche, "God is dead." Yet it would be truer to say, "He has put off our image, and where shall we find him again?" The interregnum is full of danger, for the natural facts will raise their claim in the form of various -isms, which are productive of nothing but anarchy and destruction because inflation and man's hybris between them have elected to make the ego, in all its ridiculous paltriness, lord of the universe. That was the case with Nietzsche, the uncomprehended portent of a whole epoch.

The individual ego is much too small, its brain is much too feeble, to incorporate all the projections withdrawn from the world. Ego and brain burst asunder in the effort; the psychiatrist calls it schizophrenia. When Nietzsche said "God is dead," he uttered a truth which is valid for the greater part of Europe. People were influenced by it not because he said so, but because it stated a widespread psychological fact. The consequences were not long delayed: after the fog of -isms, the catastrophe. Nobody thought of drawing the slightest conclusions from Nietzsche's pronouncement. Yet it has, for some ears, the same eerie sound as that ancient cry which came echoing over the sea to mark the end of the nature gods: "Great Pan is dead."

The life of Christ is understood by the Church on the one hand as an historical, and on the other hand as an eternally existing, mystery. This is especially evident in the sacrifice of the Mass. From a psychological standpoint this view can be translated as follows: Christ lived a concrete, personal, and unique life which, in all essential features, had at the same time an archetypal character. This character can be recognized from the numerous connections of the biographical details with worldwide myth-motifs. These undeniable connections are the main reason why it is so difficult for researchers into the life of Jesus to construct from the gospel reports on individual life divested of myth. In the gospels themselves factual reports, legends, and myths are woven into a whole. This is precisely what constitutes the meaning of the gospels, and they would immediately lose their character of wholeness if one tried to separate the individual from the archetypal with a critical scalpel. The life of Christ is no exception in that not a few of the great figures of history have realized, more or less clearly, the archetype of the hero's life with its characteristic changes of fortune. But the ordinary man, too, unconsciously lives archetypal forms, and if these are no longer valued it is only because of the prevailing psychological ignorance. Indeed, even the fleeting phenomena of dreams often reveal distinctly archetypal patterns. At bottom, all psychic events are so deeply grounded in the archetype and are so much interwoven with it that in every case considerable critical effort is needed to separate the unique from the typical with any certainty. Ultimately, every individual life is at the same time the eternal life of the species. The individual is continuously "historical" because strictly time-bound; the relation of the type to time, on the other hand, is irrelevant. Since the life of Christ is archetypal to a high degree, it represents to just that degree the life of the archetype. But since the archetype is the unconscious precondition of every human life, its life, when revealed, also reveals the hidden, unconscious ground-life of every individual. That is to say, what happens in the life of Christ happens always and everywhere. In the Christian archetype all lives of this kind are prefigured and are expressed over and over again or once and for all. And in it, too, the question that concerns us here of God's death is anticipated in perfect form. Christ himself is the typical dying and self-transforming God.

The psychological situation from which we started is tantamount to "Why seek ye the living among the dead? He is not here" (Luke 24:5f.). But where shall we find the risen Christ?

I do not expect any believing Christian to pursue these thoughts of mine any further, for they will probably seem to him absurd. I am not, however, addressing myself to the happy possessors of faith, but to those many people for whom the light has gone out, the mystery has faded, and God is dead. For most of them there is no going back, and one does not know either whether going back is always the better way. To gain an understanding of religious matters, probably all that is left us today is the psychological approach. That is why I take these thought-forms that have become historically fixed, try to melt them down again and pour them into moulds of immediate experience. It is certainly a difficult undertaking to discover connecting links between dogma and immediate experience of psychological archetypes, but a study of the natural symbols of the unconscious gives us the necessary raw material.

God's death, or his disappearance, is by no means only a Christian symbol. The search which follows the death is still repeated today after the death of a Dalai Lama, and in antiquity it was celebrated in the annual search for the Kore. Such a wide distribution argues in favour of the universal occurrence of this typical psychic process: the highest value, which gives life and meaning, has got lost. This is a typical experience that has been repeated many times, and its expression therefore occupies a central place in the Christian mystery. The death or loss must always repeat itself: Christ always dies, and always he is born; for the psychic life of the archetype is timeless in comparison with our individual time-boundness. According to what laws now one and now another aspect of the archetype enters into active manifestation, I do not know. I only know – and here I am expressing what countless other people know – that the present is a time of God's death and disappearance. The myth says he was not to be found where his body was laid. "Body" means the outward, visible form, the erstwhile but ephemeral setting for the highest value. The myth further says that the value rose again in a miraculous manner, transformed. It appears as a miracle, for, when a value disappears, it always seems to be lost irretrievably. So it is quite unexpected that it should come back. The three days' descent into hell during death describes the sinking of the vanished value into the unconscious, where, by conquering the power of darkness, it establishes a new order, and then rises up to heaven again, that is, attains supreme clarity of consciousness. The fact that only a few people see the Risen One means that no small difficulties stand in the way of finding and recognizing the transformed value.

Jung describes his search for historical parallels to the process of individuation which he was observing both in himself and in his patients.

From "The Work" MDR, pp. 192–3/200–1; 195–7/204–6

As my life entered its second half, I was already embarked on the confrontation with the contents of the unconscious. My work on this was an extremely long-drawn-out affair, and it was only after some twenty years of it that I reached some degree of understanding of my fantasies.

First I had to find evidence for the historical prefiguration of my inner experiences. That is to say, I had to ask myself, "Where have my particular premises already occurred in history?" If I had not succeeded in finding such evidence, I would never have been able to substantiate my ideas. Therefore, my encounter with alchemy was decisive for me, as it provided me with the historical basis which I had hitherto lacked.

Analytical psychology is fundamentally a natural science, but it is subject far more than any other science to the personal bias of the observer. The psychologist must depend therefore in the highest degree upon historical and literary parallels if he wishes to exclude at least the crudest errors in judgment. Between 1918 and 1926 I had seriously studied the Gnostic writers, for they too had been confronted with the primal world of the unconscious and had dealt with its contents, with images that were obviously contaminated with the world of instinct. Just how they understood these images remains difficult to say, in view of the paucity of the accounts – which, moreover, mostly stem from their opponents, the Church Fathers. It seems to me highly unlikely that they had a psychological conception of them. But the Gnostics were too remote for me to establish any link with them in regard to the questions that were confronting me. As far as I could see, the tradition that might have connected Gnosis with the present seemed to have been severed, and for a long time it proved impossible to find any bridge that led from Gnosticism – or neo-Platonism – to the contemporary world. But when I began to understand alchemy I realized that it represented the historical link with Gnosticism, and that a continuity therefore existed between past and present. Grounded in the natural philosophy of the Middle Ages, alchemy formed the bridge on the one hand into the past, to Gnosticism, and on the other into the future, to the modern psychology of the unconscious.

.   .   .   .

Light on the nature of alchemy began to come to me only after I had read the text of the *Golden Flower*, that specimen of Chinese alchemy which Richard Wilhelm sent me in 1928. I was stirred by the desire to become more closely acquainted with the alchemical texts. I commissioned a Munich bookseller to notify me of any alchemical books that might fall into his hands. Soon afterwards I received the first of them, the *Artis Auriferae Volumina Duo* (1593), a comprehensive collection of Latin treatises among which are a number of the "classics" of alchemy.

I let this book lie almost untouched for nearly two years. Occasionally I would look at the pictures, and each time I would think, "Good Lord, what nonsense! This stuff is impossible to understand." But it persistently intrigued me, and I made up my mind to go into it more thoroughly. The next winter I began, and soon found it provocative and exciting. To be sure, the texts still seemed to me blatant nonsense, but here and there would be passages that seemed significant to me, and occasionally I even found a few sentences which I thought I could understand. Finally I realized that the alchemists were talking in symbols – those old acquaintances of mine. "Why, this is fantastic," I thought. "I simply must learn to decipher all this." By now I was completely fascinated, and buried myself in the texts as often as I had the time. One night, while I was studying them, I suddenly recalled the dream that I was caught in the seventeenth century. At last I grasped its meaning. "So that's it! Now I am condemned to study alchemy from the very beginning."

It was a long while before I found my way about in the labyrinth of alchemical thought processes, for no Ariadne had put a thread into my hand. Reading the sixteenth-century text, "*Rosarium Philosophorum*," I noticed that certain strange expressions and turns of phrase were frequently repeated. For example, "*solve et coagula*," "*unum vas*," "*lapis*," "*prima materia*," "*Mercurius*," etc. I saw that these expressions were used again and again in a particular sense, but I could not make out what that sense was. I therefore decided to start a lexicon of key phrases with cross references. In the course of time I assembled several thousand such key phrases and words, and had volumes filled with excerpts. I worked along philological lines, as if I were trying to solve the riddle of an unknown language. In this way the alchemical mode of expression gradually yielded up its meaning. It was a task that kept me absorbed for more than a decade.

I had very soon seen that analytical psychology coincided in a most curious way with alchemy. The experiences of the alchemists were, in a sense, my experiences, and their world was my world. This was, of course, a momentous discovery: I had stumbled upon the historical counterpart of my psychology of the unconscious. The possibility of a comparison with alchemy, and the uninterrupted intellectual chain back to Gnosticism, gave substance to my psychology. When I pored over these old texts everything fell into place: the fantasy-images, the empirical material I had gathered in my practice, and the conclusions I had drawn from it. I now began to understand what these psychic contents meant when seen in historical perspective. My understanding of their typical character, which had already begun with my investigation of myths, was deepened. The primordial images and the nature of the archetype took a central place in my researches, and it became clear to me that without history there can be no psychology, and certainly no psychology of the unconscious. A psychology of consciousness can, to be sure, content itself with material drawn from personal life, but as soon as we wish to explain a neurosis we require an anamnesis which reaches deeper than the knowledge of consciousness. And when in the course of treatment unusual decisions are called for, dreams occur that need more than personal memories for their interpretation.

I regard my work on alchemy as a sign of my inner relationship to Goethe. Goethe's secret was that he was in the grip of that process of archetypal transformation which has gone on through the centuries. He regarded his *Faust* as an *opus magnum* or *divinum*. He called it his "main business," and his whole life was enacted within the framework of this drama. Thus, what was alive and active within him was a living substance, a suprapersonal process, the great dream of the *mundus archetypus* (archetypal world).

I myself am haunted by the same dream, and from my eleventh year I have been launched upon a single enterprise which is my "main business." My life has been permeated and held together by one idea and one goal: namely, to penetrate into the secret of the personality. Everything can be explained from this central point, and all my works relate to this one theme.

Jung's introduction to Psychology and Alchemy *is a clear summary of his views on the connection between alchemy and analytical psychology.*

"Introduction to the Religious and Psychological Problems of Alchemy" *Psychology and Alchemy*, CW 12, pars. 1–43

For the reader familiar with analytical psychology, there is no need of any introductory remarks to the subject of the following study. But for the reader whose interest is not professional and who comes to this book unprepared, some kind of preface will probably be necessary. The concepts of alchemy and the individuation process are matters that seem to lie very far apart, so that the imagination finds it impossible at first to conceive of any bridge between them. To this reader I owe an explanation, more particularly as I have had one or two experiences since the publication of my recent lectures which lead me to infer a certain bewilderment in my critics.

What I now have to put forward as regards the nature of the human psyche is based first and foremost on my observations of people. It has been objected that these observations deal with experiences that are either unknown or barely accessible. It is a remarkable fact, which we come across again and again, that absolutely everybody, even the most unqualified layman, thinks he knows all about psychology as though the psyche were something that enjoyed the most universal understanding. But anyone who really knows the human psyche will agree with me when I say that it is one of the darkest and most mysterious regions of our experience. There is no end to what can be learned in this field. Hardly a day passes in my practice but I come across something new and unexpected. True enough, my experiences are not commonplaces lying on the surface of life. They are, however, within easy reach of every psychotherapist working in this particular field. It is therefore rather absurd, to say the least, that ignorance of the experiences I have to offer should be twisted into an accusation against me. I do not hold myself responsible for the shortcomings in the lay public's knowledge of psychology.

There is in the analytical process, that is to say in the dialectical discussion between the conscious mind and the unconscious, a development or an advance towards some goal or end, the perplexing nature of which has engaged my attention for many years. Psychological treatment may come to an *end* at any stage in the development without one's always or necessarily having the feeling that a *goal* has also been reached. Typical and temporary terminations may occur (1) after receiving a piece of good advice; (2) after making a fairly complete but nevertheless adequate confession; (3) after having recognized some hitherto unconscious but essential psychic content whose realization gives a new impetus to one's life and activity; (4) after a hard-won separation from the childhood psyche; (5) after having worked out a new and rational mode of adaptation to perhaps difficult or unusual circumstances and surroundings; (6) after the disappearance of painful symptoms; (7) after some positive turn of fortune such as an examination, engagement, marriage, divorce, change of profession, etc.; (8) after having found one's way back to the church or creed to which one previously belonged, or after a conversion; and finally, (9) after having begun to build up a practical philosophy of life (a "philosophy" in the classical sense of the word).

Although the list could admit of many more modifications and additions, it ought to define by and large the main situations in which the analytical or psychotherapeutic process reaches a temporary or sometimes even a definitive end. Experience shows, however, that there is a relatively large number of patients for whom the outward termination of work with the doctor is far from denoting the end of the analytical process. It is rather the case that the dialectical discussion with the unconscious still continues, and follows much the same course as it does with those who have not given up their work with the doctor. Occasionally one meets such patients again after several years and hears the often highly remarkable account of their subsequent development. It was experiences of this kind which first confirmed me in my belief that there is in the psyche a process that seeks its own goal independently of external factors, and which freed me from the worrying feeling that I myself might be the sole cause of an unreal – and perhaps unnatural – process in the psyche of the patient. This apprehension was not altogether misplaced inasmuch as no amount of argument based on any of the nine categories mentioned above – not even a religious conversion or the most startling removal of neurotic symptoms – can persuade certain patients to give up their analytical work. It was these cases that finally convinced me that the treatment of neurosis opens up a problem which goes far beyond purely medical considerations and to which medical knowledge alone cannot hope to do justice.

Although the early days of analysis now lie nearly half a century behind us, with their pseudo-biological interpretations and their depreciation of the whole process of psychic development, memories die hard and people are still very fond of describing a lengthy analysis as "running away from life," "unresolved transference," "auto-eroticism" – and by other equally unpleasant epithets. But since there are two sides to everything, it is legitimate to condemn this so-called "hanging on" as negative to life only if it can be shown that it really does contain nothing positive. The very understandable impatience felt by the doctor does not prove anything in itself. Only through infinitely patient research has the new science succeeded in building up a profounder knowledge of the nature of the psyche, and if there have been certain unexpected therapeutic results, these are due to the self-sacrificing perseverance of the doctor. Unjustifiably negative judgments are easily come by and at times harmful; moreover they arouse the suspicion of being a mere cloak for ignorance if not an attempt to evade the responsibility of a thorough-going analysis. For since the analytical work must inevitably lead sooner or later to a fundamental discussion between "I" and "You" and "You" and "I" on a plane stripped of all human pretenses, it is very likely, indeed it is almost certain, that not only the patient but the doctor as well will find the situation "getting under his skin." Nobody can meddle with fire or poison without being affected in some vulnerable spot; for the true physician does not stand outside his work but is always in the thick of it.

This "hanging on," as it is called, may be something undesired by both parties, something incomprehensible and even unendurable, without necessarily being negative to life. On the contrary, it can easily be a positive "hanging on," which, although it constitutes an apparently insurmountable obstacle, represents just for that reason a unique situation that demands the maximum effort and therefore enlists the energies of the whole man. In fact, one could say that while the patient is unconsciously and unswervingly seeking the solution to some ultimately insoluble problem, the art and technique of the doctor are doing their best to help him towards it. "Ars totum requirit hominem!" exclaims an old alchemist. It is just this *homo totus* whom we seek. The labours of the doctor as well as the quest of the patient are directed towards that hidden and as yet unmanifest "whole" man, who is at once the greater and the future man. But the right way to wholeness is made up, unfortunately, of fateful detours and wrong turnings. It is a *longissima via*, not straight but snakelike, a path that unites the opposites in the manner of the guiding caduceus, a path whose labyrinthine twists and turns are not lacking in terrors. It is on this *longissima via* that we meet with those experiences which are said to be "inaccessible." Their inaccessibility really consists in the fact that they cost us an enormous amount of effort: they demand the very thing we most fear, namely the "wholeness" which we talk about so glibly and which lends itself to endless theorizing, though in actual life we give it the widest possible berth.* It is infinitely more popular to go in for "compartment psychology," where the left-hand pigeon-hole does not know what is in the right.

I am afraid that we cannot hold the unconsciousness and impotence of the individual entirely responsible for this state of affairs: it is due also to the general psychological education of the

---

*It is worth noting that a Protestant theologian, writing on homiletics, had the courage to demand wholeness of the preacher from the ethical point of view. He substantiates his argument by referring to my psychology. See Händler, *Die Predigt*, Berlin, 1941.

European. Not only is this education the proper concern of the ruling religions, it belongs to their very nature – for religion excels all rationalistic systems in that it alone relates to the outer and inner man in equal degree. We can accuse Christianity of arrested development if we are determined to excuse our own shortcomings; but I do not wish to make the mistake of blaming religion for something that is due mainly to human incompetence. I am speaking therefore not of the deepest and best understanding of Christianity but of the superficialities and disastrous misunderstandings that are plain for all to see. The demand made by the *imitatio Christi* – that we should follow the ideal and seek to become like it – ought logically to have the result of developing and exalting the inner man. In actual fact, however, the ideal has been turned by superficial and formalistically-minded believers into an external object of worship, and it is precisely this veneration for the object that prevents it from reaching down into the depths of the psyche and giving the latter a wholeness in keeping with the ideal. Accordingly the divine mediator stands outside as an image, while man remains fragmentary and untouched in the deepest part of him. Christ can indeed be imitated even to the point of stigmatization without the imitator coming anywhere near the ideal or its meaning. For it is not a question of an imitation that leaves a man unchanged and makes him into a mere artifact, but of realizing the ideal on one's own account – *Deo concedente* – in one's own individual life. We must not forget, however, that even a mistaken imitation may sometimes involve a tremendous moral effort which has all the merits of a total surrender to some supreme value, even though the real goal may never be reached and the value is represented externally. It is conceivable that by virtue of this total effort a man may even catch a fleeting glimpse of his wholeness, accompanied by the feeling of grace that always characterizes this experience.

The mistaken idea of a merely outward *imitatio Christi* is further exacerbated by a typically European prejudice which distinguishes the Western attitude from the Eastern. Western man is held in thrall by the "ten thousand things"; he sees only particulars, he is ego-bound and thing-bound, and unaware of the deep root of all being. Eastern man, on the other hand, experiences the world of particulars and even his own ego, like a dream; he is rooted essentially in the "Ground," which attracts him so powerfully that his relations with the world are relativized to a degree that is often incomprehensible to us. The Western attitude, with its emphasis on the object, tends to fix the ideal – Christ – in its outward aspect and thus to rob it of its mysterious relation to the inner man. It is this prejudice, for instance, which impels the Protestant interpreters of the Bible to interpret ἐντὸς ὑμῶν (referring to the Kingdom of God) as "among you" instead of "within you." I do not mean to say anything about the validity of the Western attitude: we are sufficiently convinced of its rightness. But if we try to come to a real understanding of Eastern man – as the psychologist must – we find it hard to rid ourselves of certain misgivings. Anyone who can square it with his conscience is free to decide this question as he pleases, though he may be unconsciously setting himself up as an *arbiter mundi*. I for my part prefer the precious gift of doubt, for the reason that it does not violate the virginity of things beyond our ken.

Christ the ideal took upon himself the sins of the world. But if the ideal is wholly outside then the sins of the individual are also outside, and consequently he is more of a fragment than ever, since superficial misunderstanding conveniently enables him, quite literally, to "cast his sins upon Christ" and thus to evade his deepest responsibilities – which is contrary to the spirit of Christianity. Such formalism and laxity were not only one of the prime causes of the Reformation, they are also present within the body of Protestantism. If the supreme value (Christ) and the supreme negation (sin) are outside, then the soul is void: its highest and lowest are missing. The Eastern attitude (more particularly the Indian) is the other way about: everything, highest and lowest, is in the (transcendental) Subject. Accordingly the significance of the Atman, the Self, is heightened beyond all bounds. But with Western man the value of the self sinks to zero. Hence the universal depreciation of the soul in the West. Whoever speaks of the reality of the soul or psyche is accused of "psychologism." Psychology is spoken of as if it were "only" psychology and nothing else. The notion that there can be psychic factors which correspond to divine figures is regarded as a devaluation of the latter. It smacks of blasphemy to think that a religious experience is a psychic process;

for, so it is argued, a religious experience "is not *only* psychological." Anything psychic is *only* Nature and therefore, people think, nothing religious can come out of it. At the same time such critics never hesitate to derive all religions – with the exception of their own – from the nature of the psyche. It is a telling fact that two theological reviewers of my book *Psychology and Religion* – one of them Catholic, the other Protestant – assiduously overlooked my demonstration of the psychic origin of religious phenomena.

Faced with this situation, we must really ask: How do we know so much about the psyche that we can say "only" psychic? For this is how Western man, whose soul is evidently "of little worth," speaks and thinks. If much were in his soul he would speak of it with reverence. But since he does not do so we can only conclude that there is nothing of value in it. Not that this is necessarily so always and everywhere, but only with people who put nothing into their souls and have "all God outside." (A little more Meister Eckhart would be a very good thing sometimes!)

An exclusively religious projection may rob the soul of its values so that through sheer inanition it becomes incapable of further development and gets stuck in an unconscious state. At the same time it falls victim to the delusion that the cause of all misfortune lies outside, and people no longer stop to ask themselves how far it is their own doing. So insignificant does the soul seem that it is regarded as hardly capable of evil, much less of good. But if the soul no longer has any part to play, religious life congeals into externals and formalities. However we may picture the relationship between God and soul, one thing is certain: that the soul cannot be "nothing but."* On the contrary it has the dignity of an entity endowed with consciousness of a relationship to Deity. Even if it were only the relationship of a drop of water to the sea, that sea would not exist but for the multitude of drops. The immortality of the soul insisted upon by dogma exalts it above the transitoriness of mortal man and causes it to partake of some supernatural quality. It thus infinitely surpasses the perishable, conscious individual in significance, so that logically the Christian is

---

*[The term "nothing but" (*nichts als*), which occurs frequently in Jung to denote the habit of explaining something unknown by reducing it to something apparently known and thereby devaluing it, is borrowed from William James, *Pragmatism*, p. 16: "What is higher is explained by what is lower and treated for ever as a case of 'nothing but' – nothing but something else of a quite inferior sort."]

forbidden to regard the soul as a "nothing but."* As the eye to the sun, so the soul corresponds to God. Since our conscious mind does not comprehend the soul it is ridiculous to speak of the things of the soul in a patronizing or depreciatory manner. Even the believing Christian does not know God's hidden ways and must leave him to decide whether he will work on man from outside or from within, through the soul. So the believer should not boggle at the fact that there are *somnia a Deo missa* (dreams sent by God) and illuminations of the soul which cannot be traced back to any external causes. It would be blasphemy to assert that God can manifest himself everywhere save only in the human soul. Indeed the very intimacy of the relationship between God and the soul precludes from the start any devaluation of the latter.† It would be going perhaps too far to speak of an affinity; but at all events the soul must contain in itself the faculty of relationship to God, i.e., a correspondence, otherwise a connection could never come about.** *This correspondence is, in psychological terms, the archetype of the God-image.*

Every archetype is capable of endless development and differentiation. It is therefore possible for it to be more developed or less. In an outward form of religion where all the emphasis is on the outward figure (hence where we are dealing with a more or less complete projection), the archetype is identical with externalized ideas but remains unconscious as a psychic factor. When an unconscious content is replaced by a projected image to that extent, it is cut off from all participation in and influence on the conscious mind. Hence it largely forfeits its own life, because prevented from exerting the formative influence on consciousness natural to it; what is more, it remains in its original form – unchanged, for nothing changes in the unconscious. At a certain point it even develops a tendency to regress to lower and more archaic levels. It may easily happen, therefore, that a Christian who

*The dogma that man is formed in the likeness of God weighs heavily in the scales in any assessment of man – not to mention the Incarnation.
†The fact that the devil too can take possession of the soul does not diminish its significance in the least.
**It is therefore psychologically quite unthinkable for God to be simply the "wholly other," for a "wholly other" could never be one of the soul's deepest and closest intimacies – which is precisely what God is. The only statements that have psychological validity concerning the God-image are either paradoxes or antinomies.

believes in all the sacred figures is still undeveloped and unchanged in his inmost soul because he has "all God outside" and does not experience him in the soul. His deciding motives, his ruling interests and impulses, do not spring from the sphere of Christianity but from the unconscious and undeveloped psyche, which is as pagan and archaic as ever. Not the individual alone but the sum total of individual lives in a nation proves the truth of this contention. The great events of our world as planned and executed by man do not breathe the spirit of Christianity but rather of unadorned paganism. These things originate in a psychic condition that has remained archaic and has not been even remotely touched by Christianity. The Church assumes, not altogether without reason, that the fact of *semel credidisse* (having once believed) leaves certain traces behind it; but of these traces nothing is to be seen in the broad march of events. Christian civilization has proved hollow to a terrifying degree: it is all veneer, but the inner man has remained untouched and therefore unchanged. His soul is out of key with his external beliefs; in his soul the Christian has not kept pace with external developments. Yes, everything is to be found outside – in image and in word, in Church and Bible – but never inside. Inside reign the archaic gods, supreme as of old; that is to say the inner correspondence with the outer God-image is undeveloped for lack of psychological culture and has therefore got stuck in heathenism. Christian education has done all that is humanly possible, but it has not been enough. Too few people have experienced the divine image as the innermost possession of their own souls. Christ only meets them from without, never from within the soul; that is why dark paganism still reigns there, a paganism which, now in a form so blatant that it can no longer be denied and now in all too threadbare disguise, is swamping the world of so-called Christian civilization.

With the methods employed hitherto we have not succeeded in Christianizing the soul to the point where even the most elementary demands of Christian ethics can exert any decisive influence on the main concerns of the Christian European. The Christian missionary may preach the gospel to the poor naked heathen, but the spiritual heathen who populate Europe have as yet heard nothing of Christianity. Christianity must indeed begin again from the very beginning if it is to meet its high educative task.

So long as religion is only faith and outward form, and the religious function is not experienced in our own souls, nothing of any importance has happened. It has yet to be understood that the *mysterium magnum* is not only an actuality but is first and foremost rooted in the human psyche. The man who does not know this from his own experience may be a most learned theologian, but he has no idea of religion and still less of education.

Yet when I point out that the soul possesses by nature a religious function,* and when I stipulate that it is the prime task of all education (of adults) to convey the archetype of the God-image, or its emanations and effects, to the conscious mind, then it is precisely the theologian who seizes me by the arm and accuses me of "psychologism." But were it not a fact of experience that supreme values reside in the soul (quite apart from the ἀντίμιμον πνεῦμα who is also there), psychology would not interest me in the least, for the soul would then be nothing but a miserable vapour. I know, however, from hundredfold experience that it is nothing of the sort, but on the contrary contains the equivalents of everything that has been formulated in dogma and a good deal more, which is just what enables it to be an eye destined to behold the light. This requires limitless range and unfathomable depth of vision. I have been accused of "deifying the soul." Not I but God himself has deified it! *I* did not attribute a religious function to the soul, I merely produced the facts which prove that the soul is *naturaliter religiosa*, i.e., possesses a religious function. I did not invent or insinuate this function, it produces itself of its own accord without being prompted thereto by any opinions or suggestions of mine. With a truly tragic delusion these theologians fail to see that it is not a matter of proving the existence of the light, but of blind people who do not know that their eyes could see. It is high time we realized that it is pointless to praise the light and preach it if nobody can see it. It is much more needful to teach people the art of seeing. For it is obvious that far too many people are incapable of establishing a connection between the sacred figures and their own psyche: they cannot see to what extent the equivalent images are lying dormant in their own unconscious. In order to facilitate this inner vision we must first clear the way for the faculty of

*Tertullian, *Apologeticus*, xvii: "Anima naturaliter christiana."

seeing. How this is to be done without psychology, that is, without making contact with the psyche, is frankly beyond my comprehension.*

Another equally serious misunderstanding lies in imputing to psychology the wish to be a new and possibly heretical doctrine. If a blind man can gradually be helped to see it is not to be expected that he will at once discern new truths with an eagle eye. One must be glad if he sees anything at all, and if he begins to understand what he sees. Psychology is concerned with the act of seeing and not with the construction of new religious truths, when even the existing teachings have not yet been perceived and understood. In religious matters it is a well-known fact that we cannot understand a thing until we have experienced it inwardly, for it is in the inward experience that the connection between the psyche and the outward image or creed is first revealed as a relationship or correspondence like that of *sponsus* and *sponsa*. Accordingly when I say as a psychologist that God is an archetype, I mean by that the "type" in the psyche. The word "type" is, as we know, derived from τύπος, "blow" or "imprint"; thus an archetype presupposes an imprinter. Psychology as the science of the soul has to confine itself to its subject and guard against overstepping its proper boundaries by metaphysical assertions or other professions of faith. Should it set up a God, even as a hypothetical cause, it would have implicitly claimed the possibility of proving God, thus exceeding its competence in an absolutely illegitimate way. Science can only be science; there are no "scientific" professions of faith and similar *contradictiones in adiecto*. We simply do not know the ultimate derivation of the archetype any more than we know the origin of the psyche. The competence of psychology as an empirical science only goes so far as to establish, on the basis of comparative research, whether for instance the imprint found in the psyche can or cannot reasonably be termed a "God-image." Nothing positive or negative has thereby been asserted about the possible existence of God, any more than the archetype of the "hero" posits the actual existence of a hero.

Now if my psychological researches have demonstrated the

---

*Since it is a question here of human effort, I leave aside acts of grace which are beyond man's control.

existence of certain psychic types and their correspondence with well-known religious ideas, then we have opened up a possible approach to those experienceable contents which manifestly and undeniably form the empirical foundations of all religious experience. The religious-minded man is free to accept whatever metaphysical explanations he pleases about the origin of these images; not so the intellect, which must keep strictly to the principles of scientific interpretation and avoid trespassing beyond the bounds of what can be known. Nobody can prevent the believer from accepting God, Purusha, the Atman, or Tao as the Prime Cause and thus putting an end to the fundamental disquiet of man. The scientist is a scrupulous worker; he cannot take heaven by storm. Should he allow himself to be seduced into such an extravagance he would be sawing off the branch on which he sits.

The fact is that with the knowledge and actual experience of these inner images a way is opened for reason and feeling to gain access to those other images which the teachings of religion offer to mankind. Psychology thus does just the opposite of what it is accused of: it provides possible approaches to a better understanding of these things, it opens people's eyes to the real meaning of dogmas, and, far from destroying, it throws open an empty house to new inhabitants. I can corroborate this from countless experiences: people belonging to creeds of all imaginable kinds, who had played the apostate or cooled off in their faith, have found a new approach to their old truths, not a few Catholics among them. Even a Parsee found the way back to the Zoroastrian fire-temple, which should bear witness to the objectivity of my point of view.

But this objectivity is just what my psychology is most blamed for: it is said not to decide in favour of this or that religious doctrine. Without prejudice to my own subjective convictions I should like to raise the question: Is it not thinkable that when one refrains from setting oneself up as an *arbiter mundi* and, deliberately renouncing all subjectivism, cherishes on the contrary the belief, for instance, that God has expressed himself in many languages and appeared in divers forms and that all these statements are *true* – is it not thinkable, I say, that this too is a decision? The objection raised, more particularly by Christians, that it is impossible for contradictory statements to be true, must permit itself to be politely asked: Does one equal three? How can three be one? Can a mother be a virgin? And so on. Has it not yet been observed that all religious statements contain logical contradictions and assertions that are impossible in principle, that this is in fact the very essence of religious assertion? As witness to this we have Tertullian's avowal: "And the Son of God is dead, which is worthy of belief because it is absurd. And when buried He rose again, which is certain because it is impossible."* If Christianity demands faith in such contradictions it does not seem to me that it can very well condemn those who assert a few paradoxes more. Oddly enough the paradox is one of our most valuable spiritual possessions, while uniformity of meaning is a sign of weakness. Hence a religion becomes inwardly impoverished when it loses or waters down its paradoxes; but their multiplication enriches because only the paradox comes anywhere near to comprehending the fulness of life. Non-ambiguity and non-contradiction are one-sided and thus unsuited to express the incomprehensible.

Not everyone possesses the spiritual strength of a Tertullian. It is evident not only that he had the strength to sustain paradoxes but that they actually afforded him the highest degree of religious certainty. The inordinate number of spiritual weaklings makes paradoxes dangerous. So long as the paradox remains unexamined and is taken for granted as a customary part of life, it is harmless enough. But when it occurs to an insufficiently cultivated mind (always, as we know, the most sure of itself) to make the paradoxical nature of some tenet of faith the object of its lucubrations, as earnest as they are impotent, it is not long before such a one will break out into iconoclastic and scornful laughter, pointing to the manifest absurdity of the mystery. Things have gone rapidly downhill since the Age of Enlightenment, for, once this petty reasoning mind, which cannot endure any paradoxes, is awakened, no sermon on earth can keep it down. A new task then arises: to lift this still undeveloped mind step by step to a higher level and to increase the number of persons who have at least some inkling of the scope of paradoxical truth. If this is not possible, then it must be admitted that the spiritual approaches to

*Tertullian, De carne Christi, 5.

Christianity are as good as blocked. We simply do not understand any more what is meant by the paradoxes contained in dogma; and the more external our understanding of them becomes the more we are affronted by their irrationality, until finally they become completely obsolete, curious relics of the past. The man who is stricken in this way cannot estimate the extent of his spiritual loss, because he has never experienced the sacred images as his inmost possession and has never realized their kinship with his own psychic structure. But it is just this indispensable knowledge that the psychology of the unconscious can give him, and its scientific objectivity is of the greatest value here. Were psychology bound to a creed it would not and could not allow the unconscious of the individual that free play which is the basic condition for the production of archetypes. It is precisely the spontaneity of archetypal contents that convinces, whereas any prejudiced intervention is a bar to genuine experience. If the theologian really believes in the almighty power of God on the one hand and in the validity of dogma on the other, why then does he not trust God to speak in the soul? Why this fear of psychology? Or is, in complete contradiction to dogma, the soul itself a hell from which only demons gibber? Even if this were really so it would not be any the less convincing; for as we all know the horrified perception of the reality of evil has led to at least as many conversions as the experience of good.

The archetypes of the unconscious can be shown empirically to be the equivalents of religious dogmas. In the hermeneutic language of the Fathers the Church possesses a rich store of analogies with the individual and spontaneous products to be found in psychology. What the unconscious expresses is far from being merely arbitrary or opinionated; it is something that happens to be "just-so," as is the case with every other natural being. It stands to reason that the expressions of the unconscious are natural and not formulated dogmatically; they are exactly like the patristic allegories which draw the whole of nature into the orbit of their amplifications. If these present us with some astonishing *allegoriae Christi*, we find much the same sort of thing in the psychology of the unconscious. The only difference is that the patristic allegory *ad Christum spectat* – refers to Christ – whereas the psychic

archetype is simply itself and can therefore be interpre
according to time, place, and milieu. In the West the archetype is
filled out with the dogmatic figure of Christ; in the East, with
Purusha, the Atman, Hiranyagarbha, the Buddha, and so on. The
religious point of view, understandably enough, puts the accent on
the imprinter, whereas scientific psychology emphasizes the *typos*,
the imprint – the only thing it can understand. The religious point
of view understands the imprint as the working of an imprinter;
the scientific point of view understands it as the symbol of an
unknown and incomprehensible content. Since the *typos* is less
definite and more variegated than any of the figures postulated by
religion, psychology is compelled by its empirical material to
express the *typos* by means of a terminology not bound by time,
place, or milieu. If, for example, the *typos* agreed in every detail
with the dogmatic figure of Christ, and if it contained no
determinant that went beyond that figure, we would be bound to
regard the *typos* as at least a faithful copy of the dogmatic figure,
and to name it accordingly. The *typos* would then coincide with
Christ. But as experience shows, this is not the case, seeing that
the unconscious, like the allegories employed by the Church
Fathers, produces countless other determinants that are not
explicitly contained in the dogmatic formula; that is to say,
non-Christian figures such as those mentioned above are included
in the *typos*. But neither do these figures comply with the
indeterminate nature of the archetype. It is altogether inconceivable that there could be any definite figure capable of expressing
archetypal indefiniteness. For this reason I have found myself
obliged to give the corresponding archetype the psychological
name of the "self" – a term on the one hand definite enough to
convey the essence of human wholeness and on the other hand
indefinite enough to express the indescribable and indeterminable
nature of this wholeness. The paradoxical qualities of the term are
a reflection of the fact that wholeness consists partly of the
conscious man and partly of the unconscious man. But we cannot
define the latter or indicate his boundaries. Hence in its scientific
usage the term "self" refers neither to Christ nor to the Buddha
but to the totality of the figures that are its equivalent, and each
of these figures is a symbol of the self. This mode of expression

is an intellectual necessity in scientific psychology and in no sense denotes a transcendental prejudice. On the contrary, as we have said before, this objective attitude enables one man to decide in favour of the determinant Christ, another in favour of the Buddha, and so on. Those who are irritated by this objectivity should reflect that science is quite impossible without it. Consequently by denying psychology the right to objectivity they are making an untimely attempt to extinguish the life-light of a science. Even if such a preposterous attempt were to succeed, it would only widen the already catastrophic gulf between the secular mind on the one hand and Church and religion on the other.

It is quite understandable for a science to concentrate more or less exclusively on its subject – indeed, that is its absolute *raison d'être*. Since the concept of the self is of central interest in psychology, the latter naturally thinks along lines diametrically opposed to theology: for psychology the religious figures point to the self, whereas for theology the self points to its – theology's – own central figure. In other words, theology might possibly take the psychological self as an allegory of Christ. This opposition is, no doubt, very irritating, but unfortunately inevitable, unless psychology is to be denied the right to exist at all. I therefore plead for tolerance. Nor is this very hard for psychology since as a science it makes no totalitarian claims.

The Christ-symbol is of the greatest importance for psychology in so far as it is perhaps the most highly developed and differentiated symbol of the self, apart from the figure of the Buddha. We can see this from the scope and substance of all the pronouncements that have been made about Christ: they agree with the psychological phenomenology of the self in unusually high degree, although they do not include all aspects of this archetype. The almost limitless range of the self might be deemed a disadvantage as compared with the definiteness of a religious figure, but it is by no means the task of science to pass value judgments. Not only is the self indefinite but – paradoxically enough – it also includes the quality of definiteness and even of uniqueness. This is probably one of the reasons why precisely those religions founded by historical personages have become world religions, such as Christianity, Buddhism, and Islam. The inclusion in a religion of a unique human personality – especially when conjoined to an indeterminable divine nature – is consistent with the absolute individuality of the self, which combines uniqueness with eternity and the individual with the universal. The self is a union of opposites *par excellence*, and this is where it differs essentially from the Christ-symbol. The androgyny of Christ is the utmost concession the Church has made to the problem of opposites. The opposition between light and good on the one hand and darkness and evil on the other is left in a state of open conflict, since Christ simply represents good, and his counterpart the devil, evil. This opposition is the real world problem, which at present is still unsolved. The self, however, is absolutely paradoxical in that it represents in every respect thesis and antithesis, and at the same time synthesis. (Psychological proofs of this assertion abound, though it is impossible for me to quote them here *in extenso*. I would refer the knowledgeable reader to the symbolism of the mandala.)

Once the exploration of the unconscious has led the conscious mind to an experience of the archetype, the individual is confronted with the abysmal contradictions of human nature, and this confrontation in turn leads to the possibility of a direct experience of light and darkness, of Christ and the devil. For better or worse there is only a bare possibility of this, and not a guarantee; for experiences of this kind cannot of necessity be induced by any human means. There are factors to be considered which are not under our control. Experience of the opposites has nothing whatever to do with intellectual insight or with empathy. It is more what we would call fate. Such an experience can convince one person of the truth of Christ, another of the truth of the Buddha, to the exclusion of all other evidence.

Without the experience of the opposites there is no experience of wholeness and hence no inner approach to the sacred figures. For this reason Christianity rightly insists on sinfulness and original sin, with the obvious intent of opening up the abyss of universal opposition in every individual – at least from the outside. But this method is bound to break down in the case of a moderately alert intellect: dogma is then simply no longer believed and on top of that is thought absurd. Such an intellect is merely one-sided and sticks at the *ineptia mysterii*. It is miles from Tertullian's antinomies; in fact, it is quite incapable of enduring the suffering such a tension involves. Cases are not unknown where the rigorous exercises and proselytizings of the Catholics, and a certain type of Protestant education that is always sniffing out sin, have brought about psychic damage that leads not to the Kingdom of Heaven but to the consulting room of the doctor. Although insight into the problem of opposites is absolutely imperative, there are very few people who can stand it in practice – a fact which has not escaped the notice of the confessional. By way of a reaction to this we have the palliative of "moral probabilism," a doctrine that has suffered frequent attack from all quarters because it tries to mitigate the crushing effect of sin.* Whatever one may think of this phenomenon one thing is certain: that apart from anything else it holds within it a large humanity and an understanding of human weakness which compensate for the world's unbearable antinomies. The tremendous paradox implicit in the insistence on original sin on the one hand and the concession made by probabilism on the other is, for the psychologist, a necessary consequence of the Christian problem of opposites outlined above – for in the self good and evil are indeed closer than identical twins! The reality of evil and its incompatibility with good cleave the opposites asunder and lead inexorably to the crucifixion and suspension of everything that lives. Since "the soul is by nature Christian" this result is bound to come as infallibly as it did in the

*Otto Zöckler ("Probabilismus," in Albert Hauck, ed., *Realencyklopädie für protestantische Theologie und Kirche*, Leipzig, 1896–1913 (24 vols.), p. 67) defines it as follows: "Probabilism is the name generally given to that way of thinking which is content to answer scientific questions with a greater or lesser degree of probability. The moral probabilism with which alone we are concerned here consists in the principle that acts of ethical self-determination are to be guided not by conscience but according to what is probably right, i.e., according to whatever has been recommended by any representative or doctrinal authority." The Jesuit probabilist Escobar (d. 1669) was, for instance, of the opinion that if the penitent should plead a probable opinion as the motive of his action, the father confessor would be obliged to absolve him even if he were not of the same opinion. Escobar quotes a number of Jesuit authorities on the question of how often one is bound to love God in a lifetime. According to one opinion, loving God once shortly before death is sufficient; another says once a year or once every three or four years. He himself comes to the conclusion that it is sufficient to love God once at the first awakening of reason, then once every five years, and finally once in the hour of death. In his opinion the large number of different moral doctrines forms one of the main proofs of God's kindly providence, "because they make the yoke of Christ so light" (Zöckler, p. 68).

life of Jesus: we all have to be "crucified with Christ," i.e., suspended in a moral suffering equivalent to veritable crucifixion. In practice this is only possible up to a point, and apart from that is so unbearable and inimical to life that the ordinary human being can afford to get into such a state only occasionally, in fact as seldom as possible. For how could he remain ordinary in face of such suffering! A more or less probabilistic attitude to the problem of evil is therefore unavoidable. Hence the truth about the self – the unfathomable union of good and evil – comes out concretely in the paradox that although sin is the gravest and most pernicious thing there is, it is still not so serious that it cannot be disposed of with "probabilist" arguments. Nor is this necessarily a lax or frivolous proceeding but simply a practical necessity of life. The confessional proceeds like life itself, which successfully struggles against being engulfed in an irreconcilable contradiction. Note that at the same time the conflict remains in full force, as is once more consistent with the antinomial character of the self, which is itself both conflict and unity.

Christianity has made the antinomy of good and evil into a world problem and, by formulating the conflict dogmatically, raised it to an absolute principle. Into this as yet unresolved conflict the Christian is cast as a protagonist of good, a fellow player in the world drama. Understood in its deepest sense, being Christ's follower involves a suffering that is unendurable to the great majority of mankind. Consequently the example of Christ is in reality followed either with reservation or not at all, and the pastoral practice of the Church even finds itself obliged to "lighten the yoke of Christ." This means a pretty considerable reduction in the severity and harshness of the conflict and hence, in practice, a relativism of good and evil. Good is equivalent to the unconditional imitation of Christ and evil is its hindrance. Man's moral weakness and sloth are what chiefly hinder the imitation, and it is to these that probabilism extends a practical understanding which may sometimes, perhaps, come nearer to Christian tolerance, mildness, and love of one's neighbour than the attitude of those who see in probabilism a mere laxity. Although one must concede a number of cardinal Christian virtues to the probabilist endeavour, one must still not overlook the fact that it obviates much of the suffering involved in the imitation of Christ and that the conflict of good and evil is thus robbed of its harshness and toned down to tolerable proportions. This brings about an approach to the psychic archetype of the self, where even these opposites seem to be united – though, as I say, it differs from the Christian symbolism, which leaves the conflict open. For the latter there is a rift running through the world: light wars against night and the upper against the lower. The two are not one, as they are in the psychic archetype. But, even though religious dogma may condemn the idea of two being one, religious practice does, as we have seen, allow the natural psychological symbol of the self at one with itself an approximate means of expression. On the other hand, dogma insists that three are one, while denying that four are one. Since olden times, not only in the West but also in China, uneven numbers have been regarded as masculine and even numbers as feminine. The Trinity is therefore a decidedly masculine deity, of which the androgyny of Christ and the special position and veneration accorded to the Mother of God are not the real equivalent.

With this statement, which may strike the reader as peculiar, we come to one of the central axioms of alchemy, namely the saying of Maria Prophetissa: "One becomes two, two becomes three, and out of the third comes the one as the fourth." As the reader has already seen from its title, this book is concerned with the psychological significance of alchemy and thus with a problem which, with very few exceptions, has so far eluded scientific research. Until quite recently science was interested only in the part that alchemy played in the history of chemistry, concerning itself very little with the part it played in the history of philosophy and religion. The importance of alchemy for the historical development of chemistry is obvious, but its cultural importance is still so little known that it seems almost impossible to say in a few words wherein that consisted. In this introduction, therefore, I have attempted to outline the religious and psychological problems which are germane to the theme of alchemy. The point is that alchemy is rather like an undercurrent to the Christianity that ruled on the surface. It is to this surface as the dream is to consciousness, and just as the dream compensates the conflicts of the conscious mind, so alchemy endeavours to fill in the gaps left open by the Christian tension of opposites. Perhaps the most pregnant expression of this is the axiom of Maria Prophetissa quoted above, which runs like a *leitmotiv* throughout almost the whole of the lifetime of alchemy, extending over more than seventeen centuries. In this aphorism the even numbers which signify the feminine principle, earth, the regions under the earth, and evil itself are interpolated between the uneven numbers of the Christian dogma. They are personified by the *serpens mercurii*, the dragon that creates and destroys itself and represents the *prima materia*. This fundamental idea of alchemy points back to the תהום (Tehom),* to Tiamat with her dragon attribute, and thus to the primordial matriarchal world which, in the theomachy of the Marduk myth, was overthrown by the masculine world of the father. The historical shift in the world's consciousness towards the masculine is compensated at first by the chthonic femininity of the unconscious. In certain pre-Christian religions the differentiation of the masculine principle had taken the form of the father-son specification, a change which was to be of the utmost importance for Christianity. Were the unconscious merely complementary, this shift of consciousness would have been accompanied by the production of a mother and daughter, for which the necessary material lay ready to hand in the myth of Demeter and Persephone. But, as alchemy shows, the unconscious chose rather the Cybele-Attis type in the form of the *prima materia* and the *filius macrocosmi*, thus proving that it is not complementary but compensatory. This goes to show that the unconscious does not simply act *contrary* to the conscious mind but *modifies* it more in the manner of an opponent or partner. The son type does not call up a daughter as a complementary image from the depths of the "chthonic" unconscious – it calls up another son. This remarkable fact would seem to be connected with the incarnation in our earthly human nature of a purely spiritual God, brought about by the Holy Ghost impregnating the womb of the Blessed Virgin. Thus the higher, the spiritual, the masculine inclines to the lower, the earthly, the feminine; and accordingly, the mother, who was anterior to the world of the father, accommodates herself to the

*Cf. Genesis 1:2.

masculine principle and, with the aid of the human spirit (alchemy or "the philosophy"), produces a son – not the antithesis of Christ but rather his chthonic counterpart, not a divine man but a fabulous being conforming to the nature of the primordial mother. And just as the redemption of man the microcosm is the task of the "upper" son, so the "lower" son has the function of a *salvator macrocosmi*.

This, in brief, is the drama that was played out in the obscurities of alchemy. It is superfluous to remark that these two sons were never united, except perhaps in the mind and innermost experience of a few particularly gifted alchemists. But it is not very difficult to see the "purpose" of this drama: in the Incarnation it looked as though the masculine principle of the father-world were approximating to the feminine principle of the mother-world, with the result that the latter felt impelled to approximate in turn to the father-world. What it evidently amounted to was an attempt to bridge the gulf separating the two worlds as compensation for the open conflict between them.

I hope the reader will not be offended if my exposition sounds like a Gnostic myth. We are moving in those psychological regions where, as a matter of fact, Gnosis is rooted. The message of the Christian symbol is Gnosis, and the compensation effected by the unconscious is Gnosis in even higher degree. Myth is the primordial language natural to these psychic processes, and no intellectual formulation comes anywhere near the richness and expressiveness of mythical imagery. Such processes are concerned with the primordial images, and these are best and most succinctly reproduced by figurative language.

The process described above displays all the characteristic features of psychological compensation. We know that the mask of the unconscious is not rigid – it reflects the face we turn towards it. Hostility lends it a threatening aspect, friendliness softens its features. It is not a question of mere optical reflection but of an autonomous answer which reveals the self-sufficing nature of that which answers. Thus the *filius philosophorum* is not just the reflected image, in unsuitable material, of the son of God; on the contrary, this son of Tiamat reflects the features of the primordial maternal figure. Although he is decidedly hermaphroditic he has a masculine name – a sign that the chthonic underworld, having been rejected by the spirit and identified with evil, has a tendency to compromise. There is no mistaking the fact that he is a concession to the spiritual and masculine principle, even though he carries in himself the weight of the earth and the whole fabulous nature of primordial animality.

This answer of the mother-world shows that the gulf between it and the father-world is not unbridgeable, seeing that the unconscious holds the seed of the unity of both. The essence of the conscious mind is discrimination; it must, if it is to be aware of things, separate the opposites, and it does this *contra naturam*. In nature the opposites seek one another – *les extrêmes se touchent* – and so it is in the unconscious, and particularly in the archetype of unity, the self. Here, as in the deity, the opposites cancel out. But as soon as the unconscious begins to manifest itself they split asunder, as at the Creation; for every act of dawning consciousness is a creative act, and it is from this psychological experience that all our cosmogonic symbols are derived.

Alchemy is pre-eminently concerned with the seed of unity which lies hidden in the chaos of Tiamat and forms the counterpart to the divine unity. Like this, the seed of unity has a trinitarian character in Christian alchemy and a triadic character in pagan alchemy. According to other authorities it corresponds to the unity of the four elements and is therefore a quaternity. The overwhelming majority of modern psychological findings speaks in favour of the latter view. The few cases I have observed which produced the number three were marked by a systematic deficiency in consciousness, that is to say, by an unconsciousness of the "inferior function." The number three is not a natural expression of wholeness, since four represents the minimum number of determinants in a whole judgment. It must nevertheless be stressed that side by side with the distinct leanings of alchemy (and of the unconscious) towards quaternity there is always a vacillation between three and four which comes out over and over again. Even in the axiom of Maria Prophetissa the quaternity is muffled and alembicated. In alchemy there are three as well as four *regimina* or procedures, three as well as four colours. There are always four elements, but often three of them are grouped together, with the fourth in a special position – sometimes earth, sometimes fire.

Mercurius* is of course *quadratus*, but he is also a three-headed snake or simply a triunity. This uncertainty has a duplex character – in other words, the central ideas are ternary as well as quaternary. The psychologist cannot but mention the fact that a similar puzzle exists in the psychology of the unconscious: the least differentiated or "inferior" function is so much contaminated with the collective unconscious that, on becoming conscious, it brings up among others the archetype of the self as well – τὸ ἕν τέταρτον, as Maria Prophetissa says. Four signifies the feminine, motherly, physical; three the masculine, fatherly, spiritual. Thus the uncertainty as to three or four amounts to a wavering between the spiritual and the physical – a striking example of how every human truth is a last truth but one.

I began my introduction with human wholeness as the goal to which the psychotherapeutic process ultimately leads. This question is inextricably bound up with one's philosophical or religious assumptions. Even when, as frequently happens, the patient believes himself to be quite unprejudiced in this respect, the assumptions underlying his thought, mode of life, morale, and language are historically conditioned down to the last detail, a fact of which he is often kept unconscious by lack of education combined with lack of self-criticism. The analysis of his situation will therefore lead sooner or later to a clarification of his general spiritual background going far beyond his personal determinants, and this brings up the problems I have attempted to sketch in the preceding pages. This phase of the process is marked by the production of symbols of unity, the so-called mandalas, which occur either in dreams or in the form of concrete visual impressions, often as the most obvious compensation of the contradictions and conflicts of the conscious situation. It would

---

*In alchemical writings the word "Mercurius" is used with a very wide range of meaning, to denote not only the chemical element mercury or quicksilver, Mercury (Hermes) the god, and Mercury the planet, but also – and primarily – the secret "transforming substance" which is at the same time the "spirit" indwelling in all living creatures. These different connotations will become apparent in the course of the book. It would be misleading to use the English "Mercury" and "mercury," because there are innumerable passages where neither word does justice to the wealth of implications. It has therefore been decided to retain the Latin "Mercurius" as in the German text, and to use the personal pronoun (since "Mercurius" is personified), the word "quicksilver" being employed only where the chemical element (Hg) is plainly meant.

hardly be correct to say that the gaping "rift" in the Christian order of things is responsible for this, since it is easy to show that Christian symbolism is particularly concerned with healing, or attempting to heal, this very wound. It would be more correct to take the open conflict as a symptom of the psychic situation of Western man, and to deplore his inability to assimilate the whole range of the Christian symbol. As a doctor I cannot demand anything of my patients in this respect, also I lack the Church's means of grace. Consequently I am faced with the task of taking the only path open to me: the archetypal images – which in a certain sense correspond to the dogmatic images – must be brought into consciousness. At the same time I must leave my patient to decide in accordance with his assumptions, his spiritual maturity, his education, origins, and temperament, so far as this is possible without serious conflicts. As a doctor it is my task to help the patient to cope with life. I cannot presume to pass judgment on his final decisions, because I know from experience that all coercion – be it suggestion, insinuation, or any other method of persuasion – ultimately proves to be nothing but an obstacle to the highest and most decisive experience of all, which is to be alone with his own self, or whatever else one chooses to call the objectivity of the psyche. The patient must be alone if he is to find out what it is that supports him when he can no longer support himself. Only this experience can give him an indestructible foundation.

I would be only too delighted to leave this anything but easy task to the theologian, were it not that it is just from the theologian that many of my patients come. They ought to have hung on to the community of the Church, but they were shed like dry leaves from the great tree and now find themselves "hanging on" to the treatment. Something in them clings, often with the strength of despair, as if they or the thing they cling to would drop off into the void the moment they relaxed their hold. They are seeking firm ground on which to stand. Since no outward support is of any use to them they must finally discover it in themselves – admittedly the most unlikely place from the rational point of view, but an altogether possible one from the point of view of the unconscious. We can see this from the archetype of the "lowly origin of the redeemer."

The way to the goal seems chaotic and interminable at first, and only gradually do the signs increase that it is leading anywhere. The way is not straight but appears to go round in circles. More accurate knowledge has proved it to go in spirals: the dream-motifs always return after certain intervals to definite forms, whose characteristic it is to define a centre. And as a matter of fact the whole process revolves about a central point or some arrangement round a centre, which may in certain circumstances appear even in the initial dreams. As manifestations of unconscious processes the dreams rotate or circumambulate round the centre, drawing closer to it as the amplifications increase in distinctness and in scope. Owing to the diversity of the symbolical material it is difficult at first to perceive any kind of order at all. Nor should it be taken for granted that dream sequences are subject to any governing principle. But, as I say, the process of development proves on closer inspection to be cyclic or spiral. We might draw a parallel between such spiral courses and the processes of growth in plants; in fact the plant motif (tree, flower, etc.) frequently recurs in these dreams and fantasies and is also spontaneously drawn or painted.* In alchemy the tree is the symbol of Hermetic philosophy.

The first of the following two studies – that which composes Part II – deals with a series of dreams which contain numerous symbols of the centre or goal. The development of these symbols is almost the equivalent of a healing process. The centre or goal thus signifies *salvation* in the proper sense of the word. The justification for such a terminology comes from the dreams themselves, for these contain so many references to religious phenomena that I was able to use some of them as the subject of my book *Psychology and Religion*. It seems to me beyond all doubt that these processes are concerned with the religion-creating archetypes. Whatever else religion may be, those psychic ingredients of it which are empirically verifiable undoubtedly consist of unconscious manifestations of this kind. People have dwelt far too long on the fundamentally sterile question of whether the assertions of faith are true or not. Quite apart from the impossibility of ever proving or refuting the truth of a metaphysical assertion, the very existence of the assertion is a self-evident fact that needs no further proof, and when a *consensus*

*See the illustrations in Jung, "Concerning Mandala Symbolism" (CW 9 i).

gentium allies itself thereto the validity of the statement is proved to just that extent. The only thing about it that we can verify is the psychological phenomenon, which is incommensurable with the category of objective rightness or truth. No phenomenon can ever be disposed of by rational criticism, and in religious life we have to deal with phenomena and facts and not with arguable hypotheses.

During the process of treatment the dialectical discussion leads logically to a meeting between the patient and his shadow, that dark half of the psyche which we invariably get rid of by means of projection: either by burdening our neighbours – in a wider or narrower sense – with all the faults which we obviously have ourselves, or by casting our sins upon a divine mediator with the aid of *contritio* or the milder *attritio*.* We know of course that without sin there is no repentance and without repentance no redeeming grace, also that without original sin the redemption of the world could never have come about; but we assiduously avoid investigating whether in this very power of evil God might not have placed some special purpose which it is most important for us to know. One often feels driven to some such view when, like the psychotherapist, one has to deal with people who are confronted with their blackest shadow.† At any rate the doctor cannot afford to point, with a gesture of facile moral superiority, to the tablets of the law and say, "Thou shalt not." He has to examine things objectively and weigh up possibilities, for he knows, less from religious training and education than from instinct and experience, that there is something very like a *felix culpa*. He knows that one can miss not only one's happiness but also one's final guilt, without which a man will never reach his wholeness. Wholeness is in fact

---

*Contritio is "perfect" repentance; *attritio* "imperfect" repentance (*contritio imperfecta*, to which category *contritio naturalis* belongs). The former regards sin as the opposite of the highest good; the latter reprehends it not only on account of its wicked and hideous nature but also from fear of punishment.

†A religious terminology comes naturally, as the only adequate one in the circumstances, when we are faced with the tragic fate that is the unavoidable concomitant of wholeness. "My fate" means a daemonic will to precisely that fate – a will not necessarily coincident with my own (the ego will). When it is opposed to the ego, it is difficult not to feel a certain "power" in it, whether divine or infernal. The man who submits to his fate calls it the will of God; the man who puts up a hopeless and exhausting fight is more apt to see the devil in it. In either event this terminology is not only universally understood but meaningful as well.

a charisma which one can manufacture neither by art nor by cunning; one can only grow into it and endure whatever its advent may bring. No doubt it is a great nuisance that mankind is not uniform but compounded of individuals whose psychic structure spreads them over a span of at least ten thousand years. Hence there is absolutely no truth that does not spell salvation to one person and damnation to another. All universalisms get stuck in this terrible dilemma. Earlier on I spoke of Jesuit probabilism: this gives a better idea than anything else of the tremendous catholic task of the Church. Even the best-intentioned people have been horrified by probabilism, but, when brought face to face with the realities of life, many of them have found their horror evaporating or their laughter dying on their lips. The doctor too must weigh and ponder, not whether a thing is for or against the Church but whether it is for or against life and health. On paper the moral code looks clear and neat enough; but the same document written on the "living tables of the heart" is often a sorry tatter, particularly in the mouths of those who talk the loudest. We are told on every side that evil is evil and that there can be no hesitation in condemning it, but that does not prevent evil from being the most problematical thing in the individual's life and the one which demands the deepest reflection. What above all deserves our keenest attention is the question "Exactly *who* is the doer?" For the answer to this question ultimately decides the value of the deed. It is true that society attaches greater importance at first to what is done, because it is immediately obvious; but in the long run the right deed in the hands of the wrong man will also have a disastrous effect. No one who is far-sighted will allow himself to be hoodwinked by the right deed of the wrong man, any more than by the wrong deed of the right man. Hence the psychotherapist must fix his eye not on what is done but on how it is done, because therein is decided the whole character of the doer. Evil needs to be pondered just as much as good, for good and evil are ultimately nothing but ideal extensions and abstractions of doing, and both belong to the chiaroscuro of life. In the last resort there is no good that cannot produce evil and no evil that cannot produce good.

The encounter with the dark half of the personality, or "shadow," comes about of its own accord in any moderately thorough treatment. This problem is as important as that of sin in the Church. The open conflict is unavoidable and painful. I have often been asked, "And what do you *do* about it?" I do nothing; there is nothing I can do except wait, with a certain trust in God, until, out of a conflict borne with patience and fortitude, there emerges the solution destined – although I cannot foresee it – for that particular person. Not that I am passive or inactive meanwhile: I help the patient to understand all the things that the unconscious produces during the conflict. The reader may believe me that these are no ordinary products. On the contrary, they are among the most significant things that have ever engaged my attention. Nor is the patient inactive; he must do the right thing, and do it with all his might, in order to prevent the pressure of evil from becoming too powerful in him. He needs "justification by works," for "justification by faith" alone has remained an empty sound for him as for so many others. Faith can sometimes be a substitute for lack of experience. In these cases what is needed is real work. Christ espoused the sinner and did not condemn him. The true follower of Christ will do the same, and, since one should do unto others as one would do unto oneself, one will also take the part of the sinner who is oneself. And as little as we would accuse Christ of fraternizing with evil, so little should we reproach ourselves that to love the sinner who is oneself is to make a pact with the devil. Love makes a man better, hate makes him worse – even when that man is oneself. The danger in this point of view is the same as in the imitation of Christ; but the Pharisee in us will never allow himself to be caught talking to publicans and whores. I must emphasize of course that psychology invented neither Christianity nor the imitation of Christ. I wish everybody could be freed from the burden of their sins by the Church. But he to whom she cannot render this service must bend very low in the imitation of Christ in order to take the burden of his cross upon him. The ancients could get along with the Greek wisdom of the ages: Μηδὲν ἄγαν, τῷ καιρῷ πάντα πρόσεστι καλά (Exaggerate nothing, all good lies in right measure). But what an abyss still separates us from reason!

Apart from the moral difficulty there is another danger which is not inconsiderable and may lead to complications, particularly with individuals who are pathologically inclined. This is the fact that the contents of the personal unconscious (i.e., the shadow) are indistinguishably merged with the archetypal contents of the collective unconscious and drag the latter with them when the shadow is brought into consciousness. This may exert an uncanny influence on the conscious mind; for activated archetypes have a disagreeable effect even – or I should perhaps say, particularly – on the most cold-blooded rationalist. He is afraid that the lowest form of conviction, namely superstition, is, as he thinks, forcing itself on him. But superstition in the truest sense only appears in such people if they are pathological, not if they can keep their balance. It then takes the form of the fear of "going mad" – for everything that the modern mind cannot define it regards as insane. It must be admitted that the archetypal contents of the collective unconscious can often assume grotesque and horrible forms in dreams and fantasies, so that even the most hard-boiled rationalist is not immune from shattering nightmares and haunting fears. The psychological elucidation of these images, which cannot be passed over in silence or blindly ignored, leads logically into the depths of religious phenomenology. The history of religion in its widest sense (including therefore mythology, folklore, and primitive psychology) is a treasure-house of archetypal forms from which the doctor can draw helpful parallels and enlightening comparisons for the purpose of calming and clarifying a consciousness that is all at sea. It is absolutely necessary to supply these fantastic images that rise up so strange and threatening before the mind's eye with some kind of context so as to make them more intelligible. Experience has shown that the best way to do this is by means of comparative mythological material.

Part II of this volume gives a large number of such examples. The reader will be particularly struck by the numerous connections between individual dream symbolism and medieval alchemy. This is not, as one might suppose, a prerogative of the case in question, but a general fact which only struck me some ten years ago when first I began to come to grips with the ideas and symbolism of alchemy.

Part III contains an introduction to the symbolism of alchemy in relation to Christianity and Gnosticism. As a bare introduction it is naturally far from being a complete exposition of this complicated and obscure subject – indeed, most of it is concerned only with the *lapis*-Christ parallel. True, this parallel gives rise to a comparison between the aims of the *opus alchymicum* and the central ideas of Christianity, for both are of the utmost importance in understanding and interpreting the images that appear in dreams and in assessing their psychological effect. This has considerable bearing on the practice of psychotherapy, because more often than not it is precisely the more intelligent and cultured patients who, finding a return to the Church impossible, come up against archetypal material and thus set the doctor problems which can no longer be mastered by a narrowly personalistic psychology. Nor is a mere knowledge of the psychic structure of a neurosis by any means sufficient; for once the process has reached the sphere of the collective unconscious we are dealing with healthy material, i.e., with the universal basis of the individually varied psyche. Our understanding of these deeper layers of the psyche is helped not only by a knowledge of primitive psychology and mythology, but to an even greater extent by some familiarity with the history of our modern consciousness and the stages immediately preceding it. On the one hand it is a child of the Church; on the other, of science, in whose beginnings very much lies hid that the Church was unable to accept – that is to say, remnants of the classical spirit and the classical feeling for nature which could not be exterminated and eventually found refuge in the natural philosophy of the Middle Ages. As the "spiritus metallorum" and the astrological components of destiny the old gods of the planets lasted out many a Christian century.* Whereas in the Church the increasing differentiation of ritual and dogma alienated consciousness from its natural roots in the unconscious, alchemy and astrology were ceaselessly engaged in preserving the bridge to nature, i.e., to the unconscious psyche, from decay. Astrology led the conscious mind back again and again to the knowledge of Heimarmene, that is, the dependence of character and destiny on certain moments in time; and alchemy afforded numerous "hooks" for the projection of those archetypes which could not be fitted smoothly into the Christian process. It is true that alchemy always stood on the verge of heresy and that certain decrees leave no doubt as to the Church's attitude towards it, but on the other hand it was effectively

---

*Paracelsus still speaks of the "gods" enthroned in the *mysterium magnum* (*Philosophia ad Athenienses*), and so does the 18th-cent. treatise of Abraham Eleazar, *Uraltes chymisches Werk*, which was influenced by Paracelsus.

protected by the obscurity of its symbolism, which could always be explained as harmless allegory. For many alchemists the allegorical aspect undoubtedly occupied the foreground to such an extent that they were firmly convinced that their sole concern was with chemical substances. But there were always a few for whom laboratory work was primarily a matter of symbols and their psychic effect. As the texts show, they were quite conscious of this, to the point of condemning the naïve goldmakers as liars, frauds, and dupes. Their own standpoint they proclaimed with propositions like "Aurum nostrum non est aurum vulgi." Although their labours over the retort were a serious effort to elicit the secrets of chemical transformation, it was at the same time – and often in overwhelming degree – the reflection of a parallel psychic process which could be projected all the more easily into the unknown chemistry of matter since that process is an unconscious phenomenon of nature, just like the mysterious alteration of substances. What the symbolism of alchemy expresses is the whole problem of the evolution of personality described above, the so-called individuation process.

Whereas the Church's great buttress is the imitation of Christ, the alchemist, without realizing it and certainly without wanting it, easily fell victim, in the loneliness and obscure problems of his work, to the promptings and unconscious assumptions of his own mind, since, unlike the Christians, he had no clear and unmistakable models on which to rely. The authors he studied provided him with symbols whose meaning he thought he understood in his own way; but in reality they touched and stimulated his unconscious. Ironical towards themselves, the alchemists coined the phrase "obscurum per obscurius." But with this method of explaining the obscure by the more obscure they only sank themselves deeper in the very process from which the Church was struggling to redeem them. While the dogmas of the Church offered analogies to the alchemical process, these analogies, in strict contrast to alchemy, had become detached from the world of nature through their connection with the historical figure of the Redeemer. The alchemical four in one, the philosophical gold, the *lapis angularis*, the *aqua divina*, became, in the Church, the four-armed cross on which the Only-Begotten had sacrificed himself once in history and at the same time for all eternity. The alchemists ran counter to the

Church in preferring to seek through knowledge rather than to find through faith, though as medieval people they never thought of themselves as anything but good Christians. Paracelsus is a classical example in this respect. But in reality they were in much the same position as modern man, who prefers immediate personal experience to belief in traditional ideas, or rather has it forced upon him. Dogma is not arbitrarily invented nor is it a unique miracle, although it is often described as miraculous with the obvious intent of lifting it out of its natural context. The central ideas of Christianity are rooted in Gnostic philosophy, which, in accordance with psychological laws, simply *had* to grow up at a time when the classical religions had become obsolete. It was founded on the perception of symbols thrown up by the unconscious individuation process which always sets in when the collective dominants of human life fall into decay. At such a time there is bound to be a considerable number of individuals who are possessed by archetypes of a numinous nature that force their way to the surface in order to form new dominants. This state of possession shows itself almost without exception in the fact that the possessed identify themselves with the archetypal contents of their unconscious, and, because they do not realize that the role which is being thrust upon them is the effect of new contents still to be understood, they exemplify these concretely in their own lives, thus becoming prophets and reformers. In so far as the archetypal content of the Christian drama was able to give satisfying expression to the uneasy and clamorous unconscious of the many, the *consensus omnium* raised this drama to a universally binding truth – not of course by an act of judgment, but by the irrational fact of possession, which is far more effective. Thus Jesus became the tutelary image or amulet against the archetypal powers that threatened to possess everyone. The glad tidings announced: "It has happened, but it will not happen to you inasmuch as you believe in Jesus Christ, the Son of God!" Yet it could and it can and it will happen to everyone in whom the Christian dominant has decayed. For this reason there have always been people who, not satisfied with the dominants of conscious life, set forth – under cover and by devious paths, to their destruction or salvation – to seek direct experience of the eternal roots, and, following the lure of the restless unconscious psyche, find themselves in the wilderness where, like Jesus, they come up against the son of darkness, the ἀντίμιμον πνεῦμα. Thus an old alchemist – and he a cleric! – prays: "Horridas nostrae mentis purga tenebras, accende lumen sensibus!" (Purge the horrible darknesses of our mind, light a light for our senses!) The author of this sentence must have been undergoing the experience of the *nigredo*, the first stage of the work, which was felt as "melancholia" in alchemy and corresponds to the encounter with the shadow in psychology.

When, therefore, modern psychotherapy once more meets with the activated archetypes of the collective unconscious, it is merely the repetition of a phenomenon that has often been observed in moments of great religious crisis, although it can also occur in individuals for whom the ruling ideas have lost their meaning. An example of this is the *descensus ad inferos* depicted in *Faust*, which, consciously or unconsciously, is an *opus alchymicum*.

The problem of opposites called up by the shadow plays a great – indeed, the decisive – role in alchemy, since it leads in the ultimate phase of the work to the union of opposites in the archetypal form of the *hierosgamos* or "chymical wedding." Here the supreme opposites, male and female (as in the Chinese *yang* and *yin*), are melted into a unity purified of all opposition and therefore incorruptible. The prerequisite for this, of course, is that the artifex should not identify himself with the figures in the work but should leave them in their objective, impersonal state. So long as the alchemist was working in his laboratory he was in a favourable position, psychologically speaking, for he had no opportunity to identify himself with the archetypes as they appeared, since they were all projected immediately into the chemical substances. The disadvantage of this situation was that the alchemist was forced to represent the incorruptible substance as a chemical product – an impossible undertaking which led to the downfall of alchemy, its place in the laboratory being taken by chemistry. But the psychic part of the work did not disappear. It captured new interpreters, as we can see from the example of *Faust*, and also from the signal connection between our modern psychology of the unconscious and alchemical symbolism.

Jung returned to the subject of the union of opposites in his last work of book length, Mysterium Coniunctionis, *completed in his eightieth year.*

From "**The Conjunction**" *Mysterium Coniunctionis*, CW 14, pars. 654–68

THE ALCHEMICAL VIEW OF THE UNION OF OPPOSITES

Herbert Silberer rightly called the coniunctio the "central idea" of the alchemical procedure.* This author correctly recognized that alchemy was, in the main, symbolical, whereas the historian of alchemy, Eduard von Lippmann, a chemist, did not mention the term "coniunctio" even in his index.† Anyone who has but a slight acquaintance with the literature knows that the adepts were ultimately concerned with a union of the substances – by whatever names these may have been called. By means of this union they hoped to attain the goal of the work: the production of the gold or a symbolical equivalent of it. Although the coniunctio is unquestionably the primordial image of what we today would call chemical combination, it is hardly possible to prove beyond a doubt that the adept thought as concretely as the modern chemist. Even when he spoke of a union of the "natures," or of an "amalgam" of iron and copper, or of a compound of sulphur and mercury, he meant it at the same time as a symbol: iron was Mars and copper was Venus, and their fusion was at the same time a love-affair. The union of the "natures" which "embrace one another" was not physical and concrete, for they were "celestial natures" which multiplied "by the command of God."** When "red lead" was roasted with gold it produced a "spirit," that is, the compound became "spiritual,"†† and from the "red spirit" proceeded the "principle of the world."*** The combination of sulphur and mercury was followed by the "bath" and "death."††† By the combination of copper and the *aqua permanens*, which was usually quicksilver, we think only of an amalgam. But for the

*Problems of Mysticism and Its Symbolism, New York, 1917, p. 121.
†Entstehung und Ausbreitung der Alchemie, Berlin, 1919–54 (3 vols.).
**Turba Philosophorum (ed. Ruska), Berlin, 1941, p. 119.
††Ibid., p. 127.
***Ibid.
†††P. 126.

alchemists it meant a secret, "philosophical" sea, since for them the *aqua permanens* was primarily a symbol or a philosophical postulate which they hoped to discover – or believed they had discovered – in the various "fluids." The substances they sought to combine in reality always had – on account of their unknown nature – a numinous quality which tended towards phantasmal personification. They were substances which, like living organisms, "fertilized one another and thereby produced the living being [ζῷον] sought by the Philosophers."* The substances seemed to them hermaphroditic, and the conjunction they strove for was a philosophical operation, namely the union of form and matter. This inherent duality explains the duplications that so often occur, e.g., two sulphurs, two quicksilvers, *Venus alba et rubea, aurum nostrum* and *aurum vulgi.*

It is therefore not surprising that the adepts, as we have seen in the previous chapters, piled up vast numbers of synonyms to express the mysterious nature of the substances – an occupation which, though it must seem utterly futile to the chemist, affords the psychologist a welcome explanation concerning the nature of the projected contents. Like all numinous contents, they have a tendency to self-amplification, that is to say they form the nuclei for an aggregation of synonyms. These synonyms represent the elements to be united as a pair of opposites; for instance as man and woman, god and goddess, son and mother, red and white, active and passive, body and spirit, and so on. The opposites are usually derived from the quaternio of elements, as we can see very clearly from the anonymous treatise "De sulphure," which says:

> Thus the fire began to work upon the air and brought forth Sulphur. Then the air began to work upon the water and brought forth Mercurius. The water began to work upon the earth and brought forth Salt. But the earth, having nothing to work upon, brought forth nothing, so the product remained within it. Therefore only three principles were produced, and the earth became the nurse and matrix of the others.

From these three principles were produced male and female, the

*Berthelot, *Collections des anciens alchemistes grecs*, III, xl 2, Paris, 1887–8.

male obviously from Sulphur and Mercurius, and the female from Mercurius and Salt. Together they bring forth the "incorruptible One," the *quinta essentia*, "and thus quadrangle will answer to quadrangle."*

The synthesis of the incorruptible One or quintessence follows the Axiom of Maria, the earth representing the "fourth." The separation of the hostile elements corresponds to the initial state of chaos and darkness. From the successive unions arise an active principle (sulphur) and a passive (salt), as well as a mediating, ambivalent principle, Mercurius. This classical alchemical trinity then produces the relationship of male to female as the supreme and essential opposition. Fire comes at the beginning and is acted on by nothing, and earth at the end acts on nothing. Between fire and earth there is no interaction; hence the four elements do not constitute a circle, i.e., a totality. This is produced only by the synthesis of male and female. Thus the square at the beginning corresponds to the quaternio of elements united in the *quinta essentia* at the end – "quadrangle will answer to quadrangle."

The alchemical description of the beginning corresponds psychologically to a primitive consciousness which is constantly liable to break up into individual affective processes – to fall apart, as it were, in four directions. As the four elements represent the whole physical world, their falling apart means dissolution into the constituents of the world, that is, into a purely inorganic and hence unconscious state. Conversely, the combination of the elements and the final synthesis of male and female is an achievement of the art and a product of conscious endeavour. The result of the synthesis was consequently conceived by the adept as self-knowledge,† which, like the knowledge of God, is needed for the preparation of the Philosophers' Stone. Piety is needed for the work, and this is nothing but knowledge of oneself. This thought occurs not only in late alchemy but also in Greek tradition, as in the Alexandrian treatise of Krates (transmitted by the Arabs), where it is said that a perfect knowledge of the soul enables the adept to understand the many different names which the Philosophers have given to the arcane substance. The "Liber

*Arthur Edward Waite, *The Hermetic Museum Restored and Enlarged*, London, 1893; reprinted 1953, pp. 142ff.
†See *Aion* (CW 9 ii), pars. 250ff.

quartorum" emphasizes that there must be self-observation in the work as well as of events in due time. It is evident from this that the chemical process of the coniunctio was at the same time a psychic synthesis. Sometimes it seems as if self-knowledge brought about the union, sometimes as if the chemical process were the efficient cause. The latter alternative is decidedly the more frequent: the coniunctio takes place in the retort or, more indefinitely, in the "natural vessel" or matrix. The vessel is also called the grave, and the union a "shared death." This state is named the "eclipse of the sun."

The coniunctio does not always take the form of a direct union, since it needs – or occurs in – a medium: "Only through a medium can the transition take place," and, "Mercurius is the medium of conjunction." Mercurius is the soul (anima), which is the "mediator between body and spirit." The same is true of the synonyms for Mercurius, the green lion and the *aqua permanens* or spiritual water, which are likewise media of conjunction. The "Consilium coniugii" mentions as a connective agent the sweet smell or "smoky vapour," recalling Basilides' idea of the sweet smell of the Holy Ghost. Obviously this refers to the "spiritual" nature of Mercurius, just as the spiritual water, also called *aqua aëris* (aerial water or air-water), is a life principle and the "marriage maker" between man and woman. A common synonym for the water is the "sea," as the place where the chymical marriage is celebrated. The "Tractatus Micreris" mentions as further synonyms the "Nile of Egypt," the "Sea of the Indians," and the "Meridian Sea." The "marvels" of this sea are that it mitigates and unites the opposites. An essential feature of the royal marriage is therefore the sea-journey, as described by Christian Rosencreutz. This alchemical motif was taken up by Goethe in *Faust II*, where it underlies the meaning of the Aegean Festival. The archetypal content of this festival has been elaborated by Kerényi in a brilliant amplificatory interpretation. The bands of nereids on Roman sarcophagi reveal the "epithalamic and the sepulchral element," for "basic to the antique mysteries ... is the identity of marriage and death on the one hand, and of birth and the eternal resurgence of life from death on the other."*

*Karl Kerényi, *Das Aegaeische Fest*, Zurich, 1941, p. 55.

Mercurius, however, is not just the medium of conjunction but also that which is to be united, since he is the essence or "seminal matter" of both man and woman. *Mercurius masculinus* and *Mercurius foemineus* are united in and through *Mercurius menstrualis*, which is the "aqua." Dorn gives the "philosophical" explanation of this in his "Physica Trismegisti": In the beginning God created *one* world (*unus mundus*). This he divided into two – heaven and earth. "Beneath this spiritual and corporeal binarius lieth hid a third thing, which is the bond of holy matrimony. This same is the medium enduring until now in all things, partaking of both their extremes, without which it cannot be at all, nor they without this medium be what they are, one thing out of three." The division into two was necessary in order to bring the "one" world out of the state of potentiality into reality. Reality consists of a multiplicity of things. But one is not a number; the first number is two, and with it multiplicity and reality begin.

It is apparent from this explanation that the desperately evasive and universal Mercurius – that Proteus twinkling in a myriad shapes and colours – is none other than the "unus mundus," the original, non-differentiated unity of the world or of Being; the ἀγνωσία of the Gnostics, the primordial unconsciousness. The Mercurius of the alchemists is a personification and concretization of what we today would call the collective unconscious. While the concept of the *unus mundus* is a metaphysical speculation, the unconscious can be indirectly experienced via its manifestations. Though in itself an hypothesis, it has at least as great a probability as the hypothesis of the atom. It is clear from the empirical material at our disposal today that the contents of the unconscious, unlike conscious contents, are mutually contaminated to such a degree that they cannot be distinguished from one another and can therefore easily take one another's place, as can be seen most clearly in dreams. The indistinguishableness of its contents gives one the impression that everything is connected with everything else and therefore, despite their multifarious modes of manifestation, that they are at bottom a unity. The only comparatively clear contents consist of motifs or types round which the individual associations congregate. As the history of the human mind shows, these archetypes are of great stability and so distinct that they allow themselves to be personified and named, even though their boundaries are blurred or cut across those of other archetypes, so that certain of their qualities can be interchanged. In particular, mandala symbolism shows a marked tendency to concentrate all the archetypes on a common centre, comparable to the relationship of all conscious contents to the ego. The analogy is so striking that a layman unfamiliar with this symbolism is easily misled into thinking that the mandala is an artificial product of the conscious mind. Naturally mandalas can be imitated, but this does not prove that all mandalas are imitations. They are produced spontaneously, without external influence, even by children and adults who have never come into contact with any such ideas.* One might perhaps regard the mandala as a reflection of the egocentric nature of consciousness, though this view would be justified only if it could be proved that the unconscious is a secondary phenomenon. But the unconscious is undoubtedly older and more original than consciousness, and for this reason one could just as well call the egocentrism of consciousness a reflection or imitation of the "self"-centrism of the unconscious.

The mandala symbolizes, by its central point, the ultimate unity of all archetypes as well as of the multiplicity of the phenomenal world, and is therefore the empirical equivalent of the metaphysical concept of a *unus mundus*. The alchemical equivalent is the lapis and its synonyms, in particular the Microcosm.†

Dorn's explanation is illuminating in that it affords us a deep insight into the alchemical *mysterium coniunctionis*. If this is nothing less than a restoration of the original state of the cosmos and the divine unconsciousness of the world, we can understand the extraordinary fascination emanating from this mystery. It is the Western equivalent of the fundamental principle of classical Chinese philosophy, namely the union of *yang* and *yin* in *tao*, and at the same time a premonition of that "tertium quid" which, on the basis of psychological experience on the one hand and of Rhine's experiments on the other, I have called "synchronicity."** If mandala symbolism is the psychological equivalent of the *unus mundus*, then synchronicity is its parapsychological equivalent. Though synchronistic phenomena occur in time and space they

*See "Concerning Mandala Symbolism" (CW 9i), par. 645.
†Cf. *Psychology and Alchemy* (CW 12), par. 426 and n. 2, fig. 195.
**Cf. my "Synchronicity: An Acausal Connecting Principle" (CW 8).

manifest a remarkable independence of both these indispensable determinants of physical existence and hence do not conform to the law of causality. The causalism that underlies our scientific view of the world breaks everything down into individual processes which it punctiliously tries to isolate from all other parallel processes. This tendency is absolutely necessary if we are to gain reliable knowledge of the world, but philosophically it has the disadvantage of breaking up, or obscuring, the universal interrelationship of events so that a recognition of the greater relationship, i.e., of the unity of the world, becomes more and more difficult. Everything that happens, however, happens in the same "one world" and is a part of it. For this reason events must possess an *a priori* aspect of unity, though it is difficult to establish this by the statistical method. So far as we can see at present, Rhine seems to have successfully demonstrated this unity by his extrasensory-perception experiments (ESP).* Independence of time and space brings about a concurrence or meaningful coincidence of events not causally connected with one another – phenomena which till now were summed under the purely descriptive concepts of telepathy, clairvoyance, and precognition. These concepts naturally have no explanatory value as each of them represents an X which cannot be distinguished from the X of the other. The characteristic feature of all these phenomena, including Rhine's psychokinetic effect and other synchronistic occurrences, is *meaningful coincidence*, and as such I have defined the synchronistic principle. This principle suggests that there is an inter-connection or unity of causally unrelated events, and thus postulates a unitary aspect of being which can very well be described as the *unus mundus*.

Mercurius usually stands for the arcane substance, whose synonyms are the panacea and the "spagyric medicine." Dorn identifies the latter with the "balsam" of Paracelsus, which is a close analogy of the μύϱον of the Basilidians. In the *De vita longa* of Paracelsus, balsam as an *elixir vitae* is associated with the term "gamonymus," which might be rendered "having the name of matrimony." Dorn thinks that the balsam, which "stands higher

---

*Cf. his *New Frontiers of the Mind*, London, 1937, and *The Reach of the Mind*, New York, 1947; London, 1948. The relevant phenomena are discussed in "Synchronicity," pars. 833ff.

than nature," is to be found in the human body and is a kind of aetheric substance. He says it is the best medicament not only for the body but also for the mind (*mens*). Though it is a corporeal substance, as a combination of the spirit and soul of the spagyric medicine it is essentially spiritual.

> We conclude that meditative philosophy consists in the over-coming of the body by mental union [*unio mentalis*]. This first union does not as yet make the wise man, but only the mental disciple of wisdom. The second union of the mind with the body shows forth the wise man, hoping for and expecting that blessed third union with the first unity [i.e., the *unus mundus*, the latent unity of the world]. May Almighty God grant that all men be made such, and may He be one in All.

*   *   *

It is significant for the whole of alchemy that in Dorn's view a mental union was not the culminating point but merely the first stage of the procedure. The second stage is reached when the mental union, that is, the unity of spirit and soul, is conjoined with the body. But a consummation of the *mysterium coniunctionis* can be expected only when the unity of spirit, soul, and body is made one with the original *unus mundus*. This third stage of the coniunctio was depicted* after the manner of an Assumption and Coronation of Mary, in which the Mother of God represents the body. The Assumption is really a wedding feast, the Christian version of the hierosgamos, whose originally incestuous nature played a great role in alchemy. The traditional incest always indicated that the supreme union of opposites expressed a combination of things which are related but of unlike nature.† This may begin with a purely intra-psychic *unio mentalis* of intellect or reason with Eros, representing feeling. Such an interior operation means a great deal, since it brings a considerable increase of self-knowledge as well as of personal maturity, but its reality is

---

*Cf. *Psychology and Alchemy* (CW 12), fig. 232.
†See "Psychology of the Transference" (CW 16), pars. 419ff. The incest symbolism is due to the intrusion of endogamous libido. The primitive "cross-cousin-marriage" was superseded by a pure exogamy which left the endogamous demands unsatisfied. It is these demands that come to the fore in incest symbolism.

merely potential and is validated only by a union with the physical world of the body. The alchemists therefore pictured the *unio mentalis* as Father and Son and their union as the dove (the "spiration" common to both), but the world of the body they represented by the feminine or passive principle, namely Mary. Thus, for more than a thousand years, they prepared the ground for the dogma of the Assumption. It is true that the far-reaching implications of a marriage of the fatherly spiritual principle with the principle of matter, or maternal corporeality, are not to be seen from the dogma at first glance. Nevertheless, it does bridge over a gulf that seems unfathomable: the apparently irremediable separation of spirit from nature and the body. Alchemy throws a bright light on the background of the dogma, for the new article of faith expresses in symbolical form exactly what the adepts recognized as being the secret of their coniunctio. The correspondence is indeed so great that the old Masters could legitimately have declared that the new dogma has written the Hermetic secret in the skies. As against this it will be said that the alchemists smuggled the mystic or theological marriage into their obscure procedures. This is contradicted by the fact that the alchymical marriage is not only older than the corresponding formulation in the liturgy and of the Church Fathers but is based on classical and pre-Christian tradition. The alchemical tradition cannot be brought into relationship with the Apocalyptic marriage of the Lamb. The highly differentiated symbolism of the latter (lamb and city) is itself an offshoot of the archetypal hierosgamos, just as this is the source for the alchemical idea of the coniunctio.

The adepts strove to realize their speculative ideas in the form of a chemical substance which they thought was endowed with all kinds of magical powers. This is the literal meaning of their uniting the *unio mentalis* with the body. For us it is certainly not easy to include moral and philosophical reflections in this amalgamation, as the alchemists obviously did. For one thing we know too much about the real nature of chemical combination, and for another we have a much too abstract conception of the mind to be able to understand how a "truth" can be hidden in matter or what an effective "balsam" must be like. Owing to medieval ignorance both of chemistry and of psychology, and the lack of any epistemological criticism, the two concepts could easily mix, so that things that for us have no recognizable connection with one another could enter into mutual relationship.

The dogma of the Assumption and the alchemical *mysterium coniunctionis* express the same fundamental thought even though in very different symbolism. Just as the Church insists on the literal taking up of the physical body into heaven, so the alchemists believed in the possibility, or even in the actual existence, of their stone or of the philosophical gold. In both cases belief was a substitute for the missing empirical reality. Even though alchemy was essentially more materialistic in its procedures than the dogma, both of them remain at the second, anticipatory stage of the coniunctio, the union of the *unio mentalis* with the body. Even Dorn did not venture to assert that he or any other adept had perfected the third stage in his lifetime. Naturally there were as many swindlers and dupes as ever who claimed to possess the lapis or golden tincture, or to be able to make it. But the more honest alchemists readily admitted that they had not yet plumbed the final secret.

One should not be put off by the physical impossibilities of dogma or of the coniunctio, for they are symbols in regard to which the allurements of rationalism are entirely out of place and miss the mark. If symbols mean anything at all, they are tendencies which pursue a definite but not yet recognizable goal and consequently can express themselves only in analogies. In this uncertain situation one must be content to leave things as they are, and give up trying to know anything beyond the symbol. In the case of dogma such a renunciation is reinforced by the fear of possibly violating the sanctity of a religious idea, and in the case of alchemy it was until very recently considered not worth while to rack one's brains over medieval absurdities. Today, armed with psychological understanding, we are in a position to penetrate into the meaning of even the most abstruse alchemical symbols, and there is no justifiable reason why we should not apply the same method to dogma. Nobody, after all, can deny that it consists of ideas which are born of man's imagining and thinking. The question of how far this thinking may be inspired by the Holy Ghost is not affected at all, let alone decided, by psychological investigation, nor is the possibility of a metaphysical background denied. Psychology cannot advance any argument either for or against the objective validity of any metaphysical view. I have repeated this statement in various places in order to give the lie to the obstinate and grotesque notion that a psychological explanation must necessarily be either psychologism or its opposite, namely a metaphysical assertion. The psychic is a phenomenal world in itself, which can be reduced neither to the brain nor to metaphysics.

I have just said that symbols are tendencies whose goal is as yet unknown.* We may assume that the same fundamental rules obtain in the history of the human mind as in the psychology of the individual. In psychotherapy it often happens that, long before they reach consciousness, certain unconscious tendencies betray their presence by symbols, occurring mostly in dreams but also in waking fantasies and symbolic actions. Often we have the impression that the unconscious is trying to enter consciousness by means of all sorts of allusions and analogies, or that it is making more or less playful attempts to attract attention to itself. One can observe these phenomena very easily in a dream-series. The series I discussed in *Psychology and Alchemy* offers a good example.†
Ideas develop from seeds, and we do not know what ideas will develop from what seeds in the course of history. The Assumption of the Virgin, for instance, is vouched for neither in Scripture nor in the tradition of the first five centuries of the Christian Church. For a long time it was officially denied even, but, with the connivance of the whole medieval and modern Church, it gradually developed as a "pious opinion" and gained so much power and influence that it finally succeeded in thrusting aside the necessity for scriptural proof and for a tradition going back to primitive times, and in attaining definition in spite of the fact that the content of the dogma is not even definable.** The papal declaration made a reality of what had long been condoned. This irrevocable step beyond the confines of historical Christianity is the strongest proof of the autonomy of archetypal images.

---

*This does not contradict the statement that symbols are the best possible formulation of an idea whose referent is not clearly known. Such an idea is always based on a tendency to represent its referent in its own way.
†Another example is the series of mandalas in "A Study of the Process of Individuation" (CW 9 i).
**Further material in F. Heiler, *Das neue Mariendogma im Lichte der Geschichte*, Munich and Basel, 1951.

Part 8.   Self and Opposites: God and the Problem of Evil

If wholeness or integration consists in the union of opposites, symbolized by the emergence of quaternities and mandalas, it follows that the most obvious pair of opposites, good and evil, are to be found in the self. Yet the self, as we have seen, "is a God-image, or at least cannot be distinguished from one." (CW 9 ii, par. 42) The conventional Christian view of God is dualistic, in that God is entirely good (the doctrine of the Summum Bonum), while evil is contained in Satan. Jung points out that an earlier Christian belief was monotheistic. "Clement of Rome taught that God rules the world with a right and a left hand, the right being Christ, the left Satan."* (CW 11, pp. 357–8, prefatory note to Answer to Job) All his life, Jung wrestled with the problem of the origin of evil. In his discussion of Christ as a manifestation of the self, Jung writes:

From "Christ, a Symbol of the Self" *Aion*, CW 9 ii, pars. 79–98

Just as we have to remember the gods of antiquity in order to appreciate the psychological value of the anima/animus archetype, so Christ is our nearest analogy of the self and its meaning. It is naturally not a question of a collective value artificially manufactured or arbitrarily awarded, but of one that is effective and present *per se*, and that makes its effectiveness felt whether the subject is conscious·of it or not. Yet, although the attributes of

---

**Naturally enough, theologians could not accept this view of the Deity. For discussion of the* privatio boni, *see Jung's correspondence with Fr Victor White, a Dominican priest who was a professor of theology at Blackfriars, Oxford. See especially C. G. Jung, Letters, vol. 2, pp. 58 and 71. Their disagreement led to an estrangement between the two men. See also Victor White's God and the Unconscious, pp. 75–6, n. 1.*

Christ (consubstantiality with the Father, co-eternity, filiation, parthenogenesis, crucifixion, Lamb sacrificed between opposites, One divided into Many, etc.) undoubtedly mark him out as an embodiment of the self, looked at from the psychological angle he corresponds to only one half of the archetype. The other half appears in the Antichrist. The latter is just as much a manifestation of the self, except that he consists of its dark aspect. Both are Christian symbols, and they have the same meaning as the image of the Saviour crucified between two thieves. This great symbol tells us that the progressive development and differentiation of consciousness leads to an ever more menacing awareness of the conflict and involves nothing less than a crucifixion of the ego, its agonizing suspension between irreconcilable opposites.* Naturally there can be no question on a total extinction of the ego, for then the focus of consciousness would be destroyed, and the result would be complete unconsciousness. The relative abolition

---

*"Oportuit autem ut alter illorum extremorum isque optimus appellaretur Dei filius propter suam excellentiam; alter vero ipsi *ex diametro oppositus* mali daemonis, Satanae diabolique filius diceretur" (But it is fitting that one of these two extremes, and that the best, should be called the Son of God because of his excellence, and the other, *diametrically opposed* to him, the son of the evil demon, of Satan and the devil) (Origen, *Contra Celsum*, VI, 45; trans. by Chadwick). The opposites even condition one another: "Ubi quid malum est ... ibi necessario bonum esse malo contrarium... Alterum ex altero sequitur: proinde aut utrumque tollendum est negandumque bona et mala esse; aut admisso altero maximeque malo, bonum quoque admissum oportet." (Where there is evil ... there must needs be good contrary to the evil... The one follows from the other; hence we must either do away with both, and deny that good and evil exist, or if we admit the one, and particularly evil, we must also admit the good.) (*Contra Celsum*, II, 51; trans. by Chadwick.) In contrast to this clear, logical statement Origen cannot help asserting elsewhere that the "Powers, Thrones, and Principalities" down to the evil spirits and impure demons "do not have it – the contrary virtue – substantially" ("non substantialiter id habeant scl. virtus adversaria"), and that they were not created evil but chose the condition of wickedness ("malitiae gradus") of their own free will. (*De principiis*, I, VIII, 4.) Origen is already committed, at least by implication, to the definition of God as the Summum Bonum, and hence betrays the inclination to deprive evil of substance. He comes very close to the Augustinian conception of the *privatio boni* when he says: "Certum namque est malum esse bono carere" (For it is certain that to be evil means to be deprived of good). But this sentence is immediately preceded by the following: "Recedere autem a bono, non aliud est quam effici in malo" (To turn aside from good is nothing other than to be perfected in evil) (*De principiis*, II, IX, 2). This shows clearly that an increase in the one means a diminution of the other, so that good and evil represent equivalent halves of an opposition.

of the ego affects only those supreme and ultimate decisions which confront us in situations where there are insoluble conflicts of duty. This means, in other words, that in such cases the ego is a suffering bystander who decides nothing but must submit to a decision and surrender unconditionally. The "genius" of man, the higher and more spacious part of him whose extent no one knows, has the final word. It is therefore well to examine carefully the psychological aspects of the individuation process in the light of Christian tradition, which can describe it for us with an exactness and impressiveness far surpassing our feeble attempts, even though the Christian image of the self – Christ – lacks the shadow that properly belongs to it.

The reason for this, as already indicated, is the doctrine of the Summum Bonum. Irenaeus says very rightly, in refuting the Gnostics, that exception must be taken to the "light of their Father," because it "could not illuminate and fill even those things which were within it," namely the shadow and the void. It seemed to him scandalous and reprehensible to suppose that within the pleroma of light there could be a "dark and formless void." For the Christian neither God nor Christ could be a paradox; they had to have a single meaning, and this holds true to the present day. No one knew, and apparently (with a few commendable exceptions) no one knows even now, that the hybris of the speculative intellect had already emboldened the ancients to propound a philosophical definition of God that more or less obliged him to be the Summum Bonum. A Protestant theologian has even had the temerity to assert that "God *can* only be good." Yahweh could certainly have taught him a thing or two in this respect, if he himself is unable to see his intellectual trespass against God's freedom and omnipotence. This forcible usurpation of the Summum Bonum naturally has its reasons, the origins of which lie far back in the past (though I cannot enter into this here). Nevertheless, it is the effective source of the concept of the *privatio boni*, which nullifies the reality of evil and can be found as early as Basil the Great (330–79) and Dionysius the Areopagite (2nd half of the 4th century), and is fully developed in Augustine.

The earliest authority of all for the later axiom "Omne bonum a Deo, omne malum ab homine" is Tatian (2nd century), who says: "Nothing evil was created by God; we ourselves have produced all wickedness." This view is also adopted by Theophilus of Antioch (2nd century) in his treatise *Ad Autolycum*.

Basil says:

> You must not look upon God as the author of the existence of evil, not consider that evil has any subsistence in itself [ἰδίαν ὑπόστασιν τοῦ κακοῦ εἶναι]. For evil does not subsist as a living being does, nor can we set before our eyes any substantial essence [οὐσίαν ἐνυπόστατον] thereof. For evil is the privation [στέρησις] of good ... And thus evil does not inhere in its own substance [ἐν ἰδίᾳ ὑπάρξει], but arises from the mutilation [πηρώμασιν] of the soul.* Neither is it uncreated, as the wicked say who set up evil for the equal of good ... nor is it created. For if all things are of God, how can evil arise from good?

Another passage sheds light on the logic of this statement. In the second homily of the *Hexaemeron* Basil says:

> It is equally impious to say that evil has its origin from God, because the contrary cannot proceed from the contrary. Life does not engender death, darkness is not the origin of light, sickness is not the maker of health ... Now if evil is neither uncreated nor created by God, whence comes its nature? That evil exists no one living in the world will deny. What shall we say, then? That evil is not a living and animated entity, but a condition [διάθεσις] of the soul opposed to virtue, proceeding from light-minded [ῥαθύμοις] persons on account of their falling away from good ... Each of us should acknowledge that he is the first author of the wickedness in him.

The perfectly natural fact that when you say "high" you immediately postulate "low" is here twisted into a causal relationship and reduced to absurdity, since it is sufficiently obvious that darkness produces no light and light produces no darkness. The idea of good and evil, however, is the premise for any moral judgment. They are a logically equivalent pair of opposites and,

---

*Basil thought that the darkness of the world came from the shadow cast by the body of heaven.

as such, the *sine qua non* of all acts of cognition. From the empirical standpoint we cannot say more than this. And from this standpoint we would have to assert that good and evil, being coexistent halves of a moral judgment, do not derive from one another but are always there together. Evil, like good, belongs to the category of human values, and we are the authors of moral value judgments, but only to a limited degree are we authors of the facts submitted to our moral judgment. These facts are called by one person good and by another evil. Only in capital cases is there anything like a *consensus generalis*. If we hold with Basil that man is the author of evil, we are saying in the same breath that he is also the author of good. But man is first and foremost the author merely of judgments; in relation to the facts judged, his responsibility is not so easy to determine. In order to do this, we would have to give a clear definition of the extent of his free will. The psychiatrist knows what a desperately difficult task this is.

For these reasons the psychologist shrinks from metaphysical assertions but must criticize the admittedly human foundations of the *privatio boni*. When therefore Basil asserts on the one hand that evil has no substance of its own but arises from a "mutilation of the soul," and if on the other hand he is convinced that evil really exists, then the relative reality of evil is grounded on a real "mutilation" of the soul which must have an equally real cause. If the soul was originally created good, then it has really been corrupted and by something that is real, even if this is nothing more than carelessness, indifference, and frivolity, which are the meaning of the word ῥαθυμία. When something – I must stress this with all possible emphasis – is traced back to a psychic condition or fact, it is very definitely not reduced to nothing and thereby nullified, but is shifted on to the plane of *psychic reality*, which is very much easier to establish empirically than, say, the reality of the devil in dogma, who according to the authentic sources was not invented by man at all but existed long before he did. If the devil fell away from God of his own free will, this proves firstly that evil was in the world before man, and therefore that man cannot be the sole author of it, and secondly that the devil already had a "mutilated" soul for which we must hold a real cause responsible. The basic flaw in Basil's argument is the *petitio principii* that lands him in insoluble contradictions: it is laid down from the start that

the independent existence of evil must be denied even in face of
the eternity of the devil as asserted by dogma. The historical reason
for this was the threat presented by Manichaean dualism. This is
especially clear in the treatise of Titus of Bostra (d. *c.* 370), entitled
Adversus Manichaeos, where he states in refutation of the
Manichaeans that, so far as substance is concerned, there is no such
thing as evil.

John Chrysostom (*c.* 344–407) uses, instead of στέρησις
(privatio), the expression ἐκτροπὴ τοῦ καλοῦ (deviation, or turning
away, from good). He says: "Evil is nothing other than a turning
away from good, and therefore evil is secondary in relation to
good."

Dionysius the Areopagite gives a detailed explanation of evil in
the fourth chapter of *De divinis nominibus*. Evil, he says, cannot
come from good, because if it came from good it would not be evil.
But since everything that exists comes from good, everything is in
some way good, but "evil does not exist at all" (τὸ δε κακὸν οὔτε ὄν
ἐστιν).

Evil in its nature is neither a thing nor does it bring anything
forth.

Evil does not exist at all and is neither good nor productive
of good [οὐκ ἔστι καθόλου τὸ κακὸν οὔτε ἀγαθὸν οὔτε ἀγαθοποιόν].

All things which are, by the very fact that they are, are good
and come from good; but in so far as they are deprived of good,
they are neither good nor do they exist.

That which has no existence is not altogether evil, for the
absolutely non-existent will be nothing, unless it be thought of
as subsisting in the good superessentially [κατὰ τὸ ὑπερούσιον].
Good, then, as absolutely existing and as absolutely non-
existing, will stand in the foremost and highest place [πολλῷ
πρότερον ὑπεριδρύμενον], while evil is neither in that which exists
nor in that which does not exist [τὸ δὲ κακὸν οὔτε ἐν τοῖς
οὖσιν, οὔτε ἐν τοῖς μὴ οὖσιν].

These quotations show with what emphasis the reality of evil was
denied by the Church Fathers. As already mentioned, this hangs
together with the Church's attitude to Manichaean dualism, as can

plainly be seen in St. Augustine. In his polemic against the Manichaeans and Marcionites he makes the following declaration:

> For this reason all things are good, since some things are better than others and the goodness of the less good adds to the glory of the better... Those things we call evil, then, are defects in good things, and quite incapable of existing in their own right outside good things... But those very defects testify to the natural goodness of things. For what is evil by reason of a defect must obviously be good of its own nature. For a defect is something contrary to nature, something which damages the nature of a thing – and it can do so only by diminishing that thing's goodness. *Evil therefore is nothing but the privation of good.* And thus it can have no existence anywhere except in some good thing... So there can be things which are good without any evil in them, such as God himself, and the higher celestial beings; but there can be no evil things without good. For if evils cause no damage to anything, they are not evils; if they do damage something, they diminish its goodness; and if they damage it still more, it is because it still has some goodness which they diminish; and if they swallow it up altogether, nothing of its nature is left to be damaged. And so there will be no evil by which it can be damaged, since there is then no nature left whose goodness any damage can diminish.*

The *Liber Sententiarum ex Augustino* says (CLXXVI): "Evil is not a substance,† for as it has not God for its author, it does not exist; and so the defect of corruption is nothing else than the desire

---

*Although the *Dialogus Quaestionum LXV* is not an authentic writing of Augustine's, it reflects his standpoint very clearly. (Question XVI: Since God created all things good and there is nothing which was not created by him, whence arises evil? Answer: Evil is not a natural thing, it is rather the name given to the privation of good. Thus there can be good without evil, but there cannot be evil without good, nor can there be evil where there is no good... Therefore, when we call a thing good, we praise its inherent nature; when we call a thing evil, we blame not its nature, but some defect in it contrary to its nature, which is good.)

†"Iniquity has no substance" (CCXXVIII). "There is a nature in which there is no evil – in which, indeed, there can be no evil. But it is impossible for a nature to exist in which there is no good" (CLX).

or act of a misdirected will."* Augustine agrees with this when he says: "The steel is not evil; but the man who uses the steel for a criminal purpose, he is evil."†

These quotations clearly exemplify the standpoint of Dionysius and Augustine: evil has no substance or existence in itself, since it is merely a diminution of good, which alone has substance. Evil is a *vitium*, a bad use of things as a result of erroneous decisions of the will (blindness due to evil desire, etc.). Thomas Aquinas, the great theoretician of the Church, says with reference to the above quotation from Dionysius:

> One opposite is known through the other, as darkness is known through light. Hence also what evil is must be known from the nature of good. Now we have said above that good is everything appetible; and thus, since every nature desires its own being and its own perfection, it must necessarily be said that the being and perfection of every created thing is essentially good. Hence it cannot be that evil signifies a being, or any form or nature. Therefore it must be that by the name of evil is signified the absence of good.**
>
> Evil is not a being, whereas good is a being.††
>
> That every agent works for an end clearly follows from the fact that every agent tends to something definite. Now that to which an agent tends definitely must needs be befitting to that agent, since the latter would not tend to it save on account of some fittingness thereto. But that which is befitting to a thing is good for it. Therefore every agent works for a good.***

St. Thomas himself recalls the saying of Aristotle that "the thing is the whiter, the less it is mixed with black,"††† without mentioning, however, that the reverse proposition: "the thing is

---

Augustini Opera omnia, Maurist edn., X, Part 2, Paris, 1835–9, cols. 2561–2618.
†*Sermones supposititii*, Sermo I, 3, Maurist edn., V, col. 2287.
**Summa theologica*, I, q. 48, ad 1 (trans. by the Fathers of the English Dominican Province, London, 1911–22, II, p. 264).
††Ibid., I, q. 48, ad 3 (trans., p. 268).
***"... Quod autem conveniens est illi bonum. Ergo omne agens agit propter bonum" (*Summa contra Gentiles*, III, ch. 3, trans. by the English Dominican Fathers, London, 1924–9, vol. III, p. 7).
†††*Summa theologica*, I, q. 48, ad 2 (trans., II, p. 266, citing Aristotle's *Topics*, iii, 4).

the blacker, the less it is mixed with white," not only has the same validity as the first but is also its logical equivalent. He might also have mentioned that not only darkness is known through light, but that, conversely, light is known through darkness.

As only that which works is real, so, according to St. Thomas, only good is real in the sense of "existing." His argument, however, introduces a good that is tantamount to "convenient, sufficient, appropriate, suitable." One ought therefore to translate "omne agens agit propter bonum" as: "Every agent works for the sake of what suits it." That's what the devil does too, as we all know. He too has an "appetite" and strives after perfection – not in good but in evil. Even so, one could hardly conclude from this that his striving is "essentially good."

Obviously evil can be represented as a diminution of good, but with this kind of logic one could just as well say: The temperature of the Arctic winter, which freezes our noses and ears, is relatively speaking only a little below the heat prevailing at the equator. For the Arctic temperature seldom falls much lower than 230° C. above absolute zero. All things on earth are "warm" in the sense that nowhere is absolute zero even approximately reached. Similarly, all things are more or less "good," and just as cold is nothing but a diminution of warmth, so evil is nothing but a diminution of good. The *privatio boni* argument remains a euphemistic *petitio principii* no matter whether evil is regarded as a lesser good or as an effect of the finiteness and limitedness of created things. The false conclusion necessarily follows from the premise "Deus = Summum Bonum," since it is unthinkable that the perfect good could ever have created evil. It merely created the good and the less good (which last is simply called "worse" by laymen). Just as we freeze miserably despite a temperature of 230° above absolute zero, so there are people and things that, although created by God, are good only to the minimal and bad to the maximal degree.

It is probably from this tendency to deny any reality to evil that we get the axiom "Omne bonum a Deo, omne malum ab homine." This is a contradiction of the truth that he who created the heat is also responsible for the cold ("the goodness of the less good"). We can certainly hand it to Augustine that all natures are good, yet just not good enough to prevent their badness from being equally obvious.

*

One could hardly call the things that have happened, and still happen, in the concentration camps of the dictator states an "accidental lack of perfection" – it would sound like mockery.

Psychology does not know what good and evil are in themselves; it knows them only as judgments about relationships. "Good" is what seems suitable, acceptable, or valuable from a certain point of view; evil is its opposite. If the things we call good are "really" good, then there must be evil things that are "real" too. It is evident that psychology is concerned with a more or less subjective judgment, i.e., with a psychic antithesis that cannot be avoided in naming value relationships: "good" denotes something that is not bad, and "bad" something that is not good. There are things which from a certain point of view are extremely evil, that is to say dangerous. There are also things in human nature which are very dangerous and which therefore seem proportionately evil to anyone standing in their line of fire. It is pointless to gloss over these evil things, because that only lulls one into a sense of false security. Human nature is capable of an infinite amount of evil, and the evil deeds are as real as the good ones so far as human experience goes and so far as the psyche judges and differentiates between them. Only unconsciousness makes no difference between good and evil. Inside the psychological realm one honestly does not know which of them predominates in the world. We hope, merely, that good does – i.e., what seems suitable to us. No one could possibly say what the general good might be. No amount of insight into the relativity and fallibility of our moral judgment can deliver us from these defects, and those who deem themselves beyond good and evil are usually the worst tormentors of mankind, because they are twisted with the pain and fear of their own sickness.

Today as never before it is important that human beings should not overlook the danger of the evil lurking within them. It is unfortunately only too real, which is why psychology must insist on the reality of evil and must reject any definition that regards it as insignificant or actually non-existent. Psychology is an empirical science and deals with realities. As a psychologist, therefore, I have neither the inclination nor the competence to mix myself up with metaphysics. Only, I have to get polemical when metaphysics encroaches on experience and interprets it in a way that is not justified empirically. My criticism of the *privatio boni* holds only so far as psychological experience goes. From the scientific point of view the *privatio boni*, as must be apparent to everyone, is founded on a *petitio principii*, where what invariably comes out at the end is what you put in at the beginning. Arguments of this kind have no power of conviction. But the fact that such arguments are not only used but are undoubtedly believed is something that cannot be disposed of so easily. It proves that there is a tendency, existing right from the start, to give priority to "good," and to do so with all the means in our power, whether suitable or unsuitable. So if Christian metaphysics clings to the *privatio boni*, it is giving expression to the tendency always to increase the good and diminish the bad. The *privatio boni* may therefore be a metaphysical truth. I presume to no judgment on this matter. I must only insist that in our field of experience white and black, light and dark, good and bad, are equivalent opposites which always predicate one another.

Jung continues his examination of the problem of evil in Answer to Job: *a controversial work which shocked some theologians. While he was writing it, Jung himself referred to the book as "pure poison." Jung states that his concern is*

> with the way in which a modern man with a Christian education and background comes to terms with the divine darkness which is unveiled in the Book of Job, and what effect it has on him . . . I hope to act as a voice for many who feel the same way as I do, and to give expression to the shattering emotion which the unvarnished spectacle of divine savagery and ruthlessness produces in us. [CW 11, par. 561]

Jung conceives that Job, by confronting God with his own capriciousness and ruthless cruelty, brings about a change in God's behaviour. "Job stands morally higher than Yahweh. In this respect the creature has surpassed the creator." (CW 11, par. 640) It is for this reason, Jung affirms, that God decides to become man in Christ.*

**See also Alan Watts,* Myth and Ritual in Christianity, *London: Thames and Hudson, 1953, ch. 2, "God and Satan."*

From *Answer to Job*, CW 11, pars. 579–608

The Book of Job places this pious and faithful man, so heavily afflicted by the Lord, on a brightly lit stage where he presents his case to the eyes and ears of the world. It is amazing to see how easily Yahweh, quite without reason, had let himself be influenced by one of his sons, by a *doubting thought*,* and made unsure of Job's faithfulness. With his touchiness and suspiciousness the mere possibility of doubt was enough to infuriate him and induce that peculiar double-faced behaviour of which he had already given proof in the Garden of Eden, when he pointed out the tree to the First Parents and at the same time forbade them to eat of it. In this way he precipitated the Fall, which he apparently never intended. Similarly, his faithful servant Job is now to be exposed to a rigorous moral test, quite gratuitously and to no purpose, although Yahweh is convinced of Job's faithfulness and constancy, and could moreover have assured himself beyond all doubt on this point had he taken counsel with his own omniscience. Why, then, is the experiment made at all, and a bet with the unscrupulous slanderer settled, without a stake, on the back of a powerless creature? It is indeed no edifying spectacle to see how quickly Yahweh abandons his faithful servant to the evil spirit and lets him fall without compunction or pity into the abyss of physical and moral suffering. From the human point of view Yahweh's behaviour is so revolting that one has to ask oneself whether there is not a deeper motive hidden behind it. Has Yahweh some secret resistance against Job? That would explain his yielding to Satan. But what does man possess that God does not have? Because of his littleness, puniness, and defencelessness against the Almighty, he possesses, as we have already suggested, a somewhat keener consciousness based on self-reflection: he must, in order to survive, always be mindful of his impotence. God has no need of this circumspection, for nowhere does he come up against an insuperable obstacle that would force him to hesitate and hence make him reflect on himself. Could a suspicion have grown up in God that man possesses an infinitely small yet more concentrated light than he, Yahweh,

*Satan is presumably one of God's eyes which "go to and fro in the earth and walk up and down in it" (Job 1:7). In Persian tradition, Ahriman proceeded from one of Ormuzd's doubting thoughts.

possesses? A jealousy of that kind might perhaps explain his behaviour. It would be quite explicable if some such dim, barely understood deviation from the definition of a mere "creature" had aroused his divine suspicions. Too often already these human beings had not behaved in the prescribed manner. Even his trusty servant Job might have something up his sleeve ... Hence Yahweh's surprising readiness to listen to Satan's insinuations against his better judgment.

Without further ado Job is robbed of his herds, his servants are slaughtered, his sons and daughters are killed by a whirlwind, and he himself is smitten with sickness and brought to the brink of the grave. To rob him of peace altogether, his wife and his old friends are let loose against him, all of whom say the wrong things. His justified complaint finds no hearing with the judge who is so much praised for his justice. Job's right is refused in order that Satan be not disturbed in his play.

One must bear in mind here the dark deeds that follow one another in quick succession: robbery, murder, bodily injury with premeditation, and denial of a fair trial. This is further exacerbated by the fact that Yahweh displays no compunction, remorse, or compassion, but only ruthlessness and brutality. The plea of unconsciousness is invalid, seeing that he flagrantly violates at least three of the commandments he himself gave out on Mount Sinai.

Job's friends do everything in their power to contribute to his moral torments, and instead of giving him, whom God has perfidiously abandoned, their warm-hearted support, they moralize in an all too human manner, that is, in the stupidest fashion imaginable, and "fill him with wrinkles." They thus deny him even the last comfort of sympathetic participation and human understanding, so that one cannot altogether suppress the suspicion of connivance in high places.

Why Job's torments and the divine wager should suddenly come to an end is not quite clear. So long as Job does not actually die, the pointless suffering could be continued indefinitely. We must, however, keep an eye on the background of all these events: it is just possible that something in this background will gradually begin to take shape as a compensation for Job's undeserved suffering – something to which Yahweh, even if he had only a faint inkling of it, could hardly remain indifferent. Without Yahweh's knowledge and contrary to his intentions, the tormented though guiltless Job had secretly been lifted up to a superior knowledge of God which God himself did not possess. Had Yahweh consulted his omniscience, Job would not have had the advantage of him. But then, so many other things would not have happened either.

Job realizes God's inner antinomy, and in the light of this realization his knowledge attains a divine numinosity. The possibility of this development lies, one must suppose, in man's "godlikeness," which one should certainly not look for in human morphology. Yahweh himself had guarded against this error by expressly forbidding the making of images. Job, by his insistence on bringing his case before God, even without hope of a hearing, had stood his ground and thus created the very obstacle that forced God to reveal his true nature. With this dramatic climax Yahweh abruptly breaks off his cruel game of cat and mouse. But if anyone should expect that his wrath will now be turned against the slanderer, he will be severely disappointed. Yahweh does not think of bringing this mischief-making son of his to account, nor does it ever occur to him to give Job at least the moral satisfaction of explaining his behaviour. Instead, he comes riding along on the tempest of his almightiness and thunders reproaches at the half-crushed human worm:

> Who is this that darkens counsel
> by words without insight?*

In view of the subsequent words of Yahweh, one must really ask oneself: *Who* is darkening *what* counsel? The only dark thing here is how Yahweh ever came to make a bet with Satan. It is certainly not Job who has darkened anything and least of all a counsel, for there was never any talk of this nor will there be in what follows. The bet does not contain any "counsel" so far as one can see – unless, of course, it was Yahweh himself who egged Satan on for the ultimate purpose of exalting Job. Naturally this development was foreseen in omniscience, and it may be that the word "counsel" refers to this eternal and absolute knowledge. If so, Yahweh's

*Job 38:2 (Zürcher Bibel).

attitude seems the more illogical and incomprehensible, as he could then have enlightened Job on this point – which, in view of the wrong done to him, would have been only fair and equitable. I must therefore regard this possibility as improbable.

Whose words are without insight? Presumably Yahweh is not referring to the words of Job's friends, but is rebuking Job. But what is Job's guilt? The only thing he can be blamed for is his incurable optimism in believing that he can appeal to divine justice. In this he is mistaken, as Yahweh's subsequent words prove. God does not want to be just; he merely flaunts might over right. Job could not get that into his head, because he looked upon God as a moral being. He had never doubted God's might, but had hoped for right as well. He had, however, already taken back this error when he recognized God's contradictory nature, and by so doing he assigned a place to God's justice and goodness. So one can hardly speak of lack of insight.

The answer to Yahweh's conundrum is therefore: it is Yahweh himself who darkens his own counsel and who has no insight. He turns the tables on Job and blames him for what he himself does: man is not permitted to have an opinion about him, and, in particular, is to have no insight which he himself does not possess. For seventy-one verses he proclaims his world-creating power to his miserable victim, who sits in ashes and scratches his sores with potsherds, and who by now has had more than enough of superhuman violence. Job has absolutely no need of being impressed by further exhibitions of this power. Yahweh, in his omniscience, could have known just how incongruous his attempts at intimidation were in such a situation. He could easily have seen that Job believes in his omnipotence as much as ever and has never doubted it or wavered in his loyalty. Altogether, he pays so little attention to Job's real situation that one suspects him of having an ulterior motive which is more important to him: Job is no more than the outward occasion for an inward process of dialectic in God. His thunderings at Job so completely miss the point that one cannot help but see how much he is occupied with himself. The tremendous emphasis he lays on his omnipotence and greatness makes no sense in relation to Job, who certainly needs no more convincing, but only becomes intelligible when aimed at a listener *who doubts it.* This "doubting thought" is Satan, who after

SELF AND OPPOSITES

completing his evil handiwork has returned to the paternal bosom in order to continue his subversive activity there. Yahweh must have seen that Job's loyalty was unshakable and that Satan had lost his bet. He must also have realized that, in accepting this bet, he had done everything possible to drive his faithful servant to disloyalty, even to the extent of perpetrating a whole series of crimes. Yet it is not remorse and certainly not moral horror that rises to his consciousness, but an obscure intimation of something that questions his omnipotence. He is particularly sensitive on this point, because "might" is the great argument. But omniscience knows that might excuses nothing. The said intimation refers, of course, to the extremely uncomfortable fact that Yahweh had let himself be bamboozled by Satan. This weakness of his does not reach full consciousness, since Satan is treated with remarkable tolerance and consideration. Evidently Satan's intrigue is deliberately overlooked at Job's expense.

Luckily enough, Job had noticed during this harangue that everything else had been mentioned except his right. He has understood that it is at present impossible to argue the question of right, as it is only too obvious that Yahweh has no interest whatever in Job's cause but is far more preoccupied with his own affairs. Satan, that is to say, has somehow to disappear, and this can best be done by casting suspicion on Job as a man of subversive opinions. The problem is thus switched on to another track, and the episode with Satan remains unmentioned and unconscious. To the spectator it is not quite clear why Job is treated to this almighty exhibition of thunder and lightning, but the performance as such is sufficiently magnificent and impressive to convince not only a larger audience but above all Yahweh himself of his unassailable power. Whether Job realizes what violence Yahweh is doing to his own omniscience by behaving like this we do not know, but his silence and submission leave a number of possibilities open. Job has no alternative but formally to revoke his demand for justice, and he therefore answers in the words quoted at the beginning: "I lay my hand on my mouth."

He betrays not the slightest trace of mental reservation – in fact, his answer leaves us in no doubt that he has succumbed completely and without question to the tremendous force of the divine demonstration. The most exacting tyrant should have been satisfied with this, and could be quite sure that his servant – from terror alone, to say nothing of his undoubted loyalty – would not dare to nourish a single improper thought for a very long time to come.

Strangely enough, Yahweh does not notice anything of the kind. He does not see Job and his situation at all. It is rather as if he had another powerful opponent in the place of Job, one who was better worth challenging. This is clear from his twice-repeated taunt:

> Gird up your loins like a man;
> I will question you, and you shall declare to me.*

One would have to choose positively grotesque examples to illustrate the disproportion between the two antagonists. Yahweh sees something in Job which we would not ascribe to him but to God, that is, an equal power which causes him to bring out his whole power apparatus and parade it before his opponent. Yahweh projects on to Job a sceptic's face which is hateful to him because it is his own, and which gazes at him with an uncanny and critical eye. He is afraid of it, for only in face of something frightening does one let off a cannonade of references to one's power, cleverness, courage, invincibility, etc. What has all that to do with Job? Is it worth the lion's while to terrify a mouse?

Yahweh cannot rest satisfied with the first victorious round. Job has long since been knocked out, but the great antagonist whose phantom is projected on to the pitiable sufferer still stands menacingly upright. Therefore Yahweh raises his arm again:

> Will you even put me in the wrong?
> Will you condemn me that you may be justified?
> Have you an arm like God,
> and can you thunder with a voice like his?†

Man, abandoned without protection and stripped of his rights, and whose nothingness is thrown in his face at every opportunity, evidently appears to be so dangerous to Yahweh that he must be

*Job 38:3 and 40:7.
†40:8–9.

battered down with the heaviest artillery. What irritates Yahweh can be seen from his challenge to the ostensible Job:

> Look on every one that is proud, and bring him low;
>   and tread down the wicked where they stand.
> Hide them in the dust together;
>   bind their faces in the hidden place.
> Then will I also acknowledge to you
>   that your own right hand can give you victory.*

Job is challenged as though he himself were a god. But in the contemporary metaphysics there was no *deuteros theos*, no other god except Satan, who owns Yahweh's ear and is able to influence him. He is the only one who can pull the wool over his eyes, beguile him, and put him up to a massive violation of his own penal code. A formidable opponent indeed, and, because of his close kinship, so compromising that he must be concealed with the utmost discretion – even to the point of God's hiding him from his own consciousness in his own bosom! In his stead God must set up his miserable servant as the bugbear whom he has to fight, in the hope that by banishing the dreaded countenance to "the hidden place" he will be able to maintain himself in a state of unconsciousness.

The stage-managing of this imaginary duel, the speechifying, and the impressive performance given by the prehistoric menagerie would not be sufficiently explained if we tried to reduce them to the purely negative factor of Yahweh's fear of becoming conscious and of the relativization which this entails. The conflict becomes acute for Yahweh as a result of a new factor, which is, however, not hidden from omniscience – though in this case the existing knowledge is not accompanied by any conclusion. The new factor is something that has never occurred before in the history of the world, the unheard-of fact that, without knowing it or wanting it, a mortal man is raised by his moral behaviour above the stars in heaven, from which position of advantage

---

*40:12–14 ("in the hidden place" is Revised Standard Version alternative reading for "in the world below").

he can behold the back of Yahweh, the abysmal world of "shards."*

Does Job know what he has seen? If he does, he is astute or canny enough not to betray it. But his words speak volumes:

> I know that thou canst do all things,
>   and that no purpose of thine can be thwarted.†

Truly, Yahweh can do all things and permits himself all things without batting an eyelid. With brazen countenance he can project his shadow side and remain unconscious at man's expense. He can boast of his superior power and enact laws which mean less than air to him. Murder and manslaughter are mere bagatelles, and if the mood takes him he can play the feudal grand seigneur and generously recompense his bondslave for the havoc wrought in his wheat-fields. "So you have lost your sons and daughters? No harm done, I will give you new and better ones."

Job continues (no doubt with downcast eyes and in a low voice):

> "Who is this that hides counsel without insight?"
> Therefore I have uttered what I did not understand,
>   things too wonderful for me, which I did not know.
> "Hear, and I will speak;
>   I will question you, and you declare to me."
> I had heard of thee by the hearing of the ear,
>   but now my eye sees thee;
> therefore I abhor myself,
>   and repent in dust and ashes.**

Shrewdly, Job takes up Yahweh's aggressive words and prostrates himself at his feet as if he were indeed the defeated antagonist. Guileless as Job's speech sounds, it could just as well be equivocal. He has learnt his lesson well and experienced "wonderful things" which are none too easily grasped. Before, he had known Yahweh "by the hearing of the ear," but now he has

---

*This is an allusion to an idea found in the later cabalistic philosophy.
†42:2.
**42:3–6 (modified).

got a taste of his reality, more so even than David – an incisive lesson that had better not be forgotten. Formerly he was naïve, dreaming perhaps of a "good" God, or of a benevolent ruler and just judge. He had imagined that a "covenant" was a legal matter and that anyone who was party to a contract could insist on his rights as agreed; that God would be faithful and true or at least just, and, as one could assume from the Ten Commandments, would have some recognition of ethical values or at least feel committed to his own legal standpoint. But, to his horror, he has discovered that Yahweh is not human but, in certain respects, less than human, that he is just what Yahweh himself says of Leviathan (the crocodile):

> He beholds everything that is high:
> He is king over all proud beasts.*

Unconsciousness has an animal nature. Like all old gods Yahweh has his animal symbolism with its unmistakable borrowings from the much older theriomorphic gods of Egypt, especially Horus and his four sons. Of the four animals of Yahweh only one has a human face. That is probably Satan, the godfather of man as a spiritual being. Ezekiel's vision attributes three-fourths animal nature and only one-fourth human nature to the animal deity, while the upper deity, the one above the "sapphire throne," merely had the "likeness" of a man.† This symbolism explains Yahweh's behaviour, which, from the human point of view, is so intolerable: it is the behaviour of an unconscious being who cannot be judged morally. Yahweh is a *phenomenon* and, as Job says, "not a man."**

One could, without too much difficulty, impute such a meaning

*Job 41:25 (Zürcher Bibel); cf. 41:34 (Authorized and Revised Standard Version).
†Ezekiel 1:26.
**The naïve assumption that the creator of the world is a conscious being must be regarded as a disastrous prejudice which later gave rise to the most incredible dislocations of logic. For example, the nonsensical doctrine of the *privatio boni* would never have been necessary had one not had to assume in advance that it is impossible for the consciousness of a good God to produce evil deeds. Divine unconsciousness and lack of reflection, on the other hand, enable us to form a conception of God which puts his actions beyond moral judgment and allows no conflict to arise between goodness and beastliness.

to Job's speech. Be that as it may, Yahweh calmed down at last. The therapeutic measure of unresisting acceptance had proved its value yet again. Nevertheless, Yahweh is still somewhat nervous of Job's friends – they "have not spoken of me what is right."* The projection of his doubt-complex extends – comically enough, one must say – to these respectable and slightly pedantic old gentlemen, as though God-knows-what depended on what they thought. But the fact that men should think at all, and especially about him, is maddeningly disquieting and ought somehow to be stopped. It is far too much like the sort of thing his vagrant son is always springing on him, thus hitting him in his weakest spot. How often already has he bitterly regretted his unconsidered outbursts!

One can hardly avoid the impression that Omniscience is gradually drawing near to a realization, and is threatened with an insight that seems to be hedged about with fears of self-destruction. Fortunately, Job's final declaration is so formulated that one can assume with some certainty that, for the protagonists, the incident is closed for good and all.

We, the commenting chorus on this great tragedy, which has never at any time lost its vitality, do not feel quite like that. For our modern sensibilities it is by no means apparent that with Job's profound obeisance to the majesty of the divine presence, and his prudent silence, a real answer has been given to the question raised by the Satanic prank of a wager with God. Job has not so much answered as reacted in an adjusted way. In so doing he displayed remarkable self-discipline, but an unequivocal answer has still to be given.

To take the most obvious thing, what about the moral wrong Job has suffered? Is man so worthless in God's eyes that not even a *tort moral* can be inflicted on him? That contradicts the fact that man is desired by Yahweh and that it obviously matters to him whether men speak "right" of him or not. He needs Job's loyalty, and it means so much to him that he shrinks at nothing in carrying out his test. This attitude attaches an almost divine importance to man, for what else is there in the whole wide world that could mean anything to one who has everything? Yahweh's divided attitude,

*Job 42:7.

which on the one hand tramples on human life and happiness without regard, and on the other hand must have man for a partner, puts the latter in an impossible position. At one moment Yahweh behaves as irrationally as a cataclysm; the next moment he wants to be loved, honoured, worshipped, and praised as just. He reacts irritably to every word that has the faintest suggestion of criticism, while he himself does not care a straw for his own moral code if his actions happen to run counter to its statutes.

One can submit to such a God only with fear and trembling, and can try indirectly to propitiate the despot with unctuous praises and ostentatious obedience. But a relationship of trust seems completely out of the question to our modern way of thinking. Nor can moral satisfaction be expected from an unconscious nature god of this kind. Nevertheless, Job got his satisfaction, without Yahweh's intending it and possibly without himself knowing it, as the poet would have it appear. Yahweh's allocutions have the unthinking yet none the less transparent purpose of showing Job the brutal power of the demiurge: "This is I, the creator of all the ungovernable, ruthless forces of Nature, which are not subject to any ethical laws. I, too, am an amoral force of Nature, a purely phenomenal personality that cannot see its own back."

This is, or at any rate could be, a moral satisfaction of the first order for Job, because through this declaration man, in spite of his impotence, is set up as a judge over God himself. We do not know whether Job realizes this, but we do know from the numerous commentaries on Job that all succeeding ages have overlooked the fact that a kind of Moira or Dike rules over Yahweh, causing him to give himself away so blatantly. Anyone can see how he unwittingly raises Job by humiliating him in the dust. By so doing he pronounces judgment on himself and gives man the moral satisfaction whose absence we found so painful in the Book of Job.

The poet of this drama showed a masterly discretion in ringing down the curtain at the very moment when his hero gave unqualified recognition to the ἀπόφασις μεγάλη of the Demiurge by prostrating himself at the feet of His Divine Majesty. No other impression was permitted to remain. An unusual scandal was blowing up in the realm of metaphysics, with supposedly devastating consequences, and nobody was ready with a saving formula which would rescue the monotheistic conception of God from disaster. Even in those days the critical intellect of a Greek could easily have seized on this new addition to Yahweh's biography and used it in his disfavour (as indeed happened, though very much later) so as to mete out to him the fate that had already overtaken the Greek gods. But a relativization of God was utterly unthinkable at that time, and remained so for the next two thousand years.

The unconscious mind of man sees correctly even when conscious reason is blind and impotent. The drama has been consummated for all eternity: Yahweh's dual nature has been revealed, and somebody or something has seen and registered this fact. Such a revelation, whether it reached man's consciousness or not, could not fail to have far-reaching consequences.

The bodily assumption of Mary into heaven was defined as a dogma of the Catholic faith by Pope Pius XII in November 1950. Jung, who had examined the doctrine of the Trinity ("A Psychological Approach to the Dogma of the Trinity," CW 11, pars. 172–295) believed this to be "the most important religious event since the Reformation." For the new dogma adds a fourth figure to the Trinity, converting it into a quaternity. (See also Part 7 above, prayer 287-97.)

From *Answer to Job* CW 11, pars. 748–57

The promulgation of the new dogma of the Assumption of the Virgin Mary could, in itself, have been sufficient reason for examining the psychological background. It was interesting to note that, among the many articles published in the Catholic and Protestant press on the declaration of the dogma, there was not one, so far as I could see, which laid anything like the proper emphasis on what was undoubtedly the most powerful motive: namely, the popular movement and the psychological need behind it. Essentially, the writers of the articles were satisfied with learned considerations, dogmatic and historical, which have no bearing on the living religious process. But anyone who has followed with attention the visions of Mary which have been increasing in number over the last few decades, and has taken their psychological significance into account, might have known what was brewing. The fact, especially, that it was largely children who had the visions might have given pause for thought, for in such cases the collective unconscious is always at work. Incidentally, the Pope himself is rumoured to have had several visions of the Mother of God on the occasion of the declaration. One could have known for a long time that there was a deep longing in the masses for an intercessor and mediatrix who would at last take her place alongside the Holy Trinity and be received as the "Queen of Heaven and Bride at the heavenly court." For more than a thousand years it had been taken for granted that the Mother of God dwelt there, and we know from the Old Testament that Sophia was with God before the creation. From the ancient Egyptian theology of the divine Pharaohs we know that God wants to become man by means of a human mother, and it was recognized even in prehistoric times that the primordial divine being is both male and female. But such a truth eventuates in time only when it is solemnly proclaimed or rediscovered. It is psychologically significant for our day that in the year 1950 the heavenly bride was united with the bridegroom. In order to interpret this event, one has to consider not only the arguments adduced by the Papal Bull, but the prefigurations in the apocalyptic marriage of the Lamb and in the Old Testament anamnesis of Sophia. The nuptial union in the *thalamus* (bridal-chamber) signifies the *hieros gamos*, and this in turn is the first step towards incarnation, towards the birth of the saviour who, since antiquity, was thought of as the *filius solis et lunae*, the *filius sapientiae*, and the equivalent of Christ. When, therefore, a longing for the exaltation of the Mother of God passes through the people, this tendency, if thought to its logical conclusion, means the desire for the birth of a saviour, a peacemaker, a "mediator pacem faciens inter inimicos."* Although he is already born in the pleroma, his birth in time can only be accomplished when it is perceived, recognized, and declared by man.

The motive and content of the popular movement which contributed to the Pope's decision solemnly to declare the new

---

*"A mediator making peace between enemies."

dogma consist not in the birth of a new god, but in the continuing incarnation of God which began with Christ. Arguments based on historical criticism will never do justice to the new dogma; on the contrary, they are as lamentably wide of the mark as are the unqualified fears to which the English archbishops have given expression. In the first place, the declaration of the dogma has changed nothing in principle in the Catholic ideology as it has existed for more than a thousand years; and in the second place, the failure to understand that God has eternally wanted to become man, and for that purpose continually incarnates through the Holy Ghost in the temporal sphere, is an alarming symptom and can only mean that the Protestant standpoint has lost ground by not understanding the signs of the times and by ignoring the continued operation of the Holy Ghost. It is obviously out of touch with the tremendous archetypal happenings in the psyche of the individual and the masses, and with the symbols which are intended to compensate the truly apocalyptic world situation today.* It seems to have succumbed to a species of rationalistic historicism and to have lost any understanding of the Holy Ghost who works in the hidden places of the soul. It can therefore neither understand nor admit a further revelation of the divine drama.

This circumstance has given me, a layman in things theological, cause to put forward my views on these dark matters. My attempt is based on the psychological experience I have harvested during the course of a long life. I do not underestimate the psyche in any respect whatsoever, nor do I imagine for a moment that psychic happenings vanish into thin air by being explained. Psychologism represents a still primitive mode of magical thinking, with the help of which one hopes to conjure the reality of the soul out of existence, after the manner of the "Proktophantasmist" in *Faust*:

*The papal rejection of psychological symbolism may be explained by the fact that the Pope is primarily concerned with the reality of metaphysical happenings. Owing to the undervaluation of the psyche that everywhere prevails, every attempt at adequate psychological understanding is immediately suspected of psychologism. It is understandable that dogma must be protected from this danger. If, in physics, one seeks to explain the nature of light, nobody expects that as a result there will be no light. But in the case of psychology everybody believes that what it explains is explained away. However, I cannot expect that my particular deviationist point of view could be known in any competent quarter.

Are you still here? Nay, it's a thing unheard.
Vanish at once! We've said the enlightening word.

One would be very ill advised to identify me with such a childish standpoint. However, I have been asked so often whether I believe in the existence of God or not that I am somewhat concerned lest I be taken for an adherent of "psychologism" far more commonly than I suspect. What most people overlook or seem unable to understand is the fact that I regard the psyche as *real*. They believe only in physical facts, and must consequently come to the conclusion that either the uranium itself or the laboratory equipment created the atom bomb. That is no less absurd than the assumption that a non-real psyche is responsible for it. God is an obvious psychic and non-physical fact, i.e., a fact that can be established psychically but not physically. Equally, these people have still not got it into their heads that the psychology of religion falls into two categories, which must be sharply distinguished from one another: firstly, the psychology of the religious person, and secondly, the psychology of religion proper, i.e., of religious contents.

It is chiefly my experiences in the latter field which have given me the courage to enter into the discussion of the religious question and especially into the pros and cons of the dogma of the Assumption – which, by the way, I consider to be the most important religious event since the Reformation. It is a *petra scandali* for the unpsychological mind: how can such an unfounded assertion as the bodily reception of the Virgin into heaven be put forward as worthy of belief? But the method which the Pope uses in order to demonstrate the truth of the dogma makes sense to the psychological mind, because it bases itself firstly on the necessary prefigurations, and secondly on a tradition of religious assertions reaching back for more than a thousand years. Clearly, the material evidence for the existence of this psychic phenomenon is more than sufficient. It does not matter at all that a physically impossible fact is asserted, because all religious assertions are physical impossibilities. If they were not so, they would, as I said earlier, necessarily be treated in the text-books of natural science. But religious statements without exception have to do with the reality of the *psyche* and not with the reality of *physis*. What outrages the

Protestant standpoint in particular is the boundless approximation of the Deipara to the Godhead and, in consequence, the endangered supremacy of Christ, from which Protestantism will not budge. In sticking to this point it has obviously failed to consider that its hymnology is full of references to the "heavenly bridegroom," who is now suddenly supposed not to have a bride with equal rights. Or has, perchance, the "bridegroom," in true psychologistic manner, been understood as a mere metaphor?

The logical consistency of the papal declaration cannot be surpassed, and it leaves Protestantism with the odium of being nothing but a *man's religion* which allows no metaphysical representation of woman. In this respect it is similar to Mithraism, and Mithraism found this prejudice very much to its detriment. Protestantism has obviously not given sufficient attention to the signs of the times which point to the equality of women. But this equality requires to be metaphysically anchored in the figure of a "divine" woman, the bride of Christ. Just as the person of Christ cannot be replaced by an organization, so the bride cannot be replaced by the Church. The feminine, like the masculine, demands an equally personal representation.

The dogmatizing of the Assumption does not, however, according to the dogmatic view, mean that Mary has attained the status of a goddess, although, as mistress of heaven (as opposed to the prince of the sublunary aerial realm, Satan) and mediatrix, she is functionally on a par with Christ, the king and mediator. At any rate her position satisfies the need of the archetype. The new dogma expresses a renewed hope for the fulfilment of that yearning for peace which stirs deep down in the soul, and for a resolution of the threatening tension between the opposites. Everyone shares this tension and everyone experiences it in his individual form of unrest, the more so the less he sees any possibility of getting rid of it by rational means. It is no wonder, therefore, that the hope, indeed the expectation of divine intervention arises in the collective unconscious and at the same time in the masses. The papal declaration has given comforting expression to this yearning. How could Protestantism so completely miss the point? This lack of understanding can only be explained by the fact that the dogmatic symbols and hermeneutic allegories have lost their meaning for Protestant rationalism. This is also true, in some measure, of the opposition to the new dogma within the Catholic Church itself, or rather to the dogmatization of the old doctrine. Naturally, a certain degree of rationalism is better suited to Protestantism than it is to the Catholic outlook. The latter gives the archetypal symbolisms the necessary freedom and space in which to develop over the centuries while at the same time insisting on their original form, unperturbed by intellectual difficulties and the objections of rationalists. In this way the Catholic Church demonstrates her maternal character, because she allows the tree growing out of her matrix to develop according to its own laws. Protestantism, in contrast, is committed to the paternal spirit. Not only did it develop, at the outset, from an encounter with the worldly spirit of the times, but it continues this dialectic with the spiritual currents of every age; for the pneuma, in keeping with its original wind nature, is flexible, ever in living motion, comparable now to water, now to fire. It can desert its original haunts, can even go astray and get lost, if it succumbs too much to the spirit of the age. In order to fulfil its task, the Protestant spirit must be full of unrest and occasionally troublesome; it must even be revolutionary, so as to make sure that tradition has an influence on the change of contemporary values. The shocks it sustains during this encounter modify and at the same time enliven the tradition, which in its slow progress through the centuries would, without these disturbances, finally arrive at complete petrifaction and thus lose its effect. By merely criticizing and opposing certain developments within the Catholic Church, Protestantism would gain only a miserable bit of vitality, unless, mindful of the fact that Christianity consists of two separate camps, or rather, is a disunited brother-sister pair, it remembers that besides defending its own existence it must acknowledge Catholicism's right to exist too. A brother who for theological reasons wanted to cut the thread of his elder sister's life would rightly be called inhuman – to say nothing of Christian charity – and the converse is also true. Nothing is achieved by merely negative criticism. It is justified only to the degree that it is creative. Therefore it would seem profitable to me if, for example, Protestantism admitted that it is shocked by the new dogma not only because it throws a distressing light on the gulf between brother and sister, but because, for fundamental reasons, a situation has developed within Christianity which removes it further than ever from the sphere of worldly understanding. Protestantism knows, or could know, how much it owes its very existence to the Catholic Church. How much or how little does the Protestant still possess if he can no longer criticize or protest? In view of the intellectual *skandalon* which the new dogma represents, he should remind himself of his Christian responsibility – "Am I my brother's (or in this case, my sister's) keeper?" – and examine in all seriousness the reasons, explicit or otherwise, that decided the declaration of the new dogma. In so doing, he should guard against casting cheap aspersions and would do well to assume that there is more in it than papal arbitrariness. It would be desirable for the Protestant to understand that the new dogma has placed upon him a new responsibility towards the worldly spirit of our age, for he cannot simply deny his problematical sister before the eyes of the world. He must, even if he finds her antipathetic, be fair to her if he does not want to lose his self-respect. For instance, this is a favourable opportunity for him to ask himself, for a change, what is the meaning not only of the new dogma but of all more or less dogmatic assertions over and above their literal concretism. Considering the arbitrary and protean state of his own dogmas, and the precarious, schism-riven condition of his Church, he cannot afford to remain rigid and impervious to the spirit of the age. And since, moreover, in accordance with his obligations to the spirit, he is more concerned to come to terms with the world and its ideas than with God, it would seem clearly indicated that, on the occasion of the entry of the Mother of God into the heavenly bridal-chamber, he should bend to the great task of reinterpreting all the Christian traditions. If it is a question of truths which are anchored deep in the soul – and no one with the slightest insight can doubt this fact – then the solution of this task must be possible. For this we need the freedom of the spirit, which, as we know, is assured only in Protestantism. The dogma of the Assumption is a slap in the face for the historical and rationalistic view of the world, and would remain so for all time if one were to insist obstinately on the arguments of reason and history. This is a case, if ever there was one, where psychological understanding is needed, because the mythologem coming to light is so obvious that we must be deliberately blinding ourselves if we cannot see its symbolic nature and interpret it in symbolic terms.

The dogmatization of the *Assumptio Mariae* points to the *hieros gamos* in the pleroma, and this in turn implies, as we have said, the future birth of the divine child, who, in accordance with the divine trend towards incarnation, will choose as his birthplace the empirical man. The metaphysical process is known to the psychology of the unconscious as the individuation process. In so far as this process, as a rule, runs its course unconsciously as it has from time immemorial, it means no more than that the acorn becomes an oak, the calf a cow, and the child an adult. But if the individuation process is made conscious, consciousness must confront the unconscious and a balance between the opposites must be found. As this is not possible through logic, one is dependent on *symbols* which make the irrational union of opposites possible. They are produced spontaneously by the unconscious and are amplified by the conscious mind. The central symbols of this process describe the self, which is man's totality, consisting on the one hand of that which is conscious to him, and on the other hand of the contents of the unconscious. The self is the τέλειος ἄνθρωπος, the whole man, whose symbols are the divine child and its synonyms. This is only a very summary sketch of the process, but it can be observed at any time in modern man, or one can read about it in the documents of Hermetic philosophy from the Middle Ages. The parallelism between the symbols is astonishing to anyone who knows both the psychology of the unconscious and alchemy.

The difference between the "natural" individuation process, which runs its course unconsciously, and the one which is consciously realized, is tremendous. In the first case consciousness nowhere intervenes; the end remains as dark as the beginning. In the second case so much darkness comes to light that the personality is permeated with light, and consciousness necessarily gains in scope and insight. The encounter between conscious and unconscious has to ensure that the light which shines in the darkness is not only comprehended by the darkness, but comprehends it. The *filius solis et lunae* is the possibility as well as the symbol of the union of opposites. It is the alpha and omega of the process, the mediator and intermedius. "It has a thousand names," say the alchemists, meaning that the source from which the individuation process rises and the goal towards which it aims is nameless, ineffable.

It is only through the psyche that we can establish that God acts upon us, but we are unable to distinguish whether these actions emanate from God or from the unconscious. We cannot tell whether God and the unconscious are two different entities. Both are border-line concepts for transcendental contents. But empirically it can be established, with a sufficient degree of probability, that there is in the unconscious an archetype of wholeness which manifests itself spontaneously in dreams, etc., and a tendency, independent of the conscious will, to relate other archetypes to this centre. Consequently, it does not seem improbable that the archetype of wholeness occupies as such a central position which approximates it to the God-image. The similarity is further borne out by the peculiar fact that the archetype produces a symbolism which has always characterized and expressed the Deity. These facts make possible a certain qualification of our above thesis concerning the indistinguishableness of God and the unconscious. Strictly speaking, the God-image does not coincide with the unconscious as such, but with a special content of it, namely the archetype of the self. It is this archetype from which we can no longer distinguish the God-image empirically. We can arbitrarily postulate a difference between these two entities, but that does not help us at all. On the contrary, it only helps us to separate man from God, and prevents God from becoming man. Faith is certainly right when it impresses on man's mind and heart how infinitely far away and inaccessible God is; but it also teaches his nearness, his immediate presence, and it is just this nearness which has to be empirically real if it is not to lose all significance. Only that which acts upon me do I recognize as real and actual. But that which has no effect upon me might as well not exist. The religious need longs for wholeness, and therefore lays hold of the images of wholeness offered by the unconscious, which, independently of the conscious mind, rise up from the depths of our psychic nature.

Part 9. "*Unus Mundus*" and Synchronicity

Jung, in common with other thinkers at different periods of history, believed in an ultimate unity of all existence. Using the terminology of medieval philosophy, he referred to this as the unus mundus. *This unity is outside the human categories of time and space, and beyond our separation of reality into physical and mental. In* Psychology and Alchemy *Jung writes of*

> actualizing those contents of the unconscious which are outside nature, i.e. not a datum of our empirical world, and therefore an *a priori* of archetypal character. The place or the medium of realization is neither mind nor matter, but that intermediate realm of subtle reality which can adequately be expressed only by the symbol. [CW 12, par. 400]

If our categories of physical and mental are artificial, "objective" events and states of mind may be interrelated. Jung certainly believed that archetypes manifested themselves, at least occasionally, in physical events and in states of mind at the same time. He named this phenomenon synchronicity.

From "Flying Saucers: a Modern Myth of Things Seen in the Skies" CW 10, pars. 779–80

Thus it is a fact of singular importance that number also characterizes the "personal" nature of the mediating figure, that it appears as a mediator. From the psychological standpoint, and having regard to the limits set to all scientific knowledge, I have called the mediating or "uniting" symbol which necessarily proceeds from a sufficiently great tension of opposites the "self." I chose this term in order to make clear that I am concerned primarily with the formulation of empirical facts and not with dubious incursions into metaphysics. There I would trespass upon all manner of religious convictions. Living in the West, I would have to say Christ instead of "self," in the Near East it would be Khidr, in the Far East atman or Tao or the Buddha, in the Far West maybe a hare or Mondamin, and in cabalism it would be Tifereth. Our world has shrunk, and it is dawning on us that humanity is *one*, with *one* psyche. Humility is a not inconsiderable virtue which should prompt Christians, for the sake of charity – the greatest of all virtues – to set a good example and acknowledge that though there is only *one* truth it speaks in many tongues, and that if we still cannot see this it is simply due to lack of understanding. No one is so godlike that he alone knows the true word. All of us gaze into that "dark glass" in which the dark myth takes shape, adumbrating the invisible truth. In this glass the eyes of the spirit glimpse an image which we call the self, fully conscious of the fact that it is an anthropomorphic image which we have merely named but not explained. By "self" we mean psychic wholeness, but what realities underlie this concept we do not know, because psychic contents cannot be observed in their unconscious state, and moreover the psyche cannot know itself. The conscious can know the unconscious only so far as it has become conscious. We have only a very hazy idea of the changes an unconscious content undergoes in the process of becoming conscious, but no certain knowledge. The concept of psychic wholeness necessarily implies an element of transcendence on account of the existence of unconscious components. Transcendence in this sense is not equivalent to a metaphysical postulate or hypostasis; it claims to be no more than a borderline concept, to quote Kant.

That there is something beyond the borderline, beyond the frontiers of knowledge, is shown by the archetypes and, most clearly of all, by numbers, which this side of the border are quantities but on the other side are autonomous psychic entities, capable of making qualitative statements which manifest themselves in *a priori* patterns of order. These patterns include not only causally explicable phenomena like dream-symbols and such, but remarkable relativizations of time and space which simply cannot be explained causally. They are the parapsychological phenomena which I have summed up under the term "synchronicity" and which have been statistically investigated by Rhine. The positive results of his experiments elevate these phenomena to the rank of undeniable facts. This brings us a little nearer to understanding the mystery of psychophysical parallelism, for we now know that a factor exists which mediates between the apparent incommensurability of body and psyche, giving matter a kind of "psychic" faculty and the psyche a kind of "materiality," by means of which the one can work on the other. That the body can work on the psyche seems to be a truism, but strictly speaking all we know is that any bodily defect or illness also expresses itself psychically. Naturally this assumption only holds good if, contrary to the popular materialistic view, the psyche is credited with an existence of its own. But materialism in its turn cannot explain how chemical changes can produce a psyche. Both views, the materialistic as well as the spiritualistic, are metaphysical prejudices. It accords better with experience to suppose that living matter has a psychic aspect, and the psyche a physical aspect. If we give due consideration to the facts of parapsychology, then the hypothesis of the psychic aspect must be extended beyond the sphere of biochemical processes to matter in general. In that case all reality would be grounded on an as yet unknown substrate possessing material and at the same time psychic qualities. In view of the trend of modern theoretical physics, this assumption should arouse fewer resistances than before. It would also do away with the awkward hypothesis of psychophysical parallelism, and afford us an opportunity to construct a new world model closer to the idea of the *unus mundus*. The "acausal" correspondences between mutually independent psychic and physical events, i.e., synchronistic phenomena, and in particular psychokinesis, would then become more understandable, for every physical event would involve a psychic one and vice versa. Such reflections are not idle speculations; they are forced on us in any serious psychological investigation of the Ufo phenomenon.

Jung's collaboration with the physicist Wolfgang Pauli (The Interpretation of Nature and the Psyche, *London and New York, 1955*) *led to the recognition of a shared problem. Jung repeatedly emphasized the fact that, in psychology, the observer could not be separated from what he observed, and that making the contents of the unconscious conscious altered the way in which each functioned. Modern physicists, trying to observe the behaviour of minute particles, found that their observations altered the behaviour of the particles. As Pauli writes: "In microphysics, however, the natural laws are of such a kind that every bit of knowledge gained from a measurement must be paid for by the loss of other, complementary items of knowledge." ("The Influence of Archetypal Ideas on Kepler's Theories," p. 211) Both physicist and psychologist, therefore, are up against the problem of defining an objective order of nature. Pauli also points out that scientific laws and theories are not derived entirely from the observation of the external world, but that "intuition and the direction of attention play a considerable role in the development of the concepts and ideas." (ibid., p. 151) Pauli writes: "It seems most satisfactory to introduce at this point the postulate of a cosmic order independent of our choice and distinct from the world of phenomena." (ibid., p. 152)*

From "The Conjunction" *Mysterium Coniunctionis*, CW 14, pars. 767–80

If Dorn, then, saw the consummation of the mysterium coniunctionis in the union of the alchemically produced *caelum* with the *unus mundus*, he expressly meant not a fusion of the individual with his environment, or even his adaptation to it, but a *unio mystica* with the potential world. Such a view indeed seems to us "mystical," if we misuse this word in its pejorative modern sense. It is not, however, a question of thoughtlessly used words but of a view which can be translated from medieval language into modern concepts. Undoubtedly the idea of the *unus mundus* is founded on the assumption that the multiplicity of the empirical world rests on an underlying unity, and that not two or more fundamentally different worlds exist side by side or are mingled with one another. Rather, everything divided and different belongs to one and the same world, which is not the world of sense but a postulate whose probability is vouched for by the fact that until now no one has been able to discover a world in which the known laws of nature are invalid. That even the psychic world, which is so extraordinarily different from the physical world, does not have its roots outside the one cosmos is evident from the undeniable fact that causal connections exist between the psyche and the body which point to their underlying unitary nature.

All that *is* is not encompassed by our knowledge, so that we are not in a position to make any statements about its total nature. Microphysics is feeling its way into the unknown side of matter, just as complex psychology is pushing forward into the unknown side of the psyche. Both lines of investigation have yielded findings which can be conceived only by means of antinomies, and both have developed concepts which display remarkable analogies. If this trend should become more pronounced in the future, the hypothesis of the unity of their subject-matters would gain in probability. Of course there is little or no hope that the unitary Being can ever be conceived, since our powers of thought and language permit only of antinomian statements. But this much we do know beyond all doubt, that empirical reality has a transcendental background – a fact which, as Sir James Jeans has shown, can be expressed by Plato's parable of the cave. The common background of microphysics and depth-psychology is as much physical as psychic and therefore neither, but rather a third thing, a neutral nature which can at most be grasped in hints since in essence it is transcendental.

The background of our empirical world thus appears to be in fact a *unus mundus*. This is at least a probable hypothesis which satisfies the fundamental tenet of scientific theory: "Explanatory principles are not to be multiplied beyond the necessary." The transcendental psychophysical background corresponds to a "potential world" in so far as all those conditions which determine the form of empirical phenomena are inherent in it. This obviously holds good as much for physics as for psychology, or, to be more precise, for macrophysics as much as for the psychology of consciousness.

A further extract illustrating Jung's collaboration with Pauli may help to clarify his conception.

From "**On the Nature of the Psyche**" CW 8, pars. 439–40

The application of statistical laws to processes of atomic magnitude in physics has a noteworthy correspondence in psychology, so far as psychology investigates the bases of consciousness by pursuing the conscious processes until they lose themselves in darkness and unintelligibility, and nothing more can be seen but effects which have an *organizing* influence on the contents of consciousness.* Investigation of these effects yields the singular fact that they proceed from an unconscious, i.e., objective, reality which behaves at the same time like a subjective one – in other words, like a consciousness. Hence the reality underlying the unconscious effects includes the observing subject and is therefore constituted in a way that we cannot conceive. It is, at one and the same time, absolute subjectivity and universal truth, for in principle it can be shown to be present everywhere, which certainly cannot be said of conscious contents of a personalistic nature. The elusiveness, capriciousness, haziness, and uniqueness that the lay mind always associates with the idea of the psyche applies only to consciousness, and not to the absolute

---

*It may interest the reader to hear the opinion of a physicist on this point. Professor Pauli, who was good enough to glance through the ms. of this supplement, writes: "As a matter of fact the physicist would expect a psychological correspondence at this point, because the epistemological situation with regard to the concepts 'conscious' and 'unconscious' seems to offer a pretty close analogy to the undermentioned 'complementarity' situation in physics. On the one hand the unconscious can only be inferred indirectly from its (organizing) effects on conscious contents. On the other hand every 'observation of the unconscious,' i.e., every conscious realization of unconscious contents, has an uncontrollable reactive effect on these same contents (which as we know precludes in principle the possibility of 'exhausting' the unconscious by making it conscious). Thus the physicist will conclude *per analogiam* that this uncontrollable reactive effect of the observing subject on the unconscious limits the objective character of the latter's reality and lends it at the same time a certain subjectivity. Although the *position* of the 'cut' between conscious and unconscious is (at least up to a point) left to the free choice of the 'psychological experimenter,' the *existence* of this 'cut' remains an unavoidable necessity. Accordingly, from the standpoint of the psychologist, the 'observed system' would consist not of physical objects only, but would also include the unconscious, while consciousness would be assigned the role of 'observing medium.' It is undeniable that the development of 'microphysics' has brought the way in which nature is described in this science very much closer to that of the newer psychology: but whereas the former, on account of the basic 'complementarity' situation, is faced with the impossibility of eliminating the effects of the observer by determinable correctives, and has therefore to abandon in principle any objective understanding of physical phenomena, the latter can supplement the purely subjective psychology of consciousness by postulating the existence of an unconscious that possesses a large measure of objective reality."

unconscious. The qualitatively rather than quantitatively definable units with which the unconscious works, namely the archetypes, therefore have a nature that *cannot with certainty be designated as psychic.*

Although I have been led by purely psychological considerations to doubt the exclusively psychic nature of the archetypes, psychology sees itself obliged to revise its "only psychic" assumptions in the light of the physical findings too. Physics has demonstrated, as plainly as could be wished, that in the realm of atomic magnitudes an observer is postulated in objective reality, and that only on this condition is a satisfactory scheme of explanation possible. This means that a subjective element attaches to the physicist's world picture, and secondly that a connection necessarily exists between the psyche to be explained and the objective space-time continuum. Since the physical continuum is inconceivable it follows that we can form no picture of its psychic aspect either, which also necessarily exists. Nevertheless, the relative or partial identity of psyche and physical continuum is of the greatest importance theoretically, because it brings with it a tremendous simplification by bridging over the seeming incommensurability between the physical world and the psychic, not of course in any concrete way, but from the physical side by means of mathematical equations, and from the psychological side by means of empirically derived postulates – archetypes – whose content, if any, cannot be represented to the mind. Archetypes, so far as we can observe and experience them at all, manifest themselves only through their ability to *organize* images and ideas, and this is always an unconscious process which cannot be detected until afterwards. By assimilating ideational material whose provenance in the phenomenal world is not to be contested, they become visible and *psychic.* Therefore they are recognized at first only as psychic entities and are conceived as such, with the same right with which we base the physical phenomena of immediate perception on Euclidean space. Only when it comes to explaining psychic phenomena of a minimal degree of clarity are we driven to assume that archetypes must have a nonpsychic aspect. Grounds for such a conclusion are supplied by the phenomena of synchronicity, which are associated with the activity of unconscious operators and have hitherto been regarded, or repudiated, as "telepathy," etc.* Scepticism should, however, be levelled only at incorrect theories and not at facts which exist in their own right. No unbiased observer can deny them. Resistance to the recognition of such facts rests principally on the repugnance people feel for an allegedly supernatural faculty tacked on to the psyche, like "clairvoyance." The very diverse and confusing aspects of these phenomena are, so far as I can see at present, completely explicable on the assumption of a psychically relative space-time continuum. As soon as a psychic content crosses the threshold of consciousness, the synchronistic marginal phenomena disappear, time and space resume their accustomed sway, and consciousness is once more isolated in its subjectivity. We have here one of those instances which can best be understood in terms of the physicist's idea of "complementarity." When an unconscious content passes over into consciousness its synchronistic manifestation ceases; conversely, synchronistic phenomena can be evoked by putting the subject into an unconscious state (trance). The same relationship of complementarity can be observed just as easily in all those extremely common medical cases in which certain clinical symptoms disappear when the corresponding unconscious contents are made conscious. We also know that a number of psychosomatic phenomena which are otherwise outside the control of the will can be induced by hypnosis, that is, by this same restriction of consciousness. Professor Pauli formulates the physical side of the complementarity relationship here expressed, as follows: "It rests with the free choice of the experimenter (or observer) to decide ... which insights he will gain and which he will lose; or, to put it in popular language, whether he will measure A and ruin B or ruin A and measure B. It does *not* rest with him, however, to gain only insights and not lose any." This is particularly true of the relation between the physical standpoint and the psychological. Physics determines quantities and their relation to one another; psychology determines qualities without being able to measure quantities. Despite that, both sciences arrive at ideas which come significantly close to one another. The parallelism of psychological and physical explanations has already

---

*The physicist Pascual Jordan ("Positivistische Bemerkungen über die parapsychischen Erscheinungen," *Zentralblatt für Psychotherapie*, IX, Leipzig, 1956, 14 ff.) has already used the idea of relative space to explain telepathic phenomena.

been pointed out by C. A. Meier in his essay "Moderne Physik – Moderne Psychologie."* He says: "Both sciences have, in the course of many years of independent work, amassed observations and systems of thought to match them. Both sciences have come up against certain barriers which ... display similar basic characteristics. The object to be investigated, and the human investigator with his organs of sense and knowledge and their extensions (measuring instruments and procedures), are indissolubly bound together. That is complementarity in physics as well as in psychology." Between physics and psychology there is in fact "a genuine and authentic relationship of complementarity."

In his long essay "Synchronicity: an Acausal Connecting Principle," Jung gives examples of what he means by synchronous events.

From "**Synchronicity: an Acausal Connecting Principle**" CW 8, pars. 843–5

The problem of synchronicity has puzzled me for a long time, ever since the middle twenties,† when I was investigating the phenomena of the collective unconscious and kept on coming across connections which I simply could not explain as chance groupings or "runs." What I found were "coincidences" which were connected so meaningfully that their "chance" concurrence would represent a degree of improbability that would have to be expressed by an astronomical figure. By way of example, I shall mention an incident from my own observation. A young woman I was treating had, at a critical moment, a dream in which she was given a golden scarab. While she was telling me this dream I sat

---

*Die Kulturelle Bedeutung der komplexen Psychologie, Berlin, 1935.
†Even before that time certain doubts had arisen in me as to the unlimited applicability of the causal principle in psychology. In the foreword to the 1st edn. of Collected Papers on Analytical Psychology, I had written (p. ix): "Causality is only one principle and psychology essentially cannot be exhausted by causal methods only, because the mind [= psyche] lives by aims as well." Psychic finality rests on a "pre-existent" meaning which becomes problematical only when it is an unconscious arrangement. In that case we have to suppose a "knowledge" prior to all consciousness. Hans Driesch comes to the same conclusion (Die "Seele" als elementarer Naturfaktor, Leipzig, 1903, pp. 8off.).

with my back to the closed window. Suddenly I heard a noise behind me, like a gentle tapping. I turned round and saw a flying insect knocking against the window-pane from outside. I opened the window and caught the creature in the air as it flew in. It was the nearest analogy to a golden scarab that one finds in our latitudes, a scarabaeid beetle, the common rose-chafer (*Cetonia aurata*), which contrary to its usual habits had evidently felt an urge to get into a dark room at this particular moment. I must admit that nothing like it ever happened to me before or since, and that the dream of the patient has remained unique in my experience.

I should like to mention another case that is typical of a certain category of events. The wife of one of my patients, a man in his fifties, once told me in conversation that, at the deaths of her mother and her grandmother, a number of birds gathered outside the windows of the death-chamber. I had heard similar stories from other people. When her husband's treatment was nearing its end, his neurosis having been cleared up, he developed some apparently quite innocuous symptoms which seemed to me, however, to be those of heart-disease. I sent him along to a specialist, who after examining him told me in writing that he could find no cause for anxiety. On the way back from this consultation (with the medical report in his pocket) my patient collapsed in the street. As he was brought home dying, his wife was already in a great state of anxiety because, soon after her husband had gone to the doctor, a whole flock of birds alighted on their house. She naturally remembered the similar incidents that had happened at the death of her own relatives, and feared the worst.

Although I was personally acquainted with the people concerned and know very well that the facts here reported are true, I do not imagine for a moment that this will induce anybody who is determined to regard such things as pure "chance" to change his mind. My sole object in relating these two incidents is simply to give some indication of how meaningful coincidences usually present themselves in practical life. The meaningful connection is obvious enough in the first case in view of the approximate identity of the chief objects (the scarab and the beetle); but in the second case the death and the flock of birds seem to be incommensurable with one another. If one considers, however, that in the Babylonian Hades the souls wore a "feather dress," and that in ancient Egypt the *ba*, or soul, was thought of as a bird,* it is not too far-fetched to suppose that there may be some archetypal symbolism at work. Had such an incident occurred in a dream, that interpretation would be justified by the comparative psychological material. There also seems to be an archetypal foundation to the first case. It was an extraordinarily difficult case to treat, and up to the time of the dream little or no progress had been made. I should explain that the main reason for this was my patient's animus, which was steeped in Cartesian philosophy and clung so rigidly to its own idea of reality that the efforts of three doctors – I was the third – had not been able to weaken it. Evidently something quite irrational was needed which was beyond my powers to produce. The dream alone was enough to disturb ever so slightly the rationalistic attitude of my patient. But when the "scarab" came flying in through the window in actual fact, her natural being could burst through the armour of her animus possession and the process of transformation could at last begin to move. Any essential change of attitude signifies a psychic renewal which is usually accompanied by symbols of rebirth in the patient's dreams and fantasies. The scarab is a classic example of a rebirth symbol. The ancient Egyptian Book of What Is in the Netherworld describes how the dead sun-god changes himself at the tenth station into Khepri, the scarab, and then, at the twelfth station, mounts the barge which carries the rejuvenated sun-god into the morning sky. The only difficulty here is that with educated people cryptomnesia often cannot be ruled out with certainty (although my patient did not happen to know this symbol). But this does not alter the fact that the psychologist is continually coming up against cases where the emergence of symbolic parallels† cannot be explained without the hypothesis of the collective unconscious.

Jung took over from Gnostic theology the term "pleroma," which is defined in the OED as "the abode of God and of the totality of the Divine powers and emanations." In the Septem Sermones ad

*In Homer the souls of the dead "twitter."
†Naturally these can only be verified when the doctor himself has the necessary knowledge of symbology.

Mortuos, *written during the period of mental stress which Jung experienced during the First World War, he writes:*

A thing that is infinite and eternal hath no qualities, since it hath all qualities. This nothingness or fullness we name the PLEROMA. Therein both thinking and being cease, since the eternal and infinite possess no qualities. In it no being is, for he then would be distinct from the pleroma, and would possess qualities which would distinguish him as something distinct from the pleroma. In the pleroma there is nothing and everything. It is quite fruitless to think about the pleroma, for this would mean self-dissolution. [*Sermo* I]

The opposites are contained in the pleroma, but because they are equally balanced, they are void. Although the opposites are manifested in individuals, they are not balanced and void. The individual's task is to pursue his own distinctiveness, and this involves him in distinguishing himself from the opposites.

We labour to attain to the good and beautiful, yet at the same time we also lay hold of the evil and ugly, since in the pleroma these are one with the good and the beautiful. When, however, we remain true to our own nature, which is distinctiveness, we distinguish ourselves from the good and the beautiful, and, therefore, at the same time, from the evil and the ugly. And thus we fall not into the pleroma, namely into nothingness and dissolution. [*Sermo* I]

In Answer to Job, *Jung writes:*

In the pleromatic or (as the Tibetans call it) Bardo state, there is a perfect interplay of cosmic forces, but with the Creation – that is, with the division of the world into distinct processes in space and time – events begin to rub and jostle one another. [CW 11, par. 620]

This preamble may help to clarify Jung's view as to the autonomy of archetypes.

From *Answer to Job*, CW 11, pars. 629–31

Although the birth of Christ is an event that occurred but once in history, it has always existed in eternity. For the layman in these matters, the identity of a nontemporal, eternal event with a unique historical occurrence is something that is extremely difficult to conceive. He must, however, accustom himself to the idea that "time" is a relative concept and needs to be complemented by that of the "simultaneous" existence, in the Bardo or pleroma, of all historical processes. What exists in the pleroma as an eternal process appears in time as an aperiodic sequence, that is to say, it is repeated many times in an irregular pattern. To take but one example: Yahweh had one good son and one who was a failure. Cain and Abel, Jacob and Esau, correspond to this prototype, and so, in all ages and in all parts of the world, does the motif of the hostile brothers, which in innumerable modern variants still causes dissension in families and keeps the psychotherapist busy. Just as many examples, no less instructive, could be found for the two women prefigured in eternity. When these things occur as modern variants, therefore, they should not be regarded merely as personal episodes, moods, or chance idiosyncrasies in people, but as fragments of the pleromatic process itself, which, broken up into individual events occurring in time, is an essential component or aspect of the divine drama.

When Yahweh created the world from his *prima materia*, the "Void," he could not help breathing his own mystery into the Creation which is himself in every part, as every reasonable theology has long been convinced. From this comes the belief that it is possible to know God from his Creation. When I say that he could not help doing this, I do not imply any limitation of his omnipotence; on the contrary, it is an acknowledgment that all possibilities are contained in him, and that there are in consequence no other possibilities than those which express him.

All the world is God's, and God is in all the world from the very beginning. Why, then, the *tour de force* of the Incarnation? one asks oneself, astonished. God is in everything already, and yet there must be something missing if a sort of second entrance into Creation has now to be staged with so much care and circumspection. Since Creation is universal, reaching to the remotest stellar galaxies, and since it has also made organic life infinitely variable and capable of endless differentiation, we can hardly see where the defect lies. The fact that Satan has everywhere intruded his corrupting influence is no doubt regrettable for many reasons, but it makes no difference in principle. It is not easy to give an answer to this question. One would like to say that Christ had to appear in order to deliver mankind from evil. But when one considers that evil was originally slipped into the scheme of things by Satan, and still is, then it would seem much simpler if Yahweh would, for once, call this "practical joker" severely to account, get rid of his pernicious influence, and thus eliminate the root of all evil. He would then not need the elaborate arrangement of a special Incarnation with all the unforeseeable consequences which this entails. One should make clear to oneself what it means when God becomes man. It means nothing less than a world-shaking transformation of God. It means more or less what Creation meant in the beginning, namely an objectivation of God. At the time of the Creation he revealed himself in Nature; now he wants to be more specific and become man. It must be admitted, however, that there was a tendency in this direction right from the start. For, when those other human beings, who had evidently been created before Adam, appeared on the scene along with the higher mammals, Yahweh created on the following day, by a special act of creation, a man who was the image of God. This was the first prefiguration of his becoming man. He took Adam's descendants, especially the people of Israel, into his personal possession, and from time to time he filled this people's prophets with his spirit. All these things were preparatory events and symptoms of a tendency within God to become man. But in omniscience there had existed from all eternity a knowledge of the human nature of God or of the divine nature of man. That is why, long before Genesis was written, we find corresponding testimonies in the ancient Egyptian records. These intimations and prefigurations of the Incarnation must strike one as either completely incomprehensible or superfluous, since all creation *ex nihilo* is God's and consists of nothing but God, with the result that man, like the rest of creation, is simply God become concrete. Prefigurations, however, are not in themselves creative events, but are only stages in the process of becoming conscious. It was only quite late that we realized (or rather, are beginning to realize) that God is Reality itself and therefore – last but not least – man. This realization is a millennial process.

Jung's conception of "the millennial process" referred to in the last extract may help us to understand why he believed that a profound change was about to take place in man's conception of himself and the universe. Traditionally, the reign of Christ ended with the first millennium, to be succeeded by the reign of Antichrist. This is now nearing its end, coinciding with the entry of the vernal equinox into Aquarius, and the end of the aeon of Pisces.

From "Flying Saucers: a Modern Myth of Things Seen in the Skies" CW 10, pars. 589–90

It is difficult to form a correct estimate of the significance of contemporary events, and the danger that our judgment will remain caught in subjectivity is great. So I am fully aware of the risk I am taking in proposing to communicate my views concerning certain contemporary events, which seem to me important, to those who are patient enough to hear me. I refer to those reports reaching us from all corners of the earth, rumours of round objects that flash through the troposphere and stratosphere and go by the name of Flying Saucers, *soucoupes*, disks, and "Ufos" (Unidentified Flying Objects). These rumours, or the possible physical existence of such objects, seem to me so significant that I feel myself compelled, as once before* when events of fateful consequence were brewing for Europe, to sound a note of warning. I know that, just as before, my voice is much too weak to reach the ear of the multitude. It is not presumption that drives me, but my conscience as a psychiatrist that bids me fulfil my duty and prepare those few who will hear me for coming events which are in accord with the end of an era. As we know from ancient Egyptian history, they are manifestations of psychic changes which always appear at the end of one Platonic month and at the beginning of another. Apparently they are changes in the constellation of

*"Wotan" (CW 10), pars. 371–99.

psychic dominants, of the archetypes, or "gods" as they used to be called, which bring about, or accompany, long-lasting transformations of the collective psyche. This transformation started in the historical era and left its traces first in the passing of the aeon of Taurus into that of Aries, and then of Aries into Pisces, whose beginning coincides with the rise of Christianity. We are now nearing that great change which may be expected when the spring-point enters Aquarius.

It would be frivolous of me to try to conceal from the reader that such reflections are not only exceedingly unpopular but even come perilously close to those turbid fantasies which becloud the minds of world-reformers and other interpreters of "signs and portents." But I must take this risk, even if it means putting my hard-won reputation for truthfulness, reliability, and capacity for scientific judgment in jeopardy. I can assure my readers that I do not do this with a light heart. I am, to be quite frank, concerned for all those who are caught unprepared by the events in question and disconcerted by their incomprehensible nature. Since, so far as I know, no one has yet felt moved to examine and set forth the possible psychic consequences of this foreseeable astrological change, I deem it my duty to do what I can in this respect. I undertake this thankless task in the expectation that my chisel will make no impression on the hard stone it encounters.

In a letter to Father Victor White, Jung refers to the same approaching change.

From **Letters**, vol. 2, pp. 167–8

[BOLLINGEN, 10 APRIL 1954]

The symbolic history of the Christ's life shows, as the essential teleological tendency, the crucifixion, viz. the union of Christ with the symbol of the tree. It is no longer a matter of an impossible reconciliation of Good and Evil, but of man with his vegetative (=unconscious) life. In the case of the Christian symbol the tree however is dead and man upon the Cross is going to die, i.e., the solution of the problem takes place after death. That is so as far as Christian truth goes. But it is possible that the Christian symbolism expresses man's mental condition in the aeon of Pisces, as the ram and the bull gods do for the ages of Aries and Taurus. In this case the post-mortal solution would be symbolic of an entirely new psychological status, viz. that of Aquarius, which is certainly a oneness, presumably that of the Anthropos, the realization of Christ's allusion: *"Dii estis."** This is a formidable secret and difficult to understand, because it means that man will be essentially God and God man. The signs pointing in this direction consist in the fact that the cosmic power of self-destruction is given into the hands of man and that man inherits the dual nature of the Father. He will [mis]understand it and he will be tempted to ruin the universal life of the earth by radioactivity. Materialism and atheism, the negation of God, are indirect means to attain this goal. Through the negation of God one becomes deified, i.e., god-almighty-like, and then one knows what is good for mankind. That is how destruction begins. The intellectual schoolmasters in the Kremlin are a classic example. The danger of following the same path is very great indeed. It begins with the lie, i.e., the projection of the shadow.

There is need of people knowing about their shadow, because there must be somebody who does not project. They ought to be in a visible position where they would be expected to project and unexpectedly they do not project! They can thus set a visible example which would not be seen if they were invisible.

---

*"Ye are gods." John 10:34.

Part 10. Man and His Future

Throughout his long life, Jung commented on the state of society as well as pursuing his investigations into the psychology of the unconscious. A late work, published in 1957, once again affirms Jung's belief in the importance of the individual, and suggests that individual self-knowledge and the capacity for human relationships which this brings is the only power strong enough to resist the collective dominance of the State. "The Undiscovered Self" seems an appropriate essay with which to end this selection from the works of C. G. Jung.

"The Undiscovered Self (Present and Future)" CW 10, pars. 488–588

1. THE PLIGHT OF THE INDIVIDUAL IN MODERN SOCIETY

What will the future bring? From time immemorial this question has occupied men's minds, though not always to the same degree. Historically, it is chiefly in times of physical, political, economic, and spiritual distress that men's eyes turn with anxious hope to the future, and when anticipations, utopias, and apocalyptic visions multiply. One thinks, for instance, of the chiliastic expectations of the Augustan age at the beginning of the Christian era, or of the spiritual changes in the West which accompanied the end of the first millennium. Today, as the end of the second millennium draws near, we are again living in an age filled with apocalyptic images of universal destruction. What is the significance of that split, symbolized by the "Iron Curtain," which divides humanity into two halves? What will become of our civilization, and of man himself, if the hydrogen bombs begin to go off, or if the spiritual and moral darkness of State absolutism should spread over Europe?

We have no reason to take this threat lightly. Everywhere in the West there are subversive minorities who, sheltered by our humanitarianism and our sense of justice, hold the incendiary torches ready, with nothing to stop the spread of their ideas except the critical reason of a single, fairly intelligent, mentally stable stratum of the population. One should not overestimate the thickness of this stratum. It varies from country to country in accordance with national temperament. Also, it is regionally dependent on public education and is subject to the influence of acutely disturbing factors of a political and economic nature. Taking plebiscites as a criterion, one could on an optimistic estimate put its upper limit at about forty per cent of the electorate. A rather more pessimistic view would not be unjustified either, since the gift of reason and critical reflection is not one of man's outstanding peculiarities, and even where it exists it proves to be wavering and inconstant, the more so, as a rule, the bigger the political groups are. The mass crushes out the insight and reflection that are still possible with the individual, and this necessarily leads to doctrinaire and authoritarian tyranny if ever the constitutional State should succumb to a fit of weakness.

Rational argument can be conducted with some prospect of success only so long as the emotionality of a given situation does not exceed a certain critical degree. If the affective temperature rises above this level, the possibility of reason's having any effect ceases and its place is taken by slogans and chimerical wish-fantasies. That is to say, a sort of collective possession results which rapidly develops into a psychic epidemic. Under these conditions all those elements whose existence is merely tolerated as asocial under the rule of reason come to the top. Such individuals are by no means rare curiosities to be met with only in prisons and lunatic asylums. For every manifest case of insanity there are, in my estimation, at least ten latent cases who seldom get to the point of breaking out openly but whose views and behaviour, for all their appearance of normality, are influenced unconsciously by pathological and perverse factors. There are, of course, no medical statistics on the frequency of latent psychoses – for understandable reasons. But even if their number should amount to less than ten times that of the manifest psychoses and of manifest criminality, the relatively small percentage of the population figures they represent is more than compensated for by the peculiar dangerousness of these people. Their mental state is that of a collectively excited group ruled by affective judgments and wish-fantasies. In a milieu of this kind they are the adapted ones, and consequently they feel quite at home in it. They know from their own experience the language of these conditions, and they know how to handle them. Their chimerical ideas, sustained by fanatical resentment, appeal to the collective irrationality and find fruitful soil there; they express all those motives and resentments which lurk in more normal people under the cloak of reason and insight. They are, therefore, despite their small number in comparison with the population as a whole, dangerous as sources of infection precisely because the so-called normal person possesses only a limited degree of self-knowledge.

Most people confuse "self-knowledge" with knowledge of their conscious ego-personalities. Anyone who has any ego-consciousness at all takes it for granted that he knows himself. But the ego knows only its own contents, not the unconscious and its contents. People measure their self-knowledge by what the average person in their social environment knows of himself, but not by the real psychic facts which are for the most part hidden from them. In this respect the psyche behaves like the body, of whose physiological and anatomical structure the average person knows very little too. Although he lives in it and with it, most of it is totally unknown to the layman, and special scientific knowledge is needed to acquaint consciousness with what is known of the body, not to speak of all that is *not* known, which also exists.

What is commonly called "self-knowledge" is therefore a very limited knowledge, most of it dependent on social factors, of what goes on in the human psyche. Hence one is always coming up against the prejudice that such and such a thing does not happen "with us" or "in our family" or among our friends and acquaintances. On the other hand, one meets with equally illusory assumptions about the alleged presence of qualities which merely serve to cover up the true facts of the case.

In this broad belt of unconsciousness, which is immune to conscious criticism and control, we stand defenceless, open to all kinds of influences and psychic infections. As with all dangers, we can guard against the risk of psychic infection only when we know what is attacking us, and how, where and when the attack will come. Since self-knowledge is a matter of getting to know the individual facts, theories are of very little help. For the more a theory lays claim to universal validity, the less capable it is of doing justice to the individual facts. Any theory based on experience is necessarily *statistical*; it formulates an *ideal average* which abolishes all exceptions at either end of the scale and replaces them by an abstract mean. This mean is quite valid, though it need not necessarily occur in reality. Despite this it figures in the theory as an unassailable fundamental fact. The exceptions at either extreme, though equally factual, do not appear in the final result at all, since they cancel each other out. If, for instance, I determine the weight of each stone in a bed of pebbles and get an average weight of five ounces, this tells me very little about the real nature of the pebbles. Anyone who thought, on the basis of these findings, that he could pick up a pebble of five ounces at the first try would be in for a serious disappointment. Indeed, it might well happen that however long he searched he would not find a single pebble weighing exactly five ounces.

The statistical method shows the facts in the light of the ideal average but does not give us a picture of their empirical reality. While reflecting an indisputable aspect of reality, it can falsify the actual truth in a most misleading way. This is particularly true of theories which are based on statistics. The distinctive thing about real facts, however, is their individuality. Not to put too fine a point on it, one could say that the real picture consists of nothing but exceptions to the rule, and that, in consequence, absolute reality has predominantly the character of *irregularity*.

These considerations must be borne in mind whenever there is talk of a theory serving as a guide to self-knowledge. There is and can be no self-knowledge based on theoretical assumptions, for the object of this knowledge is an individual – a relative exception and an irregular phenomenon. Hence it is not the universal and the regular that characterize the individual, but rather the unique. He is not to be understood as a recurrent unit but as something unique and singular which in the last analysis can be neither known nor compared with anything else. At the same time man, as member of a species, can and must be described as a statistical unit; otherwise nothing general could be said about him. For this purpose he has to be regarded as a comparative unit. This results in a universally valid anthropology or psychology, as the case may be, with an abstract picture of man as an average unit from which all individual features have been removed. But it is precisely these features which are of paramount importance for *understanding* man. If I want to understand an individual human being, I must lay aside all scientific knowledge of the average man and discard all theories in order to adopt a completely new and unprejudiced attitude. I can only approach the task of *understanding* with a free and open mind, whereas *knowledge* of man, or insight into human character, presupposes all sorts of knowledge about mankind in general.

Now whether it is a question of understanding a fellow human being or of self-knowledge, I must in both cases leave all theoretical assumptions behind me. Since scientific knowledge not only enjoys universal esteem but, in the eyes of modern man, counts as the only intellectual and spiritual authority, understanding the individual obliges me to commit the *lèse majesté*, so to speak, of turning a blind eye to scientific knowledge. This is a sacrifice not lightly made, for the scientific attitude cannot rid itself so easily of its sense of responsibility. And if the psychologist happens to be a doctor who wants not only to classify his patient scientifically but also to understand him as a human being, he is threatened with a conflict of duties between the two diametrically opposed and mutually exclusive attitudes of knowledge on the one hand and understanding on the other. This conflict cannot be solved by an either/or but only by a kind of two-way thinking: doing one thing while not losing sight of the other.

In view of the fact that, in principle, the positive advantages of *knowledge* work specifically to the disadvantage of *understanding*, the judgment resulting therefrom is likely to be something of a paradox. Judged scientifically, the individual is nothing but a unit which repeats itself *ad infinitum* and could just as well be designated with a letter of the alphabet. For understanding, on the other hand, it is just the unique individual human being who, when stripped of all those conformities and regularities so dear to the heart of the scientist, is the supreme and only real object of investigation. The doctor, above all, should be aware of this contradiction. On the one hand, he is equipped with the statistical truths of his scientific training, and on the other, he is faced with the task of treating a sick person who, especially in the case of psychic suffering, requires *individual understanding*. The more schematic the treatment is, the more resistances it – quite rightly – calls up in the patient, and the more the cure is jeopardized. The psychotherapist sees himself compelled, willy-nilly, to regard the individuality of a patient as an essential fact in the picture and to arrange his methods of treatment accordingly. Today, over the whole field of medicine, it is recognized that the task of the doctor consists in treating the sick person, not an abstract illness.

This illustration from the realm of medicine is only a special instance of the problem of education and training in general. Scientific education is based in the main on statistical truths and abstract knowledge and therefore imparts an unrealistic, rational picture of the world, in which the individual, as a merely marginal phenomenon, plays no role. The individual, however, as an irrational datum, is the true and authentic carrier of reality, the *concrete* man as opposed to the unreal ideal or "normal" man to whom the scientific statements refer. What is more, most of the natural sciences try to represent the results of their investigations as though these had come into existence without man's intervention, in such a way that the collaboration of the psyche – an indispensable factor – remains invisible. (An exception to this is modern physics, which recognizes that the observed is not independent of the observer.) So, in this respect as well, science conveys a picture of the world from which a real human psyche appears to be excluded – the very antithesis of the "humanities."

Under the influence of scientific assumptions, not only the psyche but the individual man and, indeed, all individual events whatsoever suffer a levelling down and a process of blurring that distorts the picture of reality into a conceptual average. We ought not to underestimate the psychological effect of the statistical world-picture: it thrusts aside the individual in favour of anonymous units that pile up into mass formations. Instead of the concrete individual, you have the names of organizations and, at the highest point, the abstract idea of the State as the principle of political reality. The moral responsibility of the individual is then inevitably replaced by the policy of the State (*raison d'état*). Instead of moral and mental differentiation of the individual, you have public welfare and the raising of the living standard. The goal and meaning of individual life (which is the only *real* life) no longer lie in individual development but in the policy of the State, which is thrust upon the individual from outside and consists in the execution of an abstract idea which ultimately tends to attract all life to itself. The individual is increasingly deprived of the moral decision as to how he should live his own life, and instead is ruled, fed, clothed, and educated as a social unit, accommodated in the appropriate housing unit, and amused in accordance with the standards that give pleasure and satisfaction to the masses. The rulers, in their turn, are just as much social units as the ruled, and are distinguished only by the fact that they are specialized mouthpieces of the State doctrine. They do not need to be personalities capable of judgment, but thoroughgoing specialists who are unusable outside their line of business. State policy decides what shall be taught and studied.

The seemingly omnipotent State doctrine is for its part manipulated in the name of State policy by those occupying the highest positions in the government, where all the power is concentrated. Whoever, by election or caprice, gets into one of these positions is subject to no higher authority; he is the State policy itself and within the limits of the situation can proceed at his own discretion. With Louis XIV he can say, "L'état c'est moi." He is thus the only individual or, at any rate, one of the few individuals who could make use of their individuality if only they knew how to differentiate themselves from the State doctrine. They are more likely, however, to be the slaves of their own fictions. Such one-sidedness is always compensated psychologically by unconscious subversive tendencies. Slavery and rebellion are inseparable correlates. Hence, rivalry for power and exaggerated distrust pervade the entire organism from top to bottom. Furthermore, in order to compensate for its chaotic formlessness, a mass always produces a "Leader," who infallibly becomes the victim of his own inflated ego-consciousness, as numerous examples in history show.

This development becomes logically unavoidable the moment the individual combines with the mass and thus renders himself obsolete. Apart from the agglomeration of huge masses in which the individual disappears anyway, one of the chief factors responsible for psychological mass-mindedness is scientific rationalism, which robs the individual of his foundations and his dignity. As a social unit he has lost his individuality and become a mere abstract number in the bureau of statistics. He can only play the role of an interchangeable unit of infinitesimal importance. Looked at rationally and from outside, that is exactly what he is, and from this point of view it seems positively absurd to go on talking about the value or meaning of the individual. Indeed, one can hardly imagine how one ever came to endow individual human life with so much dignity when the truth to the contrary is as plain as the palm of your hand.

Seen from this standpoint, the individual really is of diminishing importance and anyone who wished to dispute this would soon find himself at a loss for arguments. The fact that the individual feels himself or the members of his family or the esteemed friends in his circle to be important merely underlines the slightly comic subjectivity of his feeling. For what are the few compared with ten thousand or a hundred thousand, let alone a million? This recalls the argument of a thoughtful friend with whom I once got caught up in a huge crowd of people. Suddenly he exclaimed, "Here you have the most convincing reason for not believing in immortality: all *that lot* wants to be immortal!"

The bigger the crowd the more negligible the individual becomes. But if the individual, overwhelmed by the sense of his own puniness and impotence, should feel that his life has lost its meaning – which, after all, is not identical with public welfare and higher standards of living – then he is already on the road to State slavery and, without knowing or wanting it, has become its proselyte. The man who looks only outside and quails before the big battalions has nothing with which to combat the evidence of his senses and his reason. But that is just what is happening today: we are all fascinated and overawed by statistical truths and large numbers and are daily apprised of the nullity and futility of the individual personality, since it is not represented and personified by any mass organization. Conversely, those personages who strut about on the world stage and whose voices are heard far and wide seem, to the uncritical public, to be borne along on some mass movement or on the tide of public opinion and for this reason are either applauded or execrated. Since mass suggestion plays the predominant role here, it remains a moot point whether their message is their own, for which they are personally responsible, or whether they merely function as a megaphone for collective opinion.

Under these circumstances it is small wonder that individual judgment grows increasingly uncertain of itself and that responsibility is collectivized as much as possible, i.e., is shuffled off by the individual and delegated to a corporate body. In this way the individual becomes more and more a function of society, which in its turn usurps the function of the real life carrier, whereas, in actual fact, society is nothing more than an abstract idea like the State. Both are hypostatized, that is, have become autonomous. The State in particular is turned into a quasi-animate personality from whom everything is expected. In reality it is only a camouflage for those individuals who know how to manipulate it. Thus the constitutional State drifts into the situation of a primitive form of society – the communism of a primitive tribe where everybody is subject to the autocratic rule of a chief or an oligarchy.

2. RELIGION AS THE COUNTERBALANCE TO MASS-MINDEDNESS

In order to free the fiction of the sovereign State – in other words, the whims of the chieftains who manipulate it – from every wholesome restriction, all socio-political movements tending in this direction invariably try to cut the ground from under *religion*. For, in order to turn the individual into a function of the State, his dependence on anything else must be taken from him. Religion means dependence on and submission to the irrational facts of experience. These do not refer directly to social and physical conditions; they concern far more the individual's psychic attitude.

But it is possible to have an attitude to the external conditions of life only when there is a point of reference outside them. Religion gives, or claims to give, such a standpoint, thereby enabling the individual to exercise his judgment and his power of decision. It builds up a reserve, as it were, against the obvious and inevitable force of circumstances to which everyone is exposed who lives only in the outer world and has no other ground under his feet except the pavement. If statistical reality is the only one, then that is the sole authority. There is then only *one* condition, and since no contrary condition exists, judgment and decision are not only superfluous but impossible. Then the individual is bound to be a function of statistics and hence a function of the State or whatever the abstract principle of order may be called.

Religion, however, teaches another authority opposed to that of the "world." The doctrine of the individual's dependence on God makes just as high a claim upon him as the world does. It may even happen that the absoluteness of this claim estranges him from the world in the same way as he is estranged from himself when he succumbs to the collective mentality. He can forfeit his judgment and power of decision in the former case (for the sake of religious doctrine) quite as much as in the latter. This is the goal which religion openly aspires to unless it compromises with the State. When it does so, I prefer to call it not "religion" but a "creed." A creed gives expression to a definite collective belief, whereas the word *religion* expresses a subjective relationship to certain metaphysical, extramundane factors. A creed is a confession of faith intended chiefly for the world at large and is thus an intramundane affair, while the meaning and purpose of religion lie in the relationship of the individual to God (Christianity, Judaism, Islam) or to the path of salvation and liberation (Buddhism). From this basic fact all ethics is derived, which without the individual's responsibility before God can be called nothing more than conventional morality.

Since they are compromises with mundane reality, the creeds have accordingly seen themselves obliged to undertake a progressive codification of their views, doctrines, and customs, and in so doing have externalized themselves to such an extent that the authentic religious element in them – the living relationship to and direct confrontation with their extramundane point of reference – has been thrust into the background. The denominational standpoint measures the worth and importance of the subjective religious relationship by the yardstick of traditional doctrine, and where this is not so frequent, as in Protestantism, one immediately hears talk of pietism, sectarianism, eccentricity, and so forth, as soon as anyone claims to be guided by God's will. A creed coincides with the established Church or, at any rate, forms a public institution whose members include not only true believers but vast numbers of people who can only be described as "indifferent" in matters of religion and who belong to it simply by force of habit. Here the difference between a creed and a religion becomes palpable.

To be the adherent of a creed, therefore, is not always a religious matter but more often a social one and, as such, it does nothing to give the individual any foundation. For this he has to depend exclusively on his relation to an authority which is not of this world. The criterion here is not lip service to a creed but the psychological fact that the life of the individual is not determined solely by the ego and its opinions or by social factors, but quite as much, if not more, by a transcendent authority. It is not ethical principles, however lofty, or creeds, however orthodox, that lay the foundations for the freedom and autonomy of the individual, but simply and solely the empirical awareness, the incontrovertible experience of an intensely personal, reciprocal relationship between man and an extramundane authority which acts as a counterpoise to the "world" and its "reason."

This formulation will not please either the mass man or the collective believer. For the former the policy of the State is the supreme principle of thought and action. Indeed, this was the purpose for which he was enlightened, and accordingly the mass man grants the individual a right to exist only in so far as he is a function of the State. The believer, on the other hand, while admitting that the State has a moral and factual claim on him, confesses to the belief that not only man but the State that rules him is subject to the overlordship of "God," and that, in case of doubt, the supreme decision will be made by God and not by the State. Since I do not presume to any metaphysical judgments, I must leave it an open question whether the "world," i.e., the phenomenal world of man, and hence nature in general, is the "opposite" of God or not. I can only point to the fact that the psychological opposition between these two realms of experience is not only vouched for in the New Testament but is still exemplified very plainly today in the negative attitude of the dictator States to religion and of the Church to atheism and materialism.

Just as man, as a social being, cannot in the long run exist without a tie to the community, so the individual will never find the real justification for his existence and his own spiritual and moral autonomy anywhere except in an extramundane principle capable of relativizing the overpowering influence of external factors. The individual who is not anchored in God can offer no resistance on his own resources to the physical and moral blandishments of the world. For this he needs the evidence of inner, transcendent experience which alone can protect him from the otherwise inevitable submersion in the mass. Merely intellectual or even moral insight into the stultification and moral irresponsibility of the mass man is a negative recognition only and amounts to not much more than a wavering on the road to the atomization of the individual. It lacks the driving force of religious conviction, since it is merely rational. The dictator State has one great advantage over bourgeois reason: along with the individual it swallows up his religious forces. The State takes the place of God; that is why, seen from this angle, the socialist dictatorships are religions and State slavery is a form of worship. But the religious function cannot be dislocated and falsified in this way without giving rise to secret doubts, which are immediately repressed so as to avoid conflict with the prevailing trend towards massmindedness. The result, as always in such cases, is overcompensation in the form of *fanaticism*, which in its turn is used as a weapon for stamping out the least flicker of opposition. Free opinion is stifled and moral decision ruthlessly suppressed, on the plea that the end justifies the means, even the vilest. The policy of the State is exalted to a creed, the leader or party boss becomes a demigod beyond good and evil, and his votaries are honoured as heroes, martyrs, apostles, missionaries. There is only *one* truth and beside it no other. It is sacrosanct and above criticism. Anyone who thinks differently is a heretic, who, as we know from history, is threatened with all manner of unpleasant things. Only the party boss, who holds the political power in his hands, can interpret the State doctrine authentically, and he does so just as suits him.

When, through mass rule, the individual becomes social unit No. so-and-so and the State is elevated to the supreme principle, it is only to be expected that the religious function too will be sucked into the maelstrom. Religion, as the careful observation and taking account of certain invisible and uncontrollable factors, is an *instinctive* attitude peculiar to man, and its manifestations can be followed all through human history. Its evident purpose is to maintain the psychic balance, for the natural man has an equally natural "knowledge" of the fact that his conscious functions may at any time be thwarted by uncontrollable happenings coming from inside as well as from outside. For this reason he has always taken care that any difficult decision likely to have consequences for himself and others shall be rendered safe by suitable measures of a religious nature. Offerings are made to the invisible powers, formidable blessings are pronounced, and all kinds of solemn rites are performed. Everywhere and at all times there have been *rites d'entrée et de sortie* whose efficacy is impugned as magic and superstition by rationalists incapable of psychological insight. But magic has above all a psychological effect whose importance should not be underestimated. The performance of a "magical" action gives the person concerned a feeling of security which is absolutely essential for carrying out a decision, because a decision is inevitably somewhat one-sided and is therefore rightly felt to be a risk. Even a dictator thinks it necessary not only to accompany his acts of State with threats but to stage them with all manner of solemnities. Brass bands, flags, banners, parades, and monster demonstrations are no different in principle from ecclesiastical processions, cannonades, and fireworks to scare off demons. Only, the suggestive parade of State power engenders a collective feeling of security which, unlike religious demonstrations, gives the individual no protection against his inner demonism. Hence he will cling all the more to the power of the State, i.e., to the mass, thus delivering himself up to it psychically as well as morally and putting the finishing touch to his social depotentiation. The State, like the Church, demands enthusiasm, self-sacrifice, and love, and if religion requires or presupposes the "fear of God," then the dictator State takes good care to provide the necessary terror.

When the rationalist directs the main force of his attack against the miraculous effect of the rite as asserted by tradition, he has in reality completely missed the mark. The essential point, the *psychological* effect, is overlooked, although both parties make use of it for directly opposite purposes. A similar situation prevails with regard to their respective conceptions of the goal. The goals of religion – deliverance from evil, reconciliation with God, rewards in the hereafter, and so on – turn into worldly promises about freedom from care for one's daily bread, the just distribution of material goods, universal prosperity in the future, and shorter working hours. That the fulfilment of these promises is as far off as Paradise only furnishes yet another analogy and underlines the fact that the masses have been converted from an extramundane goal to a purely worldly belief, which is extolled with exactly the same religious fervour and exclusiveness that the creeds display in the other direction.

In order not to repeat myself unnecessarily, I shall not enumerate all the parallels between worldly and otherworldly beliefs, but shall content myself with emphasizing the fact that a natural function which has existed from the beginning, like the religious function, cannot be disposed of with rationalistic and so-called enlightened criticism. You can, of course, represent the doctrinal contents of the creeds as impossible and subject them to ridicule, but such methods miss the point and do not affect the religious function which forms the basis of the creeds. Religion, in the sense of conscientious regard for the irrational factors of the psyche and individual fate, reappears – evilly distorted – in the deification of the State and the dictator: *Naturam expellas furca tamen usque recurret* (You can throw out Nature with a pitchfork, but she'll always turn up again). The leaders and dictators, having weighed up the situation correctly, are therefore doing their best to gloss over the all too obvious parallel with the deification of Caesar and to hide their real power behind the fiction of the State, though this, of course, alters nothing.*

As I have already pointed out, the dictator State, besides robbing the individual of his rights, has also cut the ground from under his feet psychically by depriving him of the metaphysical foundations of his existence. The ethical decision of the individual human being no longer counts – what alone matters is the blind movement of the masses, and the *lie* thus becomes the operative principle of

*Since this essay was written, in the spring of 1956, there has been a noticeable reaction in the U.S.S.R. to this objectionable state of affairs.

political action. The State has drawn the logical conclusions from this, as the existence of many millions of State slaves completely deprived of all rights mutely testifies.

Both the dictator State and denominational religion lay quite particular emphasis on the idea of *community*. This is the basic ideal of "communism," and it is thrust down the throats of the people so much that it has the exact opposite of the desired effect: it inspires divisive mistrust. The Church, which is no less emphatic, appears on its side as a communal ideal, and where the Church is notoriously weak, as in Protestantism, the hope of or belief in a "communal experience" makes up for the painful lack of cohesion. As can easily be seen, "community" is an indispensable aid in the organization of masses and is therefore a two-edged weapon. Just as the addition of however many zeros will never make a unit, so the value of a community depends on the spiritual and moral stature of the individuals composing it. For this reason one cannot expect from the community any effect that would outweigh the suggestive influence of the environment – that is, a real and fundamental change in individuals, whether for good or for bad. Such changes can come only from the personal encounter between man and man, but not from communistic or Christian baptisms *en masse*, which do not touch the inner man. How superficial the effect of communal propaganda actually is can be seen from recent events in Eastern Europe.* The communal ideal reckons without its host, overlooking the individual human being, who in the end will assert his claims.

3. THE POSITION OF THE WEST ON THE QUESTION OF RELIGION

Confronting this development in the twentieth century of our Christian era, the Western world stands with its heritage of Roman law, the treasures of Judaeo-Christian ethics grounded on metaphysics, and its ideal of the inalienable rights of man. Anxiously it asks itself the question: How can this development be brought to a standstill or put into reverse? It is useless to pillory the socialist dictatorship as utopian and to condemn its economic principles as

*Added in January 1957.

unreasonable, because, in the first place, the criticizing West has only itself to talk to, its arguments being heard only on this side of the Iron Curtain, and, in the second place, any economic principles you like can be put into practice so long as you are prepared to accept the sacrifices they entail. You can carry through any social and economic reforms you please if, like Stalin, you let three million peasants starve to death and have a few million unpaid labourers at your disposal. A State of this kind has no social or economic crises to fear. So long as its power is intact – that is to say, so long as there is a well-disciplined and well-fed police army in the offing – it can maintain its existence for an indefinitely long period and can go on increasing its power to an indefinite extent. Thanks to its excess birth-rate, it can multiply the number of its unpaid workers almost at will in order to compete with its rivals, regardless of the world market, which is to a large measure dependent on wages. A real danger can come to it only from outside, through the threat of military attack. But this risk grows less every year, firstly because the war potential of the dictator States is steadily increasing, and secondly because the West cannot afford to arouse latent Russian or Chinese nationalism and chauvinism by an attack which would have exactly the opposite effect to the one intended.

So far as one can see, only one possibility remains, and that is a break-down of power from within, which must, however, be left to follow its own inner development. Any support from outside at present would have little effect, in view of the existing security measures and the danger of nationalistic reactions. The absolute State has an army of fanatical missionaries to do its bidding in matters of foreign policy, and these in their turn can count on a fifth column who are guaranteed asylum under the laws and constitutions of the Western States. In addition the communes of believers, very strong in places, considerably weaken Western governments' powers of decision, whereas the West has no opportunity to exert a similar influence on the other side, though we are probably not wrong in surmising that there is a certain amount of opposition among the masses in the East. There are always upright and truth-loving people to whom lying and tyranny are hateful, but one cannot judge whether they exert any decisive influence on the masses under the police régimes.*

In view of this uncomfortable situation the question is heard again and again in the West: What can we do to counter this threat from the East? Even though the West has considerable industrial power and a sizable defence potential at its command, we cannot rest content with this, for we know that even the biggest armaments and the heaviest industry coupled with a relatively high living standard are not enough to check the psychic infection spread by religious fanaticism.

The West has unfortunately not yet woken up to the fact that our appeal to idealism and reason and other desirable virtues, delivered with so much enthusiasm, is mere bombination in the void. It is a puff of wind swept away in the storm of religious faith, however twisted this faith may appear to us. We are faced, not with a situation that can be overcome by rational or moral arguments, but with an unleashing of emotional forces and ideas engendered by the spirit of the times; and these, as we know from experience, are not much influenced by rational reflection and still less by moral exhortation. It has been correctly realized in many quarters that the alexipharmic, the antidote, should in this case be an equally potent faith of a different and non-materialistic kind, and that the religious attitude grounded upon it would be the only effective defence against the danger of psychic infection. Unhappily, the little word "should," which never fails to appear in this connection, points to a certain weakness, if not the absence, of this desideratum. Not only does the West lack a uniform faith that could block the progress of a fanatical ideology, but, as the father of Marxist philosophy, it makes use of exactly the same intellectual assumptions, the same arguments and aims. Although the Churches in the West enjoy full freedom, they are not less full or empty than in the East. Yet they exercise no noticeable influence on the broad course of politics. The disadvantage of a creed as a public institution is that it serves two masters: on the one hand, it derives its existence from the relationship of man to God, and on the other hand, it owes a duty to the State, i.e., to the world,

*Recent events in Poland and Hungary have shown that this opposition is more considerable than could have been foreseen.

in which connection it can appeal to the saying "Render unto Caesar..." and various other admonitions in the New Testament.

In early times and until comparatively recently there was, therefore, talk of "powers ordained by God" (Romans 13:1). Today this conception is antiquated. The Churches stand for traditional and collective convictions which in the case of many of their adherents are no longer based on their own inner experience but on *unreflecting belief*, which is notoriously apt to disappear as soon as one begins thinking about it. The content of belief then comes into collision with knowledge, and it often turns out that the irrationality of the former is no match for the ratiocinations of the latter. Belief is no adequate substitute for inner experience, and where this is absent even a strong faith which came miraculously as a gift of grace may depart equally miraculously. People call faith the true religious experience, but they do not stop to consider that actually it is a secondary phenomenon arising from the fact that something happened to us in the first place which instilled πίστις into us – that is, trust and loyalty. This experience has a definite content that can be interpreted in terms of one or other of the denominational creeds. But the more this is so, the more the possibilities of these conflicts with knowledge mount up, which in themselves are quite pointless. That is to say, the standpoint of the creeds is archaic; they are full of impressive mythological symbolism which, if taken literally, comes into insufferable conflict with knowledge. But if, for instance, the statement that Christ rose from the dead is to be understood not literally but symbolically, then it is capable of various interpretations that do not conflict with knowledge and do not impair the meaning of the statement. The objection that understanding it symbolically puts an end to the Christian's hope of immortality is invalid, because long before the coming of Christianity mankind believed in a life after death and therefore had no need of the Easter event as a guarantee of immortality. The danger that a mythology understood too literally, and as taught by the Church, will suddenly be repudiated lock, stock and barrel is today greater than ever. Is it not time that the Christian mythology, instead of being wiped out, was understood symbolically for once?

It is still too early to say what might be the consequences of a general recognition of the fatal parallelism between the State religion of the Marxists and the State religion of the Church. The absolutist claim of a *Civitas Dei* that is represented by man bears an unfortunate resemblance to the "divinity" of the State, and the moral conclusion drawn by Ignatius Loyola from the authority of the Church ("the end sanctifies the means") anticipates the lie as a political instrument in an exceedingly dangerous way. Both demand unqualified submission to faith and thus curtail man's freedom, the one his freedom before God and the other his freedom before the State, thereby digging the grave for the individual. The fragile existence of this – so far as we know – unique carrier of life is threatened on both sides, despite their respective promises of spiritual and material idylls to come – and how many of us can in the long run fight against the proverbial wisdom of "a bird in the hand is worth two in the bush"? Besides which, the West cherishes the same "scientific" and rationalistic *Weltanschauung* with its statistical levelling-down tendency and materialistic aims as the State religion of the Eastern bloc, as I have explained above.

What, then, has the West, with its political and denominational schisms, to offer to modern man in his need? Nothing, unfortunately, except a variety of paths all leading to one goal which is practically indistinguishable from the Marxist ideal. It requires no special effort of understanding to see where the Communist ideology gets the certainty of its belief that time is on its side, and that the world is ripe for conversion. The facts speak a language that is all too plain in this respect. It will not help us in the West to shut our eyes to this and not recognize our fatal vulnerability. Anyone who has once learned to submit absolutely to a collective belief and to renounce his eternal right to freedom and the equally eternal duty of individual responsibility will persist in this attitude, and will be able to march with the same credulity and the same lack of criticism in the reverse direction, if another and manifestly "better" belief is foisted upon his alleged idealism. What happened not so long ago to a civilized European nation? We accuse the Germans of having forgotten it all again already, but the truth is that we don't know for certain whether something similar might not happen elsewhere. It would not be surprising if it did and if another civilized nation succumbed to the infection of a uniform and one-sided idea. We permit ourselves the question: which countries have the biggest Communist parties? America, which – *O quae mutatio rerum!* – forms the real political backbone of Western Europe, seems to be immune because of the outspoken counterposition she has adopted, but in point of fact she is perhaps even more vulnerable than Europe, since her educational system is the most influenced by the scientific *Weltanschauung* with its statistical truths, and her mixed population finds it difficult to strike roots in a soil that is practically without history. The historical and humanistic type of education so sorely needed in such circumstances leads, on the contrary, a Cinderella existence. Though Europe possesses this latter requirement, she uses it to her own undoing in the form of nationalistic egoisms and paralysing scepticism. Common to both is the materialistic and collectivist goal, and both lack the very thing that expresses and grips the whole man, namely, an idea which puts the individual human being in the centre as the measure of all things.

This idea alone is enough to arouse the most violent doubts and resistances on all sides, and one could almost go so far as to assert that the valuelessness of the individual in comparison with large numbers is the one belief that meets with universal and unanimous assent. To be sure, we all say that this is the century of the common man, that he is the lord of the earth, the air, and the water, and that on his decision hangs the historical fate of the nations. This proud picture of human grandeur is unfortunately an illusion and is counterbalanced by a reality that is very different. In this reality man is the slave and victim of the machines that have conquered space and time for him; he is intimidated and endangered by the might of the military technology which is supposed to safeguard his physical existence; his spiritual and moral freedom, though guaranteed within limits in one half of his world, is threatened with chaotic disorientation, and in the other half is abolished altogether. Finally, to add comedy to tragedy, this lord of the elements, this universal arbiter, hugs to his bosom notions which stamp his dignity as worthless and turn his autonomy into an absurdity. All his achievements and possessions do not make him bigger; on the contrary, they diminish him, as the fate of the factory-worker under the rule of a "just" distribution of goods clearly demonstrates. He pays for his share of the factory with the loss of personal property, he exchanges his freedom of movement for the doubtful pleasure of being tied to his place of employment, he forfeits all means of improving his position if he jibs against being ground down by exhausting piece-work, and if he shows any signs of intelligence, political precepts are thrust down his throat – with a bit of technical knowledge thrown in, if he is lucky. However, a roof over one's head and a daily feed for the useful animal are not to be sneezed at when the bare necessities of life may be cut off from one day to the next.

4. THE INDIVIDUAL'S UNDERSTANDING OF HIMSELF

It is astounding that man, the instigator, inventor and vehicle of all these developments, the originator of all judgments and decisions and the planner of the future, must make himself such a *quantité négligeable*. The contradiction, the paradoxical evaluation of humanity by man himself, is in truth a matter for wonder, and one can only explain it as springing from an extraordinary uncertainty of judgment – in other words, man is an enigma to himself. This is understandable, seeing that he lacks the means of comparison necessary for self-knowledge. He knows how to distinguish himself from the other animals in point of anatomy and physiology, but as a conscious, reflecting being, gifted with speech, he lacks all criteria for self-judgment. He is on this planet a unique phenomenon which he cannot compare with anything else. The possibility of comparison and hence of self-knowledge would arise only if he could establish relations with quasi-human mammals inhabiting other stars.

Until then man must continue to resemble a hermit who knows that in respect of comparative anatomy he has affinities with the anthropoids but, to judge by appearances, is extraordinarily different from his cousins in respect of his psyche. It is just in this most important characteristic of his species that he cannot know himself and therefore remains a mystery to himself. The differing degrees of self-knowledge within his own species are of little significance compared with the possibilities which would be opened out by an encounter with a creature of similar structure but different origin. Our psyche, which is primarily responsible for all the historical changes wrought by the hand of man on the face of this planet, remains an insoluble puzzle and an incomprehensible wonder, an object of abiding perplexity – a feature it shares with all Nature's secrets. In regard to the latter we still have hope of making more discoveries and finding answers to the most difficult questions. But in regard to the psyche and psychology there seems to be a curious hesitancy. Not only is it the youngest of the empirical sciences, but it has great difficulty in getting anywhere near its proper object.

In the same way that our picture of the world had to be freed by Copernicus from the prejudice of geocentricity, the most strenuous efforts of a well-nigh revolutionary nature were needed to free psychology, first from the spell of mythological ideas, and then from the prejudice that the psyche is, on the one hand, a mere epiphenomenon of a biochemical process in the brain and, on the other hand, a purely personal matter. The connection with the brain does not in itself prove that the psyche is an epiphenomenon, a secondary function causally dependent on biochemical processes in the physical substrate. Nevertheless, we know only too well how much the psychic function can be disturbed by verifiable processes in the brain, and this fact is so impressive that the subsidiary nature of the psyche seems an almost unavoidable inference. The phenomena of parapsychology, however, warn us to be careful, for they point to a relativization of space and time through psychic factors which casts doubt on our naïve and overhasty explanation in terms of psychophysical parallelism. For the sake of this explanation people deny the findings of parapsychology outright, either for philosophical reasons or from intellectual laziness. This can hardly be considered a scientifically responsible attitude, even though it is a popular way out of a quite extraordinary intellectual difficulty. To assess the psychic phenomenon, we have to take account of all the other phenomena that go with it, and accordingly we can no longer practise any psychology that ignores the existence of the unconscious or of parapsychology.

The structure and physiology of the brain furnish no explanation of the psychic process. The psyche has a peculiar nature which cannot be reduced to anything else. Like physiology, it presents a relatively self-contained field of experience, to which we must attribute a quite special importance because it includes one of the two indispensable conditions for existence as such, namely, the phenomenon of consciousness. Without consciousness there would, practically speaking, be no world, for the world exists for us only in so far as it is consciously reflected by a psyche. *Consciousness is a precondition of being.* Thus the psyche is endowed with the dignity of a cosmic principle, which philosophically and in fact gives it a position co-equal with the principle of physical being. The carrier of this consciousness is the individual, who does not produce the psyche of his own volition but is, on the contrary, preformed by it and nourished by the gradual awakening of consciousness during childhood. If therefore the psyche is of overriding empirical importance, so also is the individual, who is the only immediate manifestation of the psyche.

This fact must be expressly emphasized for two reasons. Firstly, the individual psyche, just because of its individuality, is an exception to the statistical rule and is therefore robbed of one of its main characteristics when subjected to the levelling influence of statistical evaluation. Secondly, the Churches grant it validity only in so far as it acknowledges their dogmas – in other words, when it submits to a collective category. In both cases the will to individuality is regarded as egotistic obstinacy. Science devalues this as subjectivism, and the Churches condemn it morally as heresy and spiritual pride. As to the latter charge, it should not be forgotten that, unlike other religions, Christianity holds up before us a symbol whose content is the individual way of life of a man, the Son of Man, and that it even regards this individuation process as the incarnation and revelation of God himself. Hence the development of man into a self acquires a significance whose full implications have hardly begun to be appreciated, because too much attention to externals blocks the way to immediate inner experience. Were not the autonomy of the individual the secret longing of many people it would scarcely be able to survive the collective suppression either morally or spiritually.

All these obstacles make it more difficult to arrive at a correct appreciation of the human psyche, but they count for very little beside one other remarkable fact that deserves mentioning. This is the common psychiatric experience that the devaluation of the psyche and other resistances to psychological enlightenment are based in large measure on fear – on panic fear of the discoveries that might be made in the realm of the unconscious. These fears are found not only among persons who are frightened by the picture Freud painted of the unconscious; they also troubled the originator of psychoanalysis himself, who confessed to me that it was necessary to make a dogma of his sexual theory because this was the sole bulwark of reason against a possible "eruption of the black flood of occultism." In these words Freud was expressing his conviction that the unconscious still harboured many things that might lend themselves to "occult" interpretation, as is in fact the case. These "archaic vestiges," or archetypal forms grounded on the instincts and giving expression to them, have a numinous quality that sometimes arouses fear. They are ineradicable, for they represent the ultimate foundations of the psyche itself. They cannot be grasped intellectually, and when one has destroyed one manifestation of them, they reappear in altered form. It is this fear of the unconscious psyche which not only impedes self-knowledge but is the gravest obstacle to a wider understanding and knowledge of psychology. Often the fear is so great that one dares not admit it even to oneself. This is a question which every religious person should consider very seriously; he might get an illuminating answer.

A scientifically oriented psychology is bound to proceed abstractly; that is, it removes itself just sufficiently far from its object not to lose sight of it altogether. That is why the findings of laboratory psychology are, for all practical purposes, often so remarkably unenlightening and devoid of interest. The more the individual object dominates the field of vision, the more practical, detailed, and alive will be the knowledge derived from it. This means that the objects of investigation, too, become more and more complicated and that the uncertainty of the individual factors grows in proportion to their number, thus increasing the possibility of error. Understandably enough, academic psychology is scared of this risk and prefers to avoid complex situations by asking ever simpler questions, which it can do with impunity. It has full freedom in the choice of questions it will put to Nature.

Medical psychology, on the other hand, is very far from being in this more or less enviable position. Here the object puts the question and not the experimenter. The analyst is confronted with facts which are not of his choosing and which he probably never *would* choose if he were a free agent. It is the sickness or the patient himself that puts the crucial questions – in other words, Nature experiments with the doctor in expecting an answer from him. The uniqueness of the individual and of his situation stares the analyst in the face and demands an answer. His duty as a physician forces him to cope with a situation swarming with uncertainty factors. At first he will apply principles based on general experience, but he will soon realize that principles of this kind do not adequately express the facts and fail to meet the nature of the case. The deeper his understanding penetrates, the more the general principles lose their meaning. But these principles are the foundation of objective knowledge and the yardstick by which it is measured. With the growth of what both patient and doctor feel to be "understanding," the situation becomes increasingly subjectivized. What was an advantage to begin with threatens to turn into a dangerous disadvantage. Subjectivation (in technical terms, transference and countertransference) creates isolation from the environment, a social limitation which neither party wishes for but which invariably sets in when understanding predominates and is no longer balanced by knowledge. As understanding deepens, the further removed it becomes from knowledge. An ideal understanding would ultimately result in each party's unthinkingly going along with the other's experience – a state of uncritical passivity coupled with the most complete subjectivity and lack of social responsibility. Understanding carried to such lengths is in any case impossible, for it would require the virtual identification of two different individuals. Sooner or later the relationship reaches a point where one partner feels he is being forced to sacrifice his own individuality so that it may be assimilated by that of the other. This inevitable consequence breaks the understanding, for understanding also presupposes the integral preservation of the individuality of both partners. It is therefore advisable to carry understanding only to the point where the balance between understanding and knowledge is reached, for understanding at all costs is injurious to both partners.

This problem arises whenever complex, individual situations have to be known and understood. It is the specific task of the medical psychologist to provide just this knowledge and understanding. It would also be the task of the "director of conscience" zealous in the cure of souls, were it not that his office inevitably obliges him to apply the yardstick of his denominational bias at the critical moment. As a result, the individual's right to exist as such is cut short by a collective prejudice and often curtailed in the most sensitive area. The only time this does not happen is when the dogmatic symbol, for instance the model life of Christ, is understood concretely and felt by the individual to be adequate. How far this is the case today I would prefer to leave to the judgment of others. At all events, the analyst very often has to treat patients to whom denominational limitations mean little or nothing. His profession therefore compels him to have as few preconceptions as possible. Similarly, while respecting metaphysical (i.e., non-verifiable) convictions and assertions, he will take care not to credit them with universal validity. This caution is called for because the individual traits of the patient's personality ought not to be twisted out of shape by arbitrary interventions from outside. The analyst must leave this to environmental influences, to the patient's own inner development, and – in the widest sense – to fate with its wise or unwise decrees.

Many people will perhaps find this heightened caution exaggerated. In view of the fact, however, that there is in any case such a multitude of reciprocal influences at work in the dialectical process between two individuals, even if it is conducted with the most tactful reserve, the responsible analyst will refrain from adding unnecessarily to the collective factors to which his patient has already succumbed. Moreover, he knows very well that the preaching of even the worthiest precepts only provokes the patient into open hostility or secret resistance and thus needlessly endangers the aim of the treatment. The psychic situation of the individual is so menaced nowadays by advertising, propaganda, and other more or less well-meant advice and suggestions that for once in his life the patient might be offered a relationship that does not repeat the nauseating "you should," "you must" and similar confessions of impotence. Against the onslaught from outside no less than against its repercussions in the psyche of the individual the analyst sees himself obliged to play the role of counsel for the defence. Fear that anarchic instincts will thereby be let loose is a possibility that is greatly exaggerated, seeing that obvious safeguards exist within and without. Above all, there is the natural cowardice of most men to be reckoned with, not to mention morality, good taste and – last but not least – the penal code. This fear is nothing compared with the enormous effort it usually costs people to help the first stirrings of individuality into consciousness, let alone put them into effect. And where these individual impulses have broken through too boldly and unthinkingly, the analyst must protect them from the patient's own clumsy recourse to shortsightedness, ruthlessness, and cynicism.

As the dialectical discussion proceeds, a point is reached when an evaluation of these individual impulses becomes necessary. By that time the patient should have acquired enough certainty of judgment to enable him to act on his own insight and decision and not from the mere wish to copy convention – even if he happens to agree with collective opinion. Unless he stands firmly on his own feet, the so-called objective values profit him nothing, since they then only serve as a substitute for character and so help to suppress his individuality. Naturally, society has an indisputable right to protect itself against arrant subjectivisms, but, in so far as society is itself composed of de-individualized human beings, it is completely at the mercy of ruthless individualists. Let it band together into groups and organizations as much as it likes – it is just this banding together and the resultant extinction of the individual personality that makes it succumb so readily to a dictator. A million zeros joined together do not, unfortunately, add up to one. Ultimately everything depends on the quality of the individual, but our fatally shortsighted age thinks only in terms of large numbers and mass organizations, though one would think that the world had seen more than enough of what a well-disciplined mob can do in the hands of a single madman. Unfortunately, this realization does not seem to have penetrated very far – and our blindness is extremely dangerous. People go on blithely organizing and believing in the sovereign remedy of mass action, without the least consciousness of the fact that the most powerful organizations can be maintained only by the greatest ruthlessness of their leaders and the cheapest of slogans.

Curiously enough, the Churches too want to avail themselves of mass action in order to cast out the devil with Beelzebub – the very Churches whose care is the salvation of the *individual* soul. They do not appear to have heard of the elementary axiom of mass psychology that the individual becomes morally and spiritually inferior in the mass, and for this reason they do not bother themselves overmuch with their real task of helping the individual to achieve a *metanoia*, a rebirth of the spirit – *Deo concedente*. It is, unfortunately, only too clear that if the individual is not truly regenerated in spirit, society cannot be either, for society is the sum total of individuals in need of redemption. I can therefore see it only as a delusion when the Churches try – as they apparently do – to rope the individual into some social organization and reduce him to a condition of diminished responsibility, instead of raising him out of the torpid, mindless mass and making clear to him that *he* is the one important factor and that the salvation of the world consists in the salvation of the individual soul. It is true that mass meetings parade these ideas before him and seek to impress them on his mind by dint of mass suggestion, with the melancholy result that once the intoxication has worn off the mass man promptly succumbs to another even more obvious and still louder slogan. His individual relation to God would be an effective shield against these pernicious influences. Did Christ, perchance, call his disciples to him at a mass meeting? Did the feeding of the five thousand bring him any followers who did not afterwards cry with the rest, "Crucify him!" when even the rock named Peter showed signs of wavering? And are not Jesus and Paul prototypes of those who, trusting their inner experience, have gone their individual ways in defiance of the world?

This argument should certainly not cause us to overlook the reality of the situation confronting the Church. When the Church tries to give shape to the amorphous mass by uniting individuals into a community of believers and to hold such an organization together with the help of suggestion, it is not only performing a great *social* service, but it also secures for the individual the inestimable boon of a meaningful form of life. These, however, are gifts which as a rule only confirm certain tendencies and do not change them. As experience unfortunately shows, the inner man remains unchanged however much community he has. His environment cannot give him as a gift something which he can win for himself only with effort and suffering. On the contrary, a favourable environment merely strengthens the dangerous tendency to expect everything from outside – even that metamorphosis which external reality cannot provide. By this I mean a far-reaching change of the inner man, which is all the more urgent in view of the mass phenomena of today and the still greater problems of overpopulation looming in the future. It is time we asked ourselves exactly what we are lumping together in mass organizations and what constitutes the nature of the individual human being, i.e., of the real man and not the statistical man. This is hardly possible except by a new process of self-reflection.

All mass movements, as one might expect, slip with the greatest ease down an inclined plane made up of large numbers. Where the many are, there is security; what the many believe must of course be true; what the many want must be worth striving for, and necessary, and therefore good. In the clamour of the many resides the power to snatch wish-fulfilments by force; sweetest of all, however, is that gentle and painless slipping back into the kingdom of childhood, into the paradise of parental care, into happy-go-luckiness and irresponsibility. All the thinking and looking after are done from the top; to all questions there is an answer, and for all needs the necessary provision is made. The infantile dream-state of the mass man is so unrealistic that he never thinks to ask who is paying for this paradise. The balancing of accounts is left to a higher political or social authority, which welcomes the task, for its power is thereby increased; and the more power it has, the weaker and more helpless the individual becomes.

Whenever social conditions of this type develop on a large scale, the road to tyranny lies open and the freedom of the individual turns into spiritual and physical slavery. Since every tyranny is *ipso facto* immoral and ruthless, it has much more freedom in the choice of its methods than an institution which still takes account of the individual. Should such an institution come into conflict with the organized State, it is soon made aware of the very real disadvantage of its morality and therefore feels compelled to avail itself of the same methods as its opponent. In this way the evil spreads almost of necessity, even when direct infection might be avoided. The danger of infection is greater when decisive importance is attached to large numbers and to statistical values, as is everywhere the case in our Western world. The suffocating power of the masses is paraded before our eyes in one form or another every day in the newspapers, and the insignificance of the individual is rubbed into him so thoroughly that he loses all hope of making himself heard. The outworn ideals of *liberté, égalité, fraternité* help him not at all, as he can direct this appeal only to his executioners, the spokesmen of the masses.

Resistance to the organized mass can be effected only by the man who is as well organized in his individuality as the mass itself. I fully realize that this proposition must sound well-nigh unintelligible to the man of today. The helpful medieval view that man is a microcosm, a reflection of the great cosmos in miniature, has long since dropped away from him, although the very existence of his world-embracing and world-conditioning psyche might have taught him better. Not only is the image of the macrocosm imprinted upon his psychic nature, but he also creates this image for himself on an ever-widening scale. He bears this cosmic "correspondence" within him by virtue of his reflecting consciousness on the one hand, and, on the other, thanks to the hereditary, archetypal nature of his instincts, which bind him to his environment. But his instincts not only attach him to the macrocosm, they also, in a sense, tear him apart, because his desires pull him in different directions. In this way he falls into continual conflict with himself and only very rarely succeeds in giving his life an undivided goal – for which, as a rule, he must pay very dearly by repressing other sides of his nature. One often has to ask oneself whether this kind of single-mindedness is worth forcing at all, seeing that the natural state of the human psyche consists in a jostling together of its components and in their contradictory behaviour – that is, in a certain degree of dissociation. The Buddhist name for this is attachment to the "ten thousand things." Such a condition cries out for order and synthesis.

Just as the chaotic movements of the crowd, all ending in mutual frustration, are impelled in a definite direction by a dictatorial will, so the individual in his dissociated state needs a directing and ordering principle. Ego-consciousness would like to let its own will play this role, but overlooks the existence of powerful unconscious factors which thwart its intentions. If it wants to reach the goal of synthesis, it must first get to know the nature of these factors. It must *experience* them, or else it must possess a numinous *symbol* that expresses them and leads to their synthesis. A religious symbol that comprehended and visibly represented what is seeking expression in modern man might possibly do this; but our conception of the Christian symbol to date has certainly not been able to do so. On the contrary, that frightful world split runs right through the domains of the "Christian" white man, and our Christian outlook on life has proved powerless to prevent the recrudescence of an archaic social order like Communism.

This is not to say that Christianity is finished. I am, on the contrary, convinced that it is not Christianity, but our conception and interpretation of it, that has become antiquated in face of the present world situation. The Christian symbol is a living thing that carries in itself the seeds of further development. It can go on developing; it depends only on us, whether we can make up our minds to meditate again, and more thoroughly, on the Christian premises. This requires a very different attitude towards the individual, towards the microcosm of the self, from the one we have adopted hitherto. That is why nobody knows what ways of approach are open to man, what inner experiences he could still pass through and what psychic facts underlie the religious myth. Over all this hangs so universal a darkness that no one can see why he should be interested or to what end he should commit himself. Before this problem we stand helpless.

This is not surprising, since practically all the trump cards are in the hands of our opponents. They can appeal to the big battalions and their crushing power. Politics, science, and technology stand ranged on their side. The imposing arguments of science represent the highest degree of intellectual certainty yet achieved by the mind of man. So at least it seems to the man of today, who has received hundred-fold enlightenment concerning the backwardness and darkness of past ages and their superstitions. That his teachers have themselves gone seriously astray by making false comparisons between incommensurable factors never enters his head. All the more so as the intellectual *élite* to whom he puts his questions are almost unanimously agreed that what science regards as impossible today was impossible at all other times as well. Above all, the facts of faith, which might give him the chance of an extramundane standpoint, are treated in the same context as the facts of science. Thus, when the individual questions the Churches and their spokesmen, to whom is entrusted the cure of souls, he is informed that to belong to a church – a decidedly worldly institution – is more or less *de rigueur*; that the facts of faith which have become questionable for him were concrete historical events; that certain ritual actions produce miraculous effects; and that the sufferings of Christ have vicariously saved him from sin and its consequences (i.e., eternal damnation). If, with the limited means at his disposal, he begins to reflect on these things, he will have to confess that he does not understand them at all and that only two possibilities remain open to him: either to believe implicitly, or to reject such statements because they are flatly incomprehensible.

Whereas the man of today can easily think about and understand all the "truths" dished out to him by the State, his understanding of religion is made considerably more difficult owing to the lack of explanations. ("Do you understand what you are reading?" And he said, "How can I, unless someone guides me?" Acts 8:30.) If, despite this, he has still not discarded all his religious convictions, this is because the religious impulse rests on an instinctive basis and is therefore a specifically human function. You can take away a man's gods, but only to give him others in return. The leaders of the mass State could not help being deified, and wherever crudities of this kind have not yet been put over by force, obsessive factors arise in their stead, charged with demonic energy – money, work, political influence, and so forth. When any natural human function gets lost, i.e., is denied conscious and intentional expression, a general disturbance results. Hence, it is quite natural that with the triumph of the Goddess of Reason a general neuroticizing of modern man should set in, a dissociation of personality analogous to the splitting of the world today by the Iron Curtain. This boundary line bristling with barbed wire runs through the psyche of modern man, no matter on which side he lives. And just as the typical neurotic is unconscious of his *shadow side*, so the normal individual, like the neurotic, sees his shadow in his neighbour or in the man beyond the great divide. It has even become a political and social duty to apostrophize the capitalism of the one and the communism of the other as the very devil, so as to fascinate the outward eye and prevent it from looking within. But just as the neurotic, despite unconsciousness of his other side, has a dim premonition that all is not well with his psychic economy, so Western man has developed an instinctive interest in his psyche and in "psychology."

Thus it is that the psychiatrist is summoned willy-nilly to appear on the world stage, and questions are addressed to him which primarily concern the most intimate and hidden life of the individual, but which in the last analysis are the direct effects of the *Zeitgeist*. Because of its personal symptomatology this material is usually considered to be "neurotic" – and rightly so, since it is made up of infantile fantasies which ill accord with the contents of an adult psyche and are therefore repressed by our moral judgment, in so far as they reach consciousness at all. Most fantasies of this kind do not, in the nature of things, come to consciousness in any form, and it is very improbable, to say the least of it, that they were ever conscious and were consciously repressed. Rather, they seem to have been present from the beginning or, at any rate, to have arisen unconsciously and to have persisted in that state until the psychologist's intervention enabled them to cross the threshold of consciousness. The activation of unconscious fantasies is a process that occurs when consciousness finds itself in a situation of distress. Were that not so, the fantasies would be produced normally and would then bring no neurotic disturbances in their train. In reality, fantasies of this kind belong to the world of childhood and give rise to disturbances only when prematurely strengthened by abnormal conditions of conscious life. This is particularly likely to happen when unfavourable influences emanate from the parents, poisoning the atmosphere and producing conflicts which upset the psychic balance of the child.

When a neurosis breaks out in an adult, the fantasy world of childhood reappears, and one is tempted to explain the onset of the neurosis causally, as due to the presence of infantile fantasies. But that does not explain why the fantasies did not develop any pathological effects during the interim period. These effects develop only when the individual is faced with a situation which he cannot overcome by conscious means. The resultant standstill in the development of personality opens a sluice for infantile fantasies, which, of course, are latent in everybody but do not display any activity so long as the conscious personality can continue on its way unimpeded. When the fantasies reach a certain level of intensity, they begin to break through into consciousness and create a conflict situation that becomes perceptible to the patient himself, splitting him into two personalities with different characters. The dissociation, however, had been prepared long before in the unconscious, when the energy flowing off from consciousness (because unused) reinforced the negative qualities of the unconscious and particularly the infantile traits of the personality.

Since the normal fantasies of a child are nothing other, at bottom, than the *imagination of the instincts*, and may thus be regarded as preliminary exercises in the use of future conscious activities, it follows that the fantasies of the neurotic, even though pathologically altered and perhaps perverted by the regression of energy, contain a core of normal instinct, the hallmark of which is adaptedness. A neurotic illness always implies an unadapted alteration and distortion of normal dynamisms and of the "imagination" proper to them. Instincts, however, are highly conservative and of extreme antiquity as regards both their dynamism and their form. Their form, when represented to the mind, appears as an *image* which expresses the nature of the instinctive impulse visually and concretely, like a picture. If we could look into the psyche of the yucca moth,* for instance, we would find in it a pattern of ideas, of a numinous or fascinating character, which not only compels the moth to carry out its fertilizing activity on the yucca plant but helps it to "recognize" the total situation. Instinct is anything but a blind and indefinite impulse, since it proves to be attuned and adapted to a definite external situation. This latter circumstance gives it its specific and irreducible form. Just as instinct is original and hereditary, so, too, its form is age-old, that is to say, *archetypal*. It is even older and more conservative than the body's form.

These biological considerations naturally apply also to *Homo sapiens*, who still remains within the framework of general biology despite the possession of consciousness, will, and reason. The fact that our conscious activity is rooted in instinct and derives from it its dynamism as well as the basic features of its ideational forms has the same significance for human psychology as for all other members of the animal kingdom. Human knowledge consists essentially in the constant adaptation of the primordial patterns of

*This is a classic instance of the symbiosis of insect and plant.

ideas that were given us *a priori*. These need certain modifications, because, in their original form, they are suited to an archaic mode of life but not to the demands of a specifically differentiated environment. If the flow of instinctive dynamism into our life is to be maintained, as is absolutely necessary for our existence, then it is imperative that we should remould these archetypal forms into ideas which are adequate to the challenge of the present.

5. THE PHILOSOPHICAL AND THE PSYCHOLOGICAL APPROACH TO LIFE

Our ideas have, however, the unfortunate but inevitable tendency to lag behind the changes in the total situation. They can hardly do otherwise, because, so long as nothing changes in the world, they remain more or less adapted and therefore function in a satisfactory way. There is then no cogent reason why they should be changed and adapted anew. Only when conditions have altered so drastically that there is an unendurable rift between the outer situation and our ideas, now become antiquated, does the general problem of our *Weltanschauung*, or philosophy of life, arise, and with it the question of how the primordial images that maintain the flow of instinctive energy are to be reoriented or readapted. They cannot simply be replaced by a new rational configuration, for this would be moulded too much by the outward situation and not enough by man's biological needs. Moreover, not only would it build no bridge to the original man, but it would block the approach to him altogether. This is in keeping with the aims of Marxist education, which seeks, like God himself, to remake man, but in the image of the State.

Today, our basic convictions are becoming increasingly rationalistic. Our philosophy is no longer a way of life, as it was in antiquity; it has turned into an exclusively intellectual and academic exercise. Our denominational religions with their archaic rites and conceptions – justified enough in themselves – express a view of the world which caused no great difficulties in the Middle Ages but has become strange and unintelligible to modern man. Despite this conflict with the modern scientific outlook, a deep instinct bids him hang on to ideas which, if taken literally, leave out of account all the mental developments of the last five hundred years. The obvious purpose of this is to prevent him from falling into the abyss of nihilistic despair. But even when, as a rationalist, he feels impelled to criticize denominational religion as literalistic, narrow-minded, and obsolescent, he should never forget that it proclaims a doctrine whose symbols, although their interpretation may be disputed, nevertheless possess a life of their own by virtue of their archetypal character. Consequently, intellectual understanding is by no means indispensable in all cases, but is called for only when evaluation through feeling and intuition does not suffice, that is to say, in the case of people for whom the intellect carries the prime power of conviction.

Nothing is more characteristic and symptomatic in this respect than the gulf that has opened out between *faith* and *knowledge*. The contrast has become so enormous that one is obliged to speak of the incommensurability of these two categories and their way of looking at the world. And yet they are concerned with the same empirical world in which we live, for even the theologians tell us that faith is supported by facts that became historically perceptible in this known world of ours – namely that Christ was born as a real human being, worked many miracles and suffered his fate, died under Pontius Pilate, and rose up in the flesh after his death. Theology rejects any tendency to take the assertions of its earliest records as written myths and, accordingly, to understand them symbolically. Indeed, it is the theologians themselves who have recently made the attempt – no doubt as a concession to "knowledge" – to "demythologize" the object of their faith while drawing the line quite arbitrarily at the crucial points. But to the critical intellect it is only too obvious that myth is an integral component of all religions and therefore cannot be excluded from the assertions of faith without injuring them.

The rupture between faith and knowledge is a symptom of the *split consciousness* which is so characteristic of the mental disorder of our day. It is as if two different persons were making statements about the same thing, each from his own point of view, or as if one person in two different frames of mind were sketching a picture of his experience. If for "person" we substitute "modern society," it is evident that the latter is suffering from a mental dissociation, i.e., a neurotic disturbance. In view of this, it does not help matters at all if one party pulls obstinately to the right and the other to the left. This is what happens in every neurotic psyche, to its own deep distress, and it is just this distress that brings the patient to the analyst.

As I stated above in all brevity – while not neglecting to mention certain practical details whose omission might have perplexed the reader – the analyst has to establish a relationship with *both* halves of his patient's personality, because only from them can he put together a whole and complete man, and not merely from one half by suppression of the other half. But this suppression is just what the patient has been doing all along, for the modern *Weltanschauung* leaves him with no alternative. His individual situation is the same in principle as the collective situation. He is a social microcosm, reflecting on the smallest scale the qualities of society at large, or conversely the smallest social unit cumulatively producing the collective dissociation. The latter possibility is the more likely one, as the only direct and concrete carrier of life is the individual personality, while society and the State are conventional ideas and can claim reality only in so far as they are represented by a conglomeration of individuals.

Far too little attention has been paid to the fact that, for all our irreligiousness, the distinguishing mark of the Christian epoch, its highest achievement, has become the congenital vice of our age: *the supremacy of the word*, of the Logos, which stands for the central figure of our Christian faith. The word has literally become our god and so it has remained, even if we know of Christianity only from hearsay. Words like "Society" and "State" are so concretized that they are almost personified. In the opinion of the man in the street, the "State," far more than any king in history, is the inexhaustible giver of all good; the "State" is invoked, made responsible, grumbled at, and so on and so forth. Society is elevated to the rank of a supreme ethical principle; indeed, it is even credited with positively creative capacities. No one seems to notice that this worship of the word, which was necessary at a certain phase of man's mental development, has a perilous shadow side. That is to say, the moment the word, as a result of centuries of education, attains universal validity, it severs its original connection with the divine Person. There is then a personified Church, a personified State; belief in the word becomes credulity, and the word itself an infernal slogan capable of any deception. With credulity come propaganda and advertising to dupe the citizen with political jobbery and compromises, and the lie reaches proportions never known before in the history of the world.

Thus the word, originally announcing the unity of all men and their union in the figure of the one great Man, has in our day become a source of suspicion and distrust of all against all. Credulity is one of our worst enemies, but that is the makeshift the neurotic always resorts to in order to quell the doubter in his own breast or to conjure him out of existence. People think you have only to "tell" a person that he "ought" to do something in order to put him on the right track. But whether he can or will do it is another matter. The psychologist has come to see that nothing is achieved by telling, persuading, admonishing, giving good advice. He must acquaint himself with all the particulars and have an authentic knowledge of the psychic inventory of his patient. He has therefore to relate to the individuality of the sufferer and feel his way into all the nooks and crannies of his mind, to a degree that far exceeds the capacity of a teacher or even of a *directeur de conscience*. His scientific objectivity, which excludes nothing, enables him to see his patient not only as a human being but also as an anthropoid, who is bound to his body like an animal. His training directs his medical interest beyond the conscious personality to the world of unconscious instinct dominated by sexuality and the power drive (or self-assertion), which correspond to the twin moral concepts of Saint Augustine: *concupiscentia* and *superbia*. The clash between these two fundamental instincts (preservation of the species and self-preservation) is the source of numerous conflicts. They are, therefore, the chief object of moral judgment, whose purpose it is to prevent instinctual collisions as far as possible.

As I explained earlier, instinct has two main aspects: on the one hand, that of dynamism and compulsion, and on the other, specific meaning and intention. It is highly probable that all man's psychic functions have an instinctual foundation, as is obviously the case with animals. It is easy to see that in animals instinct functions as the *spiritus rector* of all behaviour. This observation lacks certainty only when the learning capacity begins to develop, for instance in the higher apes and in man. In animals, as a result of their learning capacity, instinct undergoes numerous modifications and differentiations, and in civilized man the instincts are so split up that only a few of the basic ones can be recognized with any certainty in their original form. The most important are the two fundamental instincts already mentioned and their derivatives, and these have been the exclusive concern of medical psychology so far. But in following up the ramifications of instinct investigators came upon configurations which could not with certainty be ascribed to either group. To take but one example: The discoverer of the power instinct raised the question whether an apparently indubitable expression of the sexual instinct might not be better explained as a "power arrangement," and Freud himself felt obliged to acknowledge the existence of "ego instincts" in addition to the overriding sexual instinct – a clear concession to the Adlerian standpoint. In view of this uncertainty, it is hardly surprising that in most cases neurotic symptoms can be explained, almost without contradiction, in terms of either theory. This perplexity does not mean that one or the other standpoint is erroneous or that both are. Rather, both are *relatively* valid and, unlike certain one-sided and dogmatic tendencies, admit the existence and competition of still other instincts. Although, as I have said, the question of human instinct is a far from simple matter, we shall probably not be wrong in assuming that the learning capacity, a quality almost exclusive to man, is based on the instinct for imitation found in animals. It is in the nature of this instinct to disturb other instinctive activities and eventually to modify them, as can be observed, for instance, in the songs of birds when they adopt other melodies.

Nothing estranges man more from the ground-plan of his instincts than his learning capacity, which turns out to be a genuine drive for progressive transformation of human modes of behaviour. It, more than anything else, is responsible for the altered conditions of his existence and the need for new adaptations which civilization brings. It is also the ultimate source of those numerous psychic disturbances and difficulties which are occasioned by man's progressive alienation from his instinctual foundation, i.e., by his uprootedness and identification with his conscious knowledge of himself, by his concern with consciousness at the expense of the unconscious. The result is that modern man knows himself only in so far as he can become conscious of himself – a capacity largely dependent on environmental conditions, knowledge and control of which necessitated or suggested certain modifications of his original instinctive tendencies. His consciousness therefore orients itself chiefly by observing and investigating the world around him, and it is to the latter's peculiarities that he must adapt his psychic and technical resources. This task is so exacting, and its fulfilment so profitable, that he forgets himself in the process, losing sight of his instinctual nature and putting his own conception of himself in place of his real being. In this way he slips imperceptibly into a purely conceptual world where the products of his conscious activity progressively take the place of reality.

Separation from his instinctual nature inevitably plunges civilized man into the conflict between conscious and unconscious, spirit and nature, knowledge and faith, a split that becomes pathological the moment his consciousness is no longer able to neglect or suppress his instinctual side. The accumulation of individuals who have got into this critical state starts off a mass movement purporting to be the champion of the suppressed. In accordance with the prevailing tendency of consciousness to seek the source of all ills in the outside world, the cry goes up for political and social changes which, it is supposed, would automatically solve the much deeper problem of split personality. Hence it is that whenever this demand is fulfilled, political and social conditions arise which bring the same ills back again in altered form. What then happens is a simple reversal: the underside comes to the top and the shadow takes the place of the light, and since the former is always anarchic and turbulent, the freedom of the "liberated" underdog must suffer Draconian curtailment. The devil is cast out with Beelzebub. All this is unavoidable, because the root of the evil is untouched and merely the counterposition has come to light.

The Communist revolution has debased man far lower than democratic collective psychology has done, because it robs him of his freedom not only in the social but in the moral and spiritual sphere. Aside from the political difficulties, this entailed a great psychological disadvantage for the West that had already made itself unpleasantly felt in the days of German Nazism: we can now point a finger at the shadow. He is clearly on the other side of the political frontier, while we are on the side of good and enjoy the possession of the right ideals. Did not a well-known statesman recently confess that he had "no imagination for evil"?* In the name of the multitude he was expressing the fact that Western man is in danger of losing his shadow altogether, of identifying himself with his fictive personality and the world with the abstract picture painted by scientific rationalism. His spiritual and moral opponent, who is just as real as he, no longer dwells in his own breast but beyond the geographical line of division, which no longer represents an outward political barrier but splits off the conscious from the unconscious man more and more menacingly. Thinking and feeling lose their inner polarity, and where religious orientation has grown ineffective, not even a god can check the sovereign sway of unleashed psychic functions.

Our rational philosophy does not bother itself with whether the other person in us, pejoratively described as the "shadow," is in sympathy with our conscious plans and intentions. Evidently it still does not know that we carry in ourselves a real shadow whose existence is grounded in our instinctual nature. No one can overlook either the dynamism or the imagery of the instincts without the gravest injury to himself. Violation or neglect of instinct has painful consequences of a physiological and psychological nature for whose treatment medical help, above all, is required.

For more than fifty years we have known, or could have known, that there is an unconscious counterbalance to consciousness. Medical psychology has furnished all the necessary empirical and experimental proofs of this. There is an unconscious psychic reality which demonstrably influences consciousness and its contents. All this is known, but no practical conclusions have been drawn from this fact. We still go on thinking and acting as before, as if we were *simplex* and not *duplex*. Accordingly, we imagine ourselves to be innocuous, reasonable, and humane. We do not think of distrusting our motives or of asking ourselves how the inner man feels about the things we do in the outside world. But actually it is frivolous, superficial, and unreasonable of us, as well as psychically unhygienic, to overlook the reaction and standpoint of the unconscious. One can regard one's stomach or heart as

*Since these words were written, the shadow has followed up this overbright picture hotfoot with the Charge of the Light Brigade to Suez.

unimportant and worthy of contempt, but that does not prevent overeating or overexertion from having consequences that affect the whole man. Yet we think that psychic mistakes and their consequences can be got rid of with mere words, for "psychic" means less than air to most people. All the same, nobody can deny that without the psyche there would be no world at all, and still less a human world. Virtually everything depends on the human psyche and its functions. It should be worthy of all the attention we can give it, especially today, when everyone admits that the weal or woe of the future will be decided neither by the threat of wild animals, nor by natural catastrophes, nor by the danger of world-wide epidemics, but simply and solely by the psychic changes in man. It needs only an almost imperceptible disturbance of equilibrium in a few of our rulers' heads to plunge the world into blood, fire, and radioactivity. The technical means necessary for this are present on both sides. And certain conscious deliberations, uncontrolled by any inner opponent, can be put into effect all too easily, as we have seen already from the example of one "Leader." The consciousness of modern man still clings so much to external objects that he makes them exclusively responsible, as if it were on them that the decision depended. That the psychic state of certain individuals could ever emancipate itself from the behaviour of objects is something that is considered far too little, although irrationalities of this sort are observed every day and can happen to everyone.

The forlorn state of consciousness in our world is due primarily to loss of instinct, and the reason for this lies in the development of the human mind over the past aeon. The more power man had over nature, the more his knowledge and skill went to his head, and the deeper became his contempt for the merely natural and accidental, for all irrational data – including the objective psyche, which is everything that consciousness is not. In contrast to the subjectivism of the conscious mind the unconscious is objective, manifesting itself mainly in the form of contrary feelings, fantasies, emotions, impulses, and dreams, none of which one makes oneself but which come upon one objectively. Even today psychology is still, for the most part, the science of conscious contents, measured as far as possible by collective standards. The individual psyche has become a mere accident, a marginal phenomenon, while the unconscious, which can manifest itself only in the real, "irrationally given" human being, has been ignored altogether. This was not the result of carelessness or of lack of knowledge, but of downright resistance to the mere possibility that there could be a second psychic authority besides the ego. It seems a positive menace to the ego that its monarchy could be doubted. The religious person, on the other hand, is accustomed to the thought of not being sole master in his own house. He believes that God, and not he himself, decides in the end. But how many of us would dare to let the will of God decide, and which of us would not feel embarrassed if he had to say how far the decision came from God himself?

The religious person, so far as one can judge, is directly influenced by the reaction of the unconscious. As a rule, he calls this the operation of *conscience*. But since the same psychic background produces reactions other than moral ones, the believer is measuring his conscience by the traditional ethical standard and thus by a collective value, in which endeavour he is assiduously supported by his Church. So long as the individual can hold fast to his traditional beliefs, and the circumstances of his time do not demand stronger emphasis on individual autonomy, he can rest content with the situation. But the situation is radically altered when the worldly-minded man who is oriented to external factors and has lost his religious beliefs appears *en masse*, as is the case today. The believer is then forced onto the defensive and must catechize himself on the foundation of his beliefs. He is no longer sustained by the tremendous suggestive power of the *consensus omnium* and is keenly aware of the weakening of the Church and the precariousness of its dogmatic assumptions. To counter this, the Church recommends more faith, as if this gift of grace depended on man's good will and pleasure. The seat of faith, however, is not consciousness but spontaneous religious experience, which brings the individual's faith into immediate relation with God.

Here each of us must ask: Have I any religious experience and immediate relation to God, and hence that certainty which will keep me, as an individual, from dissolving in the crowd?

6. SELF-KNOWLEDGE

To this question there is a positive answer only when the individual is willing to fulfil the demands of rigorous self-examination and self-knowledge. If he does this, he will not only discover some important truths about himself but will also have gained a psychological advantage: he will have succeeded in deeming himself worthy of serious attention and sympathetic interest. He will have set his hand, as it were, to a declaration of his own human dignity and taken the first step towards the foundations of his consciousness – that is, towards the unconscious, the only available source of religious experience. This is certainly not to say that what we call the unconscious is identical with God or is set up in his place. It is simply the medium from which religious experience seems to flow. As to what the further cause of such experience may be, the answer to this lies beyond the range of human knowledge. Knowledge of God is a transcendental problem.

The religious person enjoys a great advantage when it comes to answering the crucial question that hangs over our time like a threat: he has a clear idea of the way his subjective existence is grounded in his relation to "God." I put the word "God" in quotes in order to indicate that we are dealing with an anthropomorphic idea whose dynamism and symbolism are filtered through the medium of the unconscious psyche. Anyone who wants to can at least draw near to the source of such experiences, no matter whether he believes in God or not. Without this approach it is only in rare cases that we witness those miraculous conversions of which Paul's Damascus experience is the prototype. That religious experiences exist no longer needs proof. But it will always remain doubtful whether what metaphysics and theology call God and the gods is the real ground of these experiences. The question is idle, actually, and answers itself by reason of the subjectively overwhelming numinosity of the experience. Anyone who has had it is *seized* by it and therefore not in a position to indulge in fruitless metaphysical or epistemological speculations. Absolute certainty brings its own evidence and has no need of anthropomorphic proofs.

In view of the general ignorance of and bias against psychology it must be accounted a misfortune that the one experience which makes sense of individual existence should seem to have its origin in a medium that is certain to catch everybody's prejudices. Once more the doubt is heard: "What good can come out of Nazareth?" The unconscious, if not regarded outright as a sort of refuse bin underneath the conscious mind, is at any rate supposed to be of "merely animal nature." In reality, however, and by definition it is of uncertain extent and constitution, so that overvaluation or undervaluation of it is pointless and can be dismissed as mere prejudice. At all events, such judgments sound very queer in the mouths of Christians, whose Lord was himself born on the straw of a stable, among the domestic animals. It would have been more to the taste of the multitude if he had got himself born in a temple. In the same way, the worldly-minded mass man looks for the numinous experience in the mass meeting, which provides an infinitely more imposing background than the individual soul. Even Church Christians share this pernicious delusion.

Psychology's insistence on the importance of unconscious processes for religious experience is extremely unpopular, no less with the political Right than with the Left. For the former the deciding factor is the historical revelation that came to man from outside; to the latter this is sheer nonsense, and man has no religious function at all, except belief in the party doctrine, when suddenly the most intense faith is called for. On top of this, the various creeds assert quite different things, and each of them claims to possess the absolute truth. Yet today we live in a unitary world where distances are reckoned by hours and no longer by weeks and months. Exotic races have ceased to be peepshows in ethnological museums. They have become our neighbours, and what was yesterday the private concern of the ethnologist is today a political, social, and psychological problem. Already the ideological spheres begin to touch, to interpenetrate, and the time may not be far off when the question of mutual understanding will become acute. To make oneself understood is certainly impossible without far-reaching comprehension of the other's standpoint. The insight needed for this will have repercussions on both sides. History will undoubtedly pass over those who feel it is their vocation to resist this inevitable development, however desirable and psychologically necessary it may be to cling to what is essential and good in our own tradition. Despite all the differences, the unity of mankind will assert itself irresistibly. On this card Marxist doctrine has staked its life, while the West hopes to achieve its aim with technology and economic aid. Communism has not overlooked the enormous importance of the ideological element and the universality of basic principles. The coloured races share our ideological weakness and in this respect are just as vulnerable as we are.

The underestimation of the psychological factor is likely to take a bitter revenge. It is therefore high time we caught up with ourselves in this matter. For the present this must remain a pious wish, because self-knowledge, as well as being highly unpopular, seems to be an unpleasantly idealistic goal, reeks of morality, and is preoccupied with the psychological shadow, which is normally denied whenever possible or at least not spoken of. The task that faces our age is indeed almost insuperably difficult. It makes the highest demands on our responsibility if we are not to be guilty of another *trahison des clercs*. It addresses itself to those leading and influential personalities who have the necessary intelligence to understand the situation our world is in. One might expect them to consult their consciences. But since it is a matter not only of intellectual understanding but of moral conclusions, there is unfortunately no cause for optimism. Nature, as we know, is not so lavish with her boons that she joins to a high intelligence the gifts of the heart also. As a rule, where one is present the other is missing, and where one capacity is present in perfection it is generally at the cost of all the others. The discrepancy between intellect and feeling, which get in each other's way at the best of times, is a particularly painful chapter in the history of the human psyche.

There is no sense in formulating the task that our age has forced upon us as a moral demand. We can, at best, merely make the psychological world situation so clear that it can be seen even by the myopic, and give utterance to words and ideas which even the hard of hearing can hear. We may hope for men of understanding and men of good will, and must therefore not grow weary of reiterating those thoughts and insights which are needed. Finally, even the truth can spread and not only the popular lie.

With these words I should like to draw the reader's attention to the main difficulty he has to face. The horror which the dictator States have of late brought upon mankind is nothing less than the culmination of all those atrocities of which our ancestors made themselves guilty in the not so distant past. Quite apart from the barbarities and blood baths perpetrated by the Christian nations among themselves throughout European history, the European has also to answer for all the crimes he has committed against the coloured races during the process of colonization. In this respect the white man carries a very heavy burden indeed. It shows us a picture of the common human shadow that could hardly be painted in blacker colours. The evil that comes to light in man and that undoubtedly dwells within him is of gigantic proportions, so that for the Church to talk of original sin and to trace it back to Adam's relatively innocent slip-up with Eve is almost a euphemism. The case is far graver and is grossly underestimated.

Since it is universally believed that man *is* merely what his consciousness knows of itself, he regards himself as harmless and so adds stupidity to iniquity. He does not deny that terrible things have happened and still go on happening, but it is always "the others" who do them. And when such deeds belong to the recent or remote past, they quickly and conveniently sink into the sea of forgetfulness, and that state of chronic woolly-mindedness returns which we describe as "normality." In shocking contrast to this is the fact that nothing has finally disappeared and nothing has been made good. The evil, the guilt, the profound unease of conscience, the dark foreboding, are there before our eyes, if only we would see. Man has done these things; I am a man, who has his share of human nature; therefore I am guilty with the rest and bear unaltered and indelibly within me the capacity and the inclination to do them again at any time. Even if, juristically speaking, we were not accessories to the crime, we are always, thanks to our human nature, potential criminals. In reality we merely lacked a suitable opportunity to be drawn into the infernal mêlée. None of us stands outside humanity's black collective shadow. Whether the crime occurred many generations back or happens today, it remains the symptom of a disposition that is always and everywhere present – and one would therefore do well to possess some "imagination for evil," for only the fool can permanently disregard the conditions of his own nature. In fact, this negligence is the best means of making him an instrument of evil. Harmlessness and naïveté are as little helpful as it would be for a cholera patient and those in his vicinity to remain unconscious of the contagiousness of the disease. On the contrary, they lead to projection of the unrecognized evil into the "other." This strengthens the opponent's position in the most effective way, because the projection carries the *fear* which we involuntarily and secretly feel for our own evil over to the other side and considerably increases the formidableness of his threat. What is even worse, our lack of insight deprives us of the *capacity to deal with evil*. Here, of course, we come up against one of the main prejudices of the Christian tradition, and one that is a great stumbling block to our policies. We should, so we are told, eschew evil and, if possible, neither touch nor mention it. For evil is also the thing of ill omen, that which is tabooed and feared. This apotropaic attitude towards evil, and the apparent circumventing of it, flatter the primitive tendency in us to shut our eyes to evil and drive it over some frontier or other, like the Old Testament scapegoat, which was supposed to carry the evil into the wilderness.

But if one can no longer avoid the realization that evil, without man's ever having chosen it, is lodged in human nature itself, then it bestrides the psychological stage as the equal and opposite partner of good. This realization leads straight to a psychological dualism, already unconsciously prefigured in the political world schism and in the even more unconscious dissociation in modern man himself. The dualism does not come from this realization; rather, we are in a split condition to begin with. It would be an insufferable thought that we had to take personal responsibility for so much guiltiness. We therefore prefer to localize the evil in individual criminals or groups of criminals, while washing our hands in innocence and ignoring the general proclivity to evil. This sanctimoniousness cannot be kept up in the long run, because the evil, as experience shows, lies in man – unless, in accordance with the Christian view, one is willing to postulate a metaphysical principle of evil. The great advantage of this view is that it exonerates man's conscience of too heavy a responsibility and foists it off on the devil, in correct psychological appreciation of the fact that man is much more the victim of his psychic constitution than its inventor. Considering that the evil of our day puts everything that has ever agonized mankind in the deepest shade, one must ask oneself how it is that, for all our progress in the administration of justice, in medicine and in technology, for all our concern with life and health, monstrous engines of destruction have been invented which could easily exterminate the human race.

No one will maintain that the atomic physicists are a pack of criminals because it is to their efforts that we owe that peculiar flower of human ingenuity, the hydrogen bomb. The vast amount of intellectual work that went into the development of nuclear physics was put forth by men who dedicated themselves to their task with the greatest exertion and self-sacrifice, and whose moral achievement could therefore just as easily have earned them the merit of inventing something useful and beneficial to humanity. But even though the first step along the road to a momentous invention may be the outcome of a conscious decision, here, as everywhere, the spontaneous idea – the hunch or intuition – plays an important part. In other words, the unconscious collaborates too and often makes decisive contributions. So it is not the conscious effort alone that is responsible for the result; somewhere or other the unconscious, with its barely discernible goals and intentions, has its finger in the pie. If it puts a weapon in your hand, it is aiming at some kind of violence. Knowledge of the truth is the foremost goal of science, and if in pursuit of the longing for light we stumble upon an immense danger, then one has the impression more of fatality than of premeditation. It is not that present-day man is capable of greater evil than the man of antiquity or the primitive. He merely has incomparably more effective means with which to realize his propensity to evil. As his consciousness has broadened and differentiated, so his moral nature has lagged behind. That is the great problem before us today. *Reason alone no longer suffices.*

In theory, it lies within the power of reason to desist from experiments of such hellish scope as nuclear fission if only because of their dangerousness. But fear of the evil which one does not see in one's own bosom but always in somebody else's checks reason every time, although everyone knows that the use of this weapon means the certain end of our present human world. The fear of universal destruction may spare us the worst, yet the possibility of it will nevertheless hang over us like a dark cloud so long as no

bridge is found across the world-wide psychic and political split –
a bridge as certain as the existence of the hydrogen bomb. If only
a world-wide consciousness could arise that all division and all
fission are due to the splitting of opposites in the psyche, then we
should know where to begin. But if even the smallest and most
personal stirrings of the individual psyche – so insignificant in
themselves – remain as unconscious and unrecognized as they have
hitherto, they will go on accumulating and produce mass
groupings and mass movements which cannot be subjected to
reasonable control or manipulated to a good end. All direct efforts
to do so are no more than shadow boxing, the most infatuated by
illusion being the gladiators themselves.

The crux of the matter is man's own dualism, to which he knows
no answer. This abyss has suddenly yawned open before him with
the latest events in world history, after mankind had lived for many
centuries in the comfortable belief that a unitary God had created
man in his own image, as a little unity. Even today people are
largely unconscious of the fact that every individual is a cell in the
structure of various international organisms and is therefore
causally implicated in their conflicts. He knows that as an
individual being he is more or less meaningless and feels himself
the victim of uncontrollable forces, but, on the other hand, he
harbours within himself a dangerous shadow and adversary who
is involved as an invisible helper in the dark machinations of the
political monster. It is in the nature of political bodies always to
see the evil in the opposite group, just as the individual has an
ineradicable tendency to get rid of everything he does not know
and does not want to know about himself by foisting it off on
somebody else.

Nothing has a more divisive and alienating effect upon society
than this moral complacency and lack of responsibility, and
nothing promotes understanding and *rapprochement* more than the
mutual withdrawal of projections. This necessary corrective
demands self-criticism, for one cannot just tell the other person to
withdraw them. He does not recognize them for what they are any
more than one does oneself. We can recognize our prejudices and
illusions only when, from a broader psychological knowledge of
ourselves and others, we are prepared to doubt the absolute
rightness of our assumptions and compare them carefully and

conscientiously with the objective facts. Funnily enough, "self-criticism" is an idea much in vogue in Marxist countries, but there it is subordinated to ideological considerations and must serve the State, and not truth and justice in men's dealings with one another. The mass State has no intention of promoting mutual understanding and the relationship of man to man; it strives, rather, for atomization, for the psychic isolation of the individual. The more unrelated individuals are, the more consolidated the State becomes, and vice versa.

There can be no doubt that in the democracies too the distance between man and man is much greater than is conducive to public welfare, let alone beneficial to our psychic needs. True, all sorts of attempts are being made to level out glaring social contrasts by appealing to people's idealism, enthusiasm, and ethical conscience; but, characteristically, one forgets to apply the necessary self-criticism, to answer the question: *Who* is making the idealistic demand? Is it, perchance, someone who jumps over his own shadow in order to hurl himself avidly on some idealistic programme that offers him a welcome alibi? How much respectability and apparent morality is there, cloaking in deceptive colours a very different inner world of darkness? One would first like to be assured that the man who talks of ideals is himself ideal, so that his words and deeds *are* more than they *seem*. To be ideal is impossible, and remains therefore an unfulfilled postulate. Since we usually have keen noses in this respect, most of the idealisms that are preached and paraded before us sound rather hollow and become acceptable only when their opposite is also openly admitted. Without this counterweight the ideal exceeds our human capacity, becomes incredible because of its humourlessness, and degenerates into bluff, albeit a well-meant one. Bluff is an illegitimate way of overpowering and suppressing others and leads to no good.

Recognition of the shadow, on the other hand, leads to the modesty we need in order to acknowledge imperfection. And it is just this conscious recognition and consideration that are needed whenever a human relationship is to be established. A human relationship is not based on differentiation and perfection, for these only emphasize the differences or call forth the exact opposite; it is based, rather, on imperfection, on what is weak, helpless and in need of support – the very ground and motive for dependence. The perfect have no need of others, but weakness has, for it seeks support and does not confront its partner with anything that might force him into an inferior position and even humiliate him. This humiliation may happen only too easily when high idealism plays too prominent a role.

Reflections of this kind should not be taken as superfluous sentimentalities. The question of human relationship and of the inner cohesion of our society is an urgent one in view of the atomization of the pent-up mass man, whose personal relationships are undermined by general mistrust. Wherever justice is uncertain and police spying and terror are at work, human beings fall into isolation, which, of course, is the aim and purpose of the dictator State, since it is based on the greatest possible accumulation of depotentiated social units. To counter this danger, the free society needs a bond of an affective nature, a principle of a kind like *caritas*, the Christian love of your neighbour. But it is just this love for one's fellow man that suffers most of all from the lack of understanding wrought by projection. It would therefore be very much in the interest of the free society to give some thought to the question of human relationship from the psychological point of view, for in this resides its real cohesion and consequently its strength. Where love stops, power begins, and violence, and terror.

These reflections are not intended as an appeal to idealism, but only to promote a consciousness of the psychological situation. I do not know which is weaker: the idealism or the insight of the public. I only know that it needs time to bring about psychic changes that have any prospect of enduring. Insight that dawns slowly seems to me to have more lasting effects than a fitful idealism, which is unlikely to hold out for long.

7. THE MEANING OF SELF-KNOWLEDGE

What our age thinks of as the "shadow" and inferior part of the psyche contains more than something merely negative. The very fact that through self-knowledge, that is, by exploring our own souls, we come upon the instincts and their world of imagery should throw some light on the powers slumbering in the psyche, of which we are seldom aware so long as all goes well. They are potentialities of the greatest dynamism, and it depends entirely on the preparedness and attitude of the conscious mind whether the irruption of these forces, and the images and ideas associated with them, will tend towards construction or catastrophe. The psychologist seems to be the only person who knows from experience how precarious the psychic preparedness of modern man is, for he is the only one who sees himself compelled to seek out in man's own nature those helpful powers and ideas which over and over have enabled him to find the right way through darkness and danger. For this exacting work the psychologist requires all his patience; he may not rely on any traditional oughts and musts, leaving the other person to make all the effort and contenting himself with the easy role of adviser and admonisher. Everyone knows the futility of preaching about things that are desirable, yet the general helplessness in this situation is so great, and the need so dire, that one prefers to repeat the old mistake instead of racking one's brains over a subjective problem. Besides, it is always a question of treating one single individual only and not ten thousand, when the trouble one takes would ostensibly have more impressive results, though one knows well enough that nothing has happened at all unless the individual changes.

The effect on *all* individuals, which one would like to see realized, may not set in for hundreds of years, for the spiritual transformation of mankind follows the slow tread of the centuries and cannot be hurried or held up by any rational process of reflection, let alone brought to fruition in one generation. What does lie within our reach, however, is the change in individuals who have, or create for themselves, an opportunity to influence others of like mind. I do not mean by persuading or preaching – I am thinking, rather, of the well-known fact that anyone who has insight into his own actions, and has thus found access to the unconscious, involuntarily exercises an influence on his environment. The deepening and broadening of his consciousness produce the kind of effect which the primitives call "mana." It is an unintentional influence on the unconscious of others, a sort of unconscious prestige, and its effect lasts only so long as it is not disturbed by conscious intention.

Nor is the striving for self-knowledge altogether without

prospects of success, since there exists a factor which, though completely disregarded, meets our expectations halfway. This is the unconscious *Zeitgeist*. It compensates the attitude of the conscious mind and anticipates changes to come. An excellent example of this is modern art: though seeming to deal with aesthetic problems, it is really performing a work of psychological education on the public by breaking down and destroying their previous aesthetic views of what is beautiful in form and meaningful in content. The pleasingness of the artistic product is replaced by chill abstractions of the most subjective nature which brusquely slam the door on the naïve and romantic delight in the senses and on the obligatory love for the object. This tells us, in plain and universal language, that the prophetic spirit of art has turned away from the old object-relationship towards the – for the time being – dark chaos of subjectivisms. Certainly art, so far as we can judge of it, has not yet discovered in this darkness what it is that could hold all men together and give expression to their psychic wholeness. Since reflection seems to be needed for this purpose, it may be that such discoveries are reserved for other fields of endeavour.

Great art till now has always derived its fruitfulness from myth, from the unconscious process of symbolization which continues through the ages and, as the primordial manifestation of the human spirit, will continue to be the root of all creation in the future. The development of modern art with its seemingly nihilistic trend towards disintegration must be understood as the symptom and symbol of a mood of universal destruction and renewal that has set its mark on our age. This mood makes itself felt everywhere, politically, socially, and philosophically. We are living in what the Greeks called the $\varkappa \alpha \iota \varrho \acute{o} \varsigma$ – the right moment – for a 'metamorphosis of the gods," of the fundamental principles and symbols. This peculiarity of our time, which is certainly not of our conscious choosing, is the expression of the unconscious man within us who is changing. Coming generations will have to take account of this momentous transformation if humanity is not to destroy itself through the might of its own technology and science.

As at the beginning of the Christian era, so again today we are faced with the problem of the general moral backwardness which has failed to keep pace with our scientific, technical, and social progress. So much is at stake and so much depends on the psychological constitution of modern man. Is he capable of resisting the temptation to use his power for the purpose of staging a world conflagration? Is he conscious of the path he is treading, and what the conclusions are that must be drawn from the present world situation and his own psychic situation? Does he know that he is on the point of losing the life-preserving myth of the inner man which Christianity has treasured up for him? Does he realize what lies in store should this catastrophe ever befall him? Is he even capable of realizing that this would in fact be a catastrophe? And finally, does the individual know that *he* is the makeweight that tips the scales?

Happiness and contentment, equability of mind and meaningfulness of life – these can be experienced only by the individual and not by a State, which, on the one hand, is nothing but a convention agreed to by independent individuals and, on the other, continually threatens to paralyse and suppress the individual. The psychiatrist is one of those who know most about the conditions of the soul's welfare, upon which so infinitely much depends in the social sum. The social and political circumstances of the time are certainly of considerable significance, but their importance for the weal or woe of the individual has been boundlessly overestimated in so far as they are taken for the sole deciding factors. In this respect all our social goals commit the error of overlooking the psychology of the person for whom they are intended and – very often – of promoting only his illusions.

I hope, therefore, that a psychiatrist, who in the course of a long life has devoted himself to the causes and consequences of psychic disorders, may be permitted to express his opinion, in all the modesty enjoined upon him as an individual, about the questions raised by the world situation today. I am neither spurred on by excessive optimism nor in love with high ideals, but am merely concerned with the fate of the individual human being – that infinitesimal unit on whom a world depends, and in whom, if we read the meaning of the Christian message aright, even God seeks his goal.

Chronology of Jung's Life and Work

From *C. G. Jung: Word and Image*, ed. Aniela Jaffé, Bollingen Series XCVII: 2, Princeton University Press, 1979.

1875
26 July: born to Johann Paul Achilles Jung (1842–96), then parson at Kesswil (Canton Thurgau), and Emilie, née Preiswerk (1848–1923).

1879
The family moves to Klein-Hüningen, near Basel.

1884
Birth of sister Gertrud (d. 1935).

1896
Death of father.

1895–1900
Medical training (and qualification) at Basel University.

1900
Assistant Staff Physician under Eugen Bleuler at the Burghölzli, the insane asylum of Canton Zurich and psychiatric clinic of Zurich University.

1902
Senior Assistant Staff Physician at the Burghölzli.
MD dissertation (Zurich University): *Zur Psychologie und Pathologie sogenannter occulter Phänomene* ("On the Psychology and Pathology of So-called Occult Phenomena," CW 1).

1902–3
Winter semester with Pierre Janet at the Salpêtrière, in Paris, for the study of theoretical psychopathology.

1903
Marriage to Emma Rauschenbach, of Schaffhausen (1882–1955); one son and four daughters.

1903–5
Experimental researches on word associations, published in *Diagnostische Assoziationsstudien* (1906, 1909) (*Studies in Word-Association*, 1918; CW 2).

1905-9
Senior Staff Physician at the Burghölzli. Conducts policlinical courses on hypnotic therapy. Research on dementia praecox (schizophrenia).

1905-13
Lecturer (*Privatdozent*) on the medical faculty of Zurich University; lectures on psychoneuroses and psychology.

1906
April: correspondence with Freud begins.

1907
Über die Psychologie der Dementia Praecox (*The Psychology of Dementia Praecox*, 1909; CW 3).
March: first meeting with Freud, in Vienna.

1908
First International Psychoanalytic Congress, Salzburg.

1909
June: moves to his own house in Küsnacht/Zurich, and withdraws from the clinic to devote himself to private practice.
September: first visit to USA, with Freud and Ferenczi, on the occasion of the twentieth anniversary of Clark University, Worcester, Mass., where

Jung lectures on the association experiment and receives honorary degree of LL.D.

1909-13
Editor of *Jahrbuch für psychoanalytische und psychopathologische Forschungen*.

1910
Second International Psychoanalytic Congress, Nuremberg.

1910-14
First president of the International Psychoanalytic Association.

1911
Third International Psychoanalytic Congress, Weimar.

1912
Another visit to USA for series of lectures at Fordham University, New York, on "The Theory of Psychoanalysis" (CW 4).
"Neue Bahnen der Psychologie" ("New Paths in Psychology," later revised and expanded as "On the Psychology of the Unconscious"; both CW 7).
Wandlungen und Symbole der Libido (*Psychology of the Unconscious*, 1916; for revision, see 1952) leading to

1913
break with Freud.
Fourth International Psychoanalytic Congress, Munich.
Jung designates his psychology as "Analytical Psychology" (later also "Complex Psychology").
Resigns lectureship at Zurich University.

1914
Resigns as president of the International Psychoanalytic Association.

1913–19
Period of intense introversion: confrontation with the unconscious.

1916
"Septem Sermones ad Mortuos"; first mandala painting.
Collected Papers on Analytical Psychology.
First description of process of "active imagination" in "Die transzendente Funktion" (not pub. until 1957; in CW 8).
First use of terms "personal unconscious," "collective unconscious", "individuation," "animus/anima," "persona" in "La Structure de l'inconscient" (CW 7, App.).
Beginning of study of Gnostic writings.

1918
"Über das Unbewusste" ("The Role of the Unconscious," CW 10).

1918–19
Commandant of camp for interned British soldiers at Château d'Oex (Canton Vaud).
First use of term "archetype" in "Instinct and the Unconscious" (CW 8).

1920
Journey to Algeria and Tunisia.

1921
Psychologische Typen; first use of term "self" (*Psychological Types*, 1923; CW 6).

1922
Purchase of property in village of Bollingen.

1923
First Tower built in Bollingen.
Death of mother.
Richard Wilhelm's lecture on the *I Ching* at the Psychological Club, Zurich.

1924–5
December: trip to the USA.
January: visits the Pueblo Indians in New Mexico; also New Orleans and New York.

1925

First English seminar at the Psychological Club, Zurich. Visits the Wembley Exhibition, London.

1925–6

Expedition to Kenya, Uganda, and the Nile; visit with the Elgonyi on Mount Elgon.

1928

Beginning of encounter with alchemy.

Two Essays on Analytical Psychology (CW 7).

Über die Energetik der Seele (various essays, now in CW 8).

1928–30

English seminars on "Dream Analysis" at the Psychological Club, Zurich.

1929

Publication, with Richard Wilhelm, of *Das Geheimnis der goldenen Blüte* (*The Secret of the Golden Flower*; Jung's contribution in CW 13).

Contributions to Analytical Psychology.

1930

Vice-president of General Medical Society for Psychotherapy, under Ernst Kretschmer as president.

1930–4

English seminars on "Interpretation of Visions" at the Psychological Club, Zurich.

1931

Seelenprobleme der Gegenwart (essays in CW 4, 6, 8, 10, 15, 16, 17).

1932

Awarded Literature Prize of the City of Zurich.

1933

First lectures at the Eidgenössische Technische Hochschule (ETH), Zurich (Swiss Federal Polytechnic), on "Modern Psychology."

Modern Man in Search of a Soul.

First Eranos lecture, on "A Study in the Process of Individuation" (CW 9 i).

Cruise to Egypt and Palestine.

1934

Founds International General Medical Society for Psychotherapy and becomes its first president.

Eranos lecture on "Archetypes of the Collective Unconscious" (CW 9 i).

Wirklichkeit der Seele (essays in CW 8, 10, 15, 16, 17).

1934–9
English seminars on "Psychological Aspects of Nietzsche's *Zarathustra*" at the Psychological Club, Zurich.

1934–9
Editor of *Zentralblatt für Psychotherapie und ihre Grenzgebiete* (Leipzig).

1935
Appointed titular professor at the ETH, Zurich.
Founds Schweizerische Gesellschaft für Praktische Psychologie.
Eranos lecture on "Dream Symbols of the Individuation Process" (expanded to Part II of *Psychology and Alchemy*, CW 12). Tavistock Lectures at the Institute of Medical Psychology, London (not published until 1968: *Analytical Psychology; Its Theory and Practice*; CW 18).

1936
Receives honorary doctoral degree from Harvard University.
Eranos lecture on "Ideas of Redemption in Alchemy" (expanded as Part III of *Psychology and Alchemy*); "Wotan" (CW 10).

1937
Terry Lectures on "Psychology and Religion" (CW 11) at Yale University, New Haven, Conn.
Eranos lecture on "The Visions of Zosimos" (CW 13).

1938
Invitation to India on the twenty-fifth anniversary of the Indian Science Congress, Calcutta; honorary doctorates from the universities of Calcutta, Benares and Allahabad.
International Congress for Psychotherapy at Oxford with Jung as President; he receives honorary doctorate of Oxford University.
Appointed Honorary Fellow of the Royal Society of Medicine, London.
Eranos lecture on "Psychological Aspects of the Mother Archetype" (CW 9 i).

1939
Eranos lecture on "Concerning Rebirth" (CW 9 i).

1940
Eranos lecture on "A Psychological Approach to the Dogma of the Trinity" (CW 11).

1941
Publication, together with Karl Kerényi, of *Einführung in das Wesen der Mythologie* (*Essays on a Science of Mythology*; Jung's contribution in CW 9 i).

Eranos lecture on "Transformation Symbolism in the Mass" (CW 11).

1942

Resigns appointment as professor at ETH.
Paracelsica (essays in CW 13, 15).
Eranos lecture on "The Spirit Mercurius" (CW 13).

1943

Honorary member of the Swiss Academy of Sciences.
Appointed to the chair of Medical Psychology at Basel University.

1944

Resigns Basel chair on account of critical illness.
Psychologie und Alchemie (CW 12).

1945

Honorary doctorate of Geneva University on the occasion of his seventieth birthday.
Eranos lecture on "The Psychology of the Spirit," expanded as "The Phenomenology of the Spirit in Fairytales" (CW 9 i).

1946

Eranos lecture on "The Spirit of Psychology" (expanded as "On the Nature of the Psyche," CW 8).
Die Psychologie der Übertragung ("The Psychology of the Transference," CW 16); *Aufsätze zur Zeitgeschichte* (*Essays on Contemporary Events*; in CW 10); *Psychologie und Erziehung* (CW 17).

1948

Symbolik des Geistes (essays in CW 9 i, 11, 13).
Eranos lecture "On the Self" (expanded to ch. IV of *Aion*, CW 9 ii).
Inauguration of the C. G. Jung Institute, Zurich.

1950

Gestaltungen des Unbewussten (essays in CW 9 i and 15).

1951

Aion (CW 9 ii).
Eranos lecture "On Synchronicity" (CW 8, App.).

1952

Publication, with W. Pauli, of *Naturerklärung und Psyche* (*The Interpretation of Nature and Psyche*; Jung's contribution "Synchronicity: an Acausal Connecting Principle," CW 8).
Symbole der Wandlung (*Symbols of Transformation*, CW 5: 4th, greatly revised edition of *Psychology of the Unconscious*).

Antwort auf Hiob ("Answer to Job," CW 11).
Another serious illness.

1953
Publication of the first volume of the American/British edition of the *Collected Works* (tr. by R. F. C. Hull): *Psychology and Alchemy* (CW 12).

1954
Von den Wurzeln des Bewusstseins (essays in CW 8, 9 i, 11, 13).

1955
Honorary doctorate of the ETH, Zurich, on the occasion of his eightieth birthday.
Death of his wife (27 November).

1955–6
Mysterium Coniunctionis (CW 14); the final work on the psychological significance of alchemy.

1957
Gegenwart und Zukunft ("The Undiscovered Self [Present and Future]," CW 10).
Starts work on *Memories, Dreams, Reflections* with the collaboration of Aniela Jaffé (pub. 1962).
BBC television interview with John Freeman.

1958
Ein moderner Mythus ("Flying Saucers: a Modern Myth," CW 10).
Publication of initial volume in Swiss edition of *Gesammelte Werke: Praxis der Psychotherapie* (Bd. 16).

1960
Honorary Citizen of Küsnacht on the occasion of his eighty-fifth birthday.

1961
Finishes his last work ten days before his death: "Approaching the Unconscious," in *Man and His Symbols* (1964).
Dies after short illness on 6 June in his house at Küsnacht.

Glossary

From MDR and *C. G. Jung: Word and Image*.

Alchemy. The older form of chemistry, which combined experimental chemistry in the modern sense with general, symbolic, intuitive, quasi-religious speculations about nature and man. Onto the unknown *materia* were projected many symbols which we now recognize as contents of the unconscious. The alchemist sought the "secret of God" in the unknown substance and thereby embarked on procedures and paths of exploration which resemble those of the modern-day psychology of the unconscious. This science, too, finds itself confronted with an unknown objective phenomenon – the unconscious.

The philosophical alchemy of the Middle Ages must be viewed in historical terms as a compensatory movement issuing from the unconscious in response to Christianity, for the subject of alchemical meditations and techniques – the realm of nature and *materia* – had been denied a place and any adequate evaluation within Christianity; it was seen rather as that which was to be overcome. Thus alchemy consists of dim, primitive mirrorings of Christian imagery and ideas, as Jung was able to show in *Psychology and Alchemy* (CW 12), using the analogy between the central concept of alchemy, the *lapis* or philosophers' stone, and Christ. The language of the alchemist employs symbolic images and paradoxes. Both correspond to the elusive nature of life and the unconscious psyche. Thus, for instance, it is stated that the stone is no stone (i.e., it is a spiritual or religious concept as well), or that the alchemical Mercurius, a spirit hidden in matter, is evasive, fugitive like the deer, for he is not to be grasped. "He has a thousand names," none of which expresses his entire being, just as no definition can capture entirely the nature of a psychic concept.

Amplification. Elaboration and clarification of a dream-image by means of *directed* association (*q.v.*) and of parallels from the humane science (symbology, mythology, mysticism, folklore, history of religion, ethnology, etc.).

Anima and Animus. Personification of the feminine nature of a man's unconscious and masculine nature of a woman's. This psychological bisexuality is a reflection of the biological fact that it is the larger number of male (or female) genes which is the decisive factor in the determination of sex. The smaller number of contrasexual genes seems to produce a corresponding contrasexual character, which usually remains unconscious. Anima and animus manifest themselves most typically in personified form as figures in dreams and fantasies ("dream-girl," "dream-lover"), or in the irrationalities of a man's *feeling* and a woman's *thinking*. As regulators of behaviour they are two of the most influential archetypes (*q.v.*).

C. G. Jung: "Every man carries with him the eternal image of woman, not the image of this or that particular woman, but a definitive feminine image. This image is fundamentally unconscious, an hereditary factor of primordial origin engraved in the living organic system of the man, an imprint or 'archetype' (*q.v.*) of all the ancestral experiences of the female, a deposit, as it were, of all the impressions ever made by woman . . . Since this image is unconscious, it is always unconsciously projected upon the person of the beloved, and is one of the chief reasons for passionate attraction or aversion." (CW 17, par. 338.)

"In its primary 'unconscious' form the animus is a compound of spontaneous, unpremeditated opinions which exercise a powerful influence on the woman's emotional life, while the anima is similarly compounded of feelings which thereafter influence or distort the man's understanding ('she has turned his head'). Consequently the animus likes to project itself upon 'intellectuals' and all kinds of 'heroes,' including tenors, artists, sporting celebrities etc. The anima has a predilection for everything that is unconscious, dark, equivocal, and purposeless in woman, and also for her vanity, frigidity, helplessness, and so forth . . ." (CW 16, par. 521.)

"No man can converse with an animus for five minutes without becoming the victim of his own anima. Anyone who still had enough sense of humour to listen objectively to the ensuing dialogue would be staggered by the vast number of commonplaces, misapplied truisms, clichés from newspapers and novels, shop-soiled platitudes of every description interspersed with vulgar abuse and brain-splitting lack of logic. It is a dialogue which, irrespective of its participants, is repeated millions and millions of times in all languages of the world and always remains essentially the same." (CW 9 ii, par. 29.)

"The natural function of the animus (as well as of the anima) is to remain in (their) place between individual consciousness and the collective unconscious (*q.v.*); exactly as the persona (*q.v.*) as a sort of stratum between the ego consciousness and the objects of the external world. The animus and the anima should function as a bridge, or a door, leading to the images of the collective unconscious, as the persona should be a sort of bridge into the world." (Unpublished seminar notes. *"Visions"* I.)

Archetype. C. G. Jung: "The concept of the archetype . . . is derived from the repeated observation that, for instance, the myths and fairy tales of world literature contain definite motifs which crop up everywhere. We meet these same motifs in the fantasies, dreams, deliria, and delusions of individuals living to-day. These typical images and associations are what I call archetypal ideas. The more vivid they are, the more they will be coloured by particularly strong feeling-tones (*q.v.*). . . . They impress, influence, and fascinate us. They have their origin in the archetype, which in itself is an irrepresentable, unconscious, pre-existent form that seems to be part of the inherited structure of the psyche and can therefore manifest itself spontaneously anywhere, at any time. Because of its instinctual nature, the archetype underlies the feeling-toned complexes (*q.v.*) and shares their autonomy." (CW 10, par. 847.)

"Again and again I encounter the mistaken notion that an archetype is determined in regard to its content, in other words, that it is a kind of unconscious idea (if such an expression be admissible). It is necessary to point out once more that archetypes are not determined as regards their content, but only as regards their form and then only to a very limited degree. A primordial image (*q.v.*) is determined as to its content only when it has become conscious and is therefore filled out with the material of conscious experience. Its form, however ... might perhaps be compared to the axial system of a crystal, which, as it were, performs the crystalline structure in the mother liquid, although it has no material existence of its own. This first appears according to the specific way in which the ions and molecules aggregate. The archetype in itself is empty and purely formal, nothing but a *facultas praeformandi*, a possibility of representation which is given *a priori*. The representations themselves are not inherited, only the forms, and in that respect they correspond in every way to the instincts, which are also determined in form only. The existence of the instincts can no more be proved than the existence of the archetypes, so long as they do not manifest themselves concretely." (CW 9 i, pars. 155ff.)

"It seems to me probable that the real nature of the archetype as such is not capable of being made conscious, that it is transcendent, on which account I call it psychoid" (*q.v.*). (CW 8, par. 417.)

Association. The linking of ideas, perceptions, etc. according to similarity, coexistence, opposition, and causal dependence. *Free association* in Freudian dream interpretation: spontaneous ideas occurring to the dreamer, which need not necessarily refer to the dream situation. *Directed or controlled association* in Jungian dream interpretation: spontaneous ideas which proceed from a given dream situation and constantly relate to it.

Association test. Methods for discovering complexes (*q.v.*) by measuring the reaction time and interpreting the answers to given stimulus words.

Complex-indicators: prolonged reaction time, faults, or the idiosyncratic quality of the answers when the stimulus words touch on complexes which the subject wishes to hide or is not conscious of.

Complex. C. G. Jung: "Complexes are psychic fragments which have split off owing to traumatic (*q.v.*) influences or certain incompatible tendencies. As the association experiments prove, complexes interfere with the intentions of the will and disturb the conscious performance: they produce disturbances of memory and blockages in the flow of association (*q.v.*); they appear and disappear according to their own laws; they can temporarily obsess consciousness, or influence speech and action in an unconscious way. In a word, complexes behave like independent beings, a fact especially evident in abnormal states of mind. In the voices heard by the insane they even take on a personal ego-character like that of the spirits who manifest themselves through automatic writing and similar techniques." (CW 8, par. 253.)

Consciousness. C. G. Jung: "When one reflects upon what consciousness really is, one is profoundly impressed by the extreme wonder of the fact that an event which takes place outside in the cosmos simultaneously produces an internal image, that it takes place, so to speak, inside as well, which is to say: becomes conscious." (*Basel Seminar*, privately printed, 1934, p. 1.)

"For indeed our consciousness does not create itself – it wells up from unknown depths. In childhood it awakens gradually, and all through life it wakes each morning out of the depths of sleep from an unconscious condition. It is like a child that is born daily out of the primordial womb of the unconscious." (CW 11, par. 935.)

Dream. C. G. Jung: "The dream is a little hidden door in the innermost and most secret recesses of the psyche, opening into that cosmic night which was psyche long before there was any ego consciousness, and which will remain psyche no matter how far our ego consciousness may extend . . . All consciousness separates; but in dreams we put on the likeness of that more universal, truer, more eternal man dwelling in the darkness of primordial night. There he is still the whole, and the whole is in him, indistinguishable from nature and bare of all egohood. Out of these all-uniting depths arises the dream, be it never so infantile, never so grotesque, never so immoral." (CW 10, par. 304.)

Extraversion. Attitude-type characterized by concentration of interest on the external object. See *Introversion*.

God-image. A term derived from the Church Fathers, according to whom the *imago Dei* is imprinted on the human soul. When such an image is spontaneously produced in dreams, fantasies, visions, etc. it is, from the psychological point of view, a symbol of the self (*q.v.*), of psychic wholeness.

C. G. Jung: "It is only through the psyche that we can establish that God acts upon us, but we are unable to distinguish whether God and the unconscious are two different entities. Both are border-line concepts for transcendental contents. But empirically it can be established, with a sufficient degree of probability, that there is in the unconscious an archetype of wholeness which manifests itself spontaneously in dreams, etc., and a tendency, independent of the conscious will, to relate other archetypes to this centre. Consequently, it does not seem improbable that the archetype produces a symbolism which has always characterized and expressed the Deity . . . The God-image does not coincide with the unconscious as such, but with a special content of it, namely the archetype of the self. It is this archetype from which we can no longer distinguish the God-image empirically." (CW 11, par. 757.)

"One can, then, explain the God-image . . . as a reflection of the self, or, conversely, explain the self as an *imago Dei* in man." (par. 282.)

Hierosgamos. Sacred or spiritual marriage, union of archetypal figures in the rebirth mysteries of antiquity and also in alchemy. Typical examples are the representation of Christ and the Church as bridegroom and bride (*sponsus et sponsa*) and the alchemical conjunction of sun and moon.

Individuation. C. G. Jung: "I use the term 'individuation' to denote the process by which a person becomes a psychological 'individual,' that is, a separate, indivisible unity or 'whole.'" (CW 9 i, par. 490.)

"Individuation means becoming a single, homogeneous being, and, in so far as 'in-dividuality' embraces our innermost, last, and incomparable uniqueness, it also implies becoming one's own self. We could therefore translate individuation as 'coming to selfhood' or 'self-realization.'" (CW 7, par. 266.)

"But again and again I note that the individuation process is confused with the coming of the ego into consciousness and that the ego is in consequence identified with the self, which naturally produces a hopeless conceptual muddle. Individuation is then nothing but ego-centredness and autoeroticism. But the self comprises infinitely more than a mere ego... It is as much one's self, and all other selves, as the ego. Individuation does not shut one out from the world, but gathers the world to one's self." (CW 8, par. 432.)

Inflation. Expansion of the personality beyond its proper limits by identification with the persona (*q.v.*) or with an archetype (*q.v.*), or in pathological cases with a historical or religious figure. It produces an exaggerated sense of one's self-importance and is usually compensated by feelings of inferiority.

Introversion. Attitude-type characterized by orientation in life through subjective psychic contents. See *Extraversion.*

Mana. Melanesian word for extraordinarily effective power emanating from a human being, object, action or event, or from supernatural beings and spirits. Also health, prestige, power to work magic and to heal. A primitive concept of psychic energy.

Mandala (Sanskrit). Magic circle. In Jung, symbol of the centre goal, or of the self (*q.v.*) as psychic totality; self-representation of a psychic process of centring; production of a new centre of personality. This is symbolically represented by the circle, the square, or the quaternity (*q.v.*), by symmetrical arrangements of the number four and its multiples. In Lamism and Tantric Yoga the mandala is an instrument of contemplation (*yantra*), seat and birthplace of the gods. *Disturbed mandala*: Any form that deviates from the circle, square, or equal-armed cross, or whose basic number is not four or its multiples.

C. G. Jung: "Mandala means 'circle,' more especially a magic circle, and this form of symbol is not only to be found all through the East, but also among us; mandalas are amply represented in the Middle Ages. The specifically Christian ones come from the earlier Middle Ages. Most of them show Christ in the centre, with the four evangelists, or their symbols, at the cardinal points. This conception must be a very ancient one because Horus was represented with his four sons in the same way by the Egyptians . . . For the most part, the mandala form is that of a flower, cross, or wheel, with a distinct tendency towards four as the basis of the structure." (CW 13, par. 31.)

"Mandalas . . . usually appear in situations of psychic confusion and disorientation. The archetype thereby constellated represents a pattern of order which, like a psychological 'view-finder' marked with a cross or circle divided into four, is superimposed on the psychic chaos so that each content falls into place and the weltering confusion is held together by the protective circle . . . At the same time they are *yantras*, instruments with whose help the order is brought into being." (CW 10, par. 803.)

Neurosis. State of being at odds with oneself, caused by the conflict between instinctive drives and the demands of one's society, between infantile obstinacy and the desire to conform, between collective and individual obligations. Neurosis is a stop sign marking a wrong turning, a summons to be cured.

C. G. Jung: "The psychological trouble in neurosis, and the neurosis itself, can be formulated as *an act of adaptation that has failed*. This formulation might reconcile certain views of Janet's with Freud's view that a neurosis is, in a sense, an attempt at self-cure . . ." (CW 4, par. 574.)

"Neurosis is always a substitute for legitimate suffering." (CW 11, par. 129.)

Numinosum. Rudolf Otto's term (in his *Idea of the Holy*) for the inexpressible, mysterious, terrifying, directly experienced and pertaining only to the divinity.

Persona. Originally, the mask worn by an actor. C. G. Jung: "The persona . . . is the individual's system of adaptation to, or the manner he assumed in dealing with, the world. Every calling or profession, for example, has its own characteristic persona . . . Only, the danger is that (people) become identical with their personas – the professor with his textbook, the tenor with his voice . . . One could say, with a little exaggeration, that the persona is that which in reality one is not, but which oneself as well as others think one is." (CW 9 i, par. 221.)

Primordial image (Jakob Burckhardt). Term originally used by Jung for *archetype* (*q.v.*).

Psychoid. "Soul-like" or "quasi-psychic." C. G. Jung: "The collective unconscious represents a psyche that ... cannot be directly perceived or 'represented,' in contrast to the perceptible psychic phenomena, and on account of its 'irrepresentable' nature I have called it psychoid.'" (CW 8, par. 840.)

Quaternity. C. G. Jung: "The quaternity is an archetype of almost universal occurrence. It forms the logical basis for any whole judgment. If one wishes to pass such a judgment, it must have this fourfold aspect. For instance, if you want to describe the horizon as a whole, you name the four quarters of heaven... There are always four elements, four prime qualities, four colours, four castes, four ways of spiritual development etc. So, too, there are four aspects of psychological orientation... In order to orient ourselves, we must have a function which ascertains that something is there (sensation); a second function which establishes *what* it is (thinking); a third function which states whether it suits us or not, whether we wish to accept it or no (feeling), and a fourth function which indicates where it came from and where it is going (intuition). When this has been done, there is nothing more to say... The ideal completeness is the circle or sphere, but its natural minimal division is a quaternity." (CW 11, par. 246.)

A quaternity or quaternion often has a 3 + 1 structure, in that one of the terms composing it occupies an exceptional position or has a nature unlike that of the others. (For instance three of the symbols of the Evangelists are animals and that of the fourth, or St. Luke, is an Angel.) This is the "Fourth," which, added to the other three, makes them "One," symbolizing totality. In analytical psychology often the "inferior" function (i.e., that function which is not at the conscious disposal of the subject) represents the "Fourth" and its integration into consciousness is one of the major tasks of the process of individuation (*q.v.*).

Self. The central archetype (*q.v.*); the archetype of order; the totality of the personality. Symbolized by circle, square, quaternity (*q.v.*), child, mandala (*q.v.*) etc.

C. G. Jung: "The self is a quantity that is superordinate to the conscious ego. It embraces not only the conscious but also the unconscious psyche, and is therefore, so to speak, a personality which we *also* are . . . There is little hope of our ever being able to reach even approximate consciousness of the self, since however much we may make conscious there will always exist an indeterminate and indeterminable amount of unconscious material which belongs to the totality of the self." (CW 7, par. 274.)

"The self is not only the centre but also the whole circumference which embraces both consciousness and unconscious; it is the centre of this totality, just as the ego is the centre of the conscious mind." (CW 12, par. 44.)

"The self is our life's goal, for it is the completest expression of that fateful combination we call individuality." (CW 7, par. 404.)

Shadow. The inferior part of the personality; sum of all personal and collective psychic elements which, because of their incompatibility with the chosen conscious attitude, are denied expression in life and therefore coalesce into a relatively autonomous "splinter personality" with contrary tendencies in the unconscious. The shadow behaves compensatorily to consciousness; hence its effects can be positive as well as negative.

C. G. Jung: "The shadow personifies everything that the subject refuses to acknowledge about himself and yet is always thrusting itself upon him directly or indirectly – for instance, inferior traits of character and other incompatible tendencies." (CW 9 i, par. 513.)

"The shadow is that hidden, repressed, for the most part inferior and guilt-laden personality whose ultimate ramifications reach back into the realm of our animal ancestors and so comprise the whole historical aspect of the unconscious . . . If it has been believed hitherto that the human shadow was the source of all evil, it can now be ascertained on closer investigation that the unconscious man, that is, his shadow, does not consist only of morally reprehensible tendencies, but also displays a number of good qualities, such as normal instincts, appropriate reaction, realistic insights, creative impulses, etc." (CW 9 ii, pars. 422–3.)

Soul. C. G. Jung: "If the human soul is anything, it must be of unimaginable complexity and diversity, so that it cannot possibly be approached through a mere psychology of instinct. I can only gaze with wonder and awe at the depths and heights of our psychic nature. Its non-spatial universe conceals an untold abundance of images which have accumulated over millions of years of living development and become fixed in the organism. My consciousness is like an eye that penetrates to the most distant spaces, yet it is the psychic non-ego that fills them with non-spatial images. And these images are not pale shadows, but tremendously powerful psychic factors... Besides this picture I would like to place the spectacle of the starry heavens at night, for the only equivalent of the universe within is the universe without; and just as I reach this world through the medium of the body, so I reach that world through the medium of the psyche." (CW 4, par. 764.)

"It would be blasphemy to assert that God can manifest Himself everywhere save only in the human soul. Indeed the very intimacy of the relationship between God and the soul automatically precludes any devaluation of the latter. It would be going perhaps too far to speak of an affinity; but at all events the soul must contain in itself the faculty of relation to God, i.e. a correspondence, otherwise a connection could never come about. This correspondence is, in psychological terms, the archetype of the God-image (*q.v.*)." (CW 12, par. 11.)

Synchronicity. A term coined by Jung to designate the meaningful coincidence or equivalence: (*a*) of a psychic and a physical state or event which have no causal relationship to one another. Such synchronistic phenomena occur, for instance, when an inwardly perceived event (dream, vision, premonition, etc.) is seen to have a correspondence in external reality: the inner image of premonition has "come true." (*b*) of similar or identical thoughts, dreams etc. occurring at the same time at different places. Neither the one nor the other coincidence can be explained by causality, but seem to be connected primarily with activated archetypal processes in the unconscious.

C. G. Jung: "My preoccupation with the psychology of unconscious processes long ago compelled me to look about for another principle of explanation, because the causality principle seemed to me inadequate to explain certain remarkable phenomena of the psychology of the unconscious. Thus I found that there are psychic parallelisms which cannot be related to each other causally, but which must be connected through another principle, namely the contingency of events. This connection of events seemed to me essentially given by the fact of their relative simultaneity, hence the term 'synchronistic.' It seems, indeed, as though time, far from being an abstraction, is a concrete continuum which contains qualities or basic conditions that manifest themselves simultaneously in different places through parallelisms that cannot be explained causally, as, for example, in cases of the simultaneous occurrence of identical thoughts, symbols, or psychic states." (CW 15, par. 81.)

"I chose this term because the simultaneous occurrence of two meaningful but not causally connected events seemed to me an essential criterion. I am therefore using the general concept of synchronicity in the special sense of a coincidence in time of two or more causally unrelated events which have the same or a similar meaning, in contrast to 'synchronism,' which simply means the simultaneous occurrence of two events." (CW 8, par. 849.)

"Synchronicity is no more baffling or mysterious than the discontinuities of physics. It is only the ingrained belief in the sovereign power of causality that creates intellectual difficulties and makes it appear unthinkable that causeless events exist or could ever occur ... Meaningful coincidences are thinkable as pure chance. But the more they multiply and the greater and more exact the correspondence is, the more their probability sinks and their unthinkability increases, until they can no longer be regarded as pure chance, but, for lack of a causal explanation, have to be thought of as meaningful arrangements ... Their 'inexplicability' is not due to the fact that the cause is unknown, but to the fact that a cause is not even thinkable in intellectual terms." (CW 8, par. 967.)

Unconscious, the. C. G. Jung: "Theoretically, no limits can be set to the field of consciousness, since it is capable of indefinite extension. Empirically, however, it always finds its limit when it comes up against the *unknown*. This consists of everything we do not know, which, therefore, is not related to the ego as the centre of the field of consciousness. The unknown falls into two groups of objects: those which are outside and can be experienced by the senses, and those which are inside and are experienced immediately. The first group comprises the unknown in the outer world; the second the unknown in the inner world. We call this latter territory the *unconscious*." (CW 9 ii, par. 2.)

... Everything of which I know, but of which I am not at the moment thinking; everything of which I was once conscious but have now forgotten; everything perceived by my senses, but not noted by my conscious mind; everything which, involuntarily and without paying attention to it, I feel, think, remember, want, and do; all the future things that are taking shape in me and will sometime come to consciousness: all this is the content of the unconscious." (CW 8, par. 382.)

"Besides these we must include all more or less intentional repressions of painful thoughts and feelings. I call the sum of all these contents the *personal unconscious*. But, over and above that, we also find in the unconscious qualities that are not individually acquired but are inherited, e.g. instincts as impulses to carry out actions from necessity, without conscious motivation. In this 'deeper' stratum we also find the ... archetypes ... The instincts and archetypes together form the *collective unconscious*. I call it 'collective' because, unlike the personal unconscious, it is not made up of individual and more or less unique contents but of those which are universal and of regular occurrence." (CW 8, par. 270.)

"The first group comprises contents which are integral components of the individual personality and therefore could just as well be conscious; the second group forms, as it were, an omnipresent, unchanging, and everywhere identical *quality or substrata of the psyche per se*." (CW 9 ii, par. 12.)

"The deeper 'layers' of the psyche lose their individual uniqueness as they retreat farther and farther into darkness. 'Lower down,' that is to say as they approach the autonomous functional systems, they become increasingly collective until they are universalized and extinguished in the body's materiality, i.e., in chemical substances. The body's carbon is simply carbon. Hence 'at bottom' the psyche is simply 'world.'" (CW 9 i, par. 291.)

Bibliography

1. Works by C. G. Jung

THE COLLECTED WORKS OF C.G. JUNG

The publication of the first complete edition, in English, of the works of C. G. Jung was undertaken by Routledge and Kegan Paul, Ltd, in England and by Bollingen Foundation in the United States. The American edition is number XX in Bollingen Series, which since 1967 has been published by Princeton University Press. The edition contains revised versions of works previously published, such as *Psychology of the Unconscious*, which is now entitled *Symbols of Transformation*; works originally written in English, such as *Psychology and Religion*; works not previously translated, such as *Aion*; and, in general, new translations of virtually all of Professor Jung's writings. Prior to his death, in 1961, the author supervised the textual revision, which in some cases is extensive. Sir Herbert Read, Dr Michael Fordham and Dr Gerhard Adler composed the Editorial Committee; the translator was R. F. C. Hull (except for Volume 2) and William McGuire was executive editor.

In the following list, dates of original publication are given in parentheses (of original composition, in brackets). Multiple dates indicate revisions.

1. PSYCHIATRIC STUDIES
    On the Psychology and Pathology of So-called Occult Phenomena (1902)
    On Hysterical Misreading (1904)
    Cryptomnesia (1905)
    On Manic Mood Disorder (1903)
    A Case of Hysterical Stupor in a Prisoner in Detention (1902)
    On Simulated Insanity (1903)
    A Medical Opinion on a Case of Simulated Insanity (1904)
    A Third and Final Opinion on Two Contradictory Psychiatric Diagnoses (1906)
    On the Psychological Diagnosis of Facts (1905)

428   BIBLIOGRAPHY

2.   EXPERIMENTAL RESEARCHES
     Translated by Leopold Stein in collaboration with Diana Riviere

     STUDIES IN WORD ASSOCIATION (1904–7)
     The Associations of Normal Subjects (by Jung and F. Riklin)
     Experimental Observations on Memory
     The Psychological Diagnosis of the Criminal Case
     An Analysis of the Associations of an Epileptic
     The Association Method (1910)
     The Reaction-Time Ratio in the Association Experiment
     On Disturbances in Reproduction in Association Experiment
     The Psychopathological Significance of the Association Experiment
     Psychoanalysis and Association Experiments
     Association, Dream, and Hysterical Symptom
     PSYCHOPHYSICAL RESEARCHES (1907–8)
     On Psychophysical Relations of the Association Experiment
     Psychophysical Investigations with the Galvanometer and Pneumo-
       graph in Normal and Insane Individuals (by F. Petersen and
       Jung)
     Further Investigations on the Galvanic Phenomenon and Respiration
       in Normal and Insane Individuals (by C. Ricksher and Jung)

3.   THE PSYCHOGENESIS OF MENTAL DISEASE
     The Psychology of Dementia Praecox (1907)
     The Content of the Psychoses (1908/1914)
     On Psychological Understanding (1914)
     A Criticism of Bleuler's Theory of Schizophrenic Negativism (1911)
     On the Importance of the Unconscious in Psychopathology (1914)
     On the Problem of Psychogenesis in Mental Disease (1919)
     Mental Disease and the Psyche (1928)
     On the Psychogenesis of Schizophrenia (1939)
     Recent Thoughts on Schizophrenia (1957)
     Schizophrenia (1958)

4.   FREUD AND PSYCHOANALYSIS
     Freud's Theory of Hysteria: a Reply to Aschaffenburg (1906)
     The Freudian Theory of Hysteria (1908)
     The Analysis of Dreams (1909)
     A Contribution to the Psychology of Rumour (1910–11)
     On the Significance of Number Dreams (1910–11)
     Morton Prince, "Mechanism and Interpretation of Dreams": a
       Critical Review (1911)

On the Criticism of Psychoanalysis (1910)

Concerning Psychoanalysis (1912)

The Theory of Psychoanalysis (1913)

General Aspects of Psychoanalysis (1913)

Psychoanalysis and Neurosis (1916)

Some Crucial Points in Psychoanalysis: The Jung-Loy Correspondence (1914)

Prefaces to "Collected Papers on Analytical Psychology" (1916, 1917)

The Significance of the Father in the Destiny of the Individual (1909/1949)

Introduction to Kranefeldt's "Secret Ways of the Mind" (1930)

Freud and Jung: Contrasts (1929)

5. SYMBOLS OF TRANSFORMATION (1911–12/1952)
    PART I
    Introduction
    Two Kinds of Thinking
    The Miller Fantasies: Anamnesis
    The Hymn of Creation
    The Song of the Moth
    PART II
    Introduction
    The Concept of Libido
    The Transformation of Libido
    The Origin of the Hero
    Symbols of the Mother and of Rebirth
    The Battle for Deliverance from the Mother
    The Dual Mother
    The Sacrifice
    Epilogue
    Appendix: The Miller Fantasies

6. PSYCHOLOGICAL TYPES (1921)
    Introduction
    The Problem of Types in the History of Classical and Medieval Thought
    Schiller's Ideas on the Type Problem
    The Apollonian and the Dionysian
    The Type Problem in the Discernment of Human Character
    The Type Problem in Poetry
    The Type Problem in Psychopathology

430   BIBLIOGRAPHY

The Problem of Typical Attitudes in Aesthetics
The Type Problem in Modern Philosophy
The Type Problem in Biography
General Description of the Types
Definitions
Conclusion
Four Papers on Psychological Typology (1913, 1925, 1931, 1936)

7. TWO ESSAYS ON ANALYTICAL PSYCHOLOGY
On the Psychology of the Unconscious (1917/1926/1943)
The Relations between the Ego and the Unconscious (1928)
Appendices: New Paths in Psychology (1912); The Structure of the
    Unconscious (1916) (new versions, with variants, 1966)

8. THE STRUCTURE AND DYNAMICS OF THE PSYCHE
On Psychic Energy (1928)
The Transcendent Function ([1916]/1957)
A Review of the Complex Theory (1934)
The Significance of Constitution and Heredity in Psychology (1929)
Psychological Factors Determining Human Behaviour (1937)
Instinct and the Unconscious (1919)
The Structure of the Psyche (1927/1931)
On the Nature of the Psyche (1947/1954)
General Aspects of Dream Psychology (1916/1948)
On the Nature of Dreams (1945/1948)
The Psychological Foundations of Belief in Spirits (1920/1948)
Spirit and Life (1926)
Basic Postulates of Analytical Psychology (1931)
Analytical Psychology and *Weltanschauung* (1928/1931)
The Real and the Surreal (1933)
The Stages of Life (1930–1)
The Soul and Death (1934)
Synchronicity: an Acausal Connecting Principle (1952)
Appendix: On Synchronicity (1951)

9. PART I. THE ARCHETYPES AND THE COLLECTIVE
UNCONSCIOUS
Archetypes of the Collective Unconscious (1934/1954)
The Concept of the Collective Unconscious (1936)
Concerning the Archetypes, with Special Reference to the Anima
    Concept (1936/1954)
Psychological Aspects of the Mother Archetype (1938/1954)

Concerning Rebirth (1940/1950)
The Psychology of the Child Archetype (1940)
The Psychological Aspects of the Kore (1941)
The Phenomenology of the Spirit in Fairytales (1945/1948)
On the Psychology of the Trickster-Figure (1954)
Conscious, Unconscious, and Individuation (1939)
A Study in the Process of Individuation (1934/1950)
Concerning Mandala Symbolism (1950)
Appendix: Mandalas (1955)

9.   PART II. AION (1951)
     RESEARCHES INTO THE PHENOMENOLOGY OF THE SELF
     The Ego
     The Shadow
     The Syzygy: Anima and Animus
     The Self
     Christ, a Symbol of the Self
     The Sign of the Fishes
     The Prophecies of Nostradamus
     The Historical Significance of the Fish
     The Ambivalence of the Fish Symbol
     The Fish in Alchemy
     The Alchemical Interpretation of the Fish
     Background to the Psychology of Christian Alchemical Symbolism
     Gnostic Symbols of the Self
     The Structure and Dynamics of the Self
     Conclusion

10. CIVILIZATION IN TRANSITION
     The Role of the Unconscious (1918)
     Mind and Earth (1927/1931)
     Archaic Man (1931)
     The Spiritual Problem of Modern Man (1928/1931)
     The Love Problem of a Student (1928)
     Woman in Europe (1927)
     The Meaning of Psychology for Modern Man (1933/1934)
     The State of Psychotherapy Today (1934)
     Preface and Epilogue to "Essays on Contemporary Events" (1946)
     Wotan (1936)
     After the Catastrophe (1945)
     The Fight with the Shadow (1946)
     The Undiscovered Self (Present and Future) (1957)

Flying Saucers: a Modern Myth (1958)
A Psychological View of Conscience (1958)
Good and Evil in Analytical Psychology (1959)
Introduction to Wolff's "Studies in Jungian Psychology" (1959)
The Swiss Line in the European Spectrum (1928)
Reviews of Keyserling's "America Set Free" (1930) and "La Révolution Mondiale" (1934)
Complications of American Psychology (1930)
The Dreamlike World of India (1939)
What India Can Teach Us (1939)
Appendix: Documents (1933–8)

11. PSYCHOLOGY AND RELIGION: WEST AND EAST
    WESTERN RELIGION
    Psychology and Religion (The Terry Lectures) (1938/1940)
    A Psychological Approach to the Dogma of the Trinity (1942/1948)
    Transformation Symbolism in the Mass (1942/1954)
    Forewords to White's "God and the Unconscious" and Werblowsky's "Lucifer and Prometheus" (1952)
    Brother Klaus (1933)
    Psychotherapists or the Clergy (1932)
    Psychoanalysis and the Cure of Souls (1928)
    Answer to Job (1952)
    EASTERN RELIGION
    Psychological Commentaries on "The Tibetan Book of the Great Liberation" (1939/1954) and "The Tibetan Book of the Dead" (1935/1953)
    Yoga and the West (1936)
    Foreword to Suzuki's "Introduction to Zen Buddhism" (1939)
    The Psychology of Eastern Meditation (1943)
    The Holy Men of India: Introduction to Zimmer's "Der Weg zum Selbst" (1944)
    Foreword to the "I Ching" (1950)

12. PSYCHOLOGY AND ALCHEMY (1944)
    Prefatory Note to the English Edition ([1951?] added 1967)
    Introduction to the Religious and Psychological Problems of Alchemy
    Individual Dream Symbolism in Relation to Alchemy (1936)
    Religious Ideas in Alchemy (1937)
    Epilogue

13. ALCHEMICAL STUDIES
Commentary on "The Secret of the Golden Flower" (1929)
The Visions of Zosimos (1938/1954)
Paracelsus as a Spiritual Phenomenon (1942)
The Spirit Mercurius (1943/1948)
The Philosophical Tree (1945/1954)

14. MYSTERIUM CONIUNCTIONIS (1955–6)
AN INQUIRY INTO THE SEPARATION AND SYNTHESIS OF
PSYCHIC OPPOSITES IN ALCHEMY
The Components of the Coniunctio
The Paradoxa
The Personification of Opposites
Rex and Regina
Adam and Eve
The Conjunction

15. THE SPIRIT IN MAN, ART, AND LITERATURE
Paracelsus (1929)
Paracelsus the Physician (1941)
Sigmund Freud in His Historical Setting (1932)
In Memory of Sigmund Freud (1939)
Richard Wilhelm: In Memoriam (1930)
On the Relation of Analytical Psychology to Poetry (1922)
Psychology and Literature (1930/1950)
"Ulysses" (1932)
Picasso (1932)

16. THE PRACTICE OF PSYCHOTHERAPY
GENERAL PROBLEMS OF PSYCHOTHERAPY
Principles of Practical Psychotherapy (1935)
What Is Psychotherapy? (1935)
Some Aspects of Modern Psychotherapy (1930)
The Aims of Psychotherapy (1931)
Problems of Modern Psychotherapy (1929)
Psychotherapy and a Philosophy of Life (1943)
Medicine and Psychotherapy (1945)
Psychotherapy Today (1945)
Fundamental Questions of Psychotherapy (1951)
SPECIFIC PROBLEMS OF PSYCHOTHERAPY
The Therapeutic Value of Abreaction (1921/1928)
The Practical Use of Dream-analysis (1934)

The Psychology of the Transference (1946)
Appendix: The Realities of Practical Psychotherapy ([1937] added 1966)

17. THE DEVELOPMENT OF PERSONALITY
Psychic Conflicts in a Child (1910/1946)
Introduction to Wickes's "Analyse der Kinderseele" (1927/1931)
Child Development and Education (1928)
Analytical Psychology and Education: Three Lectures (1926/1946)
The Gifted Child (1943)
The Significance of the Unconscious in Individual Education (1928)
The Development of Personality (1934)
Marriage as a Psychological Relationship (1925)

18. THE SYMBOLIC LIFE
Miscellaneous Writings

19. COMPLETE BIBLIOGRAPHY OF C. G. JUNG'S WRITINGS
(1976; 2nd edn., 1992)

20. GENERAL INDEX TO THE COLLECTED WORKS (1979)

THE ZOFINGIA LECTURES (1983)
Supplementary Volume A to The Collected Works. Edited by William McGuire, translated by Jan van Heurck, introduction by Marie-Louise von Franz

PSYCHOLOGY OF THE UNCONSCIOUS ([1912] 1992)

A STUDY OF THE TRANSFORMATIONS AND SYMBOLISMS OF THE LIBIDO.
A CONTRIBUTION TO THE HISTORY OF THE EVOLUTION OF THOUGHT

Supplementary Volume B to the Collected Works. Translated by Beatrice M. Hinkle, introduction by William McGuire

Related publications:

THE BASIC WRITINGS OF C. G. JUNG
Selected and introduced by Violet S. de Laszlo

C. G. JUNG: LETTERS
Selected and edited by Gerhard Adler, in collaboration with Aniela Jaffé.
Translations from the German by R.F.C. Hull.
  VOL. 1: 1906–1950
  VOL. 2: 1951–1961

C. G. JUNG SPEAKING: Interviews and Encounters
Edited by William McGuire and R.F.C. Hull

C. G. JUNG: Word and Image
Edited by Aniela Jaffé

THE ESSENTIAL JUNG
Selected and introduced by Anthony Storr

THE GNOSTIC JUNG
Selected and introduced by Robert A. Segal

PSYCHE AND SYMBOL
Selected and introduced by Violet S. de Laszlo

Notes of C. G. Jung's Seminars:

DREAM ANALYSIS ([1928–30] 1984)
Edited by William McGuire

NIETZSCHE'S *ZARATHUSTRA* ([1934–39] 1988)
Edited by James L. Jarrett (2 vols.)

ANALYTICAL PSYCHOLOGY ([1925] 1989)
Edited by William McGuire

THE PSYCHOLOGY OF KUNDALINI YOGA ([1932] 1996)
Edited by Sonu Shamdasani

INTERPRETATION OF VISIONS ([1930–34] 1996)
Edited by Claire Douglas

2. Books about Jung and Analytical Psychology

Barnaby, Karin and d'Acierno, Pellegrino, editors, *C. G. Jung and the Humanities*. New Jersey: Princeton University Press, 1990.

Bennet, E. A., *What Jung Really Said*, introduced by Anthony Storr. New York: Schocken, 1983.

Bishop, Paul, *The Dionysian Self: Jung's Reception of Friedrich Nietzsche*. Berlin, Walter de Gruyter, 1995.

Brome, Vincent, *Jung: Man and Myth*. London: Macmillian, 1978.

Franz, Marie-Louise von, *Number and Time*. London: Rider, 1975.

Franz, Marie-Louise von, *C. G. Jung: His Myth in Our Time*. New York: G. P. Putnam's Sons for the C. G. Jung Foundation for Analytical Psychology, 1975.

Kerr, John, *A Most Dangerous Method*. London: Sinclair-Stevenson, 1994.

Moreno, Antonio, *Jung, Gods, and Modern Man*. London: Sheldon Press, 1974.

Papadopoulos, Renos K. and Saayman, Graham S., editors, *Jung in Modern Perspective*. London: Wildwood House, 1984.

Samuels, Andrew. *Jung and the Post-Jungians*. London: Routledge and Kegan Paul, 1985.

Serrano, Miguel, *C. C. Jung and Hermann Hesse: A Record of Two Friendships*. New York: Schocken, 1968.

Stevens, Anthony, *Jung*. Oxford University Press, Past Masters, 1994.

Stevens, Anthony, *On Jung*. London: Routledge, 1990.

Storr, Anthony, *Jung*. Fontana Press, Modern Masters, 1973.

Wehr, Gerhard, *Jung: A Biography*. Translated by David M. Weeks. London: Shambhala, 1987.

White, Victor, O. P., *God and the Unconscious*. London: Harvill, 1952.

Index

Abelard, Peter, 160
Abraham, K., 57
abreaction, 46
active imagination, 21, 116
adaptation, 49, 59, 60-4, 102, 163, 382
   failure of (as cause of neurosis), 53, 58
   to reality (in schizophrenia), 54-5
Adler, Alfred, 18, 50, 129, 146-9, 159, 165, 167, 387
Aesculapius, 200
affect(s), 46, 91, 95, 103-4, 215
alchemy, alchemists, 19, 122, 125, 222, 225, 250, 253-86, 328
America, 368
analysis, analyst, 255, 372, 374-5, 385
ancestor, ancestral, 105, 108
Andersen, Hans, 194
anima, 87, 91, 96, 100-19, 122-3, 221-4, 299
   compensatory relationship with persona, 93, 101
animus, 87, 91, 102, 105, 109-18, 122, 221-4, 299, 341
Antichrist, 300, 345
anticipation, -atory, 216-17, 402
antinomy(ies), 335
   of God, 312
   of language, 25, 335
aptitude – subjective, 107
Aquarius, 345-7
Aquinas, St Thomas, 120, 306-7

archaic, 102, 261, 382
archetype(s), 16, 25-7, 65-6, 70-1, 79, 84-5, 87-127, 186-8, 222, 236, 247-9, 252, 260, 263, 266, 277-8, 285-6, 291, 329, 337, 343, 346, 382
Aries, 346-7
Aristotle, 306
assimilation, 180-1, 184, 188-9
Assumption (of BVM) 27, 237, 295-7, 321-9
Atman, 238, 258, 264, 267, 332
Attis, 273
attitude(s) 18, 59, 62, 97-103, 124, 147-67, 210
Augustine, St, 301, 305-7, 386
auto-eroticism, 92, 255
automatisms, 30
autonomous/autonomy
   of the unconscious, 215, 244

Ba (soul), 341
Bardo, 343
Barlach, E., *Der tote Tag*, 125
Basel, 13
Basil the Great, 301-3
Basilides, Basilidian, 290, 293
Baubo, 109
Baynes, Cary F., 226n
Benoît, P., 107, 222-3
Bergson, Henri, 51
Binet, Alfred, 30, 30n
Bismarck, Otto E. L. von, 95
Bleuler, Eugen, 13, 43
Blumhardt, Pastor J. C., 138

body, 134-5, 138-9, 296, 335
Böhme, Jakob, 237
Bollingen, J., 13
Breuer, Josef, 29
brothers, motif of hostility, 343
Buddha, Buddhism, 70, 208, 235, 267-9, 332, 358, 378
Burghölzli Cantonal Mental Hospital (Zurich), 13, 15, 17, 33

carcinoma, 206-7
Carpocrates, 89-90
Carus, C. G., 168, 213, 241
catatonia, 43
Catholicism, Roman, 23, 27, 239, 259, 269, 321-3, 326-7
causality, causal, causalistic, 26, 41-2, 155n, 172, 293, 332
centre
    of gravity of personality, 19, 20
    as goal of individuation, 278
chance, 155
character, see personality
child, children
    within adult, 194
    God's, 196
    divine, 328
childhood, 73-4, 192-6, 205, 381; see also Jung, C. G.
Christ, Jesus/Christ-image (Saviour) 26, 66, 151, 204-5, 208, 247-8, 257, 266-86, 310, 325, 344, 347, 366, 374-6, 380, 384
    a symbol of the Self, 299-309, 332
    crucifixion of, 347, 376
    incarnation of, 344
Christian, Christianity, 23, 26, 136, 196, 204, 257-61, 264-86, 358, 371, 379, 393, 402-3
Chrysostom, John, 304
chthonic, 109, 273-4

church, churches, 258, 280, 363-7, 371-80, 385, 391
church fathers, 90, 250, 266
Cicero, 240n
Claparède, E., 52, 55
coincidences, meaningful, 26, 293, 339-41
collective, 16, 18, 198-200, 205
communism/ist, 367-8, 379, 388, 394
compensation, compensatory, 17, 18, 20, 59, 93, 117, 130, 167, 181-2, 184, 210, 219, 274; (see also self-regulation)
complement, complementary, 101 (relation between anima and persona)
complementarity, principle of (in physics), 25, 334-8
complex(es), 15, 30, 33, 34, 38-40, 122-3, 144, 143
    autonomous, 40
    feeling-toned, 38
    nuclear, 48-9, 139
compulsion(s)/compulsion neurosis, 38, 43, 92
conscious and unconscious, the conscious, unconscious and individuation, 212-28
    dialectical discussion between, 254
    new centre between, 19
    relation between, 61, 180-9
    and unconscious (synthesis between), 19
    and unconscious demands, 19
consciousness/conscious mind, 16, 19, 22, 30, 38-9, 54, 61, 63, 69, 79, 82, 94, 99, 105-6, 108, 110, 111, 113-14, 116-17, 124, 145, 152, 165, 171, 180, 188, 336, 371, 375, 382, 384, 390
conscious (adj.), 16, 18, 60-3, 72, 84, 91, 92, 97-8-9, 103, 114,

117, 122, 161, 175, 180, 182, 267
Copernicus, 370
conjunction/*Mysterium Coniunctionis*, 287-97
creative possibilities, 211
Cromwell, O., 207
cryptomnesia, 67, 341
Cybele, 270

daemon, daemonic, 199-200, 209
Dalai Lama, 249
David, 318
delusion, 15, 65
    of persecution, 41, 43
    collective, 203
dementia praecox, *see* schizophrenia
Demeter, 273
demiurge, 320
Descartes, René/Cartesian, 39, 341
development,
    adult, 20
    childhood, 20
    cultural, 137
    cyclic (spiral), 278
    individual, 191-228
Devil, the, 260n, 269, 281, 299, 303-4, 310, 312-14, 318-19, 344, 375, 388
Dieterich, A., 66
Dike, 320
Dionysius, the Areopagite, 301, 306
dissociation, dissociability, 14, 39, 60, 181, 382
Dittus, Gottliebin, *see* Blumhardt
dogma, 45
Dorn, G., 293-4, 334
dream(s), 17, 18, 65, 71, 74-5, 99, 167-89, 213, 229, 248, 282, 291
    anticipatory, 173
    of death, 186-8

'big dream', 65
    compensatory, 168, 181-2
    content of, 176
    disagreement with Freud concerning, 177-8, 180-1
    initial dreams, 169, 173
    mandalas, in, 276
    organ of information, 182
    'sent by God', 260
    series, 297
    symbolism in 184-9, 282
Drummond, H., 88, 95
Duce, 192

Eckermann, J. P., 95
Eckhart, Meister, 125, 209, 259
ego/ego personality, 14, 19, 91, 96, 101, 113, 120, 123, 131, 212-26, 229, 241, 359, 378
    ego instincts, 148, 387
    crucifixion of, 300
    relation with the unconscious, 93-5, 105-9, 122-4
Electra complex, *see* Oedipus complex
Elijah, 118-19
emotion(s)/emotional (affect[s]), 91, 95, 103-4, 112, 135, 215-16, 227
Empedocles, 134
enantiodromia, 103, 126
energy, psychic, 50, 57, 132, 153
    conservation of 68-70
Enkekalymmenos (the veiled one), 115
Enlightenment, the, 201, 265
epidemic(s), psychic, 201, 350, 365
Epimetheus, Epimethean, 163
equilibrium, psychic, 130
Eros, 111-13, 115, 159
Europe, 261, 368, 395
evil, 208-9
    problem of, 266, 299-329

union with good, 270, 299-329
relativism of, 271, 280
power of, 279, 281
as *privatio boni*, 299n, 301, 305, 307, 309
as belonging only to man, 302
root of, 388
within man, 395-8
extrasensory perception (ESP), 293
extravert, extraverted, extraversion, 18, 21, 96, 129-33, 140, 144, 149, 160-5
Ezekiel, 318

fairytale(s) 124-7
faith, 278
fanaticism, 360, 365
fantasy, fantasies, 21, 46-54, 71, 74, 76, 80, 95, 99, 201, 229, 282
dreamlike, 176
infantile 48-53, 381-3
father, 108, 112, 115, 165-6, 183-4
as archetype, 270
-world, 274-5
Faust, 200, 206, 209, 221, 230n, 237, 252, 286
feeling, 18, 21, 59, 62-3, 100, 131, 133, 144, 150
feminine, female,
even numbers as, 272-3
principle, 274
synthesis with masculine, 289
Ferenczi, Sandor, 13
fixation, 46-50
Flournoy, Theodore, 138, 168, 213
flying saucers, 345-6
folklore, 65
four
in one, 284
versus three, 272-6, 289

Frazer, Sir J. G., 69
free association, 178
Freud, Sigmund, 11, 13-15, 18, 20, 29, 31, 61, 72, 75, 87, 104, 129, 138, 146-9, 158n, 159, 165, 167-9, 180, 196, 214, 372; for Jung's differences with, and break from Freud, *see* Jung, C. G.
Function(s) (the four psychological functions), 18, 62, 63, 133, 144
anima and animus, 116-17

Galen, Claudius, 134
Gandhi, 121
German(s) 367
Gnostic, -ism, gnosis, 24, 89, 119, 237, 250-2, 274, 282, 285, 301, 342
God, god-image, godhead, 20, 23, 69-70, 127, 197-8, 201, 229, 236-9, 241, 243-9, 258-74, 285, 289, 299, 305, 309-29, 342-4, 358-62, 391-2, 403
Goethe, J. W. von, 95, 130, 200, 222-3, 230n, 252
systole and diastole, 131-2, 164
Golden Flower, The Secret of the, 226-8, 238n, 251
Good
antinomy with evil, 271, 280
as value judgement, 303
reconciliation with evil, 347
Summum Bonum, 299-309
Griesinger, W., 68
Group – as opposed to individual, 200-4

Haggard, H. Rider, 107, 222-3
hallucination(s), 15, 29, 44, 66
Händler, O., 253n
Hartmann, E. von, 213, 244
Harvey, John W., 239n

Helen (of Troy), 119
Helm, G. F., 69n
Heraclitus, 70
Hermaphrodite, -ism, 271
Hermes, hermetic, 276n, 278, 295, 328
Hero(es), 70, 83, 102, 123, 154, 199, 208-9, 222, 248
Hierosgamos, 286, 294-5, 322, 328
Hiranyagarbha, 267
Hoffmann, E. T. A., 221
Hölderlin, J. C. F., 78
Holy Ghost, 70, 273, 290, 296, 323
homosexuality, homosexual, 42
Horse
    as archetype, 187-8
    Trojan, 188
Horus, 318
humours, see temperaments
hydrogen bomb, 349, 397-8
hypochondria, 157
hysteria, 14, 43, 45, 47, 51

identification, identity, 98, 101, 103
Image
    archetypal, 16, 79, 277
    as feeling-toned complex, 38
    collective, 107-8
    illusory, 108
    of instincts, 382
    primordial, 69-70, 252
    soul-image, see soul
    virtual, 107
Imago(s), 105-6
Incest, incestuous, 17, 46, 50, 58
    religious and symbolic
        significance of, 58, 294
individualism, 22, 24, 196-7
individual, -ity, 20, 22, 24, 98, 102, 191, 195, 197-8, 225, 241, 368

as microcosm, 378
carrier of consciousness, 371
plight of in modern society, 349-357
understanding of himself, 369-383
uniqueness of, 352
individuation, principium
    individuationis, 19, 20, 22, 24, 212-28, 234, 253, 284-5, 328
    definition, 212
    historical parallels to, 250
infection, psychic, 351, 365, 367
inflation, 122
instinct(s), instinctual, 117, 140, 188, 211, 378, 382, 386-7, 389
    death, 159
    ego, 148
    feminine, 105
    masculine, 105
    nutritive, 51
    relationship, 112
    two fundamental (sex and power), 386
integration, 229
interpretation
    of dreams, 167-89
introvert, introverted, introversion, 18, 21, 129-33, 140-3, 149, 160-5
intuition, 18, 21, 133, 144, 150n, 219
Irenaeus, 89-90
Iron Curtain, 349, 364, 380
irregularity
    as characteristic of absolute reality, 352
Islam, 268, 358

James, W., 138, 160, 240, 259n
Janet, Pierre, 13, 14, 29-30, 39, 51, 53, 56, 138, 168, 213-14
Jeans, Sir James, 334
Job, 309-29

Jung, C. G.
  abandonment of academic
    career, 83
  birth, 13
  break with Freud, 23-4, 71
  childhood, 22-3, 32-3
  confrontation with the
    unconscious, 71-2, 74-83,
    118-22, 129, 229-32, 250
  differing view of dreams from
    Freud, 177-8, 180-1, 185-9
  divergence from Freud, 16-17,
    20-21, 45-64
  dreams of, 74-82, 87, 234
  early work, 14-19, 29-44
  fantasies of, 74-82, 118-22, 230,
    250
  involvement with Freud, 40,
    45-64
  mandalas of, 230-5
  marriage, 13
  MD dissertation, 13, 29
  mental upheaval, 71-2, 74-83
  Pauli, collaboration with, 333
  type theory, 129-167
  visions of, 74-82

Ka, 121-2
Kant, Immanuel, 24, 61n, 168,
  332
Kerényi, Karl, 290
Kerner, J., 138
Khidr, 332
Khepri (scarab), 341
Klein-Hüningen, 13, 32
Klingsor (in Parsifal), 119
knowledge
  versus faith, 384
  versus understanding, 353-4,
    373
Kore, the, 249
Kranefeldt, W. M. 185
Kremlin, the, 347
Kretschmer, E., 139

Kundry (in Parsifal), 119
Küsnacht, 13-14

Lao-Tzu, 96, 119, 123
lapis, see philosopher's stone
Lehmann, F. R., 123, 185
Leibniz, G. W., 168
Lenin, V. I., 205
libido, 17, 51, 54-7, 59, 103, 158
life
  meaning of, 21
  senselessness and aimlessness
    of, 21, 211
  stages of:
    first half, 19; mid-life period,
    21, 24, 72, 82, 226-7; second
    half of, 74, 211
Lippmann, Eduard von, 287
Logos, 111, 113, 385
Lovejoy, A. O., 69
Loyola, Ignatius, 367
Lucifer, 195, 209
Luke, St, 89-90, 248

Magus, Simon, 119
magician
  dream of black and white
    magicians, 126-7
Mana, Mana-personality, 69n,
  122-4, 401
mandalas, 20, 229-35, 240-1,
  278n, 292, 297n, 299
Manichaean(s), 304-5
Marcionites, 305
Marduk, 273
Maria Prophetissa, 272, 275-6
Marx, Karl; Marxists, 205, 367,
  383, 394, 399
Mary, Virgin, 27, 67, 273, 295,
  321-9
masculine, male
  uneven numbers as, 272-3
  principle, 274
  synthesis with feminine, 289

mask, 96, 98, 124
Mass, the, 247
materialism, 135, 137, 333
Matthew, St, 89
Maya, 109
Mayer, Robert, 50, 68-9
meaning, 26
megalomania, 66, 113
Megara, Megaric, 160
Meier, C. A., 339
memory, 75, 219
Mephistopheles, 121, 206, 221
Mercurius, 122, 126, 276, 290-1, 293
metanoia, 376
Metempsychosis, 70
Mithras, Mithraic, 66, 325
Möbius, P. J., 151
Moira, 320
Mondamin, 332
Moses, 70
mother, 108-9, 115, 165-6
    as archetype, 84-5, 187, 273
    -world, 274-5
Mysterium Coniunctionis, see conjunction
myth, mythology, mythologem, 16, 46, 58, 65, 70, 93, 188, 274, 283, 327, 366, 402-3

Napoleon, 123, 200
narcissism, 104
Nazism, 388
Nelken, J., 214n, 222
neurosis, neuroses, 14, 17, 47-53, 60, 147, 207, 210-11, 225, 380-2, 384-7
    obsessional neurosis, 43
    present cause of, 52
    traumatic neurosis, 17
    treatment of by dream-analysis, 168-89
    value of 152-3, 167

Nietzsche, Friedrich, 25, 78, 95, 136, 151-2, 245, 247
numbers,
    as autonomous psychic entities, 332
numen, numinous, numinal, numinosity, 16, 71, 144-5, 239-40, 285, 288, 312, 372, 378

object/subject, 99-100, 131-2, 140-1
obsession, obsessional, 43
occupational therapy, 44
Oedipus complex, 17, 48, 51
one-sidedness, 19, 59, 157
opposites, 18, 25, 59, 60, 136, 159, 398
    union of 286-97, 328
    self and, 299-321
    irreconcilable, 300
    in pleroma, 342
Ostwald, F. W., 155-6, 160
Otto, Rudolf, 239
outgrowing (of problems), 227

paganism, 261
Paracelsus, 283n, 285, 293
paranoia, paranoid, 40-3, 65
parapsychology, 332-3, 370
parent(s), 105
Paul, St, 136, 240, 245, 376, 392
Pauli, Wolfgang, 25, 240, 333-4, 338
Persephone, 273
persona, 87, 93-6, 98-103
    compensated by anima, 93-6, 101
personality(ies), 18
    achievement of, 19
    as adult ideal, 193, 205
    autonomous, 31
    child's, 192-6
    collective, 98
    definition of, 195

development, 191-210, 381
dissociation, 14, 97, 220
fragmentary, 39
individual, 98-99
integration, 229
redeemer, 201
secret of, 253
splitting, 14, 40-1, 60, 97
subsidiary, 14, 31
unconscious, 29, 31, 38, 87
unity, 14
as vocation, 199
perversion, sexual, 47, 53
phenomenology, 15
Philalethes, Eirenaeus, 222
Philemon, 119-22
philosopher's stone, 289, 296
phobos, phobia, 43, 159
physics, physicists, 25, 68, 155n,
334-9, 397
Pisces, 345-7
Plato, Platonic, 136, 160, 237,
335, 346
pleroma, 24, 322, 328, 342-3
pneuma (spirit), 326
Pontius Pilate, 384
Pope, the, 26, 321-4
power, 111
Preiswerk, Hélène (referred to as
S. W.), 29-31
Prince, Morton, 29, 39, 213
privatio boni, doctrine of, 299-309,
318n
progression, 59, 60, 63-4
projection(s), 92-3, 104, 116,
242-3, 259
Prometheus, Promethean, 163,
195
Protestant, Protestantism, 258-9,
269, 321-7, 358
provisional life, 184
psyche, the, 168, 201, 215, 243,
253, 369, 390
ambiguity of, 210

healthy/sick, 151
objective, 203-4, 206
reality of, 324
self-regulating, 129-89
sovereignty of, 139
splinter, 40
stratification of, 188
psychoanalysis, 46-64
psychogenesis, 41-3
psychoid, 26
psychokinesis, 333
psychology,
analytical, 250, 252-3
educational, 193
empirical, 244, 263
experimental, 138
laboratory, 372
medical, 372
'only', 258
physiological, 138
psychopomp, 113
psychosis, psychoses, psychotic,
15
latent, 44, 350
psychotherapy, psychological
treatment, psychotherapist, 15,
44, 168-89, 207, 279-80, 354
aims of, 210-12
termination of, 254
Purusha, 238, 264, 267
Pythagoras, 136, 218

quadratura circuli (squaring of the
circle) 235-6
quaternity, 20, 235-7, 275, 321

Rauschenbach, Emma, 13, 77
reaction-time, 14, 33, 34
Reformation, the, 258
regression, 50-3, 58, 59, 60-4
religion, religious quest, 16, 46,
188, 229, 238-49, 253-85, 380
as counterbalance to
mass-mindedness, 357-63

as opposed to 'creed', 358-9
definition of, 239
impoverishment of, 265
position of Western, 363-9
repression, 14, 56, 60, 182
Rhine, J. B., 293
Ribot, T. A., 138

Sallust, 51
Salome, 118-19
Salpêtrière Hospital, 13
salvation, 278, 280, 285
Satan see Devil
scarab, 81, 340-1
Schiller, F., 144, 192, 195
schizophrenia, schizophrenic,
14-17, 40-44, 54-7, 65-6, 224,
235-6
Schopenhauer, Arthur, 24, 26,
213, 244
Schreber, Daniel Paul, 54-6, 214n
self (archetype of) 19, 20, 229,
234-8, 242, 258, 267-9, 271-2,
299-329, 331-2
The Undiscovered, 349-403
self-knowledge, 91, 113, 116,
351-3, 369, 392-403
self-realization, 24, 196
self-regulation, 17, 18, 129-89
sensation, 18, 21, 100, 144, 150n
sensitiveness, 164
Septem Sermones ad Mortuos, 24,
230, 342
sex, sexuality, sexual, 16, 17,
45-8, 50-4, 55-7, 96, 153, 185
shadow, 82, 87-93, 114, 126, 159,
221, 243, 279-82, 286, 301,
317, 347, 380, 388-9, 395,
398-400
Shankarachaya, 121, 126
Siegfried, 81-3, 87
Silberer, Herbert, 284
sin, sinner, 88-9, 258, 279-84
Socrates, 200, 237

somnambulism, 29, 97
son
of man, 371
Sophia, 322
soul, soul-image, 69-70, 97,
100-11, 137, 259, 289
religious function of, 262
spirit, spirit figures, 69-70, 124-7,
137
Spitteler, C., 105, 110
Stalin, 364
state, the, 243, 345-7, 364, 377,
383, 385, 395, 400, 403
dominance of, 349-50
opposition to religion and
individual, 357-63
stimulus, 14, 33, 35, 36
subject/object, 99-100, 131-2,
140-1
sublimation, 153-4
suggestion, 175
summum bonum, doctrine of,
299-309
Swedenborg, E., 26
symbol, symbolic, 17, 184-9,
296-7, 328, 378
alchemical, 251, 284, 296
of Assumption, 327
Christian, 277, 379
as beyond mind and matter,
331
phallic symbols, 185
sacred, 204
as opposed to 'sign', 185
of totality, 229
uniting, 225
synchronicity, 26, 235, 292,
331-3, 337-341
syncretism, 136
Syzygy, 109

Tacitus, 106
Taine, H., 138
tao, 210, 264, 332

Tatian, 301
Taurus, 346-7
Taylor, F. Sherwood, 19
Tehom, 273
Telesphoros
  as daemon of Aesculapius, 200
temperament(s), 134
Tertullian, 262n, 265, 269
thinking, 18, 21, 59, 62-3, 133, 144, 150
three (versus four), 272-6
Tiamat, 273-5
Tifereth, 332
Timaeus (of Plato), 237
Titus of Bostra, 304
transcendent function, 226
transference
  (countertransference), 148, 226, 255, 373
transmigration of souls, 70
trauma, 46, 47
totality, 20, 229, 239; see also wholeness
Trinity, the/Trinitarian, 272, 275, 321-2
Tylor, E. B., 69
types, psychological: typology, 18, 129-67
typos, 263, 267

UFO (unidentified flying object), 333, 345-6
unconscious (adj.), 14, 29, 31, 35-6, 48, 59, 60-3, 67, 84, 87-8, 93-4, 97, 99-100, 103-6, 108, 117, 122-3, 126, 161, 168-9, 176, 180, 182, 199, 202, 211, 267, 378
unconscious, the, 14, 17-24, 44, 48, 54, 62, 70, 72, 74-5, 78-9, 80, 82-3, 92-6, 99-103, 105-6, 108-11, 113, 116-18, 122, 129, 144, 147, 153, 166, 168, 176, 180, 182, 187, 201, 210,
212-26, 244, 250, 266, 275, 337, 371-2
unconscious, the collective, 15-16, 26, 65-85, 91, 116, 123, 224, 276, 282-3, 291, 325
unconscious, personal, 67, 68, 87, 91, 93, 123, 282
unconsciousness, 41, 88, 93, 104, 198, 351
understanding versus knowledge, 353-4, 373
uniqueness (of individual personality), 203, 352
union
  of opposites, 286-97
  of mind and body, 296
unity, 14, 18, 20, 25, 136-7, 229, 291, 337
  of all existence, 331
  of mind and body, 134-5, 139, 296, 335
Unus Mundus, 291-3, 331-41

Valkyrie(s), 188
Valhalla, 188
Vischer, F. T. von, 39
vision(s), 66-7, 77, 219
vocation, 199-200, 202-4, 208
Vulgate, 90

Wagner, R., 95
Watts, Alan, 310n
Weltanschauung, 367-8, 383, 385
White, Fr Victor, 299n, 346-7
wholeness, 18-19, 21, 193, 200, 203, 212, 229, 236, 241, 257, 267, 275, 279, 329, 332, 402
Wilhelm, R., 226n, 235, 251
will, 24, 154-6, 159, 213, 229, 382
  freedom of, 246
wise old man, 87, 124, 222
woman, 106-15
word-association, 14-15, 33-7
world (external/outer), 18

world (inner), 18
Wundt, W., 138

Yahweh, 301, 309-21, 343-4
yang (and yin), 286, 292
yin (and yang), 187, 286, 292
yoga, yogi(s), 79, 224, 239

Zagreus, 245
Zarathustra (Nietzsche), 245
zeitgeist, 381, 402
Zeus, 105
Zöckler, O., 270
Zurich, 13, 29, 34, 36, 120